Voyager

Janny Wurts

PERIL'S GATE

The Wars of Light and Shadow

VOLUME 6

THIRD BOOK OF
THE ALLIANCE OF LIGHT

Voyager
An Imprint of HarperCollins*Publishers*
77–85 Fulham Palace Road,
Hammersmith, London W6 8JB

www.voyager-books.com

This paperback edition 2002
1 3 5 7 9 8 6 4 2

First published in Great Britain by *Voyager* 2001

Copyright © Janny Wurts 2001

The author asserts the moral right to
be identified as the author of this work

ISBN 0 00 710108 2

Typeset in Palatino and Belwe by
Palimpsest Book Production Limited,
Polmont, Stirlingshire

Printed and bound in Great Britain by
Clays Ltd, St Ives plc

To Jeff Watson,
the guardian gryphon in charge
of technical wonders without
which more deadlines
would have been missed.

Acknowledgements

Many hands have been of invaluable assistance
on the journey to complete this creation.
Profound thanks are owed to Jonathan Matson,
Jane Johnson, Caitlin Blasdell and Jennifer Brehl,
Sara and Bob Schwager,
my husband, Don Maitz,
Lynda-Marie Hauptman,
and Devi Pillai and the rest of the staff and sales force
at HarperCollins who have stood by me throughout
the massive length of this project.

Contents

Third Book

Athera
Continent of Paravia

Age of the Mistwraithe

Legend:

- ⊠ Sorcerers' Preserve
- • Cities
- ♦ Second Age ruins
- ⊙ City that did not fall in uprising
- ⊓ Worldsend Gates
- ↑ Standing Stones
- ----- Kingdom Borders
- ∿ Rivers
- ♠♠ Forests
- ⟋ Marshes or Mires
- ∴∴∴ Wastelands
- ----- Second Age Roads
- ⌒ Trade Roads
- ⋀⋀⋀ Mountains

Scale in Leagues

0   10   25   50   100

Cildein Ocean

South Sea

Bay of Eltair

Minderl Bay

Regions and places:
Fallowmere, North Ward, Brimwood, East Ward, Earle, Rathain, Tal Quorin, Plain of Araithe, Eastern, Mathorn Mountains, Narms, Camris, Riverton, Perlorn, Crescent Isle, Valequay, Ithilt, Minderl, Adaon, Minderl Strait, Beinir's Point, East Gate, Isfar Adaw, Daon Ramon, old way, Ithamon, Lithion Barrens, Anglefen, Ward, Ishlir, Vastmark, Vastrait, Bay of Eltair, Mainmere, Narbester, halla, Shiplport, Charldon, Whitehold, Varens, Varese, Sundar, Atwood, East Halla, Melhalla, Adelion, Tirans, Kalesh, Perdith, Midhalla, Methlas Lake, Orvandir, Silvermarsh, Ithier, Durn, Sic Towers, Lissine, Thirdmark, Ghent Vale, Forthmark, Shand, Anthon, Telzen, Rockbay, Alland, Selkwood, Desert of Sanpashir, Merior, Southshire, Shaddorn, South Sea

Arithon s'Ffalenn,
called Master of Shadow!
For the sake of your crimes against our
fair city of Jaelot, your spirit shall be
delivered by sword and by fire to your
rightful hour of death . . .
– Mayor of Jaelot, decree of execution
Third Age Year 5669

I. Retribution

T he storm settled over the Eltair coast just after the advent of
nightfall. Like the worst winter gales, it stole in on cat feet.
The fitful, fine sleet dusting over sere landscape changed on
a breath into muffling snow as the temperature plunged below
freezing. The moment caught Arithon s'Ffalenn, last living Prince
of Rathain and birth-born Master of Shadow, crouched in the iced
brush of a hedgerow.

Each labored breath burned his lungs like cold fire. His sprint
was cut short, though the city of Jaelot's stone walls lay scarcely
a bowshot behind him. A skulking fugitive hard-pressed by
enemies who hunted by sword and by spellcraft, he shot a
concerned glance sidewards as Fionn Areth folded, gasping,
beside him. The young man had spent the dregs of his strength.
Even the threat of relentless pursuit could not stave off stark
necessity: the goatherd just snatched from death on the scaffold
could run no farther without pause for recovery.

'Rest,' whispered Arithon, as winded himself. 'For a moment.
No more.'

Fionn Areth's clipped nod showed resentment, not gratitude.

Yet no moment could be spared to treat with the young man's
inimically misguided loyalties. Enemies hounded their backs
without respite. Koriani seeresses would be tracking with spelled
snares. If the mayor's armed guardsmen from Jaelot prevailed
first, the pair would be slaughtered on the run.

'They'll find us.' Fionn Areth cast a harrowed glance over his shoulder. His chilled hand tightened on his sword grip as he noticed the patrol sweeping the high crenels of the battlements. The flutter of their pine brands speared rays of light through the thickening snowfall. Arithon measured their movement, intent. The alarm bells stayed mute. No outcry arose from the gatehouse. Careful to mask his own tension, he said, 'Bide easy. The mayor's guards can't know we've slipped through the walls unless the Koriathain decide to inform them.'

Nor would the senior enchantress, Lirenda, be anxious to disseminate word of her failure. Since her towering arrogance had granted her quarry the opening to escape, she would be loath to approach her male allies. Once again, her order had bungled their promise to entrap the Master of Shadow.

Left raw by the price he had paid to win back his threatened autonomy, Arithon closed with dry irony, 'From stung pride, I expect the witches will try to recoup their blunder in secret. That's to our advantage. Thick snowfall should foil their scryers and hide us, at least for a little while.'

Fionn Areth returned a poisonous glower from a face that, feature for feature, was a mirror image of the Shadow Master's. Having narrowly missed execution and burning for the crimes of his look-alike nemesis, he still suffered the morning's shock of discovery, that his appearance had been fashioned by the meddling design of Koriani spellcraft. The cruel fact chafed, that he had been used as unwitting, live bait in their conspiracy to ensnare the unprincipled killer beside him.

The betrayal stung yet. 'Never mind witches,' he gasped in spat venom to the Spinner of Darkness. 'The Alliance won't rest until you've been dismembered and burned to serve justice.'

Expressionless, Arithon refused answer. He was no less enraged at being made the political pawn in the feud that pitched the enchantresses against the authority of the Fellowship Sorcerers. Since bare-bones survival perforce must come first, he took ruthless stock of bad circumstance.

While night settled like impenetrable felt over the Eltair Bay coastline, he wrested the lay of the land from his reluctant memory. Northward, past the black spur of Jaelot's walled head-land, small farmsteads patched the land like paned glass. The occupants were suspicious and ill set toward strangers, the ancient codes of hospitality long lost since the rising that threw down the high kings. Nor did the countryside offer safe prospects. Tangled cedar windbreaks and hedgerows of red thorn

2

squared the rough, fallow fields. Two vagrants in flight from the mayor's justice dared not ply the lanes, with their drystone walls high enough to entrap, and their rutted mazes of crossroads. To the east, the salt waves of Eltair Bay thrashed a raked stretch of shingle, and a wind-razed, shelterless marshland. To the west rose the forbidding stone ramparts of the Skyshiels, sliced by ravines of weather-scabbed rock, and mantled in glaze ice and fir.

Fitful gusts already stirred the stilled air, first warning whisper of the bass-note howl yet to build to an oncoming gale. Arithon tucked frozen hands under his cloak. He held no illusions. The snowfall that helpfully covered their tracks, and disrupted the Koriani scryers carried a double-edged threat. The night ahead would bring lethal cold, and blinding, bewildering drifts. Inadequately clothed to withstand hostile elements, he and the victimized herder he had rescued could easily die from exposure.

For the storm that drove in had not arisen out of natural forces. Arithon sensed its song deep in his bones. The subliminal, whining vibration of dropped pressure came exacerbated by the imbalance wrought by disturbed magnetics. Earlier, Dakar the Mad Prophet had served him hard warning: the Fellowship Sorcerers were themselves caught in crisis, distracted by some larger upset. The illicit magics Dakar had engaged to unravel the Koriani defenses in Jaelot had assuredly added more stress to the roiled currents of lane flux. With the surge of winter solstice cresting at midnight, Arithon lacked accurate means to measure the backlash that might follow. As he chewed over that burden of worry, Fionn Areth stirred in the darkness.

Warned by a muffled, metallic ring, Arithon spun. He clamped the boy's wrist in a strangling grip and arrested the sword halfway pulled from the scabbard. 'Eighth hell of Sithaer, are you insane?'

'I should kill you here!' Fionn Areth gasped through locked teeth. 'There are widows across the five kingdoms who'd thank me.'

'They might,' Arithon agreed, his annoyance turned acid. 'But a blade in my back won't see you safe. The opposite in fact. My blood in the snow would act as a beacon for Koriani scryers. If you think you can manage to evade their spelled snares, Dakar has the food and the horses we'll need. You aren't going to find him without my guidance. Better to salve your fool's craving for justice after we've scrambled to safety.'

Fionn Areth's murderous resistance failed to slacken under restraint. Darker truth eclipsed reason. He knew this creature who entreated in pressed self-defense was unnatural, an unprincipled sorcerer whose guileful strategies had slaughtered three dedicated war hosts. Across the continent, men flocked to Lysaer's sunwheel standard and pledged to the Light to destroy him.

'Then swear me your bond,' Fionn Areth insisted. 'As Prince of Rathain, prove you meant what you said when you offered me trial by combat.'

'Very well. Accept my given word. We'll cross swords at the first opportunity, but *after* we've slipped our pursuit.' Solemnity spoiled by a stressed thread of laughter, Arithon provoked with glib melodrama, 'Dharkaron's Black Spear strike me dead should I fail you, though the point will likely prove moot. Koriathain and Jaelot's guards would end Rathain's royal line with no help from Ath's angel of vengeance.'

Fionn Areth found his sword arm released, though his volatile temper stayed unsettled. Ice showered down in cracked shards from the branches as Arithon ducked free of the hedgerow. All animal grace and dangerous focus, he cast no glance backward to ascertain whether his oath was accepted. On the insufferable assumption his young double must follow, he pursued his route across country. Brisk progress was sustained in swift bursts that utilized each quirk of terrain for masking cover.

Fionn Areth flanked him through closing curtains of wet snow, dreading the oncoming thud of hooves, and fearing, each step, the clarion cry of the gate watch's horn at his back. Led on by a felon whose motives were suspect, he nursed his distrust through the erratic sprints between hayrick and thicket and cowshed. The low-lying fields confounded simplicity. The verges were crosscut with dikes and ditches, or brush brakes riddled with badger setts. The ice-capped stone walls could turn a man's ankle. Despite such hazards, Arithon stayed clear of the cottages with their inviting, gold-glazed windows. The byres and yards with penned sheep and loose dogs were avoided, no matter the punishment exacted by chilled hands and feet and the limits of flagging stamina.

Another pause, snatched in a thicket, while snow sighed and winnowed through the frost-brittle brambles. Under lidded sky, wrapped in lead-sheeted darkness, Fionn Areth sensed Arithon's measuring scrutiny. However he strove, he could not hide his weakness. Jaelot's abusive confinement had worn him, and the relentless pace of their flight left him battered half-prostrate.

4

Each passing second redoubled their risks. The storm would grow worse, and the snow pile deeper. They struggled ahead on borrowed time, against the inevitable odds: at any moment, the town gates would disgorge mounted patrols with pine torches. Guardsmen would ride with the trained trackers lent by Eltair's league of headhunters. For the prospect of claiming the bounty on royalty, they would unleash their dread packs of mastiffs, cut mute as pups to course human quarry in silence.

In uncanny answer to brooding thoughts, Arithon whispered encouragement. 'If there are dogs, they won't scent well in snow. Can you manage? Let's go then.' He forged onward, the tenuous landmarks he steered by scarcely recognizable after a quarter century of change. Stone markers and storm-bent sentinel oaks were masked by snowfall and darkness; buildings and bylanes appeared blurred into maddening sameness. No margin remained for mistakes. A single wrong turn would lose his bearings amid the flat apron of coastal landscape. Nor did Arithon dare slacken. Koriathain might guide the mayor's patrols, intent on recouping their losses. They knew, as he did, the storm would not wait. Posed the grave danger of being outflanked, Arithon chivvied his stumbling double into the lash of the wind.

A dike almost tripped the herder. His sliding descent fetched him short in a drain ditch. The skin of ice smashed underfoot. Muddy water soaked through his fleece boots. Fionn Areth swore in grasslands dialect, his consonants rattled by chattering teeth. As chilled himself, Arithon forged ahead. The mismatched pair splashed over the slough and labored up the eroded berm. A field of corn stubble speared through the snow, rutted mud frozen underneath. Past an osier fence, they flushed a herd of belled ewes, who bolted in jangling terror.

The wind had gained force. Its bite chilled their wet feet and keened through snow-sodden clothing.

'Not far, now,' Arithon murmured, then broke off. 'Get down!'

Dazed to plodding exhaustion, Fionn Areth missed the cue. Jerked back, then knocked prone as Arithon felled him, he stifled a shrill cry of outrage. Disastrously late, he reached understanding: *the drumming he heard was not caused by the thrash of bare branches*. Flattened beneath the frail sticks of a hazel thicket, shivering under his wadded wool cloak, he held breathlessly still while the torch of an outrider flittered by.

'Well, we had to expect this.' Arithon stirred, shaking out clotted snow spooned up by his oversize cuffs.

5

With the mayor's guard now sounding the alarm, the country-side offered no haven. Uneasy farmsteaders would be out, scouring their hay byres for fugitives. They would unchain their dogs and round up their horses, and stab pitchforks through the mesh of their cornricks.

Nor did the worsening storm sustain its fickle gift of respite. The snow had already piled too deep. Once a search party stumbled across their plowed prints, they were going to become hunted animals.

'We're farther afield than they realize,' Arithon assured, to every appearance unperturbed as his extended hand was refused. While Fionn Areth struggled erect on his own, he added, 'Nor will they guess we've an ally waiting to shield us. If fortune favors, they'll keep the belief we're given to aimless flight.' For prudence, he chose not to mention that Dakar would likely need spellcraft to further mislead their pursuit.

Inured to harsh weather by his moorland upbringing, the young herder stumbled onward. The overwhelming speed of events had left him too numbed to think. Through bitter necessity, he trailed Arithon's lead through the banked snow of the sheepfold. Another deep ditch, and a slippery crossing over the logs of a stile, then partial respite as they plunged into the fir copse beyond.

Fionn Areth tripped twice before his dulled mind made sense of his jumbled impressions. In fact, they had covered more ground than he thought. The open land of the farmsteads lay behind them.

An evergreen canopy closed on all sides. The sky was blank pitch. Each gust shook crusted snow from the spruce, a mere clutch of seedlings before the towering growth that ruched foot-hills to the west. The tumbled chimney of a cottar's house jagged under the pillowing drifts, the broken yard gate a mute testament to some cataclysmic misfortune. Beyond the old steading, a ravine razed the dell, where the annual spring snowmelt roared in white cataracts to egress in Eltair Bay.

Despite the hard freeze, the crossing was arduous, the undercut banks being ice clad. Jutted rocks caved away at each step. Wet to the knees, and wrung wretched with shivering, Fionn Areth cursed the cold rivulets that chased down his boot cuffs and collar. His gloves had soaked through, the fingers inside chilled to lumps of shrill agony. Close on Arithon's heels, he panted uphill and crossed the exposed crest, harrowed each step by the howling winds off the seacoast. Descent proved as difficult, the stony soil overgrown with young firs cased in glaze ice, and uncut by even a deer path. Raked and slapped by needled boughs, Fionn Areth broke through to a clearing, too miserable to care that Arithon had reached his obscure destination.

An abandoned mill loomed on the swept shelf of snow, crooked in the oxbow bend of a stream. Its unroofed, square shell carved the gusts into dissonance. The rotted wheel canted in a rimed tumble of frozen waterfall. Nor was the ruin deserted. A stout, muffled figure emerged from its gloom, its waddling stride on the uncertain footing as ungainly as a discomposed duck.

'Dakar!' hailed Arithon, sounding weary at last. 'I want—'

'You bastard, you just about killed me with worry! Old storm rips my fixed wardspells to static, and you take a fiend's sweet time to make rendezvous!' Halted in huffing distemper, the fat prophet who served as the Shadow Master's henchman scowled. Blown snow frosted his ginger brows and his unkempt bristle of beard. 'You don't hear the horn calls? The Mayor of Jaelot's sent lancers abroad. I had just about written you both off as meat for the headhunter's mastiffs.'

'Dakar,' Arithon broke in, wrung by a shiver. 'Did you bring horses?'

'Dharkaron's black bollocks! Are you both soaked as rabbits?' The Mad Prophet flicked his irritated glance from one alike face to the other, spell-carved to match the same chiseled angles under wind-snagged sable hair. Unerringly able to discern the original, he thrust out a forearm to support young Fionn Areth. 'Yes, I managed to meet your request. We have four geldings, three hacks, and one knock-kneed packhorse. Come in. There's also a fire and hot gruel, and before you ask, yes. I've set masking runes, and have maze wards running against the mayor's riders at each of the four quarters.'

Arithon winced at the mention of ward sorceries, which, predictably, balked Fionn Areth.

Dakar jerked the boy forward in unvarnished exasperation. 'Ath preserve idiots with misaligned scruples, *come on*! His Grace of Rathain might prefer to stay outside and brood, just show me an Araethurian herdsman born with warm-blooded good sense.'

Fionn Areth resisted, given short shrift as Dakar vented his leftover tension through scolding. 'I'm damned glad you're alive and still standing to greet me, boy. That won't lift the blight of Daelion's curse off the bone-headed folly that spared you! Your prince won't have mentioned, but the risk undertaken to snatch you from Jaelot takes the prize for catastrophic stupidity.'

7

At next step, they crossed into the ring of set guard spells. Fionn Areth cried out as a sharp tingle raked his skin. He nearly sprained the Mad Prophet's wrist in his panicked effort to bolt. 'Dharkaron's bleak vengeance!' Dakar exploded. Fingers locked in the Araethurian's wet cloak, he held on, his corpulent bulk no more bothered than if he had bagged a struggling game fish. 'Koriani witches changed your *whole face* through black use of their sigils of force. What's a middling weak veil of concealment going to do, except save your skin from execution? Find the sweet reason that Ath gave your goats! Get yourself warm and dry enough to think clearly before you decide we're your enemies.'

Fionn Areth flushed, grumbled an apology in his backcountry dialect, then relented enough to let Dakar lead him into the shelter of the tumbledown mill.

The roof had caved in to a rickle of slate, but the beamed track of the log carriage for the saw still stood. The planked platform winnowed the worst of the snow. In the single dry corner, cut off from the wind, Dakar had lit a neat fire. A pot of gruel bubbled over the flames. Four horses munched hay, tied by neck ropes to the skewed post of the mill shaft, its base secured by the massive runnerstone that had ground countless harvests of barley. The animals' warmth blunted the edge from the cold. Beside three heaped saddles, acquired by means of forged requisitions and subterfuge, Dakar had blankets and cloaks and thick boots lined with lamb's wool. The collection included two buck knives, a hunting bow, and provisions fit for a trek across mountain terrain.

'Oh, well done, Dakar.' Arithon unhooked the iced clasps on his mantle, hung the sopped cloth on the sacklift, and accepted the blanket tossed into his numbed hands. Swathed like a wraith, he resumed his expert inspection. 'Where are the spirits?'

Dakar chuckled. 'Here was I, wishing the troublesome brains had been frozen clean out of your head. I've got spiced wine laced full of restoratives. If you drink too much, don't damn me tomorrow. You'll feel like your innards got packed with wet sand, with river rocks jammed in your eye sockets.'

Between helping Fionn Areth, the Mad Prophet unslung a cord from his neck and passed over a stoppered skin flask.

Arithon fumbled his effort to draw the cork. He grimaced, used his teeth, then shut his eyes in distaste and belted a hefty draught. The offensive sting made his eyes water. A husked burr of betrayal roughened his voice. 'You didn't mention lye-stripping

8

the tissue off my poor vocal cords. I won't sing a true note for a week.'

'And right blessed that misfortune will be!' Dakar shot back, scathing. 'Given the powers you've roused up in blind ignorance, we're lucky not to be cinders scattered over the Ath-forsaken dunes of Sanpashir!'

He snatched up Fionn Areth's discarded shirt, wrung out the cuffs, and hung the linen to dry. 'You'll find a clean tunic and smallclothes in the saddle pack.' At the young man's hesitation, his moon features knit into a glower fit to torch silk. 'Don't even think to protest obligation. You're the guest of your crown prince. He's oathbound by law to provide you his best hospitality.'

'We're touchy,' observed Arithon, his thoughtful gaze on the Mad Prophet's back. He rolled a sawn log closer to the fireside. As though his balance might desert him without warning, he perched. 'Has your pending fit of prescience not lifted since sundown?'

Bent over, rummaging through saddle packs like a corpulent thresher, with Fionn Areth hovering with bad humor and crossed arms, Dakar grumbled through his beard. 'I'm hungover. Jaelot's gin is a grade below horse piss – that much hasn't changed in twenty years.'

'I'm remiss.' A wry grin lit Arithon's fox features, tinged orange in the flicker of firelight. 'Why not sample your vile restorative?' He passed back the flask, while the tireless wind skirled snow devils across the darkened gap of the tailrace.

The Mad Prophet ignored both comment and offering. Straightened up burdened to the chin with bunched clothing, he foisted the pile without apology on Fionn Areth. 'Put those on.' He accepted the flask and slapped its gurgling bladder on top of a sheepskin jacket. 'As soon as you're dressed, drink up. We've got to be moving before midnight.'

Fionn Areth gaped, his arms clutching his third change of raiment since morning. 'Why can't we rest here?'

Dakar threw up his hands, eyes rolled to white rings. 'Because this is *solstice*, and the lane tides were unleashed to deliver your crown prince to Jaelot.'

When Fionn Areth looked blank, Arithon ventured a more civil explanation. 'This ruin sits on a natural watercourse. At midnight, a cresting flow of raw power will rip through the site like a conduit. Without the Paravian rituals to mitigate, the flood will rattle and shake any structure not blessed into alignment with the flow of Ath's greater mystery.'

'This mill tore to wreckage in the last causal event. And before you ask, yes, it was Arithon who sang the same powers active in Jaelot twenty-five years ago.' Nakedly worried, Dakar stowed his bulk on a saddle pack. 'The repeat performance to break your captivity might easily fell the last stones in these walls. You want to sleep under the rubble?'

'I won't sleep at all where there's sorcery afoot,' Fionn Areth retorted. Having suffered the brunt of mistaken identity, only narrowly spared execution for the selfsame sorceries raised by the hand of his nemesis, he gave each fold of clothing his suspicious inspection. If he expected copper-thread sigils worked through the seams of the hems, he encountered nothing amiss. Only sturdy, stitched hemp and plain cerecloth linings. Defeated at last by the merciless chill, he burrowed into a shirt and tunic better suited to his build than the castoffs garnered from the lady's servant who had helped them evade close pursuit.

While sorcerer and prophet shared out gruel and brisk talk, the herder buckled on his sword, then donned jacket and cloak. Leaned on a post, determined to stand guard, he declined to eat, wary lest he fall sound asleep among enemies.

The contents of Dakar's flask had a faint, metallic aftertaste. Fionn Areth drank deeply, too parched to realize that the spellcraft he reviled was in fact bound into the spirits. Grasslands ignorant, he gave no thought to question, even as the pungent restorative burned through his body and revitalized flagging, sore muscles. Restored to clear focus, warmed and eased back to comfort, he followed the conversation ongoing between the Mad Prophet of legend and the prince whose appearance the goatherd shared.

'The Fellowship knows, then?' Arithon asked concerning the defeated plot that entwined them.

'Once you crossed through Jaelot's outer wall, you broke through the ward the witches had set to forestall Sethvir's earth-sense.' Preoccupied with securing the saddle packs, Dakar shrugged. 'Better worry more for Jaelot's patrols. If I couldn't scry you, then the Koriani seers are going to be hobbled as well. Their clairvoyants can't act in full force for as long as the snow keeps falling.' The water element in the storm would maze the transmission of spells set through a quartz focus.

Arithon paused with his spoon half-raised, his level glance suddenly piercing. 'Dakar, that didn't answer my question.'

The Mad Prophet hunched his thick shoulders. Both hands stayed engrossed with the straightforward task of threading a strap through a buckle. 'Why can't you accept that I'm out of my depth?'

Arithon's expectant silence stretched taut.

'Very well, I can speculate. Sethvir's surely known about Fionn Areth's transformation for years.' Dakar gave over the truth in stark misery. 'Since the boy swore the Koriathain his free-will consent over a crystal focus, the Sorcerers can do nothing by way of direct intervention.'

'Go on. There's more.' Arithon let down his spoon, well aware his companion's diligent tidiness was in fact an outright avoidance.

Dakar jabbed the tang through the leather with a force he withheld from his language. 'For today's round of upsets, we're both in the dark. I warned you before. Something set an aberration through the lane's flux last night. Such an event on the cusp of the solstice has certainly led to an imbalance. Grievous enough to blind Sethvir's vision. *Or else your bid to reach Jaelot would have been stopped well before the Sanpashir focus reached resonance.'*

'That's old ground for argument, surely?' Arithon set his stew bowl aside, banal to the point of disinterest.

Yet Fionn Areth was not fooled. Set on edge by such casual firsthand reference to Fellowship resources and magecraft, he bristled, his unease lent preternatural spin by the spell-charged effects of the wine. Warm food and shelter notwithstanding, he noticed: Arithon had not shed his piercing wariness, either.

Nor was Dakar convinced by lame gestures. 'All right.' His capitulation exposed his threadbare fear. 'I sent for help, a plea made under the permissions you gave to be used in last line of defense. *No Fellowship Sorcerer has answered.'*

'Which doesn't necessarily mean they've been sidetracked by a catastrophe,' Arithon pointed out, reasonable, except for the sly, lightning glance to one side that gauged Fionn Areth's poorly leashed temper. 'The Sorcerers might just be allowing matters to run their due course by choice.'

Dakar glowered back, but had the good sense to keep quiet. He, too, noted the dangerous antipathy the herder showed toward Arithon.

'His Grace will have a plan,' the Mad Prophet said in a belated effort to soothe. 'At least, he passed an almighty thick sheaf of orders to the captain he left entrusted with care of his brigantine.'

'There was always a contingency,' Arithon agreed. Settled enough to have recovered his appetite, he scraped the savory last dregs from the bowl and washed out the residue with snowmelt. Just as seamlessly unperturbed, he requested an oiled rag. Then he cleared his crusted sword from its scabbard and began the deferred chore of cleaning. The fouled blade was rubbed down through an ongoing discussion of covert land routes to Tharidor.

As though fingers and rag were not crimsoned with stains from six brutally slaughtered guardsmen, Arithon concluded, '*Evenstar* should call in port there sometime before the thaws break. She'll give us secure passage to Alestron, where Vhandon and Talvish will see us safely back to the *Khetienn*, offshore.'

When Dakar looked mollified, Arithon grinned. 'Well, that was the promise that bought their hardheaded cooperation.' He gave a critical squint down his blade, the unearthly, dark metal of its forging like wet slate. The inlaid Paravian runes caught the sheen from the fire, sullen in mystery as molten glass drawn on the rod before shaping. Lined in the leaping, uncertain flame light, the thread silver edges gleamed straight and true. The uncanny temper showed no pit of rust, nor the wear left from commonplace sharpening. 'Vhandon got his chance to revisit home soil, and Talvish couldn't argue the blandishment. The s'Brydion duke can most likely be cozened to keep *Khetienn* provisioned in my absence.'

Arithon tossed the fouled rag in the flames, then companionably offered the oil to Fionn Areth, whose weapon was wet, and not kept preserved by ensorceling spells out of legend. 'You'll find out soon enough,' the Shadow Master confided. 'The s'Brydion clan are warmongering lions who judge a man first by his armament.'

'What makes you think I'll stand with you to Tharidor? Or that I care for the criminal bent of your byplays with Lysaer's sworn allies?' Fionn Areth drew himself up, braced to defiance by the spelled wine. 'On no count did I promise to stay in your company beyond Jaelot's outer walls.'

'Well then, oil your sword,' urged Arithon, agreeable. 'Because on that count we're going to fight.'

'Damn you both!' Dakar plowed erect, the stick he used to poke up the fire dropped in a shower of sparks. 'I may have wards up, but they won't protect from an outright indulgence of folly.'

As Fionn Areth accepted the invitation and the oil, and Arithon, indulgent, tore another strip of rag, the Mad Prophet howled ripe protest. 'Fiends plague, you goose-brained s'Ffalenn bastard!

That boy is scarcely past adolescence! To him, your fool mockery is serious!'

'I'm serious, as well.' Arithon's green eyes stayed imperious, their hard brilliance as faceted emerald. To the young man who ranged opposite, drawn steel in hand, plying the rag over and over his weapon's honed edge, Rathain's sovereign prince minced no niceties at all. 'Shall we cross swords? Very good. That should settle all differences. Let's please set the stakes very clearly beforehand.'

'No stakes,' Fionn Areth rebutted. 'I just want you dead. That's what drew me from Araethura in the first place.'

'I took that as given,' said Arithon s'Ffalenn. 'Now hear out my terms.' Against Dakar's furious, clashing reproof, his challenge continued, implacable. 'I say you're on our side, whether you like my morals or not. The Koriathain are to blame for your trial of misfortune, but their meddling left you with my face. Despite my list of disreputable habits, I won't stand aside and see you gutted as my namesake. Neither will I drag my close friends into jeopardy by saving you from the faggots again. The only men I trust with your safety are my own. To change that, you'll have to defeat me.'

For answer, Fionn Areth stripped off cloak and jacket and jerked up his chin. 'We'll take this outside?'

Arithon arose, all trim grace, to meet him. The blanket slipped off his squared shoulders, unnoticed, while the smoke-dusky steel in his hand flashed with a predator's confidence. 'Kill me, and the townsmen will heap you with praise. No doubt Dakar will be amazed to see how you go about claiming the hero's honors while wearing my royal likeness.'

'You can't do this.' A contrast of lumbering corpulence, the Mad Prophet shoved upright and attempted to thrust in between.

Arithon drove him back with a glance, then faced Fionn Areth, the furious temper of his bloodline a welded, unyielding presence 'Seize the opportunity,' he goaded. 'Take me down! Cast me bleeding in the mud. For the murdered children at Tal Quorin, seize the moment to claim retribution.'

Fixated, Fionn Areth stalked past the fire. 'Shall we start?' He tested the edge on his blade, prepared to cut down that light, silken voice, the withdrawn countenance and cat-footed poise of the spiteful creature who opposed him. Who wore frayed wool and linen with the arrogance of fine velvet, and whose contempt seemed to scald every private, inner wound and gall-broken dream with bright viciousness.

Dakar watched, stunned breathless, as the goatherd arose to take the thrown gauntlet. Like a moth's suicidal plunge to the flame, he resumed his plea for intervention. 'Arithon, damn you! Have you gone mad? The wards I've set weren't made to mask sound! Fight with steel, and the noise will draw guardsmen.' The Mad Prophet snatched at Arithon's sleeve and found himself shaken off.

'I want this,' said the Master of Shadow, unequivocal. His most scalding nod encompassed Fionn Areth, who paced back and forth with impatience. 'He holds my given word I would answer to justice. Since we're not going to stop, show the good sense to back off.'

'Good *sense*?' Dakar cried in shrill disbelief. 'You're the one who intends to cross steel in the dark, over glare ice and slippery footing! Not since you tried tienelle before Dier Kenton Vale have I seen you act this irresponsible.'

'Then you'll just have to trust that I have my sound reasons.' Arithon brushed past, committed.

As he rounded the fire, Dakar glimpsed the stained bandage showing beneath his left shirt cuff. Concern fanned his anger. 'Then get yourself killed! I don't want to watch.' While the prince and his look-alike stepped into the storm, the Mad Prophet turned to the thankless task of breaking camp and saddling the horses.

In the millyard outside, the raking east wind swept the snow to a thinned, brittle sheet. The pristine layer silenced footfalls as Fionn Areth and the man he pledged to destroy lined up to cross killing steel. A gust hissed down the cleared gash of the tailrace. Its funneled fury lashed at exposed hands and faces and moaned unchecked through the fir thickets. Darkness choked the impaired visibility down to an unreliable few yards.

If the man of experience now held second thoughts, no sign of hesitancy showed in the angle of the sword he raised up to guard point.

Nor did Fionn Areth shrink at the crux. Heedless that spelled wine had bolstered his resources, he stood braced to reclaim willful charge of the prophecy the Araethurian seeress had made at his birth. 'Begin,' he rang out. 'In the name of the Light, start the trial whenever you're ready.'

Arithon s'Ffalenn remained stilled, his held steel a motionless line scribed against felted darkness. 'Oh, no boy. You have your priorities dead wrong. For Alliance principles or for Morriel Prime, I won't play. If you would aspire to become Lysaer's puppet, you'll close on the same terms that he has. Just as at Tal Quorin and Vastmark, you'll have to be first to attack.'

'You think I lack courage?' Fionn Areth launched into an immediate lunge, gratified by the belling clang as his blade met his enemy's firm parry.

The slick footing demanded exacting balance. Arithon engaged the classic defense, his style and form letter-perfect. Despite adverse conditions, Fionn Areth flushed with self-confidence. His years of hard training rose to the occasion. He moved to heightened focus, prepared to carve out his own ebullient brilliance.

He blocked Arithon's strong but predictable counterthrust, and answered. Steel chimed. Like dancers engaged in partnered combat, the duelists circled, their swords a glancing point of contact between them. Fionn Areth took no chances. Deliberate in technique, he held down his hot nerves, gratified as he measured Arithon's offensive, and content to await the clear-cut opportunity to close with a lethal stroke.

Through the back-and-forth, testing exchange of first blows, he matched his antagonist's form. Not a large man, the Master of Shadow countered weight and force with neat footwork. The polished execution of each thrust and parry displayed the temper of unruffled experience. Fionn Areth gave that spare style his reasoned analysis. He had heard the exalted heights to which this man, as Masterbard, had carried his gift of music. Time demanded limitation: few men might support the same brilliance in two different arenas at once.

Engage and spring back, then sideslip; the locked patterns of combat stamped overlapped prints in the draw. Each parry cast the ring of sheared steel through the cloaking mantle of darkness. Between whining gusts, the high banks of the millrace funneled the din of each passage. Nor did the muffling snowfall do aught to mask tortured dissonance, as blade locked to blade, then screamed edge to flat upon parting.

Emerged from the ruin with the horses on lead reins, the Mad Prophet watched the exchange with worried eyes and five centuries of jaded outlook. He had seen Rathain's liege through stresses and hardship, and the bitter immediacy of forced slaughter. This unfolding encounter was a bald-faced farce. Each contemptuous movement was delivered in the snapping, crisp sarcasm that marked Arithon's inimical mockery. Nor was Dakar surprised when the moment arrived to pair action with needling satire.

'Very good, boy.' Arithon effected a lightning-fast disengage. Fionn Areth lurched through an embarrassing stagger as the expected resistance melted away and left him overextended. 'We've practiced each one of the basic attack patterns. Does your repertoire extend to intermediate skill? Go on. Come ahead. *Shall we see?*'

Backed off, breathing through tight concentration, the younger man threw off distraction. 'You won't bait me into losing my temper.'

'Bait you?' *Tap! Tap!* Arithon's sword struck, controlled to precision that mocked. 'Shall we pick up the pace?'

Fionn Areth met the devastating rush of the next lunge, wary, not yet thrown on the defensive. 'You haven't been fighting,' he accused through the clamor as his response hammered Arithon's brisk parry.

'Oh, I'm fighting,' assured the Prince of Rathain, his statement a ribbon of provocation. 'The ground's not ideal. What's the point, if I were to push my sweet luck? I might fall on my arse! This duel is *serious*. Where would the dignity be for the hero? No ballad could applaud you for striking a man when he's down, freezing the blood from his bollocks.'

'Save yourself!' Fionn Areth snarled back. Pride nettled him after all. This was his moment, his foreordained destiny. The criminal he battled should be left without leeway for crack comments on his killer's reputation. 'Indeed,' snapped Fionn Areth, 'let's pick up the pace and settle things that much more quickly.'

Through gusts and flurried snowfall, his rapid offensive battered his quick-tongued opponent into gratifying retreat toward the streambank.

Giving way before that driving rush, Arithon let his defending sword yield again and again, the resistance of his earlier style remade into a wall of substanceless air and fast movement. He skipped backward, melting away from hard contact. Fionn Areth thrust and stabbed in frenetic response to each of a dozen snatched openings. The attacks met no target. Back and back in scissor-fast footwork, Arithon gave precious ground. Behind loomed the locked mill wheel, armored in ice, a fixed barrier to choke off his options.

Gauging the distance in one snatched glance, Fionn Areth misjudged his footing. The streambank sloped gently downward, and the extended stride of his lunge landed him on a swept patch of glare ice. Sprawled to one knee, sword flung wide for balance, the herder cried out in consternation. The strong counterblow must inevitably dispatch him before he could salvage his victory.

Yet Arithon merely stood fast and waited, the dark sword in his grasp poised and still.

'*You're not fighting!*' Fionn Areth scrambled back upright, humiliated and stressed by the blazing pain of a pulled hamstring. 'Damn you to Sithaer's bleakest of pits! You give me no contest at all.'

'You wanted to fight,' said Prince Arithon, equivocal. 'I promised you one chance to test me.'

Dakar, by the mill, caught his breath as the scalding invective struck home.

'I never once gave my word I'd strike back to cause harm,' Rathain's prince added, spitefully reasonable. Then, as the goatherd hammered back in offense, he parried, sidestepped, and lagged a half beat to stoop and fling a snatched snow clod. 'So far, boy, you haven't shown me the least little cause to feel threatened.'

Struck square in the eye, Fionn Areth hissed a blasphemy. He charged up the streambank. Pressed to animal ferocity, he extended himself to deny his antagonist the chance to regain the high ground.

He encountered instead the breathtaking-fast reflex that trademarked the s'Ffalenn prince's offensive. 'No gain without sweat,' Arithon taunted. 'You wanted to make an end quickly?'

At each punitive step, through each phase of encounter, Fionn Areth's convictions were made laughingstock. He was being mauled, mouse to Arithon's cat, for sheer malice and flippant amusement. The insult struck home, fully and finally; Fionn Areth let fly the chokehold he kept on his temper.

The screaming cry of steel locked to steel filled the draw like the language of vengeance. Theirs was no longer a battle in form, restrained by the dictates of prudence. In snow and darkness, the paired blades carved wild arcs. Dakar, by the mill, mopped sweat from his brow and endured the unbearable, drawn tension. He eschewed use of mage-sight. His weak stomach refused the exactitude of his refined perceptions, lest chance death or injury drag him into the entangling fabric of tragedy. In the absence of light, the duel's progress became marked by the clangor of parries; of gasped breaths and the rasp as stiff boot soles scuffed over treacherous ground seeking purchase.

Nor had Arithon surrendered his arrogant stance. On a grievous, missed step, in irretrievably marred balance, Fionn Areth's guarding blade swung too wide. The Shadow Master jerked back his following lunge, and forwent lethal closure yet again.

'Fight, damn you!' gasped the enraged Araethurian.

A glib jab in verse, then a love tap with the blade's flat served him Arithon's blistering rejection. 'Kill me, or quit the field outright. You're not Lysaer, stripling. Desh-thiere's curse doesn't bind me. Your blood on my hands would be a cheap thrill, *and I don't like hunting sparrows for sport!*'

Fionn Areth bore in, finesse abandoned. Though he felt the searing burn of each breath, the spelled wine blunted fatigue. He smashed his clamoring, brutal attack into Arithon's graceful, quick parries. Weight and force would carry the contest in the end. Persistence must eventually wear down the blithe turn of speed that, time and again, bought evasion. The impact of steel striking steel numbed his ears. His eyes stung with running sweat. The featureless night and fine, veiling snowfall reduced his opponent to a light-footed shadow that went and came to the relentless demand of his swordplay.

The change in the match occurred without warning. In the space between heartbeats, the Shadow Master's light-handed style ripped away, immolated by driving brilliance.

Fionn Areth gasped. Scrambling to maintain a classic defense against an onslaught of innovative genius, he at last understood the prelude had been a bald sham all along. *This was a master swordsman he faced.* Anytime, even now, the dark blade could slice in and take him at will. He lived and moved on his enemy's sufferance, with no prayer for reprieve if he faltered. Gone were the mocking phrases as well, vanished like silk over flame. Lashed by a whistling, furious offensive, Fionn Areth heard Dakar shouting.

Then he shared the reason for his enemy's unveiled form: the thunder of oncoming horsemen. An armed company of Jaelot's guard charged the mill, drawn on by the belling notes of swordplay.

Rushed to elation, that despite his failed skill the sorcerer would receive his due punishment, Fionn Areth took heart. He pressed on in fixed purpose to sustain his defense until the mayor's pursuit overtook them.

Just as obstinate, Arithon extended his will to bind up his steel and disarm him. The slide of rushed footfalls scuffed off the thinned snow. Locked now in true combat, the Shadow Master and his double circled and feinted and thrust across an arena of pebbled, gray ice. Panted breath and marred balance tore gaps in technique. The raging clang of each closure sang ragged where one or the other combatant scrambled to regain slipped footing.

And still, two opportune openings came and went; even threatened with capture, Arithon abjured the disabling stroke.

Dakar shoved both fists against his shut teeth to stifle a screamed exhortation. One trip, one distraction could precipitate a fatality. Too wise to stress Arithon's rapt concentration, he recognized the moves that led into the wicked reverse stroke, and disarmament. The same sequence had once downed Lord Erlien of Alland, in a trial fought years past in Selkwood. Fionn Areth, still green, could only withstand the attacking diversion, without clue his defeat was self-evident.

But this night, on the winter-cold banks of the millstream, Arithon's skilled tactic went wrong. That stunning, last bind became slowed by a skid, then a misstep caught short of recovery. His dark steel jerked downward, unpartnered, while his left toe gave way underneath him.

Fionn Areth's missed thrust drove on, unhindered. Given no option to avoid a stabbed chest, Arithon guarded with the back of Alithiel's quilloned grip. Dakar shouted as steel screamed and slid through. Yet no outcry could arrest the following force of Fionn Areth's stripped hatred. The sword rang between Alithiel's wrought rings, and impaled her s'Ffalenn bearer's right hand.

Footing recaptured, Arithon sprang backward. Blood slicked the grasp of fingers gone strengthless. As he switched grip and fell back on a left-handed style, he was going to miss the next parry.

Yet Fionn Areth showed stubborn mettle and withheld the lunge that would have pressed the advantage. 'You have a main gauche,' he said, raging bitter. 'Why haven't you thought to use it?'

Arithon stood, hard-breathing and stilled, while the blare of a horn clove the night. An officer's bellow spurred the pounding hoofbeats on a converging course down the draw. 'All right,' he agreed. 'But let's not spoil the odds, my two blades to your one.' He flicked back his cloak, drew the evil, quilloned weapon from the sheath at his hip. 'You take the main gauche,' he invited Fionn Areth. 'I prefer my small dagger.'

As if no company of guardsmen closed in, a fast toss shied the weapon, grip first.

Fionn Areth fielded the catch in astonishment.

'Ath, no!' pealed Dakar, wide-awake to fresh danger even before his tuned mage-sense seared warning across his overcranked nerves.

This was the same main gauche that had struck Caolle down one wretched night seventeen years ago. Its steel still harbored the horrific stamp of past dissidence: the cruel death and bloodshed of a liegeman fallen for true loyalty, and a wounding of conscience that to this day stood unrequited. In an enemy's hand, fed by hot temper and the high stakes of extremity, that grievous, dark imprint might refire. In lingering resonance, old grief could allow such raised dissonance the opening to cloud Arithon's better judgment. Charged by s'Ffalenn guilt, a self-abnegating justice might complete that blade's accursed history.

But the fight disallowed any pause to broach reason. Fionn Areth bore in, sword leveled, the main gauche couched in a determinedly competent left hand.

Arithon met him, his sword tip unsteady in his maimed clasp. The weapon he retained for his left-handed guard was a suicide's choice, a slender poignard for eating. Its tanged blade had no cross guard, no length, and no leverage to outmatch the swung impetus of a sword stroke.

Dakar's rush to intervene was dragged short by four horses, planted by herdbound instinct. With raised heads and pricked ears, their curiosity had snagged upon Jaelot's approaching destriers. Dakar snarled words concerning maggot-infested dog meat.

While undaunted in the clearing, the Araethurian goatherd readied the stop thrust to murder the last s'Ffalenn prince. Restored to self-confidence, in strict tutored form, Fionn Areth held his unwavering focus. He tracked the raised sword that would fail to deflect him, and so missed the deft flick of Arithon's left hand, that launched the flat, little dagger.

The knife struck, sunk hilt deep in the goatherd's extended shoulder. He cried out, hand gone nerveless. His sword cast free, falling, sliced a glancing gash in the high cuff of Arithon's boot. Left the main gauche, but no space to react, Fionn Areth ended his thrust, still in balance, but unable to effect a timely recovery given the wretched footing.

Arithon stepped close. Stripped to desperate efficiency, he struck one sharp blow. Alithiel's jeweled pommel clubbed Fionn Areth's exposed nape and felled him, unconscious.

The horses gave way before Dakar's goading. They sidled ahead in snorting excitement, while down the choked gash of the draw the charging lancers bore in on the ruined mill. Swearing in language to raise fire and storm, Dakar reached Arithon's side.

'You've made a right mess!' he snapped, voice cracking as he stooped to assess the wound in the prostrate boy's shoulder. 'Ath on earth, man! Why did you have to choose now to indulge in a schoolboy's folly?'

Breathing too hard, his sword smartly sheathed, Arithon recovered the herder's dropped weapons from the snow. He secured Fionn Areth's bared blade through a pack strap, then reclaimed the cold burden of the main gauche. 'No folly,' he gasped, flat sober and strained. 'My given promise to meet him in challenge was made in dire straits, to make him leave Jaelot without argument.'

'Damn good that does, now!' Dakar retorted, then caught his breath at the stony expression locked upon Arithon's face. 'Don't mourn. He's not dying. Just stuck like a pig at the butcher's. He won't bleed to death. That's assuming our captors allow me the grace to set him in bandages before they drag us in chains to the dungeon.'

Arithon's relief was a palpable force. He caught the near gelding's bridle and flung the reins over the animal's plunging head. 'We aren't going to be taken.' He reached again, snapped the packhorse's lead out of the Mad Prophet's stunned grasp, then vaulted into the saddle. 'You're to keep that boy safe! Promise me! Use every means necessary, breach my private trust as you must. Just teach him that I'm not his enemy.'

Dakar missed his grab for the gelding's lost lead rein. Ever and always, he failed to keep pace with s'Ffalenn cunning through a crisis. 'Arithon, no!'

But the oncoming riders were near, and fast closing, leaving no time to argue poor strategy.

'Ward this place, now! I'll divert them.' Arithon closed his heels, spurred, pitched the horse underneath him from a standstill into a gallop. 'Given shadow, I ought to manage.' As the packhorse swerved and bolted in response, Arithon called over his shoulder. 'I'll find you, or meet you when *Evenstar* docks!'

Both horses and rider crashed into the wood, extended in flat-out flight.

Dakar stood his ground by the deserted mill. He extended the spells for ward and concealment by rote, while the horn call as the lancers wheeled and turned sounded all but on top of him. Nor could an untenable choice be reversed. Shouts pealed through the storm, fired by discovery as Arithon crossed a thinned patch of wood, or perhaps a woodcutter's clearing. He would have lagged purposefully for that brief sighting, to draw the danger away after him.

Dakar could not rejoice for the respite of safety. Naught remained but to tend Fionn Areth. That charge left the spellbinder heartsick with shame, for in fact, against the world's peril posed by the Mistwraith, the life left in his hands was the expendable cipher. Whether moved by compassion for feckless youth, or some sense of misguided loyalty, Dakar knew his excuse for inaction fell short. He had failed the primary obligation set upon him by command of the Fellowship Sorcerers.

Rathain's irreplaceable, last prince now rode alone. He carried no better protection than his birth gift of shadow, and a paltry few sigils of concealment stitched into the livery hack's saddlecloth. Whipped to zealous pursuit, the mayor's guard from Jaelot pounded hard on his trail, swallowed at length by the fall of fresh snow and the gloved ink of solstice night.

Retaliation

On the hour before solstice midnight, the vintner's shed where the Koriani enchantresses in Jaelot held their headquarters lay in flickering gloom, the reek of cheap tallow stewed through the tang of stirred dust. The flames in the dips hissed and dimmed to the drafts whining through ill-fitted shakes. Sifted snow let in by the cracks sheeted glittering residue in the corners. Only one of the circle of women who manned the crude outpost rejoiced for the upset to the order's covert plotting. Well accustomed to the ramshackle joinery that made the rough shelter a misery, Elaira lay curled in her cloak. She had finger-combed the worst tangles from her damp glory of bronze hair. Undone by the relief of Prince Arithon's escape, she slept through the first peaceful moment she had known since Fionn Areth's unjust incarceration.

Lirenda viewed her younger colleague's repose with distaste. Less inured to tough setbacks, too riled to accept the wormwood of defeat, the senior enchantress paced the shed in mincing steps and balked tension. Her hands shook. Agitated reflections snapped through her rings like actinic sparks in the flame light.

Her assigned circle of peers maintained stiff decorum. Anxious lest her shortfall brand them in shame, they endured her irritable commands in strict silence.

Lirenda rebuffed their probing questions. She gave no explanation for the monumental lapse in propriety that had allowed Arithon s'Ffalenn to bolt through Jaelot's cordoned walls.

'You must find him!' she exhorted her overworked seeresses,

23

still bent in trance over a water-filled vat once more joyously used to mash grapes.

Failure to secure the Shadow Master's capture framed a setback of calamitous proportions. In peril of ruin, Lirenda demanded another spell-driven sweep of the countryside. Her foul mood stayed relentless, as though by persistence she could expunge the memory of the branding kiss the s'Ffalenn prince had bestowed to unravel her upright character.

'You realize we waste time,' Senior Cadgia pointed out, her steadfast patience frayed ragged.

'Search wider,' Lirenda lashed back in hissed sibilance. 'I won't hear your excuse for the static thrown off by a mere winter storm. The s'Ffalenn bastard can't go far on foot in such weather. I'll know where he shelters, no matter how thorny the setbacks!'

Deliberate before such needling superiority, the elder seer addressed the frosted white image that rejected her skills in the scrying vat. The sigil she sketched with competent briskness did not frame the seals to generate ordered renewal. Instead, fingers snapping, she engaged the chaotic rune of dispersal.

The spelled binding that framed the construct for tracking dispelled as a sheet of blank light.

Ahead of Lirenda's explosive rebuke, Cadgia let fly her long-suffering temper. 'No! Enough of this foolery.' She pushed to her feet as though her back ached. 'I told you before. Your fugitives lie under Dakar's warded protection, no easy barrier for our skills to break through, even under auspicious conditions! My circle of seeresses are all bone weary. Your fruitless schemes have exhausted their strength, and I won't see them down sick by extending them further. Until this storm lifts, accept the harsh fact. Nothing more can be done.'

'How dare you ignore the Prime Matriarch's directive!' Smoothly groomed, her sable hair imperiously pinned since her demeaning affray by the wall, Lirenda advanced in a swish of damp silk.

Yet Cadgia folded broad arms, unintimidated. 'Don't start. Not now. You're behind on events. The old balance of power has shifted.'

'You've had news?' Paused as though doused by a pail of chill water, Lirenda drew a sharp breath. '*What are you saying?*'

'That when the wards you had set over Jaelot's walls were breached by the Shadow Master's passage, we received urgent word from the lane watch.' Sobered now, without petty smugness, Cadgia delivered the tidings withheld by the Prime's express command, until Arithon's escape was past salvage. 'Your hope is ashes. The succession is already accomplished.'

Lirenda blinked, gold lit as an old painting against sepia shadow. The impact of meaning took moments to crumble her adamant wall of denial. '*Prime* succession? Then Morriel lost her last faculties?'

Sensitive to the porcelain-frail note of vulnerability, Cadgia broke the shattering gist. 'Morriel is dead. We bow to the will of a new Prime Matriarch, who bears all the powers of her predecessor.'

Lirenda felt emptied, as though earth itself had dissolved from under her feet. 'Who?' she forced out in a glass-edged whisper. 'Which initiate has come to stand in my stead?'

Cadgia masked pity as she spelled out the cutting truth. 'Selidie, of course. She was the appointed Prime Senior.'

'But that's impossible!' Lirenda's disbelief uncoiled to rage, her heartbeat a drumroll within her. 'That lackwitted girl knew *nothing at all*. She never completed even a fraction of the requisite course of training!' Granted blank stares from the onlooking seeresses, who abandoned their posts one by one, Lirenda stemmed her shocked fuming. The disparities she mentioned were not self-evident. She alone had once held the candidate's position within the Koriani Order. Of all ranking seniors, only she had successfully mastered eight of the trials of initiation.

'Nonetheless,' Cadgia said, matter-of-factly. Informed by the avid stillness that Lirenda's defeat was too public, she snapped a prompt order to dismiss her subordinate seers. Mantles rustled as the women filed out. While the blast of the storm through the rickety doorway spilled in and tattered the tallow flames, the ranked senior resumed speaking. 'Should the outcome surprise you? Beyond every doubt, you failed your test here in Jaelot. I have not asked to know how the Master of Shadow managed to make his escape. Nor will I concern myself further. My seeresses tried, but their best efforts cannot salvage your gaffe. For the future, no one yet knows if Prime Selidie will renew the mandate for Arithon's capture. She has sent her summons. We are all to present ourselves for audience in the coastal city of Highscarp.'

Lirenda did nothing but close tortured eyes, a futile gesture. She had guarded against every setback but this, to be supplanted by an idiot initiate who could scarcely be trusted to silk wrap a quartz crystal; a mere child *she knew* had never progressed to the point of mastering even the least potent of the order's array of great focus stones. Still stunned by the shock of monumental betrayal, Lirenda fought to muster a civilized response. 'Go. Leave me. I need time to accept what has happened.'

Cadgia curtseyed. Her large-boned frame and careful tread crossed the dust-shafted glow of the dips. A barrage of raw wind and the clang of the latch saw her gone, leaving Lirenda to choke on the aftertaste of defeat.

She had no comforts, here; no soft carpets; no hot bath; no warm, perfumed mantle to ease the frayed rags of her pride. While the crawling spill of flame light cast overlapping haloes across the uneven floor, and the water abandoned in the scrying vat puckered to paned ice in the cold, Lirenda stood huddled in fine silk and grade wool, shivering through crushing disappointment.

The nadir to which she had fallen lay beyond words to express. Cast from the pinnacle of needy ambition into an abyss of total anonymity, Lirenda beheld the death of her most cherished hopes. She could live for six centuries on longevity spells, and at best earn the title of Second Senior. Always, *forever*, she must stand behind Selidie, whose interests she had blatantly spurned, and whose youth must inevitably outlast her.

'Life does have more than one facet, you know,' observed someone in gentle reproof.

Lirenda spun in recoil, to find Elaira awake and regarding her. The unranked initiate she had always despised sat erect in the shadows, the auburn hair she seldom troubled to plait spilled over her snugly clasped cloak. Between them, unspoken, hung the shared knowledge of Arithon's recent escape. Elaira had witnessed the despicable drama, had stood by and applauded as Lirenda's inexcusable lapse granted Rathain's fugitive prince the loophole he needed to exploit.

Yet Elaira's gray eyes held no trace of contempt; only sympathy clothed over the steadying framework of prosaic conversation. 'The Prime's seat has its drawbacks.'

'What would you know?' Lirenda snapped, all at once crushingly weary. Forgetful this once of marring her silk, she braced on the rim of the grape vat.

'Everything to do with having nothing left to lose.' Elaira tucked up her feet. Her small, marring frown came and went for the fact her ankles had numbed from the chill. 'One learns, in the streets, what cannot be taken. Friendship, courage, self-respect. The world's weave is set on a very broad loom. A single snapped thread doesn't have to mar the whole fabric.'

Lirenda tipped up her chin. 'Fine words for you. Easily said, since you never passed into rank.'

Elaira just looked at her, an odd little smile arguing the gravity of the moment. 'I can't have what I want, either. That can be supported. There are other joys, other goals, many avenues in which to seek human growth and fulfillment.'

A moment fled by, filled by the moan of the wind, while the tallow dips fluttered and streamed oily smoke, and the door shook on its ill-fitted hinges. Then Lirenda looked away. Had anyone else offered companionship through her hour of abject defeat, she might, perhaps, have loosened the grief fastening her shackled heart. But Elaira's straight tolerance did nothing but refire the memory of the s'Ffalenn prince's face, and a tenderness held in the depths of green eyes that, now and forever, would only be there for another.

Elaira had made herself outcast for a love well returned.

For Lirenda, Arithon's boundless compassion had touched and uprooted her sense of inner alignment. His cool removal left her exposed and unpartnered. 'You cannot help me,' she told the woman whose bedrock dignity eschewed refined clothes, and whose bone-simple courage surpassed her. 'I asked to have privacy. Do you mind?'

'No. Not at all.' Elaira arose. She tucked up her cloak hood and let herself into the night, in the earnest, but mistaken, belief she left her sister initiate to the healing virtues of solitude. For Lirenda, alone in the frigid isolation of the derelict vintner's shed, rage and shame far outstripped any wounding of sorrow. Truth nipped like a gadfly. If Arithon's kiss had unstrung her defenses and bared her most glaring weakness, the betrayal of Morriel's promise of redemption assuredly had preceded the bastard's flight out of Jaelot.

'Damn you to Sithaer's nethermost pit!' Lirenda cursed the lately departed spirit of the Prime. 'You had to have planned this! Why else should you contrive your passage of the Wheel while I was diverted by the pretense of proving my worth?'

Why indeed; the stabbing resurgence of logic hitched her breath. Lirenda chafed her numbed hands. A frown marred her ivory forehead, while her mind turned in bitter calculation. The events were too perfectly aligned for less than a calculated endgame. She saw, for all time, that she had become the duped butt of Morriel's manipulation. The old Prime had set her up, blindsided her with distractions, even played upon her flaws to ensure she would be distant and preoccupied through the crucial change in succession.

Lirenda reviewed the irregular facts, doused by the needling, certain awareness that her presence at hand would have posed a sure threat. Only a former First Senior could have known of Selidie's outright incompetence. The young woman had never been remotely capable of surviving a second-level initiation, far *less* the rigors of the ninth test required of all aspirants who had achieved the seat of Prime office.

'What have you done?' Lirenda demanded of the departed spirit of the crone who had wrangled and cheated her. *'Ath, oh Ath, what was your grand plan, that you dared not risk me as a witness?'*

The wind gusted, rattling the door on its hinges. Snow crystals scattered in driven bursts against the gapped board walls. Inside, ignited to towering fury, Lirenda paced, the dust lashed to billows at her back. Her cloak snagged a hook on the bottle rack. She snapped the hem free, uncaring as the lining tore with a scream of ruined silk. Her skirts with their elaborate layers of gold stitching flared to her agitation like the charge in an oncoming squall line.

No human balm could absolve her deep pain. The hate scalding through her lacked target or recourse. One stroke had cut off the prize she had pledged her whole life to pursue. The ignominy galled. Her initiate's vow to the Koriani Order would permit no release into freedom. All her days, she would suffer in dog-pack subservience for the sake of a kiss in an alley. Arithon's unconscionable intervention sealed her fate. Her name would now wear the same taint of disgrace that Elaira had borne for three decades.

'May you scream, chained in Sithaer, prince and Spinner of Darkness!' Lirenda swore under her breath. Even *still*, his near memory scalded her mind. She relived the branding, hot passion, unwilling, of her lips against his, pliant with ecstatic surrender. Damned for all time for a liaison of the heart, she reviled the love she could neither banish nor conquer.

She would suffer Morriel's most wretched revenge for that failing. Another ignominy piled on the first, when impatient ambition had driven her to break the original grand construct designed to snare the Master of Shadow.

She had not righted one shred of the balance. Arithon s'Ffalenn still ran free. Ever and always, the cipher that damned was her drawing fascination for his royal gift of compassion. His triumph had fashioned her insufferable downfall, and *oh, she knew*, might easily do so again.

Lirenda clamped her fists in frustration. She was condemned

to mediocrity, but scarcely helpless. If Arithon's wretched play on her heartstrings had destroyed her brilliant career, she had a lifetime left to exact her retaliation.

Two steps, three, her skirts snagging cobwebs from the staves of half-rotted wine tuns, Lirenda paused between strides. Miracle of miracles, amid avalanching setbacks, the tools for her use already lay in her hand.

Earlier that day, she had imprinted a sigil of command on the captain of Jaelot's garrison when the man's gruff competence had to be steered clear of her delicately plotted affairs. Yet the construct wrought at need on the street still remained fully active. Renew that one cipher of manipulative control, then key it to a geas of obsession, and Lirenda could draw the mayor's captain on puppet strings. Add a tangling net of spells, and Prince Arithon's flight could be hounded beyond reason and sanity.

The s'Ffalenn bastard would suffer for the snatched kiss that had condemned her to final failure. Lirenda vowed to seal his demise. How easily she could make him the beset hare in the path of a bloodletting hunt.

The idea took firm shape. A warm thrill curled through the enchantress's black rage. 'Oh yes, *your royal Grace*, you'll pay well for your ill-gotten freedom.'

Lirenda began by inscribing eight ritual circles to cloak her act in deep secrecy. The craft she invoked must not perturb the lane flux. Like the spider who stole from a rival's web, she worked outside strictures that governed her trained use of power. Rage snapped all restraints. In furtive steps, she laid down the sigils which ensured that the backwash of shed resonance would be absorbed within her own body. A few days of sick weakness would be worth the satisfaction of seeing Arithon s'Ffalenn hunted down like a forest barbarian.

Protections in place, Lirenda knelt by the vat last used for Cadgia's scrying. Welded to the cause of unvarnished spite, she caught the silver chain and cleared her spell crystal from her high collar.

'*An*,' she whispered, the Paravian rune for one, which opened the first stage of ritual. She traced the primary rune of binding over the membrane of ice on the water, then added in sequence the chained string of ciphers that claimed a man's will beneath the threshold of consciousness. A breath through her crystal infused her sketched symbols. The construct pulsed active, shedding harsh purple light that could burn to blindness the eyes of the careless. Drawing from the passionate well of her hatred, Lirenda laid the grand patterning, the weave of each strand and interstice as knotted silk over the maw of the vat. Fire was her natural element. The lit ruby lines of her sigil of summoning clashed into ice, scalding up whistling steam. Thawed water exploded to roiling froth, then flattened, subservient to her bidding.

The enchantress laid her dire work onto the blank sheen of its surface. Eighth-rank initiation lent her powers an edge her less-accomplished sisters would envy. She knew the forbidden lore; the annals of chaos, where natural force could be spun in linked seals to cause harm. Sign and countersign paired, each rune and sigil enchained to dark purpose, Lirenda raised a field of charged air over the mirroring water. Her will reigned supreme inside that masked space, and there, she pronounced a Name the ritual three times in summoning. An image resolved, showing the blunt, weathered features of Jaelot's veteran field captain.

An impatient man, sharpened with years to a deep-set, suspicious awareness, he handled his troops through exacting perception and a brusque, no-nonsense competence. A hard man to know, his trust was infallible. The barbed coils of a Koriani sigil of binding were going to require a specific opening to exploit.

Lirenda gave that hindrance no second thought. Like any born human, the man would have weakness. To an enchantress schooled in the high arts of observation, the seamed lines of the face formed a map of the captain's innermost character. His secrets could be gleaned through devouring survey, from the measure of resilience that sustained his vitality, to his most stubborn virtues, and his hidden pockets of vice. Each facet of self became hers to entrain in the tailor-made geas to drive him.

A flick of wrought power upstepped the spell's resonance. Lirenda surveyed the man's unveiled aura with its chiaroscuro imprint of personality. She unraveled each shadow, the petty dishonesties and shortfalls shot like mean yarn through the bright strands of courage and dedication. The unseen cords of bound energy let her interpret the bonds held between family and kinfolk. She sorted each diverse thread, the lesser ties drawn in friendship, or in strength, or in bullying authority, and gained private insight into the men who comprised the captain's command.

A half smile curved Lirenda's lips. Before her, the loom upon which she would weave her curse upon Arithon's destiny.

Quartz in hand, the enchantress entrained its spiraling axis as the focusing needle for her intent. She began stitching sigils and ciphers into the spell-summoned guard captain's aura. Ideas would seed thoughts, which would spin urgent plans, until the creature she claimed as her cat's-paw would rise and muster his troops, then press them to pursue the prey of her choosing.

Since Arithon's safest line of retreat would lie in the realm of blue water, she arranged sharp prerogatives to send Jaelot's troops to sweep the Eltair seacoast. North and south, they would quarter the flat ribbon of shoreline. Each smuggler's cove and wooded haven would be combed by sharp-eyed patrols. Reserves would be called up for active duty. Seasoned divisions would work hand in glove with the headhunters' league's best skilled trackers. Lirenda laid her linked seals like tight slipknots, ensuring which steps would be taken. Dawn would see a trained pack of hounds and mastiffs, backed by two companies of veteran field troops, set upon Arithon's back trail. Her victim would be driven due west, away from the bay, and into the Skyshiel uplands.

In winter, without resource, Rathain's prince would be coursed by hardened men who clung to his heels like the damned. If he escaped them, if he had the tenacity and cunning to survive the blizzards that raked the cruel wilds, he would find no rest and no respite. Lirenda twined layers of interlaced spellcraft to assure that his enemies would stay unshaken. No longer men, but instruments tuned to her scouring need for revenge, they would dog Arithon's trail past the limits of human endurance. They would press him through storm and ice and closed passes with the dauntless persistence of demons.

Against their harrying onslaught, Arithon would suffer exhaustion and frostbite and privation. Lirenda meshed her dark seals like linked chain. Black hatred ruled her. She would destroy his music. All the bright gifts of his s'Ffalenn heritage would be scoured away into mindless, animal instinct.

Until Jaelot's troops perished, expended like candles, they would not flag in the grip of the geas Lirenda spun through their commanding captain. They would dance their last steps to the tune of her passion, that Arithon s'Ffalenn would draw his last breath in desolate solitude. Let him rot without trace, unrecognized and uncomforted, on the wretched ground ruled by his ancestors.

Lirenda traced the last seal of closure over the construct imprinted in the vat. Moved by the venom distilled in her heart, she whispered her ultimatum. 'May you die alone, Arithon Teir's'Ffalenn. Let your accursed seed wither, and your line finish, heirless. May your feal clansmen fall to woe while your bones become stripped by the crows in the peaks of the Skyshiels.'

Delirium

Two hundred twenty-five leagues west of Jaelot as the crow flew, the Fellowship Sorcerer who served Athera as Althain's Warden lay stricken in his tower chamber. Stilled on his cot, tucked under the moth-frayed wool of the blankets he was always too harried to air, Sethvir lay like a wax effigy. His slack hands stayed crossed, his pixie-boned frame unmoved since the hour his colleague, Asandir, had laid him in repose before his pressured departure. Overtaken by crisis without precedent, Sethvir languished, his mind savaged by bursts of mental imagery, torn without order from the fragmented stream of his tie to the wounded earth.

While the magnetic lanes of the planet were skewed, the broad-ranging gift the departed Paravians had bestowed upon Althain's Warden remained whipped by the roiled flux. His earth-sense stayed deranged, a wildfire that raged and burned like loose rope snapped through his slackened grasp. Sethvir wrestled through sick, spinning senses to snatch the barrage of images back into cohesion.

Fleeting bursts showed him glimpses of Jaelot's armed guardsmen, riding head down against rising storm; in close haloes of candlelight, he saw Koriani seniors in purple robes and red-banded sleeves gathered in deep consultation. Lately given the news of the late Prime's succession, they would not yet know that Morriel's plot had upset the lane forces, a move aimed to cripple Fellowship resources and drive the first wedge through the compact.

Caught at the crux, while damaged wardspells came unraveled

across Mirthlvain Swamp, and packs of venomous methspawn stirred in their roiling thousands, Sethvir fretted behind his sealed eyelids. Predatory fish and venomed serpents might prey upon innocent lives; yet worse perils threatened. The most troubling could not be seen or touched, but lurked beyond the airless void that hung between distant stars.

Racked by sharp worry, Sethvir forced his innermind through a swift survey of the barrier ward raised to warn against an invasion of free wraiths from the dead planet of Marak. Left unguarded, the grand interstices of the construct glowed soft blue in quiescence. Yet the calm bought him no reassurance. Sethvir had no source for his gnawing concern. The circling fear chafed him, that the more evolved body of the Mistwraith left cut off beyond Southgate might move in and prey on the vulnerable world while Fellowship resources were engaged elsewhere.

Other fragmentary views showed winter's palette of snowfall and frost, and wild animals denned in hibernation. The events displayed no discernible hierarchy. The raging snarl of upset lane force had overstressed the tuned concentration Sethvir needed to refine broadscale vision, and sort the array of ongoing event that influenced the fate of Athera.

Since Morriel Prime's insidious machinations to mask her irregular succession, his Warden's perception had been whirled like a moth in a downdraft amid the spiraling disarray of the lane flux. Sethvir did not dissociate from the event, though he could have; too many guardian ward rings stood vulnerable to the effects of a magnetic imbalance. The most dangerous of these he held bound in check by direct, personal intervention. The drain of such effort bled his faculties without mercy, until tactile awareness of his body thinned to cobwebs. Moment to moment, he existed as a spark of naked will adrift on a scattered stream of imagery.

If a colleague now stood in support at his bedside, Sethvir held only the vague recognition that he was no longer alone. Words whirled between the smashed links of identity, the sound of struck consonants like flurried sparks whose meaning touched him in snatches.

'. . . no, he's not sleeping, but drawn inward.' The gusty, lecturing tone was Luhaine's, the discorporate colleague first to arrive when disaster broke the past evening. '*His sighted vision made him the only one of our Fellowship with the resource at hand to map the full scope of the damage on the hour the lanes went unstable.*'

Again, Luhaine qualified with a stone's endless patience. '*Yes, the lanes are retuned, now, except for the sixth, which sustains a remedial spell to guide it back to alignment. Since that stay should suffice, Sethvir's engaged elsewhere. He's bridging the seals that keep critical wards from unraveling . . .'*

As though spurred by suggestion, a flicker of sight framed the fortress at Methisle, where tumbledown walls no longer contained the migration of venomous creatures unsettled by shifting magnetics. Through snatched views of roiled waters, and the rustle of disturbed reeds, Luhaine's measured phrases resumed . . .

'His earth-sense is undamaged, but wielded without his full cognizance. What you ask is not possible. No other among us can track the threads of meaning and significance.' On a whiplash note of testy frustration, the Sorcerer responded to someone else present, *'Yes, in hard truth, the facts are discouraging. No. Please don't try. The Warden can't speak. His powers are spent past wise limits. The most accomplished adept in your Brotherhood could not grasp the scope of the problems he's stemming from minute to minute. Make no mistake! To disturb him at all could cast all of this world to disaster.'*

Someone proffered a gentler reply, phrasing drowned under another cascade of disturbingly fragmented imagery. Sethvir and the rest of the Fellowship understood, the lynchpin of the world yet rested on the life of the last Teir's'Ffalenn.

Nor was that spirit safe, but driven to harried flight cross-country, with an armed pack of guards at his heels. Sethvir's vision splintered through the branchings of parallel event. *He saw Jaelot's mayor ranting in targetless anger for the fact that the Shadow Master had slipped through his cordon. Then, in tied linkage, another view arose from north Tysan, of an ominous, damp stain that blackened the frost-silvered grasses where a stone basin had been recently emptied . . .*

A chill swept Sethvir, even through trance, for the tangle of energies left in dissonant imprint bespoke traces of unclean acts. *In the free wilds of Camris, his sight showed him spilled water, paned over with crystalline ice and the sick, phosphor haze of spent blood magic . . .*

The extreme sensitivity of Sethvir's earth-sense traced down that wisped remnant of energy.

'Lysaer,' he gasped in a tortured whisper. Unbidden vision expanded the connection. He beheld the fair coloring and chisel-cut face of the s'Ilessid prince. But the clean symmetry of Lysaer's features appeared subtly recast, hardened to the blind fervor of the Mistwraith's curse, which drove his headlong quest to destroy his half brother, Arithon.

'. . . without doubt,' Luhaine was saying in reassurance. 'The s'Ilessid is still in Camris. From there, he can scarcely pose a direct threat to his half brother on the east coast of Rathain.'

But that balance would change. Sethvir's earth-sense bore witness. *Cloaked under darkness, Lysaer s'Ilessid mounted a cream charger. His urgent, clipped speech exhorted an elite party of officers to ride eastward during the night.*

The man named Divine Prince by Tysan's misled masses planned to cross the Camris plain to the coast, then make rendezvous with a fast galley. Once over the narrow inlet to Atainia, he would rejoin the road to Instrell Bay and board a trader bound for Rathain as early as the next fortnight.

'We are called to serve!' Arms raised in impassioned appeal, the Prince of the Light addressed his veteran officers. 'I have received visions! Evil moves abroad as we speak! The Spinner of Darkness has returned to the continent. In Jaelot, innocent people have already suffered and died, victimized by his sorceries. I am charged by the Light to stand in defense. Ride with me! Lend your swords to bring down this minion of darkness, and be blessed in name for all time!'

'The Prince of the Light goes to muster his eastern allies,' Sethvir gasped, the words blurred into his caught breath, too faint to be understood. Against a blazing maelstrom of imagery foretelling blood and disaster, he cried tortured warning against the haze of raised voices around him. 'Master of Shadow . . . endangered . . .'

'Hush! Listen, the Warden speaks!' Cloth rustled nearby. The drafts sang of indistinct movement.

Sethvir wrestled the crazy quilt cataract of images that battered his mind beyond reason. 'Lysaer s'Ilessid knows . . .' He rammed his thoughts stable, framed intent like stamped crystal, and at last, transferred the gist of his desperate message.

While Sethvir sank back, Luhaine's staid presence assumed the task of explaining. 'Yes, we have news, an ill turn for the worse. The Mistwraith's curse does not rest while we're burdened. Lysaer s'Ilessid has discovered his s'Ffalenn half brother has dared to return to the continent. He'll muster for war on false grounds and religion. Yes, winter blizzards will slow him. But the pack of fanatics who have cast him as savior have resorted to unclean practice and dark augury. Word of the Shadow Master's presence will be sent on ahead. Sethvir foresees armed troops assembled in Darkling. Etarra has mustered for years against this hour. The field commander there will set seasoned troops on the march, well prepared for rough country and cold weather. They may not move fast, but they'll be relentless once they know Arithon's position. Until the s'Ffalenn prince escapes back to sea, his life is going to stay vulnerable.'

A second voice questioned; Luhaine settled into exhaustive lecturing, but Sethvir lost the thread as his cognizance faded back into the tangling resurgence of imagery . . .

In the wooded foothills of Tornir Peaks, an escaped pack of Khadrim flew on bat-leather wings, keening their shrill song of bloodlust. They circled a trade caravan bound for Karfael, stooped in attack, and shredded the drover's campsite. Armed guards died in flames. The screams of ripped horses and disemboweled men blended into the predators' whistles of quavering dissonance.

Sethvir sensed the bleak pain of the dying. Beyond sorrow, he curbed his flash-point anger that the clean-cut, new wards Asandir had just raised to hold the renegade packs in confinement had been utterly destroyed in the cascading flux of the lane imbalance. Morriel Prime had succeeded too well; the Fellowship was caught too desperately shorthanded to dispatch trained help to intervene.

A second scene flowered: *this one farther south, couched amid the ocher-brick towers of Lysaer's restored capital of Avenor. There, the subtle, secretive man appointed as High Priest of the Light sat awake and brooding by candlelight. In black jealousy, he pondered the name bandied in taprooms and wineshops across the city. In place of Lysaer, Divine Prince, the land's folk praised young Prince Kevor, whose bravery at the untried age of fourteen had quelled last night's pending riots. Fell portents had sheared across the clear sky, an ominous harbinger of evil to come at the hand of the Master of Shadow. Yet Avenor's unnerved people did not hail the Light, but instead drew their heart from the mortal courage displayed by the young heir apparent . . .*

Sethvir had no chance to pursue the implications sprung from that startling twist. The unformed premonition of danger dispersed like blown smoke as his view of the high priest's sanctum whirled away. Shifted sight showed *a herd of dun deer, startled from grazing the ice-rimmed hummocks of the Salt Fens due north of Earle. The does turned raised heads, while a foam-flecked black stud thundered by, its rider charged to spell-driven haste. Upon his broad shoulders, the most perilous threat unleashed by the old Prime's plotting . . .*

The Fellowship Sorcerer, Asandir, raced toward the grimward which confined the unquiet dreams of the ghost of the king drake,

Eckracken. The torn guard spells he spurred at a gallop to mend leached at Sethvir's consciousness, a burning imbalance that frayed through ordered thought with the tenacity of flung acid.

Until Asandir arrived at the site and effected full-scale intervention, the tenuous grip of the Warden's stretched resources became all that stemmed those pent powers of chaos. He had held the line firm since the deranged lane force had snarled in backlash. The stopgap spells maintained at long distance throbbed to Sethvir's heartbeat, draining his core reserves of vitality. Each minute, passing, bled more strength from him. His competent grasp on his earth-sense ebbed, while the unchecked spate of images plunged his cognizant vision into frenetic disorder.

The Warden of Althain could scarcely harness the flow. His consciousness rode the slipstream of impressions like a leaf unmoored in a gale. All his last strength was engrossed in the ties, faint but ever-present, that cast lines of spelled force like webs of wrought light across the flawed seals of *not one, but six additional grimwards*. Eleven others he watched, wary, alert for the first, crumbling trace of attrition. The stakes were unforgiving if his vigil should fail. Just one broached grimward would upend the world's order. The wild resonance of drake-dream would unleash tangling chaos and unravel the ties that bound matter.

Asandir could claim neither rest nor respite until he had tested and repaired the seals binding each grimward under Fellowship guardianship.

Another flaw in the rings holding Eckracken's haunt spat a leaked burst of static. Sethvir sensed the discharge as a pinprick of pain snagged through the whole cloth of awareness. Sensation flowered at once into vision, of a sere, winter bog, windswept under the clouded night sky. Something more than mere wind ruffled through the dry banks of the reedbeds. Sethvir knew dismay. His earth-sense scanned those contrary riffles and detected a small swarm of iyats, energy sprites native to Athera that fed upon elemental energies. To mage-sight, the creatures appeared as a mad gyre of sparks, winnowed and whirled by the insatiable hungers that drove them. They normally fed on the natural forces found in falling water, tides, and the changing dynamics of weather. Yet the tuned spirals of refined spellcraft offered more powerful fare, and inevitably lured them like magnets. Their voracious appetites were already piqued by the interference signature of the ward forces, wobbling on the brink of release. If the iyats reached the site of the grimward ahead of Asandir, they would cluster and sate themselves on the emissions let off by the lane-damaged ward rings. Like a yanked loop of knit, their feeding frenzy would unravel firm barriers into a draining breach.

Sethvir measured the drumming pound of the black stallion's hooves. He found himself faced with immutable fact: his colleague's intervention from the field would not come in time to deflect the inbound swarm of fiends. Despite sharp awareness of his prostrate state, and the frail balance of overtaxed faculties, the Sorcerer saw no choice. No other could act. He was Althain's Warden, and bound by his office to serve the Fellowship's founding purpose.

He slipped into deep trance. Oblivious to Luhaine's cry of alarm, Sethvir drew core power that he could ill spare from his already beleaguered life force. He delved into the spinning fields that bound light into matter and rewove their delicate axis into drawn cords of intent. His construct took form outside time and space, an alignment braided from will and desperate awareness. With exacting care, he paired force with counterforce, framing an intricate baffle to match the high-frequency energies leaking from the distressed grimward. Mask the source of emission, and fall back on hope that the fiend swarm would lose impetus and dissipate.

Sethvir readied his stayspell, a starburst of light whose resonant frequencies precisely canceled the signature of the grimward's skewed seal. He tapped into his earth-sense, interlinked with its tapestry, then aligned his remedial ciphers overtop of the flaw in the ward ring. The Paravian prime rune closed the contact. The grand veil of the mysteries parted, and the wrought energies of Sethvir's spell assumed anchored form in the world of Athera.

Even in trance, Althain's Warden sensed the moment of impact. His flesh felt bathed in a fissure of lava. That raging, bright firestorm seared through muscle and bone, as though living tissue rejected its ties to firm substance. Each nerve lit and blazed to a white incandescence that promised to burn for eternity. His mind, in stark contrast, was locked in cold, a chill that stopped thought and half smothered him.

There he drifted. Time and identity hung in suspension. By the depth of his isolation, Sethvir understood: the grimward was weakened, gone dangerously volatile. Should the chaos inside break through the seals, the intimate contact of his remedial stayspell would bridge a link to the seat of his being. First the life force that sustained him, then the fabric of his spirit would become unraveled, devoured by powers without mercy.

Through the sleeting, bright rain of static came fragmented voices, the echoes of words cast like flotsam amid the seething rush of a storm tide. Sethvir grasped no meaning; could not access the earth link. Effectively blinded, the Warden of Althain pitched himself to endure until the hour Asandir of the Fellowship could reach the site of the grimward, mend the stressed rings, and relieve him.

Catalysts

At the focus circle under Methisle fortress, near the hour of solstice midnight, the discorporate Sorcerer Kharadmon stands with Verrain under shimmering nets of wards, poised to bind the last of seven critically damaged lane currents back to stability; and while the pair labor to restore the earth's balance, the star wards against Marak, left unwatched during crisis, flare a strident, red cry of warning . . .

Far southward, in the Salt Fens above Earle, the Sorcerer Asandir dismounts his blown horse by the outer ward ring that contains the endangering dreams of Eckracken's haunt; in competent, brisk order, he takes over the burden of Sethvir's stayspell, disperses the questing storm of iyats, then sets about the delicate task of restoring the spells that contain the forces of unbinding chaos . . .

Still bedridden in trance at Althain Tower, Sethvir recovers command of the earth link; and, amid the uprush of restored awareness, he assimilates the near culmination of solstice, then an alarming new development that drives him bolt upright, as a nexus of forces converge on the lane tide about to rake south through the Skyshiels; 'Luhaine!' he gasps in urgent command. 'Your service is needed *at once* in Rathain . . . !'

II. Recoil

Luhaine sped forth from Althain Tower, a comet tail of urgency whose southeastward course streaked to intercept the breaking disaster Sethvir foresaw in the Kingdom of Rathain. Between patches of bare trees, under the high, horsetail clouds that preceded an inbound storm front, the discorporate Sorcerer encountered the tight-knit band of horsemen who accompanied Prince Lysaer's raced passage toward the shores of the north inlet. As unclothed spirit, the Sorcerer's refined perception could discern the auras of the men, and sort them by Name and character. As well as the burning, oath-driven presence of Lord Commander Sulfin Evend, Luhaine recognized the avid sunwheel seer at Lysaer's left hand as High Priest Cerebeld's handpicked acolyte. Sethvir's terse summary had not flinched from grim facts. Either one of those men in a muster for war promised trouble for Arithon s'Ffalenn.

Luhaine did not intervene. Since his Fellowship adhered to the Law of the Major Balance, he was bound to honor free will. Nor was he tempted by demeaning spite, though a word to the winds of the oncoming gale could have seen that select band of riders reduced to stripped bones, rusted steel, and pack canvas flogged into tatters. Even had Luhaine held license to act, the self-serving snarl of Alliance politics must bow to more pressing concerns.

The Sorcerer's urgent presence arrowed on, stepped outside the constraints that ruled time and space and the dense limitation of

41

flesh. Inside the hour, solstice midnight would unleash its tidal crest down the sixth lane's stress-damaged channel. Before then, he must shoulder a perilous mission and deliver two messages en route.

The first drove him southeast through the snowbound wastes of Atainia, then across the wind-thrashed, ebon waters that sheared rip currents down Instrell Bay. Beyond, rimed in ice, the bare crowns of Halwythwood's oaks sheltered the free-running wolf packs. As well hidden, and equally guarded in cunning, the camps of the feal clanborn sworn to Rathain nestled into the landscape. They had gathered in numbers, Luhaine observed. Through the cold of deep winter, they kept no set fires. Light on the land as the foraging deer, they adhered to strict practice, both to honor the wilds that were their pledged charge and to evade the relentless patrols dispersed by the towns' scalping headhunters.

Yet no trail-wise subterfuge could shadow the vision of a Sorcerer's upstepped awareness. The man Luhaine sought in his need stood out from the candleflame glow of his fellows as a firebrand, lashed into flaring, hot dissidence.

Left no time for manners, and less for fair warning, Luhaine of the Fellowship dropped into the lodge tent of the chieftain who bore title as *caithdein* of Rathain. There, Earl Jieret stood his strapping, full height, his arms folded, immersed in fierce argument with his only daughter, just turned a headstrong seventeen.

The infant girl that Asandir had Named Jeynsa had grown tall and resilient as willow. Her face was a study of cut angles, and her bearing, a young deer's for quick reflex. The mane of dark brown hair that licked down her back ran wild as curling bindweed. Fists set on her hips, her leathers belted with a carved antler buckle, and a baldric that hung three styles of knife and a sharpened longsword, she was a sight to give pause to any man living.

Not the father, a half a hand taller than she, and a red-bearded lion in all matters that touched on the welfare of clan and close family. His bellowed reply shook the poles of the lodge and hide walls too close to contain the bristling pair of them. 'Girl, you aren't going! Accept and be done.'

Flushed to high passion, young Jeynsa gave back no quarter. 'What do you fear, that I must stay behind?' Foot tapping, chin lifted, she surveyed his creased face with aventurine eyes that mirrored his own for sharp insight. 'Are you hiding a dream, that this time you won't come back?'

If that truth struck a nerve, Earl Jieret had faced death too many times to bow to intimidation. Clad in tanned wolfhide sewn skin side out, and bearing edged weapons with more ease than most men wore clothing, he could rival old oak for tenacity. 'My gift of Sight has nothing to do with the exercise of common sense. You are my *heir*, girl, and Fellowship chosen. You stay for the weal of the realm.'

'And Barach? He stays to safeguard our bloodline?' Jeynsa cut back, but unwisely.

Her father's hazel eyes assumed the glint of sheared iron. Scarred on hands and forearms by enemy steel in too many deadly skirmishes, he said, very softly, 'For shame, girl. Beware how you mock.' His baleful glance shifted, as though to acknowl-.edge someone unseen at her back. 'You never know who might be listening.'

'If it's mother,' Jeynsa ripped in retort, 'she can't claim I'm not just as good with a bow as the scout you took on your last foray.' Spun on her heel, Jeynsa found herself nose to nose with the image of a portly stranger who wore loomed gray robes, and whose presence shed the immovable chill of an iceberg.

'Welcome to my lodge tent, Luhaine,' Earl Jieret greeted the Fellowship Sorcerer. Vindication that fought not to show as a smile flashed white teeth through his beard as he delivered the traditional words of respect. 'How may we serve the land?'

Jolted to gaping embarrassment, Jeynsa swept to one knee. Her gesture affected no woman's curtsey, but the humility a future *caithdein* must show to acknowledge the given hierarchy of old law, that the authority of a Fellowship charter granted her s'Ffalenn liege his right to crown rule in Rathain.

Luhaine accepted her act as apology, his reproof tart enough to ease the sting to young pride. 'I'm not Asandir, lady. He's far more likely than me to sanction your hour of heirship.'

Behind her, Earl Jieret jammed his closed knuckles to his mouth, aware as his daughter surged erect that such tactful reprieve was misplaced.

'Then you're here as a messenger from Althain's Warden to send father to Prince Arithon's side?' Jeynsa flung back the hair that no one, not even her mother, could convince her to bind in a clan braid. 'Say I can go.' Eager, unscarred, she was not yet touched by the grievous sorrows her parents had known at an age even younger than she. 'I've never seen the Teir's'Ffalenn I've been pledged to serve for a lifetime.'

'Better pray that you don't meet his Grace for a good many years yet to come!' Portly and stern, Luhaine shook a schoolmasterish finger. 'Young lady, take heed. On the hour you swear fealty to

43

Arithon s'Ffalenn, the *caithdein*, your father, will lie past Fate's Wheel. That day his duties become yours to shoulder. The tradition has lasted for centuries, unbroken. The heir to the title must *never* take risks that might leave the high kingdom stewardless.'

'You stay, Jeynsa,' said Earl Jieret with granite finality. 'Barach holds the s'Valerient chieftaincy in my absence. Nor will you cross your older brother's good sense until you reach your majority.'

'Well he won't be twenty for at least one more year,' Jeynsa lashed back, unmollified. Then the heat that sustained her brash fight bled away. 'Just come back.' She clasped her father's broad shoulders, her embrace as ferocious as her brangling penchant for argument. When she left, straight with prideful clan dignity, she shed no tears. Nor did she glance behind, though she ached for sure knowledge that Sorcerer and *caithdein* would share their ill tidings without calling her mother in counsel.

After the door flap slapped shut on her heels, Earl Jieret folded his rangy height onto the split log he used for a camp stool. 'Ath bless that girl's spirit, Asandir chose her well. Jeynsa's the only one of my brood with the nerve to withstand s'Ffalenn temper.' Head cocked, his steady gaze wary in the flare of the pine torch that blazed in a staked iron sconce, he showed no trepidation, even now. 'Since you're here, Sorcerer, certain trouble rides the wind. Better say what you came for.'

Luhaine minced no words. 'You've already mustered your clansmen to arms. Had you not, we would face a disaster.'

Jieret yanked out the worn main gauche that, long years in the past, he had blooded to avenge his slain sisters. While his too-steady finger checked the blade's edge, and the relentless wind mingled the perfume of winter balsam with the brute tang of oiled steel, he addressed his worries with the same headlong brevity. 'I dreamed with Sight. This month's full moon will find sunwheel forces on the march across Daon Ramon Barrens. Sometime before thaws, the prey they course will be a lone rider on a flagging horse. The man I saw in the saddle was my oathsworn prince.'

'Let things not reach that pass.' As though a swift plea could stem fate, Luhaine added, 'I go east across the Skyshiels to give timely warning. Your liege will be urged to seek sanctuary at Ithamon. He will meet you in the East Tower, the black one, whose warding virtue is endurance, and whose binding is held by the Paravian's concept of true honor. There, guard your liege against Lysaer's forces. Prepare for a siege. We know as fact the tower's wards can stem the onslaught of Desh-thiere's influence. Sethvir believes the oldest defenses may mitigate the madness of the curse. If that hope fails, then his Grace's life will be yours to secure in any manner you can.'

'Just how long must my scouts stand down an army?' Earl Jieret placed the question with the same hammered courage that had been his father's before him.

The Sorcerer's image seemed cast from dyed glass, an uncanny contrast to the earthbound man, who listened with unvarnished practicality. 'The tower will hold, and the weather will stand as your ally. Lay in provisions to last many months. You will suffer a winter such as you have never seen, nor any of your grandfathers before you. Cold and ice will break the Alliance supply lines. You must hold fast until then.'

'Then your Fellowship is in crisis?' Earl Jieret waited through a clipped stillness, his hands on the knife motionless.

'More than you imagine. The Koriani Order tried to upset the compact in the course of their Prime Matriarch's succession.' Luhaine's confession resumed, burred rough by weariness as his image thinned toward dissolution. 'Their spells were contained, but Athera has suffered a magnetic imbalance without precedent. That's why we can promise the storms will be harsh, and the spring locked in ice until close to the advent of solstice. Summer will be short. Northern crops will be stunted. Can you manage?'

'As we must.' Earl Jieret arose, a threading of gray shot through the bonfire russet of his clan braid. 'Traithe once gave me the more difficult task.' Anytime, he preferred letting blood with forged steel to the unease of high mystery and magecraft. 'Tell my liege I will stand his royal guard at Ithamon. Say also, I'll stake him a flask of my wife's cherry brandy that my scouts will arrive there before him.'

'May we meet in better times,' Luhaine said, ashamed to give such a lame parting.

For this steadfast liegeman, who time and again had risked all for a prince most conspicuous for his absence, any tribute the Sorcerer might offer would carry a sting close to insult. Although Earl Jieret would swear that Prince Arithon's life held the future hope for his clans, in truth, the bonding between *caithdein* and sovereign ran deeper than dutiful service. Prince and liegeman shared a love closer than most brothers. For Arithon, that tie had thrice granted salvation from the drive of the Mistwraith's geas.

A fourth such reprieve seemed an omen to beckon the crone of ill fortune. Yet if Jieret Red-beard shared the same dread, his fears stayed unspoken as he wished the Sorcerer safe passage.

Luhaine left the s'Valerient chieftain to gather his weapons and muster his clan scouts for war. If the Sorcerer prayed for any one thing as he hurtled across the ice-mailed range of the Skyshiels, he asked that the price of this hour's intervention not end in bloodshed and tragedy.

Beyond the mountains, the snow fell wind-driven, a blinding maelstrom of cyclonic fury lent force by the skewed flow of the lane tides. Firsthand, Luhaine measured the building pressures Sethvir had sensed from Althain Tower. The final crest of the solstice flux would peak inside the half hour. The pending event cast a charge through the air, a dance of compressed light past the range of sighted perception. As spirit, Luhaine traced the stressed energy as a static-flash shimmer, strung in between the whiteout snowfall that was nature's effort to clear and bleed off the imbalance.

Sethvir had discerned the forked quandary too clearly. Relief could not come through the usual release, excess power sent to ground through stone and live trees, or the veins of ore threaded deep through the earth. Not since Arithon had used chord and sound to key his earlier transfer to Jaelot. His music had done more than channel raw lane force; its resonant ties to Paravian ritual had reopened the latitudinal channels. From the hour of first tide, at yestereve's midnight, through the day's dawntide, and noontide, and eventide at sundown, the land had already absorbed the burgeoning flux. Every stone and tree now rang to charged capacity. Each event cast the outflow farther afield, with the last crest at midnight still building.

Once the tide touched the quartz vein that laced through the Skyshiels, the damage inflicted by Morriel's meddling would snarl the natural flow into recoil. Ungrounded backlash would deflect into chaos, and cause undue stress on the wards confining the Mistwraith at Rockfell. Luhaine held the task of guarding the breach. As spirit, alone, he could not hope to mend the subsequent toll of the damage. The crux of that problem brought him at last to the coast north of Jaelot, in search of the Prince of Rathain.

Scarcely hampered by the mask of dense snowfall, Luhaine drew advantage from those quirks of nature accessible to him as a wraith. He was not bound by flesh to the side of the veil subject to linear time. From his upstepped perception, he could, as he chose, view events in simultaneity. Raised to static suspension, he could map Arithon's movements, past and present, and ahead through the multiple, hazy template of what might yet come to be. The future, as *now*, revealed itself as an array of free choices. Unlike true augury, each sequence branched exponentially. Images split into multiplicity, until the nexus points blurred into unformed event, and the arena of possibility thinned into an ephemeral mist too insubstantial to frame clear probability.

Though an hour had passed since Arithon drew Jaelot's mounted guardsmen in flight from the ruined mill, Luhaine easily picked up his back trail. Guided by higher wisdom and mage-sight, the Sorcerer followed, unerring, the forking tracks where the Master of Shadow had dispatched the packhorse in careening panic. The ruse had bought distance. His pursuit had bogged down in the farmlands, their zealous chase balked by timber fences, sheepfolds, and occupied bull pens. The relentless storm cut down visibility. Gusting wind filled in a shod horse's tracks and mounded the ditches in drifts. Men floundered and swore, forced to bang upon cottars' doors to recover their sense of direction.

Granted a hard-won few minutes' reprieve, Arithon happened into a pasture of hacks. He briefly dismounted to open the gate. Back in the saddle, he used the shrill whistle for fiend bane to set the freed herd to a gallop. The hazed animals melded their fleeing prints with those of his winded gelding. That ploy bought him a widening lead, until the loose livestock encountered a stud plowhorse, and the stallion's neighed challenge alerted the countryside.

The fist-shaking farmer who unleashed his mastiffs found his dogs in a thicket, snarling over the shreds of a discarded jacket. Whipped off, and urged into a wind that froze scent, the brutes were lackluster trackers. When they gave tongue at last, their master was deterred by a shadow-wrought form that convinced him the fugitive had stolen refuge within the stone walls of his icehouse.

While guardsmen converged on the farmer's hue and cry, and the dogs whined and circled over the ground trampled up by the destriers, Arithon nursed his winded gelding out of sight over the next hillcrest. He could do very little to offset the bloodstains splashed by the cornrick where he had stolen a short breather for his horse. Koriathain would assuredly seize on that slip and flag the site on their next scrying. Night and storm masked his form from the notice of men, a double-edged kindness, as the bitter chill flayed to the skin.

Luhaine ached as the immediate past converged with a desperate present. He came up from behind with no sound at all, while Jaelot's sought quarry yanked off the shreds of his glove with his teeth. Arithon fumbled open the saddlebag, fished inside, and located Dakar's spare cloak. Shivering in sodden doublet and shirtsleeves, he whispered a snatched phrase of relief as he pulled on the garment's stained folds. The wound inflicted by Fionn Areth's sword left his right hand useless. He had no chance to arrange makeshift bandaging. His awkward efforts to pin Dakar's garment plundered the last of his lead.

Jaelot's lancers bore in, hot set in pursuit.

Nerve strung and desperate, Arithon spun. Overtaken on a blown horse, he prepared to recut the darkness into nightmare shapes of illusion. His strength was long spent, to bear weapons or sword. Exposed without cover, his birth gift of shadow became his last hope of evasion.

The manifest image of Luhaine unfurled and utterly caught him aback. He sucked a hissed breath, defenses half-woven before recognition woke reason.

'Dharkaron avert!' Rathain's prince dropped his veiling of shadow with a wrenching, breathless start. 'Luhaine! Daelion forfend, I thought you were Koriathain, come to claim vengeance and gloat.' Through the oncoming pound of his mounted pursuit, he added, 'Are you here to help doubleblind witches or horsemen? I need to know very quickly.'

'Be at peace.' Luhaine loosed a swift binding to hide the scatter of bloodstains from scryers. While the snowfall laced through him, scribing gaps like flung static, he added, 'The Koriani plot's broken, and the guardsmen will pass and see nothing.' A small permission of air, a rearrangement of wind, and the pernicious cold bit less deeply. 'Bide here a few minutes. The packhorse is freed, and will find you. No guardsman's had time to pilfer for spoils. You'll recover your bow and provisions.'

Arithon propped his lamed hand on the gelding's damp crest, eyes closed as he absorbed the tactful implication that the Sorcerer lacked means to see him to shelter and safety. Too proud to plead, he still showed a gratitude that wounded for its sincerity. 'That gelding carries everything I need to be comfortable. Thank you from the depths of my heart.'

'Well, the officer who held him was foolishly negligent,' Luhaine excused, embarrassed that freeing a horse from a lead rein had been the best help he could offer.

Conversation suffered a necessary lag, while the company of guardsmen swept jingling down the lane past the hedgerow. None seemed the wiser for the Sorcerer's intervention. Over the ridge, the farmer's yells entangled with the yelps of cowed mastiffs, until wind swept the outcry away.

The reprieve did not buy this night any peace. Magnetic imbalance and building storm still spun their partnered refrain. The frenetic pull of raw force scoured the land like the tension of overcranked harp strings. Snow winnowed down like crosshatch in scratchboard through the weathered slats of the corncrib, while seconds fled, closing the interval left before midnight.

Constrained by time, the Sorcerer dashed the hope that lingered, unspoken. 'In sad fact, I bring you no other good news.'

Arithon straightened. Insight born of mage wisdom let him listen without questions until he received the raw gist.

Luhaine stayed blunt, since quickest was kindest. 'There has been breaking crisis, and Dakar is needed. I must ask if you're willing to go forward alone.'

'The setback won't come as a crushing surprise,' Arithon admitted, unperturbed. 'You know the Mad Prophet was sucking down gin to ward off a blind fit of prescience? To judge by the way he provisioned the packhorse, I expect he foresaw our escape to the coast would be forfeit.'

No sense mincing words over outright disaster. 'That way is closed to you,' Luhaine affirmed. He was loath to reveal any more than he must. Against the tenacity of Arithon's enemies, more concerns would only serve the potential for fatal distraction. 'I've already called your *caithdein* to service. He'll await you in the black tower at Ithamon. Your safe haven lies there, but you must first cross the mountains. A company of headhunters will hound your back, whipped on by a Koriani geas. Can you manage?'

'As I must.' All banal practicality, Arithon snugged his cloak hem between toe and stirrup iron. A hard snap wrenched a tear in the fabric. He worked the rent larger, then wrung off a strip to bind up his dripping sword cut. 'No, don't apologize,' he gasped through locked teeth as he knotted the ends in pained clumsiness. 'I already know you can't work a small healing. The flare would imprint in my aura. Since no tendons were cut, let's not give Lirenda's pack of scryers the free gift of a beacon to track me.'

He looked up, doubtless warned by Luhaine's tacit stillness. 'What's wrong? Dakar told me he'd had a vision that Morriel Prime had stepped outside of her body. He presumed she'd passed the Wheel. Has she left a death curse? Did she somehow strike out in malice and upset your stewardship of the compact?'

'Not yet,' Luhaine assured, relieved that the core of his business stayed obscured from the nuance of mage-schooled perception. 'Though you should be cautioned. The Prime Matriarch broke all law and precedent to arrange the transfer of power upon her succession. She caused a large-scale upset to Athera's magnetic lanes, a distraction made for the unprecedented purpose of claiming a young initiate in possession.'

'She's succeeded? Ath's mercy!' Arithon measured Luhaine's reserve, black hair torn loose by the wind flicking the drawn line of his cheekbone. To the Sorcerer's refined vision, he seemed a figure spun out of Falgaire glass. More than the shock of physical exhaustion set his faculties under siege. His fresh separation from Elaira told deepest, left him heartsore and emotionally naked. Too bone weary, this once, to question *just why* he might be directed to seek shelter at Ithamon, he cast his net of logic too close and fixed on the problem nearest to hand. 'Of course, if the Prime Matriarch's abandoned all principle, then Dakar's protection must guard Fionn Areth.'

Luhaine in hard wisdom chose not to expose the conclusion as fallacy. The s'Ffalenn prince faced a journey of terrible hardship to reach his fast refuge at Ithamon. Let him keep the false gift of his peace of mind and ride without fear that the wards over Rockfell were compromised.

'I seek Dakar next with a list of instructions. Meanwhile, time is short. Align your flight with the crest of the midnight lane tide. The tonic effects of its passage should carry you into the foothills.' The image of the Sorcerer's presence flicked out. Behind him, he left the unmarked fall of the snow, and last words, whirled in the wake of precipitous departure. 'The flux will do much to offset your exhaustion. Ath go with you, Teir's'Ffalenn. Know the seals I have set on your two horses will bolster their stamina through the night.'

Six leagues to the southeast, Fionn Areth regained awareness, wrapped in a net of blazing pain. Too fuddled to groan, he felt as if his skull sloshed with acid and stewed all his brains into jelly. His body seemed just as abusively compromised. Jackknifed, facedown, and seized by sick vertigo, he attempted to stir. Wrists and ankles, his limbs had been snugly tied. Through scattered senses, he assembled the jangled impression that he lay tossed like a meal sack over a moving horse.

His gasped protest drew no response.

The horse kept on walking. The disjointed view through its scissoring legs showed blank snow lapped against wind-torn darkness. Through a brief, sweaty struggle, Fionn Areth raised his head. That effort bought him a lashing sting, as gouged brush slapped across his bare face. Somewhere beyond view, two voices engaged in unhurried conversation, one speaker a polished, resonant baritone whose accents belonged to a stranger.

'The marker you seek lies fifty paces hence. Veer just a bit to your right.'

'Thank you,' the Mad Prophet said, testy as his toe snagged on a tree root and wrenched him into a stumble. The gelding flipped its nose as the lead rein jerked taut. Fionn Areth almost missed the next line, jostled to the beast's broken stride. 'I'd be pleased if you'd tell me what caused the delay, since I sent asking help several hours ago.'

A fir branch slashed back, dousing snow down the herder's nape. His yelp raised no sympathy. The unseen arrival, in flowery prose, gave answer to Dakar's question. 'Morriel Prime has stirred trouble beyond everyone's worst expectation. Her meddling hurled all seven lanes on the continent into magnetic imbalance. Sethvir's earth-sense was compromised. If you called, very likely he failed to hear. Worse, I've not come to help, but to ask your willing support on a problem of grievous import.'

'You think I don't have enough on my hands?' Dakar urged the burdened horse up a rise, snagged aback by its fellow, who had sidled wrong side around a fixed tree trunk. That difficulty resolved through a tug and ripe language, the Mad Prophet resumed in the same vein of bother. 'This yokel herder is rescued from death, and what does he do? He bites the same hand that dragged his arse clear of the fire!'

Another piled branch unburdened its load over Fionn Areth's strapped torso. His howl startled the horse underneath him to a jig that pummeled the pit of his stomach.

'Oh, do stop your moaning, boy!' Dakar bit back. His snap on the lead rein hauled the beast up short. It balked, then resumed its belabored pace through the deepening snowdrifts. 'Given the fiends plaguing trouble you've caused, you're damned lucky to find the breath of life still in your body. If your prince hadn't spoken, I would have gifted the fish with a millstone tied to your ankles.'

'I never asked to be saved by a criminal,' Fionn Areth ground out.

The horse underneath him stopped as if jerked. Chill steel kissed his skin. The rag ties that secured him abruptly parted, and someone's brutal, intolerant push spilled him head over heels in a drift.

Fionn Areth plowed upright, coughing up snowflakes. The

gift of erect posture provided no boon. A cloaked, portly figure observed without pity as his bashed head spun him dizzy with pain. The ignominy sparked thoughtless temper. Fionn Areth surged to his feet with bunched fists. His bandaged right shoulder hampered his swing. He lashed out, regardless, driven wild by injured pride and confusion. His blow whisked through air. Though the body he swung at seemed rotund as Dakar's, endowed with the same rooted obstinacy, his left-handed counterpunch *passed straight through*. He connected with *nothing* but an aching, dire cold that made his bones sting like struck glass.

'Do you know,' said the Sorcerer, Luhaine, offended, 'just how high the price of your rescue might come to be worth?'

'Should I care?' Shivering, Fionn Areth glared back. The apparition *was* a sorcerer. Nothing alive could mistake such a presence. The spirit regarding the herder in return was not patient, his stature restrained to a self-contained power that would stand down bared steel on a glance. Hackled by his own reckless fear, Fionn Areth lifted his chin. 'If I was a Koriani pawn before this, what am I now, but a plaything held captive by the fell forces of darkness?'

'You are much less than that,' Luhaine pronounced in frigid correction. 'Just how much less, I hope by Ath's mercy your family never finds out. The Crown Prince of Rathain might well die for his choice to indulge your adolescent ingratitude. If he does, this world could lose sunlight again without any chance of reprieve.'

That statement snapped Dakar's complacency. 'Not Rockfell!' He shoved off the gelding that butted his chest, ice melt and snowflakes snagged in his beard, and his anxiety suddenly piercing. 'Luhaine, don't say the wardspells holding the Mistwraith have somehow been thrown into jeopardy.'

'The very truth.' Image though he was, Luhaine shared the gravity of the old, leaning marker stone crusted with lichens at his back. 'When the lane tide crests barely minutes from now, the recoil set loose by Morriel's upset will dissolve Rockfell's outer defense rings. I must be well away before then. No one else could be spared to stand guard when the wards in the shaft go unstable.'

'No one?' Cracked to shrill disbelief, Dakar tugged his cloak off a thorn. 'Where's Asandir?' Rocked by the scope of unsaid implication, he advanced on the Sorcerer who faced him. 'Ath, your field strength is compromised. *That's why you need me?*'

'To travel to Rockfell with all speed, yes,' Luhaine admitted. His focus upon Dakar stayed too acute to spare second thought for Fionn Areth. 'You do understand.'

Dakar shook his head, bludgeoned to blunt terror. 'How I wish that I didn't.' He stamped his feet, fumbled the lead reins, and regarded the horses' trusting stance as though their placidity could soften his appalled disbelief. No such escape could negate the harsh truths. The defenses containing the Mistwraith were wrought to a strength born of frightening complexity. Their locked rings of power crossed on both sides of the veil. Such duality by nature required the skilled work of two Sorcerers: one in a stable state of free spirit, and one who still walked incarnate.

'Asandir's beyond reach, attending the emergency containment of Eckracken's haunt.' Luhaine's agitation shook the capped snow off the megalith as he delivered the shattering setback, that Sethvir's active resource became all that bound five other deranged grimwards to stability. 'To safeguard Desh-thiere's prison, we are left with a last, very desperate expedient: to stand a spellbinder as placeholder for Kharadmon to act through.' A stilled silhouette against the storm that roared through the tops of the fir trees, he measured Dakar's pained suspension. 'Given your help, the wards over Rockfell might be fully restored. The Fellowship asks for the partnered possession of your body, loaned for our use in free will.'

'Why not choose Verrain?' Dakar begged, tautly sober. He had witnessed the working when Asandir and Kharadmon had last sealed those dire defenses. Even the memory of what he had glimpsed sickened him to the bone. Those ranging vibrations were laid counter to spirit, counter to harmony, a dissonance coiled and barbed to revile every last linking facet of life. That cutting, mindless edge of bound chaos transcended the bounds of mortality; crossed the safe limits of solid existence to challenge the weave of creation.

Luhaine's stillness affirmed the stark fact the Guardian of Mirthlvain could not be spared from his posted vigil at Methisle. Why else would the Fellowship countenance the expedient of leaving Arithon s'Ffalenn unprotected?

'No one's watching the star wards, either,' Luhaine said, a bald-faced admission that finally imparted the shattering scope of the crisis. He was no willing messenger, to lay this crux upon Dakar's unprepared shoulders. Morriel's plots had brought desperate straits, and a peril beyond speech to encompass. The

Fellowship lacked enough hands to avert the appalling cascade of fresh damages. 'Khadrim fly and kill in Tysan, as well.'

'Oh, you have my cooperation,' Dakar burst out, bitter. 'That's given. I'll act before letting the Mistwraith escape. Who wouldn't, knowing the price of its capture?' The dread in him stemmed from the wider concern that his scant resources might prove inadequate.

Luhaine gave such uncertainty short shrift. 'Believe it, those of us who have tuned Rockfell's wardings all suffer the selfsame doubts.'

'That's consolation?' Dakar crowded into the warmth of the geldings, wishing their straightforward animal contact could lessen the chills that speared through him. Between the shrilling, furious gusts, and the shearing hiss of thick snowfall, he sensed the winding tension leading the advent of midnight. Lane forces flared and shimmered along the edge of peripheral vision. The Paravian marker stone cast a pallid corona that razed through the veil, and roused his awareness to mage-sight.

With solstice tide imminent, the Fellowship Sorcerer's need to depart pitched his instructions to urgency. 'Go to Rockfell by land. Take the route through the passes. I will wait there, holding guard, and Kharadmon will join us on your arrival.'

'What about Fionn Areth?' Unvarnished disgust for the herder's welfare the bone that stuck in the throat, Dakar added, 'I gave Arithon my word I'd look after him.'

Luhaine's cast image reflected no change, and yet his icy regard encompassed the Araethurian still standing stiff witness to what would seem an incomprehensible conversation. Too rushed to scold through a long-winded lecture, the Sorcerer made disposition. 'You are perfectly free to do as you please. Fare on with Dakar, and he'll keep his promise to Rathain's prince. Provided the problem at Rockfell can be solved, you can travel downriver to Ship's Port next spring, and reach your safe harbor at Alestron. Or you can set off alone, Fionn Areth. Should you take your own path, mind well: you will be disowned. Your liege's protection from that hour will become forfeit under my Fellowship's auspices. My personal seal will ensure the Teir's'Ffalenn never sees you this side of the Wheel. The sorry plight the Koriathain have set on you becomes yours alone to resolve. I'll take the onus of breaking the word of your death to Prince Arithon when the time comes.'

'That will tear out his heart!' Dakar objected.

But Luhaine had no mercy to spare for anything past bare

necessity. 'Athera can withstand his Grace of Rathain's broken heart. She will never again bear the risk of his compromised safety. Remember that, herder. Prince Arithon's life is a singular thread that can bind this world back to balance. Why else should Morriel design for his capture, or Desh-thiere wreak ill for his downfall?'

'He's a criminal,' Fionn Areth insisted, but softly, as though the ultimatum thrown to his discretion had sown a seed of uncertainty.

'He's a prince under curse by a Mistwraith to kill, or be killed in turn, by his half brother.' Luhaine set the stress on each syllable for emphasis. 'All of his acts, then and now, must be counted a desperate act of survival.'

'Half brother?' Fionn Areth glowered at the Sorcerer, confused. 'I never heard tell of any half brother.'

'Lysaer s'Ilessid shared the same mother,' Dakar explained, brutally short. He could not ignore the spiraling build of the lane forces prickling his nape. 'You know nothing at all, goatherd. Only the lies the Alliance presents to make puppets out of the ignorant.' To Luhaine, he added, 'Go. Now! You must. The young man will choose. I'll meet you at Rockfell as soon as I may by crossing the peaks of the Skyshiels.'

'Fare swiftly and well.' Luhaine's image dispersed, leaving darkness and snow, and the bite of a wind sharpened with winter misery.

The horses milled, restless. Their animal instinct sensed the tightening coil of the earth's rising magnetics. Dakar firmed his grasp on their lead reins, grateful a Sorcerer's wisdom had guided them to the sole nexus of balance within a radius of twelve leagues. The Paravian marker had been carved and set by the centaur guardians to channel the flux of the mysteries. Jaelot's townbred crofters had long since forgotten its meaningful connection. After five centuries of their unschooled husbandry, the network that once spanned the land like a star grid no longer remained intact. Patriarch trees had died or been cut, replaced by plowed fields and fenced pastures. Fixed stone was, thankfully, less volatile. Even marred in their settings, such ancient markers retained their dedicated purpose.

To Fionn Areth, who might ask probing questions, or even renew pointless argument, the Mad Prophet gave stiff advice. 'I don't care if you ever believe another damned thing that I say. Just pay heed to this: lane surge is in progress. Any element in disharmony caught in its path is going to get flung straight to chaos. If you don't like that thought, put both hands on that marker stone. Then at risk of your sanity, stay put! When everything settles, you'll wait for my word. I'll say when it's safe to let go.'

For a miracle, Fionn Areth seemed mollified. He assumed his place at the stone without protest, and even lent help with the horses. For a miracle, the two geldings lowered their high-flung heads. Calmed by his singsong Araethurian dialect, they eased off the lead reins that threatened to separate both of the Mad Prophet's shoulders.

Dakar had no chance to express his thanks. Across half the world, the sun's disk reached the zenith. Midnight arrived at Jaelot's old focus, and the last solstice lane tide peaked in a rush down the conduit of the sixth lane.

The channels through latitude wakened and sang, tuned into resonance by a masterbard's skills, engaged twenty-four hours earlier. The Paravian marker stone roused to the primal cry of the mysteries. Beneath the sweating palms of two humans, the torrent rekindled to fire the land's bounty licked through its interlaced carvings. As had happened for untold thousands of years, the quartz-ingrained granite resounded. The Mad Prophet was prepared as mortal flesh could be, alive as a boy when the Paravian rituals were still given active practice.

Yet the Araethurian goatherd at his shoulder had encountered no such experience. No word could prepare Fionn Areth as the surge struck the stone to a ringing crescendo. The note it sustained was downstepped in translation through the marriage of air and earth. The most subtle range of electromagnetic vibration became audible to mortal hearing. As the lane flux pealed to the chord of grand order, every formed object in Ath's creation became touched into shared celebration.

This was the raised harmony that tore down stone walls, unhinged oaken doors, and shot green, budding leaves from the hewn beams of the rooftrees erected by humans, unaware they had trammeled its path. For the second time since the Paravian departure, the solstice tide crested, aligned to an arrow of clear force. Resistances shattered. Obstructive disharmonies became swept away, immolated in bursts of flash-point heat, or else shaken asunder by vibration. Where the spate passed, the unbridled mysteries demanded no less than a burgeoning rebirth of life.

Spiraled into whirling dizziness, Fionn Areth felt as though his whole being would take flight through the top of his head. He swayed, no longer aware of his hands, touched to the tempering megalith. The Mad Prophet's shouted encouragement was lost. Fionn Areth saw and heard nothing else through that deluge of limitless ecstasy. The cascading tumult of sound unwound all reason and sanity. Hurled adrift, soaring beyond the earthbound ties of his moorland origins, Fionn Areth reeled as the boundaries framing his identity dissolved. Joy gripped him. Laughter burst from his throat, an irrepressible paroxysm that shook and rattled and shattered the fear in his heart.

In the trampling rush of abandoned acceptance, he recalled where he had heard fragments of the grand chord before this: first in the spelled cry of a sword, drawn to spare him from death and fire, and later, in the timbre of a masterbard's voice, singing to heal his torn knee. Then his last scrap of cognizance shredded. He drifted, unmoored amid the vast flux that imbued Ath's creation with life.

The suspension might have lasted one heartbeat, or closed the full arc of eternity. Fionn Areth could not finger the moment when time and space shrank him back into fleshly awareness. He understood that the lane surge was waning, the withdrawal of its tonic fire an ache beyond words to describe. He felt hollow, sucked clean, then grievously desolate, as under his hands the stone's keening cry diminished into dumb silence. The gift of its presence had been all that allowed the clay senses to share the ephemeral event. Wrenched by the dulled aftermath, Fionn Areth realized he might bear a loss for the rest of his days that his mind had no means to encompass.

The legacy was two-edged, in the way of all wisdom. Recast in the light of compassionate truth, the note of blind discord he could not sustain was his distrust of Arithon s'Ffalenn.

More than shaken, the scalpel cut of the wind on his face chasing an unwonted spill of tears, Fionn Areth leaned on chilled stone until his clamped knuckles bruised from the stress. 'I don't understand. *Who is he?*'

Out of the dark, and the harrying storm, through the jostling warmth of wet horses, the Mad Prophet gave level answer. 'He is who he said: Rathain's sanctioned crown prince, bound to serve by his oath. As you saw, he also bears living title as Athera's Masterbard.'

Fionn Areth swallowed. 'That doesn't explain everything.'

'I have answers.' Dakar for a mercy met nerve storms with patience. 'They're not simple, or short, or infallible, since at heart the man beats a fiend for complexity. He's as human as you, but his motives can be by lengths more difficult to fathom. If you wish me to speak, you'll have to stay long enough to hear through the telling.'

Fionn Areth would make no apology for an upbringing meant for the tending of goats. 'If I accept Prince Arithon's offer of protection, I deserve to know why he has criminal charges for black sorcery on record against him.'

'Ask what you will.' Refreshed by the euphoric riptide of lane force, Dakar grasped the reins of the broad-backed roan gelding and swung his bulk into the saddle. 'What I know, I'll share freely, as long as you're willing to ride. We need to set distance between us and Jaelot while we have bad weather to cover us.'

Fionn Areth mounted the lanky chestnut, his first question dropped as he closed his heels to the animal's steaming flanks. 'What actually happened on the banks of Tal Quorin?'

Dakar rolled his eyes. 'You Araethurians don't mince your words, do you?' Grateful at least that Arithon's last order gave him free permission to reply, he opened an ordered recital of facts that could wring tears from blue sky for sheer tragedy.

Yet breaking dawn cast silvery light through the diminishing veils of fresh snowfall before Fionn Areth had exhausted curiosity. He rode faced forward, staring at nothing, while the horse underneath him followed herd instinct and trailed Dakar's mount to a stop.

Silence descended like muffling cotton, sliced by the trills of a chickadee. The sky to the east gleamed lucent aquamarine between scudded streamers of cloud. In a crook tucked amid the steep-sided foothills, beneath evergreens mantled like ermine-cloaked matrons, the Mad Prophet dropped his reins and dismounted. His words fell diminished in the bitter air as he announced his intent to set up a warded camp. 'If you want to hunt game, be advised, we can't cook. Koriathain have a knack for noticing fires. Their skilled scryers can sense a dying deer if they're vexed enough for deep sounding.'

No reply; just a determined rustle of clothing as Fionn Areth reined his tired gelding around.

'Where in Ath's *name* do you think you're going now?' Dakar cracked in ill temper.

Echoes ranged back from the slab-sided hills and shook snow in heaps from the treetops.

'Back.' The Araethurian herder glared over his shoulder. 'Perhaps you speak the truth. If so, I made an unpardonable mistake.' Uncertain, in daylight, whether the event at the marker stone had been a dream wrought by enchantment to turn him, he said, mulish, 'I would know if your prince spared my life in good faith.'

'Well, you can't prove a damned thing by riding straight into the scalping knives of Jaelot's headhunters!'

For answer, Fionn Areth dug in his heels.

Quite able to move with astonishing speed, Dakar sprinted. In three bounding strides, he hauled horse and rider back to a stumbling halt. 'Nor will I let you blunder cross-country, asking after his Grace's true parentage. You'll only draw notice from meddlesome Koriathain, then bring his armed enemies after you. No. You'll do as your liege wished, and take Luhaine's advice, and accompany me straight on to Rockfell. That way, we'll both live to reach sanctuary. Once on board the *Khetienn*, you might earn the chance to ask certain questions in private. Though how you'll make up for the cost you've exacted for Arithon's bleeding kindness would leave even Daelion Fatemaster stymied.'

Star Wards

The discorporate Sorcerer, Kharadmon, was no spirit to wallow in setbacks. Reemerged from the labor of refounding the stressed chord of the sixth lane, he arrowed west on the winds of high altitude, his intent to resume the interrupted assistance he still owed the Guardian of Mirthlvain.

He arrived with his spiked style of humor intact. The prospect of labor in a bog infested with the vicious aberrations spawned by Methuri left his sarcasm honed to an edge most cheerfully pitched to flay skin. 'If I owned the keys to Dharkaron's vengeance,' he announced, downstepped through multiple octaves of vibration to condense as a current of feisty awareness above the agate focus at Methisle, 'I'd wish all the iyats in creation would bedevil Morriel's corpse. The mess she contrived to throw kinks in our work seems far too unnervingly calculated.'

'You may not have weathered the worst, yet.' His feathered blond hair lit jonquil by the ragged flame of a rushlight, Verrain stepped from the shadowed stone niche where he had stood vigil throughout the night. 'Sethvir's just sent you an urgent summons.'

'Well, blow him a kiss.' Kharadmon puffed on an irritated gust across the chamber. 'He's aware I'm much too busy.'

The flicked draft doused the rushlight. Verrain uttered a spell cantrip, and the rekindled flame showed a face drawn taut and unsmiling.

The spinning, chill nexus that was Kharadmon stalled with a snap that shocked frost over the dank walls of the chamber. 'Not about the fourth lane? I was aware Traithe needed relief.'

Verrain wrapped his muck-splashed brown cloak closer to his lanky frame. 'Ath's Brotherhood already dispatched an adept from Forthmark to help Traithe. She won't have to trek across Vastmark on foot. There's a mackerel boat tied up at Ithish with a fishing crew willing to sail her. A friend of the Reiyaj seeress arranged it.'

'The blind lizard still lives at one hundred and ten?' Kharadmon laughed. 'I'm amazed her brains haven't boiled, all those years she's spent staring sunward.'

'A daughter apparently inherited her talents, and chose to maintain her tradition.' The rushlight popped, shooting a shower of sparks. Verrain flicked off the lit embers, the scabs on his hands where marsh creatures had bitten silver-stitched by the gleam of old scars. 'Things are not well at Althain.' His black eyes swung back, concerned, toward the restless air where Kharadmon's presence hovered. 'Sethvir scarcely managed the strength to recall you. His word was delivered by the north wind.'

While the mire's pervasive, sulfurous drafts whirled off the discorporate Sorcerer still poised in a tight spin above him, Mirthlvain's guardian shrugged and addressed the concern left unspoken between them. 'Yes. The remedial spells you set for the barrier walls are going to decay over time. The flaw's not disastrous. We'll have until the spring spawning to mend them. The harsh winter's my ally. Only the mudpots need watching while the swamp's sheeted in ice.'

Which words were a half-truth to gloss over dilemma, as very well Kharadmon knew. 'I'm gone, then,' he cracked on a gusty departure. But under the space he had occupied, his classic last word: he left a green sprig of briar replete with a perfect, red raspberry.

Verrain completed a stalker's step forward, laughed, and ingested the jibe. His generous, wide mouth still dimpled with mirth, he turned from the focus and retrieved the worn ash staff left leaning against the arched doorway. At least, he reflected in grim practicality as he climbed the stairwell to resume his rapt watch over the creatures that slithered in Mirthlvain's bogs, Morriel's grand upset had ensured the thaws would come late.

Kharadmon soon shared the sorrow firsthand, that all was not right with Sethvir. He breezed into the northern latitude of Atainia and found every casement in Althain Tower's library latched tight against the onslaught of winter. The precedent jarred; always before this the Warden left one window ajar to welcome the caprice of the seasonal winds.

A transparent presence in the washed, citrine light dawning over the Bittern Desert, Kharadmon applied for entry through Shehane Althain's wardings. Where his colleague, Luhaine, would have sheared through dense stone, he preferred dialogue with air, and slipped like a thief through one of the arrow slits cut into the turret over the gate arch. Within the defenses, dour granite welcomed him. He was ushered through the matrix of ancient stone toward Sethvir's personal quarters. There, shocked surprise nearly felled him. All the clutter had been rearranged. Old bridles and snagged socks were nowhere in evidence. Every broken old artifact, each garnered stone oddity, even to the shells of land turtles and the cracked tea mugs filled with dropped feathers; every cache of Sethvir's curios had been reordered to unprecedented neatness.

Across an expanse of wine-colored carpet, a wizened little stranger in an adept's snowy robes sat on the carved stool by the hearth. His gnome-clever fingers were busy restitching the last torn strap of a horse harness.

As the poured chill of the discorporate spirit fanned past him, he glanced up and blinked mild eyes. 'Kharadmon, I presume?'

'Well, iyats don't stalk here without invitation,' said the Fellowship Sorcerer just arrived. His whirlwind review flicked the candleflames into a sputtering, pinwheel flutter. 'Were you the one who tamed raw chaos to order? If so, don't be surprised when Luhaine faints out of bliss. He's badgered Sethvir for his sloppy housekeeping for thousands of years and gained himself no satisfaction.'

'I had the help of two sisters,' the adept admitted, embarrassed. The dimpled delight of his grin burst and vanished as he gestured toward the wicker hampers piled beneath the carved dragon legs of the writing desk. 'We had to tidy up. No one could tell us where Althain's Warden had stashed his herbals for healing.' Tactfully gentle, the brother inclined his bald head toward the door of the adjoining chamber. 'You'll find Sethvir tucked in his bed. The sisters attend to his comfort.'

'I'm grateful,' Kharadmon said, heartfelt, then blazed an unswerving line of retreat to reach his overtaxed colleague.

The room beyond was kindly lit by a beeswax candle set on the sill by the casement. Its softened glow toned maple furnishings in honey and gold, and nicked glimmers off the battered bronze studs of the clothes chests. The air held the false freshness of a well-kept hospice, the perfume of lavender, sage, and sweetgrass underlaid by the bite of astringent teas, and a decoction of wintergreen for sore joints. Sethvir reclined on a mound of down pillows, his thin shoulders wrapped in a goathair blanket. His beard and his hair had been combed out like lamb's fleece, bleached and carded for spinning. The sisters who had gifted that painstaking care sat one on each side, mantled in the white robes of Ath's service, bound at the hems by metallic ciphers stitched into patterns of blessing and ward.

They arose on awareness of Kharadmon's entry, bowed their heads in greeting, then swept out to allow him his privacy.

'Should I have brought you spring lilies for a death bier?' the discorporate mage needled in opening.

Behind his closed lids, Sethvir was not sleeping. A corner of his mouth lifted in bleak humor, though his hands did not stir, and the eyes that flicked open were vacant as aqua glass. 'If you're going to ask flowers to bloom out of season, they prefer honesty to speculation. I'm only earth-blind to the fourth lane, now, and its branch meridians affect but one grimward.'

'Red roses, then,' Kharadmon amended, careful to comb his tonal range free of upset. Up and down the length of Sethvir's aura, his refined perceptions measured the patchworked, golden flares where the adepts had spun careful nets of fine energy to bridge areas rubbed thin by exhaustion. With the compassionate delicacy of a master surgeon, Kharadmon applied the keen edge of his humor to refire the dulled lines leached by pain. 'Some decrepit old layabouts will try anything to lure sweet-tempered ladies to dote on them.'

Sethvir wheezed a puffed breath, too weakened for full-throated laughter. 'Your incorrigible presence is welcome at Althain; however, the fact you've been called here when I'm unwell means the news is the black side of dire.'

'The star wards went active? I'd already guessed.' Kharadmon settled by the bedside, a revolving nexus of chill that nettled the candle to streamered smoke. 'What can you tell me?'

'Not much.' Sethvir twitched an irritable hand under the smothering bedclothes. 'I saw the guard glyphs flare red in first warning. We've got wraiths on the move out of Marak. How many, how far off, and what danger they pose lie beyond my stretched resource to answer.'

Kharadmon flicked into a wind devil's spin. 'The adepts haven't said?'

Sethvir managed a fractional shake of his head. 'If they know, they won't venture discussion. They can't intervene, regardless.'

Better than any, Kharadmon understood the implacable stance held by the white-robed adepts: the wraiths were no less part of Ath's grand creation. Even if their aberrant nature arose out of mankind's meddling, the Brotherhood by nature embraced no conflict. 'All the thorny sorts of problem fall to our Fellowship to contain, and just as well. Given nothing to do, you'd have Luhaine's confounded lectures bothering your ears day and night.'

Before Althain's Warden could answer that jibe, the discorporate Sorcerer whirled aloft. 'Don't fret. I'm already going.'

'There's no one else I could call on to send,' Sethvir whispered in depleted apology. Two images followed, ragged as ink stains on parchment. If their fuzzed edges were unlike the Warden's usual crisp sendings, their self-contained messages nonetheless carried the impacting force of slung rock: *of Asandir mending an unstabilized grimward, and of Luhaine, tied down, holding the torn bindings that secured Desh-thiere's prison at Rockfell.*

'Well, that's a fitting assignment for a boring, fat windbag.' Kharadmon laughed. 'Dour old rocks are the only wise beings who can bear his prolonged company without snapping.'

'He would say the same for your feckless badgering,' Sethvir said, his rejoinder a near-soundless breath.

'Then loose wraiths should suit my style of venom quite well.' Kharadmon shot straight up through the ceiling, his last words a shriek left imprinted on the whipped drafts. 'No apologies needed. Marak's damned spirits were my chosen quarrel long before Morriel Prime cast her lot amid the sharp teeth of ill fortune.'

Let out through a minuscule gap in the eaves too small for a nesting spider, Kharadmon sheared aloft. His haste burned a wake of stressed energies. A rolling boom of thunder ruptured the quiet over the Bittern's ribbed sands as the speed of his flight outstripped sound. He passed through the rarefied gases of the upper atmosphere, leaving a snag of whipped eddies in the jet stream winds of high altitude. His back trail showed a comet tail flare of split matter, excited to fugitive luminosity.

Then the icy dark of the void closed about him. Athera receded to a jewel-toned orb, whorled with the feathery tracks of the storms that spiraled above lapis oceans. Ahead, a spun webwork of silver-point light, spread the linked seals of the star ward. The sullen spark of ruby that had snagged in disharmony across Sethvir's broadscale awareness nestled amid the coils of spun power: the telltale guard spell strung across time and space, its watch rune aglow to provide advance warning of trouble arisen from Marak.

Kharadmon felt the chill, that the threat posed by this transmigration of wraiths might forerun the most dire peril of them all. He aligned his course for the beacon which signaled the cause of that distant unrest.

Once there, he held no illusion; the work he must shoulder lacked safeguards. No margin existed for slipped concentration, or the misstep of chance-met error. His peril embraced threat of widespread destruction, with Athera's frail balance and intricate life drawn into jeopardy with him. Enveloped by the hostile cold of deep vacuum, alone with the whisper-thin chime of the stars, Kharadmon drew himself inward. Seeking camouflage like the chameleon, he collapsed the fields of his being in stages and settled into a stillness as seamless as the quiet before Ath's creation.

The Sorcerer dissolved his very self. His presence bled into the fabric of space. At one with vast forces that abided, unseen, in the sensory illusion of emptiness, he stripped out his personal identity. Pared down to the quiescent spark of blank will, he poised, the mantle of unbridled wisdom and power smoothed into total passivity. Then, only then, he extended his inquiry into the shimmering red cipher Marak's wraiths had aroused.

The self-contained vortex of energies sucked him in. Ripped out of space-time, hurled past the annihilating fringes of chaos into the blank-glass calm that encompassed unborn possibility, Kharadmon resisted the suffocating urge to rebuild the templates of Name and character. Consumed, scoured blank as darkness itself, he became the transparent lens, a circle of focus aligned to observe without casting a ripple of distortion.

Kharadmon traced the cipher's root source back to Marak. Chilled to a patience that eschewed all activity, he recorded the foray of twelve questing wraiths, stirred to leave the voracious pack of their fellows. Without doubt, the disharmony of Morriel's meddling had whetted their predator's appetite. The resonance of that upset had predictably escaped the blanket of Athera's magnetic field through the distressed consciousness of the trees, a signal spun out like a carrier wave along the defunct path of a homing spell wrought at past need by the Fellowship.

Wraiths sensed even subtle shifts in vibration. Wedded to hatred, they savored the taste of human malice and conflict. Any breath of upheaval piqued their raw needs like the scent of freshly spilled blood. Tugged by their insatiable drive to consume, they left Marak and groped down the tenuous thread through deep space, beckoned on by faint promise of a world lush with teeming life. Other wraiths trailed in the wake of their brethren, this second wave pressured on by a rivalry that clawed tooth and nail for survival.

Kharadmon saw at once that the ongoing exodus would not dwindle into attrition. The wraiths in the lead sensed the horde crowding their heels. They would scarcely turn back, to be slashed and torn in a rage of psychic aggression. Their fellows would attack at the first sign of weakness, or the apparent uncertainty of retreat.

Gently, slowly, Kharadmon withdrew his awareness from the spelled cipher of warning. Freed at long last to react to his findings, he battled a wave of stark fear. No safe means existed to deter those wraiths strung down the back trail of spent spells. Once those pioneers sampled life on Athera, whether they encountered defenseless prey or the drawn lines of vigorous defense, their bloodlust would rise in earnest. Their frenzy would swiftly draw rampant thousands, excited by starveling need and the prospect of unconquered territory. Nor was Athera's hampered Fellowship equipped to handle an invasion with the requisite, seamless subtlety.

Alone in the icy void between stars, Kharadmon faced implacable fact. Resolution of the crisis at hand demanded no less than the diligent work of two Sorcerers: one to mask Marak, blindsiding the massed entities still seething at large on the wasted planet. Only then could the inbound wraiths be reeled in and contained, each spirit laboriously winnowed separate and Named, then restored to its shattered identity.

Nor would the next likely option bear weight, that a masterbard's talent might be pressed to assist. Arithon s'Ffalenn was already set in grave jeopardy. If his flight to reach sanctuary at Ithamon succeeded, if the ancient protections there let him stand down Desh-thiere's curse, too many unknown factors must still be put to the extreme test. Yet Kharadmon foresaw a dearth of alternatives. Paravian wards were already proved to restrain invading wraiths. In theory, a masterbard's trained gift of empathy could sound out and define the identity of misaligned spirits. Through Arithon's matured talents, the keyed tones of compassion could open the means to rename Marak's wraiths and restore their lost human awareness.

Yet until the s'Ffalenn prince achieved safety, and unless

Luhaine received the vital assistance to attend the damaged protections at Rockfell, Kharadmon could do nothing more than engage a stopgap measure to buy time.

At least he had thoroughly tested the method to meet today's raw necessity. That knowledge granted no comfort as the Sorcerer launched past the interlaced construct of wards that stood sentinel for Athera. His journey dispatched him on a spiraling course through the chartless deeps of the void. He must first intercept the wraiths' course, then deploy spells to delay them, blind them, deflect their track into intricate, stalled circles. Start to finish, with no slack for error, his work must be wrought with seamless finesse. His adversaries must never suspect their straight course had been deliberately tangled. Nor could the waylaid pack of wraiths be permitted the opening to sense the bold power that arranged their manipulation.

Kharadmon had suffered pursuit once before. Evasion had required help from Sethvir and Luhaine, their paired strengths backed by the mighty defenses laid into Althain Tower. All three Sorcerers had barely survived the ordeal with their faculties free of possession.

Nor were the stakes this time one whit less threatening. Kharadmon grasped the terrible crux. At all costs, his memories and his knowledge of arcane practice must be guarded. He must not fall to the wraiths' obsessed drive to absorb conquered victims in assimilation.

Trackers

The hour before dawn, the brick guardhouse in Jaelot held a stew of relentless activity. The clangor of metal as men sorted arms reechoed through shouted orders, and the tangle of raised voices, arguing. Just arrived on the threshold, his old man's quaver overwhelmed by the rush and commotion, the Lord Mayor of the city stood irate. Arms crossed on his chest, and both feet wrapped in flannel to cushion his limping gout, he howled at the browbeaten coachman who took the place of his usual, effete manservant. 'I don't care whistling blazes who you find to ask questions. Someone hereabouts *will* find me the guard captain, if I have to seal a writ for his arrest!'

Windburned and irritable from the buffeting storm, the coach-man gave way with ill grace. The first boy he hailed failed to hear his bull bellow through the thundering rumble of supply barrels three lackeys rolled across the plank flooring. In the maelstrom of arrivals and frenetic activity, nobody paused to note livery colors, or spared proper time to grace the prerogatives due to servants of ruling rank.

The irritated coachman was forced to jump clear to avoid being milled down, an ungainly leap that slapped his wet coattails against the spindle shanks of his calves.

The next boy he collared spun around in his tracks, staggered under a double load of horse harness. 'Let be, sir! I'll catch a lashing if the last of these bridles aren't cleaned. The riders have orders to leave at first light!'

'Impertinent wretch!' Run out of patience, the coachman

grabbed rein leather and twisted, noosing the boy by the throat. 'Do you see, over there? That's his lordship, the mayor. He's the one asking your service. Now find me somebody who can flag the guard captain's attention, or I promise, you won't live long enough to catch whippings, or carry anything, anywhere.'

The boy with some difficulty swiveled his head. His ruddy cheeks paled as he noticed the glittering personage, fuming red-faced on the fringes. 'My lord, forgive.' He unloaded the harness in a jangling heap and scampered, the coachman left cursing as he unlooped his feet from the mess of dropped headstalls and rein leather.

Through the subsequent wait, the mayor steamed, silent. The guardhouse reechoed to its hammer-beamed ceiling with the rushed noise of men under pressure. Their snappish talk came and went through the continuous dinning screel, as the armorer's boy sharpened blades and pole weapons on a pumice wheel spun by a half-wit.

At due length, a breathless equerry dashed up. Shouting, he offered to escort his Lordship of Jaelot into the guard captain's presence.

The mayor stamped a gout-ridden foot, then winced at the twinge of sharp pain. 'Damn your impertinence, it's himself should be coming to me.'

Since the harried equerry looked likely to bolt on the pretext of some other errand, the coachman entreated, 'My lord! I beg you, please follow.'

The mayor shot back a rankled glare, then embraced better sense and gave way. He waved the equerry onward and gimped headlong into the tumult.

The disgruntled party tacked an erratic course through mounds of provisions, overseen by anxious clerks busy checking off lists on their tally slates. They sidestepped, and just missed getting skewered by a man bearing bundles of furled banners on poles with lethally sharpened steel finials. Men polished armor, fitted spurs with new straps, or checked stitching on targets and scabbards. By the snatched words of conversation and the bellowed instructions that surfaced through racketing mayhem, the mayor learned that a cavalcade of five hundred prepared to ride northward at daybreak.

'I gave no such order!' he huffed over the press, buffeted by fellows lugging a field tent who failed to look where they were going.

The lanky coachman shortened his stride, belatedly reminded

that his lordship suffered from cruelly swollen feet. Worn to boredom by the incessant upset caused by the Master of Shadow, he expressed sympathy, then held the plank door in forbearance as the boy led into the candlelit closet that served as the bursar's office.

The stuffy space already held two muscled sergeants armed with chain mail and swords. They faced off against an overstrung baker who shook fat, pink fists in brisk argument. 'Damn your haste to the eighth fire of Sithaer! I can't supply a half company of men on a mountain foray at short notice! You want loaves, and not bricks shaped of flour, you'll wait. Bread dough takes time. Can't hurry that. You want your provender delivered in three hours, we can make good on half what you've listed, provided you settle for soda biscuits.'

'What foray!' bellowed the Mayor of Jaelot, ignored where he stood at the threshold. 'No such command was sealed by my hand! Who dares presume to send mounted men haring off into the Skyshiels?'

Hobnails grated as the sergeants spun volte-face. The baker squeaked and fell silent. Beyond them, a sparkling, deliberate movement, the guard captain arose from the trestle. With the shutters latched closed, sullen light from the candle lamp chased his mail shirt with glitters of reflection. Bypassing rank, he spoke first to the baker. 'Bring biscuit in casks. We'll hold the supply train, and send them along when they're loaded.'

The mayor flushed purple. Choking with outrage, he tugged at his pearl-stitched collar of state.

Before he could howl, the guard captain turned on him. Too large a man for the confines of walls, his no-nonsense manner seemed stripped away to a magma core of aggression. His weathered, flint face displayed chilling resolve, and his stare held a sharpened, fanatical intensity. 'You do want the Spinner of Darkness destroyed?'

The mayor shut his gaping mouth like a trout. Set aback under scrutiny that bored like an auger, he sucked in a shaken breath. 'We have patrols already in pursuit of the Master of Shadow.' Wary as the man who handled hot coals when he had expected an ice cube, he added, 'I've come to demand why my orders concerning the Koriani witches have failed to be carried out!'

'The messengers you sent only got underfoot.' No longer the stolid commander at arms who paid ruling rank proper deference, the guard captain's mood took on a terrifying edge. 'And the demons-accursed witches don't signify.' He kicked back his bench and stalked past the boards of the trestle. 'The watch had your warrant to arrest them last night. Wasted effort, of course. The Koriathain had gone, though the hour before, my sentries reported the good sisters seemed to be everywhere. No search will contain them. Whether or not they're inside town walls, no weapon I have can break through their wards of protection. Since they'll hide behind spellcraft and slink where they please, the larger concern should take precedence. We must turn every resource we have in pursuit of the Master of Shadow.'

The mayor advanced a gimping, short step. 'How dare you!' Flushed to his wattles, no small bit afraid, he let his shrill tirade gain force. 'Those witches allowed our prized quarry to go free! They have their own web of secretive politics, and I rue the hour we gave them our trust. We were without doubt betrayed by their senior. That small, bronze-haired healer broke her word as well, though she swore me a vow of life forfeit. I want her brought to justice for the bastard's escape. Reassign your men here. I won't sanction the authority to send our best company to break their fool necks in the mountains.'

The guard captain's baleful stillness held threat. 'I say again, do you want the shadow-bending felon taken down? Or are you not sworn to the Light, with Jaelot's resources pledged to support the Divine Prince's Alliance?'

'We're pledged, not possessed,' the mayor hedged, his gloved fingers clasped in dismay for the change that made his captain a volatile stranger. 'The s'Ffalenn pretender is criminal, and sorcerer, and likely by now, he's made his escape to the seacoast.'

'The coast is cut off. Bastard can't slip by us that way.' The guard captain advanced, the mailed fist on his sword tensed as though ready to kill. 'By my tracker's report, since the hour we flushed him, the criminal has turned northwest. He's alone, and in flight toward the high ground. We'll pin him against the ravines, or break his heart and spirit in the Skyshiels.' At the mayor's hissed protest, he flexed his hand, the sword inched from the sheath a glittering fraction. 'I won't argue further! In this case, the Light of true justice must prevail, no matter the cost of our sacrifice. Stand aside, old man! Whether the slinking fiend of a sorcerer leads us a chase through Baiyen Gap, I'll take our best lancers and hound him. No haunts, and no threat of old wives' tales will stop me. Nor will your shrinking, faint heart.'

Overfaced, whitely shocked, the mayor backed down.

His guard captain shoved past with obstinate force, the spark in his eyes the blazing flame of a lethal dedication. 'I'll do what I'm trained for, to my last thought and breath. The men I select will bear arms until the Master of Shadow lies dead.'

Winter 5670

Red Dawn

Four days after the solstice that brought the outbreak of dire portents, a wounded drover staggers into the gates of Karfael, within the crown territory of Tysan; brought before the posted Alliance officer, he delivers grim tidings from Westwood, of a caravan attacked and burned by a pack of free-flying Khadrim . . .

Several hundred leagues to the west, under the bruised colors of a cloudy dawn, the Prince of the Light and his picked cadre of field officers ride east, fired with resolve to achieve their sworn charge, and bring down the Spinner of Darkness . . .

While daylight brightens the peaks of the Skyshiels, and the blizzard disperses beneath the roaring winds of high altitude, a dark-haired royal fugitive on a stumbling horse sights a golden eagle perched on a branch; yet when he attempts a closer survey, he finds no trace of any winged being, but only the vague and lingering sense that uncanny eyes watch his back . . .

Red Dawn

III. Baiyen Gap

By morning, true to Luhaine's promise, the two horses Dakar had picked for hard journeying had exhausted the last of their stamina. Dismounted, as wearied himself from breasting the pocketed gullies and crossing ridges cloaked with stunted trees, Arithon paused to take stock. His night of brisk riding had carried him well into the Skyshiel uplands. Here, the forested foothills of the coast gave way to slab-sided ravines, notched with the gashed seams of past rockfalls and spindled thickets of fir. The relentless winds funneled through the high gaps, driving plumed streamers of snow. The steep vales yielded poor prospect of shelter, deserted except for the pine sparrows that chirped and fluttered in the branches, dauntlessly pecking for seeds.

Bone tired and chilled, with his boots sodden from crossing a fast-flowing stream, Arithon acknowledged his stark need for rest. He had descended from the scoured stone of the heights, driven by threat of exposure; the subtle inroads carved by exhaustion could creep up on a man unawares. Cold dulled the wits. Many a traveler perished in these wilds, lulled into the stupefied peace of fogged judgment. Every gut instinct for survival, and the seasoned experience of woods wisdom, urged Arithon to find a snug hollow and hunker down.

Yet the forbidding, flint spine of the Skyshiels balked preference. The terrain offered no secure cranny. He required dry ground, a windbreak, and a fire, and a fold in the hills where two horses could be tucked out of sight.

Arithon rested his forehead against the steaming crest of the gelding that had borne him through most of the night. 'Onward, brother,' he whispered. Wary, even here, since incautious sound might travel an untold distance, he addressed the back-turned ear of the packhorse lagging behind. 'I promise we'll stop at the first safe place. You'll both get the grain and the rubdown you've earned.'

He tugged on the lead rein, heart torn as the wearied animals resisted his effort to urge them ahead. Yet now was no time to hang back out of pity. Jaelot's patrols would be dogging his track. Should they overtake, the chase would be short. Exhaustion had claimed all his resources. His best chance to grant his horses reprieve lay in keeping the lead seized during the night.

With his bandaged hand cradled in the crook of his left elbow, Arithon firmed his tired grip on the reins. 'Bear up, little brothers.' He used voice to coax the recalcitrant horses and prayed he would not have to goad them. The buckskin released a long-suffering sigh, then yielded a molasses step forward. The packhorse complied out of ingrained habit, its flagging stride muffled amid pristine snowdrifts.

Arithon broke the ground before them on foot, prodded by bald-faced urgency. The wound in his hand languished in sore neglect. The angry, stinging pain of fresh injury had long since progressed to the pounding throb of edema. His stopgap field bandage was dirtied and blood-soaked, frayed the more ragged each time he bent to chip the balled ice packed in the horses' shod hooves. No wound fared well under such constant usage. He had lost the immediate, opportune chance to flush the clean puncture with spirits. Warned by the onset of harsh, fevered heat, and swelling that strained at the dressing, he fretted. Inflammation would have already set in. Arithon fought the blind urge to curse fate. His hands shaped his Masterbard's skill on the lyranthe. At the earliest moment, he must draw the infection with infusions of heat and strong poultices.

He cajoled the horses across the next ridge. Unfolded beyond lay the glacial scar of another rock-strewn valley. The space was too open, as evinced by the circling flight of a hawk, and the indignant chitters of a red squirrel startled to rage by his trespass. Overhead, the sky shone lucent turquoise, serrated by the snowcapped boughs of rank upon rank of tall fir trees. Game was not scarce. Arithon noted the lock-stitched tracks of hare. Later, he flushed an antlered stag. Beside the black current of another mountain freshet, he carved a parallel course with the pug marks left by a *khetienn*, the compact, northern leopard that hunted the deep wilds of Rathain.

The drifts on the bank lay piled waist deep. Forced to carve a tortured course back to the high ground, where the north gusts flayed off the snow cover, Arithon winced to the report of shod hooves clanging over bare granite. He cast a sharp glance down his back trail. Although he detected no sign of pursuit, he dared not bide in complacency. His narrow lead must be carefully hoarded, each hour snatched from the jaws of adversity his margin for rest and recovery.

Noon found him atop a raked notch in the foothills. The frigid air knifed his laboring lungs, and the geldings, heads drooping, puffed beside him. The vista ahead showed no promise of surcease. Downslope, and northwest, the land sheared away into weathered ledges of rimrock. The disused Baiyen trail that the centaurs had built hugged the scarp, a narrow ribbon cut into forbidding, black granite. The firs clung in pruned patches, culled by ice and storms until their whipped trunks jabbed the slopes like stuck needles. Sun sheened the drifts to pearlescent silk. Defined by the altitude's rarefied clarity, a deer could not move unseen by the eyes of a hunter.

Shivering against the cut of the breeze, Arithon searched to find a descent with some semblance of trustworthy footing. He could ill afford a turned ankle himself, far less risk laming the horses. Exhaustion had slowed his reflexes to poured lead. The smallest misstep might trip him. Unable to find a secure passage down, he veered westward, a moving target framed by clear sky, with the shod horses slipping and scrambling over the weather-stripped slabs of worn bedrock.

Two arduous hours later, he traversed a ravine bordered with lopsided hemlock. He picked his way, gasping with pain each time the horses jerked on the reins to snatch for a mouthful of forage. The needles were poison, and would induce colic. Yet the demand of their empty bellies overrode the precaution of instinct.

Beneath jutting rock, striped in the shadow of a spindly stand of birch, Arithon stopped. He broached the supply packs and scrounged out the nose bags, then measured a sparing ration of grain. The horses munched. He took stock, perils and assets, while the sun dipped in the sky to the west, and a quilting of shade crept across the timbered valley. Daylight waned strikingly fast in the high country. Already the wind gained an edge. Under darkness, the gusts turned unbearably bitter. Though to choose the sure route down the Baiyen trail would leave tracks for oncoming patrols, Arithon bowed to necessity. He had to find shelter before sundown. None would be found in this vista of steep cliffs and raked scree, which harbored no shred of ground cover.

A zigzagged descent down a snow-clad embankment disgorged horses and rider onto the ancient, shored causeway that traversed the Skyshiels to Daon Ramon. Here, the incessant blast of the wind had mercifully raked off the drifts. Arithon turned northwestward, the dry-packed snow squealing under his boot soles. The geldings followed, lackluster. Lathered sweat crusted their coats into whorls. Necks to hindquarters, they would have to be curried to free their thick guard hairs for warmth. Yet concern for that added burden of care must give way before the vast grandeur that opened ahead: the swept crown of rock held a mythic weight, instilled in all works wrought by Athera's blessed races.

Despite the worn state of man and beast, the old Baiyen way stood as a monument to evoke awe.

The trail, with its slope in graceful incline, had been a life artery through two prior Ages of history. Each massive, fitted block underfoot had been laid by Ilitharis Paravians. Their artistry still withstood the battering elements, bulwarked by the awareness of stone wakened to perpetual service. Too narrow to bear the wagons and teams that were the province of man, the stepped ledge had provided First Age Paravian war bands swift passage when marauding packs of Khadrim had made their lairs in the Skyshiels. By fire and sword, drake spawn and Paravian had waged battles over the causeway. At solstice and equinox, when lane tides ran highest, the fallen still danced in perpetual combat. Their haunts could be seen by those born with talent, silent and silver under the frost flood of moonlight. Here and there, tumbled fissures of slagged rock showed where the balefires of Khadrim had melted glassine scars in sheer granite.

Man's footsteps had never trodden here freely. When the Fellowship's compact had been sworn to answer humanity's plea to claim sanctuary, none walked where the old races forbade them, except by strict courtesy and permission. A man broke that law at risk of his sanity, Paravian presence being too bright to bear for those families whose heritage lay outside clan bloodlines. The needs of town trade had been negotiated by the long-past generations of clan chieftains, the old rights of way drawn by Paravian law into harmony with sky and earth. The sites which seated the mysteries stayed reserved in perpetuity.

Baiyen Gap was one of those crossings held sacrosanct, even

after the uprising broke charter law, and the town trade guilds ran roughshod over the established tradition of way rights. The Fellowship of Seven still enforced the strict ban against road building, despite fierce opposition, and round upon round of hot argument. Nor was the old law forgotten in the deepest wilds, where the imprint of the mysteries still lingered and centaur guardians had not taken kindly to trespass.

Arithon s'Ffalenn had little to fear, whatever the road's haunted status. By right of blood, his granted sanction as Rathain's crown prince set him as spokesman for mankind's chartered rights on the land. Wherever he walked, if he honored the old ways, the past centaur guardians would have granted him passage. He could but hope, as he set foot on the path of his ancestors, that in his hour of need the enemies riding with Jaelot's town guard would not be shown the same license.

The level footing allowed faster progress. No strange lights or haunts revisited to trouble him, or startle his flagging horses. The sheer wall of the cliff eased gradually into a milder grade crossing the broken scree slopes between mountains. Arithon traversed a succession of corries, each one thicketed in fir, and slotted with deer tracks where passing herds had paused to browse on the greenery.

Lowering sunlight burnished the high peaks. As eventide shadow tinged the snow-clad hills to a ruckle of lavender silk, he entered a vale and broke the paned ice over a tumbling streamlet. Upland silence wrapped him in the spiced scent of balsam, while the horses sucked down bracing water. Prompted by the punched spoor of a mountain hare, Arithon hitched their reins to a deadfall. A foray into the underbrush led him through the tumbled scar of a rockslide to a spring hidden within a dense copse of aspen. Fir saplings and dead briar cloaked the mouth of an oblate, scraped fissure that had once served Khadrim, and later, untold generations of wolves as a snug summer lair to raise young.

'Blessed Ath,' Arithon gasped on a breath of sheer gratitude.

He returned for the horses, then used the last hour before the light faded to sweep down the snow where his tracks left the Baiyen causeway. Twilight saw both geldings curried and fed, and a dead aspen limb chopped for fuel. The fire Arithon laid was economically small, hot enough to boil the water for remedies, but too scant to shed warmth for his body. He dared not risk the least presence of smoke to draw the attention of enemies. By the fragrant, low light of the embers, he shouldered the unpleasant task of attending his injured right hand.

The puncture had bled and scabbed many times, until the

dressing tied on in the field had to be soaked away. The wound underneath wept amid angry swelling, stuck with dirt and frayed threads. Sweating in discomfort, wrung from exhaustion and hunger, Arithon was trained healer enough to persist until the raw tissue was clean. As well, he realized he had been lucky. Fionn Areth's blade had grazed between the long bones. No tendons were severed, but the steel point had entered at an oblique angle and emerged above the heel of his hand. There, the leather-wrapped tang of Alithiel had stopped the thrust and prevented the blade from slicing disastrously home.

Arithon heated the tip of his dagger red-hot, and made his best effort at cautery. The remedy came much too late, he well knew. Already the scarlet streaks of infection ran past his wrist, drawn by the veins in his forearm. The sepsis he dreaded had already set in. Dakar's forethought had provisioned the saddle packs with a stock of healer's simples. Arithon sorted the tied packets of herbs, haunted by memory of happier hours, when Elaira had taught him the art of their use in her cottage at Merior by the Sea. The pain in his heart surpassed without contest every hurt to his outraged flesh. He wondered where the next Koriani assignment would send her; then ached for the unendurable fact of her absence through the left-handed clumsiness of fashioning a poultice of drawing astringents. To goldenrod and black betony, he added wild thyme and tansy, whose virtues would help clear the sickness from traumatized tissues.

The aftermath of the bandaging left him weakened and dizzy, the pain running through him in sucking waves that pressed him to the rim of unconsciousness. The call of that blissful, seductive darkness became all too powerfully inviting. There lay rest and peace, and the sublime balm of forgetfulness. In that hour of cold night, with the wind off the summits a whining hag's chorus, and body and mind half-unstrung, death almost wore the mask of a friend. The crossing promised oblivious freedom, and compassionate severance from care.

'I have to refuse you,' Arithon said aloud, his words forced through gritted, locked teeth. Bone weary, driven close to delirium from hunger and lack of sleep, nonetheless he clung to commitment. A blood oath sworn to a Fellowship Sorcerer yet bound him this side of Fate's Wheel.

That directive prodded him onto his feet, to paw through the packs for provender. He found black beans, which he set soaking in water. Dakar had also packed jerked beef, hard waybread, and a frozen rind of cheese. Although stress had undone inclination and appetite, Arithon wrapped himself in the damp folds of his cloak and pursued the chore of addressing survival and sustenance.

He did not intend to fall short of that goal. But sleep stole in and captured him unaware. He drifted the dark spiral into oblivion with the jerked beef and bread scarcely touched between slackened hands.

Arithon wakened, untold hours later. His mouth and throat felt packed with dry cotton; his head whirled, on fire with fever. The coals he had used to heat water for poultice were long spent. Drafts sent by the moaning gusts off the peaks had swirled through and scattered the deadened ashes. Nor had the frail links of reason withstood the onslaught as wound sickness claimed him. He did not know who he was; only where. Rock and snow framed the prison where his mind ranged, propelled into dreadful nightmare. The dark and the cold themselves seemed unreal, a fretful presence at war with the forge flame that raked through his shivering limbs. If he raved, none heard but two horses whose forms the shadows remade into creatures outside the familiar.

For hours, he saw faces, adrift in congealed blood: the dead cut down by his strategies at Tal Quorin, Vastmark and the Havens. Hands plucked at him, and whispers lamented the cut threads of lost lives. The haunts shed ghost tears, and multiplied into their legions of sad widows and fatherless children. Dead sailhands came, weed clad, out of the silted deeps of Minderl Bay. They sat at his side, weeping glittering brine and pointing bone fingers in eyeless remonstrance. Arithon addressed their silent condemnation, crying aloud for their pain. He left none of their questions unanswered, though his heart held no power to console them, nor had he the coin to purchase his own absolution. Unlike his half brother Lysaer, he claimed no grand principle; no moral truth; no lofty reason to account for the slaughter spun by Desh-thiere's curse. His apologies rang flat, and the tides of remorse ran in scouring agony straight through him.

His voice cracked. His throat was too parched for the gift of his music, and the right hand that Halliron had trained to high art throbbed and burned, and jetted rank pus through soaked bandages.

The darkness was ink and scalding misery, and finally, in a fevered, terror-filled hour, the night velvet of Dharkaron's cloak of judgment fell over him. Propped on one elbow, eyes wild and wide, Arithon faced down the ebony shaft of the Avenging Angel's Spear of Destiny.

'You've come for me,' he scratched in a desperate whisper. 'I cannot go freely, bound as I am by blood oath to a Fellowship Sorcerer. I swore to live until all resource fails me.' He wheezed through the rags of a laugh, edged in metallic irony. 'If you would claim your due vengeance of me, you must fight. Since I have no sword and no knife at hand, for my part, the contest will end at one parry. Cast your great spear against my bare fists, and be done with this life's useless posturing.'

But Dharkaron's image faded away with the unused spear still in hand. Arithon drifted in half-conscious solitude, while the winds whipped and screamed over the rock fists of the Skyshiels. Once, he opened crusted eyes and saw that the horses had broken their tethers. By sound distorted and magnified by illness, he realized they now wandered at large, browsing among the stripped trees. Thirst drove him to weak-kneed, staggering movement. He rekindled a fire with shaking fingers that could scarcely hold flint and striker. The flames melted fresh snow, which he drank. Runnels slopped down his stubbled chin, rinsing the soured salt of the sweat unwashed since his duel with Fionn Areth. Strength spent, Arithon collapsed in his cloak. In due time, sleep claimed him, ripping him open all over again as the ferocity of suppressed memories served up vengeful dreams.

He wakened to sunshine that cut into vision like the steel blade of a knife. Facedown in cold snow, his limbs sweat-drenched and half-paralyzed, he found Elaira's name on his cracked lips. Behind closed eyes, he could see her, bronze hair unreeled in combed waves down her back, and her eyes the silvered, clear gray of wild sage as the leaves shed their dew of spring rainfall.

'Beloved, don't weep,' he gasped. But her tears did not cease, falling and falling in empathic pain for his suffering.

Her caring lent him the will to flounder back into the cave. He searched out the ruckled cloth of his cloak, sought refuge under its sheltering warmth, and fell unconscious before he stopped shivering.

Lucidity returned, sealed in that ominous stillness that presaged severe winter weather. Arithon opened clogged eyes to awareness the fever had broken and left him weak as a baby. The storm scent in the air hackled his instincts to warning. Still alive through the gift of his body's resilience, he understood he had exhausted every last margin for error. Sapped as he was, he must strike a fire. Whatever the state of his sword-wounded hand, the re-dressing must wait for the more pressing priorities of bodily warmth and nourishment.

He was too spent to stand. Dizziness racked him if he so much as propped on one elbow. Reduced to the struggles of a stricken animal, he crawled, belly down, to the supply packs. He scrounged out dry tinder. Striker and flint were cast willy-nilly on the ground, along with an uneaten portion of bread, and a scrap of jerked beef spiked with hoarfrost. The bucket of soaked beans had frozen solid through who knew how many days. Arithon gave up accounting for time. He passed out twice in the course of laying a straggling fire, concerned as his efforts consumed the last sticks of wood he had gathered the night of his arrival.

The bucket of beans he thawed in the coals. He tossed the bread and meat in to soften and boil along with them, adding fresh snow to keep the gruel thin. Despite that precaution, his shrunken stomach nearly revolted. He closed his eyes, rested, his riled nerves wrapped in patience until the spasms of nausea subsided. Then he picked through the stock of simples, found peppermint leaves, and made a tea to settle his gut. Through the halting course of an afternoon, he managed in slow stages to feed himself. In cold-cast awareness, as warmth returned to his limbs, he knew he owed breathing life to the fact that Dakar had stocked the packhorse for every possible contingency.

Outside, the horses still wandered at large. They had grazed off the tender twigs of the aspens, and now pawed for moss on the ledges. Arithon whistled them in, gave them rations of grain, then restored their halters and tethers. He knew he should also cut and haul wood, but that daunting task lay beyond him. Any effort to stand straight left him reeling. If he fell in the open, or mired in the snow, he might not have the resilience to drag himself back to the cave.

The threatened storm still came on. Already, the clouds smoked over the passes. The dire, death stillness that presaged their arrival soon broke before an ominous north wind. That opening note would swell into a gale before the advent of nightfall. Arithon gathered the loose saddlecloths, his cloak, and every spare shred of clothing contained in the packs. There, also, Dakar's thorough care did not fail him. He found oiled-wool blankets, and a sheepskin jacket packed in cerecloth. Also a thick wax candle that could be used at need to heat water in a tin cup.

The saddle and pack frame, turned over, made a niche for his body, which he lined with blankets and cloak. Tucked into the fleece jacket, and comfortably warm, he drifted into a deep and healing sleep.

Hunger wakened him again just past sundown. Storm winds whined and howled down the ridge, and hissing drafts prowled through the cave mouth. Arithon chewed beef jerky soaked in warm water, then arose, a little more steady. He tended the neglected geldings. If he hoarded the barley and oats just for them, he could keep them alive without fodder at the risk that the rich diet might gripe them with colic. He mixed peppermint leaves with their ration for safeguard, his short, breathless laugh for the fact the Mad Prophet's excesses at least had resulted in horse-sized doses of stomach remedies.

Hunkered back in his nest of blankets, he peeled off the rotted remains of the poultice. His fingers were left in a sorry state of dead skin and purple swelling. The wound, back and palm, was an ugly, gaping hole ridged with necrosed skin and proud flesh. Arithon was not up to performing the task of scraping away the bad tissue. In the end, he made a scalding infusion of betony and let the injured hand soak. Then he dried and dressed the welted puncture in clean linen. The abused flesh could not heal in such state, he knew from war-trained experience. Sick at heart for his music, he forced his tired mind not to dwell on the problem. Tomorrow, in clear light, if his grip was reliably steady on his knife, he could attend to the necessary debridement.

The night passed to the shrill scream of the storm as it broke full force on the Baiyen. By the flickering spill Arithon lit, as he rose at short intervals to feed horses, the mouth of the cave became lost behind a smoking curtain of snowfall. The drifts spilled inside, shelved and sculpted by the backdrafts into layers of ice-crystal sediment. By morning, only diffuse gray light filtered through the small gap at the top of the cleft.

Inside, cut off from the wind, the cruel edge of the cold blunted by the heat of the geldings, Arithon rested. He recouped his strength as he could, in no haste to dig his way out. The thawed snow in the bucket had not refrozen, and with water and small rations of grain given often, the horses kept well enough. By the unsettled glow of the candle, he cursed his way through the hurtful process of cleaning the wound in his hand. The ache that remained after a new poultice and bandage was the healthier sting of fresh healing. He pinched out the wick to conserve precious wax, and sat, chewing jerky, in the dimness. Hour by hour, morning passed to afternoon. The blizzard's snarling gusts blew themselves out, and the light through the chink wore the golden cast of a tenuous, westerly sunshine.

Arithon dozed in his blankets, lazily aware he needed to dig out and gather fresh wood before sundown. The horses would soon require more water than the stub of one candle could thaw. If the ice was not a span thick and rock solid, he must try to lead them down to the spring. While he mulled over the list of chores to be milked from his limited strength, the bay packhorse flung up its head with pricked ears. The buckskin jerked face about on its tether, its high neck taut and attentive.

'Merciful Ath!' Arithon flung off the miring blankets. On his feet with a haste that reeled him dizzy, he launched himself through four unbalanced strides, then fell against the near gelding's neck, desperate to pinch shut its nostrils.

The horse jerked up its nose. Arithon muffled its muzzle scarcely in time, then grabbed the bay and noosed its jaw before it could blast out a full-throated whinny. Wrestling the animals' headshaking resistance, he crooned a masterbard's phrase that would quell agitation and quiet them. Shortly, he shared what their keen equine ears had thankfully detected before him. Up the Baiyen Gap from the low country came a soprano jingle of metal. Then the grate of shod hooves clipped a wind-scoured rock. A male voice bellowed a testy command, hailing a party of townborn companions to close a gap between stragglers.

Arithon shut his eyes in distress. The impossible had overtaken him as he slept: Jaelot's patrols had fared through the throat of the storm in pursuit of the Spinner of Darkness. Such relentless dedication bespoke a more sinister motive than the hatred of Jaelot's mayor. Luhaine's dire warning had proved true with a vengeance: Koriani sigils no doubt were at play, driving men to the chase past the bounds of practical sense.

Their approach was too close for flight or defense. Shaken to clammy sweat, Arithon had no choice but trust to hope that the banked snowdrift would obscure the rock cranny which sheltered him.

His first hope languished as the lead rider rounded the flank of the hillside. 'There's a crook in this corrie. Best check it out, if only to see if there's game we can flush for the stewpot.'

The snort of a horse ripped the glen's pristine quiet. In the cave's recessed dimness, Arithon kept his tight grip on the restive geldings. The bard's tricks that silenced them would scarcely serve, now. He had to force the animals to stay quiet as the small column of men turned off the Baiyen and wound their way up the gulch toward the spring.

'After five fruitless days scouring the back sides of snowdrifts, hell, it's high time we found something,' one man complained to his fellows.

Someone else cracked a jibe to coarse laughter.

'Praise fate we've seen nothing,' called another. 'Me, I'd far rather an empty trail, than stumbling across a pack o' queer lights and strange haunts.'

'No more loose talk!' reprimanded the captain. 'Next clown who so much as mentions a ghost gets dragged butt side down from his saddle.'

'Why not just press on?' someone else said, disheartened. 'Old storm's whisked away any sign of a track.'

'Demons don't leave tracks,' a companion groused back.

'Well, their horses do.' A purposeful creak of leather punched through the dell as someone else in authority dismounted. Arithon picked up the thin chink of a sword scabbard, then recognized the coastal twang of the mayor's skilled huntsman, apparently signed on as a tracker. An interval passed, filled in by the wind, while the masterful woodsman whisked off the new snow. He took thorough care, and finally encountered a hoof-trodden patch of bared ice. 'Uncanny creatures don't leave behind frozen piles of horse dung, now do they? And look here. That's broken ice. At least two beasts paused and drank at this spring. They stayed for some time. The twigs on those aspens are browsed back to stubs.'

The burred bass of Jaelot's guard captain held a ring of unnatural excitement. 'How long since he left?'

Through the hiss of a gust, the considered reply, 'I'd say the demon sorcerer moved on at least two days ahead of us.' The tracker slapped snow from wet gloves and stood up. 'Press hard, we could overtake him.'

The guard captain responded with a shouted command for the men by the spring to ride on. 'This trail threads the pass across Baiyen Gap. Once through to the barrens, the Spinner of Darkness could go nowhere else but the haunted towers that still stand at Ithamon.'

'We don't get to camp here?' the whiner said, hopeful, while his mount guzzled water. 'Just once, we could sleep out of the Ath-forsaken wind. Why not take advantage of shelter?'

'No camp!' snapped the captain before the suggestion started a pleading chorus. 'We've got maybe six hours left before sundown, and no cause to waste a clear day. Too soon, we'll be facing the teeth of the next storm.'

'Send a messenger back to guide the supply train,' the huntsman suggested, too pragmatic to waste opportunity. 'They can make good use of this campsite, and chop a few logs to bolster our store of firewood.'

'Carlis!' barked the captain above the descant jingle of bits, and the thuds as the horses were wheeled about in departure. 'Carry the word back, and warn the supply sergeant I don't want to run short of fodder!'

The noise of the retreating company diminished, combed through by the sigh of the wind. In the cave, wrung to shaking, Arithon released the noses of his two geldings. He sat, faint and dizzied, his first rush of relief accompanied by tearing anxiety. The rock lair had hidden him, just barely. Saved by the fact he was too ill to move, and sheltered behind an ephemeral veiling of snowdrift, he knew his bolt-hole could never withstand the close presence of an encamped supply train. He needed to move, and far worse than that: he dared not allow the precarious position of being caught between two hostile companies.

'Damn and damn, as Dakar would say.' His straits had gone from bad to untenable. Baiyen Gap offered the only fast route through the Skyshiels, and his pursuit, now ahead, blocked the way to his haven at Ithamon. Their armed numbers posed an unknown impediment. He could not fight through them, however few; not by himself with his sword hand crippled. Nor could he hope to outmatch their pace if he left the known gap and tried the rough passage through the storm-whipped peaks of the Skyshiels.

That problem a looming, insoluble impasse, he confronted the immediate danger of the supply company due to arrive in his lap before nightfall.

His promise to Luhaine seemed an act of blind folly. Wretched and shivering and weak at the knees, Arithon rested his forehead against his crossed wrists and fought back crushing disheartenment. Each step led him on to more bitter setback. The taint of fresh blood on his hand informed that his stopgap handling of the geldings had undone his fresh job of bandaging. A clench of nausea roiled his gut. He suppressed it, his will fueled by savage, deep rage. The prospect of what lay ahead of him sickened him more than the pain of his mangled hand. Nor would he weep, though regret burned bone deep for the words he had spoken before Asandir, years past on the desolate sands of Athir.

'To stay alive, to survive *by any expedient* . . .' he had whispered over the sting of the knife that bound him to irreversible blood-bonded surety.

The cost of Athera's need must be paid, yet again, in an untold number of lives. Rathain's prince railed at fate. His rage had no target. His heart could but cry, hagridden by the royal gift of compassion bred into the breath and the bone of him.

'Forgive,' he whispered to the stolid pair of geldings, who asked nothing more than grain and animal comfort. For there was no kind turning, no gentle release. Once again, s'Ffalenn cleverness must spin deadly traps, ever condemned to a curse-fated dance with the fervor of Alliance hatred.

'*Ath, oh Ath Creator, forgive!*' Racked by a despair beyond words or expression, Arithon forced himself to his feet. In aching sorrow, he turned his mind and scant resources to master the most ugly expedient.

The strategy he designed was disarmingly simple; and sickened him, body and mind through each step required in advance preparation.

The supply train labored, beasts mired to the hocks in fresh drifts, while their drovers startled and cursed. The Baiyen Gap was no place for the townborn. Even the wind through the firs seemed ill set, moaning in voices against them. The high peaks laddered with ice frowned and brooded, standing sentinel over the ledged ribbon of road laid by the great centaur masons. Words seemed an intrusion the gusts whisked away, and the clangor of shod hooves upon uncanny stone rang with ill-omened warning.

Nerve jumpy men glanced over their shoulders, or tripped upon ground that held neither loose rocks nor deadfalls.

'Close up that gap!' snapped the sergeant in charge to a laggard who held up the pack train. 'What's the matter? Think you see more of those blighted lights following you?'

The burly drover shook off his unease and plowed onward. 'No lights. I've got no barbarian blood in my family, to be cursed with visions of haunts in broad daylight.'

'Better we could see the queer thing that plagues us,' grumbled his bearded companion. He sawed at his reins, swearing as his sidling horse persistently shied at what *surely* was only a shadow crossing the trail. 'Worse, the creepy sense somebody's watching your back. Or you feel solid footing's about to give way, and the trail's an uncanny illusion.'

'No niche for a spy on these forsaken cliffs,' the sergeant said in snarling annoyance. 'If you fall, that's your fault for not keeping your eyes straight ahead. You want to sleep in the open? Then get that beast moving. I'll strip hide from the man who keeps us from reaching that sheltered campsite by sundown.'

The supply train reached the dell with the aspen grove under the lucent gleam of twilight. They settled in, boisterous with noise as horses and mules were stripped of packs and harness, and trees were cut to lay campfires. Jerked meat and rice were set boiling in pots, while the cold flecks of stars scattered the upland darkness. Night deepened, filled by the dirge of the winds that quashed ribald conversation. The men huddled closer to their flickering fires. On the ridges above, the wisped whirl of the snow devils seemed stirred by the restive ghosts. The skeletal tap of bare aspens framed a language too wild for mankind's tamed comprehension.

Worse, perhaps, the deep silence between gusts, vast enough to drown thought and swallow the petty, thin sounds of their presence. In this place, the bygone Ages of time lay on the land like poured crystal. The armed men and drovers clung to their fellows, uneasily aware the trail through the Baiyen did not welcome intrusion.

That moment, a deep, groaning note issued from the side of the mountain. The camp sentries spun, hands clapped to their weapons, while the men by the cookfires leaped to their feet.

For a tense, unsettled moment, the darkness seemed to intensify. Then the snowbank lapped over the rocks exploded. Flying clods and debris disgorged the forms of two galloping centaurs. Massive, immense, and bent upon murder for the trespass of heedless humanity, they drove headlong into the picket lines. Panicked horses screamed and snapped tethers. Their milling stampede swept behind startled masters, hazed into panicked retreat. In darkness, in fear, shouting in terror, men and beasts fled the corrie. The smooth trail beyond was a narrow ribbon of ice. Sliding, falling, unable to stop as their horses mowed haplessly over them, Jaelot's invaders plunged screaming and clawing over the brink of the cliff face and dashed on the fangs of the rock slopes below . . .

Braced on the rumpled snow at the rim, Arithon s'Ffalenn dispersed his wrought weaving of shadows. Trembling, he gathered his revolted nerves. His body the rebellious servant of will, he stood up. He soothed his overwrought geldings until their flaring snorts finally quieted.

The frigid night had forfeited peace, the pristine stillness of the Baiyen defiled as mangled men and smashed horses shuddered and cried. Pulped flesh and white snow commingled in bloodstains, snagged on fouled rock, and the stilled hulks of the murdered dead, fallen.

Arithon tied up the horses. Gut sick, unsure of his balance, he unslung a slim bundle from his shoulder. Then he struggled and strung the heavy, horn recurve Dakar had selected to hunt deer. The arrows were a hunter's, broad-bladed and sharp. They would kill by internal bleeding.

Unaware that he pleaded forgiveness in Paravian, his words a scratched utterance without grace, Arithon knelt in the trampled snow. Twice, overcome, he folded and rendered his gorge. Nor was his eyesight trustworthy, blurred as it was by the bitter well of his tears.

The pull of the bow pained his infected hand. Determined, he nocked the first arrow. Wood rattled against horn, tempo to his trembling, and the snatched sob of unsteady breath. Yet the will behind each move was pure iron. Integrity required that he must not falter, whatever his bodily failings. The fabric of self, curse torn and sullied, demanded no less than to finish in mercy the cruel act imposed by oathsworn survival.

At the end, as he hauled the bow into full draw, his rage at the binding proscribing his life became the fuel that set his hand steady. The ache as his mangled right hand took the strain and the sudden spurt of fresh bleeding became a pittance beside the wounding affliction of conscience.

'*Myself, the sole enemy,*' he gasped in Paravian. 'Dharkaron Avenger forgive.'

He released. On the smeared rocks below, one less voice cried out. Arithon dashed back the burn of salt tears. Again, he nocked feathered broadhead to string. Arrow by arrow, he dispatched the groaning wounded downslope. Each careful, clean shot snuffed another cry of suffering, but woke in him recall of an unquiet past, and a summer dell known as the Havens. He quashed the revolt of his clamoring mind, but could not repress the shattering screams of the dying. Pain and will could do nothing to erase final agony.

Alone in the Baiyen, against a sere mountain silence Mankind had no right to break, a night's waking nightmare dropped

Rathain's prince like a spearcast run through the heart.

At the end, the bow fell from his nerveless hands. No strength and no passion of temper remained, to hurl the hated weapon away. Arithon crumpled, brought to his knees by the anguish of immutable truth: that no centaur guardian had *ever* used lethal force against any man who offended. More wounding still, no matter whose war host harried his back, the toll of his dead had unmanned him. He could not shoulder the tactics of massacre again, except at the cost of his sanity.

Diviner

Far removed from the blizzards that savaged Baiyen Gap, and the fugitive crown prince who fled Jaelot's guard, the forerunner of war set foot on the eastern coast of Rathain. The fated arrival came deep in the night, on the decks of an oared galley rowed at forced speed through the narrows of Instrell Bay.

A fortnight had passed since the solstice. Oblivious to the flare of contention between Koriathain and Fellowship Sorcerers, untroubled by threats posed by grimwards or bindings containing the rampaging hungers of wraiths, the Mayor of Narms awoke in snug blankets. Someone who had a fist like a battering ram hammered the door to his chamber. He blinked, reluctant to complete the transition between dreams and the burdens of cognizance.

The pounding continued, relentless. 'Hell's blighted minions!' The mayor sat up. Blinking in owlish distemper, he croaked, 'Which trade guild's been raided this time?'

Two more hours remained before dawn. An ice flood of light from the waning moon threw shadow from the mullions in cut diamonds over his counterpane. Faint shouts echoed up from the courtyard. Then the door panel cracked, and his snub-nosed chamber steward peered past the jamb in fussed inquiry. 'My lord, you'll be needed. A galley from Tysan just tied up at the docks, flying sunwheel banners and bearing no less than a royal delegation.'

'*Royal*? The Prince Exalted, himself?' Narms's mayor shot out of bed, while a gapped seam in the quilt exhaled a flurry of goosedown.

Past the whirl of feathers, the house steward returned a blunt shrug. 'I'm sorry. The banners suggest so.'

'Loose fiends and Dharkaron's Black Chariot!' An unannounced crossing in the depths of winter suggested a breaking disaster. Gruff even when fully wakeful, the mayor batted snagged fluff from his beard and hushed his wife's drowsy inquiry. 'State visitors. Ring the bell for your maid. We need to be dressed very quickly.' To his steward, he added, 'Have you heard what's afoot?'

The pink, balding man bobbed his head like a turtle. 'Lord, the dock runner who fetched me knew nothing. The night watch hauls wood to light fires in the hall. There won't be time to rehang proper tapestries.'

'Well at least the trestles were scrubbed since the feast,' the wife said in acid irritation. 'Royal envoys who don't send a herald ahead will just have to bear with inconveniences.' She shoved out of bed in her night rail, a handsome woman with graceful hands who marshaled her thoughts, blinking into the flare as the servant struck light to a candle. 'The kitchen staff will be baking the day's bread. Get someone to send them notice we're receiving, and tell them how many guests of state.'

'I'll go, mistress,' the steward offered at once, then added, 'should I have the east-wing chambers refreshed?'

'Wake the master of horse, first,' the mayor amended, one foot poked half into his hose. 'If this meeting's too pressing to bide until daybreak, I'm thinking we'll be dunned for fast couriers before anyone wants hospitality and beds.'

'Yes, lord.' The steward ducked out, the door latch clicked shut with apprehensive care.

'At least we didn't suffer this intrusion two days ago.' Prosaic, the wife pinned her smoky tangles of hair, then dug in the lacquered armoire for a wrap, and the best of her fancy lace petticoats.

Stalled by a tangle snagged in his points, the mayor gave tongue out of habit. 'Our guild ministers weren't all puking drunk at the twelfth night festivities.'

'No.' The honeyed agreement that made his wife indispensable at state functions preceded her wasp sting of denouement. 'But if your Divine Prince saw all the jewels on their wives as they tried to outshine the Etarrans, we'd find his marshals dunning our treasury. Or don't you think Avenor's come begging for funds, or armed troops, or else the grain stores to mount a winter campaign on barbarians?'

'I don't know what he's come for!' Off-balance, the mayor jammed his stick shanks into his best pair of silk-slashed breeches. 'If you're going to speculate, have the good grace to wait until after I've clothed my shivering buttocks.'

'You'll sweat soon enough, on your knees before royalty.' The wife's catty tongue showed no deference to station. 'Bowing to a blood prince was bother enough, before there were flocks of sunwheel fanatics, rolling cow eyes like he's god sent.'

The mayor stretched a kink from the small of his back, startled to unwonted laughter. 'Say that to his Grace, I'll buy you new pearls.'

'I'd rather warn the unmarried chambermaids to steer clear of shadowy alcoves.' Adrift in lace petticoats, with her ribbons undone, his wife looked up in snide interest. 'Gossip from Avenor insists his Exalted Grace hasn't bedded his princess since the hour his heir was conceived.' Through a frown at her husband, who snatched up yesterday's shirt for convenience, she added, 'That's sixteen years. If the s'Ilessid's kept his manhood to himself for that long, I agree with his priests. He's not human.'

'He's not human,' the mayor affirmed, then bellowed, short-tempered, for his valet to roust up and lend help with the studs on his doublet. When the slug-headed servant failed to appear, the mayor kept talking, his elbows bent at ridiculous angles through his effort to loop rows of braid frogs on jet buttons. 'His Grace hasn't aged since I was a child, and he was presented as Prince of the West. That was before he forwent Tysan's colors for a mantle of white fox and diamonds.'

'Oh, he's aged,' the wife argued, her sharp humor fled as she stepped to assist with her husband's disgruntled robing. 'Just look at his eyes. Hard as faceted sapphire, and too driven for pity.' A break, as she perked up his wilted lace collar, then, 'You want the gold chain and ruby pendant?' Without pause for his nod, she settled the massive links over his dove gray silk. 'Whatever the Exalted Prince asks you to give, don't commit the new recruits.'

'What?' The mayor peered at his wife. 'There hasn't been heavy fighting since the Caithwood campaign failed to clear Taërlin's forests of clansmen.'

'I know.' His wife spun away in a rustle of layered muslin. 'But things change. Whatever ill wind has blown in with that galley, no man of twenty should be sent out to die before the grass greens in the spring.'

The mayor took pause, the squared links of his state jewelry dipped blood in the fluttering candlelight. 'You think the Master of Shadow's come back?'

His wife plucked up her hand mirror. One glance, and her puffy eyes half filled with tears. She slapped the silvered face down in rare and explosive anger. 'Whyever else should we be dragged out of bed before dawn?' Discomposed by the thought of exalted state company, she rebounded to blistering irritation. 'If Avenor brings word of the Spinner of Darkness, the ill news of his reiving is just going to wait until my maid makes me presentable.'

Chilled in stockinged feet, unsure how to manage the imminent concept of shadows and minions of evil, the mayor bent and rummaged through the bottom of the armoire. He fetched out the fanciest boots he could find, ones with velvet-lined cuffs and stitched patterns of seed pearls. 'I'll delay the proceedings by serving mulled wine.' He jammed a foppish black hat with peacock plumes over his short-cropped head, then sailed through the doorway, girded to balk s'Ilessid divinity and appease his wife's queer foreboding.

The hall and the stairwell were darkened by night, the pine-knot brand in the lower vestibule burned down to a flickering cinder. The light would be refreshed at the dawn change of watch, as yet several hours away.

Such lack of diligent guard was routine. Narms was no bastion of armed prowess, to draw the Divine Prince in a crisis. Its city maintained one dilapidated keep, without earthworks. Built over and around the site of an ancient Paravian sea landing, her wealth was guild owned, and invested into skilled labor. Through the centuries since the uprising, the crumbled brick quay overlooking the bay head acquired the sprawl of shanties and warehouses. Sailhands' dives lined the waterfront by the fishmongers'. The recessed cove of the harbor sheltered the industry of dyers and craftsmen, whose lifeblood was tied to town trade. Raw materials and goods came and left from the moss-crusted jetties built through the years after Rathain's last high king was slaughtered. The current garrison quartered only mounted men at arms, split into small companies to guard caravans. For the clan raids that plagued the land route to Morvain, Narms's south district offered a comfortable nest for fortune-seeking headhunters, who scoured Halwythwood for scalps that paid bounty.

By tradition, Alliance interests made landfall at Narms, then passed briskly through to hold loftier counsel at Etarra.

The mayor approached the entry to his great hall and discovered the royal delegation from the harbor already installed ahead of him. One leaf of the heavy double panel lay ajar. A spill of escaped light sliced the dimmed anteroom, strung through by the echoes of rapid-paced talk. The oddity shook him, that he felt estranged while underneath his own roof.

Anxiety bit deeper as he reached the threshold, his short-strided footsteps unnaturally loud as he entered the cavernous chamber. The hearthfire newly lit by his guard captain did nothing to lift the dank chill. Stone walls had been stripped of the star and moon tapestries unfurled each year for the solstice festivities. On a floor scrubbed bare of its formal wax polish, the replacement hangings of hunting scenes lay still rolled, not yet looped on the polished brass rods. The board trestles had been stacked by the wall during cleaning, except for the one set erect for the use of the surprise delegation from Tysan.

That rectangle stood like a snag in the candlelight, bare of linen cloth, and surrounded by men whose steel-clad intensity raised a wall of unease at ten yards. Among six, on their feet, the seated man towered, his self-contained presence a mantle of majesty that seemed bred in the flesh and the bone of him. As always, Lysaer s'Ilessid held the eye like a compass drawn by a magnet.

Golden-haired, cloaked in white, the s'Ilessid prince shone brilliant as diamond and pearl couched against the unadorned setting. The chair he occupied might have been a throne, not the tawdry furnishing the deerhounds had chewed to tattered hanks of burst horsehair. His innate nobility overshadowed his retinue, whose sunwheel tabards of gold and watered silk showed the sad creases ingrained by pack straps and sea chests.

A glance showed the mayor his game plan was forfeit. The basket of new bread sent up from the oven lay cooling, untouched, on a footstool. The carafe of mulled wine had been shoved to one side, its spiced vintage spurned for the tactical map some churl had unrolled, and impaled at the corners with the wife's best stag-handled cutlery.

'Prince Exalted,' the Mayor of Narms greeted in stiff courtesy.

His court-style bow was acknowledged by the barest, brief nod, and a glance from ice-crystal blue eyes. Preoccupied, the unlaced cuff of one sleeve stripped back to expose his immaculate limb to the elbow, the fair personage of Lysaer s'Ilessid laid his wrist in the hands of the slender young man in the priest's robe. Still seamlessly focused, he finished his answer to Narms's worried captain at arms.

'Yes. We know beyond doubt. The Spinner of Darkness has dared to return to the continent. His presence was affirmed well before the hour I set sail from Atainia.' A regal gesture invited the Lord Mayor to join his dazzling, close company. 'Very shortly, bear with me, we'll know where he lairs. My diviner will scry his location.'

Admitted to the inner circle, the mayor surveyed the prince's minimal retinue. He recognized the lean grace and searing impatience of Sulfin Evend, Avenor's Lord Commander at Arms. Three other sunwheel officers in chain mail were strangers, even the headhunter whose muscled frame wore the acid-etched poise of a predator.

Despite every evidence of prowess on the field, the seasoned men-at-arms gave wide berth to the effete priest. Set apart, that one wore the floor-length, sashed robe of a sunwheel acolyte. His six-strand chain of rank set his station one tier below High Priest Cerebeld. The gleaming gold sigil at the crown of his hood proclaimed his Light-sanctioned talent for augury.

As a diviner, he was young, a bone-skinny celibate whose cleft chin and pale cheeks showed scarcely a dusting of beard. Hands slim as a woman's clasped the royal wrist, afflicted with palsy, or else made unsteady by high-strung nerves as he unsheathed a thin ceremonial knife. 'Your Exalted,' he warned in a sugar-toned tenor, then effected a quick, neat cut with the blade, knapped from a bleached human shinbone.

Lysaer did not flinch. His arm stayed relaxed as the blood welled, and the droplets were caught in an offering bowl fashioned from glittering crystal.

The priest kissed the wet wound, then bound it in silk. His carmine-stained lips intoned blessings to the Light in a whisper that rasped like filed steel through the sigh of the fire in the grate.

Narms's mayor looked on, clammy with sweat, and bound to sick fascination. Before this, he had always thought of arcane blood rituals as tales told to threaten unruly children.

Nor did the men-at-arms appear to relish their role as close witnesses. Some shuffled their feet. Others looked elsewhere as a basin of water was tipped into the offering bowl. Blood swirled in pink patterns, stirred by the bone knife. When the mixture blended to translucent pink, the diviner placed the vessel at the center of the tactical map. He floated a wafer of cork on the water, then rubbed a steel needle with a square of black silk until it acquired a charge. There followed another incantation, an invocation to divine Light, while the magnetized needle was arranged on the cork float. The construct revolved on its bed of stained water, then stalled to oscillation on a north-to-south axis. The strangled quiet magnified the rustle of the diviner-priest's silk sleeves. Finished praying, he cupped the fluid-filled bowl. Chain mail clinked in partnered response, as Sulfin Evend adjusted the lay of the tactical map. When the poised needle and the compass rose matched up in cardinal alignment, he reset the abused table cutlery and secured the curled corners of the parchment.

The mayor strangled his self-righteous protest. Stilled as the men-at-arms, and as morbidly curious, he edged in to observe the proceedings. Tension heightened the senses. The magnified sound struck by every small movement cast echoes off stripped-stone walls. The puddled snowmelt tracked in from the street smelled dankly sharp, and the chill hung pervasive, as though the log fire in the hearth failed to cut through the cloth of a suspended reality.

Faint as the draw of air through screened silk, the diviner's sped breaths, as his fluttery hands opened a pearl-inlaid coffer and drew out a filament of gold chain. He touched his smeared lips to the copper cone affixed to the end. Blood and spittle dulled its metallic shine as he deployed the tuned weight above the map as a pendulum.

'Prince Exalted, by the blessed Light of Truth,' he intoned. 'Ask. State your divine will.'

Lysaer s'Ilessid regarded the spread parchment, his eyes honed to steel-edged purpose. 'Find the location of the Spinner of Darkness and show us his course of intent.'

Around the plank trestle, the onlookers hung rapt as the diviner-priest bowed his head. His delicate hand ceased its trembling. Settled into a trance like carved rock, with pale eyes blanked into vacancy, he quieted the listening lens of his mind. Now made the clear conduit for Prince Lysaer's destiny through the ritual link of the blood magic, he allowed the unconscious deflections of nerve and sinew to drive the dangling pendulum. The copper weight rocked to quivering life at the end of its tether of chain. Its point danced over the parchment's inked landmarks as the priest of the Light swept its progressive arcs above the mapped features of Tysan.

'Oh, come,' snapped Sulfin Evend, his annoyance a whip through awed stillness. 'We haven't just crossed Instrell Bay in dead winter to seek a quarry holed up on our back trail!'

The priest sniffed, offended. 'The Master of Shadow is the get of a demon. As prime servant of evil, he could be anywhere.'

As the Lord Commander drew breath to sneer, Lysaer s'Ilessid intervened with a glance. 'When the time comes for warfare, would you ask a diviner to sharpen your steel?'

'Point taken.' Sulfin Evend backed off, thumbs hooked like talons in his sword belt.

If his Hanshire-bred arrogance accepted dark practice in stride, the Mayor of Narms poised between welded fascination and the urge to give way to panic-struck flight. Despite creeping dread, he could not tear his gaze from the consecrated pointer tracking across the spread map. The transition struck him to a gut punch of fear when the random gyre of movement twitched into a smooth, defined swing. The diviner-priest tested, edged the chain gently northward. The arc slowed, died out; then disintegrated into unsettled shivers. Passed southward once more, the movement regained its east-to-west rhythm, as if questing the source of perturbation. Over the barrier range of the Tiriacs, along the western trade road, the copper weight's arc became agitated. Drawn across the inked site of the city of Karfael, it changed motion again, reversed in an arc toward Avenor. There, it settled at last to a rhythmically circular spin over Tysan's royal seat.

'False reading,' the priest murmured. 'Blood will call to blood, foremost through the tie of close kinship. Your royal son will shortly be bound for Karfael, did you know this?'

A dazzle of jewels marked Lysaer's drawn breath, as light nicked the studs on his doublet. 'He's fifteen years of age. Old enough to start cutting his mother's apron strings, I would say. Nor can a prince gain a ruler's discernment by staying too close to home. My garrison commander at Karfael is competent. If he can't be trusted to steer a headstrong boy from youthful high spirits and folly, we are lost before we ever raise arms against the true minion of darkness.' Through a smile of grave humor, the prince signaled for his priest to proceed with the scrying. 'Quarter the Kingdom of Rathain, if you please.'

The priest moistened his stained lips. Seized in ecstatic trance, he wet his fingers with a freshened mix of blood and saliva, then reanointed the copper weight. The chain whined, disrupted. Like a hound pulled untimely from a hot scent, the weight thrashed and trembled in confused little jerks that zigzagged without clear direction. The diviner carried on with unruffled calm, in exacting, small increments, casting across every detailed feature of Rathain. When the forest-clad coves along Instrell Bay showed him no quiver of alignment, he combed over the wastes of Daon Ramon Barrens. Next he quartered the ice-clad peaks of the Skyshiels. There at last, the pendulum deflected, then thrummed into an agitated spin.

'He's there! Oh, well done!' The Divine Prince shot erect. Shared excitement stirred through his men like a storm charge. Even Narms's mayor hung with pent breath as his Grace accosted his priest for more facts. 'Can you see where the demon is headed?'

'He won't escape this time in deepwater ships. No. You will catch him landlocked and vulnerable.' The diviner-priest hovered over his pendulum and map, consumed by the command of his sovereign to glean every detail he could from his art. 'Since landfall in Jaelot, the Master of Shadow has apparently turned inland. He's cutting a path through the Skyshiel foothills, on an angle just north of the city.'

'You know of the forbidden road that leads through that country into Daon Ramon Barrens?' Sulfin Evend supplied. 'Baiyen Gap was the ancient name for the pass. Copies of early Second Age record show the Paravian way running straight to Ithamon as the crow flies.'

While the priest rinsed and dried his paraphernalia, the raw-boned headhunter showed his contempt. 'There's no clan presence there. The site is a ruin. Why would the Spinner of Darkness be bound into such desolate territory?'

Lysaer tapped the parchment where the line of the Severnir's dry gulch snaked south toward Daenfal Lake. 'Don't for a second misjudge this fiendish creature's resourcefulness. He knows of the ensorcelments laid into the stone watch towers that stand whole amid those smashed revetments. Who can guess what evil may spring from his wiles? What if he intends to lay claim to the site and rebuild the crown seat of his forebears?'

'That's no pleasant thought,' Sulfin Evend allowed, his lean features peaked to hawkish interest. 'Those towers outlasted the assault of the rebellion. Legend holds that outsiders still need a blood prince's word to unkey the wards for admittance. The s'Ffalenn defenders besieged there in the past were said to starve to a man, their bones picked by ravens behind unbreached gates. If the Master of Shadow restores the old fortress, he could bid to revive the earth magic. We might see a canker set into our midst that could cost us dear to rout out.'

The weasel-faced captain with the axe at his belt slapped his thigh to a rasp of steel mail. 'Then we stop him. Cut off his access before he can reach his objective.'

Narms's mayor set flat palms on the trestle to brace up his spine in objection. 'It's deep winter,' he argued. 'No mounted courier can bear word to the east fast enough to make any difference. Nor can armed troops sustain a forced march that far overland without supply lines.'

Lysaer s'Ilessid straightened up from the map, his golden hair hazed in low light like a nimbus. His regard felt like touching live embers bare-handed, or staring too long at the sun. 'When else would the minion of darkness seek foothold, but amid the cruel hardship of winter?'

The mayor lacked words. He could not sustain that attentive regard, or such powerfully riveted sincerity.

'Forgive me,' said Lysaer. Recalled to the fact he conversed with a man outside his accustomed circle, he gentled the blaze of his majesty. 'Of course, you would fret for your people of Narms.' His smile was magnetic. 'Put aside all such fear. Your town will be vigorously defended.' On his feet, incandescent with purpose, he was a male form stamped from foil and light, his charisma too bright to seem human. 'We've prepared well for this hour of trial. The faithful will march on the barrens and rise above inconvenience. Terrain and cold weather can be overcome. No foul tactic from Halwythwood's barbarians will defer the arm of the Light's righteous justice.'

The mayor licked dry lips. 'I have no seasoned men-at-arms here to offer. Only those hardened few headhunters who lay over in south quarter lodgings until spring.'

Yet even the field-tested courage of such men balked at crossing the haunted vales of Daon Ramon. The woodland barbarians themselves gave wide berth to the blessed ground at Caith-al-Caen. Nor did men tread the ancient Paravian road which passed through the ruined heart of Ithamon. At the moon's full phase, and under her darkened new face, the eerie, silver-point ghosts of the unicorns galloped in silenced passage. Their dead were still seen to pace under starlight. Ethereal spirits of departed Athlien danced in the change of the seasons, and along the avenue of hallowed standing stones stitched across Daon Ramon, the east wind sang as if speaking.

'We'll face a more brutal reckoning than old haunts, should the s'Ffalenn bastard establish a presence at Ithamon.' Sulfin Evend shifted his raptor's glance to the lanky sunwheel diviner. 'How soon can you contact the priests of the Light stationed at

Etarra and Morvain? Both cities keep garrisons prepared for fast summons. We can march eighteen companies of strike troops due east, and mount twice that number from Etarra. We'll still be hard-pressed. To cordon Ithamon and crush Red-beard's war bands, we need our best men called to arms damn well *yesterday!*'

The diviner knotted his weight and chain between restless, bird-boned fingers. 'Word can be sent on the wings of a prayer ritual, or faster yet by the will of his divine Grace.'

'I'll handle this personally,' snapped Lysaer s'Ilessid. His vehemence spat glints off gold braid and diamonds as he cut off a burly officer's objection. 'By the charge of truth I'm invested to uphold, I'll suffer no minion of evil to lay his fell shadow on the land.'

Driven in dazzling, prideful magnificence, the prince clasped the Mayor of Narms by the shoulder. 'My chosen are dedicated, trained, and relentless in their commitment to uphold the Alliance of Light. Be assured of my pledge to secure your deliverance. Nothing will stand in the way of my charge to take down the Spinner of Darkness. From Narms, we'll require horses, fast couriers, and the skilled guidance of your veteran headhunters. If the Master of Shadow is to be brought down, every fighting man you have with experience in the barrens must lend his unstinting effort.'

Few men could withstand the imperative fire of Lysaer's intimate company. Those candid blue eyes saw too far into the heart, lucid with a too powerfully seductive perception. Swept beyond memory of his promise to his wife, the Mayor of Narms bowed in unreserved acquiescence. 'Prince Exalted, is there nothing my household can offer in return to grant you ease or refreshment?'

Lysaer s'Ilessid released his sure grip, warmed into touching gratitude. 'You can give me the use of a private room, and no interruptions for an hour.'

High Priest

Dedicated to his post in far-distant Tysan, Cerebeld, High Priest of the Light, was a disciplined early riser. Candles burned in his chamber before the glimmer of daybreak lit the roofs of Avenor the colors of pewter and poured lead. For the watch, shivering through the bitter misery of the night, the carmine glow from the priest's tower windows infallibly signaled the final hour before dawn. The taciturn pair of novices who attended his eminence had learned not to trouble his solitude. Cerebeld refused to have servants assist with his dress. He donned his layered white robes on arising, and arranged the seven roped chains of high office. Washed, face and hands, in the chill basin filled for his use the past evening, he followed his rigid habit of keeping devotions until after sunrise. None dared cross his threshold before his sharp clap summoned the hot bread he preferred for his breakfast.

No aspirant who demanded an earlier audience would be admitted into his presence. The novices turned petitioners away regardless of rank, no matter their reason or urgency.

Yet predawn on this day, six men-at-arms clad in royal blue tabards with the eight-point gold star of Tysan delivered an irresistible force of persuasion. The steel-strapped oak door to Cerebeld's chamber crashed back. The lead pair held the novices pinned to the wall, their mailed gauntlets and battle-trained strength overriding the howled chorus of protest. The ruffian in front still brandished the mace just used to mangle the door latch. With a flash of white teeth, the burly henchman who had rammed the locked panel refused any grace of apology. He offered his arm, inviting someone else poised in the stairwell across the High Priest's breached threshold.

A suave power who matched brute force with calculation, Cerebeld arose from the sunwheel cushion that enthroned him in meditation. He knew who had come. With Prince Lysaer away on campaign in the east, only one voice dared command the elite royal guard from the garrison.

'Her Grace, the Princess of Tysan,' announced the rogue who intruded, his sneer for the effete scent of sandalwood wafted from the priest's inner quarters.

Cerebeld looked down his axe-blade nose, his eyes colorless as rimed ice. His dark hair was slicked as a seal's coat with amber-gris. Even this early, he was ceremonially clothed, his sunwheel vestments of stainless white mirrored in the wax-polished floor. The gray bristles of his beard were trimmed to a point, accent to the wrought gold of yoked chains whose links were interlocked dragons. His beeswax complexion showed no flush of anger. Erect, unblinking, he displayed a sangfroid intimidation more effective than bluster or speech.

On that cold, predawn morning, the Princess of Tysan swept into his presence, unfazed. She shed her cloud of ermine cloak into the hands of her armed attendants. The candles on Cerebeld's locked aumbries lit her crisp dazzle of sapphire silk and wired jewelry. For this audience, the lady wore formal state trappings, the stamped brilliance of gemstones and shining gold circlet a blaze of royal authority. Unasked, she sat in the chamber's sole chair. Her skirts pooled around her demurely crossed ankles, damascened blue against her ringed hands, clasped in graceful deportment in her lap.

Doe brown eyes matched Cerebeld's hauteur with a mutual bristle of antagonism. 'I'm here on account of the prince, my blood son.'

The High Priest's plum lips thinned with distaste. 'The boy's doings are none of my affair, your Grace, unless he strays into liaison with unwholesome powers of darkness.'

Ellaine firmed her chin. Her spring-rose beauty had lost its fresh dew. The small, timeworn lines tooled into her complexion by year upon year of resignation today underscored her striking determination. 'The heir apparent of this kingdom has left for Karfael with the guard. I find your seal of approval gave him leave. He's a fifteen-year-old boy. In the company of veteran field troops, he goes armed with only a ceremonial blade, and a head full of dreams that don't match his strength, or his inept grasp of tournament swordplay. If that's not a meddling *interest* in his welfare, I'll see you clapped in irons for deceit.'

Cerebeld linked taloned hands at his waist. 'Princess, your accusation is pure hearsay.'

'The palace steward's a weasel at evasion, but he draws clear distinction against lying.' Ellaine pinned the High Priest without quarter, her retiring nature ignited to flash-point resolve. 'Gace insists that your writ gave the prince due permission to accompany the troops out on road watch.'

A presence of razor-cut, glittering white against the night-darkened panes of the casements, the High Priest of the Light checked his sigh of exasperation. 'The boy is this realm's heir apparent, if not yet a man. He can't learn to rule in Avenor sequestered behind the skirts of your chattering women.' The sharp flick of a glance cut and measured the uncowed, closed hands and tense flush of the lady seated before him. The tragic fact that the princess's late predecessor had died of a suicidal leap from the battlements above had plainly not served to intimidate. Outraged motherhood was not going to back down. 'No,' Cerebeld stated in quelling authority. 'Stay your hand-wringing, you're quite wrong. The young prince's permission arose from a higher authority than mine.'

'What, the Word of the Light?' Ellaine's contempt raked him. 'For your posturing sham of serving divinity, you've dared send my son on a winter campaign?'

'A routine patrol,' High Priest Cerebeld corrected. Attacks never ruffled him. He unclasped his jeweled fingers, his serenity built on the granite of utter conviction. 'Have you ever known me to speak false concerning your husband's divine will? My task while I wear the grace of this mantle is to hear and act for the Light. I say again, permission was served through the mouth of my office, not by my personal preference. Your son was sent to Karfael to mature his experience. He remains in the field until his royal father sees fit to send word and recall him.'

Ellaine clamped back a furious retort, too seasoned to battle the High Priest's righteous duty head-on. The brute rigors of politics had tested his primacy. Time and again, Lysaer s'Ilessid had affirmed the man's power to deliver his royal state edicts. Even Avenor's most avaricious trade ministers bowed to Cerebeld's decrees concerning the will of the Divine Prince.

Taut-faced, white-knuckled, Ellaine refused setback. 'If the heir apparent rides for Karfael, then I go as well. My train and escort will include his Grace's tutors. Two pages from Avenor's prominent families will serve the young prince as companions. Let my royal husband understand this: I will not have our son in the forests of Westwood haring after the scalps of barbarians!'

'You will not leave for Karfael, or anywhere else.' Cerebeld's velvet-clothed certainty shot dangerous currents through the spice-burdened air of the room. The edged play of the light on his sunwheel emblems gained sharpened menace as he served his ultimatum. 'The last princess before you left this city with war pending. She fell victim to the Spinner of Darkness. The Blessed Prince will not see her tragedy repeated. Dear lady, by my oath of service to the Light, you will not pass the gates of Avenor.'

Spark to struck tinder, Ellaine surged to her feet. 'Spinner of Darkness? What is he, but the name of an absent threat? I have never met him, never seen him! Nor have I stood witness to one concrete act that was his, and not some machination used to further the interests of politics. What is Arithon s'Ffalenn but convenience and hearsay that feeds the excuse for trade factions to raise arms and curb the predations of barbarians!'

'But the Master of Shadow is no longer in hiding,' Cerebeld explained after the gravid, barbed pause he used to lend weight to his arguments. 'The enemy is back in Rathain at this moment, and your husband is across Instrell Bay, raising town garrisons to challenge him.'

The High Priest waved aside Ellaine's rebuttal, that deep winter would hamper the muster. 'These are dangerous times, princess. The straits that could bring terror and woe to the innocent are just as you say: that the ports and the passes are closed in the north. No speedy warning can call cities to take arms. The years the s'Ffalenn sorcerer has lurked in obscurity have blunted the memories of his atrocities.'

Which fact was a truth without contest: beyond a bare handful, the aged veterans of Vastmark had retired from the ranks of field service.

Straight as a doll in her jeweled state garments, her bravado reduced to cosmetic paint over paraffin, Ellaine never swerved from her purpose. 'If as you say Rathain's bastard prince has returned, and the eastlands face a new war, I insist, my son should be here and not set at risk with fighting men posted to Karfael.'

For the first time in her presence, Cerebeld broke his glacial mask of objectivity. 'My lady, let me warn you.' His advancing step was a pantherish stalk, glancing candlelight struck off his silk-and-gold robes like the shimmer of sun-bathed quartz. 'Against the grand conflict of Light against Dark, nothing and no one shall come in between the Exalted Prince and his divine destiny. He is the world's ray of hope. Before his glory, and the cause that he stands for, you and your son are expendable.' A glance toward the north bank of casements lent his point stabbing edge. 'Your predecessor, the past Princess Talith, pushed that truth too far and bought tragedy. Try the same thing at your peril.'

The scrape of a hobnailed boot sole recalled the royal guards still standing in dutiful attendance. Their ranking officer cleared his throat, then ventured, 'My lady, your Grace, pay heed to the High Priest. No man in the guard can escort you to Karfael. Not now.' His ranks had not known the Divine Prince had gone to stand in defense against Shadow. Ruddy features averted in embarrassed apology, the officer added, 'You may not know the unhappy history. But when Princess Talith was abducted by the enemy, the captain of the royal honor guard lost his life in reparation. We are charged with the greater burden of your safety, and our loyal oath to your husband sets us in conflict. To support your desire to escort your son could land us with charges of treason.'

Ellaine held her fixed glare of hostility upon the impervious High Priest. 'I understand well enough that your *duty* has no heart, and no shred of human compassion. If my son goes to Karfael for the sake of the Light, and harm comes to him, on my word, I will hold both you and my husband responsible.' A cascading rustle of azure silk saw the Princess of Avenor to her feet. She paid no respects. Spun face about, she swept out with an urgency that suggested suppressed tears, but that actually curbed her rebellious need to cast off westland manners and spit on the High Priest's spotless carpet.

Cerebeld watched his royal guest leave, dispassionate as the sated snake permitting choice prey to go free. While the jingling tread of the attendant men-at-arms receded down the stairwell, he bade the rattled novices on the landing to shut the door to his chamber. Restored to solitude, the Grand High Priest of the Light murmured a purifying prayer, then resumed his morning devotions.

He thumbed open a receptacle in his wrought-dragon chain, removed the filigreed key, then turned the lock on his aumbry. 'Praise be the Light,' he murmured as he knelt. His questing touch tripped the recessed latch concealed amid the embossed gold panel. A cavity had been cunningly set into the joinery behind the whale-ivory facing glued to the cupboard door. Inside, shallow niches in a grid were labeled with the names of each city in Rathain. Most remained empty in this hour of need. But the ones for Etarra, Morvain, and Jaelot sheltered small bundles bagged in silk. Cerebeld plucked these out, his handling as reverent as though their contents were living, and irreplaceably fragile.

He transferred the cache to his personal altar, where beeswax candles, sweetened with sandalwood, burned. Four alabaster bowls held his offerings of clear water, cut herbs, and rarefied oil, and the residue of the blood shed in ceremony to reaffirm the sacrificial pledge of his person to the purpose of divine will and Light. Each day, cast prostrate across the sunwheel cushion as he begged intercession and guidance, he renewed his eternal vow.

Fervently trembling, he unwrapped the sacred bundles and withdrew their three figurines of cast wax. Each held a carved likeness, the hair real, snipped from the heads of the persons they represented. Eyes closed in prayer, Cerebeld licked his thumb. He dampened the wax face of each doll with a touch, then stilled, building the receptive inner quiet through which he would channel the Word of the Light. Minutes passed, sealed in the airborne scents of rare oils and the fragrant musk of hot candles. Predawn stillness suspended him, textureless as hung felt, until his mind unfolded into an effortless state of suspension.

Cerebeld waited, patient as the blank pool stilled to mirror the infinite.

Time brought his reward. The first tug of contact was drawn in by the ritual unreeled through the focal point of the wax dolls. Cerebeld hooked the presence of the nearest man first, the young priest who served truth in Morvain. The man slept yet, entangled in dreams, while the sea winds buffeted his casements. Awareness of the Etarran priest reached through next, tinged with the scent of patchouli he used to freshen his linen. That one was wakeful, his thought stream a sibilant murmur of prayer. The third priest, most recently dispatched to Jaelot, remained stalled in Darkling, caught in midjourney when early storms closed the passes. Asleep in a tangle of fusty wool blankets, his need to stretch travel funds kept him stranded in the smoky, dimmed chamber of a second-rate inn built for drovers.

Cerebeld cupped each separately summoned awareness within the stilled vault of his mind. Then he opened the channel that rode with him, always, through unstinting dedication to the Light.

The fervent call of Avenor's High Priest rode the failing, last shadow of night. His appeal bridged the black waters of Instrell Bay, and, searching beyond, touched the aura of Lysaer s'Ilessid.

Cerebeld immersed in the bliss of divine presence, no longer aware of the body before his draped altar in Avenor. The yawning abyss of human need, all his limiting fears of mortality fell away as he slaked his insatiable thirst for the sacred and became recharged with uplifted purpose. The Divine Prince was spark to his unfired clay. Through self-surrender, his yearning spirit escaped the torpid separation of the flesh. All dread of the Dark, and all terror of sorcery receded; lips parted with unconscious ecstasy, Cerebeld tapped into the radiant source of his avatar's strength. Abandoned to a fervor that bordered obsession, he basked in the diamond-pure stream of Lysaer s'Ilessid's just presence.

His tranced mind experienced the same agitation as his Exalted Self paced the plush carpets in the Mayor of Narms's private guest suite. Quivering now, enthralled in joined vision, the High Priest sent dutiful greeting. *'Exalted Prince? The hour is come to place the arrow of your will into the hands of your servants.'*

The reply returned by Lysaer through the link resounded with pleased satisfaction. *'My command calls for war. The minion of Shadow has dared to turn west through the Skyshiels.'*

Dropped prostrate before his altar, Cerebeld savored the intimate surge of impressions, then responded. *'Your priests stand ready at Etarra and Morvain. The one bound for Jaelot is stranded in Darkling. He is prepared to act for you there. Shine the Light of your presence through me as your conduit.'*

From the distant, closed privacy of the guest suite at Narms, the Exalted Prince raised his hand. Cerebeld trembled. Expectancy exploded to peak exultation as Lysaer s'Ilessid called down power and engaged his divine gift of light.

Seared through the eye of his inner mind, Cerebeld rocked to the surge of blind bliss. Primal pleasure burst the fragile template of identity, until Lysaer's voice rang through every chamber of his opened mind. *'Let the forces allied against Shadow arise and muster to arms! The minion of Darkness has returned to Rathain. He travels over the Baiyen from Jaelot, no doubt to lair up where the sorcerous powers still bind the old keeps at Ithamon. For the weal of the land, our duty is clear. We must launch a forced march across Daon Ramon and close ranks in strength to stop him.'*

At Avenor, the High Priest let the message channel through

him with all of its deluging glory. Unmoored by the blasting passage of pure Light, he was the nexus point, fulfilled by the dictates of Lysaer's urgent purpose. The current coursed through him, aligned to arouse three other human vessels also pledged to eradicate Darkness . . .

In Morvain and Darkling, amid shadowed bedchambers, two priests of the Alliance snapped out of sleep, touched by the dazzling burst of divine vision. The summons resounded with Lysaer's command to rise to arms and converge upon Daon Ramon Barrens. Wakeful, in Etarra, the third priest fell into a spiraling seer's dream, spun on the airy crochet of the smoke that curled off a lit stick of incense. Swept head to foot with delirious joy, he embraced the clarion call of the Light. Through his office, the Exalted Prince's will would be done. Etarra's garrison would march south with all speed to pursue the minion of Darkness . . .

The Light ebbed, then dwindled, then died. Sprawled prone on the pillow before his altar at Avenor, Cerebeld shuddered in release. As always, the limp aftermath caught him defenseless. He bit back a cry, ripped to desolation as his mind was cast into separation.

By now, he knew there existed no remedy for the dimmed prison of mortal limitation. He could only endure, drawn onward by the obdurate steel of his faith. One ritual to the next, he breathed for the moments when the exalted presence entered and claimed him as instrument.

At length, he gathered himself and arose. He felt hollow, diminished, a lackluster shell that stepped through the motions of living. Dry duty sustained him. The needs of the faithful required teaching and guidance. Their prayers must be led by rote. Amid the drab, puppet players he ministered, Cerebeld moved like the addict, perpetually craving the next golden dawn, when his being could rise and rejoice once again in communion with divine rapture.

Solstice Moon Fortnight

In the Kingdom of Rathain, the trade cities of Etarra, Darkling, and Morvain hear Cerebeld's chosen priests speak the word of the Light calling for the Alliance's faithful to muster; while on the eastshore, mounted couriers leave Narms bearing news of Lysaer's arrival, and exhorting the surrounding town garrisons to join the campaign to run down the Shadow Master in Daon Ramon Barrens . . .

In Baiyen Gap, caught critically short of supplies since the demise of his supply train, Jaelot's bespelled captain berates his sergeants rather than bow to the quandary of defeat, 'Every man present will fare on half rations! A third of the company must continue to advance. The rest will make camp and butcher horses for sustenance until a forced march back to Jaelot can arrange for another pack train to relieve us . . . !'

En route to Karfael, the royal patrol dispatched from Avenor receives a southbound courier bearing news of Khadrim attacks deep in Westwood; warned of the terror and death newly suffered by the region's trappers and farm hamlets, young Prince Kevor refuses safe return to West End, and claims his heir's right to ride at the fore, alongside the field captain's banner . . .

IV. Prime Successor

The eighty-league ride up the Eltair road from Jaelot to the city of Highscarp offered every discomfort of winter travel to the tight-knit party of enchantresses summoned for audience with the new Prime. Posthouses were few and scattered, and at this season, packed to the rafters. Day or night, the heaving waves of the bay shed chill spume, whipped on the biting east wind. Progress suffered the caprice of changeable weather. Ragged clouds and fair sky warred in crazy quilt patterns, brewed into fogs and wet snowfall as the air off the warmed, southern currents of the Cildein met the ice-honed fronts from the north. A steady onslaught of storms funneled through the Skyshiel summits, howling with shrill fury down the gorges; or they raged inland off the whitecapped bay and unburdened their tropical moisture.

As tangled were the contentions chafing the oathsworn ties of Koriani loyalty. Each enchantress bound to the initiate's purple held a different view of the Prince of Rathain's late escape. Cadgia's circle of seeresses accepted the failure with stoic good spirits, the event just another professional setback to crimp the cogs of higher authority. For Elaira, withdrawn into worried silence concerning the fate of two fugitives abroad in the Skyshiel wilderness, the affray kept its bittersweet edge of snatched victory. Whatever accounting awaited in Highscarp at the hand of Morriel's successor, her heart's love still anchored the core of her private thoughts.

Lirenda vacillated. Her porcelain-fair features flushed to rage when discussion touched upon Arithon, or else chilled to an ice-sculpture mask of balked hatred as she choked on the rags of her shame. Once past the jolting news of Morriel's death, the disparate facts sifted down to a core of disturbing suspicions. Lirenda wrestled her reservations concerning Selidie's abrupt accession alone, while the winter rigors of the Eltair coast rankled her fastidious taste for silk clothes and comfort and cleanliness.

The days passed like punishment: over roads that softened to muck in the hollows and open-air campsites left trampled by the uncouth livestock tethered on their way to slaughter. Those rare nights spent under a roof offered poorly washed linen, and smoking hearths, and stifling taprooms jammed with boisterous drovers, and bearded, swaggering caravan guards who played dice, roared jokes, and pinched doxies.

On a blustery morning twoscore days past solstice, the travel-worn group of enchantresses drew rein before Highscarp's gatehouse. Lirenda was windburned and aching tired, wrapped like the rest in mantle and gloves that reeked of woodsmoke, wet horse, and the turpentine bite of the evergreen boughs that had served her as last night's bedding. The uncivilized journey had revised her priorities. Vengeance-bent hatred of Arithon s'Ffalenn could wait on her need for a bath.

'If you're primed for hot water, we're facing a setback,' an intrusive voice broached from the sidelines.

Lirenda turned her head, fixed her smoldering gaze on Elaira, who rode with her hood blown back. The gusts played havoc with her bronze plait, streaming tendrils of flyaway hair and snagging the ends into elf locks.

Nonplussed by hot glares and glacial silences, Elaira raised her eyebrows. 'Look. Over there.' She pointed toward the swarm of beggars jostling for coin in the lee of Highscarp's outer keep, most of them missing hands or a foot from mishaps working the quarries. 'See for yourself. That's one of our initiates giving alms at the city's main gatehouse. She's looking our way. What will you wager? I say the Prime's scryers have already broken the news of our arrival. Whom do you guess they'll call onto the carpet for the privilege of the first reprimand?'

'You might pretend to an earnest concern.' Lirenda's fist tightened without thought on the rein. Her mount, in sharp protest, shook its wet crest. A spray of fine droplets snapped off its mane, laden with gravel and ice melt. 'Brute beast!' Lirenda blotted her face with her sleeve, then added a silken warning.

'The new Prime may not prove so lenient toward the weakness you bring to our order.'

'But I have no regrets,' Elaira attacked in stripped candor. 'If I must suffer for my part in Jaelot, the price will be well worth the outcome. Why not join the company of the damned with good cheer? At least bet that chunk of grade amethyst in your cloak brooch. If you forfeit your dignity, you'd have a stake to enliven the sordid end play.'

Yet if Lirenda envied her younger peer's gift to find humor amid life's adversity, the haughty set to her lips did not soften. Nor would her cynical silence relent, even as the initiate by the gatehouse abandoned her clamoring circle of beggars. Red-faced from the cold, she threaded a no-nonsense course through the traffic and accosted the sisters from Jaelot.

'Enchantress Elaira!' She delivered her unwelcome summons across the clattering rush of guild couriers and the tumult of oxcarts laden with ale casks and firewood. 'You are called to appear for immediate audience before your Prime Matriarch.'

'At least there'll be no tortured waiting.' Elaira reined her brown gelding aside, well braced for her hour of reckoning.

Drawn to a halt, with her mounted peers bunched into a staring knot amid the pressed flow of commerce, Lirenda waited for the message that would see her included. None came; her presence was dismissed along with the sisters ranked under Senior Cadgia.

The novice gave Elaira the street address where the new Prime had established her residence. 'Go at once,' she commanded. 'You're expected. One of the orphan boys under wardship will receive your horse in the mansion courtyard.'

A flock of gulls flew, tumultuous as tossed paper against the stirred clouds held over from the last snowstorm. Elaira's eyes tracked them, perhaps coveting their freedom as she parted from the safe circle of her peers.

While the brave line of the bronze-haired initiate's back disappeared into the gatehouse, Lirenda raged, her bitterness charged to sheer disbelief as further instructions were delivered to Cadgia, and a stable was appointed to provide for the company's post horses. In obvious haste to escape the stiff gusts, the Prime's novice messenger made closure. 'The rest of you are asked to take lodgings at the sisterhouse. The peeress in charge will make use of your services until the Matriarch calls general assembly.'

Dealt an unprecedented, blanket dismissal, Lirenda sat dumbstruck. Around her, the chatter of her peers rang as meaningless as the incessant cries of the gulls. Unguided, her mount trailed after its fellows through the ox-drawn drays dragging slabs from the quarries, their high, iron wheels grinding over iced cobbles and past weatherworn drivers wrapped in fringed rugs, cursing every other party inbound along Highscarp's stone causeway.

The catcalls, the pithy challenge of the guard through the wind-torn snap of the mayor's banner arose as so much patternless noise. As an eighth-rank initiate, set apart by her years of advanced training, Lirenda felt sealed into glass-walled isolation. Her fall from administrative privileges to the meniality of charitable service seemed a punishment of nightmare proportion. Cast beneath the lowliest scullion who had served on her parents' estate, she might be required to nursemaid orphaned infants, or treat scabrous beggars, or spoon-feed demented old women in the poor quarter. The ignominy rankled: as a candidate set apart for prime training, she had disdained to mingle with the low-rank initiates. The banter, the breathless laughter, the back-and-forth quips exchanged in the scullery, and the chapped hands she would earn in the laundry poured like venom through the shreds of her dreams and ambition.

'I'm going with Elaira,' she announced, her outrage driven bone deep by a background of wealth and privilege.

'Your name was not called,' Senior Cadgia reminded.

'I don't care.' Lirenda pitched her horse into a headshaking trot.

Cadgia turned in the saddle, her round, kindly features transformed from asperity to disbelief. 'Lirenda, that's folly!'

But the demoted enchantress shook off well-meant warning. Impulse had solidified into mulish resolve. She could not accept ruin in gutless defeat, falsely masked under virtuous acceptance. Lirenda jabbed spurs to her tired mount, determined to narrow the lead Elaira had opened ahead of her.

The massive, carved gate arch loomed and then swallowed her, its dank shadow bleak as her mood. By the time the wan daylight found her again, more foraging gulls had taken wing from gleaning the fish-market midden. Their shadows flicked a street jammed by workaday masses, a teeming press of patched umbers and saffron, with no trace of Koriani purple.

Elaira had passed beyond view. Set under the threat of the new Prime's authority, she would move unseen through the crowd. Her wary, street urchin's self-reliance reflexively grasped that anonymous cover for protection.

Lirenda cursed for the inconvenience.

Highscarp was riddled with twisting allies where a lone woman on horseback might vanish. Its massive breakwater skirted the foothills, a labyrinthine fortress grafted into the headland where the northbound combers thrashed into a granite coastline. The battlements were eyries that buttressed the sky, and the ramped eastern wall bore the brunt of the gales, hoary with moss between the repairs from the macerating wear of riptides and equinox storm surge. Highscarp endured, though the sea often triumphed. In a bad year, the pilings of the galley wharves became skewed and tumbled like matchsticks. Slate roofs capped by hammered lead rimmed the land, an anvil against the percussive onslaught of rough weather.

The cobbled streets Lirenda traversed smelled of fish-oil lamps, and raw turpentine, and the astringent fumes of the resin men boiled to make varnish. Here, the relentless siege of the sea was given brash challenge: backdrop to the thud of gray breakers, the dauntless clang of steel mauls, as skilled masons dressed blocks from the quarries. Nor was grace forgotten. From the striated mountains due west of the city came the opaline granite once used to lay floors in the palaces of the old high kings. Before them, the great centaurs had mined the veins of white quartz for the dolmens they chiseled with patterns to mark the lands held unspoiled for the mysteries. If the nurses' tales whispered over cradles held true, the innermost halls of the citadel had been carved before First Age history, by drake packs laired in the ledged rock.

Certainly the thoroughfares were narrow enough to suggest such ancient origins. At each crossroads and turn, Lirenda was balked by piled-up snow, street stalls swarming with commerce and stopped carts, and racing urchins playing a northcountry game with flat sticks and a stitched leather ball. By the time she clattered into the walled courtyard and dismounted before the Prime's residence, a whistling boy groom had already led Elaira's unsaddled horse to the water trough. Minutes slipped past while the animal was stabled. Lirenda slapped her slack reins in her gloved palm and fumed throughout the delay.

The house the Prime chose for her quarters commanded the view before comfort. The gabled front wing hugged the rim of a bluff, the patterned terracotta tiles of the entry chilled under the shade of the watchkeep. Gusts off the bay snapped Lirenda's thick mantle. Her tucked-up hair suffered, the frayed ends lashed into tangles. Regarded askance by the squint-eyed servant who shuffled to answer the door, she demanded to share the Prime's audience on the impetus of aristocratic breeding.

The servant gave back a draconian glower. Lirenda waited. Her imperious foot tapped. Cowed by her scathing arrogance, the servant sniffed and led off through the hush of a wainscoted hallway. Rich carpets were pooled with marigold light cast by oil lamps hung on brass chains. At home in an atmosphere tanged with the citrus of polished linenfold paneling, and admiring the beauty of claw-footed furnishings with vine-patterned ivory inlay, Lirenda surmised the new Prime had invoked some well-to-do merchant's oath of debt.

The massive, carved doors to the salon were not locked. Since the servant balked at tripping the latch, Lirenda was left the irrevocable choice of whether to proceed or turn back.

She paused, overcome. The crushing weight of the moment stalled thought. To enter the Prime's private sanctum, unasked, was to force her fate to a summary resolution. She could lose everything, sealing her plight to a lifetime of thankless servitude. The young woman now wielding Morriel's authority was a frustrating, unknown quantity.

Of all senior peers in the Koriani Order, Lirenda alone had been raised to eighth-rank training. Her knowledge would not let her gnawing doubt rest: *the new Prime's accession could never have taken the time-honored, legitimate steps*. The vacuous chit who had stood as her rival never owned the deep strength, far less the arduous self-control to bear the accession to prime power. No measure of compromise existed behind that sand grain of irritable discrepancy: desperate, even dying, Morriel might have dared an unprecedented breach, casting aside untold thousands of years of uncompromised moral tradition.

Either Lirenda lived out her days cowed by that flagrant rebuttal, or she dared confrontation here and now at the risk of her very survival.

At the cusp, outrage drove her, and the wild-card threat, that Elaira's frank testimony over Arithon's escape might prove just as thoroughly damning. Lirenda seized her chance to wrest back her autonomy and brazenly opened the door.

The panel swung into a dimly lit anteroom, curtained with tapestries in glowing Narms dyes. Dried lavender wafted delicate scent from elegant, cloisonné vases. The space appeared empty. Lirenda shed her mud-splashed mantle by the entry, startled by an unexpected movement in the corner as another travel-stained figure whirled to face the rustle of wool.

'You!' gasped Elaira. Tension sharpened her carriage. 'Are you here to make certain I don't say too much? Or shall we agree to be allies in adversity?'

Lirenda draped her stained cloak on a chairback, her eyes the pale amber of poured whiskey. 'Allies,' she responded, begrudging acknowledgment that Arithon s'Ffalenn had spun a common thread between their disparate stations. 'You don't trust me, I see. To prove my sincerity, I'll offer a warning. Throughout your audience, behave exactly as though you were examined by Morriel herself.'

Elaira weighed this through a pregnant pause, her level brows hooked to perplexity. 'Should such a threat frighten me?' In her few past encounters, the deceased Prime Matriarch had treated her with fairness, and at times a grandmotherly sympathy.

No chance remained to test Lirenda's statement. The inner doors opened, and a liveried, blond page boy called out in formal summons.

Elaira squared her shoulders. Her snagged plait an auburn flame down her back, she clasped the bronze buttons sewn for luck into the lining of her mantle, then strode resolute through the doorway. She did not glance behind as Lirenda ran roughshod over protocol and followed her.

Gloom enfolded the hammer-beamed chamber beyond. The bow windows with their breathtaking view of the bay were curtained in night-colored velvet. Nicked to gold by the flame of beeswax candles, velvet upholstery and damascened silk braid glinted from corners and lover's nooks. The furnishings were costly southern imports of Vhalzein lacquer and ebony. Carved tables and chairs wore graceful wreaths and the beardless faces of dryads. The carpets, with their twisted fringe borders, were the masterworks of skilled Morvain craftsmen. Glass and silver candlestands showed Paravian workmanship, eight centuries old, and exquisitely rare. Brought up to appreciate beautiful things, Lirenda curbed her wandering eyes and locked glances with the new Prime.

Elaira had already curtseyed to the floor. Lirenda eschewed the same rite of obeisance, instead giving the seated Matriarch on the dais her insolent, tight-focused survey.

Selidie wore silk the cream and lavender of spring irises, her supple, young limbs arranged in the austerity of a lion-bossed chair. The Prime's mantle of purple velvet with its nine bands of office had been pinned at her neck with a brooch of red gold and amethyst. Her pale, corn-silk hair was clasped in mother-of-pearl combs, not the diamond pins Morriel had favored. No question remained that she wielded the powers invested with the Matriarch's office. Her eyes watched all that moved, a sustained, nerveless focus as intent as polished steel rivets. A matched pair of ebony stands at her feet wore masked coverings, the ritual patterns of embroidered silk used to veil major focus stones. Flanking these, supported on beaten-ring tripods, were seven matched spheres of clear quartz attuned to the sixfold sigil for scrying.

Lirenda let silent seconds elapse before speaking the traditional statement of service.

Prime Selidie replied in a throaty, clipped alto, stripped of the sweet lisp affected before her whirlwind ascent to high office. 'Did you think I'd be amazed by your uninvited entry? My page has already set out a chair. You will sit. Keep silent until my interview is done, and initiate Elaira receives disposition and final dismissal.'

A prime's direct order demanded obedience. Lirenda accepted the chair, her chilled hands clasped in her lap. Elaira was left standing alone before the dais, defenseless beneath the stripping regard of those surgically measuring gray eyes.

'Come forward,' Prime Selidie commanded. 'We are private.' Yet if no ranking Senior attended her wearing the veils of Ceremonial Inquisitor, the exchange promised the razor-edged tension of an inquiry nonetheless. The outcome might easily invoke a trial, bearing stakes severe as the supreme penalty.

The victim must wait in unflinching subservience while her Matriarch posed the first questions.

'You are called to serve because Arithon s'Ffalenn is still at large on the continent.' Selidie paused, subtle in expectation.

Elaira gave away nothing, her calm stance itself a statement of blistering courage.

'There are factions marching who seek his death. You don't wonder how he fares in adversity?' Selidie leaned forward, extended an almond-fair hand, and tapped the crystalline arc of quartz spheres in sequence one after another. Power surged at her touch, waking the sigils of binding. The scrying stones flashed like turned mirrors with light, then resolved to display scenes of tight-focused color and movement.

Even from the vantage of her seat, Lirenda recognized the streaming banners of town garrisons set on winter march across the bleak territory of Rathain. Etarra's exemplary zeal had responded with eight field companies five hundred strong. Burdened with massive supply trains, slowed by freezing storms, their creeping progress advanced through the desolate terrain of Daon Ramon Barrens.

Another quartz showed Darkling's militia, armed men and laden mountain ponies breasting the chest-high drifts toward the foothills and the vale of the Severnir. The crystal adjacent displayed Morvain's bands of veteran headhunters moving apace through the deep glens of Halwythwood, where startled deer fled before them. Beyond all question, the three forces marched to a unified purpose.

'Your prince faces bad odds.' Selidie tapped the fourth quartz in its stand. That one aroused to an actinic flash: spurred on by no less than Lysaer himself, Narms fielded a smaller, fast-moving force under the sunwheel standard. They marched the old way through Caith-al-Caen, while the raised blast of Lysaer's gift of light dispelled the gossamer forms of the unicorns' memories like so much torched silk before them.

'The Alliance has raised the hue and cry, as you see. They converge on Ithamon, if trust can be placed in an estimation based on direction.' Selidie flicked the next-to-the-last sphere to life, unveiling the trials of Jaelot's pursuit through the haunted pass of the Baiyen. 'Why should Prince Arithon seek haven, do you think, in the ruin of his ancestral seat?'

Again, silence answered. Chin lifted, eyes wide, Elaira stood in squared quiet, the weight of the mantle she had not removed almost masking her small tremors of dread. Surprised to unwonted admiration, Lirenda locked clammy fingers and awaited the next step in this perilous testing of wills.

Prime Selidie stroked the last quartz in line with the chisel-point tip of her fingernail. 'Dakar the Mad Prophet is no longer free to play watchdog and royal protector.' The glass polish reflected her immaculate hand, as well as the travel-stained initiate held trapped in the lucent spill of candlelight. 'Elaira?' Selidie cajoled with a cat's concentration. 'We know that the Master of Shadow is injured. When he raves, he tends to get careless.'

'He mentions my name?' Elaira provoked in the faintest flush of first anger. She had little tolerance for playing the mouse before figures of higher authority. 'Or how else could you garner the foothold to find him?'

Selidie straightened, the last quartz left blank. 'He's the stepchild of cleverness, just as you were never a creature of subtlety.' Fine silk slithered like the whisper of ghosts as she whisked off the coverings that veiled the faceted jewels on the stands at her feet.

The first spat the glacial glimmer of pressed ice, no less than the Skyron aquamarine. The other, a faceted amethyst sphere, breathed an aura to raise the short hairs at the nape. Its surface seemed to drink in the light. Spindled glints at its heart flared to restless violet, alive with sullen rage and treacherous intelligence. Even from safe remove to one side, Lirenda wrestled the fear raised by the unshielded presence of the Great Waystone.

Elaira swallowed, the rough flush left by wind drained into chalky pallor. She would beg no reprieve. Facing the instruments of terrible, raw power that could strip her mind of free will, she managed the fiber to stop shaking. Straight in defiance, she transferred a glare like an equinox gale on the Prime in her seat of high judgment. 'We have changed from an order of mercy to one that bends lives through coercion and force? How our founders would weep. Are, in fact, weeping. Or do their venerable memories not stand here as witness, imprinted into the same matrix jewels you invoke to enact your demands?'

Which insolence snapped the Prime's patience. 'Be silent!'

'I will not betray Arithon,' Elaira stated, blunt as nails in a suicidal challenge. 'If that's what you've brought me here to achieve, let me clear the least shadow of doubt. I'll cast off my vow of obedience, even welcome the punishment that makes final end of my love as your private weapon. Never again will I be the tool to gain leverage for Koriani politics.'

Lirenda caught her breath, stunned. Against the Prime sigils, no sworn initiate held the power to keep personal secrets; Elaira had hurled down the gauntlet to compel her own immolation.

On the dais, Selidie settled back in her chair. 'You will not betray anyone,' she rebuked in flat quiet. Her oval face gave no clue to her thoughts, the lucent flesh unmarked in youth, and the disciplined iron that showed no trace of emotion. 'I am no fool, to misread the strengths and shortcomings of any initiate bound to life service. I will not abet suicide. Nor will I ruin a valuable resource over a textbook adherence to propriety.'

Shocked to naked retreat by the point-blank rejection of her tactical sacrifice, Elaira fell back on bravado. 'Swear, then.' Prompted by her razor-sharp instinct for survival, she added, 'Take oath on your personal crystal that I will never be asked to betray Arithon s'Ffalenn, nor coerce another innocent as crow bait to draw him into the hands of his enemies.'

Selidie raised a silver-toned eyebrow. 'Is your trust in my office so diminished? I have forthrightly stated my case. You are too strong a will to be wasted.' Then, as Elaira failed to relax, 'Ah, I see.' She clapped petite hands, caught remiss. 'You fear a repeat of Fionn Areth's constrained fate.' Coquettish malice touched her coral smile as she said, 'Of course, you couldn't know that plan was Lirenda's idea.'

But Elaira proved too wise to be swayed by the diversion of petty vengeance. 'Morriel's permission endorsed that mishandling.'

'As a lesson, yes, to an eighth-rank enchantress who failed to unmask the true core of the test as a trap. In due course, Lirenda proved out the flawed weakness that disbarred her from the succession.' With a girl's catty shrug, that her subject of revilement was constrained to listening silence, Selidie cupped her palms to the glowering sphere of the Waystone. 'Did you know our great amethyst can record and enforce promises?'

Elaira shivered, speared through by chills. The warning stopped breath, that this was no green antagonist who countered her moves like a predator loosed on a chessboard. 'Don't do this.'

'I require your trust,' said the Prime, unequivocal. A freezing finger of cold stirred the air, then a ripple of malice clothed in stinging power, as the Matriarch engaged her will with the wakened might of the order's most perilous focus stone. 'For the record, in duration of my lifetime, bear witness to my word as Selidie Prime: *initiate Elaira will never be forced to betray Arithon Teir's'Ffalenn in the interests of the Koriani Order.*'

Elaira shook her head, stunned. 'I need to sit down.'

The closed chamber seemed to magnify stillness, until the pearlescent gleam thrown off Vhalzein lacquer furnishings seemed a lawless intrusion of movement. Selidie uttered no word. Her eyes the dense, polished silver of hematite, she stroked the dire amethyst back to quiescence. Dainty in grace, and butterfly fragile, she inclined her head in permission.

A page pattered forward bearing a footstool. Blanched paper white and never more wary, the bronze-haired initiate groped, and caught shaky hands on the cushion. She let her knees give way underneath her. Lirenda's thunderstruck silence at her back endorsed shocking fact, that an oath on the Waystone would be held in trust by the Prime Matriarch's very life.

Limp in the juddering light of the candles, Elaira braced her stripped nerves, too aware she fenced wits with an enemy who outmatched her every resource. 'If not to lay strings upon Arithon s'Ffalenn, why should you trouble to summon me?'

'Why indeed?' Selidie loosed sprightly laughter, then dispatched her page to the kitchen to ask for a tray of tea and buttered cakes. 'Because the man is Dharkaron's own shadow to track. He's alone, and ill, and probably injured. If he's going to succumb and die in the Skyshiels, our world loses a powerful cipher. You offer the best link we have to trace him. Surely you share the same interest at heart?'

Elaira considered this. Taut fingers laced on the crossed ankles of her riding boots, she scarcely winced as the grit of dried mud flaked onto the priceless carpet. 'You won't seek to claim full advantage of his weakness?'

'Our order has no means to pluck him from the wilds of Daon Ramon, in any case. Not with five musters of Lysaer's armed allies beating the brush with drawn steel.' Selidie rearranged the sleeves of her mantle over the lion-carved chair arms. 'They wish him dead. We desire him living, but captive. You are offered the choice how you serve him.'

'I would keep him alive, but not at the cost of integrity,' Elaira admitted without heat, though the knuckles she locked on damp leather bespoke the backhanded sting of the trap barbed and set to waylay her. 'Just what service are you asking me to perform?'

Selidie regarded her disheveled wariness with a startling, frank gesture of kindness. 'You are linked to him, yes? At the outset, I ask for your help with a scrying. In exchange, I offer these safeguards. You alone will review the results. For my needs, you need share nothing except the fact of his death, or the word of his safe arrival at the ruin of Ithamon.'

'And if the issue is not black or white?' Elaira pressed. Distrust scraped through her strained fabric of hope, that the inevitable, unseen hook in the bargain must put her conflicted loyalty to a more punishing test.

Selidie answered without hesitation. 'By my oath on the Waystone, you are left free to answer his need at your personal discretion.'

Which gift was a dangerous boon. The master ciphers possessed by the Koriani Prime enabled Selidie to follow Elaira's every move; by extension, she would gain infallible means to dog Arithon's position at will.

The door latch jostled warning. Two servants in house livery entered in soundless tact. Both gave the unshielded quartz crystals wide berth. One cast a lace cloth over the claw-footed table set at Selidie's elbow. The other settled the tray of refreshments and poured steaming tea into porcelain cups.

'You're too thin,' observed Selidie. 'Why not make your choice after you've eaten some honey cake?'

'No blandishments.' Elaira had recovered the aplomb to strike back in wry humor. 'I'm no longer the starving street orphan who could be bought for the promise of bread crusts. S'Ffalenn princes have ever looked after their own, and your quarry has already proved himself as Torbrand's trueborn descendant.'

'His escape from Jaelot was no accident,' Selidie agreed, 'and you yourself honor his royal trust to the point where you won't accept bread crusts without the old-law bonds of honest friendship.'

'I'll have surety before cake,' Elaira insisted, her mettle steadfast under pressure. 'A hard ride up the coast would make anybody thin. I'll recover on gruel in a tavern, but *after* you've listed your terms of demand to offset my presumed gift of freedom.'

While Lirenda sucked in a breath of amazement, Selidie tucked her neat, coquette's fingers around the scrolled handle of a teacup. 'You should have been a merchant, the way you read nuance.' She waved the hovering servants away. Steam plumed against the dimmed fall of the tapestries as she spooned in a thick gob of honey. Her gaze stayed thoughtfully level, but not discomposed, as she savored a lingering sip.

'Merchants can't traffic in slaves or prisoners, under terms of the Fellowship's compact,' Elaira attacked. 'You need Arithon as your leverage to upset the old order, and to reach him, you plan to use me. I would have this over with.'

Selidie slapped down her cup. The furious chime of the spoon struck through silence, no less a warning than the testing tap of crossed sword steel. Robed in the Prime's mantle, and charged with the unsheathed power of her office, Selidie glared down with quicksilver eyes. 'Girl, you rankle! Don't expect I'll forgive your brash insolence. Hear your orders. Then decide what course you will take from this chamber. I will grant you the loan of a scrying quartz. You will use it to shadow the Prince of Rathain and report if he dies of wound fever. If he lives, you may engage your own powers as you will. I prefer him kept clear of Lysaer s'Ilessid and the armed forces of the Alliance.'

'No limits?' Elaira said, her voice rocked unsteady. The candlelight flared like chipped rust through her hair as she hung on the pause for an answer.

Selidie watched, snake still in her chair, while the steam twined the gloom like the half-coiled ribbons of a spell. 'No limits but one: if his Grace survives the winter, you will go to him when the thaws reopen the Skyshiel passes. You will attach yourself to his company and behave exactly as you please until such time as his life becomes threatened. Then, you will be free to intercede in his behalf. You have claimed we've forgotten our precepts of mercy. Let this prove you wrong. You are given my sanction to wield the power of the Koriani Order in the cause of Prince Arithon's life.'

'Merciful Ath, of course!' Elaira shot to her feet. 'With the usual condition *that he would owe us his personal oath of debt for our service*. Even the Fellowship must honor that stricture, no matter if the price we demand should seal his final downfall.'

Selidie inclined her head. 'We have never granted exception for royal birth or any other privilege of rank.' A brittle smile bent her lips. 'The choice remains yours, whether or not to offer your prince the option of our help. You are, as you see, the initiate best suited to carry out this mission. The only direct command you will bear is to stay involved with Prince Arithon's affairs.'

'A feat far easier said than accomplished.' Elaira drew a steady breath that laid bare the unyielding mettle of her character. 'If I don't go, I suppose you'd send Lirenda?'

'My ends can be served out of love, or from hatred,' Selidie agreed in poisoned logic. 'Which emotion will sway Arithon's fate in the straits of his uncertain future?'

'Love, of course.' Elaira shouldered the weight of that vicious irony, no less besieged by the dumbstruck antagonist who now looked daggers at her back. 'I have leave to start immediately?'

'As you wish.' Selidie raised the blank sphere from its tripod and gestured for Elaira to approach. An admonition followed as the crystal changed hands, too quiet for Lirenda to overhear. Then the audience ended. Elaira descended the dais and curtseyed, giving the ritual words of obedience. When she arose, her eyes glittered with unshed tears. Granted a terrible grace of reprieve, and the Prime's formal word to depart, she beat a tormented retreat and slipped through the outer doorway. The Prime's grant of choice held no triumph for her, but the promise of pain and a perilous, double-edged burden.

Prime Matriarch Selidie reclined in her chair, brilliant eyes closed through a moment of pleased relief. While the Waystone and the Skyron danced with the scintillant light of her ebullience, she said, 'That woman had the straight courage to refuse me. Our order's future may ride on the stunning, weak fact that she didn't.'

Lirenda cut in with acidic accusation. 'I have leave to speak? Such a love as she bears could well be strong enough to allow your chosen quarry to die.'

'Less willingly than hatred.' Selidie flexed the hand she had used to bond with the Waystone as though the stone's malice still seared an invisible burn through her flesh. 'You will learn in due time. The carrot wins better cooperation than the stick.'

Lirenda arose, a whisper of damp silk masking her stifled resentment. 'Where's the carrot, for me?'

'You were no invited witness.' Selidie met her opening advance with wide-lashed, malevolent challenge. 'Be most careful how you speak. I choose my weapons with meticulous care. When the last crisis breaks, Elaira will dance to the very same constraints that I'll use to break and scatter the power of the Fellowship.'

Lirenda tested Selidie's bitter thread of logic: that if Arithon provided a viable cipher to disrupt the grip of the compact, he must also be key to the world's future balance. Neither the Sorcerers nor Elaira would sacrifice Athera to deny mankind's rightful claim to seize dominance. A last, closing stride brought Lirenda to the foot of the low stair, her reflection overlaid in multiple imprint on the Alliance forces still marching through snow in the scrying spheres. *I thought you wanted the Shadow Master dead!* Or is his Grace of Rathain no longer a threat to Koriani continuance?'

Selidie plucked a slice of cake from the plate and licked butter icing from her fingers. 'He was a thorn in the path of Morriel's succession. That issue is ended.' She nibbled, amused, as she sensed Lirenda's probe for the crone now securely ensconced within the purloined flesh of youth. 'As you see, prime power has been transferred intact. The guard has changed. My predecessor is dead, her ashes dispersed by the rituals of due ceremony. Choose your stand on that matter very carefully.'

Lirenda regarded the creature before her with a lioness's glare and a loathing that curdled her blood. '*You* dare to warn *me*?' Challenged by an initiate who possessed eighth-rank training, Selidie must realize her unnatural state was transparently obvious. 'I'm amazed you have the bald-faced effrontery to allow me to live!'

'You weren't listening. I never, ever cast off useful tools.' Selidie shook out a napkin and whisked away a small blizzard of crumbs. 'Did you think you retained any shred of good standing to bandy high charges against me? The facts lie against you. Your ambition left enemies, particularly since you made no secret of your disdain for my novice incompetence. In Jaelot, you fumbled a major assignment. Prince Arithon went free. Tell me truth, sister.' The malice that flashed in those steel-rivet eyes held a chilling familiarity. 'Will your integrity survive the course of a formal Ceremonial Inquiry?'

Lirenda's skin rose to a violent flush.

'I thought not.' Selidie rescued her cooled cup of tea, tapping the gilt rim with a fingernail. 'Like Elaira, you must follow my bidding, even if that leaves you with lifelong penance, scrubbing floors in the Highscarp sisterhouse. Who listens to rancor from the mouth of the fallen? You are excused. Understand clearly just how low you have stooped through your weakness for Arithon s'Ffalenn.'

Trapped in the coils of her own indiscretion, Lirenda glared. Pride of upbringing choked her. Crushed under the wreckage of hope and aspiration, she found that Elaira's true spirit surpassed her. She herself lacked the insolent recklessness to cast fate to the wind for killing stakes. Her rage crumbled, impotent against the complaisance in Selidie's too-knowing regard. As Morriel, the creature had always danced her inferiors on puppet strings of indebtedness. Before her unprincipled act of possession had usurped a young woman's body, the crone would have measured and dealt with all setbacks that might steal her hour of victory.

Nor was her judgment of character inaccurate. Lirenda bent her head, unable to shoulder the shame of her outright failure. She could not follow through as Elaira had and stake the irrevocable loss of her awareness for the sake of compassionate principle.

Selidie's vile nature could not be exposed against the ruthless strength of a matriarch's hold on prime power.

Left no choice but to curtsey to the floor before her tormentor's false youth, Lirenda arose in smoldering capitulation and swept from the darkened chamber. Candles flickered and streamed acrid smoke in her wake. Their reflections flagged fire across the sere winter hills pictured over and over in the activated quartz spheres; and in the equally stony eyes of the impostor who wore the Prime's mantle on the dais.

The page boy flung open the paneled door to the corridor. Lirenda brushed past, well aware she had provoked a subtle and dangerous enemy. The cruel irony cut deepest: if not for the infamous Prince of Rathain, the Matriarch's chair would never have been tainted by the dark secret of immoral practice. Once, as entitled First Senior, Lirenda could have earned a legitimate succession from Morriel Prime without obstacle. But for Arithon's damning intervention and rogue cleverness, the wielded might of the Koriani Order should have rightfully fallen to her. With each step she took, Lirenda vowed Rathain's prince would be made to pay.

Given Elaira's permission to intervene, the geas driving Jaelot's captain could end in another failure. Arithon might survive his passage over Baiyen Gap. Lirenda ground her teeth, no less determined. Though ensuring his ruin demanded a persistence that lasted the rest of her lifetime, she would bide. The Master of Shadow would suffer the sting of her vengeance as long as he lived.

Proving

Outside the barred door to the Prime's private residence, Elaira braced her back to the courtyard wall. She sucked in steady breaths of chill air to slow the raced beat of her heart. Around her, the sounds of routine industry filed an edge on her acid-stripped nerves. She could not shake her looming sense of disaster. The facts all converged, unremitting: in the white wilds of Daon Ramon Barrens, five cities dispatched armed companies on forced march to take down Arithon s'Ffalenn. Yet no pending sense of the world's smashed equilibrium ruffled the winterbound city of Highscarp. A silvery trill of horsebells jingled down the lane beyond the gate. A servant banged open a second-story shutter and slapped the dust out of a bolster. Overhead, an ice crystal scumbling of cloud diffused the pyrite gleam of noon sunlight. The gusts turned northeast and smelled of the sea, sure signs that a gale would rage in before nightfall. The high mountain passes would lie sifted in snow, while the ridges shed their cover of drifts like fumaroles of blown smoke.

Storm and heartache came in lockstep with her mind-linked awareness: Arithon s'Ffalenn was still crossing the Baiyen, the conditions he suffered soon to become an onslaught of unalloyed misery.

As cuttingly cold, to Elaira's bare hand, was the quartz sphere Prime Selidie had given her. The binding directive attached to its custody offered no chink for compromise. The new Matriarch had matched her most desperate move, and her wits still recoiled on the outcome.

'*The bitterest enemy is myself, then,*' Arithon had once flung back when the Fellowship Sorcerer, Asandir, had pinned him on a fine point of principle.

For Elaira, who loved him, flesh as one flesh, understanding of his anguish bore down without mercy, the razor edge of her predicament resharpened by Sethvir's past assurance *that she would be party to the Prince of Rathain's final salvation or downfall.*

'Was *this* what you meant?' Her appeal to the Warden's earth-sensed awareness went unanswered, while the unkind wind off the bay tore her voiceless, and her knees refused to stop shaking.

'Oathsworn?' a boy's timid voice addressed, breathless. 'Initiate, do you wish a horse saddled for riding?'

Elaira stirred and regarded the young groom, her slate eyes still deadpan with shock.

The boy chewed his lip, then plowed ahead, gallant. 'The mare that brought you needs rest and feed. Should the house loan you a fresh mount?'

'Thank you, no.' Elaira pushed away from the wall, resolute as the first, unwanted decision snapped scattered thoughts back to focus. 'I won't be going anywhere I can't walk, but thanks for your gentleman's kindness.'

The quandary posed by her changed obligations presented a future fraught with bloodletting thorns. Where Arithon was concerned, she knew better than to trust Selidie's oath on the Great Waystone. Lirenda's warning concerning the new Prime had not been mentioned lightly. Wary of every unseen subtlety that might lurk to entrap her, Elaira chose to make her way without help. She dared not accept either post mounts or shelter from the too-open hand of the sisterhood.

'You have a mother? A family?' she asked of the horseboy.

His grin showed missing gaps where his lost molars grew in.

'Take this for their comfort.' She pressed a worn copper into the child's palm, offering the courtesy due from a guest stranger, and not an initiate sister whose order demanded unstinting service. 'Off you go,' she added, before he could shout his effusive gratitude. 'Fetch me the pack off my saddle, and see that the mare gets the rest she deserves.'

The delay to reclaim her belongings chafed at her ripe sense of urgency. Elaira gauged the entangling pressures that might offer pitfalls and setbacks. If she wished to forestall the obligations her low rank would allow the sisterhouse peeress, she must act now, before Highscarp's seniors discovered the Prime's grant of autonomy, or caught wind of her unorthodox assignment.

She descended the high road from the bluff on foot. Whipped by rising wind, she threaded between a cake seller's cart and two wagons and sheltered behind a smokehouse's woodpile. There, in brisk care, she bundled the burdensome scrying sphere into a silk scarf from her pack. Next, she counted her handful of coins, earned in the honest practice of dispensing simples and cough remedies in the wayside taverns. Two silvers, eight copper were scarcely enough to meet her critical needs. She would have to drive desperate, hard bargains to test the scope of the Prime's two-edged promise of independence.

As her first defined act to invoke that autonomy, Elaira tore off the bronze buttons she kept for luck, then gave her thick, purple cloak to the first beggar she found whining for alms in the street. 'Just turn the damned thing inside out,' she insisted, as the shivering creature fingered the distinctive color in apprehensive distrust of its Koriani origins. 'You'll stay just as warm, the lining's bleached wool, and no one will pay much attention.'

She asked for directions, found the common market, and spent her store of silver on a sturdy, used cloak of good weave that would be respectable once it was cleaned. From the smith's, for a half cent, she acquired a tarred leather bucket with a broken strap. The winds now were rising, and tasted of spume. Puddles wore glazings of rime ice. Like chalk marks under a poured-lead sky, gulls roosted on rooftrees and pilings and chimneys, breasts fluffed against inbound bad weather. Elaira pressed on to the dockside stalls, where seamy old women with crabbed hands and sharp eyes sold oddments of bone and glass jewelry, pomanders and luck charms, and the fish-scale talismans made to ward drowning prized by enlisted sailhands.

The ramshackle awnings cracked in the gusts. A shrill couple argued in the tenements overhead, while a dog pack nosed garbage in the gutter. Elaira perused tables of knucklebones and brooches, her flyaway hair tucked under her cloak, and her saddle pack guarded against cutpurses. Craftsmen and tosspots jostled their way past, and a street minstrel scraped jigs on a fiddle. At length, she found the item she sought amid a stall with tied bundles of cedar, and braided lanyards with hens' feet, and fiend bands of stamped tin and strung pebbles.

'Mother,' she said, 'I'm in need of your help.'

The old woman wrapped in faded plaid shawls perked erect, both eyes pearly with cataracts, and her arthritic hands clasped to her wash-leather satchel. 'Dearie, speak up. Henlyie's deaf as a post.'

Elaira smiled. 'I could whisper, and still you could hear me.'

The old herb witch blinked. She loosened a crabbed fist, and reached out, unerring. Her swollen fingers jinked the quartz crystal nested like a frost shard among her ragtag array of queer wares. 'Stone speaks, for you. How much can you pay?'

The ancient bronze buttons scored Elaira's clamped palm as she answered in trepidation. 'I can offer two coppers, and your pick of the rarest herbs in my satchel.'

Old Henlyie sucked a breath through gapped teeth. 'That desperate, are ye?'

Elaira shut her eyes, while the wind whined through the carved eaves overhead, and the thrash of the breakers against the seawall muttered under the boisterous shouts of the stonecutters on leave from the quarries. 'Mother, if you only knew.'

The old woman peered through fogged marble eyes, attuned to some cue beyond sight. 'Healer trained, are ye? Then ye know well enough, a true quartz will defend against lies and dishonesty. Go on, dearie. Take the crystal you need. Just give someone needy the eight silvers she's worth when you manage to mend your lapsed fortune.'

'Ath's blessing on you, mother,' Elaira replied. 'I'll see your kindness repaid tenfold.' She accepted the crystal, and left in its place a tin of her own spelled emollient, made to ease the pain of stiffened joints.

The old woman touched the tin, lifted it, and sniffed at the contents. A smile touched her face, easing the wrinkles pinched at the corners of her eyes. 'There's a boardinghouse with red shutters on Cod Street. The landlady there may let her attic for a penny, if you offer to attend the complaints of her guests.' The tin disappeared into the folds of the shawls, and a crabbed finger shook in admonishment. 'No, dearie. I have lodgings elsewhere, and no memory left for recording elaborate recipes. What meager craft I still practice is more suited to amulets, besides.'

'Then I owe you my heartfelt gratitude. Bless your days.' Elaira gathered the quartz and moved thankfully on her way.

Hungry, but in too much hurry to eat, she squeezed past the hawkers who sold bread, hot fish cakes, and sausage. The alley she descended led to the seawall.

The bay was a heaving cauldron of spindrift. Green, foaming breakers reared up, steep sides glistening, then hammered an uneven percussion of spray against the riprap that fronted the harbor. Wheeling birds landed in the sluice of the runoff, pecking for crustaceans stranded like jewels amid knots of jetsam and weed. Elaira braved the stripping brunt of the winds and filled her tarred bucket with seawater. In shrewd afterthought, she added a gleaner's harvest of kelp.

If she planned to earn bread treating quarrymens' pulped knuckles, she would need to replenish her tincture of iodine.

The owner of the red-shuttered boardinghouse was a vivacious grandmother whose shrewd glance measured the cut of her seal riding boots, then the quality tanning of the leather pack slung over her cloaked shoulder. 'One pence was summer rent,' she insisted, and held out her palm for two coppers.

Elaira gave in and paid her last coins, well aware hard-nosed bargaining would not prevail on a night with an easterly brewing. Her work required a roof over her head. Soup and coarse bread was included with lodging, and if she did not mind standing in line for the privilege, she could use the common washtub in the laundry.

'Just show me inside,' she answered, too chilled to stand on the icy stone step any longer.

The grandame regarded the brimming bucket askance, then grudgingly widened the door and admitted her. Elaira followed her shuffling step over worn runners of carpet, then up a servant's back stair. The attic landing led into a tiny room with a salt-streaked dormer window. The blankets on the truckle bed were moth-eaten, but clean. Beyond a washstand appointed with a battered tin cup and pitcher, the board floor was bare. Impressed by the size of the dust batts caught in the unswept corners, Elaira sincerely hoped the last occupant had earned her keep carding and spinning.

'Candles cost extra,' the landlady informed. 'Water's drawn from the crank well in the yard. Fetch and haul what you need for yourself.'

'Thank you.' Elaira stepped over the scuffed wooden threshold, cloak tucked against the drafts that sang through the gapped panes, and rippled the cobwebs over her head. Her breath scribed white plumes in the gray filtered light, and the basin wore armor-clad ice. She deposited her bucket of seawater and kelp, then latched the plank door after the landlady's departure. Still badly shaken, she scarcely cared that the garret room was unheated. Far worse, to try a course of questionable practice in the precinct of a Koriani sisterhouse.

'Dharkaron avert!' She was no small bit frightened by her plan to enact reckless upset to Selidie's expectations.

Elaira squared her shoulders, firmed quaking nerves, and raked the wet kelp from the bucket. She piled the mass by the frozen basin. Next, she unhooked the tin cup from the washstand and scooped it full of raw seawater. The tarred bucket remained under half-full, its handspan depth just sufficient. Elaira dug through her pack, fingers shaking. She removed the silk-wrapped weight of the scrying sphere. The dread burn of its active sigils of command cast a bone-chilling ache, even through layered cloth. In naked trepidation, on a pent breath of terror, she eased the veiled quartz into the saltwater bath in the bucket.

Sparks flew from first contact. A whine of released power threw off a hot wind as the sigils of binding tore asunder. Elaira jerked back a singed hand, while the water spat and roiled to the blast of unwound coils of energy. Crouched on her heels, her blistered hand cradled, she held on to hope that the quartz sphere could withstand the liberating force as the sigils dissolved without cracking.

'Be free,' she whispered in earnest encouragement. 'Let the spells of coercion be lifted.'

If the sphere had been loaned to help track Rathain's prince, she would employ her own skills, leaving no loophole for unasked assistance through the seals of a preset binding. There would be no fertile ground for slipped steps, no avenue left for blind snares. The Prime's bitter bargain to guard Arithon's life would not be won upon hidden traps or sly trickery. By nightfall this day, Elaira avowed she would cast off all resource upon which to hang the obligation of her order's oath of debt. If the hour ever came when for wisdom and compassion she must claim her given option to betray her heart's love, *she would use her own power by free choice*. Though she die in the effort, she would shoulder a future that relied on naught else but the course of her cognizant will.

The steps she must tread held no recorded precedent. Each minute brought dreadful uncertainty. The quartz she had cast to its fate in the pail offered no safe reassurance. While it thrashed and rattled and shook through its passage to a cleared state of neutrality, Elaira sweated and hoped. The striking eruption of violence appalled her, as the virtue of salt water stripped out the yoked power of uncounted active sigils. Every instinct shrilled with alarm. The process appeared to be lasting too long. She had been a six-year-old child when the order's seniors in Morvain had inducted her for her talents. All her Koriani arts had been learned by rote, her specialized experience aligned for an herbalist's practice.

Closed in the barren solitude of a two-penny attic chamber, the quartz sphere her need had put to the test delivered a stark lesson in humility. Elaira pressed shaken hands to her heart. 'Ath's mercy, forgive!' She realized how little she understood the coiling depths of the powers she engaged day to day, without thought, sheltered beneath the insular traditions fostered by the sisterhood.

Elaira endured, helpless and afraid as she measured the shocking scope of her ignorance. Compassionate care proved inadequate; her knowledge of healing fell woefully short. She had no advanced skills to ease the crystal through its rough passage. The efficacy of her talent fed through runes and seals, harnessed by the time-tested rituals that aligned cause to effect and bridged the veil in chained constructs that magnified will into raised power.

'Bide whole!' she entreated the traumatized sphere. 'Please. Don't let my folly lead to lasting harm.'

As though speech keyed response, the tempest in the bucket subsided. The churned water smoothed and settled to rest, with the crystal's clear structure unfractured. Elaira crouched on her heels, her limpid relief spiked through by renewed trepidation. The release just effected would not escape notice. Any flux of shed energy deflected the lane current, and the dispersal of worked sigils always released a distinct signature. The peer sister assigned to keep routine watch would recognize that imprint. She might wait until sundown and list the incident amid her routine report. Or she might be a scryer gifted with foresight and sound the alarm at the prompt of sharp-eyed experience.

Elaira wiped dampened palms on her sleeves, then unstuck the wisped hair from her temples. Time was her enemy. If she paused for one moment to nurse her faint nerves, a Koriani senior might break down her door under outraged instruction to stop her. For the willful step of blanking the scrying sphere posed but the first stage of necessity. Her next course of action was going to spark fury, if not an incensed cry for arraignment.

She shoved back to her feet. A questing sense of Arithon's awareness ranged in chills over her skin. She distanced his concern, too terrified to dwell on the chance of obstructive ramifications. Worst case, she might face the supreme punishment for oathbreaking, if Prime Selidie's promise of unfettered choice did not allow her to claim full initiative. Elaira braced against the washstand, too wrung with dread to question the price she might pay for unbending self-honesty. The tin cup with its fateful cargo of seawater all but slipped from her nerveless grasp. She forced her wrist steady. One by one, she stamped down the gathering fears that threatened to shred her resolve. Her love for Prince Arithon was caught in the breach. She dared do no less than employ concrete safeguards.

Elaira unhooked the silver chain at her neck and drew off the strung quartz that served as her personal spell crystal. Talisman for her power, carrier of the seals and sigils which held the focal point for her talent, the sliver of stone had been her companion since the hour she passed her novice initiation. Today, the flaring warmth of the stone's presence engendered no surge of confidence. Set against the Prime Matriarch's insidious designs, its familiar quiet radiance masked pitfalls and dangers. Elaira could not evade the harsh truth. The crystal itself belonged to the order. It would be reclaimed and cleared at her death, then reissued to another enchantress. The fact its possession was a borrowed resource could pose an unseen liability. Elaira poised the tin cup. Shaking, she prepared to reject the temptation that its everyday usage might serve to trap Arithon under Koriani obligation.

She would clear the quartz, living, and unbind its attunements, and bear the gamut of unknown consequences.

Poised over salt water, the crystal looked innocent, a flashy bauble that sheared light into rainbow refractions.

In reality, its function sustained an intricate balance of forces. A personal spell quartz bonded with its wearer. The complexity of its matrix evolved with use, often aligned with prerogatory directives imprinted by the will of the Prime's Senior Circle. Elaira fought ebbing courage. Twenty-eight years ago, Morriel Prime had selected her for longevity. The crystal held haplessly dangling had bindings laid into its fields that sustained and renewed living tissue. To clear out the quartz would disrupt patterned energies, with the recoiling effects of unsanctioned release rewritten in her hapless flesh.

All her experience with healing and craft lent no guidance to predict the near future. She had no grace for soul-searching thought, and no safe chance to seek deeper knowledge. The cleansing properties of salt were most final, and utterly unselective. Once the crystal was submerged, the spells of suspension that revitalized her body would unwind, then bleed away into entropy.

She could but hope, as she steeled nerves and will, that the shock of release would not kill her. To leave Arithon's fate to Lirenda's design posed the potential for outright disaster.

Eyes tightly closed, Elaira tried and failed to calm the rushed pound of her heart. The rasping itch of wool mantle against skin; the draw of each breath through her lungs; the tempestuous shrilling of wind: all subtle sensation conspired to unstring her resolve and mire her in hopeless dread. Life tied her too strongly. The looming fear of greeting death's shadow urged her to shrink from impeccable commitment. Worse, she might live, wasted or crippled by backlash thrown off as the linked sigils in her aura dispersed.

'Ath help me, I can't do this.'

Yet even as she wavered, stark honesty stung her. At the crux, she loved Arithon more. The integrity that cemented his trust crossed beyond life, went past nerve, flesh, and bone, and the bounds of sane limits and safety.

Elaira released the dangling chain. Hard braced for the shock of inflexible fate, she let her quartz take the plunge toward salt water.

The same instant, a firm hand closed over her slacked fingers. A half-sensed, fast movement, and a soft sigh of cloth intercepted the crystal's immersion. A gentle voice chided, 'There are better ways to establish the safeguards you seek.'

Elaira recoiled, instinctively too wise to scream. Her wide opened eyes met a white-robed, male figure who stood as though bathed in moonlight. His grip on her hand was warm, and not harsh. She could have pulled free on a wish, had she chosen. But the unearthly calm of his presence was not either forceful or threatening. The silver and gold ciphers that patterned his hood marked him out as an adept of Ath's Brotherhood.

'How did you get here?' she gasped, stupid and stammering with shock.

His smile lit the bare room like new sunlight. 'Sethvir of the Fellowship thought you needed help.' He released her fingers, then pried the tin cup from the frozen grasp of her hand. The fluid economy of poured water graced each move as he set the tin next to the basin. Then, his brown, almond eyes deep and grave, he regarded the spell crystal caught in the cloth-wrapped palm of his hand. 'Do you mind if I hold this?'

'By all means, be my guest.' Elaira stepped back, folded at the knees, and dropped rump first on the cot. Dust flew from straw ticking. She sneezed, blotted wet cheeks with the back of her wrist, then surveyed her uncanny visitor. 'If I had a chair, I'd invite you to sit. Since I don't, please feel free to share my perch on the landlady's mattress.'

Beyond middle age, Ath's adept inclined his head, then pushed back the folds of his hood. Graying ash hair tumbled over his shoulders. His face was strong boned, and serene as rubbed ivory, and his knuckles, workworn as a farmer's. 'Thank you. Be sure I won't stay one moment more than I'm welcome.'

'Sit then.' Elaira slid over and made room. 'Why didn't I hear you come in?'

His step on bare floorboards was light, but not soundless; his weight settled like snowfall beside her. His clothes smelled of balsam, and his laughter fell rich as the deep shade of tropical night. 'Well, you didn't because the gateway that brought me resides in the crystal you just claimed from the market.'

Elaira opened her mouth, closed it, and forcefully stilled her clamor of thunderstruck nerves. 'Then I need not be concerned that the peer seniors in my order should suspect I have mystical company?'

The initiate opened his palm and revealed her quartz pendant nestled inside a halo of grainy, gold light. 'You need fear for nothing. This room, and our words from here forward are as a dream, one step removed from the reality you know. Sigils can't breach this octave of vibration, far less carve a foothold for impact.'

'Traithe once built a fire,' Elaira allowed, too stressed and too tired to grapple nonlinear logic. 'Since your time is a gift too precious to waste, I'll let you explain without my green questions and curiosity.'

'On the contrary.' Settled at ease on his end of the cot, one shoulder braced to the wall, the adept seemed a figure loomed from ghostly silk and spun light from ethereal vision. 'Time is an illusion shaped by need and belief. The trust you have embraced for Prince Arithon's sake cannot be sustained without honesty. I'm here to open a doorway to knowledge, beginning with explanations.'

Elaira's expression of owlish thought broke under the relentless strain. She arose and paced. The cramped garret could scarcely contain the scope of the terrors that threatened to shatter her. Since the fires of Sithaer yawned at her feet, she opened the point that could catapult her into trouble. 'I made no conscious appeal to Sethvir.'

'You did not.' Ath's adept tracked her agitation, amused, but not patronizing. Aware her question scratched only the surface, he answered her core of concern. 'Your Prime Matriarch has been given no grounds to serve punishment, unless you can be taken to task for acquiring a piece of rock crystal. No rule forbids you. Yet there's a quirk in your order's history that's only revealed to those in the highest ranks. Your major focusing jewels, and all personal quartz crystals held in Koriani use, were never mined on Athera.'

Elaira poised against the ice-etched panes of the dormer, her level brows pinched with reflection. 'The stones were brought in when mankind begged sanctuary? Then those crystals won't be tied by the compact?'

'More.' Smile vanished, the adept met and matched her determined stance. 'Those crystals are not of Athera. Therefore they exist outside the scope of Sethvir's earth-sense, as well.'

The cold little garret seemed suddenly dimmer, though sundown was two hours away. Elaira tucked her fingers under her cloak to ward off a creeping chill. 'Are you telling me Althain's Warden *cannot see them at all*?'

The adept denied nothing. 'More to the point, Sethvir's gift grants him intimate contact with those crystals whose being evolved on Athera. Through the one the crone gifted, he captured the echoed cry of your tormented emotion. In his wisdom, he deduced your intent to be clear of the sigils of power your order enacts to imprint the face of creation. The step you just took on your own strength of character has opened an alternate path. Put simply, you asked. Ath's grace returns answers. My presence offers the means to pursue a gateway to higher understanding.'

Elaira swept back to her perch on the pallet, her gray eyes wide and intense. The first, incredulous tremor of excitement cut through clammy fear as she grasped the frayed threads of her courage. 'You are offering me power without strings to the order, that I might use for Prince Arithon's defense?'

'True power is neither given nor taught,' the adept said in mild correction. 'The key to the great mysteries is a gift to be claimed, arisen from wakened knowledge of the self. The course of discovery must be your own. I can serve as a mouthpiece for truth. You must draw the map. My words may affirm your first footsteps.'

Too cautious to trust fully, given her assigned charge, Elaira pounced on the glaring discrepancy. 'That's why you spared my quartz from being cleared in salt water?'

'No.' The eagle's gaze trained upon her stayed placid. 'That act was done on behalf of Sethvir.'

He would not elaborate. Ath's adepts were unyielding with

confidences, and this one volunteered no more insights. His kindly expression masked patience like rock, a firmness disarmingly gloved in compassion that would make its will known without force.

Elaira tipped her head back against the board wall, her fingers tight clasped to lock down her desperate uncertainty. She felt too tired and small for this task, and her wisdom, too young, or else bound too narrow by the didactic constraints of her order. The moan of the wind in the eaves and the distant shouts from the harborside offered no anchor upon which to hang the drift of her unmoored thoughts. If her sweating anxiety was not crisis enough, the intrusive creak of a step on the stair jolted her to alarm.

The adept quelled her panic. 'Dear one, don't worry. That's only a servant bringing the meal that comes with the cost of your lodging. The grandmother who owns this house thought you looked thin.' As the arrival knocked, he encouraged, 'Open the door, you're quite safe. The kitchen boy sent up with the tray won't see any trace of my presence.'

Elaira returned a look of raised eyebrows, then arose and crossèd the plank floor. Each movement felt awkward, all angles and noise before the adept's immaculate presence. Nor did his promise of anonymity fall short. The boy at the threshold proved painfully shy. Eyes glued to the floor, he passed her the tray with a few breathless words concerning the house tradition of hospitality.

'Please thank your grandmother for her generosity.' Elaira's warm smile raised the boy to a flush.

'Her kindness won't count if she catches me slacking.' He bolted downstairs, no doubt more unsettled by the fact she was spell trained, and a healer.

Left bearing a tray that was prodigiously laden, Elaira eased the door closed with her elbow. The bar was rendered unnecessary with an adept as her visitor. Since the room had no table, she could do nothing else but set the food on the pallet between them. Tempted by the rich odors of steamed mutton, fish soup, two loaves of brown bread, and last season's apples stewed in syrup and vinegar, Elaira recovered her humor.

'I do hope you're hungry,' she invited her guest.

'I'm content as I am.' The adept's courtesy was instinctive, as though his ear stayed more closely attuned to the scream of the wind clawing over the roof slates. 'Save what you can carry. You'll need sustenance on your journey.'

Caught dunking a heel of bread in the soup, Elaira glanced up, surprised. 'Journey? I'd thought to work healing in Highscarp until thaws.'

The adept turned his head. His desertbred eyes were unreadable in the storm gleam from the dormer, cut through the backdrop of gloom. 'You could do that. Or, if you wish to set foot beyond reach of your order, you might consider taking sanctuary. Our hostel accepts travelers. You must take the road toward Eastwall, anyway, if your Prime's charge sends you into Daon Ramon.'

Elaira bit into the bread, her methodical manner masking the bent of deep thoughts. 'My order frowns upon hostels,' she said slowly. 'Fourth-rank seniors claim that quartz crystals become altered if they are carried inside of your gates.'

The adept watched her, his settled quiet grown profound.

Tempted to walk the first steps of a riddle, Elaira rose to the challenge. 'Crystals change. Why? You will answer questions?'

'I will tell you truth,' the adept amended. 'The primary Law of the Major Balance states that where there is substance, or energy, consciousness exists also. Self-awareness in all things is Ath's unconditional gift, no matter the form of expression. Our Brotherhood keeps Ath's law before that of man. Therefore, any consciousness that finds the way inside our precinct is restored to its sacrosanct right of unfettered being.'

'Then the crystal kept under your province is set free,' Elaira concluded. The bread crust rested, forgotten in her hand, while her searching gaze sifted through the faint gold halo of luminosity released by the adept's tranquil presence. 'And what passes your gates abides first by Ath's law. Koriani power, then, cannot cross your threshold. I could enact the Prime's will concerning Arithon s'Ffalenn, and incur no tie of indebtedness to the order?'

'Those truths are self-evident, under the Law of the Major Balance. That precept holds the conscious will of all beings as sacred and therefore inviolate. I give you a parable.'

The adept paused, head tipped in tacit inquiry until he received her clear word to proceed. 'Very well. Two men rode horses into a hostel of Ath's Brotherhood. One was townborn, and his horse suffered a bridle and saddle, and was made obedient to his needs through domination and fear. The other man was clanblood, and drifter. His horse bore both saddle and rider without any bridle, or restraint by means of compulsion. Once inside our gates, both animals were stripped of their tack. They were left to do as their nature required. The townsman's horse cantered into the hills, and never returned, though a chase was mounted for days in the effort to recapture lost property. The drifter's horse remained standing at the gates. That one whinnied his glad greeting at his friend's return. One horse had a master, and the other shared a companion. Ath's freedom may be taken, or it may be given in accord with the law of free will.'

Elaira reached out of instinct and groped at the space where the quartz had hung, chained to her neck. Embarrassed, she swallowed. Beyond interest in eating, she set down the bread crust and regarded the adept who, apparently, had come at the Warden of Althain's behest.

'Sethvir believed that I needed protection. Since he acted to stop me from clearing my quartz, I need to see much more clearly. Can you lend understanding? There are complexities involved with this issue that I'm not wise enough to address.'

The adept inclined his head. 'Brave lady, had you cleared your crystal, there would have been trouble indeed. I came here as Sethvir's emissary, but I must serve as Ath's order demands. Your quartz deserves freedom, except its own will has granted you deference. It prefers to remain a Koriani tool, that you may preserve your given trust with the one known as Arithon s'Ffalenn. Stone is patient. It bides lightly in time. Count yourself honored. This crystal spirit has given you the accolade of naming you as a companion. Therefore, since you planned to relinquish your claim, I suggest you let me take the burden of carrying out its preferred intent. With your permission, I will bear the quartz back to your sisterhouse. Let it remain in the peeress's hands until you can safely resume your oathbound charge of its keeping.'

'I would be grateful, as well as content.' Self-conscious and flushed, Elaira pursued her dropped bread crust. Through the moment she required to recover her aplomb, the adept vanished without sound.

She started, glanced up, searched the shadowy space he had occupied. No visible trace remained of his presence, only a tactile patch of left warmth where he had sat on the coverlet. No small bit shaken that her spell crystal was also gone, Elaira swore like a fishwife. She had scarcely *begun* to ask questions.

Then, practical enough not to wallow in self-pity until the fish soup got cold and lost savor, she addressed the task of finishing off the perishable portion of her supper.

In hindsight, the adept had ceded her with fertile ground for new thought. Not all of her power derived from Koriani teaching.

In the course of expanding her study of healing, independence had brought her odd bits of hedge lore. She had once learned a hill grandmother's method of setting up wards using field stones. In principle, that knowledge might apply to a quartz, though the ranging of vibration directed by crude cantrips would become glass clear, and far stronger. By morning, the sphere in the salt bucket would be cleansed. She could borrow upon knowledge shared from Arithon's trained mastery and attempt to engage its Named spark of awareness. In addition, she had the untapped potential in the crystal point given by the talisman maker in the market.

If the adepts' store of wisdom might open an alternative way to access her natural-born talent, she must gather fresh courage, and against every obstacle, shoulder the risk in pursuit.

'Fiends plague and Dharkaron's Fell Chariot, but Selidie Prime and Lirenda are going to be furious!'

Raised to devilish good cheer by the prospect of being a thorn in the side of high-caste Koriani authority, Elaira mopped the last broth from her bowl. She devoured the plate of stewed apples. Then, wildly reckless, she commandeered her last cloth length of linen for bandaging and packed the leftover victuals into her satchel.

Outside, the silver-plate gleam of last daylight was already rapidly failing. Black runners of storm cloud drove in off the sea. The first, gale-force gusts slapped and battered the dormer's dilapidated shutters. The racket drummed a demon's tattoo against the bass-note pound of the surf boiling into the seawall.

At least savage weather would discourage the sisterhouse peeress from rousting the poor quarter for a renegade. Elaira stifled her wild burst of laughter as she imagined the outrage raised by Ath's adept when he knocked to deliver her spell crystal. Too bone weary to lug buckets for a hot-water bath, she steeled herself and settled for a bracing, cold wash from the basin.

Then she curled up under the blanket on the pallet and let her thoughts spiral toward sleep.

Before midnight, the storm broke. Elaira started out of unsettled dreams. She lay wakeful, strained and wary at each muted call of the watch from the street three stories below. Her overkeyed nerves would not let her rest. Worry circled her core of frustration. Over the whine of wind-driven ice, she ached for Arithon and Fionn Areth, one set on the run and exposed to cruel weather high in the Skyshiel passes, and the other gone outside her ken. While the dark fed anxieties that chafed her resolve to defeat the Prime's Matriarch's new plot, Elaira lamented her lowly third-rank status.

She had no means to access the Skyron aquamarine; nor could she breach its warded box and drag its dire weight through the gates of a hostel of Ath's Brotherhood.

If she traveled the high road to Eastwall and claimed temporary sanctuary, then Ath's order and the Law of the Major Balance might honor her born right to freedom. But the measure of reprieve from the Prime's reach and power could last only while she was sequestered. As long as the major focus crystal of the order held the bound record of her oath, she could not clear her imprinted Name from the matrix. The autonomy she had sworn into Koriani service would stay subject to Selidie's power.

Tidings

Asandir's night return to Althain Tower occurred without greeting or fanfare. He emerged from the flaring blue static of the focus circle to find the candles cold on their gryphon stands. His horse stood, still saddled, beside him. That fact served him rough warning: the pact Sethvir kept with the land's fey spirits, which normally assisted his arrivals, had fallen into neglect. He could not have encountered a more certain sign that Althain's Warden remained unwell. As the lane flux subsided to background quiescence, Asandir scanned the dungeon's chill silence. No wardings had faltered. Yet, in line with his bleak foreboding, no colleague stepped forth to greet him.

The play of raw lane force under his feet spoke of winter. He had been gone for weeks. He could but hope the supplies in the stable had not been despoiled by mice. Beyond exhausted, his rangy, tall frame was now chiseled lean from channeling the extreme, dire forces required to mend a torn grimward. He stroked the black shoulder of his equally tired horse, then gathered the reins between cinder-burned fingers. Underlit by the phosphor pallor of the runes that channeled the thrust of the lane tides, he slapped out a persistent, smoldering spark still raising smoke from his sleeve cuff. Then he addressed an eloquent apology in Paravian to his long-suffering mount, whose tail and mane had been singed to the same sorry state as his rider's tattered clothing.

Shod hooves clanged on the agate floor. The stallion trailed the Sorcerer's step off the inlaid patterns which scribed the grand rings of the focus circle. By the sidewall, Asandir unbuckled girth strap and bridle. He bundled his holed cloak and mopped the foam from the animal's face and lips, then rubbed down the sweat-drenched chest and flank, and the whorled hair left matted down from the saddle. The minor burns on fetlocks and cannon bones, he soothed with the healing of his spelled touch. When he straightened and strode into the portal which fronted the stairwell, the stallion pricked black ears and followed.

At the base of the stair, Asandir asked a permission. He spoke the true Name for his horse. The stallion whickered as though in reply, and stone responded, yielding up its fast secret.

An arched doorway melted into what had apparently been a seamless marble wall.

Beyond lay Althain Tower's snug stable, and an underground passage mazed with spelled gates that led to the fells outside. Aware he was home, the stallion shouldered eagerly over the threshold. The portal was guarded. Paravians had laid wards through the grain of the stonework. Life and movement awoke the soft sheeting flare of those latent powers. A misty light winnowed the animal's form as though testing each hair one by one. Despite mild appearance, the spell was not harmless. Had the horse still worn saddle or headstall, rope and leather would have instantly incinerated. An ill-set nail in any one shoe would have raised a snapped spark of warning.

Aware his mount's care had been measured to test his right to admittance, Asandir gave his true Name, then avowed, 'The black stallion, Isfarenn, stands surety for my given word.' As many times as this ward had challenged him, the Sorcerer still sucked a bracing breath. Then, in the respectful humility these protections demanded, he followed his horse's footsteps.

The ward forces combed *through* him and screened his integrity until he felt scoured from within. Although he experienced no painful discomfort, each nerve in his body was touched. Mind and heart were stripped bare. Paravian wards pierced through all deception, the merciless clarity imbued in their workings a violation of privacy to any creature born human. Asandir harbored no illusion. Had his horse suffered thoughtless harm at his hand, he would stand in peril of his very life.

Yet the proper permissions had been asked and given. Where hardship had taxed man and beast, the stallion Isfarenn had shared his great strength in free-spirited partnership. Asandir received his due grant of entry, untouched except for the festering blisters branded on him through his trials in the grimward.

The horse had already entered the near box stall, which had no door and no chain. Asandir fetched bristle brushes and set about grooming the animal's rank coat. When the black stud was dry, and sleek as new satin, he shook out fresh straw bedding, doled a generous grain ration, then filled the manger with clover hay.

The horse shook its crest and sighed deep with contentment.

'Rest as you can,' the Sorcerer agreed as he drew fresh water from the cistern. 'The gate to the outdoors is left open for your use. Roll on the downs as you please, but don't wander. I much doubt we'll be blessed with the option of staying in comfort at Althain for long.'

The stallion returned a companionable nose butt, then sloshed his filled pail. Asandir rubbed the intelligent, wide forehead. 'Once again, brother, I thank you.'

On departure, the stallion's true Name and contentment allowed the Sorcerer's safe return to the stairwell. While the arch faded away at his back, he swayed. Aching weariness dragged at his balance. Any bare-handed contact with grimwards wrought havoc. The insidious distortions of drake-dreams and the rip currents of primal chaos left a toll of leaching damage. The Sorcerer sensed the entropic tears laced through the ribbon-thin layers of his aura: the gadfly swarm of imbalanced energy required rest and patience to repair.

He steeled his worn spirit. Faced by the sure prospect of a swift return to the field, Asandir gathered Isfarenn's grimed tack. The saddlebags collected from the focus-chamber floor burdened his shoulder like lead. Since his life, and the world's fate, might come to hinge on his readied state of preparedness, the gear must be overhauled straightaway.

Fatigue made the stair interminably steep. Asandir paused between risers. He closed stinging eyes and, in iron fortitude, pressed his overfaced body to move on. Deadly languor enveloped him. He acknowledged the mental spur of alarm, and knew *he would have to keep moving*. The convoluted works of Eckracken's haunt had taxed him beyond prudent limits.

'For grace, and Ath's mercy,' he murmured.

A miracle answered. The burden of cinder-scorched harness was lifted out of his arms.

'In truth, Ath's mercy walks beside you, everlasting,' a voice greeted in gentle encouragement.

Asandir opened the leaden weight of his eyelids. Washed in a dazzle of soft, golden light, he made out the white-robed presence of two adepts of Ath's Brotherhood, one male, who took charge of the horse gear, and the other, a tiny, walnut-skinned woman, who extended a strong grip to brace him.

'Welcome home.' Her smile held the fire of a Sanpashir sunrise, replete with the promise of renewal.

Asandir took her hand in unabashed need. Gratitude filled his heart. Speechless, he bowed his silver head, and allowed her to tow his rangy frame up the long spiral staircase.

A wooden tub of heated water awaited in the chamber Sethvir kept to accommodate guests. Asandir had no chance to express thanks or show relief for that tender forethought. Met by lit candles and the fragrance of incense, he found himself accosted at the threshold by two more white-robed adepts. While the one with his trail gear hastened purposefully off, the new pair moved in without fuss to remove his scarred leathers and soiled clothing.

'Allow us,' urged the desertbred woman, whose tenacious grip resisted his urge to tug free. 'We were told you would thread Eckracken's maze, and leave the grimward by direct passage.'

In fact, expediency had demanded the Fellowship's field Sorcerer to do just that, his risky transfer accomplished by harnessing the dire vortex within the king drake's leviathan skull. Asandir found he lacked the strength to muster the courtesy to press the adepts for his privacy. 'Sethvir knows everybody's habits too well,' he agreed, stoic as the woman's neat touch eased off his singed shirt.

He was less able to mask his sharp flinch as the cloth scraped the blisters raised by rained cinders across his shoulders and arms. 'My dear, you know that hot water's going to sting like the eight blazes of Sithaer.'

The adept clicked her tongue and stepped back, leaving her male fellows to unlace the Sorcerer's smallclothes. 'The water is necessary to soothe your torn aura. We can reweave the ripped pattern fastest through that element. Unless you would rather be patient and rest?' Her laughter was liquid and silver, dancing antidote to Asandir's ripe flush. 'I'd thought not. If you wish to recover and ride out by dawn, you'll just have to sting, with our help.'

'How many of your Brotherhood have transferred to Althain?' Asandir asked, the concern in his tone gruffly testy.

'Six.' The female adept fetched cloth and soap, while her male henchmen helped his reeling step over the tub's rim and through the unpleasant shock of immersion. 'Bide and let go. Your colleague Sethvir is not left unattended. You shall receive a full summary of events just as soon as you regain your vitality.'

A scant hour later, refreshed and restored, Asandir dressed in a clean shirt and dark tunic, and his least-mended set of spare riding leathers. Neatly shaven, his hair a silver cascade on broad shoulders, he mounted Althain Tower's worn stair to pay a visit to the king's chamber. He went at the urgent behest of the adepts, before he looked in on Sethvir. Only the white-robed lady accompanied him. By time-honored custom, if the querent was male, a woman stood spokesman to reflect the balance inherent in Ath's creation.

'Sethvir is too taxed to share what he sees through direct link with his earth-sense,' she explained, her peppery accent spiking echoes throughout the drafty shaft of the stairwell. She wore her hood raised, the entwined ciphers of silver and gold casting soft radiance about her. 'Although in grace, our Brotherhood cannot use power to alter the way of the world, we can reflect the shape of events with the clarity of Ath's truth.' Arrived on the landing, she lifted the wrought-iron door latch. 'Go in. Behold the picked scenes Sethvir left in trust for you. As I can, I will answer your questions.'

Asandir reached out, gathered her sun-browned fingers into a hand as capable and callused as a laborer's. 'Dear lady, you've all done enough. I am grateful.' His understated touch as he ushered her aside bespoke an ironclad dignity. He was himself, his core power leashed to a presence as enduring as seamed granite. Wholly autonomous, he pushed back the oak door and entered the chamber himself.

The adept bent her head in frank homage as he passed, then trailed him inside and lit the wax tapirs in the claw-footed candelabra.

The glow enriched the gold grain of the curly maple paneling. A Cildorn carpet mellowed the plank floor, its vivid dyes muted before the jeweled silk of the heraldic king's banners. Despite vibrant colors, the chamber felt cold. No fire burned in the hearth. The scrolled, ebon pilasters and marble-topped mantel gleamed untrammeled by dust, and the high, lancet windows wore the seal of deep night. Stabbed through the perfume of citrus-oil polish, the still air gave off the uncanny, frost tang of magic.

Now wary, Asandir approached the massive ebony table, with its pedestals of standing, paired lions. His step skirted the empty oak chairs with their chased-ivory finials. Braced to neutrality, he leaned on spread hands and surveyed the circular pane of smoked glass Ath's adepts had placed on the tabletop. A sparrow perched on a chairback took wing and eerily vanished. A field mouse sat upright on tucked hind legs, whiskers pricked and attentive, while overhead its archenemy, the horned owl, blinked in disinterest from a settled roost in the rafters. Asandir showed no surprise. Such visitations occurred wherever Ath's adepts engaged a portal to tap the prime life chord.

'The glass holds those events Althain's Warden deemed important,' the lady ventured, her near presence casting a more refined light than common candleflame warranted. She perched on the seat nearest the black-and-silver leopard standard of Rathain, while Asandir, standing, absorbed the grim scenes gathered within the spelled glass.

He saw Kharadmon, far afield in the void between stars, spinning spell after spell of deflection to divert an influx of wraiths bound from Marak. 'Mercy on us,' he murmured in blanched shock. 'The worst has begun. What other ill news will you show me?'

Patient, the adept waited until Asandir had steeled his nerve to move on.

Next, the glass gave him sight of Luhaine's discorporate presence, guarding the damaged wards which secured Desh-thiere's prison at Rockfell. He awaited two others: Dakar and Fionn Areth turned their mounts loose and labored on foot through the arduous southwest passage across the white-crowned range of the Skyshiels.

He saw Arithon s'Ffalenn, asleep, huddled in a thicket; then armed companies from five cities converging on Daon Ramon, their purpose to bring war to the ancient ruin of Ithamon.

Farther south, the Master Spellbinder Verrain stood vigil at Mirthlvain Swamp. Methspawn stirred and fought beneath winter ice, feeding one on another in bloodthirsty eagerness for the release to come with the spring thaws. Traithe had left Vastmark with intent to assist him, but a flood on River Ippash would delay him.

Tension blanched Asandir's knuckles to scarred ivory against the jet grain of old ebony. 'We have no hand free to send,' he despaired, while in the glass, the events tied to Methisle streamed into the next change of scene. In northern Tysan, where Westwood's fringes thinned into a patchwork of hamlets, marauding Khadrim gorged upon the charred corpses of a trapper and his close family. 'Does this sequence get any worse?'

The adept held her counsel, aggrieved in compassion, while another view bloomed and burned across the dark face of the glass . . .

In the High Priest's chamber at Avenor, under furtive cover of night, the velvet curtains were drawn to hide the gleam of late-burning candles. There, a clandestine meeting commenced between Cerebeld and Lord Koshlin, Guild Master of Erdane, now appointed as his mayor's delegate to serve the city's close interests.

'I've maintained the appearance of keeping my Lord Mayor's instructions, and done your will without compromise,' the sly man complained. 'At every turn, I've thwarted the princess's inquiries into the death of her predecessor. Her Grace has been diverted from finding the truth so many times, she's justly begun to suspect my obstruction. Her trust is withdrawn. You must realize that leaves me exposed. At all costs, I can't risk the loss of respect should the mayor, her father, hear of her reservations.'

'I see that cost might prove a touch high,' Cerebeld agreed, his purposeful attitude undaunted. 'Therefore, we shall at one stroke change the princess's distrust to subservience.' He arose, crossed his chamber, and opened a locked chest. Gold rings glinted as he withdrew a sealed parchment. 'You shall give the lady the proof that she seeks: incontrovertible evidence that her predecessor's death was no suicide.'

Koshlin's saturnine features went slack. 'Proof?'

Cerebeld's suave manner made his scrubbed skin seem a mask of polished enamel. 'Proof, in the form of the sealed confession of the marksman whose shot sliced the rope. Lady Talith did not jump, but attempted escape on the hour she plunged to her death.'

'Volatile paper,' Lord Koshlin said. 'You dare much, to risk having her murder made public.'

'On the contrary.' Cerebeld riffled the document, nonplussed. 'The incumbent princess is distressed over her young son's assignment to ride with the field patrol. Desperation and motherhood make her mood unpredictable. Her Grace might try something regrettable. I want Ellaine cowed. She'll see how the last princess became a dead pawn, but not know the faction responsible. Fear will gag her questions. And where can this paper be taken, or shown, outside of her private chambers? She can't leave Avenor. Her guards and her handmaids are mine, every one. Her husband's kept his private distance since the heir's birth. The lady has no champion to pursue her sad cause. If you stay discreet, she'll have little choice but to retire in terrified silence.'

'Merciful Ath!' Asandir mused aloud. His seamed face turned

grim as a scarp of chipped granite, while far off, in the High Priest's closed chamber, the sealed parchment quietly changed hands.

Then the glass shifted scenes to reveal the tents of an Alliance patrol, horses and men encamped on the icy banks of River Melor.

'Sethvir has divined a threat to Prince Kevor, of course,' the Sorcerer said as his sharp glance encompassed the gold star banner flying amid the camp's standards. The blue field displayed the heraldic crown, proclaiming the presence of the blood royal among the routine, armed cavalcade.

'That boy's trueborn to his s'Illessid ancestry.' Asandir saw clear warning, that the endowment of that line's gifted justice might lead the boy to a disastrous confrontation with the pack of Khadrim seeding havoc and terror in Westwood.

'Time I went to Sethvir,' the Sorcerer announced. As the ominous record left in the glass subsided back into blankness, the silver-gray eyes raised to meet Ath's adept were recast to the glint of forged steel. 'If aught's to be done, the choice must be aired well before the lane tide rises at daybreak.'

The oak door sighed open and revealed velvet darkness. Silence greeted Asandir on the threshold of Sethvir's private quarters. The deep quiet bestowed no feeling of calm, but instead enfolded him like suffocation. The embrace of the air on his skin was too warm. Though the medicinal smell of sweet herbs was not cloying, every sense jangled warning he intruded upon something more than a sickroom.

'He's grown worse?' the field Sorcerer inquired of the adept who kept ceaseless vigil by the entry.

The gentle, aged woman turned back her hood. Her lined face a mapwork of patience, she said, 'The Warden feels no pain, nor is he unconscious. Though he might seem asleep, his state of suspension is dreamless. You may need to use Name to recall him.'

Asandir swallowed, for a moment not trusting the strength of his voice. 'Do candles disturb him?'

'Unshielded ones, yes.' Wise in her way, the adept said no more, but let Asandir enter the chamber by mage-sight. Ever so gently, she closed the oak panel to grant him full measure of privacy.

Left in darkness, his guidance the smoke-haze of spirit light, Asandir made his unerring way to the bedside. Sethvir rested amid the combed billows of his beard, the gnarled, clean hands abandoned on the coverlet too far removed from splashed inkpots and mischievous life. Ath's adepts had surpassed expectations in their meticulous care for him. The torn fissures in Sethvir's aura were reknit, the spindled gold halo without any shadow of seam. If the glow was too scant, its radiance dwindled, the cause would be Sethvir's willed choice. Minute to minute, he still poured out his vital forces for causes of perilous necessity.

Asandir paused. Upset by the pressures that demanded intrusion, he still groped for right words when a thready whisper arose from amid the piled pillows.

'Asandir? Is that you?'

The Sorcerer dropped to one knee. Through mangling emotion, he managed a reply. 'I am here. Say which grimward needs attending.'

The answer came back like a stab to the heart. 'There are five, but of those, Alqwerik's by Athir's most pressing.'

'I'll leave on the dawn lane tide,' Asandir promised, then drew a quick breath. 'No, please. Don't speak. The adepts kept their promise. I saw the unpleasant news left for me in the glass.' He need not belabor the obvious conflict, that of the multiple crises revealed, none could take precedence over the threat of even one distressed grimward. If the worst happened, and the flawed wards at Rockfell escaped Luhaine's vigilant guardianship, or if the wraiths questing from Marak slipped past Kharadmon's mazed defenses, there would be no way left on Ath's earth to recall him. No contact from Althain could cross through a drake-dream, even one spun by the ghost of a creature whose bones lay three Ages dead.

Hedged by the perils that closed on all sides, Asandir said in dire humor, 'If I meet disaster upon my return, at least I'll stand warned beforetime. You should rest.'

The stirred movement fanning through loose wisps of beard evinced Sethvir's harrowed sigh. 'No rest. Did you see? Davien's shade has left the refuge he built in the caverns beneath Kewar Tunnel.'

'Why should that surprise me? All else in creation seems ripe to breed chaos.' Just as troubled by thought of Davien's obscure motives, Asandir changed the subject. 'I saw that you fear for Prince Kevor's safety.'

'Worse,' Sethvir breathed in soft sorrow.

'Cerebeld wants him dead, that was glaringly plain.' Asandir leaned in close, elbow braced on the mattress. The other hand flexed to a fist on his knee, with his frown graven deep as worn leather. 'Beset as we are, who could stand by to help?'

'Ath's hostel at Northstrait lies along the first lane,' Sethvir pointed out, too enervated to be less abstruse.

Asandir weighed the statement, well aware that the Warden's checkered thoughts masked disarmingly shrewd ingenuity. 'Do you imply what I think?' Sharply fast to grasp strategy, the field Sorcerer clarified, 'You believe we could give Lysaer's heir a spelled talisman?'

Sethvir's eyes opened, heavy-lidded. To mage-sight, in darkness, their color shone an eerie, serene aqua that reflected a sense of vast distance. Asandir, watching, felt a bolt of black fear strike straight through him. Never before this had he seen breathing life so closely mirror the infinite. 'Tell me in words. You need grounding. I can hope speech will help.'

'The rock, chastising air?' The ghost of a smile turned Sethvir's lips as he struggled to meet the demand. 'I'd hoped the same plan might be used to spare Arithon, but the adepts refused me the use of a talisman as a bridge. They perceive very well that his Grace of Rathain's become too fated a cipher.'

'No hostels remain active in Daon Ramon, anyway. Who else could have handled the problem?' Asandir hooked a footstool, dragged it close to the cot, and assumed the unlikely perch. His lean length of limb and innate balance lent him the hunch of a wing-folded heron. 'If Prince Arithon was refused, what grounds would grant an appeal for a boy not brought up to honor the old ways? Why should Ath's Brotherhood offer their sanctuary to safeguard Kevor s'Ilessid?'

'I can't promise they would.' Sethvir's brow furrowed. '*But suppose* we created a talisman stone, imprinted with spells based in parallel with the powers that rule the scrying glass in the king's chamber. Say it was delivered by a messenger who would not be heard, unless the young prince showed the honesty of his blood heritage.'

'You mean, test him?' Asandir leaned forward, braced on crossed forearms. The idea had merit. Heirship was sanctioned along similar guidelines. 'If Kevor has the bare-bones humility to hear truth, and honors his heart ahead of the mores of his upbringing, I catch your drift.'

Sethvir's eyes closed, his flesh like worn parchment beaten by storm to its craggy template of bone. 'We could at least be sure the adepts at the hostel were made aware of his fate. Their compassion would mark his innocence, even if for a moment.'

'But a moment might suffice.' Lifted beyond pity by a glimmer of hope, Asandir traced the complex thread of logic himself. In extremity and need, the young prince might raise enough emotion and desire to engage the innate talent of his ancestry. Given the birthright of s'Ahelas descent, in theory, Kevor *could tap that stream of raw power himself.*

'Assuming that boy's gift is strong enough.' In desperation, or extreme pain, he might unwittingly waken his own talent and tear through the veil into mystery. If so, conscious forces pooled within the sanctuary *might* answer and draw him to safety. A desperate long shot. Asandir shook his head. 'Even if all those unlikely conditions were met, you know, in the hands of Ath's Brotherhood, we must lose him.'

Althain's Warden dredged up his reply, whisper faint. 'We've already lost him, entangled as he is in town politics and the thorns of Avenor's false doctrine. At best, through a talisman, Lysaer's son might be given a slim chance to claim his redemption. Would you lay the conjury into the stone as a boon, done for me?'

'You've already culled a volunteer messenger? Since I won't have to ride the west trade road in winter, I'll have the work done before daybreak.' Asandir gathered the limp hands which rested in disarray on the blanket, then gave back his firm reassurance. 'One of the river pebbles you've cached in the library will surely be willing to give us the necessary service.'

He arose on the promise he would bid farewell ahead of his departure at dawn.

Yet before he could go, the outer door cracked. A female adept he had not seen earlier asked her permission to enter. 'A message has come from our hostel in the Skyshiels.'

Asandir straightened, half-braced. 'More bad news from the east?'

The adept shook her head. 'Rest easy, no. The Warden's desire was met. One of our Brotherhood went to Elaira. Her spell quartz has been sent to her peeress, uncleared.' Which meant the order was not yet the wiser for the fact the imprinted longevity bindings on the enchantress's life had been supplanted by Fellowship crafting.

Asandir stood, eyes shut through a moment of welling gratitude. Then he regarded his prostrate colleague and sensed the frail but mischievous encouragement sent by thought across the blanketing darkness. Sparked into hope too fierce to be guarded, he dared to frame the bold question. 'You had an adept make contact with Elaira?'

'Better still,' the adept ventured, unoffended by his insolence. 'By morning, the enchantress intends to set off for our hostel in the mountains by Eastwall.'

'But that's brilliant!' His turbulent gaze still fixed on Sethvir, Asandir pondered the startling range of changed impact. Jubilation broke through his most solemn restraint. 'You're a fiendish, hard taskmaster. Why else would you hold the cheerful gossip for last?'

A hitched sigh of cloth, as Sethvir stirred under his mantle of comforters. 'You know why.' Any one of the quandaries left mapped in glass could cancel out hope at a stroke. 'The adepts will explain what has passed with Elaira. Did you want our pacts renewed with the earth sprites who tend the lower dungeon gate spells? Then leave me in peace. Or your black stud won't stand saddled and waiting by the circle on the hour you take leave for Athir.'

Winter 5670

Couriers

Covered by night in the forest of Halwythwood, a clan rider leaps from a steaming mare, bearing urgent word from the north. 'Morvain's got a war host on the march in Daon Ramon, and headhunters ride out of Narms, led by Lysaer s'Ilessid himself. Find a fast horse and a rider double quick. Lord Jieret must be told he's going to receive swarms of unwanted company at Ithamon . . .'

Two hours before dawn, Asandir twines talisman spells like fired ribbon between layers of a water-smoothed bit of quartz; once the power coils in balance at the heart of the pebble, he sets his work into concealment with a blessing rune drawn in Paravian, then places the construct on the windowsill, where an owl swoops down on silent wings, then flies off with the stone clutched in needle-sharp talons . . .

In the royal suite of Avenor's state palace, Lord Koshlin bows, ending his private audience with Princess Ellaine, and moved to pity by her terrified pallor, advises: 'Your Grace, the contents of that document are too damaging to set into a letter. I recommend that you burn the evidence at once, and trust me to bear word of the sensitive issue back to your father in Erdane . . .'

V. Spinner of Darkness

Morning broke over the Eltair coast, savaged in the black teeth of yet another onshore gale. This pelting storm struck days after the Koriani enchantress, Elaira, took her courage in hand and set forth to seek sanctuary with Ath's adepts. By then, Arithon s'Ffalenn sheltered in the ramshackle cabin of a fur trader who set traplines in the remote Skyshiel uplands. His host was a solitary, half-breed clansman who had pulled him, unconscious, from a snowdrift.

On the subject of harboring dangerous fugitives, the huge man proved cross-grained as pig iron. *'Won't see a man needy, and not take him in. You want to march out and die of the elements? Then say so. I'll show you a knife-edged cliff to fall off that'll save needless bother and suffering.'*

Two armed parties from Jaelot broached his glen. Their harrying, rude search of his humble dwelling did not change his adamant generosity. He hunted as usual, leaving Arithon the tools and new planks to repair the smashed wood of his doorjamb. The traplines replenished his ransacked larder. His rice and his millet he stored elsewhere to foil rats, and the only living creatures he refused to show welcome had hooves and smelled like horse.

The tough gelding and two extra mounts claimed as spoils

from pursuers sent to grief in the Baiyen were turned loose to graze in the deep valleys. From the hour that Arithon regained the strength to stand upright, they were thrown fodder and grain from the store left by Jaelot's decimated supply train. Today's whiteout blizzard just made that necessity harder to carry out. The valley cleft where the herd of three sheltered was silted chest deep in fine snow. The horses huddled, tail to wind, in a fir copse, visible only if a man knew where to seek them. Arithon doled out their daily ration and chipped the balled ice from their hooves.

Then he faced back the way he had come, barraged by the hags' chorus of weather. He was well clad against the assault, given leggings sewn from second-rate pelts and a hooded bear coat from the trapper. Underneath, he still wore his own fine tunic and hose, torn and repaired many times, but still prized, since silk retained the warmth under furs in peerless comfort. He carried a bow, and tinder, and sharp steel, small precautions that counted in a Skyshiel gale, when cloud and relentless snowfall mantled the high peaks, and strength and experience lent no guarantee in the brute fight to maintain survival.

Arithon plowed through a drift, the track he had broken scarcely minutes before already erased by the screaming wind. Through the worst gusts, he paused, blind and deafened. The most trail-wise of men could lose his bearings amid such extreme conditions. A wrong turn could drop him over a precipice, or send him sliding down the cleft of a ravine. Nor did he care to stumble headlong into an armed party of guardsmen.

Ruled by raw nerves and wary care, he slipped under the heaped boughs of a fir copse. Snow funneled in hissing currents around boles scoured clean of summer moss. The high-country weather spared nothing living; browsing deer had pruned the low-hanging branches, and the lichens that clawed out a lee-side existence wore hoarfrost feathers of ice. Here, deadfalls might lurk under covering snow, the stubbed ends of snapped limbs poised like spikes to pierce through a boiled-hide boot sole, or twist an ankle on an incautious step. Arithon carried a staff for safe footing, and a hand compass in a bronze case.

A gust moaned and built to a shrieking crest. Arithon sheltered his face in his hood through a flaying barrage of sheared ice. He poised while the storm's ferocity relented, as acutely aware as wild prey that the eye of the hunter would be drawn to movement. Sound reached him, instead, the chiming ring of clashed steel, broken by distant shouts. Then he caught the taint of smoke, borne down the length of the valley.

'Merciful Ath!' Arithon burst into a flat run, not back toward the horses, but ahead, in a sliding, tree-dodging charge that led toward the fur trapper's cabin.

He could make no speed. The deep drifts and precarious, iced footing combined with blinding snowfall to slow him. The healing scar on his wrist bound free movement as he cast off his staff and clawed the strung bow from his shoulder. More clumsy, the right hand: the canker left by Fionn Areth's sword thrust still oozed and bled through its tightly strapped dressing. Despite tendons that throbbed in fiery pain, and the swelling of traumatized tissues, Arithon groped for an arrow.

The tang of smoke thickened. Then the baritone voice he knew as the trapper's climbed into a shredding scream. Arithon plowed ahead, fatally slowed by the uncertain ice of a streamlet. Too late, he knew as the cry shifted pitch. However he sprinted, three hundred yards and a dense copse of fir still separated him from the clearing. He drove himself onward, a punishing effort marked by searing breaths of chill air. Once inside the trees, the low branches hampered him. He fretted, inwardly cursing the care he must take to avoid the whipcrack report of snapped sticks. Each delay cost dearly. Smoke now rolled uphill in charcoal billows, acrid with the resins of burned pine logs. Men called and laughed, and a jangle of bit rings chimed through the covering forest.

Arithon worked his way downward in sangfroid awareness that even one rolling snow clod would serve warning and set Jaelot's reivers upon him. The crackle of flame and a fanned gust of heat told him the cabin was burning beyond salvage. Past the trees, a horse snorted. An officer shouted a command, then wheeled his mount and trotted across the clearing. Through the snow-draped fringe of the firs, Arithon saw flurried movement as six more riders clambered astride and bunched back into ragged formation.

'Make that wretch sing like a lark as he dies!' someone called. The small column wheeled and moved on down the draw.

Arithon used the masking noise of their departure to close the last steps to the edge of the fir copse. Knelt down behind a thin screening of branches, he took stock.

The one-room log shack was a mass of gold flame, the roof timbers a sagging scrim of smudged embers. Amid trampled snow, splashed scarlet and pink, two men knelt over another, stretched prone. One pinned the trapper's roped wrists in restraint. The other set to with bare hands and a gore-drenched long knife, to a grunting jerk of agony from the victim. A third man stood guard, thumbs jammed in his sword belt.

'Where is he?' questioned the tormentor, his wet fist and blade on a questing course over bloodied, quivering flesh. 'Tell us, and your agony can be ended at once.'

'I trap animals, not princes,' came the ragged reply. 'I don't know any royalty.'

'Pity, then,' said the knifeman, unaware of the eyes that watched from the wood, or the hand which nocked patient arrow to bowstring and released in the lull between gusts.

Arithon's shaft took the standing guard through the throat. The man clawed once, coughing blood, then toppled.

'Bowman!' The brute wielding the knife jerked erect, then dived flat, unsure where in the trees the attacker lurked in ambush.

His companion was a half second slow to react. The next arrow ripped through his abdomen. He sprawled, screaming, over the legs of the trapper, who jackknifed and kicked out. A brutal strike with a hobnailed boot smashed the gut-shot man in the skull.

Arithon nocked a third shaft, but spoiled the release as the bowstring ripped from his lamed fingers. Before he could draw again, the wind blew a veil of snow over the clearing. The knifeman snatched his moment, and charged. His scrambling plunge into the fir thicket was met by the black steel of Alithiel, wielded with left-handed, lethal precision in a thrust through the solar plexus.

'Damn you to the joys of Dharkaron's Black Chariot!' Arithon set his foot on the twitching corpse, yanked his streaming blade free, and ended the man's ugly, whistling shrieks with a mangling slash through the throat.

Bow and sword still in hand, he thrashed out of the tree line and slid to his knees in the rucked snow next to the trapper. 'They're dead. Be still.' He raised his blade, cut the black-and-gold surcoat off the guard's corpse, and used Jaelot's lion to stanch the flow of the bone-deep gash in the thigh of the man who had given him shelter.

'Say I won't lose my leg, and that you're not royal,' the wounded man gasped through locked teeth.

'You won't lose the leg,' the Shadow Master assured, then cursed the unhealed scabs that marred his accustomed dexterity.

An interval passed, while the wind screamed and buffeted. Arithon packed a compress of snow over the knifeman's unspeakable handiwork. The injured man shivered and moaned at his touch, unstrung by shock and suffering. 'Just say you're not royal!' he hissed through blind agony.

Arithon stayed silent, but in relentless efficiency bundled him into another dead enemy's mantle. The trapper stared upward into a face of black hair and green eyes set in steep, angled features. 'If so, damn you, man! You should never have come back. Your vengeful spree of slaughter can't help but draw notice.'

Arithon laughed with an edge like smashed crystal. 'Ath, I hope so!' His tone more chill than the storm's, he added, 'By my name and ancestry, may I never condone such an act of extortion and cruelty!'

In anguish, again, 'Say you're not s'Ffalenn born!'

Arithon paused, rinsed in gold light by the flames, now chewed through the cabin's four walls. He evaded, 'There's truth to the claim I'm a bastard.'

'Go, get out.' The huge trapper cried out at the delicate probe of the fingers that explored his gashed abdomen. 'I'm a dead man. As a healer who's seen wounds, you know this.'

Arithon shook his head, tied the stripped cuff lace and torn shirt into another snow compress.

Between dizzy bouts of pain the trapper gasped argument. 'Those vultures from Jaelot are witched men, I swear, with your Grace bound as someone's prized quarry. It's unnatural. As many times as my cabin's been searched, they come back. They're out in a gale in the Skyshiels, pure folly! Even a pack of fell fiends out of Sithaer would have long since turned tail and gone home.'

'Well, they haven't discovered your root cellar yet.' Arithon applied pressure to close a slashed vein. 'My hand has scarred over. I've just proved I can hunt. Your traplines should not be beyond me.'

'Are you listening?' The trapper's weakened struggles did nothing to curb the care taken to stanch the blood flow leaking from his mauled organs. 'I can't survive.' He added the list, in graphic, hard logic, of the inexorable course of a stomach cut.

'Your fate seals my conscience,' Arithon agreed. Then, stilled and grave, his words chisel-punched through the crackle of flame, he swore the oath of sovereign prince to bound liegeman. *'For the gift of feal duty, my charge of protection; for your loyalty, my spirit shall answer, unto my last drop of blood, and until my final living breath. Dharkaron witness.'* He knotted the compress, then finished, 'You didn't betray me.'

The trapper turned away his gruff, bearded face, unprepared, and embarrassed to be touched to sentiment. 'Don't mistake your importance, prince. I wouldn't give Jaelot's dogs a stripped bone.'

'I don't leave them my wounded,' said the Prince of Rathain. He arose, yanked the cloak off the third corpse, and breathed a blessing to Ath's grace as he found the trapper slipped beyond consciousness. At least that small mercy would spare him the torment of being moved in the sling of a drag litter.

Three days later, the fur trapper used his last, labored breaths and named his next of kin to his prince: an uncle who ranged with Earl Jieret's clans in Halwythwood, and a married daughter settled with a cooper in Eastwall. ''Twas my grandame who said I'd die tended by royalty. She had clan lineage, and with that, the born gift of Sight.' A long pause, then the afterthought, trailed off in self-damning irony. 'Though I thought these mountains were as far as a man got from the finicky habits of princes.'

Arithon gathered the slack, cooling hand, his touch firm through the wracking spasms. 'My finicky habits don't run to court ceremony. But that doesn't explain the big-hearted trust that stood ground under torture to spare me.'

'Thank grandame for that,' gasped the trapper, eyes closed. 'She said I would choose if the prince who called down Dharkaron's Black Spear died beside me.'

'You failed nothing and no one,' Arithon assured, though remorse all but choked him from speech. 'I could name you hero, gild a plaque in your memory that proclaims the cornerstone for a crown will stand on the strength of your sacrifice. But the truth casts down rhetoric. A man who holds hospitality sacred is worth much more to the land than a king.'

For answer, an unearthly sweet smile touched lips already blued to corpse pallor. 'Long life, and my blessing. The Fellowship Sorcerers are right to restore you.'

Arithon bent his head. Left beggared by a giant's generosity of spirit, he said nothing through the final, torturous hour while the huge man's wracked lungs fought an exhausting passage, and the heart labored through the gasping last rattle of breath.

Nor did the ending bring peace or reprieve. Arithon arose. Though the hour was past midnight, urgency rode him. He packed satchel and saddlebags by the flickering glow of a precious stub of wax candle, then bundled his weapons and provisions outside. Around him, the night was a wind-tossed maelstrom, stars and moon mantled under the cloud of another westbound storm front. Threat of snow rode the air like subliminal lightning. Arithon ached for grief, but dared not pause for decency. He sealed the trapper's remains in the root cellar, unable to grant the small grace of a pyre, or a bard's song to honor the crossing. Not while Jaelot's patrols swept the territory in force, lashed on by their zealot captain. The sole tribute he could grant this man's sacrifice was his unbending dedication to survive.

Arithon judged his best chance was to travel fast and far as he could before daylight. The diligence of his care meant the horses would answer his whistle for feed in the dark.

The thirty-five-league passage through the Skyshiel uplands resumed and became a feat of grueling endurance, on both sides. Driven off the Baiyen trail by unsettled dreams and queer hauntings, and chased by the balefire of ghosts, Jaelot's troops scoured the high forests in small search parties. They rampaged down slopes of pristine snow, and axe-cut young trees for their bonfires. Flame was believed to drive back the haunts, and proved more reliable than the echoing dispersion of horn calls as a signal to muster or regroup.

Men quartered the gulches and ridgebacks on foot, or plowed in mounted columns through winding valleys. Despite ice and winds and bleak storm, they persisted, while their quarry slipped past like the fox. He evaded their lines, unseen and unheard, under cover of shadow, or night. The wind and the elements were his tireless ally, until the skilled trackers exchanged sullen whispers, calling him demon and fiend, an unnatural sorcerer who left no footprint on the worldly face of the landscape.

Then contrary evidence would move them to scorn, as they found frozen hoof marks and dung, or broken ice on a stream, or a swatch of young maple bearing the teethmarks of browsing horses.

Several times, a rider was spotted, crossing over a ridge. The men dispatched to investigate circled and climbed, but found only unscalable, ice-clad ledges, where neither horseman nor unmounted scout could give chase. Some claimed the sightings were apparitions designed to lead them astray; others argued that sorcerers had spellcraft which enabled them to walk upon demon-made bridges of air. Whatever the subject of carping dispute, the conclusion was self-evident: Jaelot's pursuit of the Spinner of Darkness was a harebrained feat of madness in the Skyshiels.

And yet, the guard captain held his ground, unremitting. Jaw hard, eyes narrowed, with gloved thumbs jammed in the cross belts that hung his hunter's quiver and map case, he insisted, 'Mayor'll dice my liver if we turn back without the quarry we came for. Now saddle up!'

No suggestion to withdraw was allowed thought or weight.

The order to advance stayed relentless. Each dawn, the parties ranged outward in search.

For Arithon s'Ffalenn, the nights passed in desperate flight, those days he was flushed out of hiding. Time and again he was turned from his course, or hazed between patrols back over terrain just traversed through rugged hardship. The days became patchworked fragments of memory, stitched together by dark intervals spent in furtive flight, or tension that wore like etched acid. One fair afternoon, armed riders overtook him when he went foraging for wintergreen to brew an astringent for his gelding's puffed fetlock.

Snow and fierce wind had masked their approach. Caught in the open, Arithon scrambled up rocks and snatched refuge on a cliff ledge scarcely an arm's reach over their heads. There he panted, chilled and motionless, while one man dismounted to piss in a snowdrift, and three others cut diligent circles below him. In sore misery themselves, the scouts missed the dimpled depressions of his footprints; the drifts, dry and light, were too fluffy to hold outlines. Had a man of them glanced upward, he was utterly exposed. Nor could he attack and kill all of them cleanly before someone sounded the alarm.

The rider who relieved himself mounted up, whistling, and the patrol moved off up the ridge. Arithon laid his cheek to iced stone, wrung wretched with shivering relief.

Days and nights, he endeavored to keep faith with Luhaine and reach promised refuge at Ithamon. He dogged his own hunters to steal cached supplies, then set off through seamed cliffs to the high country. Nights, under starlight, he picked his way over the scoured rock past the timberline. Shadow masked him, while his ears rang and burned to the language of wind, singing litanies over bared granite. He weathered gales in the smothered glens of the valleys, and slept under banked drifts, the warmth of his breath pocketed by the laced boughs of the firs that framed the eaves of his crude shelters.

He tracked deer, and surprised wolverine, and drank bracing waters freed from their armor of gray ice. His beard grew. The jet hair he had no chance to groom whipped in snake tangles over his shoulders. His eyes creased with the squint of haunted apprehension, and constant survey cast down his back trail. The sun shone on him, gold and glaring and without warmth, and the snows howled and stung, lashed by the bitter east wind. Higher, he ranged, into the black-stone summits of the Skyshiels, laddered with glaciers and the cobwebbed patterns of snow trapped in filed bands of sediment. Nor was he free, or alone in that wilderness that could and had torn the sinew out of all but the strongest hearts.

Against natural odds, beyond the limiting frailties of flesh, Jaelot's bewitched guardsmen tracked him. He watched them, filing like ants up the valleys, or burning fires of green fir that streamered flags of smudged smoke. He saw them break and run from the queer lights on the Baiyen, and wait, starving, for their supply lines. Like desperate, flushed game, Arithon ran before them, sometimes in the same glass-eyed panic, and other times in nerveless planning that left him as a stranger to himself.

The hand that stubbornly failed to heal grew a mass of raw, welted scar tissue. He boiled rags for bandages, and rebound the weal, and used his blades left-handed. In tight-focused effort, he mastered the pain and forced his arrow shots accurate. The few times he killed deer, they died cleanly. In their swift death, he found his sole measure of victory: his private, ongoing reassurance he had not been abandoned by mercy, and could still grant the same grace to an enemy.

Winter deepened. The high peaks wore stainless mantles of white, between storms that ripped them to bare bedrock. Always hungry, never warm, Arithon pressed northwestward, and always, his pursuers dogged him. He lost his brave buckskin down a ravine, had to sacrifice an arrow to dispatch him. Nor could he pause to salvage the meat. The gelding's scream as it fell had drawn wolves and men in a primal rush for the carcass. But the wolves adhered to natural instinct; they stopped and gorged. The men, geas driven, trampled the streambanks, but found no means to scale the high cliff face.

Safe on the rimwall, Arithon fled, while the horn calls echoed and reechoed, calling in the reinforcements that kept him dodging throughout a miserable night. Dawn found him sprawled like an animal in a khetienn's lair, while the displaced feline hissed protest, wedged into the sinkhole where the earth had caved away from a tangle of tree roots. Arithon spoke to her, the magnificent instrument of his voice burred rough with disuse. He wept then for sheer grief, that the grand resonance of his words in the ancient Paravian had lost their skilled music to calm her.

When he woke, hours later, the enraged cat had fled. Every muscle and sinew in his body had an ache, and cold willowbark tea scarcely tamed them. His trail-hardy mare had long since lost her shoes. Arithon seared the cracks in her hoofwalls with a red-heated knife, lest she split to the quick and go lame. The gelding with the puffed fetlock improved, but still could not bear a rider. He packed the supplies, uncomplaining, his coat rough and lusterless from hard use and an uncertain diet.

'When we reach Daon Ramon, you can paw for dried grass,' Arithon soothed. He ran his hands down both animals' ice-crusted legs, checking for heat in the tendons.

And the day did come finally, when the mountains relented; when the stone-clad heights receded from the cloud hems, and the trees in the valleys stretched tall and majestic with the shelter of lowering altitude. Snow sifted down, deep and smooth in the hollows, storm winds having shrieked and broken their force on the unyielding ramparts of the ridges. Arithon left the lichen-bare rock of the timberline behind him, and saw, from the north-facing gaps between ranges, the white sweep of Daon Ramon below him.

The triumph of that accomplishment was short-lived as a horn blast from behind set him under close-pressed pursuit. Arithon ran ahead, driving his tiring horses into the dense growth of a thicket. Then he retraced his steps and whisked out their hoofprints, and laid another false trail to a streambed. For a blessing, this time, the swift current had thawed. He plunged in, left the trackers the logical conclusion he had masked his trail in the water, but escaped by hauling himself into the drooping boughs of an evergreen. Tucked in the branches, he waited, unseen, while his hunters gouged the streambed to stirred silt and muck. They moved out at last, split up, north and south, in mistaken belief he would have made egress elsewhere.

Twilight fell. The drifts lay on the land like iridescent silk, tucked in folds of cobalt and violet beneath a sky deepened to indigo. Under a spattered brilliance of stars, Arithon climbed down from the pine that had sheltered him. He cut a furtive path over the snow his enemies had left trampled to confusion. Masked under shadow, he collected his horses and moved on, toward a plain that, by nightfall, unveiled the hot sparks of a dozen enemy campfires.

The despair of his straits washed over him then, a powerful force that made even the effort of hope a travail. Alone amid the whine of cold wind through acres of winter-stripped boughs, he longed for Caolle's hard-bitten advice, or Earl Jieret's firebrand tolerance. Elaira's love seemed a figment of dream, and there, too, fate denied him fulfillment. Arithon endured the dismal ache of his solitude, his relief a set litany, that this time no friend would die in heroic effort to spare him. He closed his sound hand over the frozen leather of the lead reins and sought after the comfortless shelter of a south-facing ravine.

Through the night, he lurked hidden in the deepwood, and kept sleepless watch for patrols. In a day, perhaps two, the next blizzard would roar in. While a storm masked the telltale trace of his footprints, yet again he might seize the advantage and slip past the cordon Jaelot's men cast ahead of him.

Three fortnights had elapsed since his flight on the solstice. Arithon scoured the rust from his steel, and took no false heart from the fact he had so far managed to evade capture. The windswept downs of Daón Ramon lay ahead. Thirty leagues of exposed landscape unfolded between the wooded, Skyshiel foothills and the promise of Earl Jieret's protection at Ithamon. Under deep winter, with inadequate cover, he would stand at the mercy of Jaelot's trackers. The lame horse would become a dangerous liability, and the sound one, a burden he dared not eliminate. Traveling on foot, if his enemies flushed him, he could all too easily be run down and killed, or captured by enemy riders. Jaelot's men dogged him, before and behind. Were he spotted, they need do nothing at all but close in and form ranks and surround him.

Arithon shot Alithiel home in her scabbard, then oiled his main gauche dagger. He scrounged a meal of stale biscuit and cheese, and smoked jerky from a near-emptied saddle pack. Snugged down in his cloak and his thickest fleece jacket, he measured his dwindling assets. Where Luhaine's advice had dispatched him inland, no one had factored for the driven tenacity of Jaelot's spellbound captain. Arithon found the odds on his continued safe passage had become laughably small. His broadscale use of his shadow to seed terror was now his most necessary weapon of expedience.

Spinner of Darkness, the Alliance had named him. Arithon shut his eyes, wrung to bitterness. If he survived his next crossing, the title was bound to be answered and justified.

Recalcitrant, the sky held fair through four days. Dawn on the fifth, flat cloud roofed the peaks. The air wore the whetted, crystalline sharpness that presaged another fierce storm. Jaelot's hard-bitten guardsmen watched the weather close in with trail-weary experience. The company bound to Arithon's pursuit carped over the aches dropping pressure brought to old scars. Their complaints availed nothing. While the first moaning gusts roared down off the heights, their labored progress was reduced to moving shadows amid the whirling white eddies of snowfall. They saddled their horses, formed up in patrols, and fanned out, seeking the Spinner of Darkness.

Noon rendezvous found them hunched with their backs to raw wind, while their squint-eyed tracker deliberated over the ground by the glaze of a refrozen streamlet.

'Your man fished for trout here,' he announced at due length. A jab of his stick broke through snow and revealed the buried ash of a blaze kindled out of pine heartwood that would burn fast and hot, with very little trace of smoke. 'Here's where he boiled his catch. The fillets would be dried, or packed in ice and frozen. Won't need a fire to fill his belly for at least the next several nights.'

The sergeant in charge cast away the frazzled twig of witch hazel he had plucked to scrub his filmed teeth. 'Starving or sated, may Dharkaron's Black Spear rip his vitals in twain in the afterlife. Set chains on the bastard, and we can go home. Just tell us which way he rode out.'

The tracker straightened, one gloved hand pressed to the stiff joints in the small of his back. He quartered the streambank with mincing steps, musing aloud as he sifted the scanty evidence. Always, the story had to be wrung from the s'Ffalenn demon's fastidious campsite. 'Didn't bring horses here, never that stupid. Want to know where he's bound, have to uncover the trail that leads where he had his mounts picketed.' A pause, a poke at a bush with the stick, then a drawn moment while the woodsman knelt and gently blew the new powdering of snowfall away from the sun-crusted layer underneath.

'Got him. This way.' The grizzled tracker arose and dusted his trousers, his dour face turned toward the sergeant. 'Might as well dismount now. Yon cursed spawn of evil won't belike to change his sly habits. Not for the sake of sparing your feet or your comforts.'

Never had Arithon made the fool's mistake of staking out horses where his pursuit could launch a mounted foray. He would risk the approach of no enemy horses lest equine herd instinct raise a neigh of greeting and sound a disastrous alarm.

Afternoon, the patrols were set searching in spirals, while the wind howled down and snow pelted. The west-facing slopes of the foothills soon wore a packed cowl of whiteness. The tracker forged ahead, leaned into the gusts, while his cloak cracked and slapped at his tough, stringy frame, and his beard gathered gray spikes of hoarfrost. As the men on his heels fumed and vented rank oaths, the tracker unraveled the difficult trail, patient as a spider reweaving a web from small clues strung like scattered snippets of silk.

After six weeks of balked circling through desolate territory, men muttered that Arithon s'Ffalenn walked the land far too lightly. Around fires, by night, their talk named him uncanny. By day, braced up by camaraderie and bravado, they scratched their thick beards, and boasted of how they would hang their caught quarry by the heels, and tease him with firebrands just to watch him use shadow to save his bastard's skin from the cinders.

Loudest were those who kept score by their suffering. 'As I'm born,' exclaimed one, 'I'll see the fell creature repaid for the frostbite that's blackened the tips of my toes.'

A comrade hooted. 'Who cares, for some toes? While we sleep on snow and scratch biting fleas, freezing our bollocks in this wilderness, what's to stop the wife left at home from warming the bed in our absence? We don't go back soon, I swear my sweet member will forget it wasn't made for something better than pissing.'

Someone else guffawed. 'Your *member*? Daelion's justice! That wee slippery thing that doesn't know a woman from a wet gob of spit in a mitten?' In rejoinder, chipping ice from his hobnailed boot sole, he added, 'Or aren't you the one we hear moaning behind the picket lines those nights when you draw the late watch?'

'Quiet!' snapped the sergeant. 'The pack of you ladies would flush a deaf post with your noise.'

'If there's a fugitive left in these thickets to snare, he won't be the fiend's get we're chasing,' came a sullen grumble from the ranks. 'Mark me, in this storm, the Spinner of Darkness will have snatched his chance and bolted headlong for Ithamon.'

A testy colleague elbowed the speaker. 'Would you stake your next ration of beer he's done that?'

'Be silent, fool!' cried the sergeant in rife exasperation. 'You chattering magpies let the tracker do his work. We wait on his word for my orders. If the Master of Shadow's for Ithamon, he'll be caught without any man's bet on the outcome.'

The men met his glower in foot-shuffling, sheepish quiet. They scarcely needed a tongue-lashing reminder that Jaelot's most competent officer already had a company of men positioned for ambush at the ruin.

Against the whiteout scream of a gust, the sergeant snapped his conclusion. 'Sure enough, it's our task to drive the bold rat into the trap we have waiting. But before we hare off through a blizzard on assumptions, we'll damned *well* make sure the blood-sucking sorcerer's turned west across Daon Ramon Barrens!'

'He's turned.' The tracker wormed his way out of the thicket, then winced at the shower of snow the sprung branches dumped down his collar. 'Found the hollow where he had his horses tucked up. The tracks when they left lead northwest. He's gone for the barrens in a cracking hurry. No time before this have I seen him carve a course that ran so infernally straight.'

'Move out!' The sergeant hazed his troop to form ranks. 'We go where the bastard's trail takes us.'

But the rising storm raised a morass of obstacles, with land-marks obscured, and the far-ranging patrols of outriders too scattered to be found and recalled at short notice. The wind stiffened to a lash of unmitigated misery, lent a scouring edge by the snow driven down in a hissing, whirled maelstrom of dry powder. The horses stumbled ahead, heads low and tails flattened, the men in their saddles cursing the patched skin torn off if they touched mail or weapons bare-handed.

Beyond the sheltering eaves of the forest, the fierce gusts flayed exposed flesh. Snow worked and sifted into everything, from the folds in wool cloaks to the crevices of boot cuffs, then melted into an insidious, numbing dampness that chilled a man's bones till they ached. The wet spiked the horses' coats into steaming, soaked redolence, then tipped their long guard hairs in ice. The miserable beasts shivered beneath sorry masters, who slapped sodden thighs, and cursed the name of Arithon s'Ffalenn.

Nor did the wide barrens afford man or mount comfort. The low, rolling landscape wore snagged cornices of rock, with the lee sides of the dales a morass of brush and crabbed briar. The horses ripped the fronts of their cannon bones bloody, and left streaks of pinked snow where the officers called rest halts. Iced streams and gulches snagged the lowlands like torn seams, a hazard masked over by drifts. More than one horse became wrenched to its knees in a floundering, dangerous fall. Inside of an hour, two mounts were lamed. Another had to be shot for meat, reft beyond cure by an ugly, splintered bone shredded through the thick hide of its gaskin.

While men shouldered the work to render the carcass, the officers met in harried conference with the headhunter guides and the trackers.

'Can't press on after dark, the terrain is too savage,' said the garrison quartermaster, his pouched eyes haunted, and his ruddy cheeks sadly thinned from his weeks of tribulation on the Baiyen.

'Storm's going to make the light fail early.' The sergeant slapped numbed hands, just as wearied. 'A fire and a horse roast will bolster morale.'

The head tracker held his opinion in dour silence, while the more hard-bitten headhunters insisted their wily enemy was certain to widen his lead while Jaelot's moping sluggards ate and slept.

'Would you push us on in the dark and see the next man break his neck?' The patrol captain hunched against the pelt of the storm, his nose a red knob dripping moisture. 'Hard enough to keep our bearings in this weather with the snow like a witch's curse upon us.'

'Stop now, and I tell you,' the chief headhunter argued, 'every trace of your quarry will be lost by the morning. Blizzards in this country can spin out for days. Stay on him. Press the chase. Or else throw away what chance you have left.'

Debate raged and resolved, with the patrols on the move through the gloom of a premature dusk. With the failing light, the dirge wail of the wind sawed men's nerves to uncanny tension. The lead riders lit torches that the roar of the storm fanned down to sullen embers. Their dulled, ruby glare became swallowed by murk, invisible within a few yards. No fire warmed the chill from wet feet and hands. The fresh-slaughtered meat slowly froze, a sore point for men with pinched bellies. Griped on their diet of hard biscuit and cheese, they blundered into night, harried on by a gale like a hell-bound scourge, screaming over the weather-stripped vales.

Midnight downed another horse with a torn tendon. This one they shot with a quarrel through the brain and abandoned in the gully where it lay. Fresh bickering raged over the beast's steaming carcass. On foot since the morning, the tracker was soaked through his fleece leggings, and grown testy. He questioned the reliability of what scant sign he could glean from the iced-over bogs in the hollows.

'One bad reading could turn us astray. We'd be drawn leagues off course, come the morning. Could lose our quarry for sure. Might be days before we could find his cold trail. Fresh snow's an unmerciful disadvantage.'

The chief headhunter rebutted, 'But the fugitive hasn't turned.

He's crossing these hillocks on a crow's course, straight for the towers of Ithamon. The plain fact he's not paused to lay a false trail means that he's pressed, even desperate. I say we're too close at his heels for him to attempt the precautions of a trapped fox.'

A gust raged full force, raking snow like barbed glass against the riders' bared faces. Through the misery of the moment, while men suffered unspeaking, the shrill neigh of a westbound horse rode the storm like a shred of blown rag.

'By the dark, that's none of ours!' cried the garrison sergeant, wheeling his mount. 'We've got no outriders that far ahead.' He dug in his spurs without waiting for conference or orders from his fellow officers.

Strung out in disorder, the rest of the company plunged after him. Each man in his way cursed the impulsive action. Yet to pause and deliberate was to risk separation amid the black brew of foul weather. Given scant choice, the captain in charge barked at the laggards to fall in.

The night was a wadded shroud of black felt, knit through by the forces of chaos. Ahead, amid the treacherous terrain with its rock crowns and unseen gullies, scouts picked up the muffled drumming of hooves, now sure of the beast they were tracking. The sound came and went like a phantom between gusts, a lure that kept beckoning onward. In a frenzy propelled by spell-driven eagerness, Jaelot's men-at-arms forged ahead. Whipped up to the blood-sport passion of the chase, they pursued the twisting, blind flight of their quarry until their mounts were belabored to exhaustion.

Their pace slowed to a walk, the hours passed, interminable. Cruel winds bit and snarled. Snow swirled and sifted and stung like edged sleet, the storm's onslaught continuous through air like stirred pitch. Tempers frayed. Two men came to grief, thrown from their saddles when their horses missed stride in the potholes. During the pause while the company healer set and dressed one unfortunate's broken arm, the chief headhunter returned with the unwelcome word they had spent a fruitless chase to corner a riderless gelding.

'What?' snapped the company commander, caught dismounted to examine the withers of a horse chafed raw where the saddle had shifted. 'I thought one of you scouts said he'd sighted someone astride?'

Shamefaced, the headhunter qualified. 'What he saw was a decoy, a manikin fashioned from old clothing tied and stuffed up with pine needles.'

To the owner of the galled horse, the commander said, 'Strip the mare's bridle and pack that sore with salve.' His frustration set a lash to his already sharpened speech. 'Nobody rides anywhere until we recover sound wits and a sense of direction!' Then, to the headhunter who shifted from foot to foot in the dark, 'You're here to tell me we've spent the whole night running blind circles for *nothing*?'

'We've caught a lame horse,' the man stated, shamefaced. 'The single count we've got going in our favor, our enemy has just one mount left.'

'Which does us small good. Now the fiend could be anywhere!' The commander did not need the trapper's gloomy confirmation that the fugitive's trail would now be obliterated, perhaps lost beyond all recovery. No option remained but to camp until dawn on the hope the storm would relent. Only the glimpse of the rising sun could reestablish their obscured bearings.

The men hunkered down, soaked and miserable without fires. The low brush was too thin to sustain a good blaze, and the demon gusts extinguished the sparks the field cook coaxed from dry tinder. The horses were too spent to paw for the grasses that poked spiny clumps through the weather sides of the snowdrifts. Men huddled in blankets amid punishing cold, uncomforted by the knowledge that their enemy endured and suffered the selfsame privations.

The night roared and howled, possessed in the grip of what seemed an interminable punishment. Dawn did not come. The men in their misery ached and wept pleas for the return of comfort and light. No voice answered. In vain, they held steadfast. No dark hour in memory had reigned with such force, that the advent of day should stay banished.

Early dread became whispers, spun to volatile fear. Surely this was the end. The Spinner of Darkness had worked his fell shadows and consigned his pursuit to oblivion.

As the mutters swelled toward an outbreak of panic, the officers fought to stem ebbing morale and keep a sane semblance of order.

'Are you ninnies and girls, to wail fear of the dark? No one's hurt. No one's dying. Have faith in the Light, for the dawn came again, even at Dier Kenton Vale and the maelstrom that beset the war fleet at Werepoint. We are numbers against one. This wall of shadow is doubtless no more than the work of a driven and desperate criminal.'

Men huddled together. Some sang. Others prayed. In due time, the vortex of darkness thinned and lifted to unveil a late day ripped by storm winds and blizzard. The adverse conditions would not permit tracking, nor could spent horses be forced to bear laden packsaddles and riders. The company chose the sensible alternative, and made camp in a dale where a thicket of thorn formed a windbreak. They lit fires, ate a cheerless meal of stewed horse, while their officers conferred, and decided at length to proceed for Ithamon. They would join Jaelot's guard captain there with all speed as soon as the weather relented.

'Better hope the Master of Shadow is ahead of us, bound headlong into our trap.' The sergeant slapped chips of ice from his mail and voiced his bitter conclusion. 'Else we'll be ordered to regroup and give chase when the storm clears enough to take bearings.'

Yet the snow fell at sunset, and all through the next night, a horizontal barrage that layered the landscape like draped gauze, and battened the sky in fleece scud. The brushfires burned to coals, then steamed and went out, puddled to slush and dank embers. The next cheerless day, the wild tempest blew out to thin cirrus. A platinum-pale disk spat hazed sun dogs. East, against an enamel horizon, the looming peaks of the Skyshiels notched the view in ice-clad splendor, skirted in foothills of spruce.

'Dharkaron's bleak vengeance!' the gaunt tracker fumed. 'We've drifted back eastward! Sithaer's deepest pits, we're so far astray we ought to weep as the butt of our enemy's laughter.'

'Well, he won't laugh for long.' The chief headhunter pulled out his whetstone and dragged it, screeling, along the kept edge of his dagger. 'He'll find our sweet ambush at Ithamon soon enough. May the sword of the Light and Sithaer's righteous fires drive his accursed spirit past the Wheel.'

Arithon s'Ffalenn believed himself braced for return to the haunted ruin of Ithamon. Across the sparkling, snowy vales of Daon Ramon, under sunlight like shards of white glass, he had seen spirit and sinew put to the test. Surely the three decades elapsed since the Mistwraith's capture should have allowed ample time to address the scarred wounds that remained. Yet the passage of years had done nothing to soften the old pain, scalpel-cut to the heart. No mind trained to mastery could reconcile the loss, when misuse of grand conjury in defense of his feal clans had severed his access to mage-sight. If the agonized sufferance of such a blinding could not be resolved, the cold burden of guilt could be borne. The stab of roused memory lay familiar and worn, like the ghost throb of a severed limb.

Yet when Arithon crested the knife ridge of drifts that edged the dry bank of the Severnir, he found himself grateful for the misfortune of his shuttered talent. This pass, he would be spared the visioning dream of the ghosts that shimmered and coiled through the ruin. He would see no past kings pleading for the hope of a crowned heir bringing long-sought restoration. Their gut-wrenching sorrows and their cry for reborn grandeur now lay beyond reach, safely screened from mage-gifted senses by the barriers of unhealed affliction.

Arithon would not be wrung by the tears of his bygone s'Ffalenn ancestors. Nor would he behold the searing grace of the Paravian spirit forms that sheared like bright flame through the mists.

Yet if he escaped the echoed reflections of lost glory, he could not be spared the terrible desolation of the ruins themselves. The shattered stone walls, with their smashed carvings, still bespoke the bitter violence of the uprising. The memory of dead high kings still walked moss-grown battlements. The wild winds keened through the shells of breached keeps, stones laddered in stripped ivy and an aura of tumbledown majesty.

Arithon pressed his exhausted horse northward, troubled in thought and memory. He had known these hills in the mantle of winter; had ridden, then as now, across crusted snow, with the parallel ridges carved out by gales turned the shot gold of damascened silk. A sky as lucent as aquamarine crystal reduced him to a toiling speck upon a spread tapestry of landscape. So many years since he had left this savage country in the trickle of spring thaws, savoring his last days of freedom after the arduous conquest of the Mistwraith, and before the inevitable, fated coronation that laid him under geas at Etarra. His half brother had gone mounted, pensive, beside him, while the chickadees in their solemn slate plumage had scolded over the sere fruits of last year's briars.

As if no shed blood and no curse lay between, the birds sang still in the branches. The springs burbled through their paned ice in the dells, as if only seasons had changed, and no wars strained the cloth of world destiny. Arithon paused only to water his horse. Pushed to the bone-weary limit of endurance, he wished he had less time on his hands for the morass of solitary reflection.

Too real, the chance he might fail in the mission sealed by his sworn oath to the Fellowship.

He rode with his ears sometimes ringing with fever, the relentless ache of his wounded right hand slung in a pinned fold of his cloak. Under dressings he had been too hard-pressed to clean, a raw sore leaked pus where the traumatized flesh refused to close over and heal. His chin was a stubble of uncut, black beard, and his shirts stank of unwashed sweat. By day, the sun lit flash fires in his brain. By night, the fierce stars of Athera's vast heavens pierced him with limitless emptiness.

He felt like a vessel sucked hollow of dreams, until the dread moment he chanced to look up to establish a routine bearing. His fate lay before him. Against the scribed ribbon of the horizon, he beheld the upthrust scarp of rock that bore Ithamon's ruin like the battered rim of a diadem.

Just as before, the sight struck his heart like a blow, leaving him winded and breathless. No less poignant for the forewarning of memory, the eloquent testament of smashed lives and broken dreams in the stark, tumbled stone of the wreckage. Then the four towers arisen among them, still pristine in grace, pure as a cry amid the tumbledown battlements. The ruled fall of sunlight struck their façades, raising fine sound like the chiming tap of a bronze mallet against keys of crystal and glass.

A man raised to the powers of a masterbard's art would have to be deaf not to hear. Arithon gasped, smote to the heart by that soundless chord of vibration. Four pealing notes, whose fifth register was absent, a void like a wound into darkness; for of four towers raised to anchor the tenets of virtue, the fifth one had been cast down. The King's Tower was crumbled, reduced to a weed-grown foundation on the hour a Paravian king had been murdered.

Hunched on his horse, his fist crushed to wet mane, Arithon bowed his head, shattered. He wept unabashed. The nerve in him faltered, for what lay ahead. Though blinded to sight of the spirits, the practiced maturity of his bardic perception laid him wide-open all over again. There would be no escape. He would hear in song, pouring from broken stone, the bittersweet echoes of beauty and truth, cut down by violence and bloodshed. The call would sing to him, sinew and nerve, and shackle him to the future. As the last surviving s'Ffalenn prince, his was the born burden to shoulder the promise of crown rule and restoration.

Never mind that the very thought of that role ripped him to mangling agony. The ruin sustained protest, endured against time. Its state of desecration could not alter its set law, or its ingrained fire of inspiration. Here, the unseated stones themselves rang to the foundational chord of compassion and undefiled mercy. That imprint waited with the blank patience of time, to be reclothed in its rightful, lost harmony. Arithon tasted the salt of his tears, reduced to abject humility. While he lived, Ithamon would never release its ancestral hold on the blood and the bone of him.

Torn open, exposed against silver-clad hills, with the winter's harsh grip embossed foil on black rocks, and the wind a honed dagger to flay him, Arithon fought for the necessary courage to prod his thin mare forward. The ache in his spirit would not be assuaged, nor the guilt that rode at his shoulder. There were too many dead for his name, since Tal Quorin, then those casualties multiplied manyfold more, at Minderl Bay and at Vastmark. Those ghosts would bind him to the seat of s'Ffalenn sovereignty, and hound him to desolate madness.

A more cruel moment could not be conceived, for enemy riders to sight him. Attached to the garrison men encamped by the ruin, the party of five had been sent foraging for game to ease the scarcity of supplies. Their shout of discovery from the crest of the next hilltop caught their quarry defenselessly vulnerable.

Arithon snapped face around. Shot erect by dousing, shrill fear, he took in at a glance the ragtag black surcoats worn by Jaelot's city guard. He drew Alithiel left-handed. While the enemies who charged to kill drove downslope in a spray of burst snow, he reined his mount, staggering to meet them.

'Go back!' he pealed out, a cry that distilled his raw tumult of unanswerable pain. 'Ath pity your families, desist!' Through the trained timbre of his Masterbard's voice, the hills spoke in echoes to shiver the spine.

Here, his blood tie as Rathain's sanctioned crown prince could not fail to be recognized. Where the current of the fifth lane sang through the kingdom's ancient heartland, the flux line itself bore the stamp of the Fellowship ceremony that had sealed his affirmation. The light striking off Ithamon's high towers peaked in resonance and burned, raised to a beacon flare of wild magic.

Then that errant burst snuffed out like blown flame as Arithon clapped down a defense wrought of merciless shadow. Through a darkness to freeze living flesh to dry powder, he reined about and urged his horse to a stumbling gallop.

Downhill he raced, *toward his pursuit*. To reach Ithamon, he must pass through them. His mare was too spent for a circuitous chase back through the open countryside. Heedless of bad footing, he forced reckless speed. The guidance that steered him was the jingle of mail, and the bewildered shouts of the armed men who blundered, equally blinded, to take him. If he held slight advantage for his trained grasp of sound, they were five to his one, and mounted on horses that were decently fed and well rested. Raked by thorns, slapped by branches, Arithon smashed through the gully. The heave of the horse's shoulders beneath him informed him of rising ground. Armored horsemen thrashed headlong down the slope. The shod hooves of their destriers struck red sparks from flint rocks, and their curses were all but on top of him.

Arithon sifted the oncoming barrage of sound, the whine of wind sliced across someone's bared steel, and the jink of roweled spurs, and a bearded man's labored breathing. He angled Alithiel, braced to thrust as he passed, prepared for the shock as Paravian steel sheared into armor and bone. His worst risk, the chance the blade might bind fast, and tear from his grasp in the wrench as the maimed rider tumbled.

One stride farther on, his mare misstepped, slid a foreleg on ice, and crashed sidewards. Arithon tucked into a roll before impact. He struck full force on his shoulder. The air slammed from his lungs. His grasp on the shadow screen lapsed for one second. He saw light strike through, flash in dazzling reflection off the bared runes of Alithiel, outthrust away from his body. Then the hooves of the enemy horse thudded over him, and a blow to the head sundered him into the yawning void of unconsciousness.

Whitehaven

Turned off the steep, winding road that climbed the North Gap to Eastwall, a left-branching goat track led to the hostel of Ath's adepts. The trail was narrow, a rough staircase of flint rock, hedged by the stunted firs that clung to harsh life at high altitude. Overhead, jagged summits scraped the roof of the sky, ripping the hems of the fast-moving storm clouds, or else capped by fair-weather ice plumes condensed from the sea-warmed, westerly currents that combed through the teeth of the ranges. The rare traveler attempted that route in deep winter, though the scouring north winds often razed off the drifts that mired the lower passes. Fewer still, the wayfarers who braved the upper peaks in solitude. The rigorous ascent in thin air could inflict vicious headaches and nausea, or spells of blackout faintness.

At first, Elaira presumed she had succumbed to such wasting sickness. The sheet of glare thrown off white snow stabbed like knives to the brain, distorting her overtaxed sight. Then vision failed utterly. Her perception disintegrated as though a thousand shot pinholes suddenly let in the dark.

She stumbled. Thrown to her knees, the enchantress grabbed blindly to save herself from a tumbling fall. Sharpened edges of stone gouged her shin, despite her thick hide leggings. As her outraged flesh recorded no more than the ghostly impression of bruising, she realized, through a split second of terror, that *this was no ill effect from thin air.* Then the side of her skull burst and exploded, as if someone clubbed her full force with an iron-studded bludgeon. Her cry, as she dropped, was no call for help, but the name of Arithon s'Ffalenn.

Linked by the tie of awareness between them, she shared his cold, inert sprawl on the snow-clad ground of the barrens. Then that fragile impression shattered as a gentle hand clasped her shoulder.

Vision snapped back into clarity. Elaira beheld a white mantle furred with a lining of snow lynx. Shining faint silver and fired gold, the garment was bordered with the stitched embroidery favored by Ath's adepts. Nestled within was a man as sunburned as old shoe leather, with a wire beard gathered into yellowed plaits tied off with chunk beads of amber. His voice, when he spoke, was poured honey, filled with a kindness that razed off the pain. 'Elaira?' The fact he knew her name was the natural extension of a perception schooled to reach beyond flesh. 'The hostel's quite near, just over the ridge. I can call for a litter if you feel too shaken to walk.'

Elaira gulped in the searing, cold air, unable to frame a reply. Her mind unreeled again, still tethered to a field of stained snow under the wild sky in Daon Ramon. There, a dark-haired prince sprawled inert, haplessly thrown by his leg-broken horse. The crippled animal struggled nearby, downed in thrashing agony. A pack of armed riders surrounded the rucked snow. In glass-edged focus, she saw they were unable to approach farther without risk of battering by striking hooves. Then her tortured breath stopped, while the archer among them received the crisp order to string his horn bow.

'He'll shoot the mare,' the adept explained in swift sympathy. 'Nor has the eloquent hate of the Alliance served its own cause on this day. The name of the Spinner of Darkness now inspires witless fear. Superstition will buy a delay.' The support at her shoulder was joined by a warm palm that cradled her splitting head. 'Bide now. Close your eyes. We'll have you to shelter in minutes.'

Elaira fought out a gasped protest. 'I can walk.' The rage seared her, that the one useless gesture was the limit her power could offer. She was helpless, *hamstrung*, unable to raise so much as a prayer for Arithon's plight in Daon Ramon. If she still wore her quartz crystal, even had she ranged focused spells of diversion over such distance to spare him, *she could not have done so without invoking a Koriani debt, for his life.*

Wisely, she had cut off such temptation beforehand.

Nothing left, but to regroup scattered wits; through savage

grief, she must make her unruly body take charge and resume the burden of bearing her upright. Yet even that basic discipline failed her. Anguish blurted her heart's truth aloud, a cry torn from reflexive instinct. 'Ath's blessed mercy, they're going to kill him!'

'Not yet.' The adept's sturdy grip helped her to arise. 'Listen. You'll feel him still breathing.' Yet before seeded hope could flower and buoy her, he added, 'I'm sorry, lady. Before you ask, no, our kind cannot intervene in ways that disrupt the fate of the world.'

Elaira caught back a wrenching sob. Close as she had never been to being drowned by blind terror, still, she forced the grace to ease his concern. 'Forgive me, I knew better.' She managed a step forward in spite of weak knees. Less easily, she stifled the ignominious need, to cast off respect and hound the adept to break faith with a round of tearful pleading.

'You are far from helpless,' the white brother observed. Yet if her mean thoughts had touched his awareness, his counsel came sourced in compassion. 'Belief can imprison. You are not separate from Ath's creation. Though stubborn reason may insist you can't reach past the bounds of your bodily senses, your cries for help are heard, always. Each appeal is unfailingly answered. Your inner self extends beyond all constraint, though the outer eye, attached to the world, would impose its limited state of false order.'

Now steadied enough to walk unsupported, Elaira crested the rise. Below her, nestled into the fold of the scarp, a confection of white granite and airy arched cupolas gleamed as though carved from delicate blue shadows and sunlight. The hostel of Whitehaven held a beauty to inspire the soaring flight of waking dreams. Caught by the throat as her pain dragged her earthbound, Elaira shook her head.

'I swore an oath over a Koriani focus stone,' she admitted. Through the ache of the cold drawn into her lungs, she said, bitter, 'Is that not a binding constraint?'

The adept regarded her, his expression benign, and his eyes deep as uncharted ocean. 'Does an oath chain your wishes? Your emotions? Your desires?'

'Yes, if I act on them.' Elaira slipped on an iced boulder, and recovered. 'Prime Selidie wants Prince Arithon trapped under an obligation to my order. My freedom lies in my steadfast refusal to comply, unless my distress could draw the attention of a passing Fellowship Sorcerer?' When her wild-card suggestion raised no word of encouragement, she finished her thought out of obstinacy. 'They seem able enough to act as they please, unafraid of Koriani retribution.'

'No feat is beyond them,' the adept agreed. He glanced aside, nodded in salute to the watching presence of a golden eagle, perched in mantled majesty on a broken shaft of dead fir. 'You seem recovered, now. As you choose, you may pass through our gates. One will meet you there, and escort you into the sanctuary.'

Without even a breath of disturbed air in warning, the adept blinked out of existence.

Elaira yelped, startled. In belated chagrin, she realized the snow by her side bore no trace of another set of footprints. Yet she still seemed to feel the warm grip on her arm that had braced her through the onset of breaking crisis. 'How do they *do* that?' she asked empty air.

No one and nothing replied but the wind, howling in gusts off the summits. Upslope, the stripped fir loomed empty, the eagle apparently flown. That oddity chafed. Elaira had not seen the bird spread tawny wings, or heard the whoosh of its feathers as it launched into upward flight.

Ahead, the switched-back descent to the hostel led between frost-split rock, salted with snow and the hammered-steel glimmer of glare ice. Urgency only redoubled the hazard. Elaira averted another near fall as her boot toe grabbed in a crevice. Whipped on by her worry for Arithon s'Ffalenn, she would not slow her step. She clambered down the last slope in a rush that landed her, winded and scraped, before the gateway to Whitehaven hostel.

There, despite tumult, the massive hush claimed her. She stopped short and stared, as every wayfaring traveler must who would contemplate the act of entry.

The pillars before her were cut from merled granite, veined with quartz like gouged patterns of lightning. The uncanny, whorled symbols crafted by Ath's Brotherhood marched across the faced stone, bands of ciphers that teased and confounded the eyesight: a shimmering movement that seemed wrought of light, until the blink of an eye changed the formless dance to a play of ephemeral shadow.

Elaira had experienced such carvings before, at the old hostel at Forthmark. Abandoned and reclaimed as a Koriani hospice, the stonework there was as strangely alive. On hot summer days, she had sat by the shaded walls, feasting on wild grapes, while the southern sunlight scattered chipped reflections off the shale scarps napped through the sheep fields. There, the ancient works of Ath's adepts had weathered with time, a willing ladder for climbing vines, or catch pockets for moss and rainwater. Between the arduous courses of study into advanced arts of surgery and healing, she had paused often to ponder the residual mystery.

These pillars in the lofty peaks of the Skyshiels were as old, and as gouged by the trials of the elements. Yet here, the carvings were not disused. Nor did the forces that rang through them reflect the same gentle state of neglect. The power that greeted Elaira's arrival was distinct, a delicate touch against thought and skin as precise as the point of a needle. She reeled under the uncanny impression that her clothing, and every item she carried, became subject to exacting scrutiny: as though leather and laces and oyster-shell buttons could speak, and comment on her record of stewardship.

For that unsettled instant, the frigid winds of the abyss seemed to flow straight through her. 'Merciful maker!' she gasped, driven a startled step back. 'What have I done?'

Here, fingered by the uncanny magics wielded by Ath's adepts, she understood just *how far* their knowledge ranged beyond the craft worked by the Koriani Order. Such attention to detail became frightening, that a knife or a garment might be held in the same conscious regard as a person. Broken into cold sweat, Elaira understood that all freedoms would be observed without parity inside the bounds of these gates.

Tempted to bolt to escape such a paralyzing self-examination, she held firm. The forces that probed her were intense, unremitting and precise, but not hostile. Only lies would be shredded as she crossed that dire threshold. Yet the price demanded was self, laid bare. No doubt remained that on the far side she would be greeted by someone who knew her. From her strength to her most ignominious weaknesses, she would stand fully exposed. A perilous vulnerability lay in such knowledge. Henceforward, the adepts would have gained the power to address her by her true Name.

Swept by a rippling shiver, Elaira fought down her wave of blind panic. 'Fatemaster guard me.'

Naught remained in reassurance, except to abide in trust. For time beyond memory, the adepts had adhered to their gentle creed of compassion.

Elaira stepped through, startled to find the strange pressure melted before her. She felt lifted, light, all at once more aware of the sun-carved shadows cast across crusted snow than of the pillars themselves as she passed them. Whatever strange field of spellcraft they wove, the effects absolved her of worry. Unbidden, her spirits unfolded into a rush of bubbling joy.

Once inside, as though conjured by some fey, wild trick, the promised adept hastened forward. Her host proved a tiny, wizened old man with a sparkle in his jet eyes. His smile scored his dark-skinned, bearded face into merriment and laugh lines. He enfolded her numbed hands into seamed palms with the same exuberant welcome.

'Elaira, *affi'enia*, come this way.' His peppery, fast dialect marked his descent from the insular southshore desertmen. The diminutive term he chose for address was derived from the ancient root word that meant *dancer*, although his precise turn of phrase was not known to her. 'Walk in Ath's blessing, and find ease for the heart within this hostel's sanctuary.'

He drew her forward, amused by her evident relief that his pigeon-toed step impressed footprints. 'The others you saw earlier were not flesh at all, but projections, a thought that was formed by intense concentration and focus.'

Elaira jerked to a stop. 'But they were so real!' She fingered her wrist, unable to contain sharp surprise, that the strong arm that had assisted her after collapse had been no more than an apparition. 'The one who helped me, his touch felt as solid as yours.'

The adept chuckled outright. 'I never claimed their substance was less than my own. Ath's creation is myriad.'

As she flushed, embarrassed for such an impetuous inquiry into his Brotherhood's grasp of the mysteries, he gave her hand a congenial squeeze. The spark that enlivened his eyes acquired the glint of thrown diamond. 'It is thought that spins form, not the other way around. Were you not fooled by your bodily senses, you would see the true way of the world. Thoughts and feelings combine to make dreams, and, in fact, they are the more real part of you. Did you come here to encounter the truth? Change will follow. If you wish to remain as you were, I suggest you step back through that portal.'

'I came to learn,' Elaira insisted. Consumed with dread for Prince Arithon's fate, she lacked the spare resource to argue the nature of ephemeral philosophy. Her shaken nerve was scarcely enough to hold her to steadfast courage. This place offered no shelter behind falsehood or platitude. The incomprehensible power of the gate ciphers struck home the irrefutable risk: her quest for forbidden knowledge had already cast all that she was into jeopardy.

Far more than cold air left her trembling. Chased from the shadow of self-recrimination, she acknowledged her fear. The choice to go forward might destroy all her sensible constraints, even lead her to defy her oath of obedience to her order.

Yet her love for Arithon ran deeper than cowardice. No course remained but to drown her misgiving under the tatters of courtesy. 'Please, if you will, brother, show me the way a seeker enters your sanctuary.'

The adept smiled again, his walnut-toned skin crinkled with unutterable delight. 'Dear lady, with all my heart, join our company and be welcome.'

Bone weary, and emotionally numb, Elaira trailed his light footstep over the wind-sculptured snow. Arched entry and pillared anteroom passed by as a fitful blur. She registered the impression of profound quiet, then a young man's kind hands removing the weather-stained wool of her mantles. She stared down, startled to find the reflection of a windburned face with waif's eyes gazing upward from underfoot. Then the flyaway hair snapped to snake ends and elf locks made her realize the image was her own. The tessellated marble under her step had been honed to a glossy, high polish. The surface was eerie, far too refined to have been smoothed by tools in the hand of an artisan.

Unwitting, she must have questioned aloud, for the desertman offered his cheerful explanation. 'A speaker to stone would have sung the right lines to lay the marble into alignment.' He steered her arm, gentle. 'Please follow?'

She was led down a pillared loggia. Walls and groined ceiling had been intricately carved with parallel lines of strange characters. To one who had mage talent, their presence spoke in hushed tones of sound and light. Elaira found their shapes eluded analysis by direct sight. She marveled as the effects of their presence stroked her skin and eased weary flesh like a tonic. The spiked edge to her worry softened and smoothed, gifting a detached awareness.

'You won't be separated from your feelings,' the adept reassured. He directed her toward an arched portal to one side. 'The sanctuary is a gateway to unmasked power. To enter, one must pass through the stream of the prime life chord. It is therefore necessary to calm the tumult from the supplicant's heart and mind.'

Doused in dizziness, then lifted by upending vertigo that flushed her to shivering goose bumps, Elaira caught and grasped the adept's offered arm. 'What's happening?' She felt as though the bones of her skull had dissolved, leaving her unmoored and drifting.

'You are a born talent, and a vibrantly clear one at that.' The adept steadied her wavering step. If aged features and small size lent him the semblance of frailty, his touch owned a tensile-strength confidence.

Elaira clung to him in shameless gratitude, reminded of the resilience laid by quenching and fire into a tempered-steel blade.

'The part of you that remembers harmonic balance is rising to match a higher range of vibration,' the adept explained. 'Few have the inner sensitivity to notice much more than a passing moment of faintness. If you find the sensation beyond bearing, you can choose not to enter the sanctuary.'

They had reached the high arch, raised out of dark stone, and incised with patterns that bewildered perception. The quality of the rock seemed to reject solidity, one moment the absolute black of the void, and the next, the velvet of fathomless night, scattered with pinprick white holes that were stars.

'I have to go forward,' Elaira said, desolate. Though she could not feel the step of her feet on firm ground, and her head whirled in giddy gyrations, she held steadfast. 'If I falter through faintness, please support me. Hope must lie ahead. Behind me, there is no path I know that won't lead to a poisoned future.'

'As you will.' The adept gave her an encouraging nod, then drew her across that dread threshold.

She was falling, fast and far, her flesh like a boulder dropped into a night sea. Drowning in density, her mind broke away, whirled and winnowed like a spark sucked up a vast flue. Light pierced her, blinding. She cried out, not from pain, but from startlement; fear dissolved on a breath to unbridled amazement. She had spiritwalked before, but never like this, stripped from the cocoon of Koriani discipline and the rigid array of self-limiting spells of protection.

Each thought became chain lightning, flaring and branching in all directions at once, until the building layers of reverberation framed patterns of overlaid energies. Elaira strove to quell bursting tension. Trained enough to know that unconscious terror would find resonance here, and perhaps raise a harmful backlash, she tried vainly to contain her unruly mind.

'Relax, you're quite safe.' The adept's voice served to anchor her. Mazed confusion re-formed into shapes that had meaning, and she realized he still walked beside her. His flesh had acquired a glow that shed sparks, as though his moving presence was surrounded by thousands of swarming fireflies.

Elaira wept for the sheer beauty of his face, and her tears fell as moonstones and diamonds. She glanced downward to see where they lit, or if they would splash upon landing, and saw herself changed. The sturdy boots she had worn in the mountains were gone, her leggings and wool clothing along with them. As though dreaming, she had been reclad in silk that shimmered in changing colors, now peacock blue, now green and gold, now moon silver in iridescence. Her bare feet were embraced in cool grass strung silver with dew, the flesh gone pearlescent and strange. Nor did she stand under a roof any longer. The sky overhead glimmered with starlight. Around her, a twilight grove of tall trees sheltered bell-shaped white flowers that shed a perfume of enchantment. Set like veined opal amid fragrant turf, a melodious spring trickled over a bed of white stones.

'Where is this place?' Elaira whispered, amazed. Unabashed in delight, she watched a brown-and-white thrush flit down from a branch and bathe in the shower of water.

'You stand in the sanctuary of Whitehaven.' The adept raised his hand in salute to the bird, which shook off a white mist of spray, then alit on her shoulder, singing. 'Here, power walks that will lead you to know that your dreams are the most vital part of you.'

Struck dumb with wonderment, Elaira raised a finger and stroked the thrush's flecked breast. It blinked, cocked its head, and snuggled into her warm skin, perhaps aware of the times she had shared her bread crusts with its winged brethren. 'This is my dream?' The air held the loamy afterscent of rain, and from somewhere, the crisp tang of a breeze wafted in from a fair-weather ocean.

'This is your self, wrought in symbol and metaphor.' The adept's sweeping gesture encompassed the trees, with their fey, wild majesty and their vast roots clothed over in flowers. 'The world you know outside is the same, but in this place, the innate power of your nature expresses itself more freely. The expanded resonance of Ath's presence is most patiently maintained by our Brotherhood of adepts. Here, you can ask, and perceive the connections that bind your life into patterns of pain by free will. If you wish to explore, you'll find the terrain more vast than you know, as astonishingly diverse as your wildest flight of fancy.'

'I can't ask for myself,' Elaira said, torn. Her distress carried impact. The thrush took wing and flew, and a white flower at her feet shed petals like pearls over the tips of dew-drenched grasses. She bent, contrite, and plucked up the shorn flower head. Her hands caught the dust of sifted pollen like a blush of dawn gold. 'One that I love stands in peril of his life. The Warden of Althain once spoke a prophecy that said our destinies are entwined.'

'The fate of all beings is one vast, woven tapestry,' the adept amended in mild kindness. He paused by a boulder cushioned with moss, cupped a small azure moth like a jewel, and freed her before he sat down. 'Sethvir, in his wisdom, often knows with precision how closely the threads of individual personalities spin together. Emotion drives the template of choice and thought. Those dynamic forces align the desires which bring events into manifestation.' He glanced up, his dark features graced with transcendent caring. His form shed soft radiance, even the white cloth of his robes blurring into opalescence, hazing his presence in light. 'Therefore, look to water, brave lady. The spring will reveal how your being is tied to the one Named as Arithon Teir's'Ffalenn.'

Elaira stepped forward. Water was her natural element for clear scrying. Though the immanent proximity of truth made her shrink, she was no spirit to mire herself in sheltering lies and self-blindness. Even unstrung by doubt and trepidation, she found the strength not to waver. She folded to her knees at the verge of the spring. Overcome by the muffled thunder of her heartbeat, she gazed into its limpid surface.

'Ath lend my love guidance,' she murmured, resolute. 'Let my order not gain the foothold they crave to lay claim to Arithon's freedom.' Mild chills doused her skin. Sure awareness stole through her that in this place her appeal would be heard. Given wings by the focused intensity of her thought, *something* somewhere already moved in response to deliver an answer.

No moment was given to ponder what force her need had set into motion. The springwater coalesced to a burst of white light that dazzled her vision and blinded her . . .

In the snow-clad desolation of Daon Ramon Barrens, Arithon s'Ffalenn awakened, disoriented. A murderous headache shot fiery sparks across the dark screen of closed eyelids. Crippling nausea upended his gut. Curled in a knot amid rivers of blind pain, he spewed up a gagging mouthful of bile. The return of his senses was scarcely a boon. Everything hurt. As sound touched his ears, his awareness shimmered through a needling shower of torment, those details he managed to grasp through discomfort promising small chance for improvement.

His body was dumped left side down on chill snow, wrists and legs tightly bound. The cut-leather sinew bit into his flesh. His boots were torn off. Someone's rough hands gouged and ripped at his clothing, stripping his weapons and knives.

Around and above him, the voices of men tangled in what seemed an unnatural altercation. As though fueled by spells, their unease and terror shrilled into a dissonance that charged the very air with an electrified, volatile sense of danger.

'Should kill him now!' someone pressed from the sidelines.

A gouge at his ribs, as his hunting blade was snatched from its sheath, then used to slit open his sheepskin jacket.

'Can't do that,' came the shaken reply, laced in a raw breath of garlic. 'You want a sorcerer's haunt at your back? Gut him dead, and I promise, worse trouble will stalk us. In a body that breathes, at least we can *see* where he is. If he tries spellcraft or shadows again, we'll simply bash him unconscious.'

'Do that now,' another man urged in a frightened, cracked treble. 'You know if we tie him onto a horse, somebody else has to walk! Won't reach the ruins before sundown on foot. Are we fools to risk a night in the open with the accursed spawn of evil on our hands?'

A grunt, then a pawing hand heaved him over. Arithon received a dizzied view of the sky. High above, in faint gold, he *thought* he glimpsed the outspread wings of an eagle, circling. As he squinted to be sure, a mailed fist bashed his ribs. Slammed into a coughing battle to draw breath, he scarcely felt the tug as his main gauche was yanked clear of the sheath at his hip.

A bone in the teeth of a scrapping dog pack, Arithon had no shred of strength left to raise even token self-defense. Wave after pounding wave of new pain pressed him speechlessly prostrate. He gasped in limp misery while enemies bandied his fate back and forth, caught between their cringing fear and their bristling, aggressive paranoia. 'He's skin and bones starving, with a lump on the head that should leave him dizzy till morning.'

'I don't trust that one bit,' the first man insisted, quavering with tight-leashed hysteria. 'He's Master of Shadow, who killed thirty thousand. He'd leave us all butchered and never look back.'

'Well, we haven't enough faggots to roast his fell flesh!' snapped someone who carried authority. 'Until we do, we can't finish the job properly. No sorcerer stays dead unless he's well burned. Our captain's no coward. He'll damned well want to be certain this fiend's vengeful haunt won't be able to rise up and plague us!'

Someone else howled protest on the point that a pyre in the wilderness would lose them their due claim of bounty. 'The Alliance at Avenor has pledged half its treasury in reward for the Shadow Master's capture.'

'Won't matter spit, if we're killed trying to claim it,' another man-at-arms argued.

'The demon bastard's charred skull will serve well enough as a trophy! You want better proof?' The authoritative man at last gave way to his explosive temper. 'Well, then root through the snow and dig out his dropped sword!' To a shirker who lurked on the sidelines, he bellowed, 'You there! Stop sniveling! Mount up, if you're scared, and ride back into camp. We'll stay here on guard. Ask the captain to send us an armed patrol as escort to bring in the prisoner.'

'Knock out his lights, first, he's coming around,' said the man who dismounted on orders to recover Alithiel.

Through half-cracked eyelids, Arithon saw a blurred movement. A flash of bright sun skittered off the blade of his confiscated main gauche. Then the jolt of a blow at the base of his neck brought the dark crashing down once again.

Spun back into herself where she sat by the trickling spring in Ath's sanctuary, Elaira pressed a damp hand to her face. Through the aftermath of transition, the fogs of distant spellcraft still seemed to coil through her whirling senses. An impression of lingering distortion remained, which had made the charged atmosphere seem to ring and reverberate to the cry of the men-at-arms' fanned emotions.

'That wasn't my crafting that snarled the forces of air in that way,' she gasped through clamped teeth and a tightness of throat that made even simple speech difficult. 'I'm left with the uneasy feeling that someone with talent has tampered to magnify fear in distraction. What else would provoke the guardsmen's confused thinking to hold Arithon as a live captive?'

'Your prince has attracted a powerful ally,' the adept agreed, moved from his perch on the boulder to stand in support just behind her. 'The stones of Ithamon themselves have been tuned to answer the call of that man's oath of crown service. Nor is your part diminished. Love is strung through all beings like a vast web of light. So the fire of your caring reaches all of creation, a signature wave of pure energy that raises a spike of shared resonance where like currents run in close sympathy. You attract your own destiny, in that same way. The patterns are fluid, and not locked in place, as some others might have you believe.'

A pause, filled with the splashing melodies of water tumbling over its bed of white stones. Elaira found her thoughts too dense with worry to ponder the range of that statement. 'What is my fate?' she whispered aloud. 'Where will my love for Prince Arithon lead me?'

'The spring knows,' the adept said in tacit suggestion. 'You may see, as you wish.'

Elaira never clearly decided to look. But the drifting, sweet fragrance of night-blooming flowers and the quiet of twilight stole over her. The pervasive peace crept into her heart, until the silver-braid trickle of water spellbound her scattered attention.

There followed no explosion of white fire, no visionary image of distant places. This time, she sank as though into a dream. Submersed in clear depths, soothed to reverie by the flow of the current, she gave way as the stones had, their broken, rough edges worn gently round by the water's caressing passage. Amid their smoothed company, one pebble stood out, alive with a rainbow glimmer of refraction.

Moved by the prompt of a child's fascination, Elaira dipped her hand in the water and touched.

Contact unfolded into a wild, sweet shudder of ecstasy. Like a wind from Athlieria, the connection raised a paean that chased order and reason from her mind. She cried out, swept away by delight. Around her, the night garden glittered with tiny pinpoints of light. Each one framed a dancing consciousness, weaving the tapestry of life, moment to moment in harmony. Then, stunned to stopped breath, Elaira saw the unicorn enter the glade.

The creature emerged, ghost quiet, between the hushed gloom of the trees. Her dance showered dew from night grasses. Her white coat was the ephemeral silver of spun moonbeams, and her moving grace, a beauty that seared the dross from all mortal awareness. She came, living mystery that raised song without sound out of the glade's sacred stillness, a cry of untarnished brilliance that rewove old sorrows and pain. The ache of fearful expectation uplifted, transformed into a moment of winged epiphany.

'Merciful Ath!' Elaira gasped, stuck to awe. Half-blinded by tears, she sat like struck stone, while the Riathan Paravian came, and paused, and bent her silvery neck.

Her horn gleamed, hazed in a halo of shimmering golden light. The creature stood, perhaps offering tribute, or sharing the solace of communion. The beauty of her prescience seemed too much to bear, and her warmth, too tenderly real. She was wild, her being as elusive as the sheen on a pearl, her mane snagged and tumbled like argent silk that no civilized fingers might tame.

Elaira drowned in the grace of those velvet green eyes, slit pupils narrowed like a cat's. Then the horn lowered farther, and touched her breast. Contact whirled her senses away in a rainbow shower of light.

The adept caught and gathered her senseless form into his sturdy embrace. He bowed to the unicorn. 'Shining one,' he whispered in reverence. 'We are blessed, a thousand times blessed by your willing appearance.' Then, weeping himself as though life's latent goodness had unfolded a world beyond heartache, he bent his head, overcome. When next he dared look, the unicorn was gone. Her passage left only a swath of turned grass, darkened to tarnish where the gilding of dewdrops had fallen.

He became aware of someone arrived at his shoulder. Drawn by a tentative touch at his sleeve, he glanced aside, and welcomed the adept who came to assist with Elaira.

'What happened?' she asked, her gaze searching and awed. 'Outside, we heard the stones ring like bronze chimes.'

The spry old desertman closed reverent eyes. Gladness burst through, a rush of fine chills that pierced the flesh and the bone of him. 'A unicorn came.' As the lady's heart kindled to his shared spark of wonderment, he laughed. 'In warm life, not a sending! She bowed her neck and blessed this Koriani woman.'

The female adept shook her head, overwhelmed. 'Ath grant us this day, come again!'

Under the trees, surrounded by a field of damp grass and the delicate fragrance of flowers, the man raised his wrist and blotted the tears that spilled in gilt tracks down his cheeks. 'Joy has visited. We have not seen a Paravian presence for more than five hundred years. Now, the fresh promise is given. Upon right choice of destiny, Elaira's true love for a man might one day give rise to the key that recalls the lost Riathan home to the continent.'

The woman adept reached out and tenderly stroked a slipped lock of bronze hair from the sleeping enchantress's face. The skin, chapped by mountain weather, had softened into repose; the fierce worry smoothed over as her troubled mind found its solace in dreams. 'She may not remember, on the hour she awakes.'

The adept's walnut features split into a smile of irrepressible happiness. 'Her greater being knows. Her heart has been marked. We, here, who are guardians to Ath's deepest mysteries, will safeguard this moment without forgetting.'

Midwinter 5670

Noon Lane Tide

Sight of Rockfell Peak came and went many times, in the course of a journey that led through the Skyshiel uplands. No footpath marked the jumbled succession of cleft vales and serried ridges, or switched back up the jagged flanks of the crests. Nor did strayed travelers wander these deep wilds, where the narrow valleys twined like crooked mazes, and the stands of black firs stitched the slopes, silently cowled with snow. Only the bravest of solitary trappers laid snares by the freshets that tumbled and roared over sculpted rocks and smoothed ice. Even that breed of experienced woodsmen did not hunt under the peaks that rose like dark, weathered iron to the west.

Rockfell, they said, was a place where the winds cried and moaned, tuned by the voices of haunts. The man who listened too closely went mad. In the desolation of winter, the croak of wild ravens and the creak of the snow-laden boughs might become the only sounds heard for days. Such times, the uncanny notes sung by the spirits of air drew the ear like a whispered seduction.

Dakar the Mad Prophet scoffed at such tales, until weeks of labored progress on foot brought him to make camp at the crest of a spine on the ridges. Well past dawn, with the cookfire lit, and Fionn Areth beside him, he broached the sensitive discussion concerning the uncanny difficulties ahead. If the weather was clear, the patterns of the gusts carried plaintive overtones that sawed away stamina and nerves. No comfort, since travel was not going to get easier.

Rockfell's cragged summit reared to the west. A spike jabbed above mantled shoulders of stone, the peak ruled the rickled edge of the horizon, its implacable tip slicing the clouds like knapped flint. When they resumed their descent toward the flank of the next ridge, the dread view was not going to vanish. The approach from the northeast required a winding ascent through a notch in the ranges, then threading a flume to reach the base of the mountain itself.

By then grown wary of the younger man's whipsaw moods, melancholy complaint and stoic silences broken by volte-face spasms of idealism, Dakar understood he had best not avoid Fionn Areth's touchy questions. Soon enough, the issue of unseen powers was going to become unavoidable. Crouched over a pot of venison stew, his suet-round features nipped red by the cold, he gave grudging admission that the trappers' unease was not entirely unfounded. 'The Sorcerer, Davien, laid down spells of guard that don't treat kindly with strangers.'

Fionn Areth looked up. Thin, morning sunlight flashed off the horn-laminate bow he had delicately heated to unstring. While the weapon cooled, abandoned between mittened hands, he gave that statement his inimical attention. 'We're not strangers?'

Dakar licked his thumb, fished in the pot with the peeled end of a stick, and speared out a chunk of boiled meat. He nibbled, spat, and in unhurried nonchalance wiped a driblet of grease from his beard. 'Still tough. In fact, oak-tanned boot leather might taste more savory.'

'You didn't answer my question.' Fionn Areth wrapped a sturdy forearm around his tucked-up knees. The rigors of travel had worn his face hollow. Raffish and tense as a winter-lean badger, but with no such wild creature's wise patience, he leaned into the wind that snagged tangled black hair in the wire bristles darkening his jaw. 'Dakar?'

'Avenger's Black Chariot!' Meat and stick tumbled from slackened fingers and splashed back into the pot. Showered with scalding broth, the Mad Prophet shivered, as though Dharkaron's Five Horses had trampled over his gravesite. Eyes squeezed shut, with pungent deliberation, he swore, 'May the fiend hosts of Sithaer rain flaming piss on the doings of Jaelot's guardsmen!'

Fionn Areth gave up unstringing his bow. Surged to his feet, he snatched up his quiver and arrows. 'What's wrong? What's happened?'

Hunched under three cloaks like a feather-ruffled partridge, Dakar blinked. 'I had spells of guard sewn into Prince Arithon's saddlecloth.'

The pause stretched too long. Fionn Areth yanked off his right-hand glove with his teeth and tested the string to see how much the bow's tension had slackened. 'And?'

'Put your broadheads away! You can't shoot that far. The mare wearing that blanket broke its leg. She has just expired of a mercy stroke dealt on the downs near the walls of Ithamon.' The Mad Prophet recovered his cooking stick and jabbed it clean by ramming the point with concentrated viciousness into the snowbank beside the supply packs. The weeks of sparse rations had thinned him, but now he all of a sudden looked haggard. 'No, the animal didn't just stumble and pitch herself head over heels. The arrow that bled out her life had a broad head forged by the armory smith back in Jaelot. Furies of Sithaer! If I had a flask, I'd hole up in a thicket and drink myself flat senseless.'

'What of your prince?' Fionn Areth asked, vehement. 'Do you care if he's dead? What if his enemies took him alive, or left him mortally wounded?'

Dakar bit back an uprush of spite, then sharp grief, that the Araethurian herder's fickle change of heart *could have come* at the ruined mill, before Arithon of Rathain had been forced to play sacrifice as a decoy. Yet brutal honesty choked him from speech. Often enough in the past, his own mistimed hatreds had threatened the last s'Ffalenn prince. If guilt and care would allow no forgiveness for abandoning his charge of protection, Dakar at least forced a measure of tolerance. 'Since I didn't pack gin for sweet ease and forgetfulness, any answers must be sought through magecraft. Will I get your self-righteous knife in my back, Fionn? No? Then damned *well* show me proof the use of cast spells won't raise your chicken-heart moral hackles.'

Fionn Areth flushed. 'I know goats, not much else.' A furious gust off the heights flogged his cloak, and streamered the cook-fire to ribbons. Rigid and miserable, and chilled to the bone, he gestured with obdurate sarcasm. 'Since we don't have a white kid to kill as a sacrifice, I can't very well volunteer to pin its neck down for the knife.'

Dakar hurled his sharpened stick into the coals. 'I'm Fellowship trained!' He ducked wind-borne sparks, his exasperation stinging enough to scale the rust off old iron. 'They don't work dark rites on the death of small animals. Neither did Arithon s'Ffalenn, when he still had the use of his birth-born talents. He earned his high mastery under the mages at Rauven. Whatever fools' talk you've heard in town taverns, the teaching he received regarded such practice as misuse and abomination.'

'Never mind animals,' Fionn Areth hurled back. 'Some folk insist you use men, even children and babies.' His stare level green, though the hands clamped on the horn recurve were shaking, the herder wrapped himself in the clay dignity drawn from his backcountry origins. 'Do you wonder why townborn and craftsmen are frightened? The Alliance flaunts the sealed evidence of witnesses. If the best thing I can do for Arithon's cause is to take a long stroll down the ridge, *then just say so!*'

'Stay,' Dakar snapped. 'I'd rather you saw the bare bones of the truth. Better still, why not help? You could take the tin basin. Melt down some snow since I'm going to require clean water to call in a scrying.'

For a moment, the mismatched pair locked horns, the spellbinder resigned as a tortoise bearing the weight of the world on his back, and the younger man given no civil direction to vent his heated frustration.

'Or don't help. The worst may have already happened.' The Mad Prophet shed the wadded cloaks from bowed shoulders. He arose, upended the supply pack, and from the oiled cloth satchel that stored his herbs and bottled tinctures, removed a silk-wrapped packet.

'What's in that?' Fionn Areth laid his bow aside, his truce ambivalent as he fetched the tin basin. Unbidden fear and frank curiosity pinched a frown between his jet eyebrows, *so like Arithon's*. The likeness at times raised uncanny chills, or startled queer twists of juxtaposed memory.

'You'll see soon enough.' Dakar remained too pressured for tact. Nightmares had harried his sleep once too often, where the s'Ffalenn prince stood endangered, or dead, with himself caught hobbled and helpless. 'I already gave you my promise not to keep wicked secrets.'

'That's meant to reassure me?' As though the relentless chill granted the pretense for Fionn Areth to move, he gathered his nerve and set off. His goatherd's planted, deliberate stride jarred, so unlike Arithon's instinctive, cat grace as he footed his way down the scree slope.

Grumbling the impressive invective learned in the shoreside brothels, Dakar hunkered down. Always, the cruel, thin air of the heights worked his lungs like a stranded blowfish. In rugged country or mild flat lands, he never relished the nitpicking practice of spellbinding. He had long since lost count of his cringing mistakes. For ongoing centuries, refined energies had slipped through his inept handling like spilled pins. He endured his defeats, sunk in shame and embarrassment, or shook them off with self-mocking deprecation. Often, he felt, he would have to be dead, to match even one minute of Asandir's wisdom, or rise to the standard of exacting, sure touch and utterly steadfast patience.

Nor could a man concentrate on an empty belly, with half a hundred hard corners of granite stabbing his backside like punishment. Dakar clawed underneath himself and singled out a particularly offending small stone. 'Daelion Fatemaster take pity!' He shied the fragment into the abyss that faced Rockfell in a flash-burn explosion of temper. 'Why in the name of Sithaer's sixtyscore fiends did I ever get myself born to woman' – the rock landed and plowed up a shower of snow – 'far *less* saddle myself with the cross-grained affairs of the almighty Fellowship Sorcerers?'

No natural force answered.

Overhead, frayed stringers of cloud raced over a zenith of bottomless indigo. The sun cast its dazzling patchworked light across acres of wilds, and gilded his face with scarcely a vestige of warmth. The rare glimpse of fair weather did nothing to lift the dread fastened over his heart. Dakar sucked a deep breath, and coughed. Bracing air made his lungs ache. Anytime, he preferred the sweaty, close fug of a second-rate tavern's taproom. Drowned in beer, or sunk in pumping bliss with some harlot, he would not have to care if the last s'Ffalenn prince died alone on the barrens of Daon Ramon.

'Mercy upon me,' he whispered, desperate to stem the tears scalding the backs of his eyelids. He steeled quailing nerves, stilled circling thoughts, and surrendered the comfort of his innermost mental barriers. He grasped the unruly threads of his worry and stifled their clamor in stern discipline. *For good reason* fear stalked him. He had never earned mastery, or achieved firm control over his gifted talent. Even as he invoked the calm to engage the expanded vision of mage-sight, he invited the chance that his mad bent toward prescience might resurge and rule him instead.

He might see Arithon's body, torn bloody and fallen, or worse: the dark passion of Jaelot's guardsmen. Their behavior would not be pretty as they gave free rein to their ideological Alliance doctrine. Too likely, townbred men-at-arms would satiate their terror of the dark by exacting full measure of maiming torment on the hide of their s'Ffalenn victim.

Bathed in clammy sweat, and chilled to the bone by the

hounding north winds, Dakar forced back his ravening doubts. He wrapped himself in his mantle, closed his eyes, then unreeled a line of questing thought through the vast sky arched overhead. In full daylight, he needed the Name of one star, risen high on its course toward the zenith; with that fact in hand, he must determine the precise moment the same body would cross the azimuth meridian. A Fellowship Sorcerer's majestic, poised mind could encompass an ongoing tapestry of consciousness that placed him as one point, *knowing*, in connection to all other awarenesses, seen and unseen. As an apprentice spellbinder, the Mad Prophet's skill was less facile.

Earthbound in the five senses of his mortality, Dakar, like the worm, had to grope. He turned his mind inward. Mental static subsided. He held firm until his consciousness stayed contained, a stilled pool against which the mage-sense that tracked the unseen could cast its refined reflection. Listening, Dakar cast a tactile thought into the bottomless well of the sky.

By rote knowledge, he tuned out the disparate voices of everything else: the whistle of the wind, and the rattle of storm-beaten fir branches. Their sounds in the ear were no less manifest than the voice of their being, that strand of aliveness that, interwoven, formed the fabric of all Ath's creation. Each spun thread held Name, and could be marked and traced through the realms of existence that lay open to mage-sight. A star, in that context, sang in chords of exquisite complexity. Each made itself known, an explosive, exuberant play of energies, forming and unforming in the fire dance pavane that interfaced matter and light. A pure cry of high frequency, a star's existence formed a gateway through the veil of the mysteries. Their identity crossed outside of imposed time and space; as the mind of a man might, when exactingly trained to know the elusive byways that stepped his awareness beyond the dense limits of five senses enfleshed.

Each star's patterning was self-aware, distinct in personality as no other. Dakar sifted, and puzzled, and sorted with precision. At length, he picked out the grand harmony of the constellation arisen to position overhead. Then, in a second pass, infinitely more taxing, he refined his perception to isolate the *one* star that would best serve his need. He must find it by Name, then make himself known in return, to exchange the requisite permissions. All this, he must do in the span of a moment, joined at one with the heavens that turned to the spin of Athera upon her grand axis.

A jab in the ribs knocked him rudely from trance. 'Merciful maker! Now of all times, *how can you slip off to sleep*?'

Dakar snapped open offended brown eyes. Fionn Areth stood over him, the tin basin brimming with snow clods. Rather than risk receiving the load in a cascade over his head, the Mad Prophet scrambled upright, hand clutched to his side where the young man's boot toe had rammed him. 'I wasn't asleep, you idiot goatherd!' Wrung by savage dizziness, he clasped mittened hands to his temples. 'Obviously, you've never seen a sorcerer in trance state.'

The disastrous shock to his nerves ebbed away. While his wheeling senses resettled into the sluggish couch of his body, Dakar held fast to the Name for the star he had garnered, rising barely minutes away from the overhead peak of its passage. The snow in the basin must be melted by then. Otherwise, he would lose his opening to scry. Too ugly, the chance his effort would be wasted. What use, to summon help, if Prince Arithon's predicament had already been ended by sword, then a pine torch, touched to a pile of faggots.

'Set that basin heating over the coals.' The Mad Prophet pawed through the rumpled mantle wadded over his lap, relieved to recover the silk-wrapped packet unharmed in the scrip at his waist. He had always disliked working spellcraft with an audience. Since the antagonism seeded by Fionn Areth's ignorance set him on edge all the worse, he diverted the young man with chores. 'Scrounge out a burned twig or a sliver of charcoal. Something I can use to scribe out a protective circle.'

Next, Dakar swept off a flank of raised rock, if not level, at least with a reasonably flat surface upon which to work the ceremonial array for a star scrying. He accepted the snowmelt in the basin, aware of the sun, climbing the arc toward winter noon. More seconds fleeted by as he spat on singed fingers, then tried again to grip the charcoal Fionn Areth had just raked from the firebed.

Breath plumed from his lips, streamed white in the cold as Dakar invoked a Paravian blessing to honor and hallow the ground.

'We always begin with the circle,' he explained, drawing the figure around the aligned basin. Fionn Areth watched, huddled beside the heaped coals for their warmth, or perhaps for their illusion of security. Larger worries eclipsed the concern that the venison pot had boiled dry. 'Next we mark off the cardinal directions, then intercede for cooperation from the four elements.'

Fionn Areth frowned as Dakar scratched the symbols for each point, beginning with air, at the east. 'How can you tell where due north is, precisely?'

'So you would also, if you learned to listen.' Like a vulture hunched underneath trailing cloaks, Dakar drew runes for south, west, then north on his circle. 'A good many clansmen are gifted with that awareness from birth.'

A pause, while the wind screamed and gusted. The water in the basin puckered, then hardened under the onslaught. Dakar swore, flung the charcoal aside, and scooped out a glassine fan of new ice. He would have to work swiftly. Should the water freeze over, he would lose his moment. Noon and midnight offered the most propitious times to craft an efficient scrying.

'This,' he said, stripping the tie from the silk, 'is a shred from a bandage once used to bind up a gash Prince Arithon made to seal an oath of truth for his *caithdein*. Understand, and clearly, it is my limitation that demands the use of an artifice.'

Asandir would more simply visualize Arithon's face, and by an unfailing recollection of detail, invoke a tie to his presence. A musical talent might sing in trued pitch and engage the harmonies of his Grace's Name. Since the Mad Prophet's froggy vocals would lose in a contest with a rusty hinge on a post, he resigned himself to crude methods and tore off a thread from the spotted linen. 'Just so you know the old trace of blood in this cloth will not empower this spellcraft, but only serve to hold its alignment to Arithon.'

Of course, there were subtleties beyond time to explain. Dakar cupped the ripped swatch of thread in his hand, guarded in hope that the blood pact once sworn between prince and *caithdein* could be used to touch Lord Jieret as well. Arithon had still wielded his mage-sighted talent when he had sealed binding friendship with the Earl of the North; and Jieret had inherited the s'Valerient gift of Sight. Dakar knew, as he followed each step in due order, that the rite he enacted would cast an array of hidden ramifications. By the Law of the Major Balance, each conscious act affected all others across the greater breadth of Ath's creation.

Invocations by grand conjury crossed outside the veil, past the warp-and-weft barriers of time and space that wove the world known by the senses. Spoken language fell short of description. Subjected to Fionn Areth's critical attention, Dakar fumbled to impart how a precisely tuned thought and intent could dissolve the mind's perceived boundaries. For today, he must free the reflective properties of water, and bring the element to respond to the rarefied vibration called down within the protected circle.

The Mad Prophet inscribed the linked chain of Paravian runes that ruled water. Next, he asked the requisite permission, and marveled, as he always did, as the surface smoothed over and acquired the mirror-bright sheen of pooled mercury. While Fionn Areth exclaimed, nervous and amazed, the Mad Prophet tipped his face skyward. 'Sun and star will cross the meridian, here, and fix our place of reference. This won't be easy to comprehend. But all event, past and present, is in fact simultaneous outside the bounds of the veil. For scrying, we have to establish a beacon point, a site of response for the natural forces that spell and rune will channel in answer to match our framed template.'

Dakar spoke the incantation to invoke the star, linking her portal to the one just created by circle and water. Then he cast the stained fragment of cloth into the basin, and waited the unbearable, agonized interval leading into the moment of noon.

Sweating with tension, with no second chance if he fumbled the timing, Dakar held his breath while, stubborn as any set bloodstain, the rusty clot in the thread slowly soaked through and dissolved. Mage-sight detected the delicate, smoke haze as the energies unwound in release, the trace magnetics of Arithon's identity dispersed and then imprinted into the volatile essence of water. The juncture of spellcraft reached consummation as his signature frequencies and the star's, overhead, resolved into vertical phase.

'Now!' Dakar whispered. Hope raised a flame of fierce expectation, as in response to relentless finesse his drawn rune lit to hazed phosphor, then drifted above the basin. Upon that actualized charge of prime power, the spellbinder invoked the sworn permission granted by the Shadow Master for the sake of protection and safety. Dakar followed with the Paravian command for the heightened awareness connecting spirit and flesh. *'Tiendar!'*

If Arithon Teir's'Ffalenn had not crossed Fate's Wheel, if he still breathed, incarnate, the star as it crossed the arc of the zenith would conjoin with his living self. A reflection would appear within the spelled water, unveiling his location and circumstance.

Response came, not the blank darkness Dakar most feared, but a vista of snow-clad landscape. The Mad Prophet knew the stony, rising ground, where the hillcrests cut the wind-raked sky like the etched rims of broken crystal. The site lay near the ruins of Ithamon, amid Daon Ramon Barrens. There the spell-marked water in the basin resolved a fleeting image of armed men wearing Jaelot's colors. Several conferred in a tight-knit group. Others posted a nervous guard over a bound and unconscious prisoner. Dakar received the alarming impression of bloodstained snow. The twist of black hair masking Arithon's face was snarled to his scalp, whorled into a clotted scab.

Overhead, in the Skyshiels, the sun reached station, climbed to the peak of its arc. That selfsame, meshed second, the flux of the noon tide peaked and cascaded down the fifth lane.

A burst of white light blasted off the spelled basin. The poised rune became immolated. Flash-burned, near blinded, Dakar howled an oath. His rank language entangled with a peal of wild sound far above range of mortal hearing. Yet to senses not mage-gifted, that cried note of alarm rippled across air and matter, a deep, belling toll that stirred and shook the bedrock roots of the mountains.

'What's happening?' Fionn Areth shot erect in dismay, his nape roughened to sudden gooseflesh. Hand grasped to his sword, he frantically glanced right and left while the diminishing shudder of low-range harmonics shivered the stone underfoot. 'Merciful Ath! What harm have you called down upon us?'

'No harm. Nothing demonic. Put away that fool steel, you're not going to be threatened!' Dakar spat a final, furious epithet, hands pressed to the ringing shell of his skull to damp out the lingering, persistent vibration still ranging through his mage-sense. When Fionn Areth's sword instead turned point first and threatened to skewer his neck, he shouted in exasperation. 'A plain scrying never initiates energy. This was a passive spell, drawn upon feminine principles and run through a cipher of noninterference! The event that just happened was not the effect of anything done by my conjury.'

Fionn Areth bore in until the trembling tip of his blade rasped the unshaven skin of the Mad Prophet's throat. 'Well, prove that.'

'I can't. This once, why not just believe me?' Dakar shut his eyes, snapped to ripe irritation: at least when he had suffered the same treatment by Arithon, the s'Ffalenn prince's hand did not shake. His word was no lie. Rank fool that he was, pressed by haste and concern, he had simply neglected to use common sense, or recall Asandir's basic teaching. He should have remembered the obvious step to account for his current location.

'Well, mountains don't quake for no reason, as my granduncle would say in Araethura,' Fionn Areth retorted. When Dakar's stiff silence gave him no choice but to kill or back down, still in ignorance, he sheathed his steel. Arms crossed, feet planted, he held his ground, while the fat prophet rubbed his chafed skin in scowling, ungrateful relief. 'Why should I believe the forked tongue of a sorcerer?'

'Spellbinder,' Dakar groused in correction, then grappled the steel-shod spike of a headache to form a coherent answer. 'We're due east of Rockfell, placed on direct line with the ley which crosses the Paravian circle at Ithamon.'

The herder's hard stare and blank face showed he failed to see the connection.

All but yanking his beard in martyred impatience, Dakar bit back his curses and qualified. 'When Arithon received his due sanction as Teir's'Ffalenn, a Fellowship ceremony linked his spirit in a vow of dedicated service to the land. The force that just upset our scrying was Rathain's very heartrock, responding to the distress of its threatened crown prince.'

'I saw Jaelot's guardsmen in your spelled water,' Fionn Areth admitted. Thawed enough to relax stiff ideals and his death grip on harebrained histrionics, he stood down, his stout hand released from his sword grip. 'They'll surely kill him.'

Dakar massaged his aching temples, as though gouging pressure could wrest more detail from the wisp of ephemeral memory. 'Not right away. His captors appeared too scared foolish to act. The petty officer in charge has sent for his captain and strong reinforcements. That could buy delay, perhaps until tomorrow morning.' He hesitated, pricked by the disturbing hunch something *else* of importance eluded him. Yet pursuit of that thought led him nowhere. A mental blank wall encompassed his mind, and no prompt stirred his latent prescience.

Fionn Areth regarded the suspect water, slowly freezing in the tin basin. 'Is that it? His Grace just dies? Nothing more can be done with your vaunted powers to help?'

'From here? No.' As though the appeal had not shown a stunning volte-face concerning the use of strong magecraft, Dakar shrugged. 'I was never the most gifted of Fellowship apprentices.' Where before knowing Arithon, he would have hedged, now, he just stared at his boots. 'The sad truth is, I never reached mastery.' This, despite the embarrassing centuries of Asandir's thorough instruction.

Shamed by past failings; not about to be criminally careless twice in the course of one day, the Mad Prophet attended his botched construct. He took strict steps to effect proper ritual, not speaking until he had released the hung remnants of his disrupted conjury.

While the wind bit cold through the thin, winter sunlight, Dakar rewrapped the stained scrap of linen. His care denounced fate, that within hours, the man whose blood had once soaked the cloth might be lost beyond reach, his spirit passed over Daelion's Wheel to lay down the harsh burdens of this lifetime. Savaged by regret, that a friendship whose depths had yet to be plumbed might end with such brutal finality, Dakar pitched the iced water from the basin.

Fionn Areth looked on in dull misery. Contrary creature that he was, his brooding would be sourced in a sudden resurgence of guilt.

The Mad Prophet saw, and gentled his attacking frustration. 'All hope isn't lost. Do you set faith in prayer? Then beg whatever powers will answer that the resonant cry you sensed from Ithamon will call in the attention of the Fellowship. Sethvir, at Althain, will act if he can. He may already have dispatched a Sorcerer. Last I heard, Traithe was camped in the mountains south of Forthmark. The eastern spur of the Kelhorns will resonate to the fifth lane, and despite his crippled strength, he still interprets speech out of stone very clearly.'

Yet as the Mad Prophet gathered himself and arose, he dared not voice the fullest extent of his fear. Speaking dread thoughts only lent them the more impetus, and allowed them more chance to come true. Yet avoidance could not banish the unpleasant facts: with deadly surety, the distress cry broadcast by the hills of Daon Ramon must raise the Koriathain to alert. They would plumb the cause and discover Arithon's current state of helplessness. Other Alliance enemies who employed the mage-gifted against Shadow might sense the disturbance as readily. If they knew the old lore well enough to recognize Ithamon's affirmed linkage to the oathsworn heir of Rathain's royal line, they would muster and converge on the site with self-righteous zeal and armed war hosts.

Winged

On the winter white verge of the wood lying northeast of Karfael, an old hedge woman with bundled owl feathers laced through her hair slips past the royal guard and grasps the bridle of the young prince's palfrey, pronouncing, 'Your Grace, Teir's'Ilessid! In Ath's blessed name, I am come to grant you the gift of a luck charm to ward your royal person from danger . . .'

High over the snow-covered hills near Ithamon, a golden eagle spirals in upward flight, and when he seems no more than a fleck drifting under the vaulting of cloud, he wings south and westward, his sharp eyes surveying all that moves across the sere Barrens of Daon Ramon . . .

Farther south, in an upland valley in Vastmark, a Sorcerer pauses in traverse of a shale slope, his head turned in surprise as the raven launches from its accustomed perch on his shoulder: 'You've been summoned, little brother? Then fly with my blessing, and pass on my news to Sethvir . . .'

VI. Clan War Band

On his knees in thin snow, Earl Jieret, *caithdein* of Rathain, braced his gloved hand on a sharp rim of rock to anchor his reeling senses.

'My lord, you're unwell?' said an iron, gruff voice to one side. Sidir knew him as deeply as his oldest scar, being one of the fourteen survivors of the slaughtered generation lost to war on the banks of Tal Quorin.

Beyond reply, the red-bearded clan chieftain jerked his chin in negation. His head whirled still. The nausea that had just emptied his belly yet knifed through him in dousing, white waves. He gripped the rock; waited, sure as rain the sickness that siezed him was not the result of spoiled meat.

He suffered a resurgence of disorienting darkness, then a moment of rippling confusion as his stressed senses gradually stabilized. The aftermath receded, leaving him stranded in the pallid light of winter afternoon. Above him, torn clouds cast their marching shadows across the high, ocher grasses tipped through the snow-covered barrens of Daon Ramon.

The day had utterly ceased to be ordinary: the subliminal cry that had knifed through the land resounded still in his memory. As though for one moment the rock and the soil of Rathain had been given voice to express an event of agonized extremity.

Jieret s'Valerient, Earl of the North, knew but one man for whom such an outcry would manifest. More than the realm's dedicated *caithdein*, he was also blood bond to a prince granted lawful sanction for crown rule. Their paired fates stood linked with Rathain's destiny, a tie that transcended the enactment of ceremony. Asandir of the Fellowship had himself conducted the ritual of affirmation. His was the adept command of the mysteries that had transmuted a handful of dross soil into the silver circlet that conjoined royal flesh and living earth into a lifelong partnership. A Sorcerer's seal had set the husbandry of five territories on the brow of the mortal man blood-born to uphold the high kingship.

'My lord?' whispered Sidir, strained to anxiety as the silence extended.

Jieret braced his leather-clad shoulder against the weathered slab of the rock. Still distinctly unsteady, he scrubbed his pale face with a dousing handful of snow. 'Trouble,' he gasped, as his tight throat unlocked.

He pushed off and arose. The ground underneath him felt too solid, a disjointed, unimaginable distance removed from the uncanny wave of subsonic vibration and refined light that had transmitted his prince's raw anguish. Sidir caught his groping arm in assistance and steadied the first, awkward step.

'We'll have to ride hard,' said Earl Jieret, succinct. His large hands, out of habit, checked the hang of his weapons, then jammed down his brindled wolf hat. 'If I must hazard a *caithdein's* guess, an enemy force has outpaced our intent and already made camp at Ithamon.'

'From where?' Sidir as ever showed no surprise. His stance stayed poised and quiet, except for a gray-shot wing of seal hair, that the wind flicked and lashed across his high forehead, and the stoic, deep lines etched into his windburned features.

'Jaelot, most likely, which means they're bone stubborn, to have stayed the course through Baiyen Gap.' Restored to himself, Jieret closed the few strides to his horse and vaulted back into the saddle. He snapped a curt hand signal. The swift, all-but-silent flurry of movement that drew his war band from close cover around him did not fire his usual pride and fierce confidence.

The rest of his hunch was too ugly to hazard. Certainly his gift of Sight had never before provoked sickness. Yet Jieret was no spirit to shrink from harsh facts. Survival came first. He had to weigh the frightful possibility that the Teir's'Falenn who embodied clan hopes had suffered a violent blow to the head. If the Master of Shadow was in enemy hands, not only Rathain's future, but the fate of the world rocked on the brink of disaster. Luhaine's given warning had been harshly concrete when defining the grim balance that hung upon Arithon's life thread.

'Ride!' Jieret shouted, his broad shoulders too determined to bend before the abject terror that raked him. His place was to stand at the shoulder of kings, and if need called, like his father, to die there. The anguish hurt worse than a tearing wound, that Ithamon lay fully twenty leagues eastward, on the far side of a chopped spread of ravines and rough, untenanted territory.

He might drive his company until their horses foundered, with nothing gained except grief. At two hundred strong, his hard-bitten war band could not cover the distance without rest. Nor could they forgo the short pauses to hunt, while the small, shaggy hill horses prized for their hardiness scoured the lee hillsides for fodder. They faced nothing less than ten days of hard travel, given fair-weather conditions. Even a select strike force sent in advance would reach the ruin too late to matter.

Bad odds did not reconcile Earl Jieret to the looming possibility of defeat. He would ride past the Wheel of Fate, if need be, to stand with his prince for the passage. Over the next crest, the fresh wind in his face, he counted three hours to sundown.

'Come on, you windbag sack of hot tripes!' He weathered the bucked stride as the surly hill pony flattened ears to the stab of his heels. 'You won't like the life you'll be forced to lead if my prince meets his hour of reckoning.'

When the shortest days ended on Daon Ramon Barrens, the light ebbed from the arch of the sky like water drained out of a bowl. The lingering afterglow lit a band of citrine above the cut-sable folds of the hills notching the western horizon. Early stars claimed the deep cobalt of the zenith, nicked flecks of silver that brightened and burned over the swept rock, and deep-drifted, snow-clad swales. The clan companies led by Earl Jieret called a halt to last until the late-night rise of the moon. They would let the hill ponies recover and graze, and snatch rest and sustenance as they could, while the cold settled biting and bitter, and spiked hoarfrost dusted the thickets.

No fires were lit. Posted scouts stood sharp watch on the ridges, their best assurance no trouble approached the howl of the free-ranging wolf packs.

The clan courier sent out of Halwythwood overtook them at last. Only canny experience let him spot the deep fold where they camped, thinly covered by scrub and dead bracken. He answered the sentry's crisp challenge, well aware that drawn bows would stay trained upon him until a cousin affirmed his identity. Led in by the watch on perimeter patrol, the man found Earl Jieret hunkered down on his bearskin cloak, kneading knuckles that reeked of wintergreen horse liniment into the iron-tight sinews of his neck.

Disheveled, exhausted from unimaginable setbacks, the man delivered the message he had borne like a knife in the chest throughout fifty leagues of hard travel. 'My lord, I bring desperate news from the west.'

'Sit!' Jieret ordered. 'You look ready to fall over.' He unhooked a flask from the thong on his cross belt, a silver-inlaid horn filled with neat brandy. 'Speak again when you're steady.'

The scout was still youthful, if pitifully haggard. He swayed, then crumpled, in sore need of sleep. His fur jacket was matted. Stout leathers were shreds about calves and knees, ripped to ruin on the briar. To close the long lead and overtake the clan war band, he would have run league after league on foot, one arm linked through a stirrup to spell his wearied horse. Nor had he spared time for the rites at the standing stones, to placate the ghosts that whirled thick as floss on the roadway from Caith-al-Caen. Some of their haunted light shone in his eyes as he gathered frayed nerves and related details of the Alliance armed force now mustered and marching from Morvain.

Earl Jieret snapped an oath through shut teeth. A bystander ventured a question.

'No mistake.' Fingers clamped white on the neck of the flask, the courier gasped out the disheartening gist. 'Our scouts snagged a townsman who strayed too far from camp. He talked. We know Lysaer s'Ilessid himself's south of Narms. He's got a sunwheel priest and ten veteran officers spearheading a second strike force of experienced headhunters. Ath help us, they're guided. The target of both war bands is the ruins at Ithamon. They're expecting to corner Prince Arithon.'

'Save us all, they will find him.' Jieret shot to his feet. More than strong fumes from the liniment sheened his eyes to an anguished brilliance. 'How has this happened? Jaelot's ahead of us! Morvain and Narms move abroad in deep winter. If Lysaer's involved, we have to presume they're acting in concerted strategy. We could find ourselves facing the brunt of an Alliance campaign on the wide-open ground of the barrens.'

No band of armed clansmen could stand down such numbers, not without forest or mountains to cover them. Nor could Arithon withstand a head-on encounter with his half brother. The affray at Riverton had confirmed the bleak course of the murderous insanity brought on by Desh-thiere's curse. Jieret felt all of a sudden unmoored, as though the harsh cut of the wind scoured through his hollow sense of foreboding. Far too likely, the clan company mustered from Halwythwood might not leave the barrens alive.

For of course, they must fight. Turning tail would save nothing. If Arithon died, and Alliance ways triumphed, then across the four kingdoms Lysaer held in sway, clan bloodlines would be laid waste under a decree of extermination.

His tone sparked to iron, Jieret signaled the perimeter scout, who listened, close-mouthed, at his shoulder. 'Get me Sidir. Wake the other Companions. Tell them we face a disaster.'

Unless a clan counsel could find the means to call down a miracle, Rathain's dwindled liegemen could suffer a repeat of the grief that had blood-soaked the banks of Tal Quorin.

Under the frost-point blaze of the stars, and amid icy wind in the bracken, the Companions gathered to weigh the course of their forthcoming action. Chafing chilled hands, breaths plumed in the cold, they lit no small fire for comfort. Their wary presence left almost no track on the desolate face of the landscape, with reason. These were the men of Deshir who, as boys, had survived the grim knives of Etarra's vengeance three decades and one year in the past. On Daon Ramon that night, at the side of their chieftain, were nine of the original fourteen who remained of a slaughtered generation. Three others had since died in forays against headhunters, one in Arithon's service at Dier Kenton Vale. Another guarded Halwythwood, as war captain and advisor to Jieret's family. The youngest, and least reconciled to the deaths at Tal Quorin, still maintained an obdurate presence in the endangered clan warrens of Strakewood.

The hate ran bone deep, for what they had lost. Stark as storm-weathered granite in their rawhide-laced furs and worn weapons, they huddled in darkness to answer the feud that never ceased threatening their people. No moon yet shone to reveal their expressions as the dire news was unfolded. Yet Earl Jieret could sense desperation like bared steel in Sidir's scouring silence. The same stifled foreboding was repeated in Theirid's crossed arms, and Braggen's fixed grasp on his sword hilts. Opinions were given in minimal phrases. No man disputed the need to split forces. Arithon s'Ffalenn could not be abandoned to suffer the Mayor of Jaelot's sentence of execution; nor could Lysaer s'Ilessid be permitted to savage Daon Ramon with war under drive of Desh-thiere's curse.

The relentless flaw that gutted each strategy became the unyielding reality of numbers. 'Send too few to Ithamon, we risk losing our prince to the enemy,' Sidir pointed out. His habitual, acid-etched clarity was enforced by the ramming stab of a finger. 'Send too many, and the others who ride north to set traps on the Second Age road through the barrens can't prevail. A handful won't buy his Grace any time to escape open land and reach safety.'

No one belabored the unpleasant truth, that the war band which rode to stand down s'Ilessid must shoulder a suicide mission. Earl Jieret had witnessed the firestorm of destruction Lysaer's gift of light had visited upon the war fleet at Minderl Bay. The swept, snow-clad downs of the barrens would give his clansmen no shelter. Each foray to divert the Alliance advance must be closed under ruinous disadvantage, from a state of relentless exposure.

'We're going to be targets, no mistake about that.' Theirid spat in contempt, the black-fox tails tied into his clan braid a barbaric mane down his back. 'Can't pin them with arrows, either. Not if they slink like the townbred at Valleygap, and cower beneath their supply wains.'

Braggen laughed, sour. 'Well, they can't very well cram their draft beasts under the axles beside them.' He lifted his massive shoulders in the shrug that trademarked his hot-tempered courage. 'Can't move on Daon Ramon without their supplies. To buy time for our liege, starvation will stall them. The wild game can be hazed off, as well.'

No one dwelled on discussion of the carnage that must surely follow such forays to tweak the tail of the tiger. The Caithwood campaign had left none in doubt of the Alliance intent to eradicate ancient clan bloodlines. Each back-and-forth volley of debate thrashed over which way to divide the inadequate strength of their war band.

'We sleep on it,' Earl Jieret determined at length. 'At moonrise in three hours, we'll cast final votes and decide. Dharkaron avenge, if we're wrong, we lose ground just as surely as if we waste time chasing more pointless arguments.'

'We can drink to good hunting.' Sidir loosed a brittle, snarling laugh. 'Who among us thought we would ever die abed? I never did fancy being shut inside walls through a siege.'

In a camaraderie sharpened by pending crisis, Earl Jieret unstoppered his flask and shared his last brandy amid the brotherhood of his Companions. 'May the blood on my blade be Lysaer s'Ilessid's,' he vowed as he sent them to rest.

Wrapped in the faintly rancid taint of his heaviest bear-pelt mantle, Earl Jieret crawled under a windbreak of bushes, stretched out, and closed his eyes. Like the swift, savage gusts that battered the stripped branches, his burden of worry refused to retreat. Too vividly real, the bleak possibility his prince could lie dead before sunrise. His absolute helplessness to stem that disaster crushed him to grief and despair. He felt paralyzed, numb, less alive than the lichened stone markers that gouged through the snow-silvered vales of Daon Ramon.

Jieret sucked in a bracing, cold breath and doused the ill bent of his thoughts. He must quiet his mind. Against the incessant anxiety that gnawed him, he strove to establish the stillness that opened the gateway to dreams. Like his father before him, he was gifted with Sight. Let him snatch one scant hour of peace, and he might tap into the elusive talent that gave rise to spontaneous augury. If his decision to divide the clan war band could save his imperiled sovereign, his tactics must dovetail with accurate foresight. The stakes ran too high for his limited resources; the far-flung desolation of the barrens was too vast to quarter for even large numbers of enemies. Jieret snugged down in his bearskin cloak, while the men in his company allowed him wide berth and strict silence. As well as he, they had measured bad odds. What slim chance existed for Arithon's reprieve must transcend blind luck and ride upon prescient vision.

The landscape of Daon Ramon spoke to a man beyond the veiled dark of closed eyelids. Earl Jieret lay slack, while the sough of the winds described hill and stone, and whined through their whipped stands of thorn brush. The distant call of a wolf pack howling glissandos in chorus interspersed with the call of the winter white owl. The deer who raked tines in the thickets walked abroad, to the forest-bred ear attuned and alert for the mincing, soft step of cloven hooves in the snow. Mice emerged from deep burrows to gnaw seeds and bark, tiny feet printing hieroglyph tracks.

Beyond the limits of sensory perception, the master who owned mage-sight might key into the finer pitched chant of rooted grass and the textured whisper of the black earth. Deep toned, beneath these, the vast well of existence unveiled the grand chords of harmonic resonance that bound the solidity of creation. Here in Daon Ramon, far removed from trade roads and commerce, the mysteries moved near to the surface, unchained. Where once the herds of Riathan Paravians ran in pearlescent, ethereal splendor, the terrain spoke to the listening ear and thinned the veil that bound time and dimension.

Earl Jieret never marked the second of transition between wakeful awareness and the half world of Sighted dreaming. The wind, the wolves, the nervous snorts of tethered horses seemed unchanged, until somebody swore insults in a gruff, townborn accent, and a booted foot jabbed at his shoulder.

He groaned, pulled apart by a shattering headache that he realized *was not his own.* His seer's gift had borne him to the hills near Ithamon, and folded him into the nightmare experience of Arithon's state of captivity . . .

'Bastard! You want to eat? Then wake up!' The boot came again, a spike of impatience whose agony wrenched him to breathless and dizzying nausea.

'Leave the wretch to himself,' a superior voice ventured advice from the sidelines. 'Give him gruel, he's just going to heave up his guts. And anyway, he's a lot less of a bother if he stays weak as a lamb, unconscious.'

Hostile footsteps retreated to the squeak of dry snow. The rolling, harsh spasms took longer to subside. Released to dull misery and cramping discomfort, Arithon lay in supine exhaustion. The return of full consciousness came as no boon, when hands and wrists were lashed tight with cord, and the cold gnawed with wretched persistence. The hair at his nape clung, sticky with blood, the scalp underneath tight with swelling. Pain came and went in angry, sharp throbs, and scattered his thoughts to delirium. Silted, thick mists obscured sight and blurred time as well, until he drifted, unmoored, and the phantom wings of a soaring eagle drew him back into past memory.

In another place, as unstrung by confusion and pain, he had raised his voice in denial as wounding as the bite of a vital sword thrust. '*Ah, Ath,*' he had cried to Halliron Masterbard, '*what have you given me if not another weapon for this feud?*'

Then the old man's admonition, resharpened by the unflinching veracity of the dying: '*Yes. And you will make me no promises, not to use to the fullest what you've earned. You forget. I have lived to see the sun's reemergence, and your part in the Mistwraith's defeat. If a masterbard's music can one day spare your life, or that of your loyal defenders, you will use it so, and without any binding ties to conscience.*'

The dream that linked Jieret to Prince Arithon's state of mind tore asunder, gone like rags of blown silk before the onset of prescient vision. The clan chieftain's gift tapped him into an event yet to come in the near to immediate future. The scene showed the same hills below the ruin of Ithamon, imprinted by moonlight to a landscape of sable velvet and mercury. Tucked into the snow-clad fold of a draw, Jieret saw armed guards and horse pickets, and amid these, the prone form of Rathain's prince, still bound as their prized captive. Though sprawled in the motionless appearance of unconsciousness, Arithon s'Ffalenn was awake; Jieret had observed enough wounded men to recognize the slight, subtle tension that marked a focused awareness.

The gift of his prescience granted him more: the soft, all-but-inaudible whisper of song called forth from the throat of a man trained as Masterbard.

That subliminal thread of sound swelled and grew, fashioned into a low, sustained note, richly textured with layers of harmonics. Its tonal complexities ranged beyond hearing, a living current that keyed into the true chord which accessed the world's primal mysteries. If the townsmen who paraded as sentries heard nothing, the land underneath their staid tread was not either deaf or oblivious. Answering vibrations awoke out of stone. First the pebbles and round boulders in the Severnir's bed, then the rocky crown of the hills joined with the bard's keening refrain. These in turn woke the bedrock foundations of the hills near Ithamon, until the staid granite underlying the cold earth rang to the same pitch, keyed downward to subsonic octaves.

Even removed in the solitude of dreams, Jieret sensed the hair at his nape prickle erect with foreboding. Whatever fell crafting the Masterbard spun, the effect would not leave any men inside earshot untouched by the weave of its summoning. Soon enough, the first sentry crumpled at the knees. Heedless of duty, he curled in the snow and yawned, his half-lidded eyes grown compulsively heavy until he slipped into fast sleep. One by one his companions succumbed also. Within minutes, the whole company sprawled in deep slumber, entrapped in the subtlety of the Masterbard's skill that wound a cocoon of dark sound. The slow rise and fall of their breathing became the sole sign of life left within them.

Unafflicted amid their motionless forms, Arithon rolled and wormed, belly down, toward the nearest of the fallen sentries. He paused often, nursing the pain in his head. The tender care as he extended his body became a heartbreaking testament to the intensity of his bruises. Still whispering fragmented song through locked teeth, he purloined the man's dagger, and in painstaking steps, freed his wrists. He sat up, swayed through a braced moment of dizziness, then sawed the cord binding his ankles. Still sick and unsteady as he rose to his feet, he disarmed his enemies with careful and chilling efficiency.

From the patrol's acting captain, he recovered his sword, Alithiel, his main gauche, and his confiscated hunting bow. Once only, he bent, racked through with cramps. His battered head pained him. His trained instincts as healer would warn him he should not be upright or walking. Nor could he afford to cosset his injuries, with who knew how many Alliance reinforcements inbound to take charge of a dangerous prisoner. Arithon wrapped snow into a rag as a compress. The deliberate pace of his movements bespoke a will that could dismantle mountains. Jieret's heart ached for the dream that would not allow him to offer his liege any word of encouraging comfort.

He could but watch as Arithon s'Ffalenn made his way to the picketed horses. He saddled one, then loaded the rest until his captors stood stripped of provisions. Dawnlight flooded the east primrose yellow by the hour he rode out, driving the small herd before him.

The chord raised to resonance through his Masterbard's art stayed sustained by the stone, as though the untamed fiber of the land spoke for the blood prince granted rule by the Fellowship's charter. Asleep in the snow, stripped of swords and provender, Jaelot's proud company slept oblivious, perhaps to awaken and discover their plight, or else to lie comatose until their hearts slowed, and the winter chill froze them to marble. Earl Jieret felt no shred of pity. Whether they died, or awoke to face a slower end by starvation, he prayed that Dharkaron let none of them stir before his liege was away and safely tucked into hiding.

Hunched in the saddle, grasping mane to keep balance against waves of sucking vertigo, the Master of Shadow turned northward. He did not look back. Ithamon was suspect, entrenched with camped enemies. Weak with shock as he was, he dared not reconnoiter and risk any chance of flushing more troops out to hound him.

'I'm sorry, *Caithdein*, my brother,' he pleaded, either raving, or else intuitively aware that in dream the absent earl who was his oathbound liegeman might hear his ragged apology. 'Tell Luhaine I can't keep our rendezvous.'

Whether Rathain's prince sensed the presence that rode with him, Jieret s'Valerient lost his chance to attempt a reply. The fickle thread of his prescient contact snapped under a surge of blank darkness. Through the void came the hissed sound of feathers in flight, then an ink-upon-blackness impression of form that resolved to reveal a jet raven.

The bird lit before him in a burst of white light, the whetted edge of its primaries obsidian knives that carved a haze of diffracted rainbows. The crisp rush of swept air as it folded its wings framed a Word far beyond spoken language. Jieret sensed the intelligence in its fathomless eye. Nor was the fine point of protocol left in doubt, that he must be the one to speak first.

'Do you bring me an augury?' he demanded, afraid, all too aware he lacked a schooled mage's discernment to tell if the presence before him was dangerous.

The raven shuffled its feathers as though to shake off the buffeting winds that blew far outside mortal awareness. Its clawed feet spanned a parchment scribed with a map of Daon Ramon. There, Jieret realized, its message could unveil the most critical course of the future; or the array might be the lure of a life-sucking demon, offered to tempt him to folly.

'Ath preserve, ten enemies with swords would be easier,' he snapped to himself in distaste. Yet a *caithdein* was born to spend life in royal service. Haunted by Arithon's plight at Ithamon, Jieret shook off quaking nerves and dared the risk of the next step.

'I accept you as harbinger, cruel though the news be,' he invited in ritual courtesy.

The raven that was Prophecy tipped its head to the map, then tapped its bill three times to the parchment. Vision bloomed at its touch, a daytime view of Ithamon's east-facing battlement. Beneath broken walls laced with canes of wild briar, Jieret beheld a muster of men. Their filthy, snagged surcoats bore the badge of Jaelot's snake and gold lion. Two officers argued inside their tight circle. Hot words and snapped gestures harangued against the mad prospect of tracking a captive who had escaped their patrol of outriders during the night.

Their woes were well justified. The criminal sorcerer had purloined critical supplies, and eight of their better horses. The haunts in the old ruin demoralized nerves, and the barrens offered inadequate shelter for those victims just found, and aroused out of spellbound sleep with their hands and feet crippled with frostbite. The bitter conditions that lamed them were not going to relent anytime before spring. In the deeps of midwinter, westbound storms would keep coming. Under such onslaught, even the wild deer sometimes sickened and froze on the downlands.

'What are you men, a bunch of fat farmers?' The captain at arms strode onto the scene and quashed the resolve to retreat. 'Just squat by the damned fire at the killing frost and count the acorns that fall on the roof? There's a sorcerer at large gaining ground while you whimper! I want *every* hale man in the saddle, and riding. The wounded and those without mounts are no use. They can limp in disgrace back to Jaelot!'

The small troop formed ranks, with the gruff, zealot captain still busy reviling the laggards. Lent the uncanny, keen eye of the raven, Jieret noticed an unnatural shimmer about the man's burly form. His imposing, mailed figure seemed spun about with filaments of violet light. Intuition unveiled the terrifying truth: that Prince Arithon's pursuit had been driven all along by a Koriani geas of obsession. The spirit forms that guarded the old Baiyen road, and the ghost cry of Ithamon did not daunt them. Even on short supplies, they would hound the Shadow Master's flight northward. Entrapped by the pull of strong spell seals, they were pressured to ride beyond the limit of sanity.

Jieret was granted no time to measure their plight in considered assessment. Once more he beheld the spread parchment map, with the raven's lordly, deliberate tread marking the path of Arithon's beleaguered flight northward. His Grace's evasion followed the dry gulch of the Severnir, the swale of the floodplain offering the best footing for a mounted man to make fast passage. At the broad, horseshoe loop, where the river bent east, the bird paused, its clawed feet planted between strides. It regarded Earl Jieret with mournful, sharp focus.

Then it croaked the Paravian word for the rune of beginning, and blinked . . .

A white moon rode the sky, three nights past full. Winter stars framed the hour, precisely.

A gaunt man dipped a glittering bronze pendulum in fresh blood and uttered unclean incantations through the drug-scented smoke of a brazier. One hot, scarlet droplet spattered the map, and ignited a scene of pandemonium.

'Rise!' screamed a priest in a sunwheel robe, standing guard at the site where the bloodstain had marred the inscribed terrain of Daon Ramon. His fanatic's glazed eyes beheld auguries in fire, and his shouts awoke horn calls that shattered the night calm.

'Rise and ride!' he exhorted. The banner he flourished in frenzied excitement showed the tower and mountain blazon of

Darkling. 'In the name of the Divine Prince, the faithful are called to raise swords for the cause of the Light!'

Rousted by his cries, men stumbled from sleep. They cursed, and groped through cold darkness for weapons and harness, and untied nervous horses from the picket lines. Trained hands yoked the six-in-hand teams to the supply sledges while the visionary priest bellowed his urgent tidings.

'Our allies from Jaelot drive the Spinner of Darkness in flight across Daon Ramon Barrens! For the mercy of the world, we are charged to take arms. Blessed is the steel that cuts down the enemy without quarter, and blessed the man who sends his black spirit to Dharkaron!'

On edge and watchful, Darkling's task force of three hundred advanced, westbound and primed for engagement. Through the eye of the raven, they appeared nondescript, a tinker's scrap of pins and steel filings, cast across moonlit dales. The defiles swallowed the shrill gleam of their steel. Gusting wind masked the snorts of their horses. Ahead, alone under the vast bowl of night sky, the Master of Shadow turned before them. He lashed his band of stolen geldings to flight, a tactic of graceless necessity.

Darkling's three hundred had caught him, exposed. They spurred their fresh mounts and gave chase. Vision showed their charge into the dry gulch of the Severnir. Relentlessly trapped, Arithon responded. The white moon showed his face, wrenched to wild-eyed grief, as he engaged his born gift and wrought shadow.

The bursting wave of the enemy advance plunged headlong into a well of spun blackness. The dark showed them no mercy, nor the ancient, water-smoothed boulders scabbed over with rills of green ice. The horses floundered. Rank upon rank, they tripped, and snapped legs, catapulted head over heels while their riders sprawled, dashed and broken among them. The rear guard reined back from the treacherous ravine. Valiant officers regrouped them. A brave few pressed ahead and picked out a safe crossing, only to find the unnatural darkness sucked the life and warmth from their bodies.

The terrain proved no ally, but winnowed them separate. First scattered, then cut down to groping, small groups, men blundered and circled and cursed the blanketing blindness until their wretched mounts shivered beneath them. The balking arrivals were driven on, whip and spur, until the iron bit rings froze fast to the flesh of their muzzles, and tore them to headshaking agony. Frightened riders drew rein and halted. The prudent who paused to seek wood and strike fire met their doom before moonset. The stones in the riverbed sang them to sleep, and the shadowing chill stopped their hearts.

The ones who wandered, distraught, survived, barely. When the first blush of dawn touched the white-shrouded waste of the barrens, the company that had marched from the city of Darkling numbered a scant fifty-six. They cursed the name of the Spinner of Darkness. Some wept, while hurried cairns were raised over the glass-stiff, few corpses they recovered. Others sharpened their steel for revenge, oblivious to the punishing toll their defeat must exact from the thorns of s'Ffalenn conscience. The sunwheel priest led the rites for the fallen, then accosted every man still fit enough to raise steel to press the minion of evil who had veered west to avoid them.

'We have brothers in Light marching down from Etarra. They must be warned of the ruin we've faced, lest they close unaware of the danger. The Divine Prince himself sweeps eastward from Narms. His power of Light will dispel these fell shadows. For the weal of the land, we must not falter now! Let our losses this night renew our dedication. Honor their memory! Redeem their sacrifice! Let us harry the Master of Shadow without letup. Drive him like vermin into the net the Alliance will cast for his downfall.'

Vision faded back into the form of the raven, poised like a live cipher on the map. It opened the midnight fan of its wings, then sidled northwestward, each mincing step an unembellished recounting of Arithon's marathon flight. Although Earl Jieret received no encompassing visions, he sensed sharp impressions, of punishing cold nights spent without fires, and the flaying torments of east storms. He touched, like an echo, Prince Arithon's despair, as he laired like a fox in the thickets. He shared sapping nightmares of dead men and warped music that did not dispel under daylight, but only changed form into memories as damningly punishing. The raven's cry bespoke madness and pain, intensified by the season's cruel hardships and the passage of days that extended to weeks of relentless solitude.

Nor did the map remain clear of enemies. Where the raven walked, Darkling's fragmented company pursued, vengeance bent. Earl Jieret sensed their advance on the face of the parchment, the swarming specks of miniature men mounted on ant-sized horses. He beheld the more massive incursion from Etarra, then the response to Darkling's sent courier that caused them to wheel as though choreographed. In time, a cordon closed in tight lines to box in Arithon's position.

'They know where he is,' Earl Jieret surmised, stormed by gut-wrenching alarm.

The raven regarded him through its sequin left eye. Plunged through the glistening pitch of its iris, Rathain's *caithdein* beheld the chilling confirmation of his hunch. The sunwheel priest sent as the Alliance diviner traced the Master of Shadow's each move with foul arts and a blood-drenched pendulum. His scrying would synchronize three city war bands, and see Arithon s'Ffalenn hazed like a trapped beast to slaughter. While Etarra and Darkling and Jaelot closed the noose from behind, Rathain's prince would be systematically hounded into the advance out of Narms, and into a final disastrous encounter with Lysaer s'Ilessid. The confrontation sparked to flame by the Mistwraith's curse would end in battle and agony on the frozen banks of the River Aiyenne.

Overwhelmed by sinking despair, Earl Jieret understood that the s'Ffalenn gift of compassion was going to destroy any possible hope of reprieve. The past upheld proof. Once before, Arithon of Rathain had used the full range of his mage talents in defense of his threatened people. Though his act had staved off an annihilating loss, the toll of fallen had left him shackled in guilt. His access to talent had been blinded. On the plain of Daon Ramon, his mage-sight would stay blocked; but now, inexorable training had raised the art of his music to bridge the veil and rebuild a new framework to access the mysteries.

That power could kill; had now led men to death. Entangled in the Mistwraith's geas of destruction, bound by blood oath to the Fellowship Sorcerers to seek survival by any expedient, Athera's titled Masterbard would face Lysaer and the Alliance with no other weapon to hand.

Just as clearly as Jieret knew the maiming potential of steel, he foresaw that Arithon would be forced to raise music in the cause of self-defense. Even if he survived, the fierce brilliance of his bardic gift would become crippled, as stifled to silence as the born talent for mage-sight already tragically sacrificed.

Such a blow to the heart would not be sustained. Arithon denied the expression of music posed a penalty too harsh to contemplate. Jieret ached for the quandary. Aggrieved that his war band would not be enough to stem the oncoming disaster, he cast his appeal to the raven. 'If you're sent here to guide, then how can I help?'

The bird regarded him. Black as the void, a creature born of the uncanny fusion of feather and bone and great mystery, its gaze seemed to weigh the sincerity of his heart, if not the exact sum Daelion Fatemaster placed on his living worth. Pierced through and nailed by that measuring survey, Jieret felt his courage tested as never before. Even amid the blood heat of combat, the stripped force of his will had not given way, or threatened, as now, to unravel in weakness and fail him. Only his unyielding love for his prince held him from looking away.

'How can I help?' he entreated again. Surrendered long since to the perils of the dream, and to the cruel price that could be demanded to uphold his *caithdein*'s service to Rathain, he matched the raven's dense scrutiny with challenge sprung like fire from the core of his being. 'I will not choose the life of my liege, or his sanity, ahead of my bound task to shield him. I have an heir and a sanctioned successor to carry my family name after me.'

The bird bowed to him, a tribute that touched him like pain for its unexpected magnificence. Then it cawed shrill warning, and bent its dark head, and stabbed its bill through the map where the River Aiyenne turned back on itself in a south-bending, horseshoe crook.

Earl Jieret took sharp note of the site, then wept as he grasped the significance. One chance; a precious, uncertain bid for salvation, if the men in his war band were willing to throw themselves into the breach. They might engage the armed might of Lysaer s'Ilessid in the tangling brush of the river bottom. Not to triumph; they were too few to hold out any hope of a victory. But if at the critical moment they could buy a few hours' delay, the trap jaws might be jammed from closing.

By the tightest margin, the fateful impact of Desh-thiere's curse might be thwarted. Given the slender reprieve of his sanity, Arithon s'Ffalenn might seize his opening and slip through.

If his Grace sprinted headlong for the trade road, his northern clan allies could guide him into the Mathorn uplands. Posted scouts kept tight watch over the pulse of trade traffic, waylaying town couriers for news. Born of Fallowmere bloodlines, they were specialized, skilled raiders. No one could make better speed through the mountains ahead of hostile pursuit. They knew which fishermen could be bought, and which could be trusted to have sympathy. If Rathain's prince could be spirited across Instrell Bay to make landfall on the shores of Atainia, he could claim refuge at Althain Tower by his royal right to ask sanctuary.

'I accept your message,' Jieret said to the raven, unafraid, though the losses that statement demanded would come to leave bereft families in Halwythwood.

The bird croaked out a bitten reply. Dreaming vision spun away on a breath. The flat parchment chart dissolved back into snow-clad ground, where chill gusts chased wind devils of blown ice. The stepped hills to the east wore the first, silvered blush cast by the rising moon. Jieret blinked. He tossed off the stifling weight of his bearskin and sat up to signal the watch he was wakeful.

The sight of a live raven outlined in snow shocked him still. A prickling rush of dread doused his flesh. He swallowed, locked wordless, while the bird ruffled indignant feathers against the freezing assault of the breeze. It quorked once in testy, sharp inquiry.

'Ath, I know you!' Jieret expelled a hissed breath in relief, aware all at once that guidance had come on his prince's appeal to the Fellowship. Only one Raven in Athera could transcend the veil and circumvent the earthbound paradox of time and space. 'Tell the Sorcerer, Traithe, I honor his wisdom. Give him my thanks, on behalf of my prince, and in my name as Teir's'Valerient.'

The bird cocked its head, returned a terse croak, then beat its spread primaries and flew. It did not take wing through earthly airs, amid the buffeting cold of Daon Ramon, but disappeared through a hole in the night that bent its flight through the heart of the mysteries.

The snow beneath its departure was not left pristine. In swept crystals fanned by the arc of stretched wings, stamped in miniaturized relief by the tread of its talons, Jieret surveyed a topographical map of Daon Ramon. One site was marked out by a smoking drop of blood. There lay the crossroads of the Mistwraith's staged conflict, where Lysaer s'Ilessid would face Arithon s'Ffalenn with Alliance armed forces a closed door hedging his back. Symbols denoting the phases of two moon cycles marked the hour the half brothers would do battle with Light, sword, and Shadow, unless Jieret, with his war band and his trusted Companions, gave their lives to effect intervention.

No choice; Jieret would act as his father before him, and stand ground in war for his prince.

'We ride,' he informed the scout who arrived to call him to counsel. 'Prince Arithon has effected his escape from Ithamon, and I have received Sighted guidance from a Sorcerer. We must go north with all speed and spend all our resource to hinder Lysaer s'Ilessid.'

The scout made no sound, no complaint, no murmur of consternation. He listened, stone steady, while Earl Jieret cracked out expedient instructions. 'If no man in our company stands down from this task, then I appoint Sidir to go back alone, and bear these dire tidings to Halwythwood.' A pause, while a tight throat stopped words, then the finish, 'He'll argue the assignment. But someone must serve my daughter as war captain. Of all the Companions, he knows Arithon best. Jeynsa will need his sound guidance beside her on the hour she's called to shoulder my title in succession.'

Prince Kevor

The snowball arched on a silent trajectory straight for the crown of the duty officer's helm. It struck dead center, the dulled thump of impact giving tongue like a muffled bell. Showered under a back-falling explosion of white, the field veteran shouted and spun.

His defensive crouch and halfway-drawn sword were mocked by a chorus of pealing laughter.

'Fiends and Dharkaron's vengeance, we're a sorry enough lot!' He rammed his blade home in the scabbard and straightened, dusting chunked ice from the links of his byrnie. Caught between flushed annoyance and an idiot, boyish delight, he glowered toward the pack of miscreants who still snapped twigs in the brush. 'We are the Light's sword arm, sent to take down Khadrim! Just for one moment can we behave as men on a serious mission?'

The sniggers and chortling continued without letup. The suspect frenzy of rustles moved onward through the laurel and evergreen fronting the streamlet. Someone muffled an explosive whoop. Then a scuffling fracas erupted. Amid a yowled volley of oaths, a casualty went down in a sliding tumble that splashed through the ice on the freshet. The guffaws redoubled, now laced by the victim's shrill cursing.

High spirits won out over order and discipline. The field officer chuckled. While snowmelt wicked off the ends of his hair and trickled over his earlobes, he called, 'Who's won the young prince's wager, this time?'

'Fennick, as usual,' the loser called cheerfully, probably perched on a fallen log to empty his sloshing boots.

'Well don't envy him.' The evergreens heaved and disgorged young Prince Kevor, talking over his shoulder. 'He'll wake up one day with a crick in the back, if he keeps his fool habit of stashing his silver inside the seams of his blanket roll.' His appealing, quick laughter rang through winter greenwood as another man-at-arms ankle deep in the stream called something back in rejoinder.

The devilish grin that emerged as Kevor squared up his carriage bespoke the fact the soaked wretch had not dunked his best boots by accident. The young prince's infectious temperament had won the field troop over to a man.

Nor would he escape the attentions of Avenor's women upon his return to court. Through the winter, his features had gained an angular, sure strength. If not a match for his father's unearthly male beauty, his looks held the stamped promise of character. Rawboned and gawky as an unbroken horse, Kevor showed in fleeting, stray moments of grace the tigerish poise he would carry in his maturity. His long-strided walk brought him through the trees toward the officer made the butt of his morning's antics.

He stopped, his stance square and direct as the rest of him, and ran a gloved hand through his cockscomb of russet hair. Chagrin came and went in his half-stifled smile. Unspeaking, he awaited rebuke with straight patience that was anything but a spoiled child's.

'Young master,' the duty officer began, embarrassed to feel like a pompous old fool before Kevor's disarming honesty. The snapping cold morning, or maybe the pristine blue sky, were inclined to make any rank-and-file man boisterous. Despite the ice melt running fingers of cold down the laced neck of his coif, the field veteran shrugged off his stiff effort to play the harsh disciplinarian.

'Could you lend some royal influence and get these men moving? They might, perhaps, strap on swords and get mounted?' Their orders had been to ride deep into Westwood to spare Tysan's people from predation. 'Some goodwife's babes could burn or be seized in the jaws of Khadrim while we dally.'

Kevor dropped his lanky arm to his side, the ebullience of the moment erased. In the aquamarine chill of midwinter dawn, his expression was cut steel, each line of his carriage unflinching. 'They're frightened. Understandably terrified, in fact.' He expelled a plumed breath. A small tuck cut the flesh between his brows, which were fine and dark, like his mother's.

The captain did not waste the breath to prevaricate. The best swords and mail would be little use against winged monsters that spat fire, and whose minds possessed vicious intelligence.

The young prince's lucent blue eyes again met and matched the officer's measuring survey. 'If you want my help on this matter, let the men break camp on their own. They'll find their nerves and be steadier if they're given our trust, and not pushed.'

Such moments, it was all too easy to forget that Kevor had scarcely turned fifteen years of age. The innate majesty and insight of his lineage was as yet unformed instinct, the gifted endowment that would make a strong ruler still untempered by adult experience.

The duty officer brushed off an odd grue of chill. 'If I grant your way in this, then you will promise to stay by Fennick and Ranne, and trust my judgment without swerving the next time you feel the need to play the young hothead.'

The spark of lit humor touched Kevor's eyes a split second before his quick grin. 'We'll be last in the saddle, then. Fennick just won another ten silvers. No power on this side of the Light's going to hurry him before he's cached his new hoard into his blanket roll.'

'What in the name of fell Darkness were the terms of your blighted wager?' snapped the field officer, suspicious. Given the nature of many a former contest, he winced to imagine the snowball had been tossed for a sport involving his personal dignity.

'You want to know?' Kevor's lips flexed, his smile stifled just barely in time. His merry eyes widened. 'Grace and mercy, you *do* want to know. Very well.' He glanced at the treetops, as though the first golden spatters of sun could lift his surge of embarrassment. 'Haskin insisted you'd throw your dirk at the bushes the same way you did on the day you skewered the boar.'

The duty officer flushed, since that tale involved no wild animal at all, but a squire who had unwisely brought his sweetheart on a tryst too near to barbarian territory. 'Go!' He bellowed. 'Get yourself armed and mounted, boy, and I will see after the men!'

The young prince feigned a jaunty recruit's salute, then retired straightaway to the picket lines.

Struck by the unrepentant bounce to his stride, the officer

paused. He wondered whether the mistake with the boar had been a glib ploy to distract him. For Prince Kevor had gotten himself summarily dismissed without even granting his royal promise that he would not stray from the strong arm of his royal honor guard.

Nor did the troop's overburdened commander find the chance to remedy the duty officer's lapse, caught as he was between chastising laggards, then seeing the cook's bread .oven stowed. Argumentative as crows, the lancers mounted and formed into columns. Over the silver-foil crusting of snow, Avenor's field patrol rode out, flanked by Karfael's borrowed squads of crossbowmen and archers. Steel helms and the odd lance point flared under the dollops of sun, spilled through the tall firs of Westwood.

Eight leagues from the trade road, they followed the blazed trail left by trappers and woodcutters, crossed by the punched tracks of deer and the hectic prints of small sparrows. Fresh as the breeze on that new winter's morning, the banter of the two squires who served the young prince rang over the jingle of mail, the snap of lance pennons, and the creak of saddles and gear. No one called the boys down for misconduct. The fighting clan presence had long since been cleansed from these woods. The old blood scout who still hunted here would make himself scarce, lest he find himself killed for the crown bounty. The field officers in command indulged the high spirits of the s'Ilessid heir as a boon that brightened the morale of men who rode into unprecedented danger.

Two men were entrusted to keep vigilant close watch. Fennick and Ranne had been handpicked for their post from the elite of Avenor's royal guard. Their lives were pledged to protect the young prince, though in truth no one expected this assignment to invoke that extreme, selfless sacrifice. Before leaving the walled security of Karfael, Kevor had been made to understand he could accompany the field troop only as far as the cook's camp. His Grace would not be permitted to ride with the patrols where Khadrim flew. For this winter's campaign, he would observe the command at safe remove from their call to hard action.

Still near the coast, on the fringe of the wood, the patrol followed a forester's trail cut across fir-cloaked flatlands. The scattered few clearings fed browsing deer, preyed upon by nothing more fearsome than the occasional swift-running wolf pack. The troop would cast out more scouts and outriders as the rolling ground met the rockier crags of the Tornir foot-hills.

As always, the seasoned patrol captain rode the length of the column in morning review.

'Fool horse,' he chided, as his seal brown gelding tussled the bit in high fettle. 'You in a rush to get flamed to a cinder? Go ahead, then. Just keep on acting the flighty goose. You'll be dead meat and get left as a carcass, picked over by wolves and ravens.' The horse shook its head, snorted, and jig-stepped, long since inured to the strings of mock threats crooned by its craggy rider.

Yet today, the teasing play between horse and man did not win the usual lump of molasses filched as a treat from the cook. The field captain firmed his hand on the rein and sighed through his teeth in resignation. He would rather be digging latrines as a recruit than shoulder this foray through Westwood. No bracing fight lay ahead for these men, but a madness better suited to the uncanny tricks of a Sorcerer. Since time beyond memory, Fellowship spellcraft had always contained the escaped packs of Khadrim. In the sane light of reason, no veteran company of Alliance guard with steel weapons and bows were a match for such vicious predators.

Yet the packet of orders sent by fast courier from the High Priest at Avenor had decreed the Fellowship's compact was tyranny. For profit, the trade guilds applauded the edict. Since no Sorcerer had emerged to contain the flying scourge that slaughtered at whim through the north wood, no faction in Tysan's council was likely to give the matter an argument.

Beneath the thatched shadows of Westwood's dark firs, the troop captain swore with rare venom. High Priest Cerebeld's reply to his earlier letter had all but named him craven for expressing rock-hard common sense. Nor had the directive set under the Light's sunwheel seal given him any choice. Khadrim ranged at large. The guild ministers feared the marauding packs would threaten movement of commerce over the trade roads. With the Prince of the Light away to fight Shadow, the Alliance field garrison was duty bound to step into the breach.

Securely positioned near the middle of the column, Prince Kevor cuffed away the playful blond squire who leaned from his saddle and suggestively named a court maiden. 'Oh, get away! She does not! And anyway, you're ungallant to suggest such behavior in a company of right-thinking men.'

The squire grinned, insolent, while his smart chestnut gelding skittered in response to his brash shift in balance. 'She does so! Even kisses the carpet where your foot treads, and how do you know the men in this company have one set of right thoughts between them?'

'Well, for one thing,' Kevor retorted, flushed red, 'I haven't been able to escape my palace tutors long enough to go in one brothel, far less the variety we've heard discussed every night around the campfires.' While his friend puffed his chest and drew breath to rebut him, he issued a laughing challenge. 'You've been with a lady in any of those dives? Swear? Then describe her. Surely Ranne's cousin is worldly enough to have spent a paid night there. Let's ask him to vouch for the doxy you speak of.'

The younger squire with the freckled nose stoutly defended his friend. 'That leaves your Grace as the moral example?' Paused to duck a low-hanging branch, he cast a sly glance sideways. 'What about that herb witch with the owl-feather talismans who accosted you by the roadside? Did you keep that disgusting token she gave you?'

'A small white stone,' Kevor corrected. The back-snapping branch dusted his surcoat with shed needles, and the astringent scent of green balsam. 'Clean as any other quartz pebble the innocuous old bat could rake from a Camris streambed.' Tysan's heir readjusted his reins. Turned suddenly serious in his disturbing new way of casting slight matters against a larger-scale tapestry, he finished, 'She was a harmless old woman, and a subject of the realm. As her future liege, I was merely being polite.'

The stone in fact still tumbled loose in his scrip, untouched since the moment he had tucked it away.

'Old besom's a witch,' the older squire insisted, agile enough to duck the next branch sprung on him in punitive vengeance. 'When Vorrice finds her, he'll have her arraigned for dark spellcraft.'

'Worse,' mocked the boy in the lead, twisted in his saddle to stab a self-righteous finger toward his flustered young prince. 'If High Priest Cerebeld hears you accepted her charm, he'll have you called on the carpet for embracing the forces of Darkness.'

Even set amid teasing play, the name of the High Priest tucked Kevor's features to an imperious frown. 'Let Cerebeld try!' Light temper gone as though reamed by a chill, the s'Ilessid heir pressed impetuous heels to his mount. The blooded horse bolted into a brisk canter, and left the two squires behind in a pelting shower of snow clods.

Braced by the winter breeze in his face, Kevor shrugged away the recurrent premonition that the High Priest's eyes watched his back. He had never trusted Cerebeld. The instinctive avoidance that carried throughout his childhood had catalyzed to dislike on the solstice, when the night sky had erupted in portents. That hour had brought him to take his first stand as crown prince. Every man in the city garrison knew his act had stayed Avenor's populace from running riot in fear.

The affray had aroused the High Priest's enmity, as well as the adulation of a people the s'Ilessid heir must one day rule. Now more than ever, Kevor dared not voice his bone-deep distaste for the crown's practice of burning the wretches the Light's tribunal convicted for sorcery. Often thoughtfully private, where most boys his age might indulge their outspoken opinion, Prince Kevor could but hope Gace Steward's sly scrutiny overlooked his strained bearing, each time Tysan's justice consigned the condemned to the sword and the faggots.

He had found space to breathe, away with the field troop, released from the tight expectations of royal birthright and the incessant demands of court politics. Fair mornings like this one, traveling in the company of men under the vaulting branches of Westwood, he could sometimes forget he was the Divine Prince's heir. He could snatch the rare moment and run his fine charger, and imagine himself free of obligation.

Kevor pressed his horse faster, at one with the beast as it swerved right and left, carving a track through the trees. Fir boughs and mane slapped his red cheeks, and the air filled his lungs to intoxication. The sky overhead shone a limitless blue, beckoning mind and spirit with the promise of dreams that could break every earthbound constraint.

In piquant rebellion, the prince wished the stolen moment might last until his horse was blown to exhaustion.

Responsible recognition hard followed, that his mount deserved better respect. Worse than that, if he indulged his whim, somebody else's reliable reputation must bear the inflexible consequence. Soon enough, one of his honor guard must spur his mount to overtake, understanding a boy's natural yearning for space, and apologetic for the duty his oath had lifesworn him to follow.

This time, it was Ranne's horse that thundered alongside. The guard's good-natured face was politely averted, the blunt set to his shoulders a statement clearer than speech: he had lagged behind for as long as he could stretch the reasonable limits of protocol.

Kevor reined in, too acutely aware the man would suffer the captain's displeasure if he continued to vent his explosion of youthful frustration. While the big gelding under him blew snorts of white steam and curvetted in headshaking protest, Kevor tipped back his chin and let the icy air blast down his collar. The heat in him still burned, regardless.

Ahead and behind on the quaint forest track, the field company rode armed in their polished city steel, bravely turned out in matched surcoats. They advanced uncomplaining, their banners and bearing immaculate, despite an assignment that would carry them into unimaginable peril. Sword and lance were no match for packs of creatures who breathed fire, and flew on sail wings over sixty spans wide. Their pledge to serve the Light in north Tysan must inevitably lead some of their number to an untimely, horrible death.

Kevor found, after all, he could not tame his feelings, or endure in straitlaced, princely decorum. *Who were the almighty Fellowship Sorcerers, that they should allow these staunch men to ride into the breach, and stand down the threat of Khadrim? Where were such paragons of the mysteries now? If their vaunted forces of spellcraft could avert the promise of disaster, why had they withheld their strong arm?*

'Merciful Light!' the prince ground through locked teeth. His personal aversion for Cerebeld aside, he would still have to wonder. The lives in this company felt too well set up, the un-named list of men soon to suffer and die too smoothly groomed as political martyrs. Their loss could only lend more blazing fuel to the Alliance's strident stand against sorcery. With the Prince Exalted away to fight Shadow in the east, Cerebeld and his acolytes needed no better excuse to fan the embers of war and heap more blame and condemnation on the Fellowship. The Sorcerers made ready targets, with their secretive, unbreachable powers, and their iron adherence to an outmoded law that bound growth and trade to the strangling terms of the compact.

Ranne's surprised gasp could be heard, even through thudding hooves and the noisy jangle of gear. Kevor jerked his head side-wards, flushed with embarrassment. He had never meant to blurt his viewpoint aloud. Nothing else would serve, now, but to air his thoughtless lapse into heresy. If true justice was answered, should he not be the one to pose the most searching questions? He was a crown prince with an inquiring mind. If he was ever to become the sharp statesman his father was, he must be expected to test the dangerous, harsh edges of Tysan's existing crown policy.

'Well, do you think it's right that the herb witch by the wharf in Karfael was put to death?' Kevor demanded of Ranne, low voiced. 'Go on. Why not answer? Does the memory of her screams not trouble your sleep?'

Under the resin-filled silence of the fir trees, the exchange of ideas could remain a secret between them.

'The poor woman's gone,' Ranne said in flat refusal to further the conversation.

'She burned to death in terrible agony, and for what? Now we have poor mothers dying in childbirth. Ones who don't have the coin to pay healers.' Once started, the young prince found he could not stem his blazing torrent of doubts. 'Merchants can buy fiend banes by swearing oath of debt to Koriathain. But what about the dairymaids who don't own the milk they toil to churn into butter? Should they go hungry because iyats knock over their settling pans? Tell me, how many northcountry farmsteaders are too lazy to haul their cheap tin all the way to Avenor to be warded by Cerebeld's vested acolytes?'

'Your Grace, such questions are far better posed to the Divine Prince, your father.' Ranne shrugged. His familiar, hawk profile stayed uncomfortably faced straight ahead. 'I'm a swordsman, not a state minister. It's hardly my place to make free comment on Avenor's established crown policy.'

'Those are words from the mouth of a brainless sheep, not a man with a mind and a conscience!' Kevor blazed back. 'You're better than that, Ranne, and so are Karfael's poor, who now have nowhere to turn for everyday succor and healing.' He paused. Too piqued not to make futile response, he stopped his restive horse short, his profile adamant marble, unwarmed by the strayed mote of sun that fired his hair to dulled copper. 'If my father was the avatar our people acclaim, *then why are Cerebeld's acolytes not out in the countryside dirtying their white robes, ministering to the misery in the hamlets?*'

He faced Ranne again. His blue eyes beseeched, all but brimming tears for the point he *must not for honor speak aloud*: why mortal men armed with naught else but steel should be riding against winged packs of fire-breathing monsters.

Heart torn as he shared the young prince's dilemma, the guardsman pledged to safeguard his life found no ready answers. His powerful frame seemed diminished by that failure, and his posture less sure in the saddle. 'One thing I know, boy,' Ranne said, in gruff sympathy discarding the honorifics of station, 'Best not say what you think around Fennick. He and I both gave our oaths to your father. You may hold our personal loyalty through affection, *but our first allegiance is pledged to obey the Divine Prince.'*

Indeed, Kevor knew. Each day, he lived with the shaming remorse. Two men's lives could be forfeit in public dishonor, should the integrity of their oath ever come to be questioned or broken. He held his death grip on the reins, not ready for capitulation. 'Then rest assured I will seek out my father when he returns from his war in the east.'

'Fall back, then,' Ranne pleaded. 'Before we make the field captain uneasy. He doesn't like you riding at large, not without twenty lances at the ready for your immediate protection.'

A stickler for keeping even casual promises, Kevor spun his big gray back toward the main column of the company. His earlier burst of exuberance was gone, and his subsequent anger bottled. The winter forest had lost its allure. He scarcely heard the spritely scolding of chickadees, as he fell in line beside Fennick's charger, with Ranne's a demure stride behind. The young prince rode, still preoccupied. The memory of the disturbing old woman who had grasped at his stirrup troubled him. She had worn owl feathers braided into her white hair, *that had seemed outlined in unearthly light.*

Her unsettling words lingered, along with the stone talisman now nestled among his belongings: *'For you, boy, as true a scion of Halduin's line as your s'Ilessid father is false. The wisdom of Ath lies in every small stone. This one holds a pledge wrought to keep you safe. All life is a gift. As you value yours, let this token guard you from threat.'*

At midday, the company paused to rest the horses in the yard of a charcoal burner's steading. Fennick and Ranne were allotted the privilege of commandeering hot food for the officers. The royal squires, also, enjoyed the goodwife's hospitality. The pair of them sat at her kitchen hob, wolfing down dumplings and sausage.

Kevor, as crown heir, would share the captain's table. But as often happened, something outside had snagged the young prince's attention. The place setting laid for him went unclaimed.

In the yard by the cottage, the rank-and-file lancers drew lots over who should attend to the horses. The fortunate ones who escaped duty as grooms lined up and placed wagers on an impromptu match of prowess between the troop's most skillful archers. Soon, arrows hissed and thwacked into the boles of tree targets, through a chorus of whoops and ripe curses.

Not far from the lines, Kevor perched on a stump amid the cleared glen, watching the charcoalman's young daughters sculpt a family of snow sprites. At the prince's suggestion, they had gathered small fir cones for eyes. Now, in giggling contention, they importuned him for his gold buttons to adorn the queen's balsam tiara.

'I can't carry an old bucket on the back of my horse,' Kevor demurred in his most grave and amiable courtesy. 'You'll have to trade something better than that. These buttons each have a sunwheel emblem blessed by the Divine Light himself.'

A distant shadow flicked over the sun. The posted sentry did not look up, engrossed as he was with the archers who vied for the winning point.

In the wide, sunlit dell, the smaller girl pouted with cherry red lips, and adjusted the lopsided fungus that served as left ear for the king. 'I have naught else to offer but a holly-berry necklace.' A sly glance from brown eyes to see if the prince was fool enough to accept; the berries in question decked the white bosom of the princess sprite. Gaps of raw string showed where hungry birds had pecked and stolen the pips.

Thirty leagues from the mountains, no man saw the need to set a watch against assault by Khadrim. The thundering crack of taut wing leather whistling over the trees caught Avenor's field troop in shamelessly rooted surprise.

Except for Kevor, whose untrammeled view of the sky afforded him the only clear second of warning.

'*Run!*' he screamed to the woodcutter's girls. Gold buttons scribed bright arcs in the sunlight, as he yanked off his cloak left-handed. His right gripped his sword, drawn on snapped reflex. Born to the mettle of his royal heritage, Kevor pelted into the open.

Behind him, men shouted, aghast. Their alarm was eclipsed. The Khadrim shot overhead. Black as jet with metal gray highlights struck off its sinuous, scaled body, it folded wings like webbed sails and dropped into a screeling dive. The air of its passage whistled like storm. Its talons were raked scimitars, descending.

Kevor sprinted. His vision closed down until he tracked nothing else but the narrowed red eye in the serpentine head. Drawn by unerring, predator's instinct, it fixed on the helpless smaller child, frozen in fear amidst the circle of sprites made from sticks and clumped snow.

Single-mindedly brave, brash with heedless youth, the prince called again to the girl. His cry failed to break her stunned panic. He snapped his blue cloak. The bullion thread sunwheel caught the noon light, sheeting a burst of gold fire.

The Khadrim's eye flickered and fixed on the movement. Spiked head on scaled neck snaked sidewards, refocused on the distraction.

'Run!' Kevor shouted. Sword upraised, he streamed the cloak like a flag to hold the Khadrim's killing focus. On the sidelines, the patrol recovered shocked wits. An equerry bolted into the cottage to summon the captain. Horsemen raced to snatch up idle lances. The contesting archers scrambled to retrieve their shot arrows, while their colleagues frantically strung bows.

'Fire at will!' yelled their squad sergeant, his shrill cry beaten back into his teeth by the whipping turbulence thrown off by the Khadrim's stooping strike.

The first arrows whined aloft. Disturbed air plucked and scattered them. Crossbow bolts flew faster, and more true. Their ragged volley struck armored scales and sprang off in rattling rebound. The back-fallen shafts rained earthward, each one now a threat to the young prince, who still raced straight into the jaws of peril.

'Kevor, take cover!' Fennick charged from the house, sword in hand. Ranne pounded hard at his heels. But their entreaties went unheard. One glance showed the moment's abject futility: intervention would reach Kevor too late.

No mortal man, no matter how dedicated, could possibly close the requisite distance in time. Nor could Avenor's proud field troop stave off the impending tragedy.

In that moment, also, the grisly revelation punched through. Fully and finally, Kevor acknowledged the death that descended on fang and scythed claw to take him. He was alone. Pitifully exposed in the sunlit clearing, he had no one at hand to share the dawning horror of his predicament. No coward, even now, he skidded and dodged left. He did not cry out, though heart and sinew begged for a miracle only an act of true sorcery could provide.

The men, watching horrorstruck, never knew of his nightmare fears of the fires, recurrent since the condemned witch had burned back in Karfael.

They did not hear his snatched prayer, that he might not scream as she had. The Khadrim's stooping descent blackened the sky. Under its shadow, he had time to brace his sword upright. He held firm, perhaps paralyzed before jaws rowed with needle teeth, that were going to snap shut and mangle him. The futility of his stance made seasoned men weep. The jet claws and the lean, snake-thin neck must outmatch the courage of any green boy's panicked strength.

The Khadrim closed, more swift than the wind that foreran killing squalls, its wings folded midnight against the living, steel bolt of its body.

Kevor tipped up his blanched face. At the last moment, he cast his azure mantle overhead, as though, against hope, the gold star and crown blazon of his s'Ilessid forebears might offer him binding protection.

The same instant, the Khadrim gaped its scarlet mouth and spewed an engulfing torrent of fire.

The cloak became immolated to white flame and ash, then the boy, wrapped into blinding conflagration. The Khadrim were drake spawn, and like their creators, their fire burned hotter than any wood-fueled flame. The young prince shrieked as the pain bit bone deep. His cry made no final appeal to the Light.

Instead, in extremis, Ellaine's son called on the gentle faith of his mother, whose love had guided his earliest childhood. 'For Ath's mercy save me!'

The words, tortured ragged, choked off all at once.

Then further view of the carnage was eclipsed, as the murdering drake spawn snapped out sail wings. The Khadrim braked in a flurry of sparks and fanned smoke, and touched down, its leviathan size imbued with a stunning, cat grace. Its forelimbs alighted amid the hissing steam of puddled snow, then the hind limbs, in bounding, sleek balance. Wings upraised, neck arched over the site of its kill, the creature shrilled its intent to gorge on live prey, then wreak savage havoc on the timber and lathe of the charcoalman's isolated steading.

'Shoot! Use crossbolts!' Over the shrieking hysteria of the child, through the disorganized milling of stupefied men still scrambling to order their weapons, the field troop's captain burst from the house, exhorting his archers to rally. 'As you love life, aim for the eye!'

Yet it was Fennick, weeping obscenities, who grabbed up a contestant's dropped longbow. Racing full tilt for the monster in the clearing, he snatched a steel broadhead from another man's hand. At forty yards, he threw himself sliding to his knees and snapped off a vengeful shot.

Snake fast, the Khadrim whipped around. Its neck lunged to snap, or more likely, spit fire. By stunning luck, the launched shaft hissed through its gaping jaws, and punched through the mouth to the brain. The beast threshed and fell. Massive, clawed wings scraped up arcs of thrown snow. Talons raked frozen earth. Lashed by a paroxysm of death throes, the spiked tail clubbed like a flail through the trees, snapping off limbs and pelting the glen under a rain of sheared sticks. Most men watched, dumbfounded. Ranne sprinted on. Unable to spare Kevor, he ran the battering gauntlet of slapped wings and threshing limbs, no less likely to disembowel a man in the shudders as life ebbed and ended. In rage, in blind heartbreak, that his young charge had died before his eyes, Ranne finished the task Kevor's bravery had started. He dodged clashing jaws and snatched the charcoalman's wailing little girl from the tumbledown ruin of her playground.

No man had words, as the aftermath bludgeoned them. The great hulk of the Khadrim's carcass gasped its last steaming breath and finally quivered and stilled. The shock-stricken field troop converged, too overwhelmed to react fully to the devastating impact of sorrow. Of the young prince's body, nothing remained, though men searched. Decency demanded some small token to send to the princess in Avenor, soon to weep for a son lost to the dedicated bravery bred into his ancestral lineage.

However they dug through the slurry of thawed earth, they found not one melted gold button nor any charred scrap of bone. Naught remained. Only a trampled circle of seared carbon where the dread holocaust of Khadrim fire had sheared down.

The day seemed too peaceful, and the sunlight, a bland outrage, to have borne witness to the murder of the s'Ilessid royal heir, once destined for crown rule in Tysan.

'By my life, that should have been me!' Fennick wept. Still crumpled on his knees in cold snow, oblivious to the companions who urged him to relinquish his deadlocked grip on the bow, he cast his despairing eyes skyward. 'What in the name of the Light will we say to console his lady mother?'

Mourning

Sunlight spilled like liquefied gold through the high, lancet windows at Avenor. The deep, piled carpets with their crown and star motifs spread luxuriant azure over maple parquet, waxed to the warm hue of honey. With Prince Lysaer's extended absence on campaign in Daon Ramon, no fawning advisors crowded the anteroom. The chinking spurs of impatient royal couriers did not echo off the vaulted ceilings, and hopeful petitioners did not line the benches with straight backs, against the carved backdrop of wainscoting. Winter mornings, while the frost traced gauze-lace patterns on the panes, the splendor of the royal chambers became the domain of the princess's women. They perched on the hassocks and window seats, or convened in the claw-footed state chairs, bright as plumed birds in saffron silk as they chattered over their needlework.

Lady Ellaine sat with them, set apart by her beaded aquamarine bodice, and her cincture trimmed in white lynx. Her hair had been expertly dressed. The premature gray fanned from her temples had been gently softened with cinnabar pins of carved amber. Withdrawn as she seemed from light conversation, she kept her hands busy. More than the strict deportment of her station fretted her upright posture, a manner the unobservant stranger might mistake for spiritless meekness. The short, fierce stitches laid in with her needle bespoke no such retiring tranquillity as she sewed seed pearls on a linen cap for her infant cousin in Erdane.

The confines set on her by Prince Lysaer's absence chafed her nerves, the precaution of state edict now enforced by High Priest

Cerebeld's veiled threats. Yet her sweet nature prevailed. She did not impose her dull spirits on the women who served as her ladies-in-waiting. They indulged in their gossip. Planning for the festival masques that enlivened the winter court occurred with the princess's benevolent cooperation, and her surprising, mild wit, if not her heartfelt enthusiasm. Her Grace was seen to dance at the balls, but none in her close company were fooled. Her contentment was a carefully manicured lie, and her spirit, a stifled, caged songbird's.

Since the hour of her wedding to Lysaer s'Ilessid, Lady Ellaine had been little more than a puppet played by the strings of her powerful royal marriage.

The court viewed her reliable manner with complacency, a mistake that resounded to widespread repercussions when a man's booted step approached through the marble anteroom.

Ellaine's careful needlework dropped to the carpet, limp as a wing-shot bird. Seed pearls spilled and scattered in a dancing rain. Erect in her chair, her dark eyes like bored walnut, she addressed the tall man who paused on the threshold before her ladies quite realized he was there. 'You are here for my son?'

The chatter of the women cut off as the man stepped inside.

He was dressed for the road, his boots and his spurs still mud-crusted. The mantle he wore was a swordsman's slit cape, bearing the hammer and wheel blazon of Karfael. He glanced once at the door still ajar behind him, fair and young and uneasy, his riding gloves wrung between tortured hands. Then he gathered himself. Bowed to one knee in the chill winter light that flooded the diamond-paned casements, he addressed her sovereign query. 'My Lady Princess, your son and heir died among the best of our troops, under assault by a winged Khadrim.'

A rustle of thick silk, shot through by the ping and tap as the last, forlorn pearls strayed across flooring and carpet.

The courier dared a glimpse upward. Lady Ellaine had risen, hands tucked in her skirts, while her bevy of women turned aghast faces to measure her public reaction.

'Please stand,' her Grace said, her voice level, not beaten; as though somehow she had braced in advance for an unspeakable tragedy. Only the gilt cloth edging on her collar flared to the jerk of her indrawn breath. 'Say how my son died.'

Before such straight courage, a man could but answer. 'Quickly, my lady. His suffering was brief. He charged on foot with drawn sword as the monster descended, and drew it away from a forester's strayed child. The attack caught everyone by surprise.

No scout had seen signs of the predators. By sheer misfortune, his honor guard were unable to act. The girl child survived, but at sorrowful cost. Your son Kevor died as a man, a true prince of his people. There are no remains. The Khadrim fire burned and left nothing. My Lord Mayor will bear the cost of a memorial with all honors once the thaws permit a state retinue to travel.'

Ellaine remained erect, unblinking. 'You have told High Priest Cerebeld this?'

'I have not.' The courier swallowed, the wadded lumps of his gloves fallen slack in his tormented grasp. 'His acolytes would not admit me. No one, they said, sees his eminence before he has opened his door to receive. I'm sorry. You should have had someone familiar to bring the sad tidings to you, but Ranne and Fennick travel back with the young prince's squires and all that remains of his gear. I was sent ahead with all speed, lest careless word should spread damaging, premature rumors.'

Every inch the poised princess she had never been granted the public standing to express, Ellaine held to her desperate composure. 'Your judgment is to be applauded.' She did not dismiss the courier, but added, 'Since Cerebeld is otherwise engaged, and Prince Lysaer absent, I deem it fitting that you, as Karfael's representative, and I, as the realm's princess, take immediate steps to inform Avenor's people of their loss.'

'My lady.' The courier bent his head in acquiescence.

Ellaine did not see him, but looked down in dismay at the glittering aquamarine beaded silk and white fur that jarred the air like watered light for their vibrancy. 'Meiris,' she bade, her whisper distressed. 'Fetch me a sable overrobe, and a sash and black mantle for mourning. *Quickly!*'

Through a rustle of shocked movement as the woman did her bidding, Ellaine clasped hands that broke into shaking unsteadiness. Her grief set in eclipse by pure fear, she schooled her face to white-fired enamel and sealed her hard impulse to act. 'Inwie, hurry. Tell my honor guard to arm for a public appearance. Then find a fleet page who won't pause to question. Send summons with him to the duty captain of the guard. Get him here for immediate audience.'

'My lady?' the appointed woman gasped, stunned. 'What if today's assigned officer is—'

'He will hear royal orders!' the Princess of Avenor interrupted. Jeweled silk gleamed on her form like new ice as, bare-handed, she dared seize the reins of the power implied by her title and station. *'We have crisis in Westwood!* Whichever captain of the watch is on duty, he must serve by right of my sovereignty as the mother of this realm's deceased heir.'

The thunderous knock shook the shut door to the High Priest of the Light's inner sanctum. Shrill voices clashed in deadlocked affront, the acolytes' dissonant baritones slashed by Gace Steward's yelping tenor.

On his knees before his ceremonial altar, immersed in his morning devotions, Cerebeld was jarred from the depths of ecstatic trance. He blinked, confused and disoriented. The battering assault on his door gained force. Urgent shouting rattled the blown-glass sconces, and gold fringes shivered on the draped, sunwheel cloth. The water and rarefied oils trembled in the offering bowls. Only the wax effigies of the three priests from Darkling, Morvain, and Etarra suffered the invasion, mute in their cut circle of candlelight. Their pale, molded faces stared back at him, dead, a doll's mockery of wax and cut hair, and crudely sewn snippets of silk.

The ephemeral tie invoked out of ritual had been shocked into dissolution. No connection remained with the living men in the distant wilds of Rathain.

Cerebeld arose, stiff in the knees, and charged to monumental displeasure. A large man, he moved with powerful speed, crossed the morning light spilled through mullioned windows, and wrenched open the door.

The squalling argument rocked to a stop, replaced by a scalpel-cut silence. The two acolytes sank to their knees. Left exposed, the rail-thin palace steward caught the glacial brunt of the High Priest's glower. *'How dare you!'*

Gace squeaked an insincere apology, bony hands tucked to his liveried chest like the paws of a nervous rat.

'How dare you!' Cerebeld repeated. 'Because of your meddling, our lord, the Exalted Prince, has been hindered in this day's divine work.'

'The princess,' Gace gasped. His narrow frame quivered under the azure pleats of his livery as he jerked a snipped gesture toward the east-facing bank of latched windows. 'Outside in the plaza. Go. See for yourself. Then tell me which hindrance will prove the more meddlesome to the true cause of the Light.'

Cerebeld said nothing. He strode with clamped jaw back to his altar, snatched up undone wrappings and ribbon ties, and cast veiling cloth over his clutch of wax effigies. His slicked seal hair gleamed like satin-polished wood as he stalked to the casements overlooking Avenor's grand palace of state.

The plaza seethed with the variegate colors of a gathering crowd, though the daily invocation to the Light was not scheduled to occur until noon. Some townsfolk were dressed in village motley, others in sober brocades, with the journeymen and craftsmen scattered among them still aproned from work in their shops. The gilt-roofed cupola raised over the sunwheel dais sheltered nothing except a sweeper, who leaned on his idle broom, interrupted from his daily task of tidying.

Princess Ellaine had eschewed the hallowed seat of divine office in favor of the parapet that fronted the second-story grand ballroom. She had her personal retinue and her honor guards all mantled in stark black. The captain of the day watch flanked her, jet streamers affixed to his helm. He held ten guardsmen at solemn attention, the disturbed tidings at hand evidently more pressing than keeping their post at the watch keep.

'A messenger came in from Karfael,' Gace said, lame.

Far too controlled to show his dismay, Cerebeld flicked the latch and pushed open the lead-paned casement. 'Say who has died.' He cast a commanding, uncivil glance backward, the trimmed point of his beard sky cut to the profile of a billhook.

'No one could find out.' Gace swallowed. 'The courier would not speak, except to Lady Ellaine. The boy I sent to listen at her keyhole was detained. I went myself to recover the lapse, but by then, the doors to the royal apartment were braced shut by the guard, with all of the servants inside.'

'Enough!' snapped the High Priest. Princess Ellaine was speaking, her high, clear voice riding the breezeless air. The raw gist reached the tower, broken to echoes off the saffron façades of the buildings.

Inquisitive to the bone, Gace Steward edged past the obstructive acolytes and craned his neck over Cerebeld's shoulder. 'The heir,' he whispered. 'We've lost the young prince to marauding Khadrim.'

Cerebeld gave a chopping, backhanded gesture. 'Silence, you fool!'

Snatched phrases from the princess's proclamation winnowed through the rising breeze off the harbor. '. . . go to Karfael at once . . . Royal heralds are riding this moment to bear news far and wide . . . after the ceremony to honor our loss, Avenor will succor the northern hamlets . . . other women mourn loved ones, husbands or sons . . . in Prince Lysaer's absence, hear my pledge! The depredations *of these monsters will not be permitted to continue unchecked . . . in the name of the young prince, I will dispatch two companies from Avenor's garrison . . . safeguard the defenseless countryside.'*

Gace Steward hissed an incredulous breath through locked teeth. 'She's promising armed intervention against Khadrim? Light save us all, *that's sheer madness*!'

Cheers arose from the crowd, nonetheless, a heartfelt endorsement of the princess's selfless support.

Cerebeld whirled from the casement, flushed livid. 'Madness or not, we can't stop this now. To cut her Grace down in retraction would tarnish the support of true faith, and the omnipotence of the Divine Light.'

Gace Steward pursed his lips in fidgety agitation. 'The Divine Prince will scarcely be pleased. Who gets to break the unhappy news, if the best of Avenor's trained garrison get flamed for the sake of some Karfael woodsmen?'

'The Light will receive their spirits in grace,' Cerebeld assured, more concerned by the unpredictable ramifications unleashed by the princess's wild-card bid for autonomy. 'Fetch my formal retinue!' he barked to the acolytes still frozen in stunned uncertainty. Muscles worked in his determined, square jaw as he snatched his white-and-gold mantle from the armoire.

Caught flat-footed, Gace Steward scampered to keep up. 'What steps can be taken? The princess has commandeered cooperation from the garrison troops! She's forbidden to leave Avenor, but that sanction can't be enforced while she's mourning.' His chattering monologue gained pitch and force, as he finally grasped the breathtaking scope of possible ramifications. *'Ellaine's authorized royal heralds to ride out! Who knows what dispatches they're carrying?'*

The cat had slipped out of the bag too far, this time.

Gace hopped foot to foot, hounding Cerebeld's heels as the High Priest snuffed the candles that burned on the altar. 'We can't throw a damned blanket over her Grace's head, or take back the promise she's spoken.'

'No.' One syllable, to raise the hairs at the nape for its inarguable lash of finality. Cerebeld reached the threshold, and snapped strong fingers to his remaining acolyte. 'Fetch my valet. Have him gather my ceremonial appointments and catch up. I will robe in the downstairs vestibule.'

He hastened onward, soon breasting the rush of the underlings who arrived in a panic to unfurl the sunwheel standard, and unshroud the gold-sewn, ribboned stole of office and chain of clasped dragons he wore for his public appearances.

'Well, say something!' Gace Steward shrieked in frustration as he rounded the first landing and scurried like a weasel through the press. 'What in the name of Divine Light will you do to checkrein Lysaer's harebrained wife?'

'The chit's forced our hand,' Cerebeld cracked, his venom held in savage check beneath his knifing temper. Princess Ellaine had been shown copies of a document proving the plot behind Talith's death. If this was her bid to slip the restraint of authority and bolt to Erdane to expose the information, she would be gagged. The High Priest would use the bared might of his office and travel with her royal retinue.

The stairwell ended, with the door to the vestry tucked away to one side. Ignoring the royal steward, who still yapped and fussed at his elbow, Cerebeld dispatched a waiting acolyte with peremptory summons demanding an afternoon audience with Lord Koshlin. Then, his deep thoughts contained like the seethe of balked magma, he quashed Gace's badgering with a blast of withering authority. 'Nothing's to be done, yet, you hysterical ninny! A royal son lies dead! Decency demands something more than belated words of condolence. We must make a ceremonial appearance in the square and offer her Grace's expedition to Karfael the blessing and support of the divine powers of the Light.'

Late Winter 5670

Game Pieces

In Ath's hostel near Northstrait, where the rolling boom of Stormwell Gulf's breakers smash themselves into snagged rock, an adept of Ath's Brotherhood pulls the curtain across the alcove where the motionless body lies, swathed head to foot in bandages soaked in salt water and unguent; and her sigh seems wrenched from the depths of her heart as she says, 'Khadrim fire burns deep, and the pain by itself has driven him very far from us . . .'

On the eve that Avenor's picked garrison prepares to march northward to Korias, High Priest Cerebeld receives word that her Grace, Princess Ellaine, has vanished from the palace, and though her honor guard and her ladies-in-waiting are subjected to rigorous questioning, none holds the first clue to her whereabouts . . .

Under wind-whipped tent canvas on Daon Ramon Barrens, a sunwheel priest blots fresh blood from a bronze pendulum, then straightens in triumph and taps a smeared finger on a map. 'Here, Divine Grace, the new position of the enemy. Our forces steadily close on him. Your call to eradicate the Master of Shadow may be answered inside the next fortnight . . .'

VII. Threshold

T wilight stole over Daon Ramon Barrens, sung in by bitter winds and a gauzy, thin dusting of snowfall. Earl Jieret crouched, sheltered, in the lee of a rock scarp, the hood of his bear mantle snugged to his chin, his spill of red beard shielding the gusts from his fingers. His farsighted gaze remained fixed on the gap where two hills folded into a tangle of whitethorn and witch hazel. There, on the hour past the rise of the moon, the fugitive Crown Prince of Rathain would ride through, if the prophecy sent by Traithe's raven held true to the Sighted scrying two months ago.

The scout who poised at his chieftain's shoulder chafed and blew into his cupped hands, equally tense as he received last-minute instructions.

'No noise and no light,' Jieret stated, emphatic. 'His Grace has been driven on the run since the solstice, and we can't risk him thinking we're enemies. Tell the men, hold position and stay out of sight. No one's to call out, or make an approach, unless our liege is seen to turn down a valley other than this one.'

The stakes would not forgive, if someone's ill-advised move should startle their prince to blind flight. The troops from Etarra and Darkling hazed his trail from behind, bolstered at their south flank by Jaelot's zealot trackers, whipped on by a spell-turned commander.

'Go,' Jieret finished. 'I'll signal you with an owl's call the moment I have him in hand.'

'May Ath's grace stand beside you.' The scout slapped the wadded snow from his boot cuffs and faded without sound into deepening gloom.

Earl Jieret sat alone with the dirge of the gusts, moaning over the cragged stone where he sheltered. A cold hour's vigil stretched ahead of him, less time than he wished to review his turbulent memories of service at the shoulder of Rathain's prince. The events were too few for his forty-odd years, with no single one of them peaceful. Jieret brooded, his steady gaze pinned to the draw where the shorn, winter hills meshed and met with the darkened horizon. He wondered what sort of desperate creature would ride through that gap, first set to flight through the Skyshiels in winter, then hounded across the desolate barrens, with no human contact beyond the pack of armed enemies hunting him.

Arithon s'Ffalenn at best form was a difficult spirit. No way to guess in advance how to grapple the fugitive the raven's prophecy would deliver.

The night deepened. Between gusts, the whispered tap of dry snowfall nicked through the dead canes of briar. A hare screamed, brought down by a hungry night predator; a kit fox barked in the brush. Jieret tucked anxious forearms over his knees, while the winter stars wheeled through broken clouds overhead, and the new-risen moon sliced a mother-of-pearl rim over the eastern horizon.

Precisely on schedule, a suggestion of motion ghosted through the weave of the thicket. Jieret sharpened his attention. The disturbance might be the movement of wolves, or a herd of deer seeking forage. When minutes dragged by, and no further sign met his searching scan of bare branches, he almost settled back in disappointment. No doubt he had experienced no more than a phantom wrought of overstrung nerves.

Then the shadow moved again. Snapped back to vigilance, Jieret made out the forms of three horses as they emerged in clean outline against a pristine palette of snow. Heads raised, ears tipped forward, they poised in wary silhouette and surveyed the swept valley that unfolded before them. No lead reins or bridles cumbered their heads, but two bore laden packsaddles, the bulk of their burden set close to the shoulder to free their balance to gallop. A stilled moment passed. Then the animal in the lead stepped forward, head down and blowing soft snorts. Another hushed movement, and a fourth horse slipped from cover, this one saddled and bridled, but bearing no visible rider.

Jieret bit his lip to stifle his urge to vent curses in mounting anxiety. He waited, taut strung. His eyes like chilled glass from the strain of his unblinking vigil, he picked out a shape distorting the animal's forehand.

The two-legged fugitive moved on foot, a sinuous blur at the horse's left shoulder, his stride like a stalking, male panther's.

Chills chased Jieret's spine. Never in life had he observed any man, scout or otherwise, skulk with such focused intensity. A savage, stripped grace kept each footfall economical; then the listening pause to assess front and back trail, while the gusty, thin snowfall sifted powder over scabs of patched ice, and the fanned clumps of gorse hissed refrain.

A fluid leap vaulted the rider astride, with no fumbling claw for a stirrup. He made no sound, nor delivered a visible signal. Yet his small band of horses forged ahead at an unhurried trot, the crisp crunch as their hooves punched through the snow crust diminished by the reach of Daon Ramon's vast emptiness. Down the throat of the vale, he came on like a predator, every line of him spring-wound to lethal alertness.

Jieret shivered outright. He groped, but found no words to disarm such hunted defenses. One wrong step, a chance rustle of caught brush, would flick such tuned instincts into the hair-trigger reflex of a killer. Heart pounding, he gripped a gloved fist to his sword, prepared for the frightening mischance that he might need to defend himself.

The four horses approached, the mounted one trailing. The man in the saddle stayed pressed to its mane, his presence masked from chance-met sight, and his low profile a foil for enemy archers.

At a distance of fifteen paces, he drew rein. Braced tense, he raised his head. The expression half-glimpsed under the masking, fur hood showed remote, chiseled pallor under the cloud-filtered spill of the moonlight. The face was no man's, but a specter's, pared hollow by privation and burred by the ebon tangles of ungroomed hair and beard.

Caithdein beheld his sworn liege of Rathain, reduced to a shell more unkempt than a starved, wild animal.

A gapped instant passed, wrenched from time and reason by the impact of shock and grief. Undone as he battled a weakness of nerves, Jieret could not command the steeled will to arise. The fear turned him craven, that he might discover the creature before him irretrievably lost, broken by months of desolate flight and abandoned to nightmare insanity.

Then Arithon spoke, his chosen phrase whispered in the Paravian tongue, as though week upon week of forced solitude left him accustomed to addressing ghosts. '*Ean cuel an diansil?*' which translated from the most ancient of dialects, 'Are you one who is friendly?'

Jieret gasped his affirmative in the same tongue, and in painstaking caution, stood up.

The tableau froze there, but for the wrapped hand that Arithon jerked from the snarl of the horse's mane. '*Caithdein?*' he breathed. When the bulked figure before him did not thin and fade into an apparition, the rusted grain of his voice cracked into an unstrung sob of disbelief. 'Earl Jieret?'

'Liege, I'm here for you.' Shamed for his momentary lapse into cowardice, Jieret rushed forward and caught the slight frame of his prince in a bear hug as he let go and slid from the saddle.

Too aware of the prominent bones pressed through the layers of hide clothing, Jieret sought swift distraction in talk. His rescuing words shaped the fondly shared memory, of himself as a boy who had spied on his prince from the brush. 'How did you know, this time, that somebody waited?'

'Without any telltale mosquitoes?' Eyes shut, the strain in him tempered to mercuric conditioning that ran too close to the surface, Arithon repressed the urgent need to glance warily over his shoulder. Though civil conversation must have seemed a fool's act of intrusion, he contained his raw instincts and answered. 'Your bearskin smells like woodsmoke, not new snow, and the goose grease you use to keep rust from your weapons carries a stone's throw downwind.'

'Daelion avert,' Jieret murmured. 'The most difficult points of your nature don't change.' He sensed as he spoke that the long years elapsed since their last meeting in Caithwood had not passed by without impact. Whatever the scathing scope of events, through his hands, already, he understood that his prince required a brother's attention in private. He broached the most challenging problem straight on, and hoped against nature the surprise of reunion would blunt his liege's thrice-thorny temperament.

'For a start, we'll have to attend to your wounds.' He might have laughed at the irascible draw of Arithon's breath, had their meeting been in safer country. 'Don't think to argue. You're in no fit state. My whole war band is here to support me.'

'I don't always argue with unstoppable forces,' Arithon demurred. 'Just give your promise, when you strip off the bandages, you won't cave in to demand that I should be served with a mercy stroke.'

'That bad?' Jieret said, unfazed by the reference to the bitter clan custom of dispatching the crippled before risking exposure to enemies. 'Then my scouts can be left to attend to your horses. Best we keep moving into the camp while you're still upright and walking.' Concerned for the stained dressing that showed through the torn glove on his prince's right hand, he sent the owl's call to signal his waiting companions.

The leaden, iced course of the River Aiyenne looped a meandering channel across the winter white dales of Daon Ramon. Where the lazy coils bent through layered rock, over centuries, the placid, inexorable current had carved over the deposits of petrified sediment. As ice froze and refroze through an epoch of seasons, the softer sandstones and limestone wore away until the buttressed banks became sculpted to undulant chains of hanging formations and scooped clefts.

Slack water fell at midwinter, the thaws that would swell the Aiyenne to a race of white foam a promise withheld until spring. The deeper recesses stayed dry in the cold months, and there, Jieret's war band took shelter from the flaying north winds. A hoarded store of charcoal and seal oil gave them small, smokeless fires and spare light.

A tight watch was posted. The s'Ffalenn prince just welcomed into their midst brought them a sharp increase in danger. Etarra's combined forces advanced a day's march to the east. With Lysaer's additional headhunters from Narms inbound to cap their set bottleneck, the clan war band became quarry exposed upon open ground. Earl Jieret chose not to take undue chances. Clan sentries patrolled from six outlying camps, while the hill ponies fanned over the country between in compact, separate herds, with mounted scouts set to guard over them. Cloud swallowed the new-risen moon. Night lay on the land like unpressed black felt, silted with deadening flurries of snowfall that muffled the howls of the wolf packs.

Prince Arithon was sequestered in the deepest, recessed cavern, the entry closed in by a rubble of boulders that baffled the flare of stray light. The declivity of rouged sandstone and gold ocher concretion shed false warmth in the spill of a fired-clay oil lamp. Cast shadows crawled on the sooted rock ceiling. Jieret, on his knees, nursed a pannikin of water, steeping herbs for the mash of a drawing poultice.

A grated step on loose gravel, then the subsequent absence of sound presaged the approach of a Companion. Braggen, Jieret presumed, since the man's dauntless nature most often saw him elected as spokesman for the rest. Too taxed to handle uncomfortable questions, the Earl of the North cached a cut snarl of stained dressings under the fleeces of Arithon's shed jacket. He darted a glance sidewards, reassured. Rathain's prince would stay settled despite interruption, enveloped like a lost child in the cinnamon pelt of his *caithdein's* borrowed bear mantle.

A split second later, Braggen squeezed his ox frame into the throat of the cleft. His inquisitive survey took in the pale, s'Ffalenn features, eyes closed in oblivious sleep. 'How bad is he?' The studs on his jerkin scraped in complaint as he settled on his heels in a niche, forearms crossed on the briar-scarred hide of his leggings. 'The men outside want to know. Can't pretend they don't notice the rank stink on the breeze as the aftermath of a cautery.'

Earl Jieret looked up, the ends of his beard dipped bronze by the coals just used to heat his second-best knife. 'Do they want the whole list, or just the details that are worrisome?'

Braggen snatched a glance of stamped apprehension at the dark, rumpled head engulfed in its calyx of fur.

'Say all you like. His Grace won't awaken.' Jieret shared a grin of rueful commiseration. 'I dosed him unconscious with valerian.'

'*He let you?*' Braggen's eyebrows bristled, shot upward by stunned surprise. 'By Dharkaron's Black Spear, never thought I'd see that day.'

Jieret blotted his dampened knuckles on his jerkin, unable to mask that his sleeve cuffs were spotted with blood. 'Well, you didn't see the proud flesh to be scraped away, or the tendons exposed on the back of his hand.'

'Ath, not his sword hand!' Braggen shot an appalled glance at the prone figure swathed in the bearskin.

Yet Jieret's pained nod spoke as much for the music as for concern with potential impairment of his prince's skilled use of weapons. 'Given rest and adequate time to heal over, the fingers will still function well enough to grip steel. But no simple or remedy we have in the field can reverse the damage from scarring.' The sorrow stopped words, that Athera's titled Masterbard might never recover the matchless, fierce brilliance of his performance on the lyranthe.

But Braggen had not shared Jieret's past trip to Innish, nor the summons by the Fellowship to Caithwood; along with most of the Companions from Strakewood, he had never heard Arithon play. 'His Grace is unfit?'

Jieret swallowed, returned a brisk headshake while he forced his closed throat to unlock. 'No. Except for the hand, which is serious, he has several scabbed-over gashes, some toes nipped to frostbite, and a case of nervous exhaustion.' He leaned to one side, caught up the green stick kept to stir up the embers. 'I expect a full night of well-guarded sleep should set the worst back to rights.'

'I'll tell the men.' Braggen scraped a thumb under his beard, a pinched and dubious cast to his squint as he measured the unearthly, stilled form of his prince. 'When you want relief keeping watch, cast a stone. The scout by the river will hear and send someone.'

'This vigil is mine,' Earl Jieret insisted, then swore a fierce oath as his jab to turn the coals beneath the pannikin shot up sparks that scorched a new hole in his buckskins. 'Go on. I know how you hate guarding invalids.'

'His royal Grace, anyway.' Braggen's lips twitched with distaste. 'Has a damned flaying tongue when he's hurting.'

'You remember that much?' Jieret cast down the stick as the pot spat steam and started to boil.

'Not me.' Braggen shrugged. 'My old uncle sat with his Grace after the fight at Tal Quorin. That's where he said he picked up his best collection of insults.' His teeth flashed and vanished into shadow as he rose. 'I'll leave you like the hawk set to brood on the snake. Don't expect you're not going to get bitten.'

Jieret gave back a choked snort of laughter. 'Ath grant you're wrong. If not, you owe me a fox tail as fine as the ones Theirid ties in his clan braid.'

Caught aback, Braggen poised in the cleft where the wind shrilled and sighed between boulders. 'You'd wear that?'

'Me?' Appalled, Jieret fumbled the tied packets of herbs borrowed from Arithon's saddle pack. 'Sithaer's howling furies, no. I promised I'd bring one for Jeynsa.'

'Well, she'll need more than fox tails to fill your boots, brother.' Despite his gruff humor, the worry leaked through as Braggen hitched his strapping bulk through the exit. 'Be sure you make time to sleep for yourself. We don't need you thickheaded and stupid on the hour we bearbait that daisy-faced godling's new army.'

* * *

Restored to safe solitude, Jieret kept his hands busy, nursing his small clutch of charcoal. He boiled the crusted rags of old bandages, then soaked them in an infusion of sweet herbs and tallow soap. He swabbed out the dirt ingrained in chapped skin, bathed and untangled the unkempt black hair. Nor did he stop there, but turned back the bearskin and cleansed everything else not strapped in dressings or poultices. Last of all, he honed his knife and gently commenced on the neglected tasks of shaving and trimming.

'Ath's blinding glory!' Theirid's awed comment sniped from the shadows. 'Were his Grace wakeful, he'd have some choice thing to say, if not use that wee blade to gut you.'

Jieret whirled face about, the raised steel in his hand no less than rock steady for his startlement. 'Damn you, I know that. Do you always have to sneak up on a man like you're hunting?'

Indistinct in the darkness fronting the entry, Theirid shrugged. 'Just checking up. Didn't think I'd catch you playing nursemaid.'

The Earl of the North resettled himself, exasperation and challenge in the set of his shoulders as he clipped another shoulder-length lock of dark hair. 'He can't do this himself without wetting the fresh dressings I've set on his injured hand. Nor can he very well wash his own clothes when we have to be moving by dawn.' Jieret's gray hazel eyes snagged the reflected flash off of the steel's wicked gleam. 'Look there.' He nodded to an unkempt pile of cloth, stitched through its grime with the odd satin facing, and the crimped gleam of abused silver ribbon. 'You're assigned, for impertinence. Take the good balsam soap. There's a break in the ice at the verge of the river and no lack of stones to pound laundry.'

Theirid opened his mouth, cut off from protest by his clan chieftain's snap of authority. 'His Grace kept us alive at Tal Quorin. His works since that day have come to spare every one of Tysan's clan bloodlines. We'll wash his soiled shirts, and resharpen his knives, and take pride in the hour we die for him!'

'Which won't ease your hurt in the least,' Theirid said, touched by impulse and wounding sympathy. He bent without rancor, his stalker's quiet displaced as he scooped up the ruckle of clothing. 'You're dreading the moment you'll send his Grace on, with no man at his shoulder to guard him.'

Jieret's knife jerked, rinsed bloody red by the embers. 'Fiends plague, man! Your stalking ways are quite wretched enough without picking fights with my state of mind.'

'Companion, *Caithdein*,' Theirid rebuked as he shouldered his load and edged toward the recess to depart. 'You don't stand by yourself. Each of us feels the same way.'

Then Theirid was gone, with no snatched chance for rejoinder to lighten the ache that rode on the heels of cold truth. Clansmen by nature did not indulge grief; attachments to sentiment too often abraded the inborn will to survive. Ruggedly stoic, Earl Jieret resumed his quiet work. For a brief, settled interval, rare for its intimacy, he applied his steady knife and large hands to barbering the damp strands of Prince Arithon's hair.

Peace reigned for an hour, gentled by the popping whistle of hot embers and the thrumming refrain of the winds. Jieret finished his trimming, wiped and sheathed his fine knife. While the stars above Daon Ramon wheeled and crossed a meridian masked under snowstorm at midnight, he leaned forward to discard the stray clippings in the fire.

'Save those, they'll be needed.' The acid instruction arose from the sleeper arranged in the bearskin.

Jieret jerked, startled, now watched by green eyes alert with disturbing lucidity. 'You shouldn't be wakeful. I gave you a dose of valerian strong enough to drop a young horse for a gelding.'

Arithon pushed to sit up, discovered his flesh naked, and swore with inventive irritation. He bundled his bare shoulders in cinnamon fur, then jackknifed his torso erect against the smoothed sandstone behind him. 'Mage training taught how to transmute certain poisons. In the case of soporifics, the response can become ingrained reflex.' Returned to the awkward subject of clippings, he added, 'You should mask those in silk.'

'You weren't conscious,' Jieret insisted, emphatically unwilling to be sidetracked as he folded the loose hair into a rag and weighted the packet under a rock. 'How much should I worry?' Dakar had once warned that the spurious resurgence of Arithon's talent might be provoked by Desh-thiere's curse.

'Always.' That kernel of honesty delivered, Arithon refused elaboration, but probed the new wrapping over a hand that certainly pained him like wildfire. 'Thank you,' he said through the ghost of a wince. 'I see you've been thorough. Maybe this time the injury can be given the chance to close over.'

No complaint, for the heartache of his spoiled music; just acceptance flat and hammered as lead, that spurred Jieret's concern worse than anything. Unswerving despite the smooth effort of evasion, he pressed, 'You know Lysaer's marching.'

The affirmation, too calm, 'I feel him. Northwest of here, and pressing ever closer as we speak.'

'Moving?' Jieret probed the shadowed, green eyes, alarmed as he sought the first warning of trouble. 'Not at night, surely?'

'Do you want reassurance?' Arithon as always cut past surface meaning, his head tipped to wearied rest against rippled striations of sandstone. 'We're not talking good judgment, but the drive of a curse that won't rest until one of us crosses Fate's Wheel.' An infinitesimal, strained pause, filled by the pop of an ember. A flurry of small sparks rode the draft in gyration, then snuffed into smothering gloom. 'You can't trust my intentions. I daresay that's why you're holding my sword and every last stitch of my clothing?'

Unable to soften that self-wounding analysis, Jieret bristled. 'You don't need your sword while mine's here to guard you, and your clothes, I might add, were offensive. A Companion's at the riverside, washing them as we speak.'

But the stakes were driven too high and too deep to retreat for a kindly meant platitude. 'Jieret, Caolle died because all the safeguards broke down.' Arithon's left hand clamped taut in the bearskin, the surreal, refined beauty of each rigid finger demarked by the hard gleam of bone through the skin. 'Don't ask me to take the same risks with your life! Here and now, I'm going to refuse them.'

'What will you do, then? Ride out buck naked? Let the Mistwraith's curse take you, alone against Lysaer's Alliance?' Jieret grinned. 'I don't think so. To leave this grotto, you'd first have to kill me. If you managed that much without use of your sword hand, you're a fool. Your style with a main gauche cannot defeat the best fighting blood of my war band.'

A dangerous, sheared glitter awoke in green eyes. 'Jieret. Don't provoke me. Desh-thiere's curse isn't malleable.' As though each word was drawn, white-hot, from a forge flame, Arithon forced through the finish. 'When you threaten to stand between me and my half brother, you make yourself into a nameless obstacle that exists to be struck down. With Lysaer this close, *I can hold self-restraint for only so long*. Don't spark the fell fire that burns me.'

Jieret found the good grace to break that locked stare first. Though his instinct, his love, and the yoke of ancestral duty rebelled from the pitiless fact, he affirmed the unpleasant necessity. 'I don't disagree. You will ride alone. Our task is to buy you the distance you need to stay sane as you bolt for the mountains.'

Some of the cruel tension left Arithon then. Under the snugged bearskin, his shoulders eased slightly. While the wind off the barrens fluttered the failing flame of the lamp, the rare, wry smile reserved for close friends turned the firm line of his mouth. 'I forget, you're not Dakar, but Steiven's grown son, with Dania's sharp mind to grasp nuance. This much you can trust, on my word as your crown prince. Against pride, against preference, I *must* accept the opening for survival you offer. You'll have my cooperation. Even if I wasn't bound by a blood oath to the Fellowship Sorcerers, Caolle's life left a debt I will honor. While in my right mind, I won't squander the s'Ffalenn lineage he spared to restore a crown presence in Rathain.'

The released surge of hope blazed too blindingly bright. Jieret shut his eyes to stem his shocked tears of relief. 'Thank you for that promise. Might I ask, will you marry?' The plea was ripe folly, an impulse regretted as he braced for a scalding rebuttal.

But the letdown came gentle from Arithon, this night; as ominous an admission, that this meeting between friends might very well be the last. 'Fionn Areth's ill usage at Jaelot should show you my reason why not.'

The chill in that moment bit to the bone, breathed in through the cleft off the winter white hills, where Paravians had not danced for five centuries; and perhaps, never would, in the course of an unstable future. Jieret laced chapped knuckles over his bent knee, resigned to his prince's harsh reasoning. Unthinkable, the prospect that a blood s'Ffalenn heir might be taken and used as the pawn of political expedience. For as long as Desh-thiere's curse fed the fervor of townbred hatreds, no babe born of Torbrand's lineage could grow to adulthood in safety. Fionn Areth's chance likeness had proved beyond doubt: Arithon of Rathain had too many enemies seeking just such sure leverage to entrap him.

'Any child of yours could invoke Fellowship protection,' Jieret burst out as, again, his raw longing outpaced prudent thought.

'With his fate proscribed, as a virtual prisoner!' Since his nakedness canceled the grace of retreat, Arithon used rage to buy distance. 'I'll have no get of mine entangled by the dictates of kingship and destiny. Not for a land torn to arms by the Mistwraith's cursed war, not even for the needs of the Sorcerers' compact, to save what remains of the order the Betrayer's rebellion pulled down.'

In the dim, enclosed grotto, frozen silence remained, a misery beyond the suffering imposed by the brutality of the season.

Painted in the carmine glow thrown off the embers, the *caithdein* of Rathain faced his prince. 'Even so. Or else tomorrow our shed blood will come to mean nothing.'

'Ath Creator show mercy, Jieret!' Raked on the exposed nerve of his helplessness, Arithon gave back his very self. 'I'm a man, heart and mind, not a vessel begotten to reseed the Fellowship's tailor-made bloodline. If I ever breed heirs, they will grow up in love. Sons or daughters, I would see them raised by their mother, *cherished and protected by my right arm, and the guaranteed trust of my sanity.*'

'Then you'll answer to Jeynsa,' Jieret flared, as the bared vulnerability of that naked confidence backlashed against his sworn duty to Rathain. 'Don't expect my apology, for hoping her children won't have to suffer their whole lives under threat of persecution by headhunters.'

But Arithon rejected argument, the flash burn of his fury broken to nettled impatience. 'My clothes will stay wet at least until dawn? Then we have that long to design precise tactics. I won't see you martyred. Not while there's one chance to foil the Alliance's field troops and keep you and your war band alive.'

Caught openmouthed, his adrenaline raised for a murderous row, Jieret felt as though a huge hand slapped the air clean out of his chest. From any other man, that brash-handed statement would have been needling arrogance.

Arithon Teir's'Ffalenn glared back from wrapped fur, his fox features stamped by razor-edged exasperation.

Jieret quashed the piqued reflex to scoff in disbelief. He dragged in a deep breath; cooled his boiling temper. Repossessed of his *caithdein*'s dignity, he regarded his prince long enough to unravel the lacerating entreaty twisted through the coils of s'Ffalenn conscience. He shook his head, aching. 'Caolle died, believe me, I know how that hurts.'

Arithon turned his face, the scraped shreds of his anguish buried behind the left fist still clenched in a wadded bastion of damp bearskin. 'You aren't listening.'

Chilled to a stalker's caution, Jieret tested the unspoken long shot. 'You have a plan that can save us, and still mire the Alliance advance long enough to win your clean escape?'

Still bent away, the royal profile of his ancestors all struck angles against the encroaching dark, Arithon shivered. As though weariness and uncertainty lashed a small storm through his flesh, he said, 'One chance. Not a good one. But worth giving serious thought.'

His burden of pain stayed written in silence, that too many lives had been sacrificed since the hour he had given his crown oath in Strakewood. Another friend's loss would not be endured without willful protest and fight. While the keening draw of air through hot embers scribed the midnight quiet, Jieret waited. The depths of this quandary lay outside his experience. He had no Fellowship Sorcerer at hand, to ask if his prince's reticence was straight fear, or how much was provoked by berserker's rage, that would cast away prudence before bending pride to embrace the cold wall of futility. Touched by a prickling stir of unease, he kept a cast-iron grip on his patience.

Tradition bound them. *Caithdeinen* gave their lives in the testing of princes, if no other means lay at hand.

Nor was Arithon sanguine, as he wrestled a glaring reluctance to finish. 'You are gifted with Sight. That implies birth-born talent.' The level, green eyes lifted, the dread in them unflinching. 'We might try to waken that latent potential. If we can, I haven't forgotten my training. A few simple cantrips my grandfather taught me might serve to offset the Alliance advantage of numbers.'

'Wield sorcery? *Me?*' Jieret shot to his feet, slammed his head on low rock, and swore as the pain whirled him dizzy.

'For your life, and the safeguard of your war band,' said Arithon, no whit complaisant, but cornered by grief, that a friend must weigh such a wild-card decision. His stripped apprehension matched the horror in the red-bearded chieftain who towered over him; who, as a boy of eleven years, had been bound by a sorcerer's oath to be spared from the slaughter at Tal Quorin. Twice since that day, he had stood down the brunt of the Mistwraith's possession, when Desh-thiere's curse had overwhelmed his prince.

The passage of time had not loosened that bonding. To the grown man, the sovereign prince gave his honesty, delivered with personal care and sincerity few spirits alive ever witnessed. 'No choice to make lightly. If we try this, and by sheer courage we prevail, the end play will still carry terrible risks. Not least, you could find yourself burned for black spellcraft on some crown examiner's pile of faggots. I might be oathbound to Asandir to use every means to survive. But Dharkaron stand witness, in this, I can't speak as your crown prince. First, as my friend, you would have to be willing. I won't undertake the first step of initiation without your wholehearted consent.'

Jieret swallowed, resisting the battlefield impulse to suck on a pebble to dampen a mouth dry with fear. He looked at his hands, well taught by Caolle to wield honest steel, and thickened with callus from rough, outdoor living. 'It's a difficult service I have of you, prince.'

Arithon's mouth flexed with the rueful trace of a smile. 'You'll recall, at the outset, I tried to avoid it.'

But Jieret found no refuge in banter. A practical man who respected his own limits, his courage was defined by self-confidence. At home in the wilds that framed his domain, he towered like rooted oak, unbowed by grief or adversity. The sure carriage and maturity earned through a lifetime of sound leadership came undone in that moment. Dreadful uncertainty creased new lines in his windburned face, while a gust through the defile fanned the gray streaks at his temples. Hung on the cusp of grave responsibility and a hope strung on madness and folly, he measured the chasm that yawned at his feet.

He must not tread the abyss without thought, though at Traithe's behest, in behalf of this prince, he had experienced arcane powers once before. 'I don't regret any day in your company. On the contrary. You've always done right by my trust. Do you have any sureties to offer me?'

'None at all.' Arithon absorbed the recoil that shocked through the glance held between them. 'To awaken your talents, we would first invoke chaos. Break down the mental patterns of resistance, lose the ties to your flesh, until you had no equilibrium left to perceive without taking charge of your talent. True Sight is the conscious landscape of dream. An awareness read by the inward eye, not the dense illusion that governs the outer. You would be cast adrift to unriddle the mysteries. All power moves through the higher vibrations, past reach of the physical senses. But the lowest of frequencies by their physical nature always invoke the higher harmonics. I'd give you my music to guide you.'

A ribbon of sweat licked down Jieret's neck. 'Unlike my father, I haven't been shown the day and the hour of my death.' He braced through a moment of wrenching uncertainty, then made his resolve with the same rugged character that had sustained the hard years of his chieftainship. 'I will shoulder the risk for the lives of my war band, and for my daughter, Jeynsa. Let her not swear her *caithdein*'s oath to Rathain ahead of her twentieth birthday.'

Two hours before dawn, the temperature plunged, with the snow fine as ice-tipped powder. In the grotto by the Aiyenne, new spangles of hoarfrost etched the sandstone ledges in lacework traceries of leaded silver. Reclad in his own faintly damp shirt and the ribboned silk doublet first chosen to mingle in Jaelot, Arithon looked displaced, the nonchalant elegance of his dress at sharp odds with the predatory, lean face of the fugitive. Then he pulled on his freshly brushed jacket, laced up the leathers beaten soft by the riverside, and strapped on his boots, his small knife, and the tinder kit on its hide-and-cord strap, that he kept in remembrance of the dead trapper. No fine silk showed through as he knelt and stirred up the dying coals. He could have been overlooked as a younger clan scout, prepared to range out on a routine patrol, or to lay traps for marauding headhunters.

Winter in Daon Ramon wore down all men alike. The diet of dried stores and lean game melted off summer's flesh, until bone and muscle pressed through taut, windburned skin. Touched in faint outline by the ruddy glow off the embers, Arithon seemed neither clever or dangerous as he prodded the saturated clumps of tobacco spread to dry in the warmed, iron bowl of the pannikin. The natural grace of his movements lacked symmetry. Each simple task he performed became hampered by his injured hand, its bundled wrapping held cradled from harm's way in the crook of his left elbow.

Jieret observed the course of his halting progress, unable to sleep where he lay, curled in the restored warmth of his bearskin. A liegeman forgot at his peril that this prince had been trained to a sorcerer's mastery.

Memory too often forgave the sharp edges. The Crown Prince of Rathain was nothing if not a creature of shadow and subtlety. He might appear too slight for his clothing, the left hand's clean fingers too finely bred for the sword. Yet the semblance of youthful fragility was misleading. On that day, Arithon s'Ffalenn was in fact fifty-five years of age. His black hair showed no dusting of gray. Beneath every mark of his mortal frailty ran the thread of uncanny design: his Grace had drunk from the Five Centuries' Fountain, enspelled by Davien the Betrayer to endow an unnatural longevity. The mysteries had once opened to his power of command, until the slaughter done in defense at Tal Quorin seared out the vision that accessed his talent.

Seventeen years had elapsed since the summons to Caithwood, when *caithdein* and prince had last exchanged words face-to-face. The spellbinder who had partnered the intervening absence was not here to lend counsel or valued perspective.

Blind faith remained, for a blood-bonded loyalty flawed by the Mistwraith's curse.

The trust that Earl Jieret held for the man was now asked to transcend human reason and cognizance. He could not comprehend the uncanny dangers he might face. Nor would the seasoned skills he possessed afford any shred of protection. Arithon had explained with unvarnished clarity: once started, there could be no chance to turn back.

Now, while nerve faltered, Jieret clamped his jaw hard. He thought instead of his daughter. Despite all the fire and verve of her character, she was too young for the weight of a *caithdein*'s inheritance. The difficult morass of this prince's trials was no fit burden to lay on a green girl. Let Jeynsa enjoy her carefree, sweet innocence, before she must shoulder the brute course of learning that would lead her to Rathain's stewardship.

'Jieret?' Arithon inquired gently. 'The infused leaves are now dry enough to burn. Are you certain you want to go through with this?'

Words came, with none of the heart's hesitation. 'I'm in your hands, liege.' Earl Jieret threw off the mantling bearskin and sat up, annoyed that his effort to rest had bought nothing but disgruntled misgiving and the ranging, dull ache of stiff muscles. He linked his broad hands, stretched his shoulders until his tight joints popped in protest. Weather change coming, he noted by the twinge in the forearm that had once taken a headhunter's arrow. He felt light-headed, hungry, but his prince had advised against having anything to eat. 'Let's have this thing over with.'

'I'll stand with you, each step.' Arithon scraped the dried tobacco from the pan and packed the crushed leaves into a carved stone pipe. 'I believe in your strength.'

Jieret rubbed clammy palms on the thighs of his leathers. He felt no such certainty, though the rest of the items his prince had prepared seemed deceptively unprepossessing: a handful of acorns peeled apart and hollowed out; a green length of birch twig; the hoarded stub of a beeswax candle; a flake of clear mica picked from the gravel by the riverbed. Shaved bark, rolled for spills, and a handful of quartz pebbles had been gleaned from the drift-mantled countryside. A hollowed depression in the rock held a puddle of snowmelt, and beside that, a clod of black earth still spiked with hoarfrost. The deer-antler stylus Theirid used to scratch tallies had been borrowed and resharpened into an awl.

Arithon pressed the packed pipe into Jieret's unsteady hand. 'Take this, sit down, and hold back for my signal. Certain ritual safeguards will need to be set before we can begin in earnest.' He paused, expectant, while his *caithdein* settled near the fire pit.

The coals had burned low. A bearding of ash damped the warmth that arose from the heated stone underneath. Jieret blotted the beading of sweat that sprang on his forehead and temples. 'I'm sorry,' he admitted, discomposed as Arithon's concerned gaze read and weighed each sign of his unquiet turmoil. 'Only a fool does not fear the unknown.'

'The fine line that separates idiocy from courage.' Arithon grasped his friend's shoulder in sympathy. 'I share the same doubts.' Each safeguard he set must be done from memory, with no sighted guidance to know whether an obstruction deflected his course of intent. 'We both must walk blind.'

Jieret clasped the royal wrist in stark affirmation of an honesty that commanded his respect. The clean-breasted admission that hope was uncertain served to buttress his determination. He would not back down, could not so lightly abandon the lives of his war band and his Companions. Their brave stand must confront the Alliance of Light on the field. If they took the shock of Lysaer's assault, he would risk himself first, that death not be granted the least invitation to triumph.

'For Jeynsa and Feithan, I'll see you come through this.' Arithon turned his hand, completing the traditional grip shared between adult clansmen. 'Not for my life's sake would I forfeit the bonding first sworn to spare Steiven's son at Tal Quorin.'

The winter winds spoke through the interval while the two men sustained the wrist clasp of amity. Neither one wished to break free. The past at their backs held too much strife and bloodshed, with the future before them a landscape of thorny uncertainty. Too many hopes rode upon tonight's stakes, and too many failures would cascade from false steps or misjudgment.

Then Arithon said, 'I have one wish, that we stand side by side on the hour of Jeynsa's royal oath swearing.'

Jieret tightened his hold, gripped by sudden, raw need. 'Make me one promise, that after my death you honor my daughter with the same pact you gave me as a child in Strakewood.'

'Ath!' Arithon released his hold as though burned, his skin raised to a startled, bright flush. 'She's a woman! One day she'll marry. If her man dislikes me, a blood oath of friendship would force closer ties than a kinship.'

'Even so.' Jieret smiled, a spiked twist to his humor. 'She's a vixen, sure enough, all sharp tongue and brash courage. When I'm gone, you'll become her charge as Rathain's sanctioned crown prince. As the girl's father, I'd leave her in no other hands than your own. Your first pledge was given for Steiven and Dania. Let this one be done for me.'

'For you, I refuse nothing.' Hands crossed in formality at his heart, Arithon knelt, sovereign prince to sworn liegeman. 'Take my royal oath, I'll swear lifelong friendship with Jeynsa. Accept with the understanding my mage talent is silenced. Unless that fact changes, there can be no certainty the blood tie will be joined the same way.'

'No matter.' Throat locked by a sudden, fierce rush of emotion, Jieret coughed. 'From you, my brother, one word is enough to assure your honest intent.' He rested content, the paralyzing weight of his apprehension lifted from his broad shoulders. 'Do what you will. I am ready.'

That affirmation of absolute trust made the next step most difficult to complete. Arithon broke away, green eyes too bright. He steeled his unsteady nerves. Veiled light from the embers imprinted his slight frame, swathed in crude hide and patched furs, the uninjured fingers pressed to his face, fine boned as a master's engraving. For a struck moment, he could find no words, until the wealth of his bard's gift ceded him lines from an ancient epic. *'By the grace of such subjects, great kingdoms exist.'*

Then stillness became an insupportable trial; further thought weighed too grievous to bear. Resolved to grim purpose, the Master of Shadow bent to his herb stores and tipped crushed leaves of cedar on the coals. While the fragrant, white smoke coiled upward and billowed, he snatched up the birch twig and traced a ceremonial circle within the enclosed stone of the grotto. He joined the scribed line, with Jieret and himself set inside. Eyes shut, he whispered a Paravian invocation. He blew a breath to the east, stepped a quarter turn in place, then lit the candle stub to the south and set it upon the perimeter. Faced due west, he traced a rune symbol in water; northward, the same, but with earth.

Nor was his face peaceful, or his speech unstrained as he enacted the ritual that called elemental forces to stand guard. Where once, he would have *seen* the fine blaze of light that affirmed each stage of his conjury, now, he performed by blind rote. The absence of response, the blank vacancy of senses that once had exulted in the layered intricacy of Ath's creation remade each dance step of form into punishment. The tears spilled and ran; the matchless voice faltered, seared by a fire of remorse only three living spirits understood.

Asandir had first measured the scope of the loss, six years

after Tal Quorin. Dakar, as well, had shouldered the unendurable whole, on the night of grand scrying that had shaped the tactics whose failure had seen thirty thousand dead at Dier Kenton Vale. None else but Elaira, who knew Arithon's true heart, could have foretold the bleak anguish brought on by tonight's reenactment.

Earl Jieret, as forced witness, shared the shocked revelation: the true price meted out for the clan lives spared from the sword in Strakewood Forest. Like the scant few before him, he watched Arithon lay flat his defenses. The focused purity of intent softened the severe s'Ffalenn features, left them exposed to a child's stripped wonder of expectation. Then the moment of crux, when a lifetime's honed talent launched in flight, and failed to cross through the veil. Base matter stayed obdurate. Sealed vision froze all the world's dazzling majesty to the drab planes and angles within range of self-limited eyesight.

Nor could the lamed spirit vised in the breach shield his bared will from the harrowing. Arithon's vulnerable longing transformed, remade on a breath into ripping loss outside grief or tears to describe; as though light itself lost its luster to limitless darkness, or a dreamed, perfect pearl dimmed to crude gravel at the mere brush of a hand.

Arithon drew in a tormented breath. His face, his whole posture seemed wracked out of true, as though the living heart had torn out of him, and Ath's gift of life made his body a prison pinched out of songless clay.

That moment, Jieret would have begged sky and earth to be anyplace else on Athera. He had seen scouts die of lacerating wounds, but not suffer such agony as this. The bitter understanding sucked him hollow with dread, that no mortal who touched the core of grand mystery could emerge from the crucible unchanged. Any subsequent break in connection left a scar which cut deeper than transient hurt to the flesh. Hard on the heels of unwanted recognition, he knew drowning fear, that he had agreed to embark on that journey without any grasp of the consequences. He had never glimpsed the irreversible sorrows, if tonight's course of expedience succeeded, and he survived the first trial of initiation and cast his conscious awareness into the unseen realms past the veil.

Too soon, Arithon s'Ffalenn knelt before him, his regard a set mix of flint determination and empathy, and a lit spill in his trembling hand.

Just as racked by regret, Jieret accepted the offering. He raised the stone pipe, packed with the tobacco that had been soaked in an infusion of crushed tienelle leaves. 'Whatever may come, keep your safe distance from the fumes as you promised!'

Stripped to sincerity, Arithon said, 'On that point, I won't bend.'

Amid myriad risks, untrained use of tienelle might prove the most unforgiving. Though spiked tobacco was too mild to be lethal, Jieret received warning: the herb's myriad poisons would induce a withdrawal of sickness and cramping. The bystander who breathed tainted smoke could succumb. Arithon could not transmute the effects, reft as he was from his mage talent. The bard's art he offered to guide Jieret's progress relied on his voice, and even slight nausea would stress the control he required to sustain an exacting, true pitch. Beyond physical ills, the herb's visionary properties would unshutter the gates of the mind. Every damaging event held in memory would break free, an unbridled reliving too virulent for conscious awareness to grapple. Under such influence, the Mistwraith's geas might emerge in full force and smash the ties binding sanity.

Lysaer s'Ilessid and the Alliance were too close at hand. Any such misstep would invite a swift fall to disaster.

'Don't dwell on distractions,' Arithon cautioned. 'They'll only unbalance you. As you ease into trance, you don't want to fall into the reflected morass of your fears.' He retreated to the side of the circle by the cleft, where the influx of fresh air would sweep off the narcotic.

Jieret settled against the support of the boulder. Flame fluttered as he lit the pipe. A curl of blue smoke stung his nostrils. Even weakened, the tienelle bit swiftly. An answering frisson shot a flash-fire reaction the length of his overstrung nerves. He whispered a final plea to Ath's grace, that his lineage should stay safe. Then he set the stem to his lips and drew in a lungful of smoke.

The scent overwhelmed him, acrid and keen as the cutting winds of high altitude. His thoughts jerked, and then eddied, tugged as the first, wild rush of expansion combed through the lens of his senses. His hearing exploded. The smallest sounds magnified into a whirling barrage of raw noise. Jieret gasped, flicked to vertigo, as his skin went on fire. He felt every current of breeze stroke his flesh, while the plain weight of clothing bore him down like prolonged suffocation.

'Steady, hold steady,' Arithon encouraged, his voice a cool current of calm through a lit conflagration of air.

Jieret forced a grip on slipped courage, sucked down another breath. The smoke ripped, as it passed. His throat and his windpipe felt lye-stripped. His eyesight dissolved into rainbow sparks, while the merest sigh of the draft pummeled his eardrums like thunder.

'Arithon, I feel lost.' This experience held none of the spiraling, smooth uplift he recalled from his journey with Traithe.

The reply came back mangled as hearing imploded. Jieret gasped, the frayed cloth of his mind sucked down and tumbled by the raced flow of blood in his veins. The sensation of the bare stone at his back raised a sleeting, bright tingle, distinct as a silver-tipped hail of needles. His awareness floundered, broken winged as a bird encased in a skull of cast lead.

'Arithon, blessed Ath, I'm going to go mad.' Jieret cringed as his note of raised terror stormed back, an onslaught of echoes that hurled him into a kaleidoscopic maelstrom of chaos.

The bard's voice returned reassurance. 'Take in more smoke. One more breath, maybe two, and your physical senses will stop overloading and shut down.'

Before panic set in, that such loss would unmoor him, Arithon gently clarified. 'You'll still feel, still hear. But instead of responding to substance through flesh, the inner eye of the mind will begin to perceive through the range of higher vibration. The true sight of mages, Jieret, will be found as a tapestry wrought of the colors that lie beyond visible light. Don't sink into fright. Relax, let the tienelle raise you.'

The stone pipe weighed like poured lead in the grip of stump fingers. Silver smoke swirled a ghost serpent's dance on the drafts. Beyond that fascination, the deep waters beckoned, twined with the whispers of family and friends gone beyond Daelion's Wheel.

'My sister,' Jieret whispered, drawn into the cold by the shimmering image of a girl child's fire-seared hand. 'Edal?'

A note sang out of nowhere and speared him. Sound shattered the dangerous allure of the shadows and razed the dead spirits from the smoke. Snapped back to himself, Earl Jieret found the stone pipe still lit in the welded grip of his fingers. He forced the hot stem between his numbed lips. Weeping for grief and the rags of old anger, he inhaled another draft.

Pain followed breath and set hooks in his heart. He felt upended, then dangled, hung like a gutted carcass of game on the prongs of a headhunter's hatred. The air wore a luminous mist of red blood, alive with the faces of enemies. Seized by a lust to rend and kill, Jieret shouted. The need for a sword in his hand cut like pain, an exquisite, fine agony that promised him ecstasy, once he gutted the brute Etarrans who had slaughtered his family in their march up the banks of Tal Quorin.

'Jieret!' Arithon raised true song. His clean line of melody tore through blind rage like a clarion cry in white light. Into that breach, a stream of fast words quenched ugly memories to quiescence. 'Beware. Before you discern mage-sight, *you will perceive thoughts as form.* Your own mind can spin traps and pitfalls. Don't bow to illusion. Stay calm. Touch the earth. Stone itself will help ground and center you.'

Jieret forced in a whistling, taxed breath. He was running vile sweat. The tienelle fumes made objects seem to startle and flash, as though form was remade into shapes of self-contained movement. His head felt cracked open. His addled perception leaped and recoiled like whiplash, too volatile for plodding reason.

'Steady,' urged Arithon. His calm soothed and anchored. 'The key is to stop thinking, stop remembering. Your personal beliefs will just serve to bend and distort the fine energies. *Just be.* True sight cannot be imposed from within. You must allow. Invite higher order to manifest what *is.*'

'Merciful Ath, I'm not made for this,' Jieret ground out in tight protest. One glimpse at his hands showed his scars as fresh wounds, welling bright scarlet by firelight. The blood there was other men's, shed with his own. He had no means to tell if the Sight was past reliving, or prescience.

'*Your stroke must kill cleanly,*' exhorted Caolle. His irascible shout seemed much too alive to arise out of fragmented memory. '*Miss your mark through an opening, your enemy will rally. Best way I know to wind up stone dead before you can sire a child to continue the name of s'Valerient.*'

'You are more than your past, brother, more cherished than your bloodline,' Arithon broke in, insistent. 'Love and worth are not measured by adherence to duty, but for a friend's generosity of spirit.' When his razor-clear note of gentleness failed to settle, he insisted, 'Here. Let me show you.'

But Jieret heard nothing, drowned as he was in the hardships imposed by his ancestry. Jeynsa's face filled his sight. Her hands clasped his shoulders, pleading. 'Father, just come back.'

Jieret opened his lips to ease her distress, then screamed as a shock like cold steel lanced his flesh. His vision exploded through showers of light, then sucked through a riptide of darkness.

Loss

The wind hissed over the iced vales of Daon Ramon. Its snarling passage through low brush and briar beat a whipcrack refrain, thrumming the tent's guy ropes and slapping the loose ends against the taut drum of pitched canvas. The drafts found their way through the weave of wool blankets. On winter campaign, the cold nights became a marathon of bitter endurance. For the men in Lysaer s'Ilessid's company, encamped on the wild vales between the old Paravian way and the serpentine loops of the River Aiyenne, the grinding misery of discomfort was not the least problem. Here, the fourth lane flowed over the land, swelling to meet the ancient nexus at Caith-al-Caen, where age upon age of Paravian dancers once summoned Athera's living consciousness into a quickened presence. The currents of the mysteries still ran near to the surface.

The tuned powers aligned in each pebble and stone tumbled in spate with the sun tides. Midnight, dawn, sunset, and noon, the flux could break with stunning force into the unwary mind, seeding burning, bright dreams, or awakening visions like tapestry woven from light. Where a mage-sighted talent, or persons of clanborn descent, might discern the searing beauty of the spirit forms bled through from the past, those ordinary others confined to five senses suffered sharp nerves and jumpy behavior. Seasoned veterans startled at shadows, chafed raw by the constant reminder that unseen powers stalked every move attempted by breathing, warm flesh.

At dark phase and full moon, a man could go mad, simply trying to sleep.

Sulfin Evend posted guard over the Divine Prince himself on such nights, unwilling to trust the wits of the sentries allotted that duty by roster. Always, he stood his turn of watch unpartnered. Though allotted a bear rug under sheltering canvas, he preferred not to rest, but perched on the box that contained the sunwheel seal and the chart cases, a sword's length from his sovereign's bedroll. His presence was that of a hooded falcon: too stilled to seem dangerous, and cloaked in a stalker's unobtrusive quiet that melted back into the shadows.

Royal birth had long since accustomed Prince Lysaer to having his privacy shared by crown servants, loyal men chosen for deferent silence and sophisticate, steel-clad discretion. Yet since the hour he had stood against Shadow at Tal Quorin, he insisted on sleeping alone. That night of full moon, under gauze snowfall and torn clouds, he sat wakeful, as loath to retire as his vigilant Lord Commander.

He occupied the tent's only camp stool, a chart of Rathain unfurled over his knees. His head was propped on an informal hand, long fingers with their splintering flare of gemmed rings shoved through his corn-silk hair. He was not drowsing. Sulfin Evend had enough past experience with Koriathain to discern the subtle difference. Despite the wayward, fierce currents of lane force that surged across Daon Ramon, the Blessed Prince had slipped into a light trance. Persisting through several disrupted attempts, he had managed to establish communion with his High Priest at Avenor.

The candle lamp, burning, cast an aureole over his elegant shoulders. If the surcoat he wore was no longer stainless white after long weeks in the wilds, costly elegance lingered, a marble tableau picked out by the shine of gilt braid where the flame light wakened reflections. As Sulfin Evend watched, those golden sparks flickered, then shuddered to jarring motion.

Lysaer shot straight, his indrawn breath sounding coarse as a tear in cloth.

Sulfin Evend twitched not an eyelash. With every nerve in him already primed for instantaneous action, his speech kept its laconic character. 'Bad news?'

The Exalted Prince released knotted fists. He masked his face behind his spread hands, elbows braced on the chart, which buckled under his careless pressure. Unsteady enough to display his fine trembling in the shimmering flare of his diamonds, he announced, 'My son is dead.'

A pause. Sulfin Evend waited. His war-trained tension uncoiled, since no overt peril threatened life and limb within the pitched tent in Daon Ramon.

A drawn moment later, Lysaer looked up. 'Kevor.' No tremble of inflection; his voice still struck blank from shock, he elucidated, 'Burned to a cinder with the field troop, apparently dispatched to hunt down Khadrim.' The eyes on his Lord Commander were an open, dilated black, rimmed in gemstone azure. Yet their depths reflected a wound so deep, thought could scarcely encompass the recoiling agony. Lysaer fought for recovery, as awareness mapped the imprint of a loss beyond any rational acceptance.

Staring, locked, at that intimate profile of raw grief, Sulfin Evend felt himself speared by transfixing chills. As long as he had served as the Alliance Lord Commander, he had never once glimpsed the depth of his prince's humanity.

'Kevor's gone!' Lysaer gasped. Disbelief strained his words to a whisper. 'My son, taken before he could achieve his manhood. He'll never find the mature stature, now, to heal the blight that Shadow and Darkness laid like a curse on his birthright.'

Sulfin Evend possessed the quick mind of a strategist, no boon in the crux of this moment as he found himself made the voice for Lysaer's tormented conscience. 'You could never permit that boy to know how much you cared for him.' The bitterest price, paid by s'Ilessid for the toil of a thankless, divine service. 'As the Light's given arm to defend the innocent, you dare not love.'

Though the cold ran through flesh and branded, bone deep, Lysaer admitted in searing simplicity, 'What can be done? That is my fate.' Behind the fire and passion, a hopeless measure of pain underpinned the framework of autocratic sovereignty. Few men had ever seen past the mask. That privileged handful had all been struck down, Sulfin Evend realized, touched into ripping epiphany. They had died in the wars fought by warped sorceries, at the hand of the Spinner of Darkness.

The s'Ilessid prince regarded his helpless, clamped fingers, now cradled upon the inked vista of Daon Ramon Barrens. As though the creased landscape stood surrogate for the violence wreaked on his spirit, he added in beaten sorrow, 'Any tie of the heart, no matter how guarded, might fall into binding use by the enemy.'

The moment of bludgeoned vulnerability was ill omened, for the hour when Alliance field troops closed the cordon to take down the Master of Shadow. Nor was interruption any more welcome, as coarse canvas scraped warning, and the door flap slapped open. A blast of chill air billowed into the tent, snapping the ties on the pennons. In strode the stick-thin, obsequious seer Sulfin Evend regarded with instinctive, bristling distaste.

The pale creature bowed. His large hood as always shadowed his face. White cloth lent him the aspect of a starved wraith, exacerbated by the fingertips snipped from the fine silk mesh of his gloves. He would avoid untoward stains as he practiced, the affectation an odd contradiction for a man who adhered to the shady side of his profession. His knurled hands trembled with evident eagerness as he unveiled his bronze offering bowl and unsheathed his sacrificial knife. Mouthing his incessant, ritual prayers, he raised the bone blade like a flaked shard of ice.

'Jeriayish, not now!' Sulfin Evend's concerned gaze stayed fastened on the Blessed Prince. Through this terrible hour, divine duty could wait. Though his Grace seemed himself, the inbred reflex of state poise apparently beyond reach of all pain, Lysaer's stripped heart betrayed otherwise. The man just made a bereaved father still reeled in wordless shock. He deserved the humane consideration of privacy.

The diviner-priest paused. His hooded head turned toward the Lord Commander, every draped fold in his mantle a statement of rigid fanaticism. 'Best that you leave.'

Sulfin Evend held fast, a leashed tiercel poised on a perch. 'At Lysaer's order, not yours.'

When the Divine Prince gave no gesture of dismissal to break their deadlocked wills, the priest minced a step forward. He placed the bronze bowl on the trestle next to the camp cot. 'I know Cerebeld's news.' His thin lips flexed downward, their wax pallor touched gilt by the ragged flare of the candle. 'Our hunt for the Spinner of Darkness is too near consummation to let up for the sake of a mortal tragedy.' He kissed the bone knife, and murmured, 'Lord Exalted?'

Lysaer stirred, moved, his arm offered as though by rote. Dragged by its own weight, the gold-embroidered cuff tumbled back. The blood-flecked binding underneath offered the uneasy testament that such rites had grown frequent as an addiction.

Assured of his authority, the priest closed his jittery fingers over the royal wrist.

Lysaer jerked back, sparked to sudden offense. 'Leave me!'

Jeriayish huffed with exasperation. 'But Cerebeld's priests need to know—'

Cat fast, Lysaer spun in recoil. His forearm raked the trestle and sent the sacrificial bowl flying. The clangor belled through his raised voice as the vessel clashed and rolled across the field armor laid in readiness over his clothes chest. 'I said leave!' His cool presence shattered. Lysaer stood, the humanity in him a towering force that cried out in raw pain for reprieve. 'For the sake of my son, who has died for his people, Cerebeld's priests can wait for an hour.'

Jeriayish narrowed his eyes. The knife still held poised in his persistent grip, he accused, 'If you take any pause to grieve as a father, your Alliance forces from Etarra and Darkling cannot respond if the enemy turns or doubles back in midflight.' He advanced again, already dismissing the Lord Commander's watchful presence behind him. 'You risk much. Let one boy's death allow Arithon of Rathain to escape, and all of mankind will remain in bondage to the powers of Darkness!'

Sulfin Evend witnessed the shift at close hand: saw the bastard's dread name trigger recall of the Light's divine purpose. Prince Lysaer's living flesh struck a tensile pause, reforged by a power beyond bearing. His eyes flared, just once, as though racked by mute protest. Then paternal need became smothered out, pinched off like the hapless flame on a candle. What welled up in place of that natural grief was ice chill, as fixed in its purpose as any steel blade whetted for bloodletting combat.

'I know *precisely* where the Spinner of Darkness makes camp.' Each consonant was edged glass, and each vowel, a note of undying conviction. 'We are that close, *I can feel him, each breath*.' Lysaer regarded his shrinking priest, his magnificence the forged beacon of altruistic inspiration. 'I require no man's impertinent reminder to fulfill the task laid before me! While the enemy lives, I can have no peace. His evil is a thorn in mind and flesh, a gall that won't ease until his demonic spirit has been cleansed from the world and consigned to its final damnation.'

Struck dumb by the price a man paid to be god sent, Sulfin Evend shuddered. His sharp intelligence and courage fell short, to endure the scope of such sacrifice. Nor did he possess the sheer, hard-core will to suppress his earthborn humanity. He laid his light hand on the hilt of his sword, humbled as never before. The concept that Lysaer had once scraped his knees in the carefree innocence of boyhood seemed unreal. His fertile mind failed to imagine the crucible that could mold a child to mature with the heartless strength to endure such a burden of inflexible responsibility.

As Jeriayish stumbled a quailing step back, Lysaer struck with a hammering fist and crushed out the dribbled stub of the candle. Even amid freezing darkness, his driving will made itself felt. He was welded force, both template and channel for the cause of divine purpose. Such power could reshape men and cities, and as surely, the destiny of Athera herself. 'We march inside the hour. Before dawn, as we pause to refresh the horses, you'll be given your chance to cast a divination to satisfy Cerebeld's priests.'

The diviner bowed and fled, too cowed to grope after his offering bowl. His scuttling retreat through the tent flap just missed collision with the squire called in to assist with the royal armor and surcoat.

'Go!' bade Lysaer s'Ilessid to the stilled presence of his Lord Commander. The change in his manner posed a terrible dichotomy. No shadow of the bereaved father remained in those enameled blue eyes. First eclipsed, and then canceled, grief stood demolished, flesh and bone become the drawn sword of dedicated ferocity. 'Rouse the camp. Have the men armed and ready to ride out at my order.'

Crossing

Jieret crumpled, caught by his liege's quick grasp before he crashed onto cold rock.

'Brother, damn you, bear up!' Lungs on fire with the need to draw breath, holding Jieret's limp weight crushed into a slump against his shoulder and neck, Arithon quartered the ground. He retrieved the stone pipe, left-handed. Still holding his throat closed, he managed to stoop and empty the bowl of white ash. Poisoned smoke whirled around him. He staggered, off-balance. The dragging burden of his liegeman all but felled him as he ground the spilled embers under his heel. Wary as he was of the last, wisping fumes, close proximity itself posed grave danger. He was still flicked into reeling dizziness by the taint of the volatile oils ingrained in his *caithdein's* hide clothes.

Yet Arithon dared not chance the moment to invoke more prudent precautions. He snatched up the guard candle from the north quadrant, thrust the flared flame toward the face he held cradled at his shoulder. Eyes of gray hazel stared up at him, sightless. The pupils stayed black and distended.

'Daelion show mercy!' Slid to his knees, Arithon bent, the bronze head eased to rest against his thighs. He tightened fierce fingers in Jieret's red hair, spun to fine white at the temples. 'Don't surrender. Not without showing some fight!'

No response; Arithon cupped the slack features of the man who had spared him Desh-thiere's triumph, who had, under the cold sobriety of given orders, broken his crown prince's will to preserve an integrity that, for need, must outlast s'Ffalenn compassion. He pressed his cheek close, listening for a faint trace of breath. The hair reeked of tienelle and smoke. The flesh sprawled, inanimate as death.

'Daelion's bane on me, Jieret. Not this,' the whisper a stripped plea that did nothing to rouse any sign of vitality.

Head bowed, eyes tight shut, Arithon steeled his jagged nerves. Then he dealt the stilled face under his hands a sharp slap with his uninjured hand. '*Aletier!*' Awake! he cried in Paravian.

Jieret jerked, a spasm of reflex that did not touch the eyes, still sightless and wide in the flickering glare of the candle.

Arithon pinned the strong wrists hard to the stone, ready for what must follow. He held the man down with all his fierce strength through a harrowing fit of convulsions.

That moment, a slight noise intruded, where the winter gusts howled through the gap in the boulders. A spattered grate of footsteps crossed the loose gravel and ground to a frantic stop. 'Merciful Ath, was that Jieret's scream?'

Then the damning, split-second assessment, as whichever scout had arrived caught sight of his chieftain, bucking and thrashing under the pinioned hold of a sorcerer who gave no civil answer. Instead, he spoke words in fluent Paravian over what seemed a struggling victim.

'What have you done?' Steel screamed from a sheath. 'Is this how loyalty is answered by a prince undone by Desh-thiere's curse? By unspeakable acts of black spellcraft?'

'He is alive!' Arithon refused the overriding instinct to look up, face around, and address the new threat at his back. Though the voice of the scout was not one he recognized, the lethal combination of fear-blinded rage framed a timbre his Masterbard's ear must acknowledge. In the white heat of crisis, he cleaved to one truth, that he feared for his liegeman's life more.

Nor had his efforts brought about a recovery. Jieret's struggles subsided again into the torpor of unconsciousness. Arithon locked his hands, both the sound and the wounded onto the younger man's shoulders. He refused to relinquish the gaze of sightless eyes. 'You hear me, Jieret! *I'm with you, each breath.*'

'What have you done to him?' Studs grated on stone as the scout pressed through the cleft and fully entered the cavern. Touched by the dying glow of the embers, his upraised sword skittered hellish reflections across the shadowed rock walls.

More scuffling steps arrived from behind. A bass voice burst in, breathless, 'I heard Jieret scream. *What in Sithaer has happened?*'

'A curse-born atrocity.' Checked by shocked fright and agonized betrayal, the first scout edged aside. 'See for yourself.'

The scene he exposed offered no shred of contrary testament. A fool could not miss the pungent scents of rare herbs, or fail to measure the items laid out for ritual spellcraft. Caught in the flickering flame of the candle stub, *a prince who should have been prostrate with valerian* knelt over their chieftain's felled form. The fresh wrap on his hand showed a spotting of scarlet, as though his blood had been let with deliberation. Jieret's ginger hair spilled in disordered waves over Arithon's unsteady forearms, as though he had engaged some ugly ritual of dark magecraft to revitalize himself in exchange for the life drained from his liegeman's slack body.

The newcomer drew steel, shaken to terror, and unable to refute grim conclusion. 'Why would his Grace kill, unless driven by the curse?'

'On my life as your crown prince, I am in my right mind.' Arithon bent, his ear pressed to Jieret's chest. No faint sound of breath; frantic, the Shadow Master snapped, 'Find Theirid. He knows. He'll explain.'

But the plea might as well have fallen on deaf ears. These were the Companions, the child survivors of Tal Quorin who had grown up motherless. Alongside Earl Jieret, they had shared the terrible burden of ensuring the next generation, most of them orphaned themselves, but more desperately cherished by grief-stricken fathers whose families and wives had been slaughtered. Each one had seen sisters broken and violated by Etarra's campaign of butchery and wrought fire.

Mere boys, they had piled stones on the grave cairns of their parents and siblings, while the crown prince those massacred kinfolk had died for slipped away in unremarked anonymity. Arithon to them was a figure of hearsay, not seen since, for whose sake their chieftain was wont to depart for months upon dangerous courses of travel, and for whom Caolle had taken his death wound upon foreign soil

Panicked to uncertainty, the first scout declaimed, 'Theirid's gone on patrol.'

'Then send for him!' Unable to listen undisturbed, Arithon straightened. He laid chilled fingers against Jieret's throat, his urgency a dammed-back scream as he felt the fast, thready pulse turn ragged under his touch. He gathered himself again, slapped the flat of his hand down hard on his *caithdein's* motionless chest.

'Breathe, Jieret, damn you, man! Don't fail me and quit.' To the clamor of outrage arisen as more men packed like wolves in the cleft, Rathain's prince said, 'Stand down! Let me finish what's started!' If he failed to act swiftly, the chance would be lost, to bind the unmoored spirit of the man back into his flaccid, drugged flesh.

'Your chieftain is alive,' he repeated, emphatic. 'I beg you, don't meddle through ignorance!'

'Then rise on your feet!' interjected a third voice, the bark of impatient authority surely Braggen's. 'Prove what you say. Draw Alithiel against us. If your cause is just, if you're not possessed and lying, the Paravian starspells will waken as surety.'

Arithon jerked his head in stripped negation. '*I don't have my blade.* Jieret took charge of her. Even if he hadn't, the sword would not waken. Not unless I fought you in earnest. That won't happen. Can't.'

Continuously busy, the Shadow Master set his crooked knuckle against the skin above the bridge of Jieret's nose. Schooled by Elaira to know healing arts, he applied steady pressure on the meridian point which stimulated the central nervous system. Under his ministration, Jieret's limp form shuddered. His chest heaved as he dragged in a hoarse gasp of air.

Eyes closed in flooding gratitude for that tentative sign of reprieve, Arithon sought once again to placate the distrustful Companions. 'I'll raise no weapon against you. Charter law binds me. By my oath to Rathain, sworn on my knees before Steiven, you are my charge to protect. Over the steel of your fathers, I pledged you my service as crown sovereign, *unto my last drop of blood, and until my final living breath.*'

He sang out a note pitched to a clear F, then pressed his ear flat against Jieret's torso. If the heartbeat had steadied, the lungs under his ear screamed like an overstressed bellows. Arithon chafed the chieftain's slack wrists, then grabbed his chilled fingers and massaged the palms on the line that revitalized the diaphragm. He spoke as he worked, his tender inflection at unnatural odds, forged on raw will and concentration. 'Brother, don't let go and fall into the darkness. The light shines. I'm with you still. *The nightmares you suffer are not real.*'

Yet if the unseen torment of the mind posed the more terrible enemy, the immediate threat enacted by living men in the grotto was perilously still unfolding.

Braggen snapped first. 'By Ath, no mouthing of law can excuse this!' Ox shoulders tucked, he charged forward. Gravel grated, churned underfoot as other scouts surged at his heels. Their bared swords were leveled in rigid hands, their faces torn by a volatile mix of worry and vindication.

Arithon whirled like a cornered fox. 'You must not cross the circle!' His voice cracked to alarm. 'Heed my word! You tempt dangers you cannot possibly imagine. A mistake made now with the best of intentions could kill your chieftain, or worse, draw in the might of our enemies.'

The quandary stopped thought, that he could not stand against the scouts' surge to take him without leaving Jieret abandoned. Split second in decision, he rejected his own safety. If breaking the ritual circle drew notice, there would be no respite from the bloodbath to come without a live chieftain to restore the frayed chain of command.

Arithon stayed unmoved on his knees, as the blundering rush of his well-meant opposition scuffed across his exactingly drawn rings of protection. Metal spoke first. The drawn swords contained iron, whose grounding nature razed holes through the set frame of his intent. His bard's gift picked up the high, thin whine as the first line of laid energy sundered. By that sign, he knew: *the wards had been active.* Whatever questing power had been engaged and probing his sealed defenses, no barrier remained to deflect its hostile presence. The price of that misstep could not be measured; its penalty would fall in the future.

He cradled Jieret's head between his fixed hands, disregarding the vehement sting of the hurt palm too recently cauterized. His patient touch neither jostled nor flinched, even as the turbulent press of the men scattered the joined remnants of his precautions to oblivion. He disregarded the rough hands which bore in and touched pricking steel to his sides and his back, with Braggen's, most fierce, at his throat.

He raised his chin, adamant; kept his voice vised to calm, keenly aware the least note of upset would lend spin to the nightmares that pinned Jieret at the rim of Fate's Wheel.

'Fetch me Sidir or Eafinn!' Arithon swallowed, the sweat at his collar painted in glistening streaks. 'They served at my side at the Havens. Entrust them to judge me for falsehood.'

Braggen spat. 'Eafinn's gone, killed by scalpers last spring. Sidir's sent to Caithwood to guard Jeynsa.'

Hedged by the nervous pressure of six swords, Arithon grated, 'Then wait here for Theirid!'

'What, and watch Jieret die, sucked dry of life to fuel some spell brought on by Desh-thiere's fell purpose?' Braggen shivered, caught aback by the appalling courage of Arithon's adamant passivity. 'The High Earl said himself, he'd drugged you unconscious with valerian. If you were innocent as you claim, and had worked no dire spellcraft, you wouldn't be up on your feet!'

Shaken, bone white, cranked under stress to the limit of breaking, Arithon battled for hold on his stressed self-control. His effort drove him to the blank-faced, withdrawn concentration of the trapped beast, who gave over all struggle to husband its drive for survival. Rathain's prince held, obdurate, to his preferred course. Jieret's welfare came first. His touch on slack flesh remained gentle and steady, until the wrenching dichotomy of his pose seemed unnatural; as though flesh and bone were not man, but demon, inhumanly bound to a purpose beyond the compass of human frailty.

'Mercy, for Jieret's life!' The care in his hands struck sharp contrast to his words, a masterbard's peal of command. 'I have no other proof to offer as bargain!'

'For your life?' Braggen said. High emotion suffused his saturnine features. 'To stay my hand, liege, show us sane common sense. You need do no more than stand aside!'

Amid that locked tension, Jieret's breath caught and faltered. Arithon moved to lend succor, caught short by the bristling thrust of Braggen's sword against the pit of his neck.

The green eyes blazed then, sparked to desolate fury. 'Then betray your clans! Render Caolle's death useless! Break the trust of *my caithdein*, and cut me dead in cold blood. But beware if you murder. Jieret will be lost. For his sake, I will have given you my life as the last Teir's'Ffalenn. Dharkaron Avenger stand as my witness! If I die at your hands, I will have crossed the Wheel in unbroken service to *all* my feal liegemen of Rathain.'

While the bystanders watched, horrified, he leaned into the steel.

Braggen held firm, his skin drained sick white. The fixed point dimpled skin. Stressed tissue let go without sound, and parted under the pressure. A welled drop of scarlet sprang and flowed from the puncture.

Now trembling, Arithon pressed on inexorably. As the sword's tip encountered the banded cartilage of his windpipe, he gasped, 'Jieret!' his raw anguish a brother's. Eyes shut, in tormented disregard of the hostile steel ranged against him, he addressed his prostrate liegeman with the compassion that formed the very fiber of his heart. 'Forgive me.'

'Stop this!' someone shouted. Another bystander broke down weeping.

Braggen alone confronted the crux. He must pull his blade, or risk that Arithon's bearing onslaught would snap before his fixed steel inflicted fatal damage.

'His Grace is oathsworn to our earl by a sorcerer's blood pact,' a new voice entreated from the cleft. 'Braggen, put up! He can't stand down, though you kill him.'

Braggen's confounded consternation might as well not exist, for all the heed his liege paid that cry. Nor did he back down, or beg for a stay of clemency.

For Arithon s'Ffalenn, no pain of the flesh could unseat his agony of mind, that he may have overestimated Jieret's inborn strength, or worse, his natural talent. The horror that threatened *would not be borne*, that his error of judgment should have led the son of Steiven s'Valerient into jeopardy. 'Jieret! I swore on my blood to hold your life sacrosanct. You won't escape what that means.'

For the sake of this one life, he had spared Lysaer at Strakewood. The irony of that hour would not lose its cruel edge: that the price of love and integrity had come at excoriating cost. Had he allowed the Mistwraith's curse free rein then, had he immolated his half brother years ago at Tal Quorin, the geas of enmity would have ended, fulfilled. *Tens of thousands of dead men would still be alive with their families.* Nor would the Alliance war hosts have been given the purposeful reason to muster. Lacking the fuel of self-righteous zeal to ignite the cause of town greed, the gold pledged for bounties, which had set clan continuance into jeopardy across the breadth of two kingdoms, would never have swelled the headhunters' coffers.

A movement, a sudden shifting of shadows as parted bodies winnowed the candleflame.

'You will hear me, Jieret!' Rathain's Prince insisted. His wide, opened eyelids scarcely flicked in acknowledgment as Braggen gave way and stepped back. Arithon rejected all thought of the men who surrounded him. Lent the exacting self-discipline of the mage-trained, he exhorted for Jieret's hearing alone. 'I will give you the full measure of your worth, brother. Stand tall, my *caithdein*. Own who you are, or die craven.'

While fresh-runneled blood striped his collarbone scarlet, he raised a new song. Each note poured out of his stinging throat framed an edged contradiction of dissonance.

Nor did he take notice that a sent runner had finally summoned in Theirid. The influx of raised voices, as argument raged over the damning appearance that he had engaged in fell sorcery, did not move him. He sang, heart and spirit, with an artistry focused to stop breath and word in midsentence.

The clansmen fell mute. Stunned to awed stillness, they had no choice but listen as the bard's song for Earl Jieret s'Valerient framed a power of forced testament. Whether or not the masterful melody masked some heinous act of dark magecraft, the unalloyed majesty of Arithon's voice could and did bind each hapless listener into thrall. The soaring web of captivation undid distrust. Doubt unwound. First shamed, then ripped into mangling remorse, the scouts with drawn steel sheathed their weapons. They crept back, caught breathless, and gave the bard space to recall Earl Jieret from deep coma.

The snare of cruel memory *must* lose its hold before that fired influx of sound. Seamless melody entrained a sweet, tuned perception that unlocked every closed, hidden door of the heart. Shown Jieret's Name in a language of trued harmony, given view of his selfhood, exalted to poignancy through the eyes of a friend, the Companions wept to a man. They knew their chieftain, none better: the patience that hardship could recast as intolerance; the care that strong character held in denial, to anneal the courage that enabled year upon year of unyielding defense by the sword.

Nor was Arithon himself untouched by the sacrifice. Blind with remorse, he hurled all that he was into song, each line in sere a cappella a spearcast flung hard to the mark of exacting pitch. His humility wrought art to a pinnacle of command that cried primal light across darkness.

His gift flowed like spun dream, love and will distilled into razor-edged clarity. But delay set the penalty. Through the lagged minutes of dissident distraction, Jieret's awareness had drifted too far.

Arithon extended his voice and his mind across every barrier of limitation; and still, his rare talent was not enough. He could not bridge the gap. Notes bundled and strung in single formation were too threadbare a loom for the tapestry. Jieret's ears were sealed clay. His beleaguered senses had ranged beyond reach, lost in the grand weave of subliminal vibrations beyond the bounds of the veil.

Arithon sensed the limit through the vibrating air and the slack flesh held cupped in his hands. The heartbreak undid him, that the kindled flame of his care could not unbind the sealed gates of the mysteries. Around him, the scouts stood in lacerated shock.

Silence reigned as the bard acknowledged the blank wall of his failure, and his melody faltered and faded. His face twisted, desolate. No recourse remained. The musician had no access to the harmonics he could have called forth, effortless, from the strings of the lyranthe left behind in Sanpashir. Nor would men in a war band have any substitute instrument. Scouts on campaign carried nothing but weapons, and the joyless necessities of survival.

The wail of the wind seemed to grind on the quiet left by the melody's cessation. Arithon opened his eyes, half-unhinged with distress, the fight in him catapulted into mad-dog desperation. 'Fetch my sword!'

His whiplash command jarred and broke the diminished grip of spellbound reverie. Wakened to reason, recoiled to distrust, the scouts by the cleft stirred, while Braggen's bellowed refusal clashed outright with Theirid's cry for patient tolerance.

'Find me Alithiel, *do it now!*' Arithon's urgency cut like a blade. 'Braggen! As you love your chieftain, stop arguing. Just let Theirid past. Allow him to give back my sword.'

'We daren't.' The protest was Theirid's, rough with tormented uncertainty. 'Earl Jieret left firm orders. That blade is all the surety we have against you if Desh-thiere's curse sunders your sanity.'

'Then bind my hands!' Arithon snarled back. 'You will do as I say, *now*. Unsheathe my sword. Lay her lengthwise, point down, with her hilt over Jieret's heart. Damn you for cowards, lash my wrists all you like. For this purpose I need not touch the weapon!'

Against deadlocked stillness, a scraped stir of gravel; a scout pushed through from the rear ranks. Just arrived from patrol, his clan braid pale flax against the striped fur of a badger hat, he appealed, 'Leave his Grace free! Were my father alive, he would have given his trust.'

'You're Eafinn's son?' Arithon's taut features eased into startled gratitude. 'Theirid's right. For Desh-thiere's curse, Alithiel should not be given into my charge. For your faith, I give you my honor to guard. For pity, step forward and tie me.'

Cord was found, amid somebody's kit. Lanky and competent, despite flushed embarrassment, Eafinn's son knelt at Arithon's offered back. 'Forgive the necessity.' He looped the knots expertly tight, well trained in the skill of handling dangerous captives.

The young man arose. His curt nod summoned Theirid, who tested the lashings himself. Only then did the older Companion allow the Named steel to be brought in and drawn from her sheath.

Alithiel's blade glistened like dipped jet, the refined silver tracery of Paravian runes reduced to dulled mercury in the close-gathered gloom. No sparkle of starspells spun gossamer light as Theirid laid the steel at flat rest upon Jieret's laboring breast. Each jagged, snatched breath ripped the stillness like rent canvas, the stopped intervals now grown irregular, each one more frighteningly prolonged.

Arithon remained on his knees at the clan chieftain's head, his arms bound immobile behind him. No word from him was needed to spur haste. His patience itself framed a cold-cast warning to the scouts who completed his rapid directions. They tucked the bear-pelt cloak under Jieret's nape, then folded the slack hands over Alithiel's smoke-dark quillons.

'Stand away.' Rathain's prince bowed his head. For a terrible instant, he seemed to gather himself, as though he wrestled his crippling doubts, then coiled them into vised stillness. His last instructions framed a hammered command. 'Snuff out the candle. Once I have started, for Ath's mercy, stay clear. We'll have no second chance if I falter.'

Once again he raised his voice into song. The first line of melody invoked the sword's Name, a phrasing that extended beyond the three syllables in Paravian that tagged her earth-forged identity. This clear strand of harmony spoke first of star-fallen steel, then of coal fire in a cave, and the dedicated artistry of the centaur smith who had poured out his masterful skill as a craftsman in expression of love for his son. Arithon reached deeper, tracing out the unseen. He sang the sword's birth, and the delicate complexity of the Athlien spells, which had spun its fine-tuned enchantment using the chord which had Named the winter stars. Then, in darkened tonality, the thralled listeners tasted war and death, and blood spilled in tragedy as Durmaenir s'Darian fell. Arithon's skill encompassed the sorrow of Ffereton's grief. His tears streamed in sympathy, though the instrument of his voice remained sure, wedded to the stark demand of his art through a jarring transition in key.

Now the very rock in the walls of the cavern cast back his full-throated appeal: Arithon of Rathain gave his own Name and ancestry. As Alithiel's bearer, he asked to be heard in his hour of need. His melody underwent a towering transition, as he translated his love for Earl Jieret into free-ringing sound. Line upon line, he poured out his heart, a detailed account of what he stood to lose if his sworn *caithdein* slipped past Fate's Wheel.

The clan scouts who heard him shed silenced tears, for the depth of their misunderstanding. Given, firsthand, the steadfast integrity of their chieftain, wrapped like white flame in the gratitude of s'Ffalenn compassion, they realized that the sons and daughters of Deshir who had died in defense of their prince were remembered, each one. Cherished, such that their loss for the cause of s'Ffalenn survival had left their sworn prince indelibly wounded in spirit. Arithon begged, in eloquent pain, that Earl Jieret not be asked to suffer the same sacrifice. The cost of one life could come too high. As a spirit beggared beyond hope of restitution, as a prince indebted to his liegemen's dedication, the bard cried aloud for reprieve.

His humility touched Braggen with stunning force, until the huge man covered his face in shame, massive shoulders bowed and shaking.

The tension raised to an unbearable pitch. Such unfolding purity of expression in song *could not* be sustained for much longer.

Yet the bard did not falter in his delivery.

He arose to the impossible, climactic effort, and phrased the opening notes, one by one, of the chord that would waken the Paravian starspells.

First, nothing; the fluid beauty of Arithon's voice became flawed by a burr of rough anguish. He gathered himself, sang the sequence again, as though he might squander his living essence to fuel his expression in sound.

A faint shimmer glanced the length of the blade. A bystander loosed an awed gasp. Arithon hung on the last, powerful high note, heart and mind joined as the dimmed cavern burst and burned under an explosion of sound and white light.

Alithiel woke. Her cry was the grand chord of glorified illumination that seared reason away in a burgeoning blast of wild joy. While each mortal listener became swept headlong into unbridled rapture, the bard alone held to his purpose. Lent a near-to-inhuman concentration by the strength of his desperation, he wrapped his own song in counterpoint to that blaze of primal mystery. Through Alithiel's unbound might, he sang Jieret's name, interlinked with his own plea for mercy.

Harmonics awoke, born out of the melody twined with the dance of the starspells. The air quivered like stressed glass. The gathered scouts felt, to a man, as though their heartstrings might wind taut and burst. Arithon held, his face ribboned with silvered light, where the sword's burning brilliance lit the wet tracks of his tears.

Then the crescendo passed. Sound faded, diminished to a whisper that died away into a cavernous silence.

'Jieret?' Arithon said, desolate.

Yet under the dimmed flame light, the gray hazel eyes had reopened. Jieret sucked in a stressed breath. He coughed. Choked up by a throat stung yet from the tienelle, he gasped back a coherent answer. 'Blessed Ath, I feel scoured from one end to the other in forces impossible to bear.' He stared upward. The reverberation of remembered awe gained fresh impetus as changed senses took in the experiential vision of newly roused mage-sight. Yet the wonder of that sacred moment came marred by a welling burst of emotion.

'Arithon, for mercy,' Jieret gasped in iced clarity. '*Is* this *what you forfeited for our sake when you spared Deshir's clans on the banks of Tal Quorin?*' He surveyed the form of his liege looming over him, the impact of that hideous truth vised behind the mute grip of Arithon's stillness.

His *caithdein*, in that instant more painfully vulnerable, could not match the strength of that effort. His aquiline features shuddered and broke, torn into lacerating pity. 'If so, *how do you bear it?*'

'Son of Eafinn!' Arithon snapped in a harsh change of subject. 'Sheathe Alithiel. Let Theirid carry her out of my presence. Once you have that assurance, I ask you to cut me free.' He raised stunned eyes to take in the others, still staring, locked into paralysis by the drama unfolded before them.

'Leave us,' pleaded the Prince of Rathain, his voice frayed hoarse from strain and exhausted gratitude.

For mercy, this time, his heartsore appeal was obeyed. The clansmen who were his sworn liegemen departed, abashed. Eafinn's son stayed alone, to stand guard by the entry. As a gesture of profoundly inadequate apology, he was left the black sword, Alithiel, entrusted to his steadfast hand.

Late Winter 5670

Commitments

Two hours before dawn, in the hollow where the Alliance company takes pause to allow the diviner-priest his scrying, Jeriayish breaks from his trance, dazed incoherent and weeping; given his tearful confession that spellcraft and music have unbound his oath to the Light, Lysaer consults Sulfin Evend. 'Allow the cavalcade a brief rest. The priest's madness won't matter. I can sense the enemy by my own resource. He's not more than five hours' march distant . . .'

Clouds break from storm over the Skyshiels, leaving skies of rinsed blue above blanketed ridges, where the guarding shade of a Fellowship Sorcerer watches two diminutive figures inch up the trackless slopes toward their long-sought destination: the black scarp of Rockfell, thrust upright like a wracked tang of iron, and bearing the shaft of Desh-thiere's prison . . .

In Whitehaven hostel, Elaira attends the adept who has answered her earnest request to study the mystical properties of quartz; and his features stay shadowed by concerned reservation as he opens with a grave warning, 'First you must recognize the crystal you partner is a living, free consciousness. That truth you will honor, but at a high cost. For you will be set into headlong conflict with the practices of your order . . .'

VIII. Evasion

Restored to the solitary company of his prince, Earl Jieret shut his eyes, overwhelmed. The shift wrought out of the fires of the tienelle trance had reforged the landscape of his mind. Sense and perception were overturned into change, until he could scarcely orient to any aspect of his surroundings. Ordinary objects had acquired a complexity beyond grasp of thought or reason. Solid rock seemed to shimmer with motion, while the air wore its currents of draft and convection in confusing, transparent overlays.

Jieret discovered that closed lids relieved nothing. Darkness itself seemed sheared into rainbows, each color a dancing glory of undying celebration. The drawing pull posed by that play of fine energies in fact owned a perilous fascination, a splendor that might hold a man mesmerized until he forgot the driving force of his birth-born identity.

Worse, the *caithdein* feared to look again at his prince, whose form now wore an aura of pale gold, streaming like needles of refined fire against a backdrop of shadow that *lived* in ways beyond language to express. Jieret reeled, still shocked to awe by a majesty he had never dreamed might exist underneath the day-to-day weave of creation. His heart felt all but torn asunder by the magnetic draw of powers that spoke as a layered tapestry of song.

The bewilderment dizzied. Jieret rested his head against Arithon's knees, helpless as a babe, while waves of rapture burned him to a dichotomy that remade the weight of his body into a shackling burden. 'Do you suppose this is how our ancestors felt after an encounter with Riathan Paravians?'

'Perhaps,' his liege ventured. The bard's voice wore its gifted richness as a tuned instrument, wakening an answering range of vibration. Reverberations streamed past the veil into mystery, transformed to expression as pure light. Such fullness of vision made a bothersome effort of hearing plain words, far less discerning their mundane meaning. 'Your senses have expanded past the limits of flesh,' Arithon qualified. All tender patience, he well understood not to rush his charge through the awkward process of assimilation. 'As the tienelle's effects wane, you'll be able to filter those added perceptions at will.'

'I feel like soft clay that was mashed into pieces, then fired with everything set in the wrong place.' As if a wind had punched gaping holes through his brain, admitting a range of alien sensation, Jieret balked at the opened gateway to new knowledge. If he wished, he could pick out the individual consciousnesses twined through the air, or laced through the matrix of stones. No part of Ath's vast creation was inert. In despair, wrenched to nausea as a shudder of reaction coursed through him, he agonized, 'How in the name of my oath to the kingdom am I going to handle a sword?'

The mere *thought* of killing while gifted with mage-sight posed a desecration beyond horror to contemplate.

Shaken, and badly, Jieret shivered again. He forced his eyes open, made himself look up into the dazzling presence of the man who braced him in steadfast calm. 'I never understood, until now, what my father asked of you when he charged you as Rathain's prince to uphold our defense at Tal Quorin.'

'The Fellowship knew,' Arithon said, his reassurance swept clean of rancor. 'Don't forget, they were first to take my oath of accession, binding me to the kingdom.' Some concepts lay utterly beyond words to express, among them, the terrible reverse, that Earl Jieret must soon endure the same nightmare for the sake of his liege's escape.

Arithon shifted, caught a horn dipper of water, and added a pinch of powdered root from his remedies. Then he raised Jieret's head in support and offered the bittersweet contents. 'Drink until you can't take any more. The marshwort will cause sweats. The tienelle poisons must be flushed from your body, or you're going to be wretchedly ill.'

The ice touch of the water raised an explosion of sensation, actinic as lightning flung in branching arcs across Jieret's already traumatized eyesight.

'It's all right,' Arithon soothed, his grip eased to allow the recoil as his chieftain yanked back from the contact. 'Water carries strong electromagnetic properties, a useful tool for a mage who knows how to harness them.'

'Fatemaster's mercy!' Jieret exclaimed. 'The whole damned *world's* gone crazy.'

'It's been that way all along,' Arithon contradicted. 'Enveloped in the flesh, most of us simply never sharpen the ability to see.' He offered the water again, not quite smiling in sympathy as his chieftain mastered tight nerves, propped himself on one elbow, and drank. 'Rest if you can. Everything's raw, and too fresh to integrate. The gifts you have wakened will settle with sleep, and the aftereffects of the tienelle won't lift for another hour.'

'I don't think I can sleep,' Jieret protested, hating the thin, lost tone of his voice, slapping back forlorn echoes from the sandstone walls of the cavern.

Arithon caught his hand and gripped back in encouragement. 'You will. You must. I can help.' Spent though he was from his earlier effort, he engaged his bard's gift and cast song into phrases that gently compelled the overtaxed mind into quietude.

Jieret wakened, disoriented. Lapped in a languid, warm peace that left his limbs battened in lassitude, he had no wish to move, though his shirt and hose were glued to his body by a film of sticky sweat. The prodding need to empty his bladder at length made him open his eyes.

The sandstone cavern seemed awash in a silver-gray light that rendered his surroundings desolately colorless. Disjointed by grief, as though something priceless had been jerked beyond reach, Jieret caught his breath with a cry. The sudden, stabbing hurt ran clear through him, for a world turned unexpectedly dull and lifeless as ashes. Caught by the throat by a fierce urge to weep, he said through locked teeth, 'I thought you said sleep would help me adjust!'

'It has.' Arithon's solace was immediate, and nearby, a razor's edge of alertness. 'If you think you've gone blind, look again. You'll see I've extinguished the candle to save wax.' As Jieret blinked in disoriented confusion, he phrased his explanation with delicate care. 'It's barely past dawn, and no light shines in here. If you find you're not in total darkness, what you're seeing are the spirit forms of your surroundings.' A movement of clothing sighed to the left as Rathain's prince shifted position. 'That's astral mage-sight, Jieret. You've triumphed.'

'But the colors,' Jieret gasped, still wrung by their loss. He felt reft, his heart all but shredded with yearning to somehow restore them.

'Not gone.' Arithon's reply carried an imprinted echo of shared pain, that for him, his forfeited access was permanent. 'You've shed the augmented influence of the tienelle, which lends the illusion things have changed for the worse. In fact, you'll be able to exert self-command. Once you've calmed down, I'll show you. With practice and discipline you'll soon perceive the higher levels of vibration at will.'

'Well, such lofty happenings will have to wait until after I've gone out to piss.' Jieret cast off the mantling bearskin, then wrinkled his nose at the reek of sour sweat in his shirt. 'Dharkaron's Five Horses, I stink as though I've slept all night in a midden.'

'Your sense of smell has been sharpened,' Arithon agreed. His *caithdein*'s ripe oath clashed with his laughing devilment as he added, 'The gift isn't always an advantage.'

'If you die with no issue, prince, believe this,' Jieret grumbled. 'My curse will ride Fate's Wheel and hound you on the other side of the veil.' Still manfully swearing, he stepped out, one hand braced against the rock cleft, and the legs underneath him shaky and unreliable as a newborn's.

The Earl of the North felt stronger by the time he returned, shirtless and dripping from a bracing scrub in the river. If his physical well-being seemed somewhat restored, his mental equilibrium still suffered an array of unsettling tricks. His vision stayed strange. All solid objects wore a phosphorescent haze, lending their appearance an eerie double image. When light touched their edges, he found himself dazzled, as strange flares of reflection fractured into unexpected, prismatic rainbows.

Inside the cleft, cut off from sunlight, he sensed other powers alive in the earth clamoring at his raw senses. He strove to bear up, aware as he rose to the unfamiliar challenge that he felt no piercing regret. Truth walked in the mysteries. Now that the film had been lifted from a blindness suffered since birth, he shuddered to think of the price to be paid, should he ever be forced to step back into the dimmed realm of common perception.

Again, the swift recognition of grief, that Arithon of Rathain had met such a fate and found strength to go on living. Jieret walked softly, moved to awed respect as he rejoined his prince's presence.

Arithon had kindled the candle stub. The finer blaze cast off his aura seemed like spindled gold wire amid the hot orange glow of the flame light. Jieret had to squint to discern his friend's purposeful hands, busy cleaning the meats from the acorns that Theirid had been sent to gather last night. Sundry other items rested amid several packets of dried herbs from his healer's stores, those the least reassuring: silk threads unraveled from Arithon's frayed sleeve cuff now tied the cuttings of black hair into neatly laced bundles.

Chilled by more than the frost on the air, Jieret wrung icy water from the end of his clan braid. He forced his numbed fingers to work and began dragging the snarls from wet locks. 'What fell bit of craft are you spinning with that stuff?'

Arithon's glance lit to a glint of pure wickedness. 'In theory, Morriel's ugly little tactic with a fetch can be used in reverse, against Lysaer.'

Jieret locked his hands in the soaked auburn tangles. Through the spiking, sweet moment, while an almost unbearable hope pierced his heart, he somehow held on and recovered the calm to restart his breathing. 'You mean you can haze the enemy into the mistaken belief there's actually more than one of you?'

'I can't. You will. The setting seals must be yours, since my sighted talent won't answer.' Arithon picked up one of the quartz pebbles, then reached out and unsheathed his main gauche. 'I don't like the method, but in case Lysaer's scryers use blood magic, we'll choose the one that's reliable.' He set the blade to the inside of his wrist and jabbed a small nick. The stone was dabbed with a small drop of blood, then thoughtfully nested inside the hollowed-out shell of an acorn.

Touched by a queer grue, that a line had been crossed beyond which no safety existed, Jieret held silent and finished replaiting his clan braid.

'I chose eight, for the symbolism,' Arithon said. 'In all workings of craft, such things by their nature lend clarity to intent.' The admission sparked an evil ring of irony as he qualified his decision. 'That's the dread number of Sithaer's blackest pit, and also the closing note in the octave whose resonance, amplified, lets demons take solid form on this side of the veil.'

'Ath bless!' Jieret threw off his unease long enough to grin through his beard. 'That's bound to seed unholy mayhem with your half brother's arse-kissing priests!' He shook out his damp shirt, undecided if he dared take the time to hang-dry it. 'You'll force the Alliance to split forces?'

'Well, I can hope so.' Arithon coiled one of the tied strands of hair, packed it over the smeared quartz, then jammed the cap of the acorn back into place over the contents. Lastly, he secured the small package with pine pitch and a pliable strand of silver wire filched from Alithiel's scabbard. 'Plants pass on their qualities, when used in a construct. In this case, I picked oak for its strength, endurance, and longevity.'

Jieret snorted. 'You're thinking to teach me the ways of such fell tricks?' He grimaced, hesitated, then decided to pull on the damp cloth of his shirt. Outside, the sun was still too low on the horizon to have warmed the hoarfrost from the scrub brush. Enemy troops now closed on three sides, with the watchful eyes of their front-running patrols far too near to risk even a scout's tidy fire. Under clear sky, a spire of smoke would be seen for leagues in every direction.

Left clammy by worse than the clasp of wet linen, Jieret pressed, 'What needs to be done, we'd better get started. My perimeter guard already argues we've been in one place for too long.'

Arithon looked up, his green eyes piercing. 'We have maybe two hours.' A frisson of chill seemed to rip through his frame. His masking effort as he reached for the next acorn made an insufficient diversion to offset his *caithdein*'s sharp scrutiny. 'After that, I can't guarantee any leeway. Let my half brother come too close, and the driving pressure of Desh-thiere's curse will swell to unmanageable proportions.'

'You feel him already?' Jieret demanded, aware as he spoke that the shadow of *something* unwholesome swept across Arithon's aura.

At least his liege had the grace not to lie. 'A constant thorn in my side.' He paused, as though snagged into vicious inner conflict. Only a man who knew him to his depths could observe the near-to-invisible struggle as he battled and reaffirmed his precarious hold on self-possession. After a fraught moment, his aura burned clear. A shade paler, his hands a trifle less steady, he resumed packing the next acorn. His glance of bright inquiry took in the distress behind Jieret's scowling expression.

'You saw that?' Too mortified to suffer the inevitable reply, he shrugged off what, for him, had to be an excoriating storm of embarrassment. 'As you say, time grows short. Please, don't interrupt. You aren't going to like the strategy I've planned, but while you were sleeping, I measured the options. Here's how I believe we must play this.'

Long before noon, the scouts who kept watch from the hilltops overlooking the Aiyenne dispatched runners with urgent word. The first advance columns of townsmen approached, plowing their arduous way down the vales to the north and east. The contingent from Narms, closing off free escape to the west, was led in by the savvy experience of headhunters.

'No sign of them yet, but that's a false reckoning,' gasped the rider sent back to the riverside camp with the news. Given the league's specialized knowledge of the land, an approach spearheaded by seasoned professionals was bound to be cunningly circumspect. 'May not spot them at all, till they're crawling all over us.' Dismounted to ease his laboring mount, the man tucked his reddened hands out of the wind and cast an anxious glance backward. 'Theirid's had all the ponies brought in. They've been saddled, in case, and the war band's armed also. Everyone's waiting for Jieret's orders.'

Still on guard at the mouth of the cleft, crouched on his knees on swept stone, Eafinn's son squinted down the shining edge of the blade he had just finished resharpening. 'High Earl will give orders whenever he's ready.' As glacially cool under pressure as the father whose loss the past spring had cost the war band its most wily captain, he flipped back a fallen hank of pale hair, then deliberately slid the weapon home in its sheath. 'At his Grace's pleasure, he'll come out.'

The messenger scout cracked in jangled impatience. 'I don't care blazes *what* they're doing in there!' The fringes on his stained buckskin jacket snapped to his vehement gesture. 'If we don't move out fast, our prince risks disaster. Do you want him trapped like a rat in that grotto? Then pass him my message in warning.'

With long-limbed, quick grace, Eafinn's son stood. 'I was charged to guard his Grace's privacy.' Under late-season sunlight that hoarded its warmth, his bare head shone like burnished platinum. The competent fingers clasped to Alithiel's black hilt stayed as nervelessly set in their purpose. 'My prince holds my promise. No way I'll let you risk crossing his will after what happened last night.'

'See sense, man!' The scout runner spun, his agitation increased as his keen ear detected the inbound drumroll of hooves. He scanned the mottled hills, patched brown and gray where weathered outcrops of sandstone punched through the ice-crusted mantle of snow. He pointed to the low ground at the verge of the river, left flattened by the silted burden of sediment laid down each year in spring flood. 'That's our rider, inbound. I'd lay spit against the red blood of my ancestors he'll bring word that the headhunter troop with s'Ilessid has been seen on our western flank. Press things any later, we won't have a chance. It's haul our liege out by the scruff of his neck or get speared like stoats defending the ground where we stand.'

Loose stone chinked as Eafinn's son planted his stance. 'Even so,' he insisted, though he had not missed the disturbing fact that the inbound rider slid his horse on its hocks down a gravel bank rather than lose precious minutes on a safe but more roundabout route. 'I'm not the man to judge what's at stake. Don't ask me again to break my given word or ignore the command of Rathain's sovereign prince.'

'That won't be necessary,' Earl Jieret interjected from behind, as he squeezed his way through the cleft. Reclad in his studded brigandine, and armed with his father's belt and throwing knives, he looked bleak enough to scale iron at twenty paces. To the overwrought rider, now flushed to embarrassment, he snapped, 'No questions! I need the Companions here, *now*!'

The rider vaulted astride in relief, wheeled his mount, and pounded away on the errand.

Rathain's *caithdein* stepped from the rocks. Fully emerged into daylight, he stretched his broad shoulders as though to throw off binding cramps. The leonine bristle of his beard failed to mask the startling change undergone during the night. He looked something more than worn to distraction: a fey, wild spark lit his glance from within. Through his frowning pause as he ascertained that the camp on the riverside was packed and ready to move, the otherworldly light in his gray hazel eyes took on a glint like the reflection off rain-beaten metal.

Struck that he looked like a man who kept too slight a hold on breathing life, Eafinn's son found himself moved to a queer stab of pity. 'Don't say his Grace had no plan to save us.'

'He has a plan,' Jieret affirmed, agonized. Through the distanced clatter as the inbound rider reined across the icebound span of the riverbed, he added his heartsick opinion. 'If this war band is spared, it will happen because Arithon will have courted disaster and taunted the turn of Fate's Wheel ahead of us.'

'Then how can I help?' Eafinn's son asked, sharply driven to try to relieve some the source of the tension.

'Leave the sword in my care.' As Alithiel's burdensome weight changed hands, Jieret delivered a bitten string of instructions. 'Fetch the horses his Grace brought in last night. They're faster than our ponies. Check them for soundness. If Cienn reshod them as I asked, bring them here. Have the three fittest ones saddled and bridled.'

'You want supplies also?' Given his chieftain's clipped nod of assent, the young man evinced the resilience of his family heritage. 'I'm gone, then.'

His light step scarcely stirred the loose rocks as he ran downstream on his errand. Jieret drew in a deep breath. He was given no moment of privacy, nor space to contain his trepidation before the Companions arrived: Theirid with his black-fox tails streaming in the stiffening gusts from the north; squat, muscular Cienn, replacing a snapped tie on his bracer; Braggen, his heavy brows bristled, and his short, scrappy steps reflecting a pique like dammed magma. The others checked weapons, or swore at the uncooperative, clear sky. Two-legged and dangerous, they were a leashed wolf pack, fretful of the delay, and explosively primed for an action they knew must court failure.

'My brothers,' Rathain's *caithdein* addressed as he met each man's eyes in bleak honesty. 'The charter law of the realm, your children's future, and the guardianship of the free wilds stands or falls upon how we carry the day. Prince Arithon has given all in his power, and more, to lessen the odds set against us. If his strategy prevails, some will survive. Whether you face life or death for his cause, by your oath of fealty as his clanborn liegemen, *I ask* that you not fall short.'

No time, for lingering last words or commiseration over shared risks; no time to seek praise or encouragement that might bolster morale or raise heart; no time at all to acknowledge or honor the binding, close ties of a lifetime. Nor did one Companion among them complain of the lack. Jieret in that moment could have wept for the gift of their outright trust. He battled his sorrow, that such shining strength of character should become nothing more than a ready weapon on this hour, upon which hung all the hopes of the next generation. These eight true spirits, who had known grief and bloodshed too young, as grown men could reliably perform without sentiment.

Wrung by the urgent necessity that must see them sent out, some to die in the maneuvering sacrifice of game pawns, Jieret knelt. He drew his knife, and scratched a crude map on the sandstone. From somewhere he mustered the necessary speech. 'Here is what your prince asks of you.'

Against the cry of the wind, he produced the spelled acorns, explained how each was a proxy. One by one, he outlined their destined use. He named each appropriate bearer. Called by name, the Companions stepped forward. The moment as each man accepted his fate cut deepest, for unkindly brevity. The shared glance, the fleeting brush of warm flesh as the talisman was transferred to a competent hand. Jieret raged, the scream in him silenced, that for many this might be the last parting on the earthly side of Fate's Wheel. His sore regret was not eased, despite all that his liege had done to spare his *caithdein*'s raw conscience.

The burden of conferring the hardest choices had been made by Arithon's command, under Rathain's vested crown authority.

For the grace of that studied gesture of reprieve, the heart must not shrink from its office. Jieret forced down the unbearable pain. He stifled his awareness of pending tragedy, the most wounding detail sealed under time's urgent pressure: that the formidable, compassionate perception which had plumbed the worthy character of each Companion in scarcely an hour of contact would not in turn be understood by these men, who must bear the realm's fate by their actions. They accepted the risk to life and limb for a prince they assumed was a stranger. Jieret bore up, cut to solitary grief by the solid affirmation *that their Teir's'Ffalenn knew them. His was a mage-trained awareness, schooled to acknowledge individuality. He had raised that gift to a masterbard's empathy, that heard and embraced the unique splendor of song, braided through each man's identity. No time to explain how his Grace would mourn each one lost, all the days that his life should outlast them.*

The eighth and last acorn was dispatched to Eafinn's son, just arrived with the saddled horses. 'The honor is not truly mine, but my father's,' he said as he tucked the spelled construct safely away in his scrip. Flushed faintly pink, he clasped wrists with his chieftain. 'Give his Grace my regards, if I cannot.'

The leading reins of the horses passed into Jieret's broad grasp, and the young man departed, straight as the ash spear he had inherited from the kinfolk who had died, so long past, at Tal Quorin. From the vantage by the river, his neat clan braid stood out, burnished flax against the drab buckskins of the scouts he selected to ride in his squad.

Only Braggen remained, the result of fierce dispute that his liege had resolved by enforcing his sovereign right. Of eight Companions, just the one had not received a spelled acorn. Touched through his new mage-sight by the bearing pressure of the huge man's simmering temper, Jieret secured the horses to a nearby deadfall. In the face of Braggen's blistering, stiff silence, he scuffed wet snow over the map and scrubbed the scraped lines off the rock. Tired to the bone, and anxious for what lay ahead, he held off his final set of instructions as the mounted scout plunged up the near bank of the Aiyenne and hauled his lathered gray to a headshaking stop.

'Lysaer's force approaches! They're using the available cover like ticks. Can't tell you numbers yet, but their advance is no more than six leagues off.'

'Let them come unhindered,' Jieret instructed. 'You'll answer to Theirid, he'll be on the east flank. Eat now, if you have to. The war band will be riding within the hour, split into eight squads, to bait the enemy into a mazing pursuit.'

The scout scraped at the caked mud on his face, smeared in streaks for the purpose of camouflage. He checked his sword, dubious. 'You've found a way to make the Alliance split forces?'

'Yes.' As the scout reined around and departed, Jieret shook himself out of a moment of odd, inattentive hesitation, as though his sight played untrustworthy tricks where the sunlight patterned the ridges of sandstone underfoot. He added, a near whisper under his breath, 'Just pray the plan works.'

He shook off rising dread. Through the silvery glare cast off rotten, patched ice, under slanting sunlight leached of all warmth by the rampaging, unnatural winter, he was left alone to tame Braggen's volatile mood of contention and dauntless courage.

'Was there no place for me?' the huge man asked, forlorn. Confusion sat ill on his strapping, broad frame. Accustomed to act with decisive competence, he confronted his chieftain unflinching. The shame tied him in knots, that this day found him wanting. That the other Companions must carry the hazards of crisis without him demeaned his manhood too much to bear.

And time, once again, denied Jieret the chance to measure his course with due care or finesse. 'On the contrary. Arithon asked for your service by name. We are left, you and I, to shoulder the most dangerous share of our prince's intricate strategy.'

Braggen's axe-cut features cracked to stark surprise. 'We *two*?' Gruff embarrassment burned a flush through creased skin. After his attacking provocation last night, he had presumed his liege would show him no more than the favor of civil tolerance. Now granted an unlooked-for forgiveness, even grounds for an unbroken trust, the Companion scrubbed his face with gloved hands. Fast as he moved, his response failed to mask the startled, bright shine of his tears.

Jieret averted his glance, stunned to awe. As always, the bard's fierce insight surpassed him. He, who had handled Braggen's irritating bluster all his life, had expected outspoken resistance.

Yet Arithon's compassion saw the overlooked truth: of all men, this one now had something desperate to prove. He would stand by his charged orders, ferocious in grit, determined not to meet the Wheel's turning stripped of the honor that sourced his self-worth.

Braced by the vehemence in Braggen's character, the last assignment became almost painless to complete. As Rathain's *caithdein*, shadow behind a throne to be held secure for the future, Jieret set the cold weight of Alithiel into the last Companion's stunned hands. 'By the power vested in me under charter law, as given by the Fellowship of Seven, I'll have your oath on this blade you won't falter.'

In the absence of the crowned heir, his sworn purpose was to guard the well-being of the kingdom. Jieret assumed the burden of that stewardship, spear straight, while Braggen knelt on the stony ground and set his crossed hands, then his forehead, to the black metal of Alithiel's cross guard.

'My oath, on this sword, may Dharkaron strike swiftly should I fail or fall short.' Braggen's rough, dark head remained bent in submission as the hand of his chieftain forbade him to rise.

For a chill, prolonged moment, the only voice in the world was the wind, sheeting over the brush of the barrens. Under glacial sky, the snaked bed of the Aiyenne wore its jumbled rickle of grayed ice. The two clansmen poised on the scoured rock ledge seemed diminished, resolute mortal will reduced to a mote wrapped in transient flesh against an enduring and desolate landscape.

The crown prince whose sovereign word might reverse that one moment's critical act and consequence had already passed beyond argument.

Jieret flung back the bronze length of his clan braid. Chin tipped to sky, he drew a chilling, deep breath, and sealed his final decision. 'His Grace asked you to carry the most difficult proxy of all.' The ninth and the last, bearing the number symbolic of death, rebirth, and redemption. The Earl of the North threw off his shiver of wretched foreboding. 'Yet for the good of the realm, I see fit to change his Grace's instructions. His chance of survival, and ours, will be greater if I carry forward the burden he assigned to you. Can you accept this? Will you stand in my place?'

'Your honor, my earl, has always been mine.' Braggen looked up, brown eyes stark with appeal. 'Was there ever a question?'

Jieret found courage from somewhere to smile. 'Never. Rise,

Braggen. In my stead, you must be the liegeman who stands guard at Prince Arithon's side.'

'He'll argue,' Braggen snapped, once again set off-balance by bristling incredulity.

'He would,' Jieret agreed. He clapped the other man's muscular shoulder, in no doubt at last that his impulse was merited. He gestured for Braggen to follow, then reentered the cleft, his voice dampened by the encroaching stone as he ducked through the narrow passage. 'His Grace is in no position, as you'll see. Nor will your service escape complications. The risks you must handle won't necessarily be the sort you can solve with brute force and edged weapons.'

Inside the cavern, the candlewick burned down to a drowned and flickering stub. Under the uncertain, flittering light, half-mantled in crawling shadow, Braggen made out the form of the s'Ffalenn prince, tucked prostrate in the muffling fur of the high earl's favorite bearskin. The sharp s'Ffalenn profile was stilled as carved wax. The hair his *caithdein* had trimmed with such care spilled in onyx disorder over one angled cheekbone and the river-washed boulder that cradled his head.

Braggen paused, horrified. 'Ath, he's out cold.'

'More,' revealed Jieret from the uncertain dark. 'He worried the drive of the Mistwraith's curse might overcome his last strength. Rather than lose his will to insanity, he decided to spiritwalk. A dangerous precaution, but one he hoped would also displace his half brother's awareness of his presence.' Sensitive to the Companion's mulish uneasiness, since he harbored the same doubts himself, Jieret hastened to qualify. 'His Grace was mage-trained, remember! The risks are well-known to him. In addition, we agreed on the expedient safeguard of binding his unmoored self to Alithiel.'

Braggen regarded the sheathed steel still in hand, his hard features set with dumbfounded distaste, or else fear that chilled metal might burn him.

'That step isn't done yet,' Jieret reassured. He resisted his sharp urge to consign the cursed twists of s'Ffalenn ingenuity to the nethermost bowels of Sithaer. As much the unwilling victim of circumstance, he withstood Braggen's riled unease and wiped sweating palms on his leathers. 'I'm sorry if you feel cast out of your depth. The truth is, the man appointed to Arithon's side must assist with the final stage of the ritual.'

Booted feet planted, Braggen clutched the black sword with

the delicacy of a man who handled a venomed serpent. 'I well understood why Caolle spat curses over the subject of magecraft.'

Jieret hesitated, swallowed, forced himself steady despite a trepidation far worse, that he, with his sighted talent just wakened, must enact the distasteful conjury. 'Someone should be left to seek Fellowship help in case the spells fail.' The whelming fear was too monstrous to silence, that his inexperience presented a thousand stray loopholes. 'Dharkaron avert, I begged his Grace not to go through with this madness! *The whole harebrained tactic could go wrong.*'

'It won't. It can't.' Braggen folded his arms. The dulled studs on his bracers a rasped note of disharmony against the uncanny Paravian sword. Unashamed for the clay in his nature, he was first to brace up failing nerves. 'We'll just have to set trust in our liege's wisdom and follow through as he asks.'

Jieret stifled his rampaging thoughts of disaster. In punishing truth, every passing second diminished a margin that Arithon could ill afford to lose. More stressed than the hour he pledged marriage to Feithan, Deshir's chieftain made himself survey the arcane framework already laid down under Arithon's meticulous guidance. The unsealed gift of mage-sight unveiled the glimmering figures like chalked light, surrounding the prince's stilled form, then the harder, bright line of the circle of protection that shielded his naked spirit from the outreach of hostile intent. The trace smoke from the cedar burned to hallow the space still dusted the air with an ephemeral shimmer of indigo. Confined by the blazing barriers of intent that imbued the charged line of the circle, Arithon's spirit paced, naked of flesh, a translucent vessel in refined human form, hazed in the delicate, striated gold of the unshielded aura.

'*You won't fail me, Jieret,*' he insisted, a voice without sound heard in the mind of the *caithdein* whose oathbound service had enacted the defenses that both protected and bound him.

'You can't know that,' Jieret whispered, well aware the change of roles he intended would shortly make Arithon furious. Yet duty to kin and kingdom came first. 'My liege, forgive.'

His gut remained tied into battlefield knots as he began the irrevocable last steps of the safeguard that would either spare Arithon's sanity, or else strip him defenseless for the enemy sword that would seize opportunity and kill him.

'Stand there,' Jieret instructed, amazed that his voice should sound steady. With his heart locked against his prince's cry of dismay, he grasped Braggen's elbow and guided the Companion's step past the spelled lines that ungifted eyesight could not discern. 'Unsheathe Alithiel and hold the blade upright. Whatever happens from here forward, you can't let the steel touch the earth.'

Faint as the distant chiming of bells, Arithon's shade pealed wild protest. *'Jieret! My brother, we're blood bound by oath. By the mercy of Ath, don't break that trust. I hold your life sacred! Don't spurn the integrity that lies between us, not like this!'*

Jieret's jaw flexed, spiking the chestnut ends of his beard. He said nothing in answer, while his steadfast Companion assumed his position three paces from the boundary that contained Arithon's scarce-breathing flesh.

'No, Jieret.' Imprisoned by the flux of preset limitation, Arithon's spirit swirled like whipped fire, spiked to savage, trapped sparks of irritation. *'I've wept for Caolle too long and too hard!'*

'As you knew Caolle, you'll agree he would approve.' Deshir's adamant chieftain took up the cut-birch stick. To Braggen, who stared in perplexity, he explained, 'I'm addressing my liege, who's making his sovereign displeasure plain as scat in rough language. You don't sense him?'

Braggen shook his seal-dark head. 'I don't. The birth gift never ran strong in my family. Our women always claimed our lineage survived the Paravian presence through bear-stubborn will, and an ironclad core of stupidity.'

'Well, right now, that's your blessing,' Jieret said in chagrin. 'His Grace isn't sanguine. Had he the means to recover his talent, he'd blister my hide for presumption.'

'Then be sure I'll get flayed for your insolence later,' Braggen shot back in sour irony.

'That's Torbrand's lineage,' Jieret agreed. 'Vindictive when crossed as an iceberg-bred kraken dumped spitting into a lava pit.' His smile too grim, and his hand faintly shaking, he went on to inscribe the requisite patterns of protection.

The first circle sealed the confines of the cavern against outside interference. Jieret marked the cardinal points of direction, recited the clear words of permission and intent, then lit the cedar brand and fanned the sweet smoke to clear the laid ground of any disharmonious imprints. To the reviling oaths that sang through his mind, he said calmly, 'I have sons and a daughter raised to maturity. Consider that proof you have kept any promise you once made to Steiven and Dania.'

'Damn you!' snarled Arithon, impotent as a whirlwind balked

by a pane of caulked glass. *'That doesn't excuse your obligation to Feithan, or cast off your ties as a father!'*

While Braggen looked on, stunned still with embarrassment, the High Earl straightened up, stricken. The second circle was just barely complete, linking the Companion, himself, and Arithon's vacated body.

'Arithon, look at me,' Jieret insisted, his voice strangely tight. 'Yes, look! A change has been wrought.' Stripped of defenses, laid bare of subterfuge, the shift became all too apparent. The strange, distanced glint in his gray hazel eyes reflected that eerie, unworldly detachment given to those who had journeyed too far past the veil.

'Do you know what I saw in the tienelle trance?' Soft as a plea underlaid by the razor's edge of a scarcely buried suffering, Jieret addressed the space where the disembodied spirit of his prince paced in searing frustration. 'I met my sisters and mother in a place of pure light, and they were unspoiled and beautiful. There was joy in that reunion. There, I could find closure and healing for a grief that has blighted my peace for nigh onto thirty years.'

A drawn, sharp pause, while Arithon froze in shock, and Jieret gathered up an unprepossessing flake of mica.

No longer trembling, Deshir's chieftain grasped the unsheathed knife laid out for completion of the ritual. 'Don't let me end this without your understanding. A true brother would give me that much.'

'No word of understanding I could ever deliver will explain my breach of trust to your daughter.' Behind the evil, glittering line that shackled his heart's cry for action, Arithon's sorrow shone pale as crystal, etched into a rebuttal that gave no ground to defeat. *'For the love that I bear you, which is all I hold for bargain, I reject this bitter gift. I withhold the grace of my royal blessing. The cost of a crown can come too high! Jieret, don't leave me the wretched legacy of a life bought in blood. I won't endorse a survival founded upon the sacrifice of our vital friendship.'*

Jieret regarded his prince, no longer torn. His blunt features had refigured to a tender sorrow, bespeaking a care that extended beyond fragile ties to mortal life. Gently, he shook his leonine head. 'For the sons of my sons, liege, you'll see that I must.'

Silence, of a depth to make the mind ring to the cry of an unexpressed agony.

Jieret used the birch stick anyway, laid down another shining circle that contained nothing more than the ringed cipher holding Arithon's shade, and himself. A small flash, as he cupped the flake of mica and asked for the permission to serve his great need. Then, unflinching, he bent and swept a gap in the primary circle that held his prince's confined spirit in separation.

One circle contained them. *Caithdein* and prince faced off as a pair. Jieret, in warm flesh, and Arithon, whom he had been born to serve, a bristling imprint wrought out of spirit light in the poised stance of a duelist. Yet no offensive was possible, naked spirit pitched against an entity sheathed within the protections of the body. Nor could any act his Grace might conjure revoke the free-will permissions he had left in trust with Jieret s'Valerient. His royal consent, given to his liegeman, by its nature had been unconditional. No regret, even one wrought from untenable grief, could cancel the binding set upon him.

Arithon could but watch, agonized, as, each move deliberate, Jieret tipped the flake of mica and captured the reflection of his unshielded spirit.

Steadied as steel, the Earl of the North invoked the words of binding that would marry Arithon's image into the mineral's matrix. As the Shadow Master had promised through a morning of cursory instruction, mage-sight clearly showed the moment the spell sealed and meshed. The common fleck of mica heated and flared, then burned into configured light. The mercuric blaze of its presence became augmented with the signature essence of Prince Arithon's living aura. For all intents and purposes, the mirror spell of illusion merged his live presence with the stone and made them one and the same being.

Into the wondering triumph of the moment, as Jieret spoke the rune to seal his flawless execution of grand conjury, Arithon s'Ffalenn used his silence like weaponry to wear down resolve and compel space for second thoughts.

Jieret stayed unmoved. He tucked the spelled mica amid the packed contents of the last acorn without fumbling. 'For the love I bear you, Arithon, I return the gift of life you gave me as a boy on the banks of Tal Quorin.'

Such drilled quiet could have burned, for its baleful intensity. Jieret reaffixed the acorn's cap, careful not to mar the minute chains of ciphers scratched over the seed's oiled surface. He secured the end with pine pitch, spoke the name for the Paravian rune of ending, then wrapped the finished construct in a loose twist of silk. As he tucked the fated bundle into the breast of his jerkin, he concluded, 'You're not free to refuse, liege. Not before you have tasted fulfillment, as I have: conceive an heir in marriage with the woman of your choice and raise Rathain's next crown prince to maturity.'

Silence, from the Teir's'Ffalenn, as the realm's acting steward arose to his lanky, full height. Sketched in the failing light of the candle stub, he loomed large as his father, his broad hands as capable, and his carriage as self-assured as he shouldered the deliberate next step.

Braggen watched, seized dumb, as Jieret struck the flint and lit the spill of herbs left bundled and waiting. He reinscribed the line of the circle holding the Teir's'Ffalenn. No vital step omitted, he cut himself separate from Arithon's ward of containment, then sealed the new circle behind him with a crisp incantation and a powdery trail of warmed ashes.

Arithon tried again, spoke Jeynsa's name with each syllable of appeal pronounced with a masterbard's attacking clarity.

Jieret fielded the strike, placid. 'On the hour my daughter swears her oath as *caithdein* she'll embrace the steel of her heritage. She has been raised strong. As the Fellowship's marked candidate for my succession, she'll rise to her inheritance and forgive us both for what comes of this day's work.'

'*If she might, I won't.*' Half-unmanned by his failure, Arithon faltered, his gift for glib satire broken by strain into vindictive desperation.

'You forget,' Jieret answered. 'I know you too well. However you bristle and snap, your compassion can seed no rancor. For that, you've forgiven me already. It's your conscience that's hounding you past reach of peace. Have done, brother. For my sake, and yours, let it go.'

Inarguably firm, he asked Braggen to hand him Alithiel's empty scabbard.

'*I'll renounce you,*' threatened Arithon. '*Your family, your heirs, everything you stand for! I'll turn my back. If I survive, they'll watch me walk away, forgetting the names of your father and mother, and every misbegotten offshoot of your lineage.*'

'You wouldn't, and you can't,' Jieret contradicted. 'If the truth hasn't moved me, your lies just demean you.'

Rammed against an unyielding defeat by the High Earl's immovable courage, the conflicted presence of Arithon s'Ffalenn whirled in raging bitterness. The fabric of his very self all but came undone as he saw his bluff called. Never before this had his arsenal of threats been so savagely reduced by bare honesty. Even had Jieret not known his true heart, a blood-pacted friendship sworn under the sighted strength of his mastery was utterly beyond his present power to revoke.

He could do nothing, *nothing but rage*, as his *caithdein* laced the scabbard in the black silk cord pulled from his ripped-off shirtsleeve. Warded word, and arcane sigils laid down at each crossed junction, remade the battered leather into a spelled prison to bind him. Then the parallel lines, drawn by the birch twig, and sealed with dry ashes, framed the path that would join the connection.

Braced to finish the final stage of the ritual, Jieret asked for the sword. Deaf to pity, he sat with the blade's icy length pressed between his fixed palms. He made the incantation, flawless and sure, that traitorously transferred his liege's Named permission into the warded black metal.

Against silence like a cry, he returned the weapon to the hands of his waiting Companion. 'Braggen, on my word, you will raise the sword Alithiel and thrust her blade through the circle of ash that holds Arithon's spirit form captive.'

The victim found his voice, a peal of blazing torment that raised sympathetic resonance from cold stone. Vibration cast back in subliminal echoes, to lift the hair at the nape. *'Jieret, no, don't do this!'*

Made aware by Braggen's bounding start that the plea had sheared within range of hearing, Jieret stiffened to adamance. He confronted his prince, his hewn features drained pale, and his voice racked to stark desperation. 'Even if, in my place *you know well you would do the same thing*?'

'Still, I ask you, I beg you, *don't do this. Bear the spelled sword yourself. Stay at my side as we planned.*' A stricken pause, then the admission, delivered with stripped human need, *'After you, there is no one else but Elaira. Can't you see how your loss would diminish me?'*

A long look, exchanged between *caithdein* and sworn prince; a stretched second, fractured from time by pure heartbreak. In speechless communion, the locked conflict between them encompassed a love beyond words. The bonding first made with the boy at Tal Quorin had grown to mean more than blood, more than duty, more than the gift of breath and life.

The one moment was too unutterably fleeting to carry the hope and the pain that should have endured to the peaceful, quiet parting of old age.

'No,' Jieret gasped, his tone flattened and final. 'I see too well I've made the right choice. You might give too much, if I rode beside you. The temptation to spare me might drive you to jeopardize your survival. Caolle would have endorsed my fair judgment. Braggen's better with the sword, always has been.' After a frightful, shuddering pause, he mastered himself enough to manage the echo of his most wicked smile. 'You'll live to be crowned as Rathain's next king, or else leave s'Ffalenn progeny. In memory, I'll still stand beside you.'

Cruelly isolate within the spelled circle, Arithon's spirit form lashed back in emphatic rejection. *'You can still change your mind! Cast the mica construct into the running waters of the Aiyenne. Jieret, you'll have done far more than your duty to Rathain on the instant you've won a diversion.'*

And again, Deshir's High Earl gave back his refusal, sealed by a *caithdein's* irreproachable integrity. 'The crown charter we guardian can't stand on the foundation of our mortal attachments.'

'Bedamned to the law, if it strangles the care that gives our wretched existence its meaning! The weight of royal sovereignty is as much my bane as any warped destiny bound by the curse of Desh-thiere.' Shattered, unable to weep for the fact he was helpless, Arithon recoiled at last against the tenacious thorn of his character. *'I am not reconciled,'* he insisted.

And yet, Teir's'Ffalenn and Torbrand's lineage to the very bone, he gathered the bleeding shreds of rent pride. In thankless torment, he strove to embrace the left burden of an insupportable tragedy. *'Meet my death well, Jieret. Swear to me! Promise! Make Lysaer strike you down fast and clean in the open! By the tenets of clan custom, you won't let his Alliance fanatics seize their chance to take you alive.'*

'Ath keep you safe, liege,' was all Jieret said. 'On the hour, when it comes, I'll give Caolle and Steiven and the others who have loved you all of your heartsore regrets.' At the crux, only tears slipped his ironclad control. Scalding drops traced his cheeks, their soundless agony absorbed into the graying strands of red beard that had made his name the scourge of the Northern League of Headhunters.

Jieret had the rest of his nerves kept in hand as he nodded his signal to Braggen.

Nor did man or sovereign flinch through the devastating instant of parting. Eye to eye, heart to heart they endured the shearing grief as Braggen carried out his called duty.

The black sword sliced the circle. Hungry spells set into the metal by unbending design first swallowed the scintillant golden aura, then the defiant, bright spirit and vital personality of Rathain's last sanctioned crown prince.

Darkness remained, scored ghostly phosphor by the lines of spelled circles, and the less ordered flare of the struggling candleflame.

'Sheathe the weapon,' Jieret instructed. His split-gravel command splintered the horrific silence wedged like a gap in stilled air. 'The cord ties hold all the protections wrought to shield him.' Freed now to release the dammed flood of his sorrow, he fumbled with palsied hands and found the strip of fine silk torn away from Arithon's shirtsleeve. 'Hold the weapon up. The hilt must be wrapped. Otherwise, his Grace's naked presence will offer a beacon for scryers on the instant we break the outer circle.'

Braggen did as he was asked. His own need to weep all but choked the labored breath in his throat. He stood fast, while Jieret set the last wards and bindings, and swathed Alithiel's black cross guard in the frayed length of silk. Nor could he avoid a harrowed glance sidewards at the body which lay, much too still, amid its calyx of bearskin. 'You court the very edge of disaster,' he husked as he received the harsh weight of the sword.

'I know. If we fail, we lose everything.' Jieret refused to dwell on his own coming trial, but delivered his rapid instructions to the last remaining Companion. 'You have one day, and *no more than three*, to see Arithon out of this territory. Once the sword's drawn, all the spells will disperse. Our liege will awaken, restored to his flesh. Keep the blade always at hand. If Lysaer prevails, see that his Grace dies free, beyond reach of the Mistwraith's cursed madness. Keep his horse tied to yours, that if mishap befalls, you won't separate.'

Time again stole the moment to exchange speech or encouragement. In silenced efficiency, *caithdein* and Companion swept out the used circles. They picked the cavern meticulously clean of every slight sign of their presence. The herb satchel was packed, the knife oiled and restored to its place in Prince Arithon's saddle pack. When the horses were loaded, the two clansmen gathered up the limp form still wrapped in the mantle of bearskin. Together they bore their liege out of the cleft. He weighed very little, a rag doll whose touch seemed incongruously warm for the corpse-slackness of limbs and body.

Under the pallid, platinum sun, buffeted by winter that raked the land with unnatural tenacity, they securely lashed Arithon's unconscious frame on the back of the fittest gelding. Then Braggen mounted. Still stripped to his jerkin and his lightweight, studded brigandine, Jieret set foot in the stirrup as well. Only the wide-open sky of the barrens bore witness to their rushed parting.

'Good hunting,' said Braggen, self-consciously brief, and no artist with speech under pressure.

'Guard my liege well.' Jieret found no more words to send back, on the chance his Companion survived him. He had none for Jeynsa and his two sons, that the raising of them had not spoken. For Feithan, he trusted her woman's wisdom to know the strength of his lifetime affection. His prince received a swift touch on the crown of the head. No help for the fact the distanced mind would not feel or retain any trace of remembrance.

Jieret set determined heels to his horse, and reined its blazed head firmly westward.

Moved to blind tears as the animal sprang to a canter that scattered a spray of loose gravel, Braggen called out, 'Ath keep you close!'

Then, at a whisper sawn through by raw grief, he addressed the unconscious prince whose life now became his given charge to protect. 'I could not have done as he did. Perhaps for an enemy I hated beyond life, but in love, I could never have spurned the appeal torn whole from the depths of your heart.'

Observations

Darkness extended beyond measure, a limitless binding that swallowed awareness of time and identity. Elaira fought down rattled panic. Her streetwise tenacity rejected the defeatist belief that she had been trapped unaware. She held Prime Selidie's promise of noninterference. Ath's adepts had assured her, again and again, that no hostile spellcraft might cross the wardings that guarded the sanctuary of their precinct.

Plain logic insisted the black void engulfing her must originate from inside her circle of intent.

Pure night surrounded her. Its environs revealed no loophole, no form, impenetrable and featureless as black glass. Elaira reclaimed her slipped hold on deep patience. She banished her terror, one clinging strand at a time. When no solution presented itself out of calm, she formed the desperate mental image of a sigil asking for guidance.

At last, through the murk of undermining uncertainty, she heard a far-off voice, faintly calling her name.

She turned toward the sound, traced its musical resonance like a drowning soul thrown a rope.

The stark blackness wavered, then shattered into light. Elaira found herself restored to the warm, sun-washed alcove that Ath's adepts used for their stillroom. Nothing appeared out of place. Her shaken, deep breath brought the heady, ripe fragrance of sweetgrass and dried flower petals. The rows of brass canisters gleamed with brilliant polish above the marble font kept continually filled with fresh water. The wall, banked with herb drawers, each bearing its neat scripted label, and the scales, mortars, and pestles remained, every one, in right order. Nothing threatened from the shelves where the unfamiliar ingredients were stored. As well as exotic roots and distilled salts, the white brotherhood employed recipes of advanced complexity involving crushed minerals, essences pressed from the oils of fresh plants, and ritual infusions of words set in light, absorbed from the sun or the moon.

To her intense disgust, Elaira discovered her collapse had upset the pestle she had been using to crush powdered charcoal for ink. Her wrist, sleeve, and cheekbone wore striking black smears. The lay brother on duty noted her riled disarray, his bearded lips turned with barely stifled amusement.

'Don't dare say I fainted,' she stated, hot in defense since she had no reason at hand to explain her peculiar behavior. The queer upset had subsided. Elaira repressed the rank urge to swear, braced back to stability by the spiced scents of willow bark and astringents. The remedies still steeped in the warm paraffin and suet used as base for the salves being packed into tinware containers.

'You didn't faint,' the lay brother agreed. His white teeth flashed through his close-cropped beard as he gave way to acerbic merriment. 'If you had, I couldn't have recalled you by Name.'

He stopped smiling, warned as Elaira froze in the act of wiping her smeared cheek on her sleeve cuff. Prepared for her stopped catch of breath, he tracked her dismay as she recovered the source of the blackout that had suddenly ruined her morning.

'Dharkaron's black bollocks!' she burst out, her exalted company forgotten as the shock struck through. *Her empathic link to Arithon s'Ffalenn had cut off, vanished away into nothing.* Unthinking as reflex, she hurled her mind inward, seeking; and again, the suffocating dark erupted from nowhere and engulfed her searching awareness.

This time, the lay brother moved fast enough. Lunging past the trestle, he caught her wrist and stayed her collapse before she spiraled away into the yawning expanse of the void. His voice, ever gentle, held sympathy as he urged, 'Elaira! Let go. Pull back.'

'Arithon!' she gasped, awash in raw dizziness. 'What's happened?' All night long, she had sensed the Teir's'Ffalenn's signature patterns ebb and resurge. She had tagged the flux as involvement with magecraft, no cause for concern. Rathain's prince had been rigorously trained. The intensity of focus that distanced their shared linkage had affirmed the engagement was made by free will. No warning had presaged the wrenching, sharp horror of feeling his presence cut off. Distressed to a panic that scraped her tone raw, she added, 'Had his Grace died, I should have felt his transition as he passed over Fate's Wheel!'

'Sit,' urged the lay brother. Inarguably firm, he guided her into the secure nook of a diamond-paned window seat.

She could not stop shaking. The flooding warmth of the sun seemed unreal. The nub of the wool tapestry cushion beneath her felt insubstantial as mist.

'What's happened?' Elaira demanded, unable to settle. Equilibrium failed her. Despite years of experience, and the well-practiced discipline of restraint, tension hardened her hand to a strangling grip over the lay brother's sleeve cuff.

'Be at peace. We'll know shortly. I've summoned an adept who will help you.' He gently disengaged the grasp of her fingers. 'You'll want a restorative, meantime.' The lay brother left her, selected an herb mix, then lifted the honey flask from the trestle. He drizzled a dollop into a flagon of cool water, then stirred in a selective pinch of crushed leaves.

Elaira accepted the draught, unsteady as she assayed a small sip. 'Thank you. For this, and for the calling. If you hadn't responded, no doubt I'd have battered myself to gibbering shreds.' For a mercy, the remedy eased her terror a fraction. She was able to think, and compose her fraught nerves, though very little could be done for the charcoal dust that blackened her tumbled bronze hair.

'What herbs did you choose?' She asked as much to gain knowledge as to ground herself through the balm of workaday detail. Raw leaves without heat to effect their release made too weak an infusion to explain the draught's heady potency.

'I used betony and starflower,' the lay brother explained. 'The essences lie in the oils. That's why they act quickly Those particular plants have fine energy properties that address the disharmonies in the aura.'

Too disturbed to pursue the bent of her interest, Elaira declined to sound the contents of the flagon for precise understanding of the trace energies binding the restorative's efficacy. Six weeks of applied study at the hostel had expanded her natural vision. Her work with free crystals had extended and deepened her knowledge of spellcraft, and daily chores in the stillroom had enriched her skills as a healer. The inhabitants of Whitehaven sanctuary practiced a refined lore far beyond the specialized teaching once gained from the sisters at Forthmark. The adepts' understanding of life and regeneration surpassed the reach of the wisest Koriani herbalists, even those who had worn their gray-banded sleeves over centuries of hospice service.

Throughout the winter, while gales spun snow like smoke off the bleak upper scarps of the mountains, Elaira had seized on the rare opportunity to heighten her craft. Now ripped by a shiver of gut-deep unease, she wondered whether the lure of such learning had caused her to shelter too long.

'The passes through Eastwall are icebound anyway,' the lay brother pointed out in response to her gnawing uncertainty. Settled as pooled rain in his slate-colored robes, he resumed his interrupted task at the trestle, weighing packets of herbs on a balance scale of antique, verdigris bronze. 'No one can pass westward by land until spring.'

If his words implied other means of travel existed, Elaira's agitation foreclosed her usual curiosity. Chilled through her fleeced-leather leggings and wool smock, she huddled in full sunlight, sipping watered honey and herbs in fraught silence and strained apprehension.

At length, the promised adept ascended the tower stair in spry steps. He burst into the stillroom, a willowy old man clad in flowing white wool who shed radiance like autumn sunlight. The silver and gold ciphers stitched on his hood scattered the chamber with small rainbows and ambient reflections. 'Your prince is unharmed,' he assured without query, his olive-skinned features crinkled with laugh lines. 'Nor is he endangered, at present.' Aware his raised hand could not stem the tortured rush of Elaira's questions, he smiled. 'Come along. You can see for yourself. One waits for you beside the sacred spring. As you wish, you might ask him for help.'

Elaira abandoned her perch on the window seat and replaced her emptied flagon on the trestle. 'Another adept? But I thought your Brotherhood didn't use power to act.' If her question was impertinent, she hoped the old man would forgive. Words could not express how profoundly distressing she found the prospect of a return visit to the spring.

'Your visitor is not one of us,' the elder chastised as he held open the door. He watched closely, assured as her color returned in the icy draft of the stairwell. Though no crisis could warrant a white brother's intervention, he kept stride alongside Elaira, guarding her fragile state of balance throughout the winding descent.

'Well, what might befall the Prince of Rathain while I visit the spring in your grove? How do I know I won't fall unconscious like I did the first time?' Breathing the thin, icy air in swift gulps, Elaira balked on the lower landing. 'I awoke three days later, and still can't recall where I went.'

The adept paused also, a scintillant presence who chased the deep gloom from the base of the stairwell. Patience stilled his gnarled hand on the latch that fastened the outer doorway. 'Brave lady, you must walk alone in this matter. Our creed will permit nothing else. The spirit your need has drawn to our hostel has been known in the past as a meddler. Yet he in his wisdom would be first to agree: only you can decide whether to go, or to stay. Free choice remains yours. You can embrace or refuse congress with those forces called into the fate you create by your actions. This arrival is yours, though its cause and effect may lie outside the scope of your present understanding.'

Elaira swallowed. The awareness bore down, that time taken to ponder the adept's abstruse counsel might deliver an unforseen cost in grave consequences. 'Lead on, brother.' Of all things she feared, the unforseen at least held the potential to defer the paralyzing despair of rank helplessness. 'I may as well take the easy plunge into hot water. Whatever I've called here, I'll find strength from somewhere to face it.'

The adept nodded, tripped the latch, and ushered her into the sun-washed glare of the courtyard. 'You have a true heart. The power drawn in by the cry of your need would be most unwise not to grant you every due measure of respect.'

Arrived at the end of the marble loggia, the adept stopped and bowed. 'Lady, at this point I must leave you. Proceed on your own as you choose.'

The black-stone pillars loomed just ahead, darker than midwinter night. The uncanny patterns incised on their surface flared and glittered, randomly bright as the rainbowed glints chipped off of sun-caught diamond. Elaira surveyed the threshold between. From two steps away, the archway led into what seemed an innocuous cupola, apparently lit by unseen skylights cut through the dome overhead. The high polish of the tessellated marble floor appeared impeccably solid. Yet Elaira had learned to grant no credence to the untrustworthy illusion of eyesight. To advance was to cross an invisible boundary and forfeit all earthly experience.

Suddenly unsure, she drew breath to ask questions. But the adept had gone, unseen and unheard, leaving a silence as sealed as a tomb. Turn back, and he might reappear to escort her. Ahead resided the heartcore of a mystery beyond mortal understanding. Threatened by sudden, rushing vertigo, Elaira reached out to brace herself; a mistake. The carved patterns altered the very nature of substance. Her touch met a riling, sharp tingle of energy, as though her hand had dissolved into stone to the wrist.

Her startled outcry cast back no echoes, an eerie anomaly in this place of groined ceilings and high-gloss marble floors.

No choice, but to go forward alone. Heart pounding, Elaira regrouped her frayed nerves. She closed her fingers around the three coins worn for luck since her childhood days as a street thief.

'By Ath, prince,' she muttered. 'Whatever scrape you've fallen into, you'd better pull yourself clear before we all find ourselves entrapped into debt by my order, or worse: waken some dire power better left undisturbed like the sleeping dog out of proverb.'

She stepped forward, resolute. Just as before, her senses betrayed her. The transition that dissociated both space and time closed down without seam or bias. She emerged through the arched portal into the sweet mildness of a midsummer night. A forest glade surrounded her, moon-washed grass dipped pearlescent with dew. The shadows cast by the soaring crowns of the trees lay as deep as razor-cut velvet. A fountain burbled over white stones, juddered with star-caught reflections.

Against the silvery fall of clear water, a man's figure stood out like a displaced fragment of autumn.

Expecting her, he arose. The burnt orange and sienna cloth of his doublet rustled, a flame backdrop for his fox brush hair, streaked at both temples with white. He was clean-shaven. Neat in movement, fastidious in each detail of dress and grooming, he had peat-dark eyes, and a presence of ruthless, clear focus as he greeted, 'Elaira *anient*?'

Jarred as much by his soft, smoky baritone as by the queer, Paravian phrasing, Elaira responded with a startled question. 'Why call me *"the one"*?'

'For truth.' He gathered her hand in long fingers, his touch warmly confident. She noticed a ring inset with citrine, and a trifold insignia of crescents that flared to a mercuric flash of caught moonlight. Up close, his angular features showed dichotomy: the enigma of a secretive presence, touched by a smile that was electric, and brimming with inquisitive curiosity.

'Sorcerer,' she whispered, her perception alive to the leashed power in him, an unstated air of subtle command shared by none but the Fellowship. Revelation burst through, couched in shock like a dousing of ice. 'Ath above!' Elaira gasped. 'You could be no less than—'

'No!' His interruption came sharp. 'Have a care. In all caution, let's leave that identity unspoken.'

He released his grasp, not before she had encompassed the impression of flawless flesh and bone vibrancy. 'You are quite the master of convincing illusion.'

'Am I?' Fleeting bitterness sliced through, self-defined as his stance in cool grass. While he sat at his ease once again on the piled white stone rimming the lip of the spring, his eagle's gaze tracked her, unswerving.

'Only a fool would respond to that sort of baiting question.' Pragmatic under the bearing assault of the Sorcerer's observation, Elaira advanced. 'Everyone said you were rendered discorporate.'

'Truth,' her controversial visitor allowed. He laced his long fingers over his knee, his posture nonchalant, and his honesty a dagger of sly insolence.

His bottomless depths and his well-masked emotion stayed opaque to her highly skilled training. Elaira dipped her hands into the chill fall of the water. She managed to ignore his probing regard long enough to splash her hot face. The dousing eased back some of the hollow uncertainty wrung through her displaced equilibrium. She straightened, blotted damp hands on a skirt that breathed an herbalist's blend of dried lavender and birch root into the breezeless quiet. 'Why have you come here?'

He raised both eyebrows, not surprised, but for emphasis as his raking gaze held her. 'Your directness blisters. Are you always abrupt as Dharkaron's cast spear?'

She regarded him back, unmoved by provocative rhetoric.

His quick laughter burst through then, spontaneous and sultry as heat lightning. 'Your order might think you a troublesome burr, but I take delight in your company. You asked for guidance, remember?'

Smiling, he waited for her stiff acknowledgment, as she recalled the mental sigil she had sketched in wild panic when the flooding darkness had overwhelmed her awareness.

'Therefore, I came with an invitation. Like the fresh breeze, you might accompany me on a flight of reconnaissance.' He extended a lean-fingered, beautiful hand, his palm at ease and turned upward. 'Would you care to pay a visit to Daon Ramon Barrens?'

Elaira fought past the tight fear in her chest, and finally managed strained speech. 'You know what happened to Prince Arithon.'

The visitor's moment of levity faded, not into the withdrawn graveness of Traithe. This Sorcerer towered with an incisive confidence that a lesser presence might misinterpret as braggadocio, or worse, an affronted, bristling challenge. 'Nothing occurs on Daon Ramon Barrens that the stones of the earth don't bear witness. Their secrets are plain, to those willing to listen.' He stood once again, his hand still extended. 'Yes, I know of Prince Arithon. His fate is unfolding. Come along. If you care, you can observe and perhaps even share in the outcome.'

'If you promise I'm not making a mistake,' Elaira said, her words a wry prayer as she clasped her chilled fingers over his in tacit acceptance.

'Oh, life itself's a mistake,' murmured the Sorcerer whose past acts had earned him the title of Betrayer.

He returned a warm squeeze, his pleasure a gift that touched the heart for its mischievous spontaneity. Then the moment ended, too brief. The masked flux of power within him unfurled, demarked as a terrifying ring of forged purpose that commanded a rippleless silence. Centered in a storm without tumult or movement, form and flesh whirled away. His shape as a man re-formed on a breath into feathers and wings, edged in a haze of gold light.

Elaira felt her awareness netted up and enfolded. Gathered into a hold as implacable as steel gloved in trappings of velvet, the seat of her consciousness became snatched from her body. Pale moonlight dissolved. The random melodies of the springwater receded as she arose into air, at one with the eagle whose powerful downstroke lifted, then hurled her up and out of the glade, and into the icy winds of high altitude . . .

Under the pallid, cerulean sky, the hills of Daon Ramon wore snow rime like snagged silk around weathered rims of bared rock. Experienced trackers avoided the crests, where no cover grew to mask movement. Such country became a commander's nightmare. Knives of fragmented flint studded the frost-burned mosses and nestled amid the wind-raked tangles of gorse. The low country between ridges cupped a warren of deer paths, unreeled like string through the peat bogs and hummocks, with their winter-dried tassels of grasses. Stands of dense brush welcomed no man's passage. Witch hazel and brambles choked the throats of the gullies, an intertwined mat loomed by years of wild growth that hid fox earths and badger setts. The veteran headhunters who led Lysaer's strike force were wily enough to shy clear. Past forays through the barrens had taught them the untrustworthy ground was snaked through by streamlets gushing into the Aiyenne's looped coils. A horse could break legs, and a man, twist his ankles, where the fast, hidden currents ran armored with thaw-rotten ice.

That left the pitched ground of the slopes, flayed bare by the winds, or else piled with the leavings of storms, drifted snow the day's sun softened to silver-point lace, refrozen by night to filed iron. Rugged as their mapless territory, the clan war band wore leggings of boiled elkhide and rode range-toughened ponies with thick skin and well-feathered fetlocks.

Townborn pursuers who lacked the advantage of stout leathers drew steel and hacked through obstructions. Their zeal stayed unblunted. Whipped on like hounds on the scent of close quarry, they wrapped the scraped legs of their horses in flannel. At night, resigned, they plied needle and thread, for the obstinate brush tore the stoutest loomed canvas to tatters.

None petitioned to turn back. They ate hardtack, shot deer and hare as they could, and cheerlessly cursed the land under them. Amid their dour ranks, all memory of the golden, wind-rippled grasslands had faded away into legend. Only stone, sleeping under the raced gusts of wind, retained the imprinted glory of past Ages. Apparitions and ghosts were all that remained of the Paravians who had once danced to raise the mysteries to grand harmony. Long gone were the days when their rituals called down the lightning-struck fires that cleared the hills of rank growth and renewed the exhausted soil.

Chafed more than he liked to admit by that lingering presence of history, Sulfin Evend completed his morning review of the company under his command. He found the men fighting fit. Despite the arduous weeks of chapping cold, buffeting gales, and a desolation fit to break sanity, they kept their faith. Triumph lay within reach. Dismounted at noon to water and grain horses, they picked clinging burdock from their kit. Others, just returned from the rigors of scout duty, wistfully discussed sharing beer in the celebrated taverns of Etarra.

Under Lysaer s'Ilessid, their force rode in readiness. No matter the past scores of death and disaster, this specialized strike force was made the forged weapon to hunt down the Spinner of Darkness. Rathain's last prince was their charge to reap; s'Ffalenn lineage would die, unmourned as the haunts of the ancestors who lurked like caught cobweb amid Ithamon's razed stone and smashed bastions. Each man had trained in rigorous preparation for the field that would bring the just fruits of their victory.

Sulfin Evend enjoyed no such cocky surety from the post of commanding authority. He had remained at the Divine Prince's right hand, his night sleepless. Long after sunrise, when Jeriayish's mad face still ran with tears of rapt bliss, Prince Lysaer had ordered the raving priest bound and silenced. Sulfin Evend attended the distasteful task himself. The issue raised by the uncanny defection was far too sensitive to entrust to even his most stolid officer. Unsettling enough, that the priest stayed unfazed through the course of uncivil handling. Rumpled and subdued in his soiled white robes, he crooned into his gag, trembling in witless, transported ecstasy as Lysaer's strapping squire bundled him onto the back of a docile horse.

Sulfin Evend clenched his jaw and smothered irritation. Bred to Hanshire's tradition of liaison with Koriathain, he knew of no arcane binding that should leave the priest shaken so thoroughly out of his senses. Whatever queer force his blood scrying had encountered, one instant's contact had destroyed his right mind.

A Fellowship Sorcerer might wield such power. Under the pallid sky of Daon Ramon, Sulfin Evend slammed his fist into the palm of his left-hand gauntlet. He barked orders to ease and water the horses, then mounted himself, prepared to ride out and collect his reports from the front line of headhunter trackers. Taciturn face turned into the east wind, he strangled his doubts. Whether or not his proud company held the mettle to destroy the demon Prince of Rathain, faith had blinded them, utterly. They had gone too far to turn back.

The barren land guarded its secrets too well. He saw no trace of enemy movement. Chilled by more than cold, feeling exposed despite his battle-honed weapons and chain mail, the Alliance Lord Commander swept the mottled folds of the hills. Emptiness met him. The morning advanced, with the wind-scoured flanks of the ridges persistently vacant. The front-rank scouts had encountered the hoof marks of unshod ponies, but the troop's sharpest trackers could not reach an agreement. One insisted a scant few clan horsemen had recrossed their own tracks. The other argued a larger force had split into flight in small groups. The mishmash of prints on the streambanks revealed no clear line of pursuit.

Amid frayed uncertainty, the chief headhunter from Narms met setbacks with squint-eyed suspicion. 'Red-beard's no fool. He won't make mistakes.' Deshir's war band knew the lay of this country too well, old knowledge refreshed through the years of Etarra's purging campaigns. Dour as the briar-scarred gelding he sat on, the bountyman spat in contempt. 'You want the harsh truth, friend?'

His measuring glance matched the Lord Commander's taut quiet with worldly understanding. 'I worry we haven't seen any traps. That's unlike any clanblood bastard I've scalped, not to leave nasty pitfalls or garroting snares, or slip nooses that trip a man's horse by the fetlocks.'

'We've kept the slinking vermin too pressed,' Sulfin Evend dismissed, though the prick of his instincts belied such a pat explanation.

'Better hope so.' The headhunter scratched at his greasy black hair, then dug in a spurred heel to forestall his horse, which bared yellow teeth at the Lord Commander's wiry gelding. 'Me, I'd be worrying what other mischief Red-beard's plaguing fiends've brewed up.' That said, he reined his irritable mount volte-face to resume his delayed patrol. 'Sure as fish swim, I'd say that gibbering priest didn't cast off his faith for anyone's natural causes.'

'Double the scouts who ride in the skirmish line,' Sulfin Evend cracked back, too trail-wise to stew over morbid fears and formless, circling supposition.

'Done, then.' The veteran headhunter took his leave, too pragmatic to say if the change had settled his own store of reservations.

Through the interval while the main company with Prince Lysaer ate trail rations on the sheltered side of the crest, Sulfin Evend lingered on the hilltop. A searching, sharp sweep from that desolate vantage did not shake his recurrent suspicion that he did not ride alone.

'Grace and Light!' he hissed under his breath. 'Will you breeding fiends just begone!' A man did not move in Daon Ramon Barrens, that spirits did not hound his tracks. At length, in disgust, since no shade could wreak lasting harm beyond headaches and unsettled thoughts, Sulfin Evend adjusted his slackened reins. His round of inspection would not be complete until he had checked on the pack train, and arbitrated the day's fresh complaints from the drovers in charge of the baggage.

At first stride, he hauled his mount back to a halt. Something *did* watch his back: a massive golden eagle perched amid the dead limbs of the scrub. Its flat, amber eyes seemed to *look right through him* in that brief instant of shared contact.

Then the raptor unfolded shadow-dark wings. On a powerful downstroke, it launched into flight, the gust whipped up by its passage a lashing slap against the Lord Commander's cold-reddened cheeks. Sulfin Evend blinked back stinging tears. When his blurred vision cleared, the uncanny creature was lost beyond sight.

In its place a messenger on a lathered horse tore up the scree slope, urgently shouting. 'You're wanted back, now!'

Sulfin Evend pressed his mount down the slope. He heard the gist, moving: how the sunwheel priest had collapsed from his fit without warning.

'His heart stopped, they say, though no one's hand touched him,' the messenger gasped through the clatter of scree churned up under cantering horses. 'Prince Lysaer assayed a blood scrying after that. Now he's bid for a change in strategy. You're needed to oversee the division of our forces. By command of the Light, we've now got to run down what looks like eight separate fugitives.'

'Decoys?' Fastened on the gist of the problem, the Alliance Lord Commander set urgent spurs to his mount. He chose to plow through the next stand of brush. Clawed like fell vengeance by the dense canes of thorn, he vented his grim disbelief. *'You're saying the shadow-spinning bastard's found a way to fabricate false leads that foiled the cast sigil of a blood scrying?'*

'Apparently so.'

Sulfin Evend kept his balance as the horse scrambled over a patch of bad footing and recovered. That dire news drove his spiking dread down to the marrow of his bones. 'Then you know what we're facing is a sorcerer's maze created with fell signs and black sorcery.'

'Divine Grace will prevail,' said the messenger, breathless.

'Even so,' Sulfin Evend snapped back, 'I'll place my trust in steel before prayer.' He kept pace with the messenger's flying mount, now grappling the firm evidence that the stakes were likely to turn for the worse. Lysaer s'Ilessid would not retreat before evil. Riding in the footsteps of his slaughtered predecessors, Sulfin Evend could not shake the ugly foreboding: that the cocksure hunters in their sunwheel surcoats were now being nose-led, the traps for them set by one desperate and dangerous mouse.

A speck against sun glare, the eagle circled. Where a mortal bird might have flapped, unable to rise on the weak winter thermals off the slopes, this raptor soared, unimpeded. His high-pitched cry communed with the winds and invited their dancing partnership. The frigid north air whistled through knife-edged feathers, ruffling the russet-and-gilt hackles on his neck, but causing him no inconvenience. Avid, he watched. His awareness interpreted far more than an avian creature hatched from an egg, and his farseeing gaze missed nothing.

Where the definitive signs of clan presence could be hidden from two-legged eyes, the advantage of height unveiled every stray movement against the crumpled tapestry of Daon Ramon's stark landscape. In eight tight-knit enclaves, Earl Jieret's war band prepared for their imminent encounter with the Alliance armed forces. The dulled glint of steel through clumped brush told where leather-clad scouts crouched in ambush. Of the spring traps, the nooses, the deadfalls with trip springs, set where oncoming troops would soon tread, no sign showed; the ground seemed untouched by disturbance. The snares had been laid before the past snowfall, some set under the clairvoyant guidance of Jieret's dreaming, and others by hunch and conjecture.

Yet the eagle's uncanny perception read beyond surface appearance. His sweeping overview revealed dangers a man's earthbound senses would miss. Death awaited the Alliance's sworn faithful, cunningly placed on rock-strewn hillcrests, or under the innocuous snowdrifts, and on the brush-choked, silted banks of the meandering creek beds. No matter how vigilant, the armed ranks who invaded the sacrosanct wilds would pay with their lives and their blood.

Mage-wise, the eagle discerned the subtler tactics, as well. His peerless vision detected the flaring light of Prince Arithon's signature pattern, stitched as a fetch into the thin shells of acorns by thread-fine chains of spelled ciphers. He knew the Names of the men chosen to bear the sealed constructs. Moment to moment, he could have listed the ones most likely to die, as the shifting templates of causation and intent laid the map of the unwritten future above the range of etheric energies.

Nor did the bird's survey miss the lone rider who chivvied two saddled horses on lead reins. He unlocked, in an instant, the arcane connection between one horse's bundled-up burden, and the silk-wrapped weight of the Paravian-made weapon strapped to the mounted man's back. What the eagle knew, the Koriani partner he carried in linkage understood just as clearly: his awareness encompassed Elaira's stricken dismay as she unraveled the import of the Teir's'Ffalenn's desperate strategy.

For reply, the raptor circled into the wind and spiraled his flight path still higher.

The horizon rolled back, the earth a broad platter seething with bellicose industry. To the north spread the toiling lines of the Alliance companies from Etarra, their trampled back trail a dimmed swath straggling southward over the snow. Eastward coursed the pack of Darkling's light horse, streaming through thickets and brush, and relentless as hounds in full cry.

To the south glimmered the entangling snarl of compulsion cast over Jaelot's spellbound guard captain and the hard-bitten remnants of his company. The weak or faint-hearted by now had been left by the wayside. The strong-minded and practical voices among them, who had argued the folly of a suicidal advance, were long since dispatched, sent homeward bearing insatiable demands for relief supplies and reinforcements. The zealot survivors had abandoned all reason. Time and close contact had extended the spell's reach, infecting them with the driving obsession borne by their luckless commander. Beneath the eagle's expanded scrutiny, their heads seemed entangled in a sickly orange web. In contrast, their bodies appeared queerly darkened, their forms traced like moving shadows against the vibrant aspect of their surroundings.

No hedging protection could mask the blighting signs of dark practice from the probing sight of a Fellowship awareness. The cast sigils that warped them through the discipline imposed by their captain's chain of command stood out clearly as strung foil on the hazeless, cold air.

Elaira's shock of recoil was genuine, as her linked vision recorded sure evidence of Koriani meddling in the men's state of unkempt self-abandonment. She had not known, then; the Sorcerer clothed in the form of the raptor saw into her heart, and was satisfied. If the enchantress also recognized the hand that had wrought such offensive craftwork, her thought remained masked; that license was permitted. In respect for the fact she could not break integrity in betrayal of her order's vows, the eagle did not pry, though the clean winds of the thermals wafted the taint of that sorry usage: of matted hair rancid with unwashed sweat, and grease from the seared horse meat the men had consumed when supplies ran low, and the lean, barrens deer failed to yield enough fat for subsistence. Like mad animals possessed by some ravening need outside the bounds of their nature, they would course their live prey with insane disregard for survival.

The great eagle quartered the winter-bare landscape. His raking flight swept over the sunwheel banners cracking above Lysaer's personal troop. On the cusp of the moment, while Sulfin Evend lost his passionate argument against dividing the Light's forces for a change in tactics at the ninth hour, Jieret's clan war band wove their desperate, last-minute strategies, aware they could not prevail. Their thin lines of defense could do no more than to stall and deflect, or kill with ruthless invention. Encounter would set off a dog-pack fray of brief but manic intensity.

To the eagle's prescient perception, the freshets in the hollows would soon run fouled and red. Combatants who fell here would never return home. Rathain's clanblood stood to lose irreplaceable family lines; townborn would be shown no mercy. Winter itself would cause losses. Distinction would blur between the hacked dead. *The fallen would be beloved fathers and sons, alike as brothers in abandonment. Their scattered remains would be devoured by scavenging wolves, then picked over by ravens and crows.*

The gusts moaned across Daon Ramon Barrens that day, alive with the wisped forms of Paravian spirits, who mourned for the sorrows of war come again. Though the eagle's rarefied hearing could have shared their plangent lament, its purpose lay with the living.

'*Whom would you follow?*' the creature inquired of his Koriani guest. His words were not spoken, but arose as whispered sound braided into the wind hissing over its silken feathers.

'*His caithdein,*' came Elaira's reply, a thought as steadfast as an iron rod to the eagle's nonavian mind. Shrewd even through her paralyzing worry, the enchantress had taken the tactical choice: named Earl Jieret over the dour-faced Braggen, riding alone, with a laden horse and the dire burden of a silk-wrapped Paravian sword.

The eagle returned caustic admiration. '*Brave lady.*' He wheeled, his power and grace like the shimmer of storm-charged lighting. '*You don't flinch from necessity, do you?*' Sorcerer that he was, he endorsed her conviction: the Koriani Prime would be assiduously tracking every small move that she made. By granting the more believable decoy the branding tag of her interest, she would mislead them; but at the cost of relinquishing Prince Arithon's fate through his hour of critical risk.

'*Cringe, rather,*' Elaira returned, wry. Her stab at humor was empty bravado. Her consciousness felt stretched, cast over such a vast distance, the mortal burden of flesh and bone gone liquid and unreal as water. Detached from the body, her visceral fears became magnified by the merciless fact she had lost every outlet for distraction. '*My sisterhood plays for stakes far more lethal than Lysaer's compulsion to kill.*'

Lirenda's failure had fanned coals to flame in the order's entrenched desire to trap Arithon. Elaira could not conceal her deep dread from the Sorcerer who bore her along. For herself, and for her beloved, the stakes riding on a misjudgment promised ruin without parallel.

She knew, as no other: Koriani spellcraft coiled through crystal could be made to bind the free spirit and impose an imprisonment to outlast a lifetime.

Late Winter 5670

Invalid

The half world that swallowed him fueled nightmares, unending: of fire that seared him, skin and muscle from bone. His suffering brought agony that licked every nerve end, an acid-walled prison without cease. He slept little. The grinding weight of his damaged body abraded away his awareness. Cohesive thought became ripped to delirium. Each breath that necessity forced him to draw whistled into his body, tormenting seared tissue with inescapable repetition.

The pain wore him, tore him, snatched away the requisite peace he must have to seek a quiet passage out of life. He wept with longing for the turn of Fate's Wheel and the oblivion of final release.

Who he had been mattered far less than what he had become, which meant the voice calling his name repeated itself for an immeasurable span of time. Words and syllables seemed only meaningless noise amid a cacophony of chaotic sensation. The insistent throb of his flame-ravaged flesh disallowed him the focus to respond. Minutes flowed past, unmeasured, spiked at odd intervals by motion and touch that set off a conflagration of raw torture.

He would have screamed then, had the fires of the Khadrim not scarred his throat beyond the capacity for speech. Because he had no will and no choice, he endured, in animal misery.

For unfathomable days, the voiced phrases flowed around him, over him, through him, eliciting no response.

'. . . his consciousness may have left his body, but not detached . . .'

'. . . could use Name and recall him. At least then he could remember himself, and recover his birth-born identity . . .'

'. . . adepts have refused that. He asked for help, but whether to live or to die remains at issue still. Until he garners the presence of mind to decide, nothing more can be done. Have patience and tend him. His youthful strength and resilience are considerable. Though he suffers, he's not yet outmatched . . .'

The words washed over him, flooding and receding, less meaningful than the reflex pull of the moon dragging the ebb and flow of the tides.

Until one string of phrases spiked through, shattering the fog like a stone cast through paned glass: '. . . well, the waiting makes no one suffer but him. His lady mother believes he is dead . . .'

His royal mother believed he was dead. The mere thought of Ellaine's tears scalded conscience: a solitary love that strung the sole thread of her joy, snapped and gone with his spirit. Her loneliness blazed like a cry in the night, and his anguish could not be deafened. Grief exploded and smashed through his physical pain, a wounding a thousand times deeper.

On the pallet in the white-stone ward of Ath's hostel at Northerly, Prince Kevor s'Ilessid dragged in a terrible, hitched breath and reclaimed the power of his voice. 'Help me,' he rasped, the barest, scraped whisper lost under the pound of Stormwell Gulf's breakers, sheeting white spume against the vicious rocks of the coastline. Hurled spindrift misted the chamber's high-tower windows, until leaded panes wore a frosting of salt, spindled with crystallized patterns.

Kevor tried and failed to force his eyes open. By the dull, muffled burn, he presumed there were bandages soaked with strong salves masking his face.

He could not know the truth, that the covering of cloth made no difference. Were the wrappings removed, the flat glimmer of afternoon light lay beyond his fire-scorched eyesight. He tried again to frame speech, and discovered the horror: the passage of air through his ruined mouth and throat could not shape clear words to release the scream in his mind: 'Help me, I beg you! For my mother's sake, I would live.'

'Blessed Ath lend him grace!' someone cried in relief. 'He's found his way back to self-awareness.'

Then, as though his anguished thoughts had been heard, an explosion of white light deluged through his being, blinding him to the ceaseless erosion of pain. He drifted. Tenderly clasped in a river of calm, he was soothed, the raw wound of his torment cocooned. The bright current that buoyed him disturbed not a thread of his being, but lent him the gift of serenity. He could pause, and recoup, and rebuild shattered consciousness from the haven of sheltering peace.

Out of clear calm, a whisper arose, and Named him in utmost compassion. 'Prince Kevor s'Ilessid!'

The call of that summons hurled him into a dizzying, upward spiral that wrung him, spirit from flesh. For the span of an eyeblink, he was not here, nor there, but all places, and all things, a thought without limit, spun through the weave of creation.

Then he woke as if from a dream.

He found himself standing in the shaded, summer twilight of a forest glen. Small flowers bloomed in the long grass, drenching his bare feet with dew. Birds took flight, and somewhere, a nightingale sang. A fox watched him, forefeet extended in a lazy, luxuriant stretch. Beneath its paws, bare inches from its muzzle, a field mouse crouched washing its whiskers. The unnatural absence of the small creature's fear did not seem out of place. Nor did the trilling splash of water welling up from some sourceless spring in the rocks require the encumbrance of logic to source its continuous renewal.

Naked, reborn, Kevor stood in that place of enchantment and gasped. He felt no self-consciousness, no sense of shame. Only the riptide wave of pleased wonder ran through him, alive with untamed abandon.

'You expressed your desire to heal,' someone prompted from behind him.

Unstartled, still wrapped in amazement, Kevor turned around and saw the white-robed woman who regarded him, her long, fine hair spooled gold on her shoulders, and her eyes soft as moss on a streamside.

His curiosity escaped before thought. 'Who are you?'

As though his lapse of courtesy meant nothing, the lady's smile came quiet as moonlight. 'An adept of Ath's hostel, here to assist, but only as free will dictates.'

Touched by a distant remembrance of fire and the searing trauma of attack by Khadrim, Kevor waited for the shiver that never came. He felt whole. His memories were complete, yet somehow excised from the impact of terror or pain. Horror had been denied its cutting edge. He discovered he could examine his past with an unparalleled freedom. 'I was maimed,' he stated, an unemotional truth. 'Have I died, then?' The grief of loss caught him unprepared, as though his current emotions gained an additional spin from the shedding of prior encumbrances. 'Is this vale on the path to Athlieria?'

The adept's smile faded into a gesture of gentle negation. 'You have not cut the tie to your body. Not yet. You need not, if you feel the life that hangs in the balance still holds meaning and value.'

'You can send me back?' Distracted by a momentary flicker of movement, Kevor glanced sidewards. Wonderment touched him. The languorous fox had been joined by a tortoise, while a luminous moth with mother-of-pearl wings flew from flower to flower, dusting a gold haze of pollen. He might have become lost in rapt fascination, had the adept's grave remonstrance not called back his strayed attention.

'You could heal yourself.' She knelt to the tortoise, which ambled forward and shared silent concourse at her knee. She thanked it politely. Then she nodded her dismissal and restored her wise gaze to the young prince who watched in stilled patience. 'To that end, I can offer you counsel.'

Robed in fair skin and his natural dignity, Kevor held out his hands. 'Am I not healed already?'

The adept arose, saddened. Her hair caught the light, moon-touched to the chill gleam of platinum. 'No. You are dreaming. The body you remember holds to life by a thread. The Khadrim's fire left crippling damage.'

Kevor shivered, overwhelmed all at once. The uncanny place, with its deep-running current of mystery, was too strange to quell his uncertainty. Cast out of his depth, he fell back on his breathtaking gift of raw courage. 'Say how I should start.' His voice shook, as again, the thought of his mother left alone in Avenor raked over his heart like cold fingers.

The adept clasped his hand. Her touch felt warm, too real for a dream figment, and yet, her sincerity could not be faulted as she led him toward the lip of the spring. Her voice was clear as poured honey, over the bubbling uprush of water through stone. 'First you must honestly answer what caused you to set your life into jeopardy.'

'But that's simple.' Kevor let himself be drawn into the pool. Cool water burbled up through his toes, and splashed over his ankles and shins. 'The forester's daughter was going to be killed, and I was the one standing in the nearest position to act.'

Her hand released him. The subtle absence of touch became the first indication that his integrity was set on trial. 'If that were all, you would not have seen harm.'

'But—' Kevor's protest died away unspoken as the water in the pool rippled and fractured into vision: showing him alongside his two honor guards, and one of them prepared with a bow and a timely arrow. Showing him again, with the presence of mind to exhort the children to scatter, then himself, spinning to run in the *opposite* direction, which caused the Khadrim a fractional hesitation, as it was forced to discern, and choose between three possible targets. Showing him again, hurling his cloak as diversion, then rolling to hide underneath the snow-covered log he had sat on.

'Something undermined your commitment to life,' the adept pointed out. Her velvet admonition came tempered in honesty that probed his intent like honed steel. 'You acted to spare someone's child, that is true. But your own purpose faltered. You allowed your own death in the outcome.'

Kevor swallowed. His chest felt stone heavy, and his mind flinched from direct encounter with the weighty revelation that gnawed at the edges of consciousness.

The adept read his reluctance. Her compassion was immediate. 'You are given free will. No one but you can name the moment when you pass across Fate's Wheel. The complexity lies in the way you lose your true self in the maze of your own awareness. Healing is an energy that arises from within. If your choices, your feelings, and your fears lie in conflict, the channel of your will becomes clouded. To cross back, to return to the other side of this divide and reclaim your right to wholeness, you must first understand the choices that set your life into jeopardy.'

Kevor lifted his head, faced her square on, though the roil of raw nerves made him dizzy, and his spirit shrank from the impact of the cruel facts that arose out of darkness to meet him. Once he had skirted that edge of harsh truth to Ranne in the winter wood. The questions still held locked in his heart must find voice, though the cost would be written on a shrouded future, wrought of unformed event on a landscape of shapeless menace.

'I was afraid,' he confessed. 'I knew if I broached the uncomfortable question, I might uncover more lies. The answers I found might run deeper than a corrupt influence in Avenor's high council.'

Kevor faltered. The adept waited, patient, as he assimilated his sorrow and defined the fell demon that rode him. 'If I examined each issue, and followed the logic of mercy, I realized I might expose my father's call to the Light as a fraud. Worse still, I saw the possibility of a more callous cruelty: that the men who rode with me were being sent to their deaths for the purpose of a political manipulation.'

Once spoken, the ripple of dread rolled over and through him. Chills puckered his skin. He was naked, stripped beyond privacy, inside and out. The shame burned Kevor red, first for the taint on his s'Ilessid name, then oddly, for the fact the ugly truth freed him. He could act. Now, he could face the worst, and not let the core of his own hidden dread stalk him out of the shadows.

His young will took fresh fire, rekindled by the knowledge that if Tysan's high council had a rotten core, his born gift of justice must prompt his return. He would confront his father and rout out the canker. No son worthy of his royal lineage could leave Lady Ellaine alone to face the possible threat of Avenor's internal corruption.

His resolve must have shown in his face and changed bearing.

'You should be warned,' the adept added in tender precaution. 'In this place, you walk very near to the seat of your true power. You will choose to live, but the fires you call down to transfigure your maimed body cannot do other than remold the foundation of your being. Your flesh will be made anew in the passion of your will. But the man who steps forth shall be changed.'

Kevor replied with the bright-edged impatience of youth. 'Then I must take that chance.'

'No chance, but a certainty.' The adept regarded him and saw no weakening of his resolve. 'Immerse in the pool. Make your choice with your heart and the whole of your mind. Then allow what occurs. You will awaken and arise if you can accept the gift of your own grace, healed or still scarred by the tenets of your conviction. If you cross the Wheel, one will assist. If you regain awareness, I will be there, standing vigil at your bedside to offer you comfort.'

Kevor gave her his smile, which had won him the loyalty of men, and the love of Avenor's populace. His resolve showed the steel-clad fiber of his heritage. A shining commitment to justice that, *in another set of circumstances, with no premature blight cast on the path of his destiny*, would have earned him the Fellowship's sanction for high kingship.

Tysan's true prince bowed amid the safe haven of the grove. 'Lady, my gratitude will last for as long as I live to draw breath.'

His grace in that moment as noble as his ancestry, he bent to his knees, drew breath in an eagerness mixed with trepidation, and plunged into the mystical flow of the water.

For a moment, nothing happened. The spring lapped around him in a swirling caress, cool and impersonal in its peace. Then all at once his awareness of form seemed to melt. Current that was power itself brushed his skin, then touched through him in tacit contact. Kevor shivered, quelled his spasm of hesitation, and opened his spirit in welcome.

The trickle swelled into a thundering spate that roared through him. He was blinded, deaf, made the focus of a cataract that ripped open the fabric of his being and hurled all that he was into light.

He knew of no time, no space, no beginning, and no end. No solidity anchored him. Kevor shouted with no voice as he found himself cast headlong into the sea of possibility, whose mystical fires kindled the crucible of change. Adrift on the flux of prime power, he lit and blazed, at one with the chord that sustained Ath's undying creation.

At the last instant, before his awareness dissolved into that dance of eternal celebration, he realized the adept's warning had surpassed all imagining. On the day he chose to separate from the flux and return to earthly awareness, he would no longer be the idealistic young prince, but something else altogether. Here, limits dissolved, and bold wishes held impact. The constraints of duty and obligation lost meaning. He could remold himself on the wings of free will, and arise annealed to become whatever he chose . . .

Late Winter 5670

Fluctuations

Recalled from the deeps between stars by Sethvir, the Sorcerer Kharadmon knots one last twist in the maze he has spun to deflect Marak's free wraiths; grim in the hope his work will delay their incursion through the unavoidable span of his absence, he arrows across distance toward the mottled blue fleck that comprises the world of Athera . . .

At Avenor, the royal guard rides out in glittering force to search the hamlets in the countryside; galleys comb the fishing coves on the coastline, and the inner cabal meets under candlelight to report all comings and goings from the city; yet frantically as High Priest Cerebeld drives the search to recover the missing princess, he fails to find any trace . . .

A fair spider in a spun web of spellcraft, Prime Matriarch Selidie confronts the sisterhouse prioress: 'You are required to stand witness,' she pronounces, her command lent incised clarity by the phosphor array of fine sigils surrounding the enabled Great Waystone. 'Earl Jieret must be tracked. As Rathain's *caithdein*, he now bids to secure the Master of Shadow's escape. I hold the firm hope that adverse circumstances will draw Elaira in as accomplice . . .'

Late Winter 5670

IX. Caithdein

With the consummate care that marked the skills of a forest-bred clansman, Earl Jieret urged his winded pony into the stand of a hazel thicket. He broke no twigs. The respect his kind tendered toward all growing things gave apology to the frozen moss crushed under his silent step. His knowing instinct avoided loose rock. Since he had never asked more than the pony could give, it followed with herdbond trust.

The stillness man and beast wore like a cloak wove them as one with the landscape. Jieret's dull leathers blended into the gully that seamed the swale. As the pounding roll of inbound hoofbeats neared his exposed position, he stilled all fear. He did not withdraw, or huddle up and shrink inward. His woodwise heritage used Paravian wisdom, and expanded the fabric of his awareness outward, merging his humanity with the fabric of Daon Ramon until his poised presence wore the staid patience of stone.

Versed in the lore of his people since boyhood, Jieret used such ancient skills to make himself seem invisible. He stilled all thought, all concept of danger, as the band of Alliance trackers crested the barren ridgetop. Through the bustle and commotion as they overtook and swept past him, his mentor the hunted hare, the *caithdein* relied on thin camouflage: the ceaseless thrash of the wind through bare twigs broke the outline of his motionless form. Whining gusts over gorse and rock masked his horse's labored breathing. Crouched low, his face tucked deep in the hood of his

337

mantle to shadow the tone of pale flesh, he stood his ground as two enemy riders clattered a spear's length to either side of him.

Headhunters, both, the men did not speak. Vigilant and thorough as hungry predators, they quartered the ground on patrol, thrashed through the gulch, then clambered up the lichened scree that crowned the low rise beyond.

Jieret waited, immobile after they passed. He listened for the cheeps of foraging sparrows to mark the moment he could safely emerge. The triumph bought by his minuscule victory brought no smile to his set lips. Now slipped inside the vanguard of Prince Lysaer's company, his peril would vastly increase. A chance sighting or an unlucky encounter would see him cut off with no line of retreat.

He still seized a moment for the time-honored word of respect, giving thanks to the scrub growth and cragged rock whose presence had granted him shelter. He left the requisite token of offering: a strand of hair nipped from his clan braid. Yet on this day, when necessity brooked no delay and the future course of the kingdom hung on the thread of its crown prince's safety, the traditional rituals that honored the balance triggered a barrage of expanded awareness.

A wave of indescribable sensation flowed upward out of the earth. Startled by a tingling rush that blasted away equilibrium, Jieret reeled. Embraced by the clarity of conscious being, he shared the impact of his own gratitude, as plant and soil and stone acknowledged the human need in his thanks. Each spirit responded by its true nature, as doubtless it always had. Only now, the latent talents of the mage had crossed the threshold of initiation. His retuned ear heard the voice of the land speak with a living presence.

The reedy stems of dry grasses now whispered the language of wind, their summer green memories aged into wisdom. Frozen streambeds promised the cascade of fluid emotion, and their power, the catalyst to key unformed expression to the alchemy of creation. As Jieret gasped, dizzied with shock, stone steadied him, earth's presence giving the love of a mother, guiding her child's first footstep. Jieret marveled, entranced as the cradling embrace of the hazel boughs cherished him in a communal embrace.

A man could lose himself amid the loomed threads of Ath Creator's diversified joy. No singer, Jieret felt the wild urge to open his throat in a burst of unfettered laughter. As though every nerve had been painlessly stripped, he became deluged in a lucent gold sleet, as the forces inlaid through sunlight and air whirled him into their dancing spiral of regeneration.

Overset by the lure of a dangerous fascination, Jieret fought back the sweet waves of abandon. He drew a succession of steadying breaths, aware he must recover his concentration. The wonders he witnessed already blurred his prudent discernment. Under mage-sighted influence, he would regard an enemy's bared steel as a friend, seeing no more than a sorrowful ignorance in the hand that acted with hatred and malice. Temptation tore him. He could so easily marry his thoughts to the wind, casting aside the bothersome needs of survival.

Jieret shivered, jostled as his pony butted him in impatience. Perhaps the creature understood by herd instinct that its rider grazed too near the razor's edge of stark peril. A man cloaked in mage-sight perceived how a wrong word or thought could be crippling. At one with the mysteries that nurtured his very being, he faced the interlocked recognition that the mere influence of his will could unbind. Jieret realized he must disengage from his state of heightened awareness, yet the shift must be done with delicate care. His state of connection lent every choice the brute force of a sharpened impact. If he shut down the cataract of sensation through fear, his mind would accept his perception of threat, and reseal the open door after him.

He risked being blinded. Without access to mage-sight, he could never complete the worked plan that enabled Prince Arithon's escape.

'Merciful maker,' Jieret whispered. He floundered far out of his depth. Arithon had opened the keys to the mysteries, with no time given to enact proper safeguards or begin the basic sound teaching to use them.

Jieret squeezed his eyes shut. No improvement; masked sight only wakened his inward, seer's vision sprung from his talent for prescience.

Caught in unalloyed solitude, Deshir's clan chieftain crumpled to his knees as his outer perception dissolved into silvery dreamscape. Like trained adepts who could forecast at will, his refined gift reattuned to match the cascade of the lane currents. Ancient powers became manifest. Jieret beheld the vibrant, living matrix of the earth, which combed through the land in bright channels, with himself as a being of shadow and flame embedded within the flux.

His confused thoughts cast shimmering, concentric ripples. The rings fled away and collided, entangled with other sets roiling from elsewhere, their vast confluence a sea of quivering, mercuric energy. Man and beast with their stirred-up moil of emotions impressed that smoothed flow into moving spikes of interconnected response.

Jieret experienced each singular disturbance as a feather brush down his scraped skin. Split away from the familiar, solid world he had known, he felt the tug of a burgeoning undertow as senses he never knew he possessed transmitted the warning of pending danger. Unease ripped his gut as the converging flows revealed Lysaer's Alliance allies as they closed their advance to take Arithon.

Fear refined that raw vision. Jieret perceived the blood shadows of dark magics that sent the seer priests the simultaneous command to re-form their massed ranks for battle. Suspended in earth's energy like an insect on a pool, he traced the sinister change in the lane currents as armed companies paused and mustered into coordinated patterns of assault.

Ripples became arrowed waves of raw force: this marring flow from the south the ragtag guard troop from Jaelot, haltered in the tangle of the Koriani sigils that drove them under geas to attack. Farther east, another influx lit by rage and sharp vengeance, the survivors from Darkling's garrison advanced, hazed on by the comet-blaze of conviction raised by a fanatical priest.

Sharp knots in their path, the determined bands of clan scouts, standing ground to obstruct where they could. The lane's flux revealed their inadequate numbers; without mercy exposed the futility of their fierce dedication and bravery.

Desperate with grief, Earl Jieret buried his face in his hands. Though the horsy taint of his deerhide gloves touched his senses with near-painful clarity, his Sight did not change. His awareness found no firm foothold. Terror washed through him, snagging static through the flux, as again, he fought to reorient. Entrapped in deep vision, he was left vulnerable as a babe to the enemy. Though he worked himself dizzy, he found no relief. Inner sight only shifted his vantage.

Northward, he sensed the elite sunwheel companies dispatched out of Etarra. The trained ardor of the Light's foremost field troop had knit the lane's flow into an axe blade of unified purpose. Its passage razed onward, distorting all patterns found in its path. A wall of sharp minds, brought to welded purpose, eclipsed the webbed traceries of rocks and plants under a stain of penumbral shadow.

Before them, like hapless prey set to flight before the assault of beaters and hounds, the fired spark of purpose that was Braggen and three horses, bearing the spelled sword, Alithiel. His plight appeared hopeless, snagged as he was between Lysaer's advance and the inexorable crush of the Alliance's closing forces.

Jieret battled despair, that his night of high risk and desperate planning now seemed an act of futility. The rage all but seared him, that his liege's painstaking strategy might send valiant men to their deaths, all for naught.

Too late, he recalled his connection to the mysteries, as the bursting dam of his anger incised the live flux of the lane force. Instant impact slammed him to jangling discord. The crosscurrents tumbled him. Plummeted downward, as though his awareness plunged from great height, he drowned, immersed in a vast ocean of feeling.

As stone, as plant, as the body of Athera herself, he ached from the vibration of townborn feet. As the interlocked weave of sand grains and soil, he flinched to the pained grunt of spurred horses. Empathy savaged him, as thorn branch and mosses shrank from shared awareness of plant cousins callously trampled. Sucked under by the whorled tumult of distressed energies, Jieret suffered direct pain, a burning recoil lashed through mind and spirit where the companies of sunwheel men-at-arms forced their self-righteous passage. Bursting panic could not break the sequence of altered perception. His senses wheeled free. Reft from his humanity, he experienced with utmost, faithful clarity, as the wind-raked, barren hills of Daon Ramon responded in kind to the drama of hunter and prey.

Earth was anything but blind or deaf to the deeds of her two-legged inhabitants as enemy met enemy in first contact.

The moment erupted in graphic display, the whirled sparks of each man's individual being fanned into explosive conflagration. Hatred and fear launched their savage attack. The staid hills resounded to the pound of sped hearts, each flesh-and-blood drumbeat mirrored threefold in the sensitive purl of the lane pulse. The event scored the flux as a fraught cry of light, tortured to raging disharmony. Scattered before the fury of the charge, ephemeral as moving shadows, Jieret recaptured the dedicated purpose of Rathain's fleet-footed clan scouts.

His throat closed in anguish. Haplessly trapped, he stood as eyewitness, shaking with impotent grief. The Companions who survived the fell slaughter at Tal Quorin had replaced the kinship of lost family. Tragedy bound them closer than brothers. Wrung by their plight, Jieret felt the torment of hearts pressed to bursting. He ached with the burn of each desperate, fast breath. His inner mind blazed with the pain of shared fears. Fired by sympathy, his mage vision flowered into Sight.

The immediate influx of smell touched him first, a musk of sweat-lathered horses. He felt the wind next, a raw blast of biting cold. Before him, etched into a clarity like torture, he beheld his war band's best scouts, standing their ground for Rathain. Jieret braced to endure as the staunch spirits his ironbound duty had sent into trial were called to play out the sacrifice.

The moment engulfed him, as Eafinn's son's party burst out of cover as decoy, their assigned task to lure the fanatics from Darkling into a preset array of spring traps. Jieret's pulse leaped to the panic of hill ponies pounding across frozen ground. He heard the shouted command as the townbred captain wheeled his mounted lancers. The hammer of shod hooves bearing down in pursuit rocked his mind, until all other senses rang, deafened.

His gift rode him, relentless, while new mage-sight exposed the blued fire of spirit light, warped and muddied by the savagery of human will bent upon killing destruction. He flinched with the shock of steel meeting steel; felt the wrenching jar of the first woundings. Around him, the stark horrors of death and the fierce passions of the chase exploded to blazing chaos. The fury of Sithaer itself was unleashed as plant, and dumb animal, and motionless stone ignited in subtle recoil.

The warriors enclosed in the clay blindness of five senses saw only the deadened reflection: the impacting force of their actions escaped them. Snapped bone and burst flesh became as crude overlays, masking the lights of more subtle energies, whose existence played through all form. Their voice was not dumb, but mistaken for empty silence. Through the window of mage-sight, their racked pain resounded, octave upon octave above the fixed range of flesh-bound, mortal perception.

Jieret experienced the unseen devastation firsthand, felt the spill of torn life crying out for cessation and peace. But hatred stopped ears, even to the screams of the wounded who writhed dying on the chill ground. Whipped on by self-righteous convictions, the townborn poured down the ridge in a frenzied rush of pack violence. Not one checked his mount as the first horse seemed to trip on its forelegs. It tumbled, kicking. None noticed the sharpened stake through its gut, until the heightened thrill of the hunt changed to horror as the next concealed snares dropped their prey. Sharpened wood, notched with barbs, had been lashed to green saplings, bent to the ground in brute tension. No trace of tampered ground granted fair warning: the sun-crusted face of the drifts shone pristine over the buried release strings.

Earl Jieret, who had helped lay those snares himself, now

suffered the mage-sighted shock of his handiwork. He wept without voice, that he could not cry warning to enemies. By ruthless design, the trigger ropes mired the destriers' oncoming strides. Rope traps whipped taut. Horses hurled head over heels with noosed fetlocks, and their riders crashed, crushed and broken. They screamed, the potential invention of intelligent humanity reduced to burst organs and snapped bones. Their blood stained the ground as they whimpered. Enraged beyond mercy, the rear ranks rode over them, a howling storm that would not be assuaged, except by quenching cold steel in hot vengeance.

Jieret fought to breathe. Crushed under the milling storm of his visions, undone by the scope of shared suffering, he crouched, unaware, his face pressed to the earth. He could not detach. Nor could he endure, as the unraveling burn of torn life force marred the unseen world like a blighting, white mist, and the lane's pulse imploded to disharmony.

The killing raged on. Jieret suffered the full gauntlet of sorrows that left him unmanned and weeping. Each rag doll in armor who perished had Name; each crushed moss and lamed horse and chipped stone sang in pain, as death by willed violence sliced black wounds through the interlocked heart of the mysteries. Guilt choked Jieret's throat, a revulsion so deep the world's gift of free breath seemed to brand his rank tissue with self-hatred.

Nor were his personal ties dimmed or lost in the throes of expanded vision.

Earl Jieret sensed the individual desperation of the clan scouts his engineered tactics set to rout. He tasted the bitter courage of the archers waiting in ambush, who held to their obdurate discipline; who set aside fear and girded themselves with the love they held for their families. Their chieftain knew them, each man. He called their Names, helpless, while they fired their last arrows to unravel the enemy's charge. He felt them, each one, taking fatal wounds upon lance point and sword as their positions became overtaken.

Their deaths were quick, but not kind. Each man passed the Wheel aware that his sacrifice would not spare his fleeing companions. Cut down, abandoned, they spiraled into final unconsciousness, knowing their spilled blood snatched no more than the hope of diversion.

Time for Braggen with his burdensome custody of Alithiel to seize chance for the opening to slip Lysaer's cordon. Time that might win another precious league of distance for the hunted Prince of Rathain.

Earl Jieret muffled his choked-off sobs, as Eafinn's son met the same death as his father. As brave, that true spirit would pay his respects to Daelion Fatemaster twenty years younger than his late sire. Nor did his release at the turn of the Wheel absolve him of this life's responsibilities. He breathed his last agony upon ice-chill ground, unable to know if his wife of three months had quickened with the seed of a child to succeed him.

That peal of unquiet pain did not cease with the young scout's death. His sorrow endured, a cry of imbalance, recorded by stone in the stained ground beneath his torn corpse. The creatures who dined upon carrion would partake of that essence, and the winds that swirled over the site would be tainted, their song soured by unfulfilled purpose. Once, such lingering malaise had been cleansed by the rites of Paravian dancers. Now, Jieret perceived with a poignancy that striped his chilled cheeks with fresh tears: the path that promised to right the land's balance yet relied on the hands of Rathain's restored high king.

To that end, more clanblood must soak frigid earth.

'No!' The tormented whisper of Jieret's rebuttal ripped through vision and, finally, shocked him awake. Shivering in clammy runnels of sweat, he recovered his senses, curled on his knees on cold ground. For a long, wrenching moment, he could do nothing but weep for his lost equilibrium.

By the father and mother slain on the banks of Tal Quorin, he had never imagined the day he might face the temptation to reject his oathsworn heritage. 'Ah, Caolle,' he gasped. 'I never understood why you abandoned your post, until now.'

Only wind answered. Nearby, his strayed pony browsed with its reins snagged over a branch. Earl Jieret pushed to his unsteady feet. He raked up the fallen cloth of his hood, every joint in him aching.

Sore irony burned him, that he must go on, though the role his last choice had set into motion now posed an unthinkable horror. He could not turn back. Another patrol would sweep his position inside a matter of minutes. Jieret recovered his pony. He unsnarled the reins with shaking, numbed fingers, set foot in the stirrup, and mounted. A lifetime of hard training and brutal war had done nothing to harden him for the punishing crux of this moment. To gather himself and set heels to his horse required an act beyond courage.

In Daon Ramon, alone, Earl Jieret s'Valerient wrestled the shadows of blighting uncertainty. For the first time since boyhood, the demon fear gnawed him: that he might fall short as his father's son and disgrace the name of his lineage. Too real, the chance he might fail to uphold his *caithdein*'s vow to safeguard the kingdom. In Rathain's most critical hour of need, he questioned whether he lacked the fiber to master the same crisis his crown prince had faced years ago at Tal Quorin: whether he, too, could summon the will to draw steel, and kill with his mage-sight unblinded.

A league of hard riding won no foothold for peace. Earl Jieret felt as though the chill blew clear through him, where he knelt on the flint stone of a rise. Light-headed as smoke that might disperse to the wisp of a wrongly drawn breath, he tightened his left-handed grip on a shard of white quartz. The prankster gusts whipped him, starched with the forerunning hint of new snowfall. Their force slapped a reddened bloom to his cheek and wisped loosened hair from his clan braid. Rathain's *caithdein* closed the inaugural spell circle against the assault of undermining uncertainty. Across the bared rock of Daon Ramon's heartland, he enacted the rune ring Arithon had shown him in the last, darkened hours before dawn.

Jieret shivered, beyond regret for his hazardous change in decision: that his Teir's'Ffalenn had designed his instructions under the strict presumption the work would be done at safe remove from Alliance front ranks.

Regardless of placement, the lines must stay exact. Each quadrant of the inscribed figure held meaning, lens and focus to anchor his conscious intent.

'*You're laying down the steps of a ceremony,*' Arithon had said, his spare words chosen for clarity. '*My grandfather spoke this truth: that symbols created in sequenced awareness align the will on three planes. Mental, emotional, physical, your actions create the templates for thought and desire to enable manifestation. For the initiate mage, the drawing of runes sets the self in accord, preparing the channel through which invoked power will flow.*'

Yet mere language could not touch the indescribable beauty that bloomed at each stage of completed connection. Given sight to invoke the hidden fires of grand conjury, Jieret trembled, struck breathless as the heart of the mystery responded. The precisely scratched ciphers under his hands flared into actualized being. Their flame was not separate. Around him, stone and tree and iced snowdrift, the greater web of creation resurged to the spark of his human invention.

Jieret sensed his own impact, heard his sacred self in the chord of Ath's unity, a Named vessel of awareness cherished in celebration by the undivided paean of whole consciousness. Truth became etched through the nerve and the bone of him. He perceived the Wheel of Fate, birth to death, as no closed hoop, but an open spiral whose expanding coils encompassed the untamed gyre of eternity.

A man exposed to the scope of such knowing must fight to keep his hand steady. Jieret blinked back his tears, all but swept away as the thundering currents of prime power conjoined through the poised axis of his being.

The spelled circle surrounding him was little more than a crude framework made for the purpose of binding and holding an illusion. Yet its geometry held the echo of the majestic, universal design. Through its interlocked quadrants, Earl Jieret glimpsed the shimmering weave of the snake that devoured its own tail. Death and rebirth married into continuous reunion, as unseen light and consciousness danced the steps which sustained living form.

Shaken afresh by the ugly need that had set such forces in motion, Jieret sealed the outer band of the construct with invocation of the Paravian rune, *Alt*. Moment to moment, the destructive purpose he must enact became ruinously harder to sustain.

He glanced up, apprehensive, saw the flicker of movement he expected amid the patched stands of the brush. Already the ranked lines of Alliance horsemen advanced down the cleft of the valley. Men and beasts as exalted by life as himself, whose patterns of expression were unique on the loom of Ath's creation. The core truths disclosed by his opened mage-sight were not going to spare him the heat of the crucible.

Torn into anguish, Jieret sought solace in cherished memories of Strakewood. The care ran bone deep, for his clan's ancestral ground with its tangled tapestry of evergreen, its fir and its vales of broad oak. He must bend with the winds of ill fortune, even as the graceful willows which knotted their gnarled roots in the riverbanks he recalled from his boyhood.

The men today's effort must lure to their doom were whole beings who chose to embrace a dangerous ignorance. Their misled practice must never be permitted the free rein to triumph. Were the old ways to fail, Rathain's charter would be riven. No high king's rule would maintain the law and the balance. The forests that preserved Paravian mystery would fall to the stroke of the axe. Acres of greenwood would be shorn for the plow without blessing or regard for the weal of the sacrosanct wilds. The land's bounty would be broken to fuel creedless towns, whose inhabitants salved their self-blinded fear through the limitless maw of their avarice.

The unveiled face of the mysteries themselves underscored the fragile thread binding the future. Paravian presence had withdrawn. Outside the eyes of the mage-trained, or the wisdom of Ath's adepts, the high kingship's justice alone gave protection to all living things – man, animal, insect, fish or plant – as equal parts of a whole cloth. Oathsworn for life to uphold that order, a *caithdein* had no choice but to act. Jieret stamped down his heartsore reluctance. For the s'Ffalenn crown prince who carried the Fellowship's sanction; for the land he defended through selfless service, he unclenched shaking fingers and drew out the bundled silk veiling the ninth acorn, imbued with Arithon's Named essence.

He unwrapped the string ties, well warned that he handled the seeds of impending disaster. Ripped by his need to embrace Jeynsa and his sons once again – to kiss Feithan's lips a last time – Jieret cupped the swathed construct and began the innermost circle of ciphers that would frame the heart of the construct.

A minute flowed by. Another. Jieret invoked the requisite words of release, that changed binding into free partnership; schooled by a heritage of oral tradition, he made no mistakes as he traced the glyph that would call in the powers of the air. Hunter's instinct prickled his nape, insistent warning of the closing proximity of his enemies. He cut off the distraction.

Whatever occurred outside the circle must not deflect him, now. His trial by fire that morning had taught him: listen too closely to subtle intuition, and mage-sight would crash down all barriers. The hilltop where he worked had been selected for its conductive resonance. If he heeded the wayward pull of his heart, he risked being swept away by the intimate, wrenching details as his war band was reaped like chaff before the might of the Alliance advance.

For each casualty fallen, the earth mourned alike. Pressed by the destruction sown on three sides, with the force under Lysaer s'Ilessid himself closing the fourth side of the square, Earl Jieret held fast. He persisted, though the lane tides tugged and swirled, the silvered flux wracked like gale-blown ribbons to the dance of men locked in violence.

More than once, Sighted impressions leaked through. Each brought a vignette of tragedy. Jieret resteadied his shaking fingers. He gripped the quartz, and quashed back his wild grief, while three leagues to the west, Theirid's band fought a bitter engagement to win opportunity for a scant handful of scouts to slip through. Men who would scatter and lose themselves in the trackless barrens, then fight afresh for survival amid the relentless winter elements.

Jaw clamped in stark effort, Earl Jieret focused his scattered attention. He unslung his bow. From his quiver, he drew out a wrapped arrow whose point had been consecrated for revenge. Though his taste for such violence had soured beyond recourse, he freed the black shaft from its deerhide covering. Time had not warped the walnut-stained wood. The razor-steel point retained its keen edge, and its message, engraved and sealed with his own blood.

Son of Steiven s'Valerient and Dania, he had a personal debt to repay, a grim score left unsettled since Deshir's wives and children had been violated, their massacred bodies broken and burned beside Tal Quorin over three decades past. Jieret rested the arrow across his bent knees, then mustered the brute will to survey the landscape before him.

The oncoming horsemen filed down the gulch, a moving flurry of pebbled steel helms, cloaked and hooded in drab cloth and leather. The advance guard was followed by Lysaer's main company. Not a large force, but a field troop of headhunters welded by experience to mobile and deadly efficiency. They understood the terrain. Jieret noted their avoidance of scrub growth that masked sucking bogs and poor footing. They employed no voiced orders, but used hand signals alone to part ranks for an iced-over gully.

Their silent, seamless advance chilled the blood far more than the ceaseless north winds.

Moved by wary reflex, Jieret reviewed his surroundings. High overhead, a dark eagle circled, a speck against lucent silk sky. Behind, he felt as though hidden eyes watched him. Though his studied search caught no one lurking, his creeping unease would not rest. His mage-sight unveiled a queer, subdued blight cast over the rocks and bare bushes. As though the awareness of stone and live root shared his acid foreboding, and sought anonymity by dimming their essence of spirit light.

Jieret faced forward. He could ill afford to fret himself stupid over the spurious prompt of some haunt. The men in the vale would not wait on his doubts. They came on relentless, the gleam of bared steel like the glint on a reptile's scales, half-glimpsed through the thickets and bracken. This was no troop led by pedigree dandies, but a strike force of hardened killers. The officers' mounts were not plumed or caparisoned. They spurned war medallions and trinkets. For their badge of prowess, the headhunters from Narms preferred a fringe of cured clan scalps sewn to the edge of their saddlecloths.

Only an act of impeccable timing might disarm such ruthless dedication.

The riders were now a long bowshot away. Jieret could discern faces, bearded chins tucked into wool mufflers. He could count weapons. Some carried short bows tucked into scabbards hung from the horns of their saddles. Others preferred lightweight lances, or bludgeons to brain fleeing quarry from a gallop. Jieret had seen every ugly way to die, written into the flesh of kinsmen and friends cut down for the claim of town bounties. Clammy sweat slicked his shirt to his skin. Any crack archer who handled a horn recurve might spot him for an exposed target. Jieret hunkered down with his back to the hillcrest, trusting thin cover and stillness to hide him. He held his ground, locked in stonecast patience, while the gaps in the gusts brought the jingle of mail and the snorts of the enemy horses.

Nor did his selected prey stay elusive: the gold-sewn, light figure set at the troop's forefront shone through the drab brush like white flame.

In arrogant disregard for the savage terrain; a bald-faced declaration that eschewed every sensible tactic, Lysaer s'Ilessid rode resplendent in glittering gold braid, spurs and bullion trappings buffed to a brilliant, high polish. The effrontery mocked. His palace courtier's dress offered the open invitation to make his sunwheel surcoat a target. Cut the head off the snake, and the coiled hatreds that drove Alliance policy would lose their coordinated purpose. Arithon of Rathain would be set free, with Desh-thiere's curse deprived of its focus.

Even without the conflicts of mage-sight, Jieret would not have succumbed. Clan marksmen from Tysan had been first to learn that the Divine Prince could raise light in protection against mortal arrows. Today's blinding opulence offered the brazen invitation to display such invincible power.

Jieret laid bow and arrow within easy reach, well aware the success of his effort now hinged on the powers of grand conjury.

He must act by rote, steered step by step by his trust in Arithon's trained knowledge. Any unforeseen departure, no matter how slight, could unbind the plan laid to spare the prince and Rathain's clan survivors. Jieret picked up the quartz shard and scratched out, one by one, the innermost circle of figures. He sensed energies like pressure, grazing his skin. Small winds licked heat at his fingers. Though aware of the vortex of unseen movement turning inside the marked space, he lacked understanding of the forces he handled. For the strike prearranged to deflect Desh-thiere's curse, the delicate strictures of check and balance had been instilled into formula. The steps framed a summons of appeal to the elements, a linked chain of command dangerously harnessed to the quickened awareness of powers so raw, their rising punched Jieret's gut like a fist.

Vertigo raked him, tinged by nausea. His ears seemed to crackle with subliminal sound, as though strayed pulses of charge played over his aura. He felt saturated. Like the slosh of a bucket brimful of stirred liquid, the primal potential of unformed event threatened to shatter his inner balance.

More terrified of that strangeness than of straightforward death by enemy steel, Jieret laid his petition to engage the winds into the central ciphers. He asked a permission, then observed the startling wonder of his need, granted. A flare of fine light flowed in from the scribed mark at east, and spread subtle fire throughout the hoop of laid runes. The experience raised a shudder of gooseflesh. Jieret resisted the seductive pull of an awe that whirled him to distraction. Within a thickening glue of poised forces, he invoked Prince Arithon's Name. Then he asked the power of wind to conjoin with his plea and become catalyst in defense of Daon Ramon.

A gust flicked his cheek, sharp affirmation his appeal had drawn a response. One last step, and the ending rune of release would engage the finished construct; the dire coil that Arithon's trained mind had conceived, and which now relied on his *caithdein's* talents as cat's-paw to enact into manifestation.

There, Jieret languished, doused in a cold sweat. He could not avoid one last, fatal glance to gauge the pace of the advance riders. They were close enough, now, that line of sight could pick out their individual preferences: the jaunty set to this man's chin, and the wry laugh of another who joked to chaff at a disgruntled companion.

Jieret caught back his breath in wringing dismay. At the cusp of the moment, he could not shake the horror of the act his given word must commit. He could not dissemble, or evade the harsh truth, that the horsemen were sadly misguided. Despite hatred and prejudice, they were no less a part of the splendor of Ath's creation. They had mothers and daughters and brothers and wives, just as the forest-bred war band who fled from their weapons of slaughter. The fine difference, that clanblood could treat with Paravians, scarcely justified the violent rending of life.

In the wholeness of mage-sight, a man was a man, no matter the choices that shaped his beliefs or his origins.

Teir's'Valerient though he was, sworn to a blood-bonded legacy, Jieret found himself utterly unable to seal the spell's final closure. The forces of deception and death hanging poised offended all life, not just these victims who marched under Lysaer's sunwheel banner.

A stunned second passed, followed by another. A fleeting few moments, and the opening would pass to enact the sole course of strategy. Jieret cursed through locked teeth. Necessity demanded. Lives stood at risk. Even the certainty of Prince Arithon's death failed to sting him back to conviction. His grip on the quartz shard went nerveless and numb.

The memory resurged and stabbed through like vengeance, that once, he had drawn the black sword Alithiel and compelled his liege to complete an equally untenable strategy. Unmanned by horror, Arithon had pleaded; and for the ugly charge of an oath to guard his liege's given integrity, Jieret had used the sword's power and broken him.

Now, when the drive of Desh-thiere's curse threatened more innocent lives, no implacable hand bearing the threat of spelled steel pricked at the *caithdein*'s back. Jieret stood alone. Against stripping doubt, he had only Arithon's trust, the sworn covenant of a mage-bond, and shared love of a measure to humble. The clan chieftain knelt, his head rested on his slack forearms. Unable to master himself, he could not recoup his sapped will, even to raise his strung bow. He coughed back bitter tears. The shame rocked his core, and past record seemed inconceivable: *that his prince had owned the magnanimous heart to forgive him for forcing his unwilling hand to an act of slaughter and mayhem.* When, to avert a disastrous war, the fleet brought to bear Lysaer's war host to Merior had been charred to ruin on the waves of Minderl Bay.

'Move, call out, touch a weapon, and you die!' cracked a voice in townborn accents.

Jieret started. He suppressed the raw reflex to rise, just barely. Instinct had been accurate. *He had been watched.* At the corner of his vision, he picked out the whipcord-lean captain sighting him over the glint of a spanned steel quarrel. The man had dark hair and eyes like chipped ice. The commander's badge stitched to his shoulder seemed merited. Jieret must defer to the ruthless, cool poise in the hands that aimed the cocked crossbow.

'Stand up. Very slowly.' No fear in that order; only competence that made retribution a certainty.

Acute peril shattered Jieret's deadlocked indecision. Finality faced him. If he crossed the Wheel, cut down by a quarrel, his fall must seal Arithon's death. Pulse racing as panic threatened to darken the pitched sensitivity of his mage-sight, the Earl of the North bent his head. No need to feign the shock of defeat as he tightened his hold on the quartz shard. His shaking limbs would not let him stand upright. All options were forfeit but one. Jieret inscribed the Paravian cipher for ending and closed the inner, spelled circle. Then, as though pleading for Dharkaron's deliverance from the enemy holding him cornered, he whispered the last words of release.

'Stand up, I said!' barked the townborn commander. 'Or lie there stone dead with my steel through your neck. You won't gain by delay. Your henchmen can't save you. My trackers made certain before I closed in. You're alone, Red-beard, and bound for your overdue reckoning at the hand of the Blessed Prince.'

Jieret sealed the incantation. He lifted his head. Turning his body in feigned surrender, he masked the critical, trailing finger that snagged off the loose twist of silk. The acorn imbued as the Teir's'Ffalenn's fetch rolled free of its protective covering. The cleared charge of its presence keyed the spelled circle active. The kick of connection as bound force locked with catalyst flared through Jieret's body, a brief, leaching burn of meshed energies.

The man bearing the crossbow stiffened. Perhaps rankled by an unsettled shift in the breeze, or a hint of latent talent, he somehow marked the shocked, lucid moment as the elements aligned before cataclysm.

Earl Jieret stood erect, a weaponless target. Blind instinct screamed warning: his harmless appearance would not disarm the adversary now primed to kill him. Through a howling force like a vast, indrawn breath, and the cry of raised mysteries, mage-sensed, he provoked, 'Have Lysaer take my personal reckoning, instead.'

The crossbow twanged in release. Timed to the same second, the ritually laid circles relinquished the amplified signature of Arithon's Named presence to be winnowed on the random play of the winds.

Light answered.

Not the gentled fires of raised spellcraft, but the annihilating blaze of Desh-thiere's curse unleashed in ferocious hatred.

Already set on hair-trigger edge, Lysaer s'Ilessid lashed out with his gift on the surge of animal reflex.

The coruscation ripped through the winter air like forge-heated steel plunged screaming into white ice. The bolts struck too closely spaced to assimilate. Rattled by the drumroll concussion, shaken bone from bone by the booming reports as the hills rocked and slammed under punishment, Jieret scarcely knew whether the crossbolt ripped over his head, or if wood, feather, and forge-sharpened steel had been reduced by instantaneous immolation.

For that moment, Lysaer's fury consumed all the world. His howling screams meshed with the shriek of hurled balefire. Spurred by the illusion, driven wild by the surety that his half brother's being *surrounded him*, the Blessed Prince gave vent to the full range of his powers. Again and again, the bright levin bolts rained down. The teasing winds bearing their illusion whirled and parted, unmoved by the turmoil as he extended himself to obliterate his nemesis in a murderous fit of possessed hatred.

The blasts seared across Daon Ramon's seamed hilltops. Jieret cowered, knocked flat by their unleashed violence. Though the protection of the elements raised to guard point within the outermost ring of his circle spared his life, he could not dissociate from the killing shock to the land.

Snow sheared into steam. Brush and briar torched in conflagration. While the concussive reports slammed and battered the ground, ancient bedrock exploded and burst. Fragments kicked aloft, smelted to run lava that fused into teardrop nuggets of black slag. The grip of Desh-thiere's curse subjugated its victim with a force that canceled all mercy. More than once, Jieret had borne witness to horror: he had seen the last trace of humanity extinguished from Arithon's eyes.

Lysaer was all the more sorrowfully vulnerable, lacking the course of arduous self-discipline Rauven's mages had instilled in his half brother. The s'Ilessid prince had no resource to grapple the twisted obsession that drove him. That pitiless consequence Arithon had foreseen, and turned to his hand as a weapon. His knowledge and Jieret's fresh talent had been conjoined to raise fiendishly inventive devastation. 'The sense of my presence will prod from all sides, an irresistible provocation. Desh-thiere's geas will triumph at a stroke. Lysaer will lose all reason. He might well be pressed to expend himself until he drops from exhaustion.'

The massive assault did not recognize limits. The rage stirred to life by the windblown essence of the fetch kept up its jabbing aggravation, invoking the cursed mind to still more desperate response. Lysaer went mad. Trusted friends assumed the appearance of foes. No matter how loyal, the neat ranks of Alliance horses and men were shown no grace of reprieve. The light razed their brave ranks at a stroke. Jieret coughed on blown smoke. His stomach clenched from the stench of charred meat.

'Ath show them mercy!' he ground out through a flattening spasm of nausea.

Yet no piercing regret could ever reverse the consequence of his action. On all sides, the land raged in wildfire, stitched through by sheet lightning and levin bolts. Narms's headhunter company was already consumed. Memory and flesh, their corpses were winnowed to carbon and ash, lost before they could draw breath and scream.

More mercifully dead than the raped clanswomen and girls, once burned alive in Deshir; yet peace did not come. The last bolt whiplashed the sultry sky. Its harsh, slapping echoes rolled over the hills blasted to waste and black char, and then faded. Stillness returned, more dreadfully empty than the stunned quiet after an earthquake. Jieret propped himself on one elbow. For the sake of the incised black arrow that waited, he dared to survey the vista left by his handiwork.

A lone fleck, pristine white against ravaged landscape, Lysaer crouched, undone. At some point, he must have dismounted. Collapsed on his knees in dangerous proximity to the skittering hooves of his charger, he still clutched his reins out of habit. The gold sunwheel emblazoned on the breast of his mantle invited the arrow that would finish him.

Jieret swallowed. The merest thought of drawing his bow stitched his gut into wrenching distress.

The remorse in the hunched s'Ilessid shoulders was too human, the fair face laid bare by revulsion that damned with too honed an edge of stark truth. Despite the past cruelties embedded within the campaigns launched at Tal Quorin and Vastmark; regardless of proof, that Lysaer's brilliant statesmanship could effortlessly reclothe ugly facts in self-righteous lies, the *caithdein* of Rathain could not evade his own callous manipulation. The s'Ilessid gift of justice and Desh-thiere's warped curse had become his ready tools to cast his own drama of purging destruction.

Even for Rathain, the price came too high. The leveling unity exposed by his mage-sight unstrung the illusion of vengeance.

Amid blighting drifts of smoke and whipped ash, through the actinic flares left scored by each light bolt's aftershock, Jieret beheld the wisped haze of spirit light ripped out by the trauma as each victim perished. Like a lingering malady, he tasted the acid despair of every man's unfulfilled dreams. He ached for their grief, crying their wordless woe for the beloved families the Alliance crusade of false justice had left abandoned and fatherless.

His throat knotted, Jieret called on the force of bare will and closed his hand on the strung bow. His integrity as *caithdein* was the lynchpin for a kingdom, in a strategy that must not fail. If he folded to shame, these deaths would become but the first wave of casualties in an unraveling chain of disaster. Compassion for life could not exonerate him. He guarded the very threshold of hope, a short step from the act that would free his crown sovereign from the perils of Desh-thiere's vengeance. One stroke would secure Prince Arithon's safety, and unshackle a future that relied on restored charter law.

Jieret reached in resolve. He touched the black arrow, and cried out, jerked back by the burn of his own hatred. The energy coiled like unclean filth into the steel of the broadhead. He saw rage and cruelty: long years of unreleased grief for his mother and sisters, slowly twisted into a whispering poison. The taint stained the fiber of feather and twine, a man's dark domination of innocent wood, whose place in Ath's order served no cause and no purpose beyond an abiding peace without word for suffering bloodshed.

The dichotomy snapped him. Convulsed in a silenced, agonized sob, Jieret abandoned the arrow. He could no more have wielded the bow in his hand than he could have knifed his own child.

No moment could yield a more wretched exposure as the muffled clank of a crossbow's cranked ratchet sawed through drifted smoke and stunned quiet.

Jieret flung himself prostrate. Tear blinded, near helpless, he realized his enemy must have sheltered beneath the rock rim of the hillcrest. He lay flat, pulse racing. Torn nerves and outraged senses still stressed him to gasping vertigo. He could not grip his sword. One attempt, and his gut seized to cramps at the barest touch of forged steel. Ripped prostrate by gagging spasms of nausea, he realized muscle and nerve would not harken to the bald-faced demands of survival. Defenseless as a babe before the thundering chord that called him to rejoin Ath's unity, Jieret wept for his daughter and wife. His tears fell as bitter for the prince yet to pay the fatal cost of his weakness.

'Brother, forgive me,' he whispered in shame.

For answer, a loose rock scraped at his back. The shriek of steel cable as the crossbow released tore through the blameless song of the breeze. Jieret accepted the hammering whap as the bolt ripped into his shoulder. Smashed facedown on chill stone, the let flood of his bleeding a tortured echo struck through the weave of the lane flux, he found the grounding spike of raw pain an almost welcome relief.

He coughed, spitting gravel. Dizziness raked him in beating, black waves. Through ebbing senses, he heard his enemy's footsteps stumble upon his array of scribed runes and spelled circles.

'Don't cross the line,' Jieret warned, eyes pinched shut against the spasm of agony that wrenched him to shuddering paralysis. 'Enough killing's done.'

But the sunwheel officer's stunned exclamation overrode his whispered protest. 'Light save us all! You're no clan fugitive, but Shadow's damned henchman, and a sorcerer!'

'Don't cross the circle,' Jieret begged. If he would die a failure, let him not go with more spell-wrought deaths on his conscience.

'I'll do more than cross,' his enemy snapped back. 'I'll erase every unclean line of your works, and destroy the fell seed of your conjury.'

Movement; a grate of kicked gravel, then an eddy of breeze acrid with carbon brushed across Jieret's exposed cheek. Then mage-sight exploded in a shower of sparks as the armed towns-man scuffed out the first line, with the command for a ritual cleansing. 'Avert!'

'No,' Jieret protested, to no avail. The first circle was breached. The second was already half-scrubbed away under his enemy's industrious heel. Shortly only the innermost circle remained, with the acorn construct left forlorn on its bed of weathered stone.

'Don't.' But the *caithdein*'s desperate plea passed unnoticed.

The Lord Commander of the Light's faithful erased that final, frail barrier. Protective spells crumpled, a sheet-thin failing of light unveiled by the torn shreds of Jieret's mage-sight. He saw no explosion, heard no clap of backlash. Yet around him, the barrens went utterly still as the mazing runes that had masked the location of Arithon's conjured fetch broke away.

Absorbed by his crude exorcism of spells, Avenor's Lord Commander never glanced down the hillside. The change passed unnoticed, as the white-clad figure straightened up from devastated collapse. If Sulfin Evend heard his Blessed Prince's ravaged cry, he paid no more heed than he gave the gasped warning from the barbarian chieftain his quarrel had wounded.

As the sparking burn of Lysaer's raised light once again seared across the sky and earth, blinding Jieret's dazed sight, the Lord Commander raised his spurred boot. He stamped down on the acorn. The fragile shell smashed. Its delicate, spelled contents sprang into release, and a rune of stasis unraveled. Grand conjury met and matched preset patterns of intent, as the intricate, wound spring of Arithon's last line of defense spells unfurled, beyond any man's power to recall.

Eagle's Eye View

Shadow erupted, a scrolled spiral of jet ink that uncoiled in release from the remnants of the crushed acorn. From the eagle's high vantage, circling above, the darkness expanded, whirling into a maw that encompassed Lysaer's deluging blast like caught magma. Light, shade, and the inset directives of masterfully laid magics interlocked with a bestial howl. Unlike other clashes provoked by Desh-thiere's curse, the darkness did not seek to smother the coruscating bursts. This counterflare of shadow had been tempered by spelled ciphers that bent and funneled the light bolts with capturing force. Lysaer's assault became whirled into a needlepoint focus as it struck its intended target: the eggshell remains of the acorn, and the mica construct bound in black hair that wore the pattern of Arithon's Named essence.

That blasting intervention became all that spared the two enemies locked in their crisis of contention. Both the Alliance commander and the clanblood chieftain shot down by the bolt from his crossbow escaped the horror of instantaneous incineration. Swathed and shielded under those veils of risen dark, they were the fortunate ones.

For the light hammered into that conjured bait did not disperse into flash-fire heat. A crafty intervention by set wards of grand conjury grappled the aggressive impetus of Lysaer's unsheathed gift and engaged a locked glyph imprinted with its matched opposite: the barbs of compulsion Desh-thiere's curse had twisted through Arithon's aura. Hate fused with like hatred. Across space and time, the light bolts exploded, raging. The spelled lure that drew them raised the unslaked fury of years to a storm of mindless annihilation.

Across the winter hills of Daon Ramon Barrens, eight other acorn constructs responded. Fused into unity outside the veil, the fetches of Arithon's presence responded as *one*. The blind-fold directive of the Mistwraith's geas could not discriminate between states of existence to separate one clever construct from the next. Nor had Lysaer's intent as he struck encompassed the possibility that his marked quarry would be split *manyfold*.

Yet the eagle's lofty perspective unveiled the full breadth of the defenses wrought by Rathain's prince and his *caithdein*. The conjoined finesse of a master's trained knowledge, and the fresh exuberance of Jieret's wakened mage talent, diverted Lysaer's attack across time and space. The blasting coruscation smashed with obliterating force into each of the eight enspelled acorns. Their bearers, fallen, or living and hounded to flight, bore the flash-burn brunt of the impacts. Whether flying in retreat, or locked in mortal combat, men were razed, willy-nilly, where they stood.

The sprawled, broken body of Eafinn's son ignited, along with the sly-faced tracker from Darkling, paused to harvest a barbarian scalp and cash in on the mayor's bounty. The headhunter band with him danced, set aflame, horses and humans screaming in raw-throated agony.

Two leagues farther east, the spelled company from Jaelot became torched. Their unfortunate officer had cut Theirid's clan braid. Paused to stuff the trophy in his saddle pack, he died, blazing, along with his mounted escort. Not a dead man among them ever guessed the acorn tucked into the rag knotting the barbarian's hair had been anything more sinister than a talisman worn as a luck charm.

Of the southbound ranks from Etarra, none perished; but the well-knit course of their advance burst into harrowed disarray as other acorns planted across their line of march erupted to rocketing sheets of white balefire. Wind-borne sparks seeded a wall of burning brush across the countryside. Some of Jieret's clan war band escaped through the gaps, saved by the opportune evasion as the enemy's scorched ranks came unraveled. Others in pitched battle seized on their chance as the roiling pall of smoke broke the nerve of well-disciplined mounts, and hazed the Alliance host into reeling retreat. Others died in the merciless, red rage of skirmish. Sword to sword, closed into a jostling ring, the townborn locked weapons with screaming clan foes left no choice but to fight to the death. Jieret's scouts stood their ground, back-to-back. They cut and slashed, grimly knowing, as the air in their midst exploded to shrieking flame and bright lightning. The ten who still stood on their weary feet burned. Irreplaceable lives set forfeit to buy the most bitter of victories: they charred, having lured their Alliance enemies to share terrible doom through their oathbound ties to the Light, and the darker obsessions of battle frenzy and bloodlust.

Where no spelled acorn had been set to cause mayhem, the ranks of the townborn scattered in wailing fear, unsure if the levin bolts might strike them next. They cowered, or fled, or wept where they stood, unmanned by their terror of treacherous black sorcery, and the rampaging conflagrations that had unraveled their stern strength and immolated brave officers and companions.

High above the smoke, and the fires, and the screams, where the winds blew untainted, the golden eagle still circled. His farsighted vision tracked the hellbound flight of clan riders, and singled out the furtive bearer of a spelled sword wrapped in leather. That one drove two saddled remounts at a relentless gallop, his determined course bent northwestward. A blink, and the bird watched man's doings no more, but traced the distressed lane forces purling across the smoldering vales and scorched earth. His Sorcerer's perception soon found what he sought: a dissonant, edged whine that sawed through the barren's chill silence. The eagle banked, following.

Landscape unreeled beneath each driving wingbeat, tracing that streamer of strayed energies back to its original source. The disturbing current emanated from a gap between hills, an unclean residue left in the wake of the fires still charring the bones of Jaelot's ill-fated garrison. The geas of forced intent that had warped their behavior now drifted free, left unmoored when the slain captain's spirit crossed over Fate's Wheel.

This time, the enchantress whose awareness rode under the eagle's protection raised thought in shocked distaste.

'That's an uncleared remnant of a Koriani sigil! No doubt some botched effort of Lirenda's to avenge herself on Arithon s'Ffalenn. Her attempt to cause harm using preemptive spellcraft was certainly never sanctioned.'

The eagle returned a stripped fact in reply. *'Your Prime Matriarch was displeased enough to reassign the enchantress to a stint of unranked service at Highscarp's sisterhouse.'*

'Did she?' Elaira's rejoinder shimmered with rueful amusement. *'Well then, Lirenda's unlikely to humiliate herself further by petitioning the old peeress there for the leave time to disperse these embarrassing remains.'*

Sorcerer and enchantress were both well aware those loose ends posed a potential danger. Unless ruled by a banishing, such unattached sigils could settle upon a man wit-lost in drink, or attach to some unguarded traveler. A forge-fire spark touched the eagle's sharp eyes. His opinion came razored with sarcasm. *'Shall we provoke? I'd say your colleague deserves a comeuppance for slipshod practice and arrogance.'*

The question did not beg any grace of permission. Without pause for Elaira's considered response, the bird banked again. Icy winds keened through taut feathers as he abandoned his lazy circling. The seared, corpse-strewn landscape unreeled beneath his sharp plunge.

A fast-moving scrap of suncast shadow, the eagle swooped down upon snow-patched hills, then over the smoldering waste of acres blackened to carbon. The steady beat of his wings whipped the brush, still streaming the sulfurous smoke of spent wildfires. His path leveled over the gulches where the maimed and the fallen still bled, writhing in nooses and spring traps, then skimmed toward the razed hillcrest where Rathain's wounded *caithdein* lay sprawled at the feet of an Alliance commander. In wicked certainty that Elaira's presence would be the tracked lure for Prime Selidie's scryers at Whitehold, Davien bent the roundabout course of his passage directly across the keening roil of Lirenda's illicit spellcraft.

In far-off Highscarp, a single lit candle challenged the gloom in the Matriarch's chamber of audience. The daylight flooding the wide, breakfront windows lay muffled behind velvet curtains, while six senior seeresses tracked Davien's flight through an oval obsidian mirror. Following each twist and turn of his progress, Selidie Prime stiffened in sudden censure.

She expelled a hissed breath, then flicked a finger to the prioress standing as witness. 'What is initiate Lirenda's assignment on the sisterhouse duty roster?'

'She assists our fifth-rank senior sealing fiend banes.' A small, wizened woman rendered bone thin by strict service, the aged prioress had outworn her tolerance for inferiors with rival intelligence. Years of jostling for rank had resharpened her antagonism to a consummate arsenal of tact. 'An eighth-rank's trained knowledge has been a great blessing to Saytra, whose hands suffer pain in cold weather.'

Selidie stroked the delicate nail of her forefinger down the curve of one flawless cheek. 'Lirenda's discipline, sadly, does not match her abilities. When this scrying finishes, you'll send summons in my name and appoint another assistant for Saytra. Lirenda will be referred to me for an audience. Henceforward, I will take on the selection of her assignments.'

'Your will,' murmured the prioress, disconcerted and unsure whether the change had gone in her favor.

Like every ranking senior at Whitehold, she had learned to step softly before the Matriarch's quicksilver temperament. One moment Selidie might order the attentive company of a dozen seniors; at the next breath, she was likely to send them all packing with a peremptory demand for privacy. No way to forecast which way the storm blew; the clear, girlish features saffron lit by the candle were an immaculate, expressionless doll's. Selidie had depths to her no one dared touch. From the shining, pinned knot of her marigold hair, to the tip of each manicured finger, the new Matriarch bore the weighty mantle of prime power with inscrutable, adamantine authority.

Today's close examination of events in Daon Ramon showed no sign of cessation.

'Stay with that eagle,' Selidie commanded her assembled circle of scryers. Tight focus restored, she resettled herself on her tasseled hassock, the gleaming gold sigils stitched into her overskirt set adrift on a tissue of silver muslin. The grape-colored velvet of the garment beneath melted without seam into a darkness that swallowed her slippered toes. At the Prime's knee, surrounding the dusky polish of the scrying slab framed in its lion-foot stand, the six seniors who shouldered her bidding remained submerged in linked trance. Their faces set wax in congealing shadow, they breathed in tuned unison against a silence that hung dense as soaked felt.

The entrained flow of images they channeled from Daon Ramon described a horrific contrast of destruction and tumult. Where the eagle's flight skimmed, the raised fires of Lysaer's wrath had fanned a scorched vista, strewn with the smoking, charred ribs of hapless small animals and deer. The seared meat of downed horses pinned the grisly, scorched corpses of riders with faces beyond recognition; men fallen with blackened, fragmented finger bones still obscenely wedded with the melted lumps of steel weapons. The worn stone of the hills had been blasted to slag, a feat not seen since the wars in the Age of Dragons.

'Such bald-faced effrontery!' Selidie murmured. 'He won't escape consequence, this time.' The back of one hand pressed to her mouth to mask a spasm of sickened distaste, she chose not to qualify which male offender had provoked her scathing comment. She might have condemned the hand of the killer, or the ferocious cleverness of the plan that had engendered first provocation, or even, the Sorcerer masked in the form of the eagle who steered his willful course through the carnage.

If Davien was her malefactor, he showed no concern. A powerful wingbeat drove him beyond the crest where Earl Jieret was presently being bound hand and foot by his Alliance captor.

Neither man had come through the conflict unscathed. The obsidian mirror showed singed clothing and livid weals where exposed skin had scalded to blisters. Jieret squinted and cringed, as though blinded. The grate of the embedded bolt in his shoulder drove him near witless with pain.

Sulfin Evend fared better, since his placement at the moment the light bolts had struck had set him at the nexus of the spell that released Arithon's contained shielding of shadow. His immediate belongings had not escaped. The wooden stock of his crossbow had subsumed to hot coals. His horse was cooked meat for the crows. The scrying mirror flung back his ripe curse, spiked with his pedigree Hanshire accent.

'Ah, excellent, we can hear them.' Selidie's triangular smile showed teeth, and her view of the glass, a hungry cat's fascination.

'Why not just kill me?' Earl Jieret provoked in a forced gravel whisper. 'I won't walk one step, though you force me, and I'm too awkward to pack on your back.'

'You'll be dragged, then,' Sulfin Evend snapped, surly as he discovered his spoiled boots, holed through by hot ash and cinders. 'Death here and now is too tidy for you, Red-beard. You'll taste the fire and sword as a sorcerer, but before that day comes, we'll be bargaining. Let's see what value you bring as a hostage to reel in the Spinner of Darkness.'

'Wasted effort,' Jieret insisted, broken off by a grunt of taut pain as his enemy rolled him onto his back, then looped his tied forearms with a half hitch. 'His Grace of Rathain is far beyond reach, and unlikely to return as your sacrifice.'

'So we'll see.' Sulfin Evend adjusted the drag rope over his shoulder, then leaned into the burden of hauling the chieftain behind him as deadweight. 'If nothing else, there are merchants in Etarra who would pay in gold coin for the spectacle of your execution.'

Selidie clapped her hands in sharp glee. 'Oh, excellent! We might see this bait taken.' She gave the Highscarp prioress's blank look the contempt of her explanation. 'If Elaira breaks down and frees Earl Jieret, she'll disarm the new threat to Prince Arithon. But then we'll have Rathain's *caithdein* bound to us under a Koriani oath of debt. We, and not Lysaer, will hold claim on the pawn to draw in and trap the s'Ffalenn bastard.'

'Should we trouble?' Despite the chill in the fireless chamber, the prioress found her palms sweating. 'The wretched royal bastard's already doomed, set to flight like a rabbit in Daon Ramon.'

'But you're wrong,' Prime Selidie contradicted. A fair spider centered within her spun web, she stroked the enamel face of the scrying glass with eager satisfaction. 'The Master of Shadow has become this world's most powerful bargaining chip. Take him, and we'll break the Fellowship's will, then wrest our order free of the compact.'

Hostage

Earl Jieret endured the jouncing, rough transit, too dazed with pain to separate the scrapes of sharp rocks from the raking gouge of razed roots as the Alliance Lord Commander towed his captive bulk over the gulches. If the thorns of furze scrub and briar ripped him bloody, the burns inflicted by his grazing encounter with Lysaer's light bolts overwhelmed every other sensation. The raw flesh of his face raged and stung as though put to the torch. Each slight breath of wind, even the wan spill of winter sunshine, hazed his seared skin and lashed up a flood of bright agony. Faint from shock and blood loss, Rathain's *caithdein* bit back shredding screams as the bite of the crossbow bolt grated and lodged deeper into the bone of his shoulder.

The rare patch of iced snow left him scratched, soaked, and gasping. No horror of war had ever savaged him like this. The few times he blacked out, the mercy was brief. Through spinning, patched senses, his awareness ebbed and surged back into brutal, clear focus. The unending blindness did not lift. The ghastly realization undid him, that the conflagration must have spoiled his eyesight. Scouring tears welled through his shut lids like white lye, beyond any power to subdue.

Hope died, that he could find any reprieve. The death that might save him lay pitifully beyond reach. Jieret struggled, dazed as a fish on a line. Exhaustion drained him. The unbearable interval ground on and on, filled by the abrasive buffet of wind, the unending barrage of his agony strung through by the chink of Sulfin Evend's roweled spurs.

The cessation of movement brought no relief. Vertigo made the ground seem to heave underneath him. He lay, sick and panting, while hearing delivered snatched fragments of speech that his paralyzed mind could not fathom. More helpless with misery than any man born should endure and still keep breathing life, he sprawled limp. Every muscle felt pulled, and each tendon, flayed bare. Pain mantled him under a suffocating blanket, until the pressed weight of his suffering drilled his skull like a sieve and scattered his thoughts like spilled water.

Then hands grasped his clothing. He was propped partly upright. The explosion of hurt left him heaving and stupid. The world spun, with his body soaked clay, nipped and tugged by demonic fingers. Cold kissed his skin, then the tip of a knife blade probed like a ruby-hot poker.

'No choice,' snapped a voice. 'We'll just have to tend this.'

His shoulder was pinned in a grip like locked shackles. He flinched and whimpered, too wretched to choke back his animal screams as the buried steel bolt was cut free of the muscle, then the flange of the point pried from its wedged seat in his collarbone.

The brutal round of cautery that followed half killed him. For time beyond bearing, Jieret lay on his side, heaving and panting and broken past sanity by the stink of his own seared flesh.

Footsteps went and came again. Ruthless handling pried his mouth open. A tin cup rapped his teeth. Ice-chilly water slopped into his mouth, bitter sharp with the taste of ashes and the rusted tang of rinsed blood; evidently he had bitten his tongue, unawares. He choked; received a pounding slap on the back that cleared his throat and forced the unwilling reflex to swallow.

'Dharkaron's black vengeance!' he gasped through the ache as the cold reamed a pit in his belly.

'Damned well not!' snapped the Lord Commander in his clipped, Hanshire accent. 'Light as my witness, you hell-spawned demon, I'm going to see that you live.'

Jieret lay limp through the jostling discomfort of bandaging. Even without sight, he was astute enough to recognize an expert field dressing. The last chance extinguished, that he might pass Fate's Wheel by the grace of inept treatment and wound fever.

'My liege, forgive,' he implored as his senses revolved and slid over the brink, into spiraling darkness. Hindsight blistered with undying shame, that he had not thought to turn steel on himself and take the clean end that Arithon's last words had pleaded.

*   *   *

Jieret drifted in and out of pain-soaked dreams and brief periods of blackout sleep. When he woke, stiff and aching, the gnawing cold told him full night had finally fallen. The wind had shifted. Rising gusts from the north wore the keen scent of storm beneath the pall of charred brush. A crisp dryness burned his nostrils, clear warning of impending snowfall. Still bound hand and foot, he lay on his side. A wool blanket mantled his throbbing shoulder, soaked in the heat thrown off by a nearby campfire. To judge by the lessened sting to his skin, his burned face had been eased with grease salve, and a wet cloth swathed his light-scalded eyes.

Hearing informed him he was not alone. Another casualty moaned and shivered to his left, apparently delirious with fever. To judge by the oaths spat in flat Hanshire accents, the Alliance Lord Commander disliked his role of nursemaiding disabled prisoners.

Jieret heaved in a taxed breath. Though his parched larynx felt lined in ground grit, he made a rasping effort at speech. 'You could simplify matters, and just cut our throats.'

'Sithaer's demon minions!' came the ripping reply. A deadened thump shook the ground, as though a saddle or horse pack was cast down in a burst of irritation. 'I don't like spooning gruel, and I won't have your lump-head barbarian opinion concerning the fate of your betters!'

Made thick by discomfort, Jieret took a moment to unriddle the cause of the Hanshireman's pungent language. 'Oh, that's rich.' He wheezed, unable to stifle his barked laughter. The fit was short-lived. Aggravation wakened the ache in his shoulder and seized up his laboring chest. When the spasm unlocked, he resorted to words, which hurt just as much. 'You couldn't be suggesting that your daisy-faced godling has collapsed from overexcitement?'

'Let him hear you say that, he'd clip out your tongue!' The flint snap to Sulfin Evend's response gave rise to a revelation.

Jieret understood, with bleak joy, that he was not helpless after all. Amiable as the shark set at large among fry, he prodded, 'Why? Should s'Ilessid fear my voice? Or did his fair coloring mislead even you? Surely you know the sordid truth.'

The clink of Sulfin Evend's spurs hesitated, as though he froze between steps.

Into the dawning suggestive pause, Jieret punched out his surgical riposte, 'No one told you that Lysaer s'Ilessid is half brother to Arithon s'Ffalenn?'

A hard, disturbed silence, filled by the wail of fell winds, then the sickbed whimper of the invalid alongside, *who had to be Lysaer*, stricken prostrate by massive overuse of his gift. Presupposing that backlash had inflamed the s'Illessid to an imbalanced state of high fever, Jieret goaded, 'You never heard that Avar s'Ffalenn got his son on the mother of your Blessed Prince?'

'Bastard! Pirate's get!' A riled disturbance as blankets were tossed off, and the invalid rose to the baiting. 'My mother's shame and a sorcerer's game piece!'

Sulfin Evend's growled oath entangled with a scuffle, as he leaped to wrestle his royal charge flat. Lysaer's enraged words emerged through the fracas, deranged and deadly with spite. 'What is the man, but the cursed seed of an enemy bred and born just to gall my royal father to blind rages?'

Jieret suppressed a wicked thrill of glee. 'Ath's truth! A blood kinship exists between your false avatar and the one you name Spinner of Darkness.'

'No kin of mine!' snarled Lysaer in delirium. He fought, cursing Sulfin Evend's restraint, all the while railing in affront, 'What is the s'Ffalenn wretch but a criminal condemned for the wreck of a fleet? His damned sorceries, you know, were what sent me to exile!'

'Not divine calling, after all,' Jieret agreed.

'Stop this!' A heaped pile of faggots overset with a clunk, hard followed by a commotion across the fire pit.

Then a rasp of loose stone bespoke lightning movement. Jieret was slammed down by a clout that skewed the bandaging over his eyes. Stunned dizzy, he battled the fingers that clamped in sharp effort to silence him.

'Want a gag for your pains?' Sulfin Evend ground out. He mashed his victim's burned face to the snow. 'You've caused his Exalted Grace undue distress with your slander.'

Still vigorous, Jieret twisted his head and jerked free, then gasped on a scraping breath, 'Ah, I see! His exalted self might not care to discuss family history when he's flat on his back, sick and raving. A delicate quandary. Would the trade guilds still pay for his war camps and diamonds, or will they decide to expose his grand cause as a fraud?'

'Clan cur! You blaspheme!' Sulfin Evend used expert force and manhandled his barbarian antagonist facedown on the frost-hardened ground.

'Do I?' gasped Jieret, though his mouth filled with slush and the gritted tang of mulched leaves. 'Princess Talith learned better, during the weeks she spent in Prince Arithon's company. Perhaps that's why some well-placed jackal in Avenor's high council made certain she fell to her death.'

'She was a suicide, and already condemned. Her conviction for adultery and high treason stand as a matter of public record.' An unpleasant, short skirmish saw Jieret's maimed shoulder slammed down, then ground beneath the mailed weight of Sulfin Evend's bent knee.

'Murdered,' gasped Jieret. 'Why not collar Avenor's inner cabal and ask for the truth?'

'Enough, damn you!' The Alliance Lord Commander twisted sidewards. He snatched up his knife, hacked a seam, then shredded a strip from the edge of the blanket. 'I'll bind your mouth. Knotted rope would hurt most, but the nicety will have to wait.'

'Indulgence of cruelty won't change the unsavory facts. You zealots at Avenor are no better than string puppets played for a blood feud.' Breathless, near fainting, Jieret turned his face just in time.

The punch of Sulfin Evend's studded fist grazed his cheek, plowing pain from his scarcely scabbed burns.

'Coward!' Jieret kicked out his lashed ankles. The wrench ripped him out of his enemy's grasp just long enough to invite, 'Why not ask Lysaer which one of us abuses Ath's grace with presumptions?' Unable to gauge Sulfin Evend's reaction without eyesight, Rathain's *caithdein* risked all and provoked, 'Or are you afraid you've bent your pedigree neck to a mortal man who's a liar?'

'Honorless scum! I said, *that's enough!*' A scrambling lunge spat a spray of loose gravel. Enraged, but far too controlled to indulge the reckless urge to kill outright, Sulfin Evend rammed into the barbarian's back and neck and trounced him flat in a snowbank.

Jieret thrashed, tried to roll. His lips split, ground into frost-cracked rock and ice. Helpless to fight back, he prayed for the swift slice of a blade at his throat. Again fortune jilted him. He received instead a shattering slam, as a wood billet cracked his nape like a bludgeon and cast him adrift into darkness.

Earl Jieret roused, gagging. The copper-sweet scent of blood clogged his nostrils. His mouth gushed. The drowning sensation of tepid liquid flooding his gullet wrenched him double. He choked, curled into a spasm of coughing. He tried to spit and clear his mouth. Yet the horror did not subside. The effort stunned him to wounding pain and a shocked surge of dizziness.

When he gathered himself and sorted the damage, the uncouth discovery unstrung him. His outcry of rage was reft wordless. Revolted body and mind, he curled in a knot, while appalled revulsion grasped his gut with barbed hooks and twisted him witless with nausea.

Had he known any way to stop reflex, he would have willed his ruined flesh to cease breathing.

'Your tongue was cut out,' said a steely voice from a point not far overhead. 'My Lord Commander, Sulfin Evend, wielded the knife. Had he not addressed the matter forthwith, you would not have been spared. The same act would have come at my command.'

Blind, now reft dumb, Jieret clamped bloodstained teeth. If he must weep, the bandages masking eyes hid his shame. No such kindly recourse existed, for hearing. He refused to cringe, or whimper like some pitiful, trapped beast as the speaker addressed him again.

'Surely you realize your worth as a hostage?' Such seamlessly detached majesty could only belong to Lysaer s'Ilessid himself. 'If you regret your insulting, brash words, you'll have no more chance to complain.'

A pause, while Jieret fought his spasming throat to locked silence.

The Divine Prince leaned closer, his magisterial tone shaded to contempt. 'Try to write, and I promise, both your hands will be put to the sword. The foul rumors you broached were not only ugly, but dangerous.'

Degraded beyond bearing, unable to avoid the slimy puddle of his own filth, Jieret turned his face to the ground. He raged to lash back that such goading was moot. Crushed and bleeding, overwhelmed by abject despair, he could write nothing at all with bound hands. The hurt squeezed his heart, that he should have lived to become a tool in the hands of his enemies.

Prince Arithon must be left free to prevail, unimpaired by encumbrance or hostages. The outside hope waned, that Sulfin Evend could be moved to question his unbending loyalty. The small seed of destruction that Jieret had planted had found no fertile ground, to have earned a vindication of such vile proportions.

Footsteps approached, tagged by chiming spurs. 'At least dose him with poppy,' suggested the Lord Commander. If he felt any pity at all, his following line came dry with laconic practicality.

'You want a live prisoner, we'll need to do something humane to ease his condition.'

'He's a meddling black sorcerer!' snapped Lysaer s'Ilessid. 'There will be justice served for that, and the longer list of civil crimes committed against my city of Etarra.'

Sulfin Evend abandoned his argument. A matter of firm record, Red-beard's marauding raids had preyed upon innocents for years. The Northern League of Headhunters kept a damning tally of the number of caravans with drovers and draft animals slaughtered. By Etarran account, this slinking clanbred assassin had shot the marked arrow that cost Lord Mayor Pesquil his life. Worse, he had stood as the Master of Shadow's collaborator when the fleet burned at Minderl Bay.

The finish carried the cold ring of finality as the Blessed Prince made disposition. 'Let the murderer languish. His trial of nightmares and suffering will answer for each of our men who has died.'

Tortured awareness was all that remained.

Jieret was left sprawled upon stony ground, condemned to a grinding extension of life that promised indescribable agony. His bound limbs had already stiffened with chill, until every joint ached with persistence. A blind man could not mark the passage of nightfall. He could wrest no comfort from measuring the critical three days of grace, through which Arithon s'Ffalenn might sustain his perilous refuge under the masking spells holding his spirit apart from his flesh.

Minute to minute, the uncertainty racked Jieret, that his liege's survival might lie beyond all redress.

Caithdein of the realm, he wept then, a silenced outpouring of grief. He could do *nothing*, only beg for the descent of Dharkaron's Black Spear to lay waste useless flesh and bring him the surcease of release.

He received no deliverance. Only Sulfin Evend, with a bitter decoction of willowbark and betony. 'His Blessed Grace is resting. Bedamned if I've taken this much trouble just to sit by and watch you succumb out of shock.'

Jieret averted his face and refused the strong drink.

'Devil!' his tormentor gasped under his breath.

Locked teeth were pried open and the remedy dribbled into the prisoner's lacerated mouth. Reflex made him swallow. Fed gruel and rebandaged and cleansed of his own filth, Jieret struggled, cuffed and pinned down like a puppy until the dregs of his pride lay in tatters.

He sprawled listless afterward, too spent to move, while the virtues of healing herbals slowly dampened his rioting pain. His poisoned, trapped thoughts now ranged free of distraction, gnawing his spirit without surcease. Guilt raked him, that Arithon's parting word had been a plea to die fast and cleanly.

Jieret tipped his head toward a clouded sky his ravaged eyes could not see. Light snowfall dusted his bandaged cheek. His other companion, a prankish southeast wind, tossed him scraps of conversation. His deprived mind seized on those fragmented bits, a hunter's skill Caolle had drilled into his being until he reacted by instinct.

'. . . no other survivors,' Sulfin Evend was saying. The clipped chink of rowels told of purposeful strides toward the picket where, by the smell, Lysaer's horse had been tied. 'Just myself, and your mount . . .' A gust tore a gap, then, '. . . can't last three days on the rations left in my pack.'

Lysaer's response was spiked with testy consonants.

Avenor's Lord Commander gave him back unsympathetic practicality. 'Well, there's not much alternative. Unless you care to share carrion with the vultures?'

A ripped intake of breath, then a curt phrase from Lysaer, from which the word 'sorcery' stood out with etched clarity.

Leather harness creaked. A girth buckle clanged upon rock. Sulfin Evend evidently saddled the one horse. His exasperation wafted through a snort as the animal shrank from the embrace of cold trappings. '. . . foolish belief you could match mortal troops against the Spinner of Darkness unscathed! I've said fifty times, do I need to repeat this? Meddle with a demon who's been trained to mastery, you've no choice at all but to defend with arcane protections!'

A shrill hiss masked the following line as snow was dumped on the hot ring of stones where the fire burned. '. . . rejoin the Etarrans,' Lysaer ended, his cool equanimity restored as the coals subsided to steam and wet ashes. 'Their priest has dispatched a half company to meet us. The rest have been told to stay encamped until the ones who are scattered can regroup.'

'Then we should wait here for them,' Sulfin Evend objected. His voice strengthened as he turned back toward camp and shook out the white stallion's bridle. 'Forgive my presumption, my Lord Exalted. But we have no scouts and not a standing man for protection. The wise course is to lie low right where we are. Let the Etarran trackers find us.'

Silence, from Lysaer, who perhaps had sat down. The rustling friction of wool cloth and silk mantles became lost in the rise and fall of the wind.

'Bedamned to your sacred mission to destroy the minion of Shadow!' Sulfin Evend resumed, apparently undaunted by what must have been a scathing glare of displeasure. 'We are as two straws amid a burned landscape that doesn't have spit left for landmarks!'

No response, just the magisterial bustle of hands, stubbornly repacking a saddlebag.

Sulfin Evend's tirade resurged in earnest. 'Have you gone mad? A storm's moving in. You're not recovered. In harsh fact, you look likely to measure your length if you stand up to empty your bladder. This horse has singed legs. He can't bear two riders. Let me tell you, that barbarian prisoner's too injured to shoulder a journey on foot. We've thwarted the last reason he has to keep living. Push on, strain him further, he'll tip over the edge. Might as well draw your sword and just kill him.'

Stillness descended, the wind's wail touched through by the whistle as an ember expired in the fire pit. Lysaer never moved. When he spoke, his collected tone held the dangerous tang of sheared iron. 'What will be said to the widows at Narms, if we make no effort to pursue? Could you tell them the Spinner of Darkness went free for the sake of a road-raiding murderer's safety? We break camp, *no matter the cost*. If you think the barbarian hostage too weak, then I'll fare on foot. Let him be the one to go mounted.'

The eagle circled high overhead, a stealthy shadow knifing through spangling flakes of light snowfall. He observed the racking indignity as Jieret was hauled upright and lashed to the back of the horse, while the unseasonal, cold wind hissed down from the north and tweaked the brushed bronze of his feathers. Over the land, patched charcoal and white, the late winter closed in, the iced freshets gnarled like twists of wrapped steel through frost-hardened soil that languished for sign of coming spring.

'*It's due to lane imbalance,*' Davien supplied, the enchantress whose awareness rode with him sharing his relentless reconnaissance. '*Weather can't break until the winds shift their pattern, a cycle unlikely to see change before the midsummer solstice.*'

That bit of ill news would bring famine in the north. Late-planted crops might have no time to yield, before next autumn's frosts spoiled the harvest.

Yet Elaira was unable to focus for long upon worries concerning the future. Far beneath, an ant figure in byrnie and helm, Sulfin Evend slogged ahead. The burdened stallion plodded on a lead rein at his heels, its coat smirched ivory against the watered-milk flurry of snowflakes. Lysaer s'Ilessid accompanied on foot, morose in his soot-grimed finery. The gold-and-white sunwheel mantle now hung ragged at the hem, irretrievably soiled by cinders. Storm and gloom cast his gilt trappings in tarnish, and his steps betrayed stumbling unsteadiness.

'He can't last an hour,' the Sorcerer reassured. A downbeat of wings skimmed him on a quarrel's straight course through a gust. 'If you want, we can wager when he'll collapse. Double stake, if Sulfin Evend can manage to catch him before he lands on his face.'

Yet even the bite of corrosive humor failed to raise any quip in response. Elaira's anguished attention remained fixed on the blanketed form strapped over the drooping horse.

Distance and altitude failed to mask the details of Jieret's relentless defeat. He still wore his leathers, the soft buckskins Feithan had tanned with such love streaked and torn where the light bolt had grazed him. Bloodstains blotched his wounded shoulder, bound up in frayed strips of rag. The russet braid that had once rallied his war band like a banner dangled down, clawed to napped tangles by each grabbing thorn branch. Wind flicked and snapped the stained ends of the dressing bound over his ruined eyes.

The ignominious certainty must sting like rubbed salt in the sore of his misery, that shortly his cut clan braid would be nailed to Lysaer's sunwheel banner as flaunting proof of his capture. In a day, Lysaer's cause had undone a lifetime's unassailable dignity. A s'Valerient son who should never have failed in his charge as Rathain's *caithdein*, his proud build and stag's strength had been purposefully broken. The horse bore him on like a ragpicker's haul, bundled for two-penny salvage.

While the snow swirled and winnowed, and the eagle sustained its grim vigil, Elaira's held presence erupted to fury for Lysaer's self-righteous cruelty. 'Ath's deathless mercy, I dare not move to help him! How much worse, as caithdein if he became forced to betray Arithon under the obligation of a Koriani oath of debt?'

The eagle bristled the hackles on its crest. 'Meddle in the fate of a sanctioned crown prince? No Prime Matriarch ever dared!'

'You've been out of touch,' Elaira revealed, her acid thought shaded to sorrow. 'Selidie's predecessor already set precedence. Morriel laid claim to Cattrick that way, and spoiled Arithon's machinations at

Riverton.' She had the respect not to press home the point, that Koriani politics had grown more aggressive through the years, with Fellowship numbers and resource left erosively curtailed.

The eagle shook out its ruff. The sharp lift of the wind screamed through taut pinions as it circled. '*You've the same flaying tongue as Kharadmon, even if female wit is more subtle.*' ·

A spark of grim humor leaped through the contact, a flicker that might have been laughter had Elaira's awareness been couched in its housing of flesh. '*I've no guile at all, as your colleague Kharadmon already had the poor grace to find out.*' A pause, while the snowfall thickened to pearl. The wind-whipped procession below stalled for parley, then turned off the trail to seek shelter and rest in a gully. While the gelding shook the caked ice from its mane, and the captive was unlashed from its saddle, Elaira bit back in acerbic honesty, '*Are you going to act?*'

The eagle folded broad wings and plunged in a whistling descent. He leveled off mere yards above the iced tips of the brush. The veiling scrim of the snowfall that obscured a clear view of the valley scarcely troubled his silken glide. '*I am guile itself. Knowing that, and informed of my reputation, would you care to strike a bargain?*'

Elaira's self-contained pause wound into taut trepidation. '*This won't be a contest concerning how long the s'Ilessid takes to fall down.*'

The Sorcerer's silence seemed an ominous affirmation.

Below, the horse slipped and scrambled down a bank of loose scree. A bloom of bright red showed that Jieret's ripped shoulder had opened and started to bleed.

'*The choices are ugly,*' the enchantress returned, agonized. Yet the fierce heartbreak engendered by pity ruled her more powerfully than fear. '*Speak first. I can't weigh the decision without knowing your terms.*'

Davien flapped, the strength in his wingbeat no natural bird's, that drove without effort through the rough gusts of low altitude without buffeting. Nor did his yellow, predator's eyes show emotion as he fixed on the party of three men and the horse, now jammed into a huddle in the thicketed lee of an outcrop. '*As* caithdein *of Rathain, Earl Jieret is entitled to ask Fellowship help. I can, perhaps, arrange the opportunity for the man to enact that fine point of law in free will. In return, I require your presence. You need do nothing else, lady. No act of yours shall touch Jieret's fate. Just lend me your company as living witness for the duration.*'

Elaira knew better than to ask what stakes might be played by a Sorcerer named as Betrayer; rankest folly to think she could second-guess the least clue to Davien's underlying motivations. Pragmatic by necessity, she considered the clan chieftain, and the devastating cost that would be extracted for his untimely survival. *'Can you assure me that Jieret will see release and live out his days a whole man?'*

No liar, Davien did not play on false hope. *'I can promise nothing concerning a mortal man's destiny. Earl Jieret's own choice must prevail. What can be restored is his power to act. He alone must decide how he'll use it.'*

Wrenched by the sight of the limp form being manhandled off the steamed horse, aching for the crimson stain slowly soaking through the ill-tied layers of wool bandage, Elaira cut off debate. For Arithon's sake, as well as Earl Jieret's, the stakes riding on her refusal posed the more deadly predicament.

The misery of inaction would torment her far worse than flinging all caution into the winds.

'Very well, here's my word.' Brought up driving hard-handed bargains with thieves, the enchantress phrased her matching bid in shrewd language. *'If there's a chance Earl Jieret can escape the entrapment of serving as bait to draw Arithon, I accept.'*

Near and Far

Crouched over her scrying mirror at Highscarp, Prime Selidie gasps in stunned joy to the prioress, 'Mother fortune, we've been blessed! Davien the Betrayer has just made a serious misstep. He can't know we've reclaimed our Great Waystone from Sethvir's keeping at Althain Tower, or he'd never dare seal a bargain with an initiate who's bound under my sigils of prime power. He's vulnerable, don't you see? The great amethyst can entrap his discorporate spirit, lent access to him through Elaira . . .'

At Avenor, High Priest Cerebeld addresses the Light's inner cabal, his gold-and-white robes tainted crimson by the failing light through the tower casement, 'I know there's been war, with blood spilled on both sides. The Master of Shadow is flushed, but not taken. Further word from Etarra's high priest says that our Blessed Prince moves to join the dedicated arm of his sunwheel companies, and renew the pursuit with sharp vigor . . .'

On Daon Ramon Barrens, under lashing snowfall, the scattered survivors of Earl Jieret's war band huddle in fireless cold, unable to know how many kinsmen their desperate strategy has kept living; and they pray that abroad in the howling darkness, a sword-bearing liegeman still braves the storm, driving three horses and standing staunch guard on the cloak-wrapped burden of Rathain's unconscious crown prince . . .

Late Winter 5670

X. False Step

The storm churned the night to a black maelstrom, snow lashed horizontal by howling winds armored with flaying, chipped ice. Harried in flight by the fury of the elements, the eagle banked in descent. He folded long wings and settled to roost on the gnarled root of a deadfall. Ephemeral as a shadow cast on dark felt, he fluffed gold-tipped feathers and kept unseen watch on the campsite a stone's throw away.

There, Lysaer s'Ilessid sat huddled before the whipped warmth of the fire that Sulfin Evend maintained with hard labor and dogged persistence. Dry hardwood was scarce on the barrens; green sticks of hazel and ice-crusted rowan would not take a spark in such weather. The blaze was kept fueled by scrub evergreen needles and a scavenged collection of pine knots, streaming vile smoke and shot sparks from the high content of volatile resins. Naught else could withstand the blizzard's wild onslaught. Twice in an hour, Lysaer roused and shook piled snow from his shoulders.

Despite his meticulous care to mask weakness, he showed all the suffering signs of a backlash provoked by overextension. The massive flux of energies he had channeled in blind rage had upset his auric balance. Vertigo skewed his senses. He started at ghost movement and sprang tense as phantom sounds grazed his hearing. Subject to bouts of spinning faintness, followed by shuddering palsy, he handled himself with eggshell tenderness and kept still as much as he could.

The gloved fingers tucked in his lap were still trembling. Nor did the incursion of Paravian haunts fade for the sake of infirmity. Lysaer felt them, sometimes pressured by an intimacy that made him gasp as they grazed his sensitized skin. His untrustworthy vision failed to dismiss the discomfort, but tended to remake the darkness and blown snow into patterns of leering ghosts. Minute to minute, the day's toll of dead seemed to hound his presence in reproach. Their hands, clothed in wind, plucked at his clothes, and their gaping mouths moaned for vengeance.

Lysaer rejected their burden of grief. The ruler who bogged himself down with past failings inevitably lost his vision. A man's death, or a company's, must be measured by how many others their sacrifice could keep safely living. The Shadow Master pinned under pursuit in this wasteland meant the blameless, walled cities were spared. The strong heart must not falter in chastisement of evil. Only stern measures could wrest the future away from the influence of fell shadows and sorcery.

The Narms headhunters had not given their lives to no purpose. Today's slaughtered dead had sprung the first line of the Master of Shadow's defenses. A vigorous scouring of Light had cleared the landscape of lurking barbarians. Now, arcane subterfuge broken, the quarry was stripped of defenders. Lysaer huddled under the damp silk of his mantle and counted the effort a victory. If his searing assault had spared any clansmen to stand in the enemy's defense, they would be scattered and few. Set on the run, they would lack the stamina and resource to turn the flower of the Alliance: crack troops he had groomed from a decade's summer musters, and marched well equipped from Etarra.

Sustained on taut nerves and anticipation, Lysaer regarded the gust-snatched streamers of flame. If his trembling sickness relented a little, his blue eyes burned too fearfully focused and bright. While the drive of his cause consumed every thought with an addict's obsessive intensity, he weighed the tactical worth of the captive, tucked against the rock outcrop.

The clan chieftain still lay where his knees had buckled. His great frame shuddered in a shivering daze, listless since Sulfin Evend had bound his ankles. More stout lashings anchored his wrists. Stretched spread-eagled between two stunted alders, he could not crawl away. The afternoon's stint on horseback had exacted a punishing cost. Despite the Lord Commander's brusque ministrations, and a second round of cautery to stop the fresh flow of bleeding, Jieret languished. The throb of his injuries pressed him to silenced misery. By the fireside, Lysaer could have counted each one of his laboring breaths.

'Relax and stop frowning, he's not like to die on you.' Wet and tired himself, pitched to a moody alertness that promised no tolerance for setbacks, the Alliance Lord Commander slogged in from his latest scavenging foray into the brush. 'Give him a night's rest to let his wounds close, he'll be past the worst danger of bleeding.'

Sulfin Evend unburdened his bundle of cut pine boughs; then the prize of his search, a twisted branch snapped from a scrub oak. While Lysaer tracked each movement with eyes like chipped sapphire, his officer brandished the stick like a wand and inscribed a circle around the fire. Lips moving as though in prayer or incantation, Sulfin Evend sealed the crude figure that enclosed himself and the Blessed Prince.

'What foolery is this?' The rough indignity of the setting stole nothing from Lysaer's regal authority.

'Protection, plain and simple.' Sulfin Evend poked the stick upright into the flank of the snowdrift beside him. 'Koriani witches employed by my father say a circle drawn with cut oak, and spoken over with words, will turn aside the simpler forms of dark spellcraft.'

Prince Lysaer bridled, his attack the strung reflex of a spider caught on a jerked strand of web. 'You feel yourself threatened?'

Sulfin Evend paused. Cat tense on his feet, he snapped a gesture toward the chieftain he had bound captive. 'He's clanbred, and sired as well by a bloodline not to be trifled with.'

When that terse explanation failed to lift Lysaer's censure, the Lord Commander beat the ice from the folds of his mantle, and sat, riled to a pang of rare temper. 'What, did you think I would cut a man's tongue for sheer spite?' He sustained his prince's displeasure and pressed back in deliberate sarcasm. 'You can't believe that I buckled before the trifling fear that some fool might be swayed from the Light by a spurious claim that the Spinner of Darkness could possibly be your close kin?'

Lysaer averted his face, a sharp break that gutted the offensive from the bearing assault of his scrutiny. 'But the enemy *is* my half brother, more's the pity. The sordid fact's not well known.'

Sulfin Evend's determined jaw sagged, stupidly open with shock. Then he closed his mouth, gathered himself, and strove to assimilate the impact of what he had heard.

A gust dulled the flames. For one fickle second, storm and illusion prevailed: the wet hair plastered against Lysaer's turned cheek appeared tarnished, his invincible shoulders bowed down by the ache of a grinding human weariness.

On a ragged note far strained from his usual poise, the avatar who bore title as Prince Exalted delivered his distasteful explanation. 'The infamy happened when I was three years of age. My mother was raped by a brigand. Her get of that union became a living aberration, raised and trained at the knee of an unprincipled sorcerer. At the outset, the nightside of power was needed. You'll have heard how my gift of light was interwoven with spelled shadow to restore Athera's choked sunlight.'

'I was a child,' Sulfin Evend admitted. 'The news we received at Hanshire was embellished, a wild tale of supernatural acts, bought in blood sacrifice and enacted by foul pacts with demons. Most folk believed such. For a year or more, my nurse scared me silly by using the sun as a threat to forestall my penchant for mischief.'

'She'd claim that overexposure to light would eat into your flesh until nothing remained but a skeleton? I heard that one as well, though in my case, from irate citizens who blamed my hand for the frightening change in the weather.' Lysaer's warmed, lifting humor ebbed away, unveiling a gravity as jagged with pride as chipped flint. 'No bloodshed happened, in fact. No one's act of conjury raised demons. But the use of black practice engendered corruption. The s'Ffalenn bastard proved as morally derelict as the blackguard who fathered him. When the mist was defeated, he cozened the Fellowship Sorcerers to endorse his claim to royal birthright. In conspiracy with his clever machinations at Etarra, they sought to insinuate a reign of terror and darkness.'

The damped embers rebounded. In the gold wash of flame light, Lysaer's determined composure seemed touched to etheric sorrow, the fallible mold of bone and flesh sustaining a spirit that burned too pure for the clay of mortality. 'What use to weep? My gift of light became rededicated as this world's hope and shield.' His scarred past sustained by a reserve of stark courage, he finished, 'Athera is now threatened, and kin ties lie forfeit. My given charge is to destroy an aberrated creature who should never have seen birth, or lived to draw breath in the first place.'

The tragic history, so long silenced, had been presented uncolored by melodrama. Annealed by his years of solitary shame, Lysaer never softened his commitment to defend. His staunch quiet disallowed the inner ache of betrayal; before the festering sore of a mother's violation, he displayed no weakness of human character. He met stoic self-sacrifice with matchless grace, until the observer who shared his secret burden of pain could not escape feeling awestruck.

Lysaer *was* Light, a being of quickened inspiration whose

magnificence was not dimmed, but lent force and weight by the contrast of tawdry blankets, and the earthbound drape of his snagged and cinder-burned clothing.

Unshrinking, the Blessed Prince faced his Lord Commander. With the attentive humility that melted stone hearts, he gave his sad past a swift closure. 'I surely owe you an apology.'

His blue eyes maintained their unwavering sincerity as he unlaced the gloved fingers locked over his tucked-up knees. 'Athera is not the world of my birth.' His contrite gesture encompassed the marked circle in the snow that earlier had raised his contempt. 'I've disparaged your effort, presuming clan rule was deposed for reasons of tyranny. The sorry practice of raiding and headhunting led me to believe the atrocities were the offshoot of feuding hatreds handed down since the uprising. Your action, tonight, bespoke more than prejudice, and your remark on clan heritage perhaps sprang from a threat that's outside my awareness. What has you concerned? If your fear has substance, then why has the reason been quietly held in obscurity?'

'Avenor's records were destroyed.' Discomposed to embarrassment by the sympathy in Lysaer's diligent regard, Sulfin Evend took an awkward moment to rise to the change in subject. 'Like most old towns, the royal seat of s'Ilessid was burned. Later, in case any fugitives survived, armed zealots came back and leveled the walls, stone by stone.' He cast an uneasy glance at the barbarian prisoner, roped like a steer by the outcrop. 'Wait. First let me dose Red-beard with a posset. Sorcerers and seers always hear what concerns them. If we're going to broach ancient history in depth, I don't want to feel that one's eyes boring holes through my back.'

'Seers?' Lysaer's startled wariness raised a shiver that ran, head to foot, through his seated frame.

Sulfin Evend raised ice-flecked eyebrows, unamused, while the tireless wind whirled snow like white gauze between them. 'You never suspected? Barbarian lineage inevitably carries a strong latent measure of mage talent.'

Lysaer jammed rigid hands through his hair. As though the strain all at once overwhelmed him, he demanded, 'How do you know this?'

'By well-established fact, though for years the remembrance has fallen into obscurity. Dark spellcraft can use ready fear as a weapon. Now the victim of their own paranoid silence, most town councils have long since forgotten.' Granted the nod of permission he required, Sulfin Evend dug the tin flask from the saddle pack. In straightforward competence, he set about mixing a soporific he kept at hand to speed healing. Storm filled the interval as he arose. Shrieking gusts deadened the grunting scuffle as he forced the bitter draught upon the captive.

Returned to the fireside, the Lord Commander piled more evergreen onto the embers. Smoke boiled up, pricked sultry with sparks, as the resinous flames flared and crackled. 'It's a close-kept secret,' he began, 'but my family carries the strain of an ancient bloodline from Westwood. Not prevalent, mind. We've had generations of outbreeding since the ancestor who got a child of rape on a captive. But now and again the traits of that heritage resurface, sometimes in force. You've admired Raiett Raven, even leaned on his talent. The most prosaic Mayors of Hanshire have ruled by uncanny instinct. We still retain a Koriani seeress to advise our high council.'

Lysaer's rapt regard became piercing to sustain. 'You yourself bear more than a trace of the taint?'

'The old lines breed truest,' Sulfin Evend admitted. Restless or self-conscious, he reached, caught a pine bough, and cracked off needled twigs with brisk fingers. 'In the first years of the compact, the clan forefathers and -mothers were selected for talent. A sworn covenant with the Fellowship has kept their marriages all but pure for a span of five thousand years.'

'An inhumane practice, the controlled breeding of dynasties,' Prince Lysaer said, thoughtful. A fresh tremor shook him. 'No wonder the citizens revolted.'

But Sulfin Evend jerked his chin in rebuttal. 'When outcrosses happened, there were no reprisals. The myth may persist, but actually, the archives that survive attest that no babes were ever put to death.' He tossed the stripped handful of fir needles in the flames, his hawkish features branded in flaring light as he qualified. 'If the town parent raised the offspring, quite often the Koriathain claimed the girl children for training.'

Lysaer stirred. The soaked gilt braid on his surcoat threw off a subdued glitter as he brushed settled snow from his lap. Sharpened to insight, he ventured, 'Is that why relations with the sisterhood soured?'

'Not at all. To become an oathsworn initiate in past years was considered the highest honor.' As though the conversation nipped close to the bone, Sulfin Evend busied himself, rummaging through the supplies in the saddle pack. He pulled out a linen-wrapped packet of flour and two leathery strips of dried meat. 'Their midwives keep meticulous records of birth, even now. They must snatch their girl novices as they can, from the pool of available throwbacks. Oh, never doubt, the witches still know which gifts the clan lineages foster.' He paused, hissed an oath against Shadow, then lamented, 'The flat griddle's lost with the pack train. We'll have to fall back on the headhunter's practice of toasting salt bannocks on the tread of a stirrup iron.'

Not deflected one whit, Lysaer levered off the saddle he employed for a seat. Snow spangled his shoulders like gemmed lace, and his leather-gloved fingers shook alarmingly. He masked the infirmity abetted by the covering darkness as he fumbled to unfasten the cold buckles. The gusts hounded his effort as he pried the damp-swollen leather from the tangs. Unwilling to attract a measuring survey of fitness from his Lord Commander, he passed over the freed stirrups with the provocative comment, 'What became of male children left at large in the towns?'

'Most returned to the clans. A partbreed of any generation could bid for reacceptance, had he the courage to test his inherited talent.' Sulfin Evend scooped out a pannikin of flour. He drew his belt knife and stirred in a dollop of snow, then shaped the thickened dough with the same fussy concentration that made him a superior marksman. 'In fact, all clan children underwent the same rite of passage, to ensure that their lineage bred true.'

Sulfin Evend cast about, but found no object handy to dangle the stirrups over the fire pit. He rejected the convenience of using a sword blade, since heat could spoil the steel's temper.

'Never mind. I'll take my bread blackened.' Lysaer snugged his forearms under the blanket, then pursued the original topic. 'What was the trial?'

'Exposure to the living presence of the Paravians.' Sulfin Evend placed two bannocks on the bars of the stirrups, then nested the precarious array amid the coals. When he looked up and caught Lysaer's sheared gaze still upon him, he bristled, 'What other test would be valid?' It went without saying that those lines kept purest posed the least risk of breeding up aberrant stock.

'What was the penalty for a failure?' Lysaer pressed, not about to back down before the bent of his inquiry was satisfied.

'Madness. Or a yearning of spirit too overwhelming to remedy, that would waste the flesh unto death.' Resigned as he watched the wind-ripped flames lick their meager dinner to carbon, Sulfin Evend shrugged muscled shoulders. 'The insane could take charitable refuge in the towns. Others found peace in Ath's Brotherhood. Those branch lines died off, as a rule. Even today, the adepts shun the attachment of children.'

'Powers of Darkness!' Lysaer shoved to his feet. 'Are you suggesting the rogue mage talents that riddle our society *all originate through the inherited taint of clan forebears*?'

Sulfin Evend hefted his knife, stabbed up a burned bannock, and extended the smoking morsel as offering. 'Even so.' His flint-pale eyes nicked with reflected firelight, he added the razor-edged irony, 'You never wondered why Hanshire's mayors don't fraternize with Erdane's council? Or why High Priest Cerebeld and his acolytes are decidedly unloved by the secret factions who pressure town politics? Their flow of gold helps proliferate the leagues of headhunters, and their sworn purpose is to hound the old blood to extinction.'

'I won't traffic in prejudice,' Lysaer said, firm.

And Sulfin Evend snapped back, 'You already have.' Confronted by Lysaer's inimical outrage, the Lord Commander had no choice but to outline the truth. 'Erdane is a stewpot of secretive, old hatreds. Best look to the men who come to your court smiling, and bearing gold as ambassadors.'

Chilled as the impersonal mask of vested sovereignty shuttered Lysaer's blanched face, Sulfin Evend risked his life for addressing sedition: he set brazen truth before nicety and ripped the decorum off the underlying canker of his doubt. *'The cream of your priesthood is already gifted.* If you want spells and sorceries expunged from Athera, you'll one day be faced with turning on friends and cleansing an innocent populace.'

Lysaer sat back down. Even in rage, civil grace did not leave him. He accepted the bannock, halved its crumbling crust, then loosed a startling, sharp gasp of laughter. 'You and Raiett have the testing guile of snakes. Is this your latest attempt at persuasion? If I don't plan to stamp out all the offshoots of talent, you want me to use fire to fight fire?'

'You'll have to,' Sulfin Evend forced out, his throat bound in desperate tightness.

Lysaer flicked crumbs from his glove, his fastidious gesture at odds with the fury forced into civilized speech. 'You think I should found my own coterie as a weapon of self-defense and hurl enemy sorcerers to perdition?' He bit into the charred gob of dough, his glance like honed steel, and as dangerous.

Sulfin Evend could not match that damning, bright gaze. He speared the other bannock, then selected his words with the care of a man crawling headfirst down a wolf's den. 'An assault by shadows and black spellcraft has just slaughtered our company to a man. If we join the Etarrans, what good can that do? How else can you hope to stop the same evil from destroying their best troops tomorrow?'

'Light prevails over darkness,' Lysaer reminded. 'By my law, which is just, only those born with talent *who practice their craft upon innocents* need fear the sword and the fire. My priests, who are trained, use their skills for the purpose of tracking the Master of Shadow. If they might one day raise wards to protect, the first guiding rule cannot change. Their oath to the Light is made punishable by death, should they stray and use magecraft for harm's sake.'

Sulfin Evend expelled his pent breath. Versed in hard statecraft, war trained to respond under pressure, he moved deliberate, swordsman's fingers and rolled out another wad of dough. 'Then you won't raise a campaign of extirpation to cull all trace of talent from Athera?'

'You fear I would put all your relatives to the sword? Surely not.' Lysaer tossed the gritted crumbs of the bannock into the heart of the fire. His expression stayed graven with offense as he said, 'I am the Light and the just arm of defense sent here to protect the innocent. Whether or not the Paravians ever return, whether mankind could be driven to madness among them, as you claim, I would not see born talent wantonly slaughtered. Quite the contrary. Those gifted with mage-sight who embrace the Light shall be nurtured. When the minions of Shadow are cast down in defeat, we'll need their help to break the yoke of the compact. Our people must stand to enforce their right to claim the free wilds for their children.'

Sulfin Evend yanked back singed fingers from the coals, too incredulous to pause for a lapse into carelessness that may well have blistered his sword hand. *'You would take arms and challenge the might of the Fellowship Sorcerers?'*

Sugared snow flew as Lysaer resettled his tucked blankets. 'For the welfare of civilized settlement, yes, I will wrest those proscribed lands out of sanctuary.' His back braced against the saddle to doze, he shut his eyes, and said, sanguine, 'Lives must be held sacred. No farmsteader will freeze for want of cut wood. I would see no child starve for the sake of a grasslands that could have been plowed up for barley.' The crowning point was delivered with astonishing assurance. 'Today's losses will fire outrage. Enough outcry will finally mow down the objections and reverse the town councils' distrust of magecraft. Never fear. Once the mayors prove ripe for acceptance, my high priests will have their skills ready.'

'We adapt in reaction,' Sulfin Evend said, bitter, his strategist's instinct for constructive aggression given no outlet to vent his frustration. 'Are we always to lag one dance step behind the enemy's deadly innovation?'

Lysaer shook his head. His expression of repose unmarred by the rancor that had, seconds past, made him dangerous, he offered his startling confidence. 'The man who learns by example never turns. Our enemy has no scruple, and his clan following is bound to his cause by survival. Set against such dedication we need an Alliance annealed beyond reach of politics. I will match that challenge. At my back, I will have total commitment, an unbreakable unity forged by a threat irrefutably defined in blood and lives, as need be.'

Then the wounding retort, as Sulfin Evend's weary grief ripped restraint. 'Then I can no longer shoulder this command!'

Unspoken, the censure he had carried since the dark night in Camris, when he had witnessed the unsuspecting inhabitants of Avenor cast into jeopardy as a ploy to loosen the purse strings of frightened guild councils.

'My foresight proved sound.' Lysaer opened his eyes. Their blue depths were terrifying for their serenity, and the confidence self-contained in his presence, a force to leave lesser men cowed. 'No trade ministers were browbeaten. The coin that will fund our future campaign will be freely given, not pried from tight fists by a tax.'

Wildly angry, Sulfin Evend stood his ground. Although Avenor's merchants had been hazed into emptying their coffers for the cause, today's fallen had been thrown to the mercy of poor planning. Their families deserved honesty, first, and a better memorial than a ploy to recast them as victims of abstruse manipulation. 'Well, I'm tired of seeing red-blooded men killed for the sake of arse-kissing politics!'

That snapped Lysaer's patience, though his resting hands kept their stillness under the blanket. 'We are all no better than game pieces given the illusory power of choice.' His censure held no rage, only a wretched weariness that seemed sprung from the marrow of his bones. 'If you think you are different, or you know a better way, then walk in my shoes! Tomorrow, the Etarran troops will be yours. Command as you please. I will follow. Let's see you bring the Spinner of Darkness to his knees by the vivid heat of mortal inspiration.'

While Lysaer settled into an exhausted sleep, Sulfin Evend paced the camp, attending small chores to stay wakeful. He repacked the saddlebags. Since thick snowfall now blanketed the available fodder, he poured out a ration of grain for the horse. Last, he checked on the prisoner. Each small move he made was marked by the eagle, unseen and still perched with unnatural vigilance on the cragged root of the deadfall.

The great bird watched with the vision of a Sorcerer, which saw beyond form and shadow.

The electromagnetic surge of the storm filled the air with sparkling currents. Against the bright, static spray of falling snow, the warding circle traced out by the oak branch cast a faint lavender glow, smeared dark where the Lord Commander's busy footsteps had crossed its ephemeral boundary.

The eagle shifted weight from one mailed foot to the other. He clashed his armored beak, impatient, until the Koriani enchantress whose consciousness partnered him posed her perplexed observation. *'Why should you want him to refresh his scribed line? He's not trained to the discipline of focused intent.'* Her disparagement stemmed from the fact that the warding raised by Lysaer's officer could deflect very little beyond a hedge witch's charm of ill favor.

'Bide with me.' The eagle roused his feathers to dislodge tickling snow, then surveyed the campsite, first through his right eye, then through the left, his avid analysis a clear indication the changed viewpoint carried significance. *'The circle's potency scarcely matters. My purpose requires only that it should exist.'*

Less given to patience than to the intuitive hunch that she had been subtly warned off, Elaira shied from disturbed recollection: of the Sorcerer's gaze, meeting hers in Ath's hostel. His eyes had been shadowy, fathomless brown, their secretive depths well beyond her Koriani skills of analysis. Elaira quashed back her insatiable urge to ask questions. Her word had been given. She had sealed her commitment. For the sake of Rathain's *caithdein*, she had chosen to follow a Sorcerer's lead into the irrevocable unknown. If she would unmask the Betrayer's intent, she must stay the course of unfolding event.

No change seemed imminent. Storm lashed the night with a hag's chorus of wind and a torn lace curtain of snowfall. The drifts sifted deep in the lee of the rocks. A whiteout blanket smothered the char in the valleys. An hour crawled past, while Sulfin Evend scrounged more fuel to nurture his lagging fire. He sat down and meticulously oiled his sword, then secured the salvageable parts of his crossbow, and in due course progressed through a lethal collection of knives. The white horse dozed with its head down. Lysaer stirred in and out of unsettled dreams and broken sleep.

Daon Ramon's stark savagery relented for no man. If peace could be garnered amid the rampaging splendor of the elements over untamed landscape, the invasive certainty that the Master of Shadow lurked abroad stalked the heels of each unguarded thought.

Sulfin Evend exhaustively polished his weapons. He wiped down the horse harness to the last strap, then cast about for something else to occupy purposeful fingers. By that hour, the blizzard had started to slacken. Lysaer, between dozes, raised the suggestion that his Lord Commander would spoil his judgment by morning unless he stood down to rest.

Gray, falcon's eyes swept the golden-haired prince in the blankets, meting out critical inspection. 'You're not fit to keep watch.'

Lysaer rolled onto one elbow and gave a suggestive shrug. 'Against what? If the Spinner of Darkness ventures this way, my inner guidance will warn me. Should barbarians ambush, the snow cover's too thick to hear their murdering footfalls. The horse will smell the presence of enemies before we do, and the fire can be left to burn out.'

'Sunrise can't be far off.' Sulfin Evend measured commonsense wisdom against the clamor of his strategist's instincts, and gave in. For far too long, he had battled the depleting fog of deep weariness. Since the gale was relenting, he appropriated one of the prisoner's blankets, then recovered his oak stick and recast the circle around his immaculate campsite.

Earl Jieret lay motionless as before, his form cut outside the ephemeral tracery, faint as a ribbon of lavender foil dropped glimmering over the snow.

'*Now, we play chess,*' the eagle pronounced on a devilish frisson of pure joy. He did not wait for Sulfin Evend to lie down, but unfurled broad wings in the darkness and launched himself off his perch.

'Now, in truth,' echoed the Koriani seeress. Stationed in the Prime's private chambers at Highscarp, she tracked the same scene, avid as any huntress set after cunning winged prey with poisoned bait and a net. She stroked her quartz scrying sphere, teasing out the full range of its virtues, then scribing fresh sigils to fine-tune her surveillance to utmost, ruthless clarity. 'The Betrayer has started making his move.'

As the night advanced, more than the sisterhouse peeress stood attendance on Selidie Prime. Now the chamber accommodated a joined ring of twelve seniors, already settled into deep trance where they knelt in formation on the wooden floor. Inside their linked circle, the parquet had been chalked with a massive array of twined sigils. Their combined force sustained an inner quadrant demarked by four more enchantresses, stationed at the cardinal directions. The least of these wore four bands of earned rank on her sleeves, colored scarlet to denote their administrative service. Each clasped an enabled quartz wand the length of a tapered candlestick.

Prime Selidie crouched at the center of the conjury, a gown of eggplant purple puddled over her slippered feet. Her blonde hair had been braided into a rope, laced with lavender ribbon. Immersed in a state of forbidding concentration, she completed the lines of an elaborately protected squared circle. She exchanged the white chalk for a black wax stylus, then laid down the eightfold sigils of binding at each corner. To the enchantress on vigil at the scrying sphere, she announced, 'The trap is almost complete.'

Reassurance came back, whispered through shadow grained with the smoke of burned herbs, and the more acrid bite released by tobacco spiked with a tienelle infusion. 'The Betrayer appears to be in no hurry.'

In fact, the seeress went on to explain, he had made ingenious use of Sulfin Evend's crude ward to evade infringing the Law of the Major Balance. Lysaer's Lord Commander had drawn the ring with intent to deflect an outside interference; Davien perforce had respected free will. The quartz sphere reflected his avian form, a gliding dark shuttlecock on the loom of the air. Each pass threaded spellcraft, knitting a clever veil of illusory affirmation that nothing untoward should transpire *inside* the rim of the circle.

Outside, the Sorcerer could do as he liked, beyond concern that either Lysaer s'Ilessid or Sulfin Evend should perceive his industrious activity.

'He's alighted on the outcrop above Earl Jieret,' the seeress gave dutiful report.

The coral curve of Selidie's lips showed delicate satisfaction. She crossed the last cipher, set the rune of ending, then laid aside the wax stylus. Flushed by the sped pulse of excitement, she arranged a silver, lion-foot tripod just above the rim of her construct. Last, she unwrapped the amethyst Waystone.

Its bared facets unleashed a flood of chill air, and the warning, charged scent of ozone. The bronze candlestand with its burning wick shot tangles of ruby reflection through the shadowy heart of the stone. Each movement reverent, the Prime settled the sphere in the wrought ring with its sigils of warding and guard. She fussed, bringing its central axis to alignment above the geometrical figures of binding restriction. She rotated the jewel widdershins in its cradle, testing and tuning its position by increments until she ascertained its optimum orientation.

Lastly, she checked: the silk scarf sewn with the ninefold copper sigils of imprisonment lay within instant reach, tucked underneath her left sleeve cuff.

The last steps were complete. Despite trained restraint, Selidie Prime shuddered to the raw thrill of anticipation. She embarked on a feat no Koriani Matriarch before her had ever dared to attempt. If she met success, within the next minutes, she would hold a Fellowship Sorcerer pinned under the power of the Great Waystone.

'Stand ready to anchor me,' she bade the four wand-bearing seniors awaiting, their even breaths settled in preparedness.

A final exhale, and Selidie engaged her own iron discipline. Her mind spiraled downward into deep calm. Eyes closed, she cupped her palms over the Waystone. The amethyst's cool surface became faintly clouded with moisture under her animal touch. Quiet settled, as though a sealed bubble surrounded her person through the eerie suspension as the jewel awoke to her presence.

That stillness deceived, the velvet glove concealing the knife. As always, the jewel's awareness slammed active with no warning, a buzzing wasp storm of rage that lashed through every sensitized nerve. Selidie endured, her resistance passive. Fear and bright agony ripped past without foothold as the Waystone's barbed spite spewed like a maelstrom through her mind.

The flood tore at her, shrieking, a ferocious, seeking assault that pried to find foothold in weakness. Should the torrent breach even a pinhole flaw, or hook any chink of insecurity, Selidie would be lost. Her consciousness would drown in that roiling, mad spate, bound hostage along with many another matriarch who had failed the stone's testing before her.

The jewel laid traps, offered false turnings and ambush; it lured and lulled, teasing her guard with illusory bouts of quiescence. As often as the Matriarch had threaded the maze, no passage was ever the same. Dewed with perspiration, she withstood blows and blandishments, until the wave of the great amethyst's malice reached a crest. On the poised instant between flood and ebb, she threaded the precisely tuned sigils that suborned wild might into mastery.

Peace descended, a bursting jolt of pure ecstasy that never failed to stun the mind for the space of a heartbeat. Selidie smiled, ceded a focus of clear power that would act on the breath of her whim.

Her living palm wielded the poised axis of a force that could imprison the shade of a Fellowship Sorcerer. No talent on Athera could move to prevent her. Davien had betrayed his colleagues before. His seclusion within the caverns at Kewar had extended for centuries, a withdrawal so deep, his colleagues were unlikely to miss him. Selidie aligned the Great Waystone to the Prime's sigil of command, the symbol that held mastery over every initiate sworn to the Koriani Order. At her call, Elaira must answer. The Betrayer was discorporate, his sealed word a direct and binding attachment to his unshielded spirit. His promise to Elaira would hold him in linkage; and like the jessed raptor tied to a creance, the Matriarch could reel him in.

Her figured square with its sigils of confinement had been well laid to receive him. Selidie's smile displayed perfect, white teeth. Ripe for the challenge, she addressed the seeress, 'Davien's still engaged? Excellent. He'll be taken unaware. For safety, the moment has come to disperse your spells of scrying.'

Silk rustled across the hushed chamber as the seeress bent to her quartz sphere. Her raised hand overshadowed the scene it depicted, of the great golden eagle, landed in the soft snow beside the stilled form of Earl Jieret. Her traced cipher of release dispelled the connection. As the image faded, Davien's musing thought to Elaira bled through, a ghost's whisper carried across time and space as the contact dwindled, *'When this is over, you'll just have to trust me to safeguard the life of your prince . . .'*

'The connection is severed,' the seeress confirmed.

Selidie drew herself erect, then raised her right hand from the Waystone's chill surface. Eyes closed, her left palm still in contact, she extended her forefinger and traced the cipher of prime domination over the facet framed by her touch. The crystal responded. A spiraling wind of raised force filled the chamber, tuning the air like a soundless chord and lifting the hair at the nape to a clamor of instinctive warning.

Spider still as she bided in wait for the gathering power to peak, Selidie savored the rapture of her unbridled anticipation.

Once the Betrayer lay at the order's mercy, she could seize the Named imprint of his consciousness. Given that template, she could then craft the specialized sigil to rule him. His formidable power would become hers to milk. With Asandir absent, and Sethvir laid low, the Prime Matriarch would stand unopposed. She could unleash the old knowledge she guarded. Within the next minutes, she would claim the sure leverage to free the Koriani Order and lead mankind back into ascendancy.

The Waystone reached resonance. Embraced by a pall of silvery light as its field of charged forces surrounded her, Selidie closed and sealed the last link that enabled the squared circle of entrapment. Then she spoke the name of Elaira three times over the prime sigil of command.

The summons crossed the barriers of time and distance. Reaction was instantaneous: Elaira's spirit was netted in by main force from her far-off sojourn in Daon Ramon. Selidie sensed the moment of contact; felt the spelled directive cast its taut mesh over the enchantress and the Fellowship Sorcerer that folly had tied into partnership.

The Great Waystone heated against Selidie's clasped hands. 'We have him!' she crowed as the sigil clamped down, its barbed hooks deeply set into her hapless quarry. 'May he well rue the day that his kind bound our sisterhood under the compact!'

Without the bone and flesh of a body, Davien would have no foothold to anchor him at the instant of flux.

The crystal's charged matrix served as ladder and gateway, spanning the axis of existence. Selidie kept watchful contact, light fingers tracing the pulse as her array of keyed spellcraft thundered to enable the threshold opened within. Inside the holding, split second of recall, she grazed against the full awareness of the Sorcerer's being. Davien's presence loomed vast, power chained into knotted complexity beyond mortal thinking to grasp. He was leashed might and lightning, dark unknown and gold light, a conscious pavane of moving energy, the essence of which strained away through her grasp like blown smoke.

'No!' Stunned by the sense of his substance eluding her, Selidie cupped the Great Waystone in a convulsive grip. Already hot, the stone lit to burning, polarized in return by *something* that did not bleed away as Davien's awareness departed. Along with Elaira's oathbound spirit, the Prime detected a packaged bundle of energies. She could not tag its signature. Its presence was a puff of movement and air, an impression half-formed as a spell weave of runes caught up like a burr in the transfer.

The Prime received warning, but no time to react. Before thought could respond and snap the connection, the fragment of malice the Betrayer delivered lodged inside the sealed well of her trap.

The Waystone rang like a bell. The inbound vibration raised a standing wave that could not be damped at short notice, tuned as it was into phased resonance with the prime cipher of command. To force the calibration awry was no option. The interlocked currents would turn lethal with imbalance. Only through controlled care and a ritual sequence of steps could the power be bled off in harmless dispersal.

White ice under pressure, Selidie stamped down rattled nerves. She could outface this crisis. Strong enough not to be hazed into panic, she uttered the first cantrip to discharge the prime cipher.

Too late; already a silver jet of possibility erupted within the circled square. Then the tendril became manifest. Orange flame licked up the silver legs of the tripod and engulfed the Waystone still clasped between the Prime Matriarch's hands.

Singed to blisters, she yanked back, then cursed the thoughtless speed of brute reflex.

The lapsed contact had broken her rapport with the jewel. Cut off from access, she had lost her means to steer the amethyst's roused might to quiescence.

Although the disbanding of the prime cipher had granted Elaira's spirit an immediate release from the summoning, the crafted lines of the construct to imprison a Sorcerer still glowed on the hardwood floor. The eightfold sigils of binding remained fully active, a ranging force laid down with all but indelible potency.

Selidie cradled reddened hands to her breast, her curse a cracked note of frustration as she encompassed the scope of expanding dilemma. The Waystone's raised matrix was linked to the spells. She could not breach their warding from outside to quench the fire, which was real, a ridiculous crudity kept fueled by wax polish and blackening walnut parquet. To intervene would unleash the Waystone's raised field, inviting an uncontrolled backlash that would kill every enchantress caught within range. Nor was delay feasible. The flames nipped and crackled, hot enough to shatter the great amethyst. The jewel's loss was unthinkable, a blow that would cripple the order's best strength and destroy an irreplaceable reservoir of stored knowledge.

'Dharkaron's Black Spear strike us all to perdition!' Selidie howled in black fury. The ignominious simplicity enraged her, that the Betrayer should have balked her bold play with no more than a commonplace firestorm. Not only was the Great Waystone at risk, but the building heat of the conflagration *was melting the dark wax that defined the eight ciphers of containment.* Another minute would see the wards breached from within, likely seeding a spiraling holocaust.

Prime Selidie fell back upon crude expedient, and snatched the silk stitched with the ninefold sigils of imprisonment from her sleeve cuff. Cast the cloth over the Waystone, and its ties to the construct would be cut. The wards in the silk could withstand its raised power. Wrapped and pulled to safety, the stone could stay masked, the forces of backlash held in abeyance until the irritating threat of the fire spell was resolved.

Driven frantic as she snapped the folds from the cloth, Selidie called instructions to the four seniors standing as anchors. 'Scribe a fresh circle! We're going to need a new set of wards laid down underlaid by the forces of water!' The construct would close a catchframe of containment and stay the spread of the flames. 'Act swiftly!'

Within a scant second, the wax ciphers binding the original squared circle were going to puddle and give way, spilling who knew what chaos of Davien's to the caprice of the four winds and beyond.

Selidie cast the unfurled cloth over the dark facets of the Waystone. The licking blaze snapped and ignited the hem, then flared up the gauze-thin silk. Selidie cried out as the sewn copper sigils liquefied in the heat. A searing rain of metallic droplets pattered over her wrists and hands. Scalded, she gasped out a whistling breath as the ephemeral cloth wisped to ash.

'Maker preserve, we're in trouble now,' wailed one of the watching enchantresses.

'Be silent!' Weeping tears for the setback, shaken with pain, Selidie wrestled to center her distracted mind. Disaster beckoned. She had less than a heartbeat to act. No choice remained, *no choice at all*; she must surrender burned hands to the fire and reforge her snapped link with the Waystone.

Once she harnessed the amethyst's matrix, she could wield its empowered focus. The construct for containment and Davien's sent spell could both be doused at one stroke.

But she had to subdue the roused Waystone first. Already lashed into unbridled resonance, the jewel would strike with instantaneous force. Its assault would be unrelenting. Selidie would have no moment of preparation, no interlude of testing quiet in which to compose her riled nerves. Worse still, she must distance every distraction. The risk was unilateral. She could not divide her resources, even to set the most basic protection to safeguard her unshielded hands.

While she battled the Waystone, the fire would burn her. In peril of her very survival, she must yield no thought to the horror, must stand unmoved by torment. Fail in rigid discipline, and the spite in the amethyst would claim her. Personal consciousness would be dragged under and shackled, a living imprisonment more final than Daelion Fatemaster's damnation.

Too many of her predecessors had been lost in times past, never to see rescue or recovery.

Not courageous at all, but ruled by the gauntlet of duty, Prime Selidie spread trembling, blistered fingers. She thrust her arms through the fire, screaming out her raw fear. Then, her dread vented, a hold like cold death clamped over her traumatized mind, the Prime Matriarch groped for the Waystone.

Eyes closed, consumed by unflinching purpose, Selidie refused to acknowledge the stink of her own charring flesh. The actinic flare of outraged nerves reamed her through, then became stripped of meaning by the bared lash of her will. She held herself shuttered. Entombed in a bastion of self-imposed calm, all her focused resource pitched to wrestle the Waystone's ferocious peril, she blundered toward her objective. Her weeping skin made contact with a searing hiss. Now wedded to the amethyst's deadly, dark facets, she would either immolate herself, or wrest out an avenue of yielding surrender through which she could impose dominance.

Crowded, battered, pummeled by the maelstrom of the stone's viciousness, she lost all thoughts but the one that secured her self-identity. Time lost cohesion. She could not stay the onslaught to know whether the wax sigils had melted, or if the squared circle had breached. All details became immaterial: whether her hands became crisped to the bone did not matter, or whether the great amethyst would shear into cracks and shatter to fragments from heat stress.

Nor dared she acknowledge the gibbering cries of lost primes, their ghost presence turbulent about her as they mocked, or gabbled their insane advice. Slaved consciousnesses, all, they were part of the Waystone's imprinted core, a storehouse of past wisdom and historical detritus, evolved into sentient malice.

As crystal, the amethyst could not access itself; insatiably hungry, it craved to add Selidie's awareness to its purgatory of trapped spirits. Those assimilated human thoughts and emotions provided the enlivening seeds, enabling its matrix to evolve through interactive conception.

Selidie resisted the siren cries. She deafened her being to the melting enticements that promised her pleasures unimaginable. She faced down the threats, arisen like dragon's teeth, that browbeat her resolve with vistas of limitless pain. She broke through the clamor of illusions insisting her autonomy had been broken in defeat.

Obdurate, Selidie braced through the ordeal. Exposed, stripped naked by the shot arrows of a thousand barbed energies, she held fast. Her stance must *be* strength, without desperation. Inner balance must prevail in the face of rank chaos, though earth itself should give way and crumble under her feet. She must not think, must not feel. Lose her grip on resolve, and the grinding mill of the Waystone's stewed rancor would sweep her under. She resisted as rock, hammered and smashed and pummeled by currents that wore at her reserve with the blind rage of a cataclysm.

Damned faces streamed by, claiming to be mother, father, sister, or brother. Selidie kept her true memories wrapped silent, abjured all temptation to refute the snared spirits. To acknowledge them at all, even as impostors, was to trip and fall into a morass of hostile energies that would flay her. The Waystone's pack of captive spirits demanded, then howled. They tore with tooth and nail, hurling fragments of ancient spellcraft in their effort to wrest her spirit from its housing of breathing, warm flesh.

More patient than the most cold-blooded predator, Selidie maintained her beleaguered pocket of calm. She resisted the falsehood, that the scope and force of the conflict had hurled her beyond time. Centuries, or mere seconds, the elapsed interval *must not matter*. If she succumbed to any small thread of distraction, she would become lost forever.

Then the opening presented. Her inner sight picked up a split-second rift through the snarling legions of ghosts. Into that breach, she rammed the first sigil configured to rule the Great Waystone. One axis of four stood cleared of obstruction. Given that foothold, that abatement of ranged power, the Koriani Prime oriented her awareness within the dark heart of the sphere. Riding on spatial instinct and the hardened reserve of experience, she tapped into the amethyst's matrix, then lashed back, her will focused diamond, and her mastery unerring. As the other three sigils swept chaos before them, she achieved the stunning release. Unified peace descended as the crystal opened in limpid surrender.

Her senses rushed back. Slapped blind and breathless by an onslaught of lacerating pain, Selidie maintained her trembling hold. She tapped the Waystone's tamed focus to steady herself, then forced open smoke-stinging eyes.

Restored to awareness, she crouched, bent and weeping over the charred wreckage of her hands. The fires beneath had somehow extinguished, a mystery she had no scrap of resource to pursue. From whatever source, the intervention had come too late to spare her from ruin. Blackened stubs of stripped bone, stuck with scorched meat and tendons, remained clamped with welded tenacity to the Waystone.

The jewel was still hot. Smoke purled reeking wisps from the crabbed remnants of her fingers. Underneath, the heartcore of the jewel was uncracked; its facets still gleamed, the spiked core of the matrix glimmering with needles of poised force.

Limp, all but broken, Selidie croaked the command to restore the grand focus to quiescence. As the jewel's powers ebbed, then finally deserted her, she shuddered under the assault of a pain beyond all rational endurance. Overset by reaction and visceral horror, Prime Selidie tore her flaking flesh free.

She would have collapsed, had two ranking seniors not rushed forward and caught her. Their trembling grasp shored her up, a staunch presence bracing her shoulders.

'Come,' someone said. 'Let us get you away.' Then, 'Just lean back and breathe. Asya's already gone to the sisterhouse. She's bringing a third-rank healer to help straightaway.'

Selidie dragged in a coarse, moaning breath. Through a nightmare of agony, she struggled for speech: how had the fires of Davien's conjury extinguished? An inarticulate whimper rasped from her throat, weak as a newborn kitten's.

The seeress used her crystal, tapped her gift of empathy, and read her Prime's balked intent. Her neutral voice answered and resolved burning need. 'The Betrayer included a limiting rune. His fire spell dispersed by itself.'

Which meant, all along, *there had been no danger*. Amid greasy smoke and the scorched waste of her wardspell, Prime Selidie absorbed the cruel truth: that the squared circle would not have been breached; nor would the Great Waystone have cracked under stress. Had she held back, taken one cool moment to weigh risks, she could have escaped with no further harm than a few scalded blisters.

'Oh, mercy, my hands,' she groaned through locked teeth. Her head lolled back, singed hair tumbled loose, as her attendants bore her up and assisted her tottering step. 'Burned to the bone, and for nothing.' She wanted to howl, that she had been wantonly crippled by tricks, the victim of her own cleverness.

She understood Davien's promise with Elaira had been nothing more than fiendish bait all along.

Like a headstrong, green fool, she had succumbed to assumption, and treated with the Betrayer as though he was an unshielded spirit.

'You know what this means,' she gasped, excoriated by trapped rage and humiliation. Shocked, spinning on the verge of hysteria, she pulled up short, and cried out to the devastated sisters who tended her, 'What in the name of Ath's creation has this Fellowship meddler become?'

As a discorporate entity, Davien should not have possessed the means to evade her laid snare!

'Hush,' soothed the seeress. 'Never mind. Keep you still.'

Another initiate burst in with soaked towels. Solicitous hands eased the Prime down on a cushioned divan and started the tender task of wrapping the seared bones of her fingers. Soon after, Selidie lost her last wits to the pain.

A dimmed voice of protest funneled to her through a roaring storm of torment. 'Mercy on her, can't this wait for a posset?'

Then at last, someone kind forced a rag to her mouth and muffled her mindless screaming.

Back on Daon Ramon Barrens, naked to the skin, the Sorcerer Davien rubbed his hands down the lean, muscled line of his flanks. Then, bothered by the nagging pull of a cramp, he clasped his immaculate, artist's fingers and stretched linked arms over his head. The flex of his lips held both sorrow and irony as he cast a glance eastward, and murmured, 'My dear, the lesson was harshly unpleasant, but needful. You will certainly think twice before you wield the power of your order, or poke prying hands into Fellowship business again.'

Supremely untroubled by the blasting wind, or by the last, wisping snowfall that dewed his pale skin and flecked spangling flakes amid tumbled, cinnabar hair, Davien closed his dark eyes.

He dispatched a ranging thought to the east, and assured

himself that Elaira's spirit had returned without harm to her body. She would waken shortly in the hostel near Eastwall, secure within the adept's sacred grove, and none the worse for her spiritwalk in Daon Ramon.

Then, freed to attend to more pressing matters, the Sorcerer regarded the blanketed form of Earl Jieret, lashed wrist and ankle before him.

Davien's knife-sharp brows gathered into a frown. He bent, his questing touch light as a ghost's, and ascertained the clan chieftain was unconscious. Pulse and breathing were regular. The *caithdein's* condition was stressed, his body dehydrated from blood loss, but in no threat of imminent collapse. Faultlessly gentle, the Betrayer turned the man's head. He straightened the snarled clan braid, then stroked the soot-streaked, snake locks of loosened hair from the chieftain's cheek and forehead. 'Brave one, take my promise, you won't suffer alone any longer.'

Last, his formed will made manifest as an intricate tracery of light, the Sorcerer imprinted the cipher to summon Traithe's raven against the *caithdein's* stilled brow.

He added a whispered blessing, then finished, 'Act wisely and well.'

Davien straightened up. His flesh by now stung to a blush by the cold, he tipped back his head. The aquiline jut of his profile formed a stamped cameo against the black rock of the outcrop as a poised second passed. Then a soundless explosion of light ripped his male figure into formless static. The sparks winked and faded. In their place, an eagle shot upward, winging purposefully northward into the waning night.

Behind, flurried in a backwash of winnowed snow, the raptor left the elegant, clear imprint of two naked human feet.

Shortly there came a gyrating wind, which blurred their edges, then fully erased them.

Second Dawn

Winter's latest rank blizzard slowly wore itself out. Early daylight painted the cloud banks over Daon Ramon to a sea of raging vermilion. The muffled hills were loaf sugar beneath, veined black where the swift, open streamlets carved through the meandering seams of the gullies. For Braggen, holed up under the clotted boughs of a thicket with three blown-out horses on lead reins, the storm's ending increased the potential for lethal setback. He had been forced to pause in his flight with Prince Arithon since several hours before, as the heavy drifts piled too high.

No horse could gallop, mired to the chest. Set to awkward flight, he could not risk becoming a slow-moving target for Etarra's crack teams of archers. While the blizzard tapered off, he had shivered in wait, hoping the lessening snowfall would mask his rucked trail, plain as a plowed furrow across the pristine curve of the swales. Braggen took stringent steps to evade chance discovery. He blindfolded the horses. Then he smeared their nostrils with a wintergreen salve and strapped on burlap nose bags to smother their keen sense of smell. Should mounted riders close in, he could ill afford the prompt of a whinny if his small herd called in challenge. The country was too riddled with headhunter trackers to countenance the exposure. If he chanced to be flushed, the prince in his charge would be doomed; even to inexperienced eyes, the drifts disclosed each sign of disturbance as cleanly as inked lines on a manuscript.

The day brightened, affirming as fact that Braggen's restraint had been nothing but stark necessity.

Beyond the screening lattice of caked branches, the stitched tracks of several mounted patrols scored the hillsides, basted with the zigzagged game trails of deer and the skipped prints of winter-furred hare. The clansman resigned himself. He had no choice but bide. At least the ditch where he sheltered was snagged in wild briar. The tangle formed a vicious bulwark of thorn, nearly impassable to a horse, and for a man, a snagging trap that invited scored flesh and ripped clothing.

Braggen had needed spur and whip to drive his three animals through. That harsh foresight, and his hunter's instinct for weather, had let him seek cover in time. The prints of his back trail lay well buried before the snow dwindled and the gusts backed down to a breeze.

Through the inactive hours, the gruff clansman did what he could, shifting his gear onto the cream gelding and rubbing down the tired animal he had ridden. The horse bearing Arithon could not be relieved. The far ridge had sparkled with torches, before dawn. By now the Alliance scouts ranged out in force, the deep-winter silence marred by the occasional snatched fragments of their hailing shouts. Should a passing patrol flush him from cover, Braggen refused to be set on the run with his prince caught in the change between one mount and the next.

For a mercy, the royal body wrapped in Jieret's bearskin was warm, if scarcely breathing. Now and again, Braggen bared the pale face, inanimate as death in repose. Not even an eyelash would flicker when he dripped melted snow to moisten the slack-jawed mouth. The blued eyelids stayed closed, and the unbandaged hand remained slack in the bindings that secured the scarred forearm against the horse's wet neck. The fine, sculptured bones and spare symmetry of each knuckle gave graphic testament to the disastrous confrontation that had so narrowly missed costing Earl Jieret his life. What liegeman could behold the startling grace of those fingers and not grasp the tragic truth: that this prince was not and never had been a man made for wielding the sword.

'My liege, I am sorry,' Braggen whispered, though he harbored no fondness for sentiment. Yet even against his hardened sensibilities, he saw that Arithon s'Ffalenn should be nowhere near this brutal setting. The crime lay beyond words, that a bard of his stature had been born at the crux of a conflict. Such talent as his should have been cosseted in comfort, surrounded by gentle company. Throughout a long lifetime, this Masterbard should have shouldered no other burden than setting his matchless voice to the extraordinary gift of his music.

Discomfited, Braggen coughed behind his wet glove. For a nerve-wracked moment, he faced away. Then, with bearded lips compressed to a dogged line, he checked the wounded right hand to make certain no stains had leaked through the dressing. Jieret's cautery had been thorough. The measure was holding despite rough usage and the desperate, jolting ride.

'Give his Grace no sustenance,' the High Earl had told Braggen, though the instruction seemed queerly unnatural. That any creature could survive in suspension, apparently more dead than alive, made this charge an unsettling watch duty.

Braggen folded those too-eloquent hands under the generous cover of the bearskin. A man of visceral emotion who had been molded to austerity by bitter experience, he ate his biscuit and jerked meat stubbornly facing the hills. Bare survival demanded his unswerving attention. He tried not to dwell on the royalty strapped to the back of the horse like a sackful of raider's booty.

Late morning, a changed wind swept the sky to clear cobalt. Braggen aroused from a catnap with sun in his eyes, and cursed the untrustworthy weather. Risen temperature had already laddered the clumped ice on the branches to plinking, glass droplets. The snow silvered also, glazed to a crust where the shade fell. Even the slight thaw brought conditions from ugly to worse. By nightfall, the drifts would be armored with ice, an outright gift to a tracker since an old trail would seal with the freeze. The fluffy light snow and churned clods where horses breasted a fresh passage were going to become impossible to conceal.

Braggen saw no alternative, had already faced the flat recognition that he could not remain tucked in hiding. Each passing hour let his enemies close in, among them Lysaer s'Ilessid. Only two days remained of the grace period that allowed Arithon's spirit to stay safely bound in the sword blade. If the Teir's'Ffalenn was not carried beyond range of Desh-thiere's curse before then, the disaster that followed would lie beyond all hope of mending. Braggen fretted, weighed his dearth of unlovely options, then committed his resource to the one that looked the most promising.

The Alliance patrols combed the brush for clan fugitives. His best chance of upset lay in contrary action: he would not give them a skulking target.

Committed to peril, Braggen waxed the string and bent his yew longbow. While the sun slowly climbed the arc to the zenith and dipped past the high mark of noon, he subjected each one of his arrows to an exhaustive inspection. The ones with worn fletching and uneven shafts, he discarded. The rest, he punched into the snow in neat rows, the best ones ranked nearest to hand. An old hunter's trick, he slit a thread off the cuff of Arithon's silk shirt and snagged it to one of the branches. The streamer would act as a telltale to read every minor shift in the wind.

He checked the blindfolded horses again and filled their nose bags with grain. Lastly, he waited. Not temperamental when his task involved raiding, he held his nerves vised to a serpent's cold patience. He stood his ground, stilled, with only the day's shadows moving.

The next patrol happened by in the late afternoon, a half dozen of Etarra's elite troops whose field experience included the reiving habits of headhunters. As the curve of the hill steered their progress, Braggen could see bloodstains pinking the sweat on their horses' flanks. Each man's saddlecloth wore a fringework of scalps, the ripped hide raw red where some late victim's clan braid had been hacked off as a trophy.

Nearer, the six came. Their course was going to pass the thicket quite closely. Braggen held fast, unafraid of detection. Around him, for clear yards on all sides, the drifted snow lay unbroken. The trampled passage of two earlier patrols crossed the slopes, right and left, an imprinted reassurance that nothing untoward had entered the vale since the scouts had made their last sweep.

The men bearing in, their reins looped at a walk, had just survived a fresh skirmish. If their bullish senior officer looked bothered by saddle sores, his underlings were cocky, loud-mouthed with high spirits and victory. They moved upwind as well; their horses were not going to be first to scent the bunched geldings masked in the thicket. The party drew nearer. Engrossed in a moment of jocular pantomime, they entrusted their mounts to pick their own footing. Predictably, their track skirted the far rim of the gully where the wind-razed dusting of snow offered easier passage for animals whose legs were scraped raw from punching through ice-crusted drifts.

The late sunlight picked out detail with merciless clarity: of clotted swords jammed into scabbards, uncleaned, and saddle packs bulging with booty. Braggen recognized one of the braids, the seal brown one with the black-diamond snakeskin knotting the end as a tie. He had seen that marsh krait tanned by a young girl from Halwythwood as a gift to bring her sweetheart fair luck.

She would grieve to learn that Dame Fortune had looked elsewhere this sad morning on Daon Ramon Barrens.

His rage locked and barred behind cold-blooded purpose, Braggen firmed his grip on his bow. His movement stayed imperceptibly slow as he caught up the first, flawless arrow. He nocked the end to the string. Patient as a plaster-cast statue, he held. Coiled in a state of light, relaxed balance, he watched the oncoming riders whoop and boast, laughing as they described the favors they would claim from the ladies at home, once their purses jingled with bounty gold.

Deadly silent, Braggen bent back his bow. As locked on his course as the draw of moon and sun, raising the unstoppable tide, he sighted his mark through the lattice of crusted branches. The steadfast word of apology he whispered was the same one accorded the deer he brought down for the stewpot. 'Forgive.'

He released. His shaft took a rider in the middle of the pack at point-blank range through the throat.

Another arrow; another shot, and the man behind tumbled from his saddle. The rear guard reined up in shouting surprise. A third arrow, released, slammed and folded the officer as he spun back to address the confusion.

By then, the last man in line had belatedly noted the launching site of the bowfire.

'There!' he screamed. 'In that thicket!' Flattened against his horse's neck, with a stout companion sharp at his heels, he charged downslope and drove his mount into the gulch.

Ruled by nerveless experience, Braggen ignored them. His fourth arrow tracked the cool veteran on the bank who had kept his head in the crisis. No fool, that one jabbed spurs to his chestnut with intent to seek reinforcements. His good sense was hampered by his officer's mount, left riderless in his path. The beast wheeled and crow-hopped, both forefeet snagged in dropped reins.

A disastrous, forced check on the part of the veteran; and Braggen's bow thwapped in release. The man fell, transfixed in the groin through the slit hem of his mail shirt.

The other pair who had rushed to attack had dependably mired in the gully, their horses bucking the chest-deep drifts. Braggen had time to measure his shots. The trailing man was cut down, wounded, as his mare foundered, stumbling; the companion ahead clawed up the near bank under cover of his mount's neck, to be tossed forward at the shuddering pitch as the horse under him sharply missed stride. The animal went down hard, the shaft nestled into its seal-dark coat buried to the fletching behind the jaw. As its gurgling scream shattered the quiet, the rider kicked free of his stirrups. Trained in countless drills, he cast free, running; and tripped, both ankles noosed by Daon Ramon's vicious coils of briar.

Sword out, pale with the awareness he sprawled at the mercy of the hidden clan marksman, he dropped flat and tried to kick free.

His killed horse cost a small penalty. The blindfolded animals at Braggen's back now snorted and sidled in alarm. In jeopardy of being jostled if one broke a tether, the clansman slipped forward. At the verge of the thicket, he nocked his next arrow and took aim with exacting care.

He wounded the last man, also. Again, on a fleeting word of apology, he shot and fully dispatched the expiring horse.

Then, another shaft ready to draw, he waited. The two men he had deliberately crippled floundered and thrashed through the snow. Five horses, cast loose, circled and chuffed, and finally bunched up, facing the strange herd in the thicket. They snorted and tossed heads, the sharp smell of blood warring with herdbound curiosity.

Braggen watched only the felled men. One sprawled still in a stain of spreading crimson, determinedly playing dead. The other, moaning through clenched teeth, made no effort to shout and bring help; as sure a sign as a raider would get that no allies lay within earshot. These had not been outriders, but routine scouts, with no company marching at hand.

Braggen lowered his bow. He bundled his last arrows back into his quiver, then soothed his unsettled geldings, a difficulty: reaction to his late round of butchery left his hands badly unsteady. Lilting soft nonsense, he untied equine blindfolds and stowed the nose bags to let the animals breathe unimpaired. Then, in no hurry, but without wasted motion, he picked his way from the thicket. His thick, stag-hide leathers let him plow through the thorns with small penalty beyond a few scratches. An ugly but unavoidable cruelty, he adhered to his plan by strict order of priority.

Both the wounded were disarmed. The man with the arrow through his thigh cursed him steadily, until faintness rendered him speechless. Braggen stood by, wretched and clammy with his own distressed sweat, until blood loss finally drove the man senseless. Then he snapped off the arrow shaft and bound up the wound. The other man did not quiet until he was forcibly gagged. He was left where he lay, while Braggen attended the loose horses, catching the one which had entangled its bridle, then mounting to herd in the others. He secured all five, then tied three to a scrub tree, while the one he sat and another in hand were wheeled and trotted this way and that. Before long, the torn snow in the gulch wore a mishmash of overlaid tracks. Braggen reined up satisfied when he judged the site wore the appearance of a hard-fought skirmish.

Shaking now, chilled to the bone as the ripping winds robbed the warmth from the lowering sun, the clansman dismounted. He had little time, and no chance at all, if another patrol happened by and flushed him before his grisly round of artifice was finished. The dead he stripped to the skin, rings and clothing. He ripped out the shafts that had killed the first two, leaving a reiver's toll of cut throats and sword wounds. As though the officer's corpse had been clanborn, hacked down by headhunters, he drew his knife. Retching, he forced himself to follow through. He bludgeoned the face and hacked off the scalp.

The hair he jammed under a sizable boulder, and the clothes left too blood-soaked to disguise. He saved one blotched shirt, used the linen to bind up the head and face of the gagged man. The wretch slowed his progress with useless struggle, until a kick in the belly dropped him limp. While he choked through an unnerving interval of recovery, Braggen lashed him, wrist and ankle, and secured him across his own horse. The stout companion received the same treatment. Limp from his draining wound, that one draped like a sack, stertorously breathing and pale. His less-damaged comrade thrashed and moaned, while the chestnut mare under him stamped and sidled, jibbing against the lead rein looped around her high-set neck.

Braggen barred his heart against mercy. Their lives against Arithon's, his choice was clear-cut. He left them. Bearing an armload of filched clothing, he burrowed back into the thicket. A handful of minutes, and he reemerged, clad in the weapons and clothing of an Alliance man-at-arms. He had done the unthinkable and cut off his clan braid. His stout leathers and furred cloak were stuffed as additional booty in the saddle pack borne by one of the Etarran horses. The officer's sunwheel mantle now covered Arithon, the bearskin beneath kept for warmth. A last touch, the royal feet dangling from the hemline no longer wore soft-soled boots. Those, too, had been shoved in the supply pack and replaced with square-toed black ones, too large, and buckled with an engraved set of roweled spurs.

His Grace had been splashed with blood. Since he was not bearded or gray, a stained dressing swathed his mouth and jaw, and all of his raven hair. The few strands which spiked through were gore-soaked, and whitened, a piece of invention done with a filched lock clipped from one of the clan trophy braids.

'A more honorable end,' Braggen snapped to himself, a bit breathless. Strung-up nerves and the effort of swallowing back nausea were turning him faintly dizzy. Numb in the feet since the largest man's boots were too tight for his muscular calf, he banded the horses together and set off. He rode up the ridge line, to every appearance an Alliance survivor whose patrol had been set upon, with himself left to bear up the wounded and drive in their salvaged mounts.

Just past sundown, he was challenged at the first checkpoint. The cleared air by then had brought in vicious cold. Each stinging breath feathered tendrils of hoarfrost on beard and hood. A northerly wind sang over the hills, stamped calcine white under flooding moonlight. The men at the posts were permitted no fire. Every miserable one of them huddled on watch, faces cowled in wool, and backs turned to the punishing chill.

The halberdiers who barred Braggen's way were loath to stand out in the wind, or brandish their steel-studded weapons.

'Password!' snapped the sergeant as the disorganized cavalcade shambled toward him. He wore a blanket under his cloak that covered the oiled links of his hauberk. His gauntlets were left off for comfort. On a night too cruel to sustain suspicion, he tucked his gloved hands beneath his crossed arms and held back, keeping his numbed feet well clear of maceration as the horses with emptied saddles shoved and stamped, barging against the ones burdened.

Braggen wrangled with the reins, engrossed by the trials of keeping the three mounts bearing bodies clear of the jostling press. 'I'm sorry,' he apologized, his phrasing slurred to sound townborn. 'I don't know the watchword.' The deception enhanced by the loosely wrapped cloth of his muffler, he affected a show of self-conscious embarrassment. 'I was griped from bad meat, had the runs in the ditch. Wasn't listening up at the time we rode out, for the worry I'd brown my own breeches.'

As one of the halberdiers masked a snigger, he tipped his head toward the motionless form sheeted under the sunwheel mantle. 'Dorik knew.' Helped by the grace of Etarran vanity, Braggen had found the fallen officer's name stamped in gold on his saddle.

'The eighth patrol's Dorik?' A tall man shoved from the press of his fellows, his gloved hand clenched to his sword grip. 'He's dead, then?'

'Probably will be,' Braggen answered, resigned. 'He wasn't good when I pulled him out of the snow. We were ambushed,' he added in redundant afterthought. As though stupid with shock, or chilled witless by cold, he hunkered against the vicious barrage of the wind. 'I was going for a healer.' Eyes shut in forbearance, though every nerve crawled, he forced himself still as someone else shoved his way into the packed mass of horses. Enemy hands pulled back the cloak hood. Arithon's wrapped head was examined in the darkness, with no chance of reprieve if the ruse with stained bandages roused the watch officer's suspicion.

'Head wound,' someone murmured. 'It appears to be Dorik, and yes, he's breathing, just barely.'

Braggen let his horse feel the kiss of a spur, then reined its startled bound short with impatience. 'I've said Dorik's hurt badly. Hold me up, and you'll throw away his last chance if he can't hang on.'

'Where did this happen?' the sergeant demanded, cutting through the distressed clamor as other men crowded around.

'His pulse is too sluggish,' the observer reported. 'Won't see the morning, most likely.'

Braggen jabbed another rude heel to his horse, on the far side, where no one would see. Obliging, it sidled. The speaker was driven back before any further examination unmasked his desperate subterfuge.

But the sergeant was not so easily discouraged. 'Where did this happen?'

The milling horses lent Braggen the excuse to be terse. 'Back there, a touch over three leagues, in a gully. You can't miss the bodies.'

That moment, the other prisoner gagged under the splashed bandage aroused and started a round of muffled screaming.

'Light's grace! Let me ride, he's in pain,' Braggen begged.

Another man with a bristle of blond beard elbowed the onlookers back in sharp pity. 'Let the man pass! If that's Hadge, Dorik's tracker, he's got a pretty wife who's going to be grieving.'

'Can we leave?' Braggen snapped. 'Else I'll be hauling three stiffs for my pains. Where's the main camp? Someone point me toward a warm tent and the hands of a competent healer.'

The gruff sergeant relented. 'We'll do better. I'll dispatch an escort to take you.'

'The barbarian dogs had crack bowmen,' Braggen cautioned. 'Might need your men here, in case I was followed. I'd feel better if you used your damned escort to run down the murdering bastards.'

'The more reason not to send you on alone,' the sergeant insisted.

A nerve-wracking delay, while Braggen was offered a drink from a flask, and the man to ride with him was chosen. To save time, the Etarran-bred horse with the least bloodstained saddle was cut from the bunch for his use.

'Hurry on, man. Catch up as soon as you're mounted.' Before the scout who came forward could settle astride, or adjust the length of his stirrups, the disguised clansman spurred away at a canter.

Beyond the next range of hills Braggen sharply reined up. 'Here,' he called, while his escort fell in, breathless with annoyance alongside. 'Come and take charge of some of these lead reins.'

'Well, didn't I just try?' The fellow edged his gelding into the press, leaned out and extended his arm to shoulder his share of the burden.

He received no gift of reins, but Braggen's mailed hand on his wrist, and a yank that dragged him half out of his saddle. While his horse plunged and jostled at the sharp shift in weight, he sucked in a gasped breath.

The knife took him before he could yell, a punching stab through the neck. He struggled, gagging, while the blade's point sawed deep and sliced through the artery under his jaw.

Rushing dizziness followed the hot jet of his blood. The jolt of pure panic raced his heart and sped the ebb of his dying strength. He bled out his life, choking through a hacked windpipe, helpless to vent the undignified rage of being tied like killed game to the neck of his distressed horse.

'Ath's mercy, let you be the last of them,' Braggen pleaded when the victim he strapped down had ceased breathing. Now informed where the camp was, he made swift disposition and cut loose the bay laden down with the corpse. The two others with their burden of wounded, he freed also. A sharp smack with the flat of a sword drove them off at a violent gallop. Let them lay down confused trails for the trackers. With luck the needy wretches they carried would preoccupy the patrol who finally chased down the strays.

Bone chilled, and wretchedly trembling, Braggen wiped clean

his sticky knife. He sheathed the weapon, then dragged at the lead reins, towing his remaining band of horses north and west. He risked precious time, keeping the animals' pace to a prudent trot. A few he let loose at intervals when he pulled back to a resting walk. These obliged by seeding meandering loops and a jagged chain of back tracks. On short notice, this was the best could be done to suggest the whole band made their aimless way without riders.

Once he judged he had passed well beyond the Alliance encampment without drawing the perimeter scouts, he changed horses and veered due north.

The cold settled in. A crystalline clear sky lidded the downs like a jar of rare indigo glass. Braggen hunched against the buffeting gusts, chilled to relentless discomfort. The spilled blood of the killed man on his forearm and shoulder froze the cloth to crackling stiffness. The damp sleeve beneath did not dry, but let the remorseless cold burn straight through to the skin. He understood he would need to get dry, or else suffer crippling frostbite.

He drew rein under an outcrop, dogged by the hagridden certainty that each passing second of delay would later come to cost dearly.

Yet if his right hand became too numbed to grasp weapons, no lead he could wrest would be enough to draw his prince clear of armed enemies. Without pause to dismount, Braggen did as he must: unstrapped the silk-wrapped sword from his shoulder. Clutched in an agony of strung tension, he peeled off the sodden Alliance cloak, then the tunic and shirt with its gold ribbon and sunwheel badges. Eyes roving the horizon, each sense primed and listening for the patrol that could trap him in this moment of vulnerability, he crumpled the fine cloth, blotted sweat from his horse's neck and rubbed down his gore-stained skin.

The wind lashed his bare flesh. The cruel stinging was recorded by each exposed nerve. The risk as he dressed half unhinged him with fear. His hands, uncooperative, had long since lost the dexterity to contend with bone buttons and laces. Wrapped shuddering at last in the reclaimed comfort of his original garments, Braggen caught the sword back. Spurred by desperate haste, he slung its silk-clad hilt once again close to hand's reach. Then he ducked his head before the ceaseless, sharp wind, and swung his mount northward again, driving the remounts ahead.

The gelding entrusted with its sunwheel-wrapped burden he kept strapped in tandem with his own.

Setting moon rimmed the hills to the west in cobwebs of ghostly light. The brush and scrub trees had long since rattled clean of the past night's tracery of snow. The curved backs of the drifts wore a sheen of faint silver. Under the ongoing hooves of the horses, the bite and crunch of packed ice punched through the risen scream of each gust. Smashed fragments of crust skittered downwind like thrown cullet. Braggen pressed on with his head turned, face shielded behind the furred rim of his hood. His feet were feelingless lumps in the stirrups. His hands fared no better buried wrist deep in his gelding's tangled mane. If danger arose, and he needed Alithiel unsheathed, he would be forced to cut through the silk wrappings to draw her. The slipknotted bindings Jieret had tied were beyond his fumbling cold grip.

The threat at his back seemed an abstract dream, but for the caked stains on the sunwheel mantle cast over Arithon's body.

Braggen moved by brute will. He prodded his tired horse onward, guided by the yellowed, setting moon until its wan lamp extinguished behind by the fretted hills to the west. The sky overhead was black enamel and chipped diamond, the rock-clad gullies smoothed over by night, treacherous as deadfalls underfoot.

Not long past moonset, Braggen had to cut loose the roan mare. A stumble had lamed her. Despite the pain of a severely wrenched fetlock, she refused to be left, breasting the deepest footing three-legged. Shredded by pity, Braggen found her a sheltered gulch. There, he paused to let the other mounts drink from the black current of an open streamlet. He could do no more. The surcease from the wind offered the mare blandishment to stay, and trailing willow fronds provided her browsing.

He dismounted to blazing pain in both hips from too many hours astride. Limping and stiff, he performed the chore of changing mounts, while the gusts roared over the lip of the ravine and hurled slivered ice through the rattling branches. He stamped circulation back into his feet and dug out a meal of dried meat and biscuit. While he chewed, he checked Arithon. The slow breathing masked under the gore-crusted dressings remained reassuringly warm and regular.

Braggen transferred his prince's slack weight onto the back of a fresh horse. The bandaged hand was still dry, though the bindings keeping his Grace in the saddle had chafed a sore in one wrist. Braggen eased the raw patch with salve, then wound a torn strip from a dead man's shirt around the cord to make padding.

By the time he set foot in the stirrup and remounted, his pulse raced. Fear and tension had filmed him in clammy sweat that was going to chill bitterly, later. Worse, the horses stopped short in refusal to leave the protected ravine. Shrinking himself, crying curses for the necessity, Braggen lashed their balked rumps with the ends of his reins and drove them to forsake their sound instincts.

For now the cold posed an enemy more deadly than any two-legged tracker the Etarrans might set on his back trail. Weariness compounded the incessant chill, hazing the mind toward dozing sleep and leaching away better judgment. Braggen bludgeoned his thick wits, agonized between choices: whether to stop and seek shelter, or press onward into the terrible wind, at the risk of fatal exposure.

Overhead, the stately turn of the stars told him three hours remained before sunrise.

Braggen scraped the frost rime from his beard, his breath a white plume in the darkness. A glance backward showed the rumpled swath of his passage. The scarred prints stitched over the pristine hills left a beacon for enemies to follow.

He made his decision in grim understanding that Daon Ramon's bitter cold at least posed an element of uncertainty. The threat at his heels held no sweet ambiguity. If a company of Etarrans came on in pursuit, and caught him dismounted to rest, he and the prince he was charged to safeguard would be dead in a matter of minutes.

In the end, the torments of unremitting winter lent the gift that spared the s'Ffalenn lineage from extinction. For when the past night's bloody ruse was unraveled, and the slaughtered patrol left unhorsed in the gulch had been tracked down and accounted, only one party of Etarran men-at-arms was dispatched to ride out and retaliate. The accounts matched the evidence with inarguable impeccability: the task force was assured they pursued a lone killer, burdened down with a wounded henchman. Because their presumed quarry was likely no more than a scout strayed from Jieret's war band, they avoided the savage discomfort of mounting the chase until dawn broke.

Under the knives of pallid new sunlight, the patrol of ten lancers saddled up and turned windward. They broke ground, pushing hard, inside a few hours covering the same ground that Braggen had passed through the night. They recognized the lamed mare they found in the ravine, and also, to an outbreak of curses and threats, the stained cloak jammed in her saddle pack.

Enraged, primed for vengeance, they thundered ahead, plowing the barbarian's insolent trail into ripped gouts of torn snow.

The prints they were following yielded no fugitive, but diabolically converged with the chopped slurry of the Mathorn Road.

The patrol pulled up, milling. Amid frozen ruts, the trampled mishmash of cart tracks, and the ice-rimmed hoof marks of galloping couriers riding post from the inland cities to Narms, they could not decipher which way, east or west, their benighted quarry had turned.

'Sithaer's breeding fiends!' cracked the distempered officer, compelled to draw rein and split forces. His men dispersed under orders to detain and question every wagon and rider they encountered. Yet no merchant's caravan reported anything untoward. The message couriers who might have distinguished the barbarian were long since away down the road.

The search party encountered no other loose horses; none bearing a bearded and bandaged officer, and none ridden by a reiving clansman disguised in a bloodstained town mantle. Nor did they find any telltale sign that the fugitives had turned off the thoroughfare. The pair might have slipped northward into the mountains, or swung south again in fiendish deception, to hide in the boggy, briar-thatched bottomlands carved by the frozen Aiyenne.

The officer hammered an enraged fist into his horse's wet neck. He swore until he ran short of breath, not one whit appeased when his unhelpful scout suggested the clansman was quite likely a Companion from Deshir.

'A right demon for cleverness, and worse, on this route, he'll be a well-seasoned raider.' The veteran slapped his whip against his gloved palm in balked fury. 'Send too many men to beating the bushes, we could see them blunder into a right mess of set traps. If not, very likely you'll see what slender evidence he's left become ground underfoot and obliterated.'

The sergeant shut his mouth, his frown like strapped lead. Inexcusably, this setback was going to serve him a serious delay. 'Call the patrol in, then!' he snapped in the teeth of his exasperated scout. 'Find our three fastest men. They go back to fetch trackers. Tell them, better blister their butts at a gallop! Each minute we hang back, that clan butcher's widening his lead. I could strip *hide* for the blighted night watch and their pussyfoot shirking! We're not going to close on this murderer now without help from the headhunters' damned dogs!'

Penalty

The Prime's summons reached the sisterhouse in the early afternoon, with Lirenda immersed in the distasteful task of rendering sulfur for plague talismans. Highscarp's wealthy merchants preferred such wards for their southbound trade ships. Naught else, they believed, would repel the suborned humors that carried the virulent summer pestilence that plagued galley crews sent around Scimlade Tip.

Lips tucked in grim distaste, her patrician nose wrinkled under the assaulting odor of rotten eggs, Lirenda batted away a fallen strand of jet hair with the back of a humid wrist. Detesting the stench, left rumpled and sweaty from the heat thrown off by three boiling pots set on braziers, she would have given the plump, beringed customer the sharp side of her tongue, had he stood there: that the eight-penny casks filled in the marshes by the Ippash delta caused more running flux than any seasonal change in the air. The pinchfisted fool could have saved the bother of talismans, and spared the silk guild a needless oath of debt had he underwritten the silver to pay for clean water drawn from the city cisterns.

Immersed within her black cloud of irritation, Lirenda failed to notice the liveried page at the doorway until he had spoken in direct address.

'Initiate Lirenda, you are asked to present yourself to the Prime.'

Called in the act of weighing an ounce of ground sulfur piled on a twist of rice paper, the enchantress who had fallen from

416

senior privilege startled abruptly erect. Her sleeve snagged the chain suspending the scale pan. A chiming spill of tipped weights clattered across the sheets of stamped copper on the tabletop. One struck the glass flask, and the sulfur upset. Arisen with her lap streaked with reeking yellow powder, Lirenda all but spat the requisite words of formality. 'You may lead me to the Matriarch.' Bristled with anger to be caught in a common laborer's state of disarray, a frosty edge sharpened her aristocrat's hauteur. 'I shall follow the moment I've refreshed my appearance.'

'You'll come now,' an icier voice interrupted. Arrived behind the page, her cowled robe missed in the gloom of the corridor, Senior Cadgia touched the boy's shoulder in kindly dismissal. No such softened sentiment eased her brisk manner as she surveyed her former superior. 'I have been sent as your escort this time. The Prime is ill disposed, and will not be kept waiting on a charge of disobedience.'

A moment, while threat flooded dread like poured ice through her veins; Lirenda bent her head. The onyx sheen of her hair dipped into the shadow as she grasped the tongs and emptied the coals from the braziers into the fire pail. Steam billowed in clouds of silvery vapor that drafts from the high windows dispersed. Her tawny eyes an unblinking tiger's upon her triumphant elder, Lirenda said, 'I bow to the Prime's will on the matter, of course.'

The audience was not held in the customary ground-floor chamber, with the wide, breakfront windows overlooking the whitecapped vista of Eltair Bay. The doubled doors to that room were latched closed as Lirenda was ushered past. Muffled by the carved panels of curly maple, she heard the scrape of industrious brushes, as complaining drudges inside scrubbed and waxed the parquet floor. An acrid odor hung on the air, reminiscent of recent smoke. Had the enchantress not been consumed by the need to stifle her rising anxiety, she might have asked after the irregularity. But Cadgia's tread hustled her down the wainscoted hallway, then up the stair with its brass rods and red runner. A clipped gesture warned Lirenda to follow without pause, sure sign any questions would be rebuffed.

An acrid bite of charred wood also lingered along the upper passage. Smoke had grayed the groined ceiling. Pallid light fell through the lancet windows and struck bladed rays through a film of blue haze. The leftover smell bore a nauseating reek of singed meat, poorly masked by the purging fragrance of herbs.

Through the delicate perfume of sweetgrass and gardenia, sharp as filings, Lirenda noticed the bracing tang left by an infusion of tienelle. That trace scent of seersweed awoke damning proof: something more than an act of deep conjury had transpired behind those shut doors late last night.

Snapped from self-absorption, Lirenda took stock of the overlooked details and noted the undue tension that stilted her colleague's self-righteous carriage. Speculation rekindled, igniting the predatory glint in the depths of her tawny eyes. She had heard that a Senior Circle had met, filled by members of the Koriani Council. She had not guessed, nor had stirring rumors yet ruffled the routine affairs in the sisterhouse, that their works had gone drastically wrong.

Lirenda smiled, sparked to provocation. 'I'm not being called to mop up the spilled broth?'

One brief returned glance brushed her off in contempt. Yet the stunned, secret silence that stilled Cadgia's tongue bespoke a far-reaching disaster.

Lirenda had no chance to probe whether the setback could be milked for advantage. The older enchantress turned down a molded gilt archway, set her pink, matron's hand to the latch, and clicked open the door to the Prime's private apartment.

The anteroom, with its dark, tasseled tapestries, and its low, cushioned divans, lay empty. Stale air and closed-in dust suggested the casements had not been opened for freshening. The plush rugs, bordered with sigils of guard, had not been brushed up by the servants. The purple wool pile bore the crushed imprint of many feet, coming and going. An overbearing taint of tansy salve lingered, the rancid musk of the goose-grease base intermingled with the dried lavender the past Prime, and now her young successor, preferred to sweeten her closets.

The Prime's bedchamber door was also closed, with the thick velvet curtains gathered over the lintel drawn across to muffle sound.

Curiosity prickled too sharply to quell. 'Selidie's unwell?' Lirenda demanded in a disbelieving whisper.

Cadgia regarded her, again without answering, the chill deep as layered ice in blue eyes. She brushed back the curtains, gently tapped. As the page inside responded and inserted a key, then unlocked the oiled-wood panel, she gestured for Lirenda to enter. 'You're expected.'

The disgraced enchantress straightened, chin raised. She needed no refined skills of observation to sense that looming peril awaited her beyond. Her dignity regal despite her wisped hair and the sulfur streaks marring her skirt, she crossed over the threshold to answer the mandatory summons.

The curtains over the windows were drawn.

Under gloom deep as night, scented candles burned in tiered ranks from silver holders atop the armoire. More tapers blazed from bronze stands, set on both sides of the raised bed. The furnishing itself was massive and old, of black Valzein lacquer, gleaming with citrus oil, and inlaid like white fire with floral patterns in costly mother-of-pearl. The tied-back folds of the bed hangings were purple, the sumptuous Narms dyes dark enough to seem black. The warding sigils stitched in copper and gold thread, whorled in patterns of hold and bind, bespoke an exhaustive, even desperate strength. The chained ciphers described no pattern of protection Lirenda had ever been taught.

All but overcome by the sudden, shrill instinct that urged her to drop dignity and flee, she clung to decorum. Step by trembling step, she advanced. The figure propped amid the pillows regarded her, the cold eyes pale azure, not jet. Yet with her lush hair bound under a headdress of white linen, and her porcelain skin pale as a snowfield, Prime Selidie for one unnerving moment seemed as wasted as the ghost of her late predecessor, Morriel.

Shaken by that uncanny impression, Lirenda reached the throw rug spread at the foot of the bed. Deportment sustained her. She curtseyed. Yet even as she drew breath to pronounce the formal words of obeisance, another woman's voice interrupted; someone whose presence had been shielded behind the strategic dazzle of candles.

'You will not address her,' informed the sisterhouse peeress. 'Nor will you otherwise speak, except in reply to set questions.'

Lirenda lost poise, her gasp of sheer terror like a rip in the absolute quiet: for this summons was no formal audience, and no straightforward reprimand. She had been called to the ritual, closed trial reserved for initiates who had transgressed their vow of obedience.

The peeress's presence had passed unseen because she would be veiled and gowned in black for her role as Ceremonial Inquisitor.

Heart hammering, drenched in the sudden, sour sweat of a fear of suffocating proportion, Lirenda shut her lips against protestations. The order's strict form would not permit questions. By ancient custom, the Koriani Prime could refuse to speak to outsiders. As an initiate placed on trial for infraction, Lirenda was forced to rely on the inquisitor to stand as her intermediary.

'You will kneel,' instructed the peeress. Even her judgmental nature showed distress for the gravity of the charge. Also aware of the unspeakable horror that attended the supreme penalty, she visibly struggled to uphold her office with the semblance of neutral decorum. 'Face your Prime.'

Lirenda did as bidden. Worse than afraid, she shifted her gaze and confronted the Matriarch enthroned on the bed.

Selidie's regard encompassed her with frigid dispassion. The eyes beneath her delicate, arched brows were placid, clear as the glaze on the gentian glass blown by a Falgaire artisan. She appeared settled, in full command at initial, first glance.

Yet the fine-grained, young skin wore the faint stamp of circles beneath masking layers of rice powder. The experienced eye read the signs: the Matriarch was spent from some hard rite of spellcraft, her febrile exhaustion betrayed by the light, kept low to ease sluggish pupils. Composed as she seemed, the hands in her lap lay concealed in the frothy, voile lace of a shawl.

Her tone as she spoke was blunted and languid, as though she had been dosed with strong possets. 'Inform the accused there will be no questions. Her guilt is already proved.'

Lirenda jerked back from retort just in time. Any speech, any appeal would compound her disobedience, closing forever the last loophole in due procedure, that her sentence had not been pronounced. Under the burden of unbearable tension enlivened by panic, she could feel every fiber of the pile rug digging into her knees; each fan of draft across her damp skin. The scent of the air, laden with unguents and the medicinal sting of turpentine, all but overwhelmed her strained senses. Lirenda swallowed, choked mute. Despite every effort, her body betrayed her: once she began shaking, she could not stop. Humiliation stained her cheeks as the long, raking tremors built and built, then swept beyond hope of concealment.

A word from the Matriarch would seal her fate for all time. She could be condemned as a witless one, pinned down and marked with the oathbreaker's brand on her forehead. That cruel debasement would become her last conscious memory before her core self became forfeit. By Koriani law, the mind of the forsworn was routed out by spelled forces channeled through a major crystal until her last shred of identity became stripped.

Selidie said nothing.

Through the hideous pause, the candles kept burning. The boy pages in their gold-and-violet livery maintained their assigned post by the door. Under the muffling veils of the Ceremonial Inquisitor's regalia, the peeress scarcely breathed. Her long fingers clasped white knuckled at her waist, the only detail picked out of the shadows to reveal her silenced distress.

Raked over the coals of a reviling helplessness, Lirenda sustained under torture. Her sole voice was the lifetime result of stern training: a will that let her endure in raw courage. She held herself, kneeling, just shy of collapse, quiet in the threadbare pretense of a calm that had long since been shattered.

Selidie stirred finally. Her head tipped back to rest amid the pillows sewn with sigils in metallic thread. She slanted a glance toward the Ceremonial Inquisitor. 'What should be the punishment for acts of vengeful spellcraft inflicted upon a company of unsuspecting guardsmen from Jaelot? That harm cost their lives.' Her voice dulcet, she added, 'The geas of pursuit that drove them to ruin *was not done by my order!*'

Forbidden to answer unless the question was addressed to her by name, Lirenda stayed silent. Pinned under the Prime's devouring regard, she still wrestled her risen distress. Her body refused the same self-command. Perspiration stippled her brow and rolled in drops down her temples. Frozen as the mouse before the coiled snake, she dared not even wonder how the Prime had discovered the details of her transgression. She had set rigorous sigils of guard against scrying. A linked construct tied in by masterful invention should have kept the spell's signature from imprinting any telltale traces on the lane flux.

The Ceremonial Inquisitor also was reft speechless, while the ranked candles burned, the white beeswax run liquid and refrozen in grotesque, clumped driblets.

Selidie Prime held her blazing regard on Lirenda. Her stilled quiet stayed absolute, the linen mantled over her as freezing white as the shimmer off a distant ice field. At length, she snapped a command to her pages. 'Fetch the Skyron crystal.'

Brittle as blown glass, drained sickeningly hollow, Lirenda fought not to faint. Mercy upon her, *she was not sentenced yet!* But the desperation, the looming fear of annihilation, threatened to break her before time. If this were Morriel she faced, *everything that transpired was a test.* The penalty confronting her was not pronounced; its severity could yet be mitigated. But not if she snapped or lost her head. Lirenda hung on beyond reason and will, her soaked clothing plastered against quivering flanks. She closed her dry throat against pleading until the tears she refused to shed brimmed the shelves of her eyelids.

'The accused has schooled herself to a superb self-control,' Selidie observed, while the page who filled her request came forward and raised the lid of a bronze-bound coffer. 'A great shame she could not show the same character regarding her personal feelings.'

The prioress herself could scarcely withstand the bearing pressure of those glacial, blue eyes. She curtseyed, her black robes and veil a sigh of stirred draft in the stillness. 'Given a stay of clemency, the accused might yet learn.'

Selidie's delicate features showed no change of expression. 'She has been shown quarter. Was, in fact, granted an earlier reprieve in the form of a trial of recompense.' Contempt like a whipcrack infused the last line, and the chill gaze blazed back, to flick over Lirenda, from her raised, rigid chin, to her cramped, slippered feet, tucked under her buttocks as she knelt in ruthless suspense by the foot of the Prime's raised bed. 'She failed the test, and in rebellious fury, committed the act that has brought her here to face sentence. This time, no plea will be heard.'

The prioress bent her head, chastened. 'Your will be done, Matriarch.'

'Bind the wrists of the accused with stout cloth,' Prime Selidie commanded the page who remained by the door. No gesture accompanied her ringing, hard words. 'Then bring her before me.'

To the Ceremonial Inquisitor, she instructed, 'Take up the Skyron crystal when the boy retrieves the small coffer. You will unveil the stone. Raise its active focus, then hold the channel open for my use.'

Lirenda shut her eyes, a fractional break in control, but one impelled by necessity. Dizzied and faint, she could not stay upright for another moment without easing her spinning vision. Sound continued to reach her, the remorseless train of forward events marked out through a swimming, self-imposed darkness: the approaching step of the page, then his hesitant touch as he grasped her. She must not resist, must not flinch at the tightening bite of the cloth as he knotted her wrists behind her back.

Nor did that ignominy blunt the clink of wrought brass as the prioress unlatched each one of twelve fastenings on the box holding the Skyron aquamarine.

Although this focus stone did not emanate the overwhelming aura of the Great Waystone, its unveiled presence could be felt, a dire current flooding through the sharp taint of ointments, and the musk of Lirenda's terrified sweat. She fought her turned senses, roused deadened flesh to respond as the page's prod at her back signaled her to arise. Stumbling against the boy's inexpert touch, she mounted the low step to the Prime's bedside.

There, she was again bidden to kneel, this time on bare floor. The wood hurt her knees. The discomfort compounded the raced thud of her heart, and the shuddering weakness that remorselessly threatened to unstring her.

'Ath's pity upon you,' the peeress breathed, her whisper in Lirenda's ear surreptitious as, relentlessly bound to obedience, she was told by the Prime to touch the enabled aquamarine against the neck at the base of the accused's skull.

The contact burned, colder than arctic ice and tingling with a charged corona of power.

Lirenda would have collapsed then, had the peeress's stout knee not braced her back from behind. What lay ahead would be worse than unpleasant. Twice in her career as First Enchantress to the Prime, Lirenda had been the one asked to bear the live focus stone while a condemned initiate was rendered witless.

Prime Selidie knew as much. She observed her victim's stifled panic, remote in disinterest as a reptile.

She has not read the sentence, even still, Lirenda reminded herself. The stress climbed unbearably, while the cloth ties she reflexively fought in tight jerks chafed her skin red, and terror all but overmastered her.

Yet no reprieve came. Step by step, the process resumed as the Prime demanded the surrender of the accused's personal quartz crystal. Lirenda bit her lip to throttle her urge to whimper as the page came forward, dug under her tight collar, and caught up the stone's silver chain.

Head turned aside, Lirenda choked back a gasp as the quartz pendant was lifted away.

'Remove the covering from my hands,' Selidie directed the page. 'Then turn the accused's crystal over to me.'

White lace was lifted away, releasing the cloying stench of styptic powder, unguents, and herbs. The hands, now revealed, were a grisly ruin, all cracked, charred flesh, and brittle ends of seared bone.

Lirenda stifled a gagging shriek. Suffocating under the night-mare web of anticipated experience, she needed her last shred of will to stave off total breakdown. Second to second, she battled hysteria with the fact that *she had yet to be sentenced.*

The creeping suspicion stayed all but drowned under her blasting fear: *that whatever power had upset the Prime's conjury had acted on a scale unimaginable.* Never before in the order's long history had Fellowship Sorcerers broken through the wards of the Great Waystone. Ath's adepts, or Paravians, none else were capable.

Lirenda latched on to the faint breath of hope, that such a crisis meant she was needed. Perhaps after all, tonight's brutal trial was no more than a course of chastisement.

Prime Selidie refused the humane course in any case. She did not soften or speak outright. In punishment, surely, for the past folly of Lirenda's insinuations at Whitehold, she followed the irreversible steps that would sunder the condemned from personal volition and memory. The Matriarch accepted the quartz and chain into her crippled hands, despite a pain which snatched her breath ragged. She hissed through her teeth and unbent crabbed fingers, then traced the Prime's sigil of command over Lirenda's crystal.

The accused felt the force of that binding lock over her. Vised in its hold, body and mind, Lirenda became powerless to move. While thought and feeling raged on untouched, shackled within helpless flesh, she felt the first, sawing tingle of the Skyron stone thrumming its invasive vibration through her skull. All her barriers were stripped. The fire of impelled presence poured in liquid torment along the trapped channels of her nerves. Nausea followed, ripped by spinning dizziness. Unable to seize even the animal relief of letting her stomach wring itself empty, Lirenda heard every word as Selidie pronounced the formal lines of her sentence.

'For the crime of disobedience, for causing willful harm without direct orders from a Koriani senior, the accused will wear the brand for the rest of her natural life.' The Prime Matriarch leaned forward. The raised crystal, its dangling chain gently swinging, was touched to Lirenda's brow.

Dread flowered from the contact, a desperate, suffocating panic that snapped reason like so much spun thread.

Cut off from survival's most primal instinct to flinch, Lirenda longed for her wheeling senses to shut down. Relief lay beyond reach. She could not faint. The Skyron aquamarine charged with the Prime's master sigils denied her any small respite. The sickening stench of Selidie's roasted flesh enveloped her like a cloud. By force, she endured the corpse-touch of bare bone, a prick alongside the chill point of the quartz crystal bearing on her sweating skin. She smelled the Prime's breath, sour with herb tinctures, as the incantation was spoken.

Then the blinding, hideous pain, as the powers of prime command were unleashed through the crystal, searing the indelible mark of shame on her forehead. Then the figure was completed, the branding accomplished. The quartz point rested still upon Lirenda's brow, driving a rod of coruscating agony into the depths of her cranium. She heard more words, felt the faint snap of connection as the smaller stone became joined into resonance with the overbearing currents raised through the Skyron focus.

Merciful Ath, the worst was to happen. She would be made witless and finish her days as a drooling husk. Lirenda breathed in snatched whimpers, lost now, about to be broken beyond hope. Through abject terror came wretched relief, that within a few moments, the numbness would come. She would not feel, would not think. Though the body would survive, her humiliation would be ended, all personal awareness erased into peace for the rest of her life.

'Inform the accused,' said Prime Selidie above her, inexorable as Daelion Fatemaster, whose dispassionate decree dispatched all doomed men to Sithaer. 'She will not be made witless. As eighth-rank, in these times, her high knowledge and training are assets that cannot be spared. Therefore, since her integrity is not to be trusted, her free will shall become bound over to me.'

A ghastly spear of ice thrust through skin and bone, raw power cast out of the Skyron crystal as sigils were formed and the stone responded in tuned resonance. Lirenda felt all her bones turn to water. Yet she was not permitted to fall. Racked upright by the hold of spelled forces, she could neither move nor blink. Above her, the voice of her Prime tolled on.

'No spell will the accused cast that does not move through my auspice. She will not speak, unless my voice questions her, or unless my instructions allow. If she ever departs from my presence without leave, her life ceases, her breathing and heart to be stopped. Since her post is to be at my side, day and night, she will act as my personal servant. So must it be.'

The rune of ending slammed down with annihilating force, a closure like the knell of doom struck through Lirenda's caged being. She found herself crying. The tears streamed down her numbed cheeks, splashing over her silk clothes and the violet sheen of the coverlet.

After what seemed an eon, the Skyron aquamarine was drawn away by the peeress's unsteady hands. The power of its binding did not ebb with its touch. Selidie's wrought geas stayed fixed through live flesh, deeply set as the thrust of a sword blade.

Lirenda's fury could do naught but beat helpless wings against the slammed door of her mind. The finality crushed her, that this spelled enslavement was going to be permanent; the secret of Selidie's unconscionable transgression would stay locked into oblivion within her.

The centuries of life bequeathed by her longevity stretched ahead, framing a bleak and desperate future. Lirenda cursed the air in her lungs, then reviled her reflex to keep breathing. Through that moment, and the next, and the next after that, against the grinding purgatory of stolen years yet to come, the fall of Dharkaron's Black Spear would have been a welcomed kindness.

Instead, shaken hands caught her elbows, lifted, and resettled her puppet's frame on a stool. Someone's cool industry untied her wrists. Still, the sobs shook her, deep wrenching gasps all the more terrible for the fact that Selidie's punishment throttled them vocally silent.

Through her desecrated misery, Lirenda was scarcely aware of the bustle as two healers with the gray bands of charitable service returned to minister at the Prime's bedside. Stepping past and around her, they attended the Matriarch's cracked, ghastly hands. Their scolding distress over the folly of movement fell muted, lost into the shadows and scintillant light cast by the bright-burning candles.

Then one of the healers bent over Lirenda. Her competent touch clasped one wrist and measured the imprisoned, fast race of her pulse. 'She ought be given a sedative to settle the strain.'

The Prime granted permission.

A nearby clinking of glass, then the chill rim of a cup pressed against the condemned's numbed lips. Unable to wince as the bitter soporific ran over her tongue, helpless to raise the natural objection that should have risen her gorge, Lirenda swallowed.

Spiraling darkness arose, dense as felt. As she sank toward an oblivion that promised no respite, she heard Selidie's formal address to the peeress, dismissing her from the role of Ceremonial Inquisitor. Then the page boys were given rapid instructions to see Lirenda's clothing packed into trunks for an immediate sea journey to Forthmark.

The choice made sense, Lirenda understood, sluggish thought fueled by the last, drowning flare of her embittered rage. The irony cut cruelly. Too late to fight, she understood why the dread sentence had not allowed mercy, or sealed her escape into the abandoned peace of the witless.

Prime Matriarch Selidie had spoiled her hands. She therefore needed a highly trained proxy to enact the steps of her advanced conjuries. How bitter the rage for the price of her mishap, that all the power and young vigor of her body had been hobbled in one crippling setback. She had acted to ensure an uncertain future, in the face of disastrous setback.

The comprehensive damage to her burns could not be assessed or remedied without exhaustive and expert help. The healers in Shand were the finest in the Koriani Order, and the only ones versed in the balanced use of opposing forces. Both the sigils of death and forced regeneration would be needed to restore any semblance of function to the Matriarch's ravaged fingers, if indeed, the feat could be accomplished at all.

Burning with smoldering, savage fury as she sank into the numbness of drugged sleep, Lirenda cursed the name of Rathain's importunate prince. Had she never met Arithon Teir's'Ffalenn, she would not be unstrung, or enthralled as the puppet for the cause of Selidie's balked plot against the Fellowship Sorcerers.

Elsewhere

Beneath the spired stacks of Rockfell Peak's cornices, as two specks against its laddered ice and the sweep of pristine snow-fields, Dakar and an argumentative Fionn Areth make their last camp before starting their arduous ascent to the ledge where Luhaine awaits, preoccupied with sustaining the damaged wards guarding the Mistwraith's captivity . . .

In Ath's hostel near Northerly, under the assiduous touch of the adepts, unguent-soaked bandages are unwound with care to reveal muscle and bone undergoing the start of a healing regen-eration; and the lady adept weeps for joy, her face raised to her fellow attendants, 'Ath bless, his young Grace has made himself whole in spirit. As he chooses, the body may follow . . .'

At Avenor, immersed in his sundown devotions to the Light, Cerebeld sees Lysaer s'Ilessid reunite with the Etarran troops in Daon Ramon; yet the peace of finding his Blessed Prince safe sits uneasily on glittering shoulders, as, robes swirling, the High Priest paces the carpet, his thoughts continuously agitated by Princess Ellaine's confounding disappearance . . .

XI. Nightfall

The heavy soporific Sulfin Evend had given released Jieret
from black sleep by midmorning. He did not rouse at once.
Scarcely conscious, he realized at length he was strapped to
the back of a horse. The creature was moving. That fact seemed
detached, a detail of little importance. He suffered the burn of
cold winds and the deep ache of injuries at strange remove, as
though the dense weight of his flesh-bound being belonged to
another existence. The more vital part of himself that was spirit
drifted still, unfettered and free.

Enveloped by peace that reached past mortality, contained in
that self-sustained state of winged lightness, Jieret dreamed.
Merged with the air, his awareness unreeled over the land,
guided in flight by a raven.

The bird did not speak. In this hour, she did not offer symbols,
or gesture at inked, parchment maps. On outstretched, coal
wings, she skimmed on the wind's breath, over the snow-clad
hills of Daon Ramon. Rock and ice, the scenery glittered like
damascened silver under the varnishing glaze of thin sun. The
rough brush lay bejeweled, with the deer and the hawk, the
winter owl and the hare, set as moving masterworks amid
the vast breadth of the Creator's interlocked tapestry.

At odd moments, the brown pelts of the stags seemed recast in
spun light, as if the ghost presence of bygone Paravians aroused
to the touch of hoofed herds on the game trails. Other times the

winds recalled the lost resonance of a centaur guardian's horn call, whose belling harmonics had once sounded a paean of joy to awaken the slumbering stone in the outcrops. Past and present merged, a living dynamic that flowed in balance with the dance of four elements, wearing the changing face of four seasons.

The raven was not bound to the ribbon of time. She had flown these skies in the Age of Dragons, and also knew the dark blank of the void in the era before the earliest formation of matter. Spirit bound to the enchanted bird's course, Jieret followed her lead ever deeper into the layered realms of mage-sight.

The limitless well of the creature's jet eye held the language of wisdom, the silent unknown that encompassed all things. Raven flew beyond fear of death. She knew each crossing and gateway; she possessed the key to all portals. Peerless navigator, the stuff of the bird's very self was wrought of primordial darkness. The black rainbow shine as the sun struck her feathers knit the shroud of Ath's mysteries: all shape and form pooled as latent energy, the infinite source of the unbirthed potential that could, and had, formed whole, complex worlds at the mere flick of a thought.

The raven flew, her wings bridging the veil, and Jieret followed. Sustained by the gift of his talent, he traced every twist and turn of her course. Through raven's ears, he heard the speech of the air as the unbridled breath of dawn that gifted the listening mind with inspiration. He experienced the illumination of sun, moon, and stars, and felt the raw fire of passion that could wither or seed resurrection. The water in the streambeds channeled the flow of his feelings, and the love at the heart of him, raised and nurtured to cherish the land. In stone, he was shown the enduring commitment that shaped the firm dictates of will.

Through the raven's sight, Jieret beheld marvels: the lattice of energies sustaining all being and the strung flare of the lanes that balanced the currents of change. Passion, inspiration, love, and commitment, he tracked the spun forces within his core being. He forgot the slack body Sulfin Evend dragged north, lashed to the back of a horse. Form lost its priority. Thought and breath, desire and emotion, his clay presence was founded in transience. Granted the gift of raven's perception, Jieret threaded the labyrinthine path across the next threshold. Ancient knowledge opened through that gateway of initiation. Like the soundless spin of a black feather, fallen, the first key to grand conjury settled into his outstretched grasp.

Change bore him into a soaring lift of expansion. Rathain's *caithdein* beheld the truth in the land embodied within himself, and himself, mirrored back in the body of the land; one cloth, and one thread, wrapped and woven upon the warp-and-weft loom of the elements.

Raven's knowledge recast all form as flux, vibration and energy cast into illusion as varying states of solidity. Set against the grand backdrop of the mysteries, the momentary present ran fluid. A mountain stood unveiled as a monument of promise; and a river, the expressed voice of emotion. Drawn into connection by the bird's peerless patience, Jieret wept, touched by the purity of the joy that sourced the vast dance of creation. Suspended upon the primal chord of Ath's mystery, failure lost its cruel sting. Death was rerendered as meaningless.

Peace returned. For an hour, Jieret slept, dreamless, wrapped in primordial darkness. The swish of the raven's wing strokes soothed his throbbing hurts, and the beat of its heart timed his breathing.

He roused when hands shifted him off the spent horse. Sudden shock and raw hurt cut through like a blade and sheared off his access to mage-sight. Plunged back under the suffocating shadow of blindness, he first cried aloud out of loss, then with heartsore longing to kick free of the pain-ridden flesh that racked his senses and threatened to break him.

No succor answered, only the vicious teeth of the troubles that bound him unwilling to life. By then, tenacious, his training took over. Forest-bred clansman, he would not give way to captivity with no show of fight. His mind could be dredged from the shoals of despair. Beleaguered awareness could be compelled to sift through the broken mosaic of impressions. By blistering discipline, against trying lethargy, Rathain's chieftain recovered his bearings.

Voices exclaimed over him, none of them friendly. Jieret sorted their tones of contempt, and their clipped Etarran accents. One man's baiting comment concerning triced enemies raised gales of unpleasant laughter, then a companion's rejoinder cut short by an officer's reprimand. Boots sucked and splashed through puddled mud. Rough cloth sighed over metal. As the circle of detractors made way for another arrival, the wool-musty smell of their campaign-soured bodies admitted a shearing feather of wind.

The breeze off the hills was not scoured and clean, but came burdened by the sweat taint of horses, oiled metal, and smoky cookfires boiling links of hard sausage.

Set on unsure feet in the mushy snow, Jieret had no strength to reject the enemy arms that supported his upright posture.

'No nonsense!' cracked Sulfin Evend, nearby. 'We keep him

alive. That means tender handling and a healer.' His impatient spate of orders faded and resurged, as some busy horseboy gathered slack reins and led off his lathered mount. 'The barbarian will be housed under guard alongside the Blessed Prince. Yes, inside the captain's campaign tent! Now move! You sluggards can't see he's in desperate straits? I want the man flat on his back, *now*, and cosseted like a sick sister!'

Before Jieret could be hefted and slung across the most burly guard's shoulder, a small fellow reeking of unguents and dried blood shoved declaiming into the press. 'Dolts! Fetch a litter! There's been an arrow removed from that shoulder, I'm told. Hoist him like that, you'll rip the wound open. Sure as the Avenger's Black Spear, that would kill him, low as he is with shock and excessive blood loss.'

By then, the hooding blackness had started to spin. Jieret fought the rush of trembling weakness, then shuddered to the touch as hard fingers clamped down on his jaw. He recoiled into someone's mailed fist, felt his clan braid caught and held as the inveterate camp healer examined his cloth-wrapped face. Hot breath brushed his cheek, thick with the odor of onions, as some henchman pried open his mouth and exposed the ghastly, maimed stump of his tongue.

The din of the voices receded, became the shrill calling of gulls over a storm sea of surf. Jieret never noted the litter's arrival, or felt the brusque handling that caught him short of collapse. Surrendered back into the peace of unconsciousness, he slumped against the townbred captors who eased his tall frame off his feet.

He woke out of nightmare. Not yet fully aware, Jieret reacted on instinct, already fighting the new coils of rope looped over his ankles and wrists. A sharp grip caught his shoulder and wrestled him down.

'If you thrash,' someone snapped, 'they'll come back for sure and strap you down to the pallet.'

Jieret turned his head right and left, the weight on his chest invasive as poured lead, and his breath tight and fast with desperation.

The guard who pinned him flat on the ticking turned out to be rarely perceptive. 'Relax.' He flicked something limp as a tassel against Earl Jieret's flushed cheek. 'There, do you see? No one's chopped off your clan braid, just yet.'

On a groan of relief, Rathain's *caithdein* subsided. His mouth had been treated with a salve of camphor and cloves. The astringent sting scoured the membranes of his nose, and caused his seared eye sockets to water through whatever numbing wash had been used to curb the incessant pain. His shoulder had been stitched and tightly rebound. The blankets spread over his scraped limbs were loomed of fine wool and, against every precedent, dry.

Too spent to argue, Jieret settled back. His scalp thumped into the sandbags the healer had used to wedge his head still, a practice that suggested a hovering assistant, probably under instructions to force broth or possets down his unwilling throat. Since he had also been stripped of his leathers, he was grateful at least that indignity had occurred during his late bout of unconsciousness.

The greater ache in him could find no relief. The maimed limits of his sensory perception and the confines of a wounded body now became an unbreakable prison. Jieret sprawled, bound and helpless, unable to express the towering rage that flared to each beat of his heart. The remedies dispensed by Lysaer's camp healer had dulled the razor-sharp edge of his mind. He burned for escape. Beyond reason, he craved the climbing, high song of the stars and the moon, abiding within the realms of pure light that lay past the closed doors of his mage-sight.

The slow minutes passed, every second prolonged agony. Time hung. The sentries posted at the campaign tent stamped their numbed feet. Outside, a man-at-arms upbraided a page for a sloppy job cleaning his boots. The camp cook baked the day's bread in his ovens, and soldiers complained of the grinding misery that passed for life in a field camp.

Taxed into lassitude, Jieret gave way to the leaden exhaustion that made every slight movement a trial. Even discounting the stout, knotted cords, he doubted he could have mustered the strength to roll his battered frame over.

'All right, then.' The guardsman's grip lightened up on his shoulder, then trustingly withdrew. 'Keep on using good sense, my orders say I won't have to call someone in to knock you down with valerian.'

Blinded and tongueless, kept as Lysaer's prize trophy, the clan chieftain harnessed the dregs of his resource and measured his current surroundings. Candles burned, expensive ones made from beeswax, though the rancid reek of commonplace tallow dips still clung to the canvas that billowed overhead. Oiled steel, goose grease, bark-tanned leather; one by one, he identified the scents attendant upon campaign warfare, and the stockpiles of a camp armory. The tent headquarters seemed spacious; probably had a partition, with the sleeping area curtained off from a trestle layered with tactical maps.

To Jieret's left, the varnish taint of ink and parchment bespoke a lap desk kept to write dispatches. Strained hearing picked up the muffled murmur of voices, then Sulfin Evend's impatient query demanding to know in searching detail of the outlying patrols and deployment.

The replies were perfunctory, given without excitement. Hide creaked, near at hand. Left to bored duty, the guard by the pallet presently unsheathed his knife. Jieret counted seconds to the whispery patter of scrolled shavings and breathed in the mild spice of birch.

From the feverish shadows of memory, he all but heard Caolle's disparaging comment, that a fellow who dared to pass his time whittling had better be a tried veteran carrying rank. *'Someone who won't find himself digging latrines for his idle amusement while on duty.'*

Jieret wondered whether his deceased war captain had known the same bitter despair, trussed and wounded as he had been near the end, a cipher retained among enemy hands while still bound, unwilling, to the wrong side of Fate's Wheel.

Pragmatic to the last, Caolle had not stood down. The clan chief his able teaching had raised was honor bound to do nothing less. Against grinding humiliation, and the inconsolable grief that yearned for release into the rapturous refuge of mage-sight, Jieret fought. He rejected the suffocating void of futility and forced his tormented mind to wring meaning from every detail of his surroundings.

Activity from the Alliance encampment filtered through the tent wall. An invalid could track the banter and complaints of men on campaign and keep count of mentioned numbers. He could listen for inbound and outbound patrols, and between the dinning clang of a blacksmith's hammer, discern the individual neighs of picketed horses. Jieret strained through the chatter of the water boys thawing ice in the cauldrons, then the querulous bark of an officer demanding if Skannt's prized pack had been fed. No hounds bayed or barked; these dogs would be trackers cut to run silent, a deadly danger should they be yoked into couples and set on the trail of a fugitive.

In time, a disturbance unraveled the established pattern of routine. A scout just arrived on a lathered horse brought word of a raiding clansman. The reiver was assigned the fresh blame for five dead, and two victims, grievously wounded.

'. . . the same devil who slipped through the checkpoint, disguised. Yes, he got through! Who wouldn't have passed him? He used the pretense of bearing our own wounded officer on to the care of a healer.'

Last night's watch captain answered the predictable inquiry with a professional's clarity. 'A patrol was dispatched several hours before dawn, under orders to trap that barbarian.'

The day's duty officer returned his harried confirmation, that the killer had not yet been found. Between the ongoing demands of rotating scout teams and sentries, of settling disputes, and attending the loose ends of the half dozen bothersome skirmishes with clanborn holed up in thick brush, he and his overworked staff had been further beset by Sulfin Evend's scouring tongue.

Lysaer's Lord Commander had cut them no slack, but adjusted the trim of a discipline blunted by unremitting weeks of Daon Ramon's rough country and the harsh winter's recurrent foul weather. The recoil was ongoing. Men scurried, shamefaced, still caught aback by the colossal upset of receiving the Divine Prince's presence in a war camp not groomed to host royalty.

The dissent outside the command tent eddied nearer, the barked voice of the officer clashing against implied reprimand. 'Then wear my boots, curse you! Damn bastard sorcerer's henchmen are demons, wicked as lightning to catch.'

Jieret lay like lumped wax on the pallet, unwilling to betray the least sign of sharp wits to the watchful eye of the guardsman.

'Very well, horseman, let's have your report. Short and sweet, is the wretch sent across Fate's Wheel? Then how did your sergeant's blundering negligence manage to let him escape?' The approaching footsteps squelched through the muck beside the campaign tent, and on a blast of iced draft, burst inside.

Cut off by the slap of the canvas door flap, the breathless messenger delivered, '. . . only one barbarian, lordship, still on the loose. Wind itself couldn't corner him. He's got remounts in tow.' His excitement flowed into detailed recitation as the arrivals stamped through the curtained partition to consult the tactical maps. 'Damned fugitive's already reached the trade road. Can't read which direction he turned. Too many wagons have scoured the tracks. If we're to find where he took to the hills, we'll need a skilled tracker and handlers with a dog pack.'

'I'll give you twelve men, and six couples of hounds,' the day's watch officer snapped in decision. 'Take the second-best tracker. I want the one Skannt trained kept in reserve, for the hour we flush out the Shadow Master.'

'No. Send Skannt's man, now,' Sulfin Evend countermanded.

'But, your lordship, that's overreaction, surely?' Present all the while, perhaps dozing after his superior's blistering review of the camp, the Etarran captain arose to a slither of cloth and the creak of a pegged wooden camp furnishing.

Avenor's Lord Commander slapped down his protest. 'If the clan wretch has remounts, he'll be moving for some purpose. The second-rate tracker might lose him.'

'One man?' scorned the watch officer, all gruff disbelief. 'Sending Skannt's tracker's like using a catapult to peg down a damn fool rabbit.'

'Get this much, and clearly!' Sulfin Evend broke in. 'By my command, no murdering clan bastard will be given any such quibbling advantage. He might snatch that margin. Your Blessed Prince doesn't want his kind left free to breed up clutches of children! Bring him in living to answer my questions, or else drop him, dead. Fail in this, and somebody here loses his officer's badge! Take my word, *captain*, you don't want to put me in that kind of thrashing bad mood.'

The commotion raised as the chastised men left masked Sulfin Evend's cat step across the tent. Whether by instinct or the refined intuition of mage-sense, Earl Jieret felt the bearing pressure of the Lord Commander's regard rest at last upon him; as though somehow, Lysaer's dedicated Hanshire captain suspected some trick of binding spellcraft had allowed the Master of Shadow to slip through his line of Etarrans. His inimical survey could almost be felt, a steel probe slicing through skin.

The experience stayed unpleasant. Jieret knew visceral, crawling dread, the unnerved anticipation an animal at slaughter must feel, when stunned and stretched for the knife. The clan chieftain endured in harrowing darkness. His hold upon life had grown tenuously light. Death at the threshold would come as a friend on the hour when fate chose to knock. The last fear he harbored was not for himself, but for his crown prince's survival.

The flooding anxiety raised for Arithon's sake snapped the shackles over his mind. Jieret seized that opening and escaped. Swept into an eerie detachment by the gift of the raven's teaching, his sensitized talent granted him vision beyond the limits of sight. In altered perception, he mapped the looming presence of the Lord Commander beside him. He watched in turn, as the pale, steadfast flame of Sulfin Evend's oathsworn loyalty blazed up like the flare of fierce-burning phosphor.

Earl Jieret garnered the uncanny insight, that the man before him was hagridden. His bold, Hanshire arrogance masked a consuming concern, that his plans would be balked despite the extreme measures taken. Frustration spurred Sulfin Evend like live sparks, as though the hunch rode him, that *somehow* this victim, disarmed, broken, blinded, and mute, would contrive to slip through his fingers. The contest he waged with Rathain's bound *caithdein* now trod on intangible footing.

The Earl of the North need do no more than stop breathing to triumph. His worth as a hostage to curtail the clan war bands would dissolve with his death, leaving Lysaer s'Ilessid no more than a rotting carcass.

No fool, Sulfin Evend apprised the spider-silk filament binding Jieret to life. 'I want the captive dosed with a posset,' he snapped. He would use every dirty tactic at hand, twist even the tools of the healer's trade to forestall any chance of defeat. 'Find whatever the camp bonesetter's got in his stores to scatter the prisoner's reason, or better, submerge his awareness in sleep.'

'My lord?' The guard dropped his carving in reflexive protest. 'What under the Light do you think the sorry wretch can accomplish wrung limp as he is with grave injuries?'

'He can think,' Sulfin Evend replied. 'That by itself makes him dangerous.'

The coarse scrape of mail and the jinking of spurs marked off his step to depart; then a pause, as he offered a rare explanation to steady his doubtful guard. 'You're too fresh to recall, man.' Heightened prescience showed the bound man on the bed that Lysaer's Lord Commander recalled the harsh lesson of Caolle's last legacy. 'But Deshir's last clan war captain was once kept alive by Koriathain after a fatal wounding. Even dying, he managed to take over three ships. Refitted them as the Shadow Master's prizes, to the ruin of our southshore sea trade. That dog trained this one. Never doubt, we'll still thrash the fiendish get of s'Valerient lineage long after the sire's been dispatched to Sithaer.'

Jieret fought, first the bonds holding him, then the camp healer's zealot assistant, arrived to carry out orders. He bit the knuckles of the hand that forced his mouth open. The first posset the Etarrans sought to pour down his throat spilled in the ferocity of the struggle, soaking the blankets and also the fresh bandage strapping his wounded shoulder.

'Blazing furies!' cracked the bite victim, his curse gritted rough as he took stock of the fingers laid open. 'Barbarian's deranged as a rabid wolf. Somebody else can change that damned dressing and give up their dry blankets to cover him.'

'Orders,' insisted the guardsman, laconic, while Jieret lay pinned, sweat streaked, and panting amid the rucked wads of his bedding. 'We're to keep him alive, no matter how cross-grained.'

'Well, my master can treat him, and bleed for the privilege!' The offended assistant snatched up his satchel and stamped off, trailed by the exasperated yell from the guard as he stormed on his way through the tent flap.

'Better yet, send back the lads who doctor the oxen. They'll have the muscle to hold the brute down. We'll clean up the mess once your tincture takes hold. If you want, you can smash out his damnable teeth once he's meek as a babe and knocked senseless.'

Footfalls went and came again, this time in heavyset force. Rammed flat by strong hands, Jieret smelled mud-splashed boot leather and the mustier fust of fabric stained pungent with iodine.

'This time, we'll use poppy,' the healer announced, surly for the disruption keeping him from his rounds. 'Triple the dose. Leave his teeth in his mouth. The drug won't be kindly. Dharkaron Avenger will send yon clan devil his torment in the form of harrowing nightmares.'

'Light avert!' gasped the guard, no benediction spoken for Jieret's sake, but a reflexive protest to cancel a heretical oath that invoked the ancient powers.

Incensed by that faith in Lysaer's false cause, as well as the grinding ignominy of a life fallen prey to Alliance usage, Earl Jieret strained in redoubled effort. As his pack of armed keepers swayed off-balance, he burst a knot, tore chafed skin, and jerked one of the ties off his wrist. The victory won him no satisfaction. His blind strike at the guard was curtailed by mailed fists. Then the heavies who bullied the ox teams arrived, and he was knocked breathless and spread-eagled.

'You loutish fools, you've reopened his shoulder!' the healer carped from the sidelines. A knife blade was jammed between Jieret's closed teeth, his jaws pried apart to a chipped grate of enamel. Someone wearing spiked gauntlets crammed a paste ball of poppy through his lips, then clamped his mouth shut by main force. Whether he swallowed or not never mattered. The wound that remained at the root of his tongue flooded the remedy into his bloodstream.

Pain faded first. The rambunctious talk of the enemies crowding his pallet subsided into a spray of meaningless noise.

Under the bandages wrapping his eyes, Jieret wept for the

loss. He could do nothing, *nothing at all*, but tremble in assaulted outrage. The drugged juice whirled him dizzy, then pitched his awareness down and down, into the ink darkness of Sithaer's nethermost pit.

After that, nothing touched him: not the fresh round of cautery to staunch his torn shoulder, or the hands which turned his head, set a knife to his nape, and hacked off the russet length of his clan braid. By then, he traversed a landscape of dream, cast beyond reach of physical pain, and whirled outside of bodily awareness.

The raven came. She folded jet wings, all the colors of night, and stood on his chest like a sentinel.

'Help me,' Jieret begged. 'Let me not die enslaved.'

The bird regarded him, first with the left eye, then swiveled her head in fixed gaze with the unwinking right. As though she tested his plea for sincerity, she wasted an interval, preening.

Shackled in darkness, Jieret screamed for release. 'Let me not break the blood bond I hold with Prince Arithon. On his life, my oath of service to the realm stands or falls. He is my sons' and daughter's irreplaceable stake in the future.'

The raven flapped her wings once and cawed, sharp and shrill with impatience.

'By my Name,' Jieret begged. The cry of his spirit swelled and cast rolling thunder across the cavernous vault of his dream. 'Let the Fellowship Sorcerers rise to meet Rathain's need. I grant free permission. Let them to do as need dictates. For the heritage of my forebears, I will bear the cost and the sacrifice.'

For one instant, the raven regarded him again, a chipped jet figure of limitless majesty. Then she dipped her head in salute, bent, and hammered her beak straight down into Jieret's chest.

The blow punched through skin and muscle and bone, and pierced the core of his beating heart. He felt no pain. When the raven withdrew the black awl of her bill, there came no fountain of blood; no trauma of outraged sensation. Fear dissolved. Enveloped in a moment of childlike wonder, Jieret was consumed by a transcendent peace that blazed into a paean of welcome.

Then the raven spread dark wings and flew. A rising, spiraling giddiness arose, as the sucking wind of the void blew and whistled through the hole her presence left behind. As though some tangible mooring had been cut, Jieret felt a release. Caught like a sail in an updraft, his awareness launched upward and partnered the raven's free flight.

The cloth wall of the tent posed him no barrier. Objects were not solid by the dictates of mage-sight; recast as loomed energies, the canvas became as substanceless as cloud vapor. Creature of wild magic, the bird passed straight through, and the man, a spirit unmoored from his laboring flesh, followed its swooping lead skyward.

The hills of Daon Ramon unfolded below, clothed in velvet snow. Brush brake and briar seamed the gullies like black stitching, with the muddy sprawl of the Alliance encampment a marring rickle of trampled ground. The sky overhead was a rinsed, gentian blue, and the cries of the officers, strident. Laced through the joined fabric of winter landscape, under its lid of clear air, the purl of lane forces glimmered and waned, a sparkle of tinseled embroidery.

Then across that tableau, an inflamed streak of scarlet, where dogs with no voice had been leashed into couples by human handlers to track down unnatural prey.

Jieret's sight snagged on that thread of disharmony. The activity ignited the wish of his heart: *that he should know whose footsteps they hunted*. He beseeched assurance that the quarry hounded to flight was not the last Prince of Rathain.

A wingbeat ahead, the raven glanced back, the sunlight a sheen of metallic filigree on the edges of wind-riffled feathers. Creature of magic, the bird sounded the measure of the spirit she had drawn in tow, her eye an unwinking jet bead.

Then the black gaze swelled and swallowed all the world, hurling Jieret's altered vision headlong into his gift of prescient Sight . . .

The first enemy patrol had not found Braggen because he had holed up under the cobwebbed, black timbers of a posthouse mule shed that had twice been damaged by fire. The neglected thatch leaked. The rest of the structure stayed standing through shoddy repairs because the grandame of the head hostler was a simples woman who knew a few spells to bind wood. Since her mother before that had been clanborn, her grandson was known to the scouts who raided the Mathorn trade road. For gold or for payment in contraband spirits, the man would sometimes harbor their wounded, or provide a fresh horse to a man pressed under closing pursuit.

At lawful need, the mule shed was used for overflow stabling, as shelter for hot-tempered stallions, or for mares in fresh heat who kicked and squealed, damaging stall boards while teasing the insolent geldings.

For that reason, nobody troubled to question the hoof marks leading to and from the inn's gatehouse and the main stable.

By midafternoon, within the same hour as six couples of hounds, two appointed handlers, and Skannt's best headhunter tracker left the Etarran camp and streamed over the hills toward the trade road, Braggen was touched gently awake.

He opened his eyes. Patches of afternoon blue shone through the singed thatch, and under them, the tousled brown hair and inquiring, grimed face of the hostler's second-string groom.

'The remounts you asked for are saddled and ready,' the boy informed his illicit guest.

Braggen rolled and sat up, a gruff set to his lips for the twinging protest raised by his stiffened limbs. If the mere thought of straddling a horse felt like agony, he lacked time and resource to waste his breath in complaint. Expressionless, he brushed a stuck stem of timothy from his cropped bristle of beard. His blunt fingers had not lost their dexterity as he caught up the silk-wrapped sword he had slept on. A second glance reassured him: the bundled form of the prince still lay quiet beside him, packed safe as a goblet of Falgaire glass in a piled twist of straw bedding.

'Provisions?' he asked.

'Packed in the saddlebags, along with a flask of neat spirits.' The boy shot a strained glance over his shoulder. 'There were riders, this morning,' he admitted. 'They stopped for mulled wine and asked after a man who'd pinched clothes from a sunwheel officer.'

Clad in his own forest leathers, Braggen finished the thought with gruff bluntness. 'Nobody expected us, and so no one searched.'

But the next party who came making inquiry would not be as slack, or as trusting. If the posthouse was honest, the head hostler had a long nose for trouble. Friend to the gold the clans paid in exchange for his blind eye and his covert assistance, he likely sensed today's fugitives were not routine scouts on a raid to lift some town courier's state dispatches.

'Don't worry. We'll be deep into the foothills as soon as may be.' Braggen accepted an offering of tough bread and sausage from the boy. He chewed with tense economy, caught Arithon up, and arose from the straw, his Grace draped like a meal sack over his shoulder. The readied horses stood in the mule shed, two of them grain-fed post mounts, shod with steel caulks for sure purchase on ice, and three others, slope-shouldered mountain ponies with tough legs and feather-clad hooves.

The head hostler hauled up the billets and tightened the last girth. At Braggen's approach, he looked around, a man with a face like cracked shoe leather, and knuckles rouged as cherry wood knobs from the persistent cold. 'Your man looks dead,' he observed, clipped to exasperation as he strode to Braggen's side. Tight buckles and stiff harness were his stock-in-trade. His chapped fingers made swift work of strapping the Prince of Rathain astride the restive mare chosen to bear him.

Under the crusted dressing, and the wisps of blood-clotted gray hair, the subject under discussion never moved. His breaths came shallow and too widely spaced.

Braggen said, emphatic, 'If you're caught under questioning, then assuredly, he's dead. Or best still, he hasn't ever been here.' To the hostler's startled glare, he shrugged without sympathy. 'That's why you get soft taking risk pay.' Braggen took the reins of the unmarked bay gelding, adjusting the stirrups for his stout length of leg. The metal irons, with wise foresight, had been muffled with flannel. One less detail of two that might slow him; he broached the other forthwith. 'The liver chestnut mare with the crooked blaze I brought in, did you mask her?'

'Used walnut dye. Won't anybody see that marking at all till she sheds to her summer coat.' The hostler watched Braggen mount, a critical crook to his mouth as he satisfied himself that his fastest gelding would be carrying a man who could ride. Inspection complete, he passed over the laden horse's lead rein. 'The ponies aren't stupid, either,' he resumed, his brown eyes seamed with reproach. 'Should follow your lead without a restraint, as long as their bellies stay full. Let them get hungry, they'll find their way back here, no matter if they're tied or not.'

But Braggen was too shrewd to be hooked into pointless talk. He would not be raiding couriers, or harrying the road, but bound at a hagridden clip straight upcountry. Above the Mathorn foothills, blooded mounts would be useless, and a tied pony became staked kill for the wolves. Draped against the bay's neck to clear the low-slung rafters, he gathered his reins, prodded with light heels, and wheeled his responsive horse toward the shut doors of the shed. 'When you're ready.'

'You were the one who insisted on leaving before sundown.' The bay snapped its head as though the rein had been jerked, and the hostler sourly relented. 'Our morning string is let out to pasture this hour anyway. Serving girls are eating, and the Narms coach isn't in. You get seen leaving now, it's sheer rotten luck.'

Braggen slapped his fist to his belt knife, his beard split in snarling agreement. 'For eighteen royals, gold, we leave during daylight, and luck has no part of the bargain.'

Surly now, his rough cheeks leached white, the hostler set the boy to peering through a knothole. Given the signal the yard was still empty, he slipped the bar in one motion. The doors swung open on soundless, oiled hinges.

His square features frown lined, and his pinched shoulders huddled into his hay-sprinkled jacket, the hostler saw Braggen through, then closed and bolted the crossbuck doors behind him.

'He'll breach the pasture fence,' he informed his shivering horseboy. 'When he does, we aren't going to notice until some-time past sunrise tomorrow.'

Together, the pair watched the taciturn clansman spur away, masked almost at once by the striped fall of sunlight through the straight trunks of the aspens. Hard on the bay's heels, the string of ponies flattened furry ears, forced to a brisk trot up the steep trail to the meadow.

The old hostler shook his head, touched by a foreboding that clenched sour knots in his belly. 'That man's not from Halwythwood. Sure as foals suckle milk, if he's of northern lineage, he knows something dangerous we don't.'

The horseboy stopped pressing nervous patterns in the snow with his boot toe. 'The risk pay is serious? You think we're going to be questioned?'

The hostler pursed his lips. 'Sure hope not. But I suggest you take a nap in the hayloft, just in case. Don't stop drinking the beer I send up till you're knocked puking flat and stunned witless.'

'Sithaer's blazing furies, man!' The boy rolled his eyes. 'Last time we did this, I had to chase strays with a tongue like mulched straw and a headache!'

'You'll have much worse,' the hostler promised, his foreboding pressed beyond avarice to open regret. 'I'll cut the switch myself and warm your arse to match, if hell breaks loose after that fugitive!'

Braggen did not need to smash through the fence. Surrounded by the curious herd given their hour of turn out, he found a cracked board half-screened by dead brush at the north end of the meadow. The damage had been pegged with a rusted, bent nail. Still astride to avoid marking two-legged tracks, the clansman jockeyed his gelding through the milling horses. He laid his mount and Arithon's alongside the weak fence and lashed out, his booted foot still in the stirrup. The split board slithered free with scarcely a thump in the unruffled covering of snow.

The mountain ponies became more than man's match for devilment, nipping and crowding their larger fellows. To ripe squeals and kicks, the harassed herd shouldered past and poured through the gapped fence.

The mare bearing Arithon plunged on her lead rein, more than anxious not to be left. Braggen curbed her rank fuss, his bay gelding steadied between iron legs. He drove firmly upslope, his trail masked by horses that careened and cavorted about him. The ponies frisked back through the mêlée, well content to follow the saddle pack holding the grain sacks.

Braggen set a determined pace, spaced stints of steady, slow trotting to cover the maximum distance. Flanking the trade road, the terrain was mild, the hills lightly forested, with thin soil laid over slabbed granite unable to support stands of miring undergrowth. Sunlight speared through pale aspen, and evergreen, and birch, and punched the snow to lacework dollops and filigree. Flocks of pine sparrows flitted and chirped. Despite the hard winter, the valleys guttered and trilled with boulder-choked streams, splashing under drilled rimes of ice.

Footing was best on the south-facing slopes. Bearing northward, Braggen chose the least arduous passage, as a horse might, who carried no rider. The loose ponies obliged, crossing and recrossing the path of their bridled companions. At due length, the clansman reached scoured rock, baked dry in the afternoon sunlight. He chose the straight course. Horseshoes with caulks would leave telltale score marks, but the scent would not hold for the dogs. If Alliance pursuit was delayed beyond nightfall, the trail would be harder to find in the dark than a dimpled track left in snow.

By the hour the sun dipped, the hillcrests arose into ridges of jagged, seamed rock. Braggen crossed game trails cut by elk and deer, and once, the print of a great cat. Higher, even small game was scant, beyond the white ermine with black-tipped tails, cavorting in the deep snowdrifts. A raven soared against lucent sky, its wingspan as broad as a hawk's. Behind, the low country spread like sugared burlap, sliced by the undulant, muddied scar of the Mathorn trade road.

Ahead, upright cornices reared like etched planes of snapped crystal, and the high mountain summits buttressed the northern horizon, snagged at their peaks with flossed cloud. Braggen took his fixed bearings on the ranges, then bent his course more to the west. Clan raiders kept outposts between Etarra and Narms, and maintained well-stocked caches to allow furtive travel. From these foothills, they staged raids with swift strike teams, lightly burdened, that roved like wolves through the deep seams of the glens.

Since luck had not favored an early encounter, Braggen toiled upward, guided by natural markers. Scouts from a manned outpost must eventually notice the rider at large in their territory. Once that happened, the Prince of Rathain would receive their expert help to speed his flight over the mountains.

Braggen stroked the bay's soaked neck, his legs firmly pressed to its heaving flanks to steady it over snagged footing. If he begged fate for any one favor, he asked that his roving, northern kinsmen discover his presence quickly. For if he was overtaken by townsmen, he must stand down the enemy alone. Let him not be forced to draw the black sword, and recall his prince back to waking consciousness before time.

Slim odds could be lengthened, if his liege could stay cloaked from the Mistwraith's geas through the next day and night. That grace alone might buy enough time to shake off Etarra's diligent company, if not the trained headhunters whipped on by the curse-tainted cause of s'Ilessid.

Near sundown, the mare stumbled and cast off a shoe. Braggen eased her along on gimping, short strides, sore for the fact the rocks bruised her. He preferred to dismount and shift her unconscious load, but dared not leave any obvious signs to flag the eyes of a tracker. Sweating at the delay, his forward progress slowed to a crawl, he wove through a stunted thicket of evergreen. Westward, the sun set, washing the upper peaks carmine. Twilight fell, purple and shadowed. Before the light failed, Braggen found the swept patch of scree he had searched for. South-facing exposure had melted the snow, leaving clean stone and packed gravel. The site offered no shelter. Wind swooped and hissed down in bone chilling gusts, moaning through the storm-broken hulks of blanched deadfalls left piled in the wake of a slide.

Weary enough to sleep where he stood, Braggen slid from the saddle. He hitched his reins to a boulder, then undid the cords that secured Arithon with fumbling, cold-stiffened fingers. He transferred his limp prince to the bare back of the hardiest pony, and snugged Jieret's bear mantle overtop. Long beyond needing the disguise of stained bandages, he unwound the caked cloth, then bundled up the fouled, cut hanks of gray hair and crammed the litter into a saddlebag.

By then, early stars pricked the azure zenith. A fast meal, oats for the horses, and a rapid check to be sure of his weapons, and Braggen stripped the bay's headstall. Leaving the saddle and pack with the grain bags, he looped a rope to its neck, then shortened the bridle to fit one of its small, shaggy cousins.

'Sister, I'm sorry,' he soothed to the lamed mare. 'Find your way home to your stall as you can.' Amid deepening darkness, he stripped off her tack, ditched her saddle in a snowdrift, then dusted the site smooth with a pine switch. Dogs would nose out his scent, no help for it. The detail was likely moot. Once Skannt's trackers came this far with hounds, they would not be searching blind, but chasing down quarry in lethal earnest. Too slender to hope that the clever old hostler could keep Lysaer's prize field troop beguiled. Once the worst happened, Alithiel must be drawn. Desh-thiere's curse would resurge with Prince Arithon's awakening and tag his present course like a beacon.

'Give me my lead until daylight tomorrow,' Braggen whispered as he muffled the bit rings his new mount seemed hell-bent on jinking with her tongue. He remounted bareback, sought out the argent spark of the pole star to ascertain his bearings. Then he kicked his fidgety pony due north, and prodded the one bearing Arithon. 'Just twelve hours,' he begged of the world's unseen powers. 'By then, let Deshir's scouts find us.'

In harsh fact, he received less than one, and no help from his kinsmen at all.

By then, rugged riding had carried him above the high foothills. Before him, the midrange peaks sliced the wind, their rocky slopes stepped with fir. The valleys narrowed, seamed with silvered streams, the rimwalls and snagged ramparts like snow-covered bastions scraped by the dark scars of slides. The ponies proved surefooted on hard-packed ice. They managed the strewn fields of tumbled boulders, where the long-legged bay bred for speed as a road mount moved from stumble to scrabbling stumble. Working upcountry in careful, tight switchbacks, Braggen drew rein and attended the inevitable necessity of turning the animal loose.

Full night had fallen. The mountains climbed upward, sawtoothed as black flint, with the sky a breathtaking backdrop of sequined sarcenet above. Behind, the land dropped away in desolate, rucked folds. Mottled forest frayed into the salt white of cleared glens, then the far-off, shaved square, yellow under the glimmer of lanterns hung in the posthouse coach yard.

The glinting flicker of flame light between stood out like a cry in the darkness.

'Black angel of vengeance!' Braggen's clipped oath snagged steam like gauze in the cold, while the chill in the wind reamed straight through him.

That the expertise of Skannt's trackers now trailed him lay beyond any reasonable doubt. Townborn trappers avoided these wilds, traditionally guarded by clansmen. Fine ermine pelts were not worth a cut throat, and the bold handful of woodcutters who pilfered the verges never ranged far from the road, nor would they dare fell a tree in the dead of the night.

Braggen measured the distance. The weaving string of brands crawled upslope not even an hour behind him; which meant dogs had been on his trail just past noon, with the ruse at the meadow no more than an hour's impediment. He counted six torches. By headhunters' form, that meant a dozen armed men, a tracker, and two kennelmen moved against him. The stark dearth of options could be weighed on a split second's thought. He could not run; the easy ground lay behind him. Against that disadvantage, which allowed his pursuit to close his lead far too quickly, he had spare mounts to lay down a false trail. One inadequate tactic, with nothing else in reserve but two recurve bows and his sword arm.

Since the outset, he had ridden with the chance he might fail. Now, Braggen stared down the throat of bad odds, each passing second another strike fate would be counting against him. He must swiftly accomplish what had to be done, with no chance to fish for alternatives.

Braggen dismounted. He unstrapped his own saddlebags, spare quiver, and bow, and hung them on the breast strap and surcingle shortened to fit the loose pony. He changed the bridle as well, then peeled back Jieret's bearskin, robbed the cloak underneath from his liege's back, and knotted the hood through the stirrup iron of his gelding's vacant saddle. He left the hem trailing. A hard shove drove off the stripped pony, then the bay gelding bearing the grain sacks. If the pair ran fast and far enough, the cloth would act as a drag and leave tempting scent for the dogs. Braggen replaced the bear cloak over Arithon, then mounted the last, laden pony.

Moving again, he reined toward the ridge, where he could keep watch on the torches closing behind him. He drove the game little gelding beneath him, used its strength without mercy to breast the deep drifts or pick safe steps on the uncertain footing. Over the granite ledges, he muffled the beasts' hooves. Sound could carry for leagues in the clear winter air; and did, when the tracker's dogs caught the fresh scent at his heels, and slewed off at a leash-pulling tangent. Faint over distance, the voices of men called out excited encouragement.

Grim, his jaw locked, his rapid breath drawn through cold-reddened nostrils, Braggen picked through the scrub timber and boulders atop the high scarp. Apprehension prickled the hair at his nape. Below, he watched the streamers of flame judder and wink through the trees, nearer, and steadily gaining. Time had come for his next disposition. He dismounted again, transferred the provisions and spare arms onto Arithon's mount, then jammed his cloak through the neck strap of the pony that had gallantly borne him.

'Fly, brother,' he urged, and dispatched the animal at a clattering run downward, into the bowl of the next valley. With luck, the tactic might buy him an hour, with trackers and dogs mired in deep drifts, chasing a trail that went nowhere.

Alone with the tough chestnut bearing his prince, Braggen rechecked the packs that secured the provisions. He strung one of the bows, made sure knife and sword hung unhindered and loose in their scabbards. Then he drew his small dagger and sawed through the cords holding Arithon, except for the rag ties that bound his Grace's wrists around the pony's thick neck. All but shaking with haste, Braggen unhooked the silk-wrapped sword from his back and clambered onto the burdened pony. A snatched whisper of apology; then he asked the beast for its heart, to carry its double burden across the swept rock apron under the spine of the ridge.

So began the last leg of his journey from the banks of the Aiyenne, where he had accepted the vital charge his chieftain laid on him to finish. In darkness, under the cold scattering of stars, with no movement about him but the mournful north wind in the scrub pines, and the steam of the pony's puffed breath, Braggen dug in his heels. The surly beast under him surged onward at a jolting, short-strided trot.

His warmth shared with Arithon's, one hand on the bridle reins, and the other clasped to the weight of Alithiel, the clansman traversed the iced spur of the rimrock that gashed the steep face of the hillside. The cold air held the clarity of liquid glass. Bare granite rang to the strike of bare hooves as the overburdened pony scrabbled for purchase. The crux was a cruel one, which risk told the worse: whether the noise would hasten discovery, or whether a descent into muffling snow would trade silence for crippling penalty. Beside miring swift progress, the inevitable fresh trail must reveal their scant resources to the enemy tracker.

Braggen forged upward. Frequent sharp glances cast down his back trail marked the progress of his pursuit. He wrung what inadequate comfort he could from the fact that only one patrol hounded him. Had the Alliance commander realized his men coursed something more than a renegade clansman, the slope at his back would have been swarming with brands. As things were, in twelve hours, the valley would seethe with the tramp of advancing armed troops. Braggen threaded the scraped rock of the heights on the scant reassurance that no horn calls sounded. No shouts of alarm shattered the still night at his back.

In time, one of the torches disappeared, then blinked back into sight, meandering through the low ground in tortured pursuit of the pony. The wily tracker in charge was no fool. He had split his pack; two torches still clove to the ridgetop.

Battling to maintain his narrowing lead, Braggen dipped over the far side. Protected under the lee of the scarp, he slapped the rein ends to smarten the pony's pace until a copse of dense fir forced him to slacken. The snow deepened, silted where trees had broken the wind, and set drifts carved to whale-backed hillocks. Plowing breast deep, the pony bucked to make progress. By now, the obvious trail would not matter. Ahead, the dark seam of the cliff wall hemmed in the sequined span of the sky. Between its raised rampart, too high to scale, rose a narrow cleft like an axe cut.

For Braggen, the site marked the end of the trail. He would find no more favorable a position for defense. He must make his stand here and balk the encroaching patrol if he could.

'Go!' he cried, breathless, as the pony cleared the last drift and clambered up the rising ground. 'Reach the gap, little sister, your load will be lightened.'

Pressed to Arithon's back, man and game beast clawed past the low, needled branches and broke through the last, thinning trees. Heavy snow mantled the approach to the notch. Rather than muscle his mount through the difficult, deep footing, and blaze a cleared path for his enemies, Braggen reined right. The pony scrabbled upslope at an oblique angle, reached the south-facing scar of pebble and moraine melted bare by for-tuitous sunshine. In clattering haste, the clansman wheeled, cutting back across the broken ground skirting the base of the cliff rim.

The pass loomed ahead, a twisted seam gouged through vertical rock and polished by eons of weather. Gusts screamed through the narrows, funneled to buffeting dissonance. The cold knifed through clothing with searing force, snapping loose strap leather and chilling the sweat streaking the pony's whorled coat. Braggen dismounted, the wrapped length of Alithiel cradled left-handed. Head down against the sting of the wind, he guided the blowing mare into that jagged rock gateway. The sky narrowed overhead, reduced to an indigo ribbon pinpricked with scattered stars.

Plunged into deep darkness, Braggen shrugged off a bristle of gooseflesh. A live presence seemed to brood over this place, as though history watched in attendance. No doubt, the steps of countless Paravians had trodden this pass through the course of forgotten ages. Whether the rift had once been hallowed ground, if the kinder breezes of high summer still rippled the hidden mirror of a rock pool or the gushing cleft of a sacred spring, winter hoarded the land's ancient secrets. The clatter of stone shards and the chink of steel weaponry tore the grace of that mystical peace, casting back the sharp echoes of thankless intrusion.

Braggen found shelter in a natural cavern formed under a tumble of fallen boulders. There, with time his worst enemy and no moment to ease his laboring breath, he drew his small dagger and sliced the last ties binding Arithon's slack wrists.

'Hold you steady,' he murmured to the pony. Spurred by necessity and hammered resolve, he crouched, laid the swathed length of the sword on his knee, and nicked through the cross-laced string ties. One frantic jerk tore off the silk binding.

'Merciful Ath guide your footsteps, my prince,' Braggen murmured in heartsore appeal. Then he grasped the bared hilt in nerve-deadened fingers and yanked the black sword from its scabbard.

The blade pulled free with a crackle of white sparks. A shearing snap followed. The shock of wild sound ascended, risen into a keening whine far above audible sound as the spell-sealed wards tore asunder. Braggen felt the flare of an uncanny heat spike through the steel in his hand. The sensation accompanied a ringing vibration that lifted his hair.

Then, on the pony, Arithon stirred. He drew in a shuddering breath. A frisson rippled the length of his frame, and both hands spasmed closed into fists. Words passed his lips, a snatched, lyric phrase in Paravian cut short by a racking, dry cough. There followed a transitory moment of forgetfulness, blurring the edge of transition.

'Jieret?' the prince murmured. He lifted his head, his inquiring features yet veiled in fallen strands of black hair. 'Are we clear? Did the ruse with the fetches spare the worst blow to your war band?'

Braggen averted his face. Ripped into misery by that note of blind trust, half-crushed by the pending weight of an inevitable disappointment, he could not bear to witness a sorrow whose memory would brand him forever.

To Arithon's credit, there came no shocked gasp; no outcry against the wounding stab delivered by fate's latest cruelty. Only the soft rustle of disarranged cloth, as the Teir's'Ffalenn propped himself upright. By instinct, he settled his balance erect on the back of the pony. When he spoke, his inquiry fell gentle, the very soul of compassionate tact. 'Braggen? Forgive me. If you're ready, please say what has passed in my absence?'

No time to break the unpleasant news kindly, or appease the raw brunt with condolence. Braggen swallowed, turned, met his prince's taut state of calm with no saving poise to cushion the drive of necessity. His words held all of his gouging, rough pain and embarrassed humiliation. 'Jieret stayed. None could stop him. I was charged to stand at your back in his place. Your Grace, you must ride, and at once. A tracker with hounds is hard at our heels. He leads a patrol of crack veterans from Etarra.'

For a mercy, the Shadow Master bowed to the blow that Earl Jieret's decision had dealt him. 'How long was I down?' He accepted the deadly weight of Alithiel from his clan liegeman's urgent hands. 'Do you know how far my half brother's troop lags behind us?'

'You were out for two days. I don't know about Lysaer,' answered Braggen in ragged haste. 'We passed through the lines of the enemy last night. The way's open, northward. Please, liege, just listen! You've got provisions for a tenday, grain just for three. The pony's not fresh. I've left you a bow, half my good arrows, some tinder. Keep Jieret's cloak, and my spare in the saddle pack. Where I'm bound, I'm not going to need it.'

A brief, hurried wrist clasp, exchanged in the dark. 'Fare you well, liege. Stay free. Grant my sons a crowned heir for Ithamon.'

Braggen spun, snatched the bow from his shoulder, and bolted.

Head down, he sprinted back toward the mouth of the gap. He could not see, for the tears that welled in his eyes. Yet the wind, and the stumbling slap of his footfalls over raw stone did not cheat him.

He heard the parting line of his prince with utmost, terrible clarity. 'No man better, to have filled Jieret's shoes. Shoot straight, Braggen. More than my gratitude, you'll spin the thread of posterity with your courage. For tonight, know the truth, that I am as worthless, while you hold the weal of Athera between your two hands.'

Had Braggen glanced back for even a brief moment, he would have seen that the prince he dismissed to seek safety had no intent, then or ever, of leaving him.

Late Winter 5670

Shadows Behind
the Throne

The raven blinked.

Dream ruptured, casting Earl Jieret out of the web of prescient Sight. The image of the high gap in the Mathorns dissolved, and with it the vision that had witnessed the parting between Rathain's crown prince and the staunch Companion sworn to his defense. Yet Jieret did not recover full waking awareness with the release of his seer's talent. Instead, he found himself oddly adrift, his disembodied awareness still cast in suspension above Daon Ramon's vast landscape. The hour was twilight. From his overhead vantage, the snow-covered vales rolled away, frozen spume on a storm-tossed sea.

Preternaturally attuned to the passage of time, Jieret understood he had suffered a fit of prescient vision. *Alithiel had yet to be drawn from her wrapped and warded scabbard.* The confrontation in the mountain foothills would not come to pass until several hours past nightfall. Arithon's anonymity rested on that scant margin. The risky protection safeguarding his sanity from Lysaer's closing proximity became the sole factor to stall the drive of Desh-thiere's curse.

The realm's *caithdein* was not resigned. Regret gouged him to relentless guilt. The accursed fact galled, that he should still breathe after his late string of failures.

The raven cocked her head in midflight, her intelligent regard turned piercing. *'You are alive. Since every man is the Fatemaster's partner in choosing his moment of death, your spirit remains on this side of the Wheel for a compelling reason.'*

Disembodied in dream, Jieret's frustration erupted in silenced explosion. *'For what purpose, if I am left helpless?'*

'But you are not helpless,' the raven cracked back, the downstroke of her wings whiplash curt. *'The thread of your consciousness is part of the life-weave that anchors Athera's existence. Every thought you have, every whisper of feeling, every desire you hold in your heart carries a distinct, measured impact.'* Her eye a bright bead of sheared obsidian, the bird concluded, *'No matter what straits, or how dire the circumstance, only the fool disowns his vested power to respond.'*

Presented with Jieret's dumbstruck distress, the raven trimmed her ink pinions and shot forward. *'You disbelieve? Then behold, your own Sight will show you the truth. You have already looked out at your world. Yet the greater mystery will not stand revealed unless you allow what exists to see you.'*

The land unreeled beneath Jieret's focused regard, stone and snow and hill and brush alive with the glimmerance of enhanced vision. The intricate patterns encompassed more than one layer, as though he discerned time and space through a series of stacked, colored templates. The sheer complexity stunned and confounded. Yet even without trained experience, or practice, he could intuitively grasp small details. Here, he discerned the bright spark of an owl gone to roost with fluffed feathers in a thicket. He watched the glittering, poured stream of a hunting wolf pack, and the placid emanations of deer. Daon Ramon unfurled secrets like a tapestry below, the life of all things animate and inanimate strung on the spooled flow of the lane flux. As an unseen observer, Jieret felt secure from a peril half-sensed, and beyond any language to express.

'Will you dare?' provoked the raven, a punch-cut black shape sailing light as a leaf, at her heart the vast chasm of eternity.

'Death would be simpler,' Jieret reproached. Bodiless, he still felt the pull of trepidation. Yet his shortfall had never been cowardice.

Given the choice between helpless captivity and passing the gateway of unknown fear, he embraced his decision. He cast off the innermost barrier of his selfhood and threw open the floodgates of consciousness, until he stood naked before every facet of Ath's vast creation.

The spun envelope of awareness that held him apart dissolved like gauze ripped by a gale.

His awareness exploded with contrary sensation: rising, falling, spinning, imploding, expanding. He had expected to forfeit his individuality, but no such oblivion befell him. Instead, all that he was, and had been, became *more*. Jieret tumbled in the maelstrom of forces that spiraled the limitless spectrum of wrought form. Nowhere became everywhere; darkness became light. He was wind, then fire, then water, then earth. He beheld the boundless space of infinity in a stone, then the space of the void packed into honeycomb vaults of energetic activity. Epiphany flooded him, that vision extended beyond the realm of perceptible light. To the thrum of a heartbeat, on the flap of the raven's outstretched wings, awareness smashed past the bounds of the limited mind.

Jieret s'Valerient perceived his own Name. Hard on the heels of that understanding came expansive recognition: that all Names in existence were contained within the imprint of his personal consciousness. Each mote and thread in the tapestry of Ath's being reflected the sum total of himself. *He was the past, where Paravians danced at solstice, and he was the branching multiplicity of futures, where all possibilities existed, based on each ongoing moment of choice.* He held the key to the hour a s'Ffalenn prince was crowned high king, *as well as* the hour the Mistwraith's curse triumphed, bringing down darkness beyond all redemption.

Both outcomes deployed from the palm of his hand. Two fates, for Rathain, strung on the balance of his unwritten destiny. At today's crux, as Rathain's sworn steward and acting *caithdein*, Jieret seized his chance to leave both futures open. The fork in the path would be left to posterity. Triumph or tragedy, the unclaimed legacy would remain, lodged in the web of unresolved possibility.

'*Will you dare?*' prompted the raven again.

From a point that was nowhere, and everywhere at once, Jieret s'Valerient answered. '*I have seen your promise that I am not helpless.*'

'*Then my task here is finished.*' The dark harbinger banked on spread wings, doubled back, and flew *through* him, leaving her parting fragment of mystery: that Traithe and Sethvir had always been heard to address her presence as '*brother*'.

In that eyeblink of time, Earl Jieret felt his awareness drawn back into resharpened focus. The part of his being that answered his Name gently drifted to rest above the slack form of his body.

Passing time had changed little. His inert, drugged flesh still lay senseless and bound within the Etarran command tent. The hour was past sundown. Lamps had been lit, their oil-soaked wicks casting a soot haze of smoke. The carnelian light flecked glints of reflection off oiled metal and the battered accoutrements of war: the racked swords and lances; the rolled pennons with their sunwheel finials; the horse harness with chased stirrups and bits. Nearer at hand, traced in gloom and spiked highlights: the brass corners of the locked chests; and the hanging flagons with their stamped tin necks plugged with rolled-leather stoppers.

Jieret's scarce-breathing form lay faceup on the pallet. The posted guard had been changed, his replacement no less than the Alliance Lord Commander.

Sulfin Evend had stripped off his field cloak and surcoat. Still clad in the pebbled gray links of his byrnie, a snagged pair of trunk hose, and boots ringed with damp from his tour of the camp, he had removed his fur-lined helm. His head was left bare, dark hair spiked and matted where the steel had pressed wayward cowlicks. His lean hands were stripped of scaled gloves as he bent keen inspection upon an arrow's repaired fletching. The activity was ongoing. Three sheaves in waxed quivers leaned at his knee. Cast underfoot, a loose scattering of shafts had apparently failed to pass muster.

Jieret's disembodied presence drifted amid the throes of a mild dispute. Across the tent, the curtain enclosing the tactical maps stood open; with deceptive nonchalance Sulfin Evend answered the query just spoken. 'Yes, Lord Exalted.' If he was overawed by the personage in the glittering, bright mail, overlaid with a jeweled, white surcoat, his level tone conveyed only emotionless flint. 'My order dispatched the best tracker we had on that errand.'

'Why?' Lysaer s'Ilessid's return query also held unflawed patience; but the rings on his fingers snapped curt sparks as he laid both hands, forced and still, on the layered maps spread over the trestle.

Sulfin Evend raised eyes like dark smoke with held fury. 'More likely to bring in his quarry, that's self-evident.'

The gold braid and bleached lamb's wool might have clothed a stone statue, under the flare of the lamps. 'To chase a clan fugitive, traveling alone?'

'But one who kills with the premeditated force of ten of my best-trained veterans.' Sulfin Evend thumbed the resharpened point on a broadhead. His glare a raised challenge, he turned over his hand, then shaved the fine hair from the back of his wrist to test the whetted edge. 'Against that breed of fugitive, I send out the best. That way, our skilled soldiers come back to us, living.'

'You're in command,' Lysaer reassured. Above the ranked counters representing armed men, his eyes shone the chaste blue of cornflowers. 'Though I must say, I've never done anything so barbaric as tying a man's severed plait to my standard.' His lips flexed in distaste. 'You know that's quite likely to make my poor bearer a target?'

'Then the bearer will ride at my stirrup.' Sulfin Evend tapped the arrow in his hands, his placating smile a needle of sultry irritation. 'That way, we'll flush the best of the clan archers. I'd sooner have the barbarian cut down before you're at risk of his skills. Do you think me a fool?'

'I think you are ruthless,' said Lysaer s'Ilessid. 'The fool is going to become the poor wretch who's asked to carry my banner.'

Sulfin Evend lifted his stubbled chin and laughed, his release as much humor as relief. 'He'll be the man who botched last night's patrol, of course. You don't like my handling when an officer's inept? Is that the fine point you're stripping my sad hide to make?'

'I don't like the fact that he's Minister Sorchain's favorite cousin,' Lysaer amended with sharp delicacy. 'He's got Etarran pedigree longer than your arm, and I'll face a political brangle, if he dies here.'

'Should I worry?' Sulfin Evend selected another arrow, closed an eye with the same steely glint as his mail shirt, and sighted the length of the shaft. 'If I dispatch the Master of Shadow for you here in Daon Ramon, I could retire. Then you and cousin Raiett can devote all your days in the lion's den, soothing your pride of Etarran ruffled tempers.' The arrow proved warped beyond saving. The Alliance Lord Commander snapped it over his knee. The crack of dry wood fell like a shout against sudden, blanketing silence.

Prompted by instinct, Sulfin Evend looked up. Lysaer remained in his seat at the map table, his posture struck to a listening stillness of deep and disturbing intensity. The Alliance Lord Commander felt a prickle of warning lift the hair at his nape.

Then Lysaer s'Ilessid shot to his feet. His camp stool crashed into a pile of shields, while map counters bounced in a jostled cascade from the tabletop.

'What's amiss?' Sulfin Evend cast down the halved arrow and clapped a fist to his dagger. 'Are we threatened?'

His questions stayed dangling. The spasm of hatred that warped Lysaer's face disallowed civilized speech.

A disembodied presence, unseen and unnoticed, Jieret s'Valerient also sensed the crux when the black sword Alithiel was fatefully drawn from her sheath. Though Braggen's action occurred twelve leagues distant, in the high notch of the Mathorns, the vulnerable second of transfer as Arithon's spirit rejoined its seat of warm flesh flicked a ripple across the unseen chord of world life force. The event was unsubtle. Though the tie to his drugged body had frayed to a thread, Jieret felt as though a thin, heated wire had just jerked the length of his spine.

'Muster your front-rank officers! Do it now!' Lysaer shouted. 'Light bless whatever instinct you followed. I think your best tracker's just flushed the Spinner of Darkness himself.'

'The bastard's unmasked?' Bolt upright in one bound, Sulfin Evend strode over the discarded arrows and snatched up his damp surcoat and cloak. 'Where? We've got trouble if he's already north of the trade road.'

Undaunted by that possibility for setback, Lysaer seized the officer's horn from the weapons rack by the tent flap. 'That's rugged country, but the passes are snowbound. The Master of Shadow surely can't cross the divide.' Jewels flashed to his frenetic haste as he thrust the horn into Sulfin Evend's reaching grasp. 'Sound the alarm. You've got three companies of my crack Etarran troops, well seasoned at harrying clan scouts. Cut off the hills to the Instrell coast. We'll drive the criminal to the ground in high peaks. He won't slip through, *I can sense his position,* and we hold Red-beard captive, a bargaining chip to effectively muzzle his allies.'

'Well, keep a tight guard on him!' Sulfin Evend cracked back as he shouldered head down through the tent flap. 'The Mathorns are known as a bolt-hole for raiders. If I'm still in charge, then the field scouts ride point. Damned if I'm going to spearhead a foray doomed to march into a trap.'

'Forget torches,' Lysaer said, too driven to abide the delay. 'Tonight, we're not going to need them.'

Earl Jieret's clear sight tracked the pair's progress beyond the command tent. Cast adrift by the raven, he experienced the freedom of a discorporate spirit. His expanded awareness of the mysteries revealed the aligned pull on the elements as Lysaer s'Ilessid tapped into his birth gift.

The effort held none of the trained master's subtlety. A willed state of mind punched a vortex within Lysaer's auric field. Light flowed from the aperture framed by his hand, two threads of harmonic resonance pulled from the grand chord and bidden to manifest as white fire.

Earl Jieret extrapolated that Arithon's grant of shadow might draw from a power akin to the raven's: the negative absence of kindled energy that accessed the spectrum of unborn possibility.

But speculative thought had no chance to flower as the Blessed Prince burst the night with his display of raw force. Stars and moonglow became utterly blasted away by the whiteout, coruscating explosion. Every man in camp was slapped to full alert, dazzled blind at their posts, or else wrenched from sleep by the crackle of stress-heated air that fountained off Lysaer's closed fist. Horses surged and plunged on the picket lines. Voiceless tracking dogs clawed at the bars of their cages, distraught to shivering anxiety.

The upset was not limited to animate life. Granted the scope of a sorcerer's sensitivity, Jieret saw plants and mosses recoil from the untimely flare, their diurnal rhythms and patterns of seasonal dormancy cascaded into imbalance. Stone resounded to the stressed shift in vibration, and disrupted harmonics shrilled a jagging flare through the gleaming web of the lane's flux.

A ghost print drifted in overlay, unveiling the altered course of the probable future: within a matter of hours, the brute sinew of war would snarl Daon Ramon to moiling conflict. Rathain's *caithdein* arose in response, and awarded the land his last service.

He touched awake the enduring part of himself reflected within each facet of Ath's creation, and offered the gift of his conscious voice. By direct intent, Jieret ceded the inanimate world the measure of his self-expression; yet his comprehension of grand conjury lacked detailed depth. He failed to realize that his blood pact with his liege would also involve the ties of a crown prince sworn to safeguard the realm under sanction by Fellowship Sorcerers.

Air spoke first, a cry on the wind to stun the listening mind for its aching expression of sorrow. Stone resounded, adding notes to the chord, until the ground underfoot rumbled with building vibration. The upwelling wave swelled and suddenly flowered into a peal of spontaneous harmony. The struck tone sustained. Through its belling tumult, the shrill shouts of the Etarran officers rousting the men sounded thin as the cheep of young birds.

Sulfin Evend attempted to reimpose order by blowing the brass mouthpiece of the ram's horn. Yet the tone that emerged was not the bull bellow his seasoned troops knew and expected. As Jieret's impetuous grasp of the mysteries opened a tear in the veil, the ancient past bled into the present, and irrefutably tangled. This trumpeting blast resounded across time, overlaid by the mightier flourish from the dragon-spine horn of a departed centaur guardian.

Then, in a feat that smashed credibility, that call became answered by its echoed twin. The response arose from the desolate hills beyond the camp's guarded perimeter.

Men snatching up weapons glanced into the night, the rushed pace of their muster blunted by creeping unease. Lysaer brightened his flare of wrought light. Illumination leaped skyward. The dazzling geyser burned back the darkness, and wakened a flurry of movement.

Daon Ramon's array of Paravian ghosts now gathered to answer the land's injured cry of distress. Armed men quailed before them. Seasoned headhunters convulsed into huddled knots or took to their heels in confusion.

No less stunned, Sulfin Evend dropped the ram's horn from shocked fingers. The bronze-capped end clashed at his feet, all unnoticed. Blunt reason rebelled against what his eyesight recorded: that one of the specters was not a pale wisp of spirit light. He stared, with Lysaer beside him no less stupefied, as the apparition his horn blast had summoned strode boldly into his war camp.

The Ilitharis Paravian towered above the scurrying humans. Even the stout trio of mounted sentries were dwarfed, as they wrestled their shying horses in a courageous attempt to oppose him. The centaur came on, his advance undeterred. His staid pace carried him *into the swords upraised and slashing to gut him. As though he were smoke, he passed through the spears, then the impediments of cook tents and guy ropes.* Yet he was not any mere figment of illusion. Lysaer's bursting shower of light utterly failed to dispel him.

'Mercy upon us!' the lance captain screamed.

For the centaur came on, *as though solid matter held no form and no substance before the wild majesty of his presence.*

Maned and bearded in leonine splendor, he had chiseled, teak features countless seasons had weathered to angles. His antlered head was crowned by a circlet of oak, the leaves autumn gold, with new acorns in clusters that gleamed like peridot jewels. His torso was bare, his adornment simple: bracers of scaled bronze on his forearms, a starburst medallion of worked turquoise on his chest, and a great sword in a russet-leather harness. He also carried a double-headed axe slotted through a braided thong loop at his shoulder.

His imposing appearance first obscured the queer fact that his cloven hooves left no track.

'Look, he's not real.' Lysaer's gesture encompassed the paste of slush and merled mud, bearing only the blurred imprints of heeled boots.

'Illusion, perhaps,' allowed Sulfin Evend. He rubbed his eyes hard, and still, his unruly knees remained turned to water by an awe that shattered his intellect. 'Has to be.'

Beside him, the Blessed Prince clamped a desperate grip on his crumbling state of composure. He stood his ground by ingrained royal bearing, his stance like rigid marble. The sheer effort taxed him. His breathing came shallow and quick, as he wrestled the pull of emotions beyond the pale of prior experience.

For if the creature who invaded his camp was a sending, or some other ephemeral fetch, neither cold steel nor light carried any power to banish it. As the centaur approached, the actinic brilliance fell on him without inconvenience. He was not blinded. On the contrary, his arrival made the very air burn bright gold, the halo about him not unlike the shining emanation that marked Ath's adepts in dark places. For the Ilitharis Paravian, the effect was intensified, a blaze of fired glory to kindle the heart and lift the mind into rarefied ecstasy.

The unleashed dazzle of Lysaer's gifted might seemed diminished against such refinement, a display crude as candle flame before the grace that walked in the guardian's presence.

Fully armed veterans backed away weeping. Other men crumpled to their knees and covered their abashed faces. The bold few still holding the front ranks were wrung faint. More than a few cast themselves prostrate in terror. Others were driven out of their senses by a radiant, pure beauty beyond reach of their wildest dream. The mounted sentries dropped their lances, ashamed, as the horses beneath them gentled to listening stillness. First one, then another, raised nickers of greeting.

The Ilitharis viewed them like lost little brothers, his massive fists crossed in salute at his chest, and his nod of acknowledgment regal. His fetlocks of gleaming, flaxen feathers unsullied by snowmelt or mud, he halted foursquare before Sulfin Evend and the light-bearing form of Lysaer s'Ilessid.

His massive size overshadowed them. Tall though he was, Lysaer's burnished head reached no higher than the centaur's muscled equine shoulder. Nor could his pale brilliance outshine a coat the color of shelled autumn chestnuts.

Lysaer drew himself straight to issue a challenge, and found that his voice had failed him.

The centaur did little more than gaze downward, his eyes the flecked green of moss on rinsed granite. '*I speak for the land of Rathain, and these hills of Daon Ramon, which are not open to trespass. No seal has been granted, and no marker stone has been removed to give mankind the right of free passage.*'

'Illusion, just illusion,' Sulfin Evend muttered, over and over like a litany. He stayed erect by main force, and clenched his loose bowels, while his quivering skin broke into drenching sweat. Whether the reaction was due to a figment of spun spellcraft or some sending tricked out of the past, the Paravian apparition overwhelmed him. Mind and war-trained discipline escaped him. Sulfin Evend squeezed his eyes shut, too wrung with nerves to close his hand over his sword grip.

'But I am not illusion,' the centaur rebuked. Touched into sympathy by his saddened reproof, the stone underfoot sang aloud. 'Yet the fact that I do not fully stand in your time does not alter the truth.'

Not the words themselves, but the tone behind them ripped Sulfin Evend to tears. With a terrible mercy that probed through his deepest reserve, and laid bare his vulnerable self, the centaur resumed his address. 'Beware what you spurn, son of the sons of a daughter, who was stolen away from her birth-born heritage in Westwood. My form is a parallel echo from the past, no less real than you are, in Name.'

Through an effort not a man in the camp could have matched, Lysaer s'Ilessid held firm. His will hammered steel, he recovered his voice and his shielding armor of outrage. 'Your kind have passed from here,' he said in peremptory dismissal. 'Return whence you came, before you are sent with a banishing!'

The Ilitharis Paravian turned his antlered head. He regarded the s'Ilessid, not with contempt, but with a compassion that held even ugliness sacred. 'Outcast,' he Named him.

As Lysaer s'Ilessid stiffened, incensed, the centaur's grave speech wrought a binding to silence all protest. 'Mourn the day,' the creature abjured in fierce sadness. 'In formal judgment at Althain, you once received sealed renouncement of your right to Fellowship intercession. Remember the choices that compelled that harsh step. For Paravian law is not revoked, or even held in abeyance. Mankind walks here by the grace of the compact, while the Sorcerers yet guard that trust. They have oathsworn your half brother to uphold Rathain's charter, and for shame!'

Where a lesser man would flinch, Prince Lysaer endured, light raised aloft in denial. Mortal clay before unearthly magnificence, he staunchly refused to stand down.

Arms outflung, the centaur tipped his bearded face to the sky, as though in appeal to the stars and moon to soften that act of rejection. 'You have raised an armed force, and cajoled with smooth lies until a kingdom's born subjects would hunt down and murder the crown prince who stands as their sovereign! Arithon Teir's'Ffalenn serves the land's justice, and I am come as the voice of the soil your unclean warring would desecrate.'

'The Master of Shadow has become the sworn servant of evil!' Lysaer insisted, his conviction a drawn line of defiance. Although his pale skin was running with sweat, he flourished his beacon in challenge. 'Stand aside, or believe this, I will march despite you.'

'Stand down,' urged the centaur. He did not threaten, despite his vast strength, and the leashed power of the mysteries that rang through his being like mute thunder. 'Be yourself, son of Talera.' In kindness, he exhorted, 'Abjure your clinging need to hide behind vanity and acknowledge the sorrows set on you by Desh-thiere's curse.'

Lysaer lifted his chin, head tipped back, that he could meet and sustain the direct gaze of the Ilitharis Paravian. The effort cost, terribly. Sulfin Evend, beside him, had long since given way to a power beyond mortal knowing. Disbelieving, he watched his Blessed Prince shoulder the contest: to stand naked before that mighty a presence and maintain the flawed frame of human identity.

Lysaer possessed inborn stature; had been raised a blood prince of a noble and time-proven lineage. Since childhood he had learned to place personal needs behind the demands of his people. Only once had he lost himself, to Talith's love. He had weathered the sacrifice and the mourning, his priorities rigid as he realized his care for her had forged a weakness his enemy might use to break him. He put her aside, had survived in separate torment all her days and through the grief left by her dying.

The marring devastation, the deep pangs of remorse, he had kept masterfully hidden. No one saw the dreams that stole in uninvited, ripping his sleep into silenced torment. None shared the tears he dared not shed, even under the cover of darkness.

His servants were bidden to leave candles burning, not due to the curse, or his hatred of shadow, as common hearsay supposed; but because any moment of unobserved privacy threatened to shatter the bulwark of his integrity.

Before this hour of trial, Lysaer had faced down Fellowship Sorcerers. He had withstood even the sublime blandishment found in an enclave of Ath's adepts.

But this night's confrontation was inexpressibly worse. As though all the scars of his past had torn open, the pain became fresh and still bleeding. Under the centaur's regard, a man saw himself mirrored, each excoriating detail a crippling blow to the unquiet heart. Lysaer reexamined every base longing. He faced his known flaws, but magnified beyond bearing. Every loss, every tortured regret, even the branding burden of the thousands of lives cut cruelly short in his service bore him down until he felt crushed under shackles and chain.

The wounding horror of the unadulterated truth would have reduced him to sobbing shame had the visitation been fashioned to break him. But the great centaur's wisdom saw past limitation. His purpose knew nothing of punishment.

Against the raw balance of personal shortcoming, Lysaer s'Ilessid was shown its shining opposite: himself washed clean of all stain. The Ilitharis Paravian reached out with both hands in forgiveness. His steadfast promise extended the offer of an unconditional redemption. One step forward, one touch of the mystery contained in the creature's free majesty, and Lysaer understood he would be enfolded by the limitless peace of Ath's welcome.

He would transcend his mortality and receive instantaneous release from all suffering. Bend his neck in submission before the shining grace the Paravians carried, unsullied, and he could arise reborn. Wearied flesh could be shed like an outworn sleeve. The dark knots of subterfuge, his suffocating web of entangling choices could all be unraveled at a stroke. Unimaginable longing consumed him, to be uplifted on wings of white light. This being might bear him past the bounds of the veil and grant him the untarnished recall of a lost paradise.

One word, and Lysaer could reclaim a beauty that eluded the language of dreams.

'Come home,' invited the centaur, and bespoke him by Name. 'Be reunited with the limitless seed of mankind's original heritage.'

The temptation to accept became overpowering. Even the

Divine Prince's unmatched dedication could scarcely withstand the assault. His pale features twisted, ripped to punishing torment, though his wide-lashed blue eyes never wavered.

Still present, still a permeable awareness laced through the cloaking night, Jieret s'Valerient's unmoored spirit bore witness to the confrontation. He could not be unmoved by the lordly magnificence of the apparition his summons had drawn from the far past to speak as his voice. Nor could he spurn the grim strength of s'Ilessid, warped by Desh-thiere's geas, and the ironies sprung out of conflicted character that maligned his royal nature.

Sulfin Evend wept outright. Locked into sympathy, battered by the struggle parsed out in the suffering draw of each breath, he sweated in shared pain as Lysaer s'Ilessid sustained that stripping exposure. Brute endurance robbed every pretense of privacy. Here stood no Lord Exalted, no avatar, but a man whose most inviolate secrets became ruthlessly plowed to the surface. Alongside his sundered affection for Talith, other specters arose to revile him: a mother's betrayal that cast him to exile and a lifetime of binding commitment; a wronged young woman wedded for expedience, and a son lost to deadly danger too young. Within Lysaer's being each separate tragedy had branded its wretched mark.

Divine purpose had never reduced his humanity. Lord Commander and *caithdein* shared the same understanding as they saw him labor through shattering distress. Again and again, with no hope of redemption, the prince who stepped forward in humanity's defense had offered himself as a living shield without regard for the cost to himself.

The prospect seemed impossible, that a mere man could resist the centaur guardian's gift of ecstatic peace. Braced for total loss, Sulfin Evend masked his face with mailed hands. He could do nothing, only try to shut out a capitulation he lacked the staunch courage to witness.

Hearing still served him with tortured clarity. The rough, hard-fought rasp of Lysaer's breathing bespoke a contest that surpassed the breaking point of surrender. Sound detailed the agony of a will pressed beyond extreme limits, to survive an unbearable pressure.

'I refuse you,' Lysaer forced out. Scraped raw with grief, he added, 'My task here is unfinished. Athera has no champion to take up my sword if I should abandon my purpose or falter.'

The centaur's reply resounded with sadness, and pity to wring the heart helpless. 'You are bound by a curse. Nothing less, nothing more. Admit that, and you take the first step to claim back your lost honor.'

'If you're right, then I'm damned!' Lysaer hurled back. 'My list of dead will be mourned. Across Fate's Wheel, they will be freed to accept your vaunted redemption.' Beyond desperation, he choked back his tears, clinging to the ripped shreds of conviction. 'But if you're wrong, if your race is demonic and your illusions are lies, then I become worse than damned. I would forfeit salvation before taking the chance of abandoning mankind to the darkness. For the wives, for the mothers, for the children unborn, the least risk is too terrible to contemplate.'

'The darkness you battle is none but your own,' the Ilitharis said in mild correction. 'If you find demons, they will be nothing less than *i'methient*, the rank creation that springs out of ignorant hatred. I leave you a warning: Daon Ramon is protected by Paravian law, as set forth in Rathain's crown charter. You and your following embrace no grand cause, but enact wanton ruin and trespass.'

'Your law is extinct,' Lysaer insisted. 'On my sword, hear my promise: mankind's justice succeeds you. Begone from this place, you are powerless.'

'Living Paravians still inhabit Athera!' The stamp of a hoof, and a bass thrum from bare stone issued a warning like distant thunder. 'I am a shadow called from the past, bearing no more than a shadow's influence, scion of Halduin. My spirit has departed this world of Athera, and now walks the far realms of Athlieria. Beware, should you challenge my living relations. Even bearing the blood of crown lineage, you shall not stand in defiance before them.'

Faster than Lysaer could frame a response, Sulfin Evend felt a sharp blast of wind strike his cheek. He uncovered his eyes, looked up, beheld the centaur guardian risen into a towering rear. Cleft forehooves lashed sky, stars shining above like wan sparks cast through the radiance of a presence far above an earthbound comprehension. Eclipsed by the creature's vast shadow, Lysaer's sunwheel banner snapped and flagged, a white blur in cold darkness with the limp russet trophy of Earl Jieret's clan braid spiked on the golden finial.

Still rampant, the centaur cried out, 'Be it known, this desecration has been done to a Man who is as my brother!' He turned his head to the side, exposing a braid in his mane. The strand count and pattern precisely matched Jieret's, the badge of regard an ancestral grant awarded to the lineage of s'Valerient. The guardian met the offense with aggrieved rage. His shouted command rang across the night hills in the lyrical cadence of Paravian. *'Fiaidliel! Ei lys cuen sheduanient i'an!'* Fire-Light! I call you to cleanse this!

The clan braid exploded in a blast of bright flame. Without sound, with no trace of wisped smoke or ripe stink, the degraded remnant was immolated. The Alliance banner beneath flapped pristine, its sunwheel emblem untarnished.

'You are a marked spirit,' the centaur guardian addressed Lysaer s'Ilessid in parting. 'The blood of one *caithdein* stains your hands already. Woe betide you for the price you shall pay if you dare to murder another.'

Lysaer remained adamant, his proud head thrown back, and his hair like stuck floss against the damp skin of his temples. 'I will meet any price and execute any criminal to wrest mankind free from the wiles of demons and sorcery.'

'Then expect you'll bear consequences. The land here will grant you no welcome.' The centaur apparition brought from the far past raised his dragon-spine horn. Face tipped skyward, Daon Ramon's winter starlight like crowning jewels strung through his circlet of oak leaves, he winded a resounding note.

The primal vibration reechoed through rock and soil, and also through the flesh-and-bone substance of every man within earshot. Ranging harmonics pealed forth and mustered the wind, which arose into whirling gyration. The white banner streamed and snapped back on itself until gold silk and fringe frayed and shredded. Tent canvas billowed like sails and snapped guy ropes. Weapon racks became hurled to the ground. The horses lunged and tore loose from the picket lines. Tracking dogs succumbed to berserk rage and clawed free of their osier cages. Bowstrings snapped. Steel swords suffered stress cracks, while the horn call achieved resonance and belled to an unbearable crescendo.

Athera herself roused to the centaur guardian's trumpeting summons. Through expanded awareness, Earl Jieret saw the lane forces wax bright and flow molten silver over the hillcrests. As the energy gathered, then surged toward release, the ground trembled and heaved, flinging tent poles helter-skelter, and toppling stacked supplies and wheeled drays like flung toys. Barrel hoops snapped. Restraints flew unraveled. Men wearing amulets or luck charms ripped them off as the seals flared with heat and burst into singeing flame.

Worse, the tin fiend banes guarding the camp border exploded, flinging showers of violet sparks.

Lurking iyats descended to feed on the disturbance. Havoc erupted, a pelting, hammering maelstrom of projectiles as loose pebbles and stray gear whirled aloft. No object escaped the maniacal invention of a fiend storm's exuberant play.

Loose daggers or sticks, bits of harness, or stacked cookpots, even Sulfin Evend's discarded arrows, the iyats seized on whatever they found with no shred of discrimination. Natural order unraveled. Torn canvas whooshed flat as tent stakes uprooted. Laces slithered through eyelets and crawled on the ground like live snakes. The cook's wagon swarmed with airborne utensils, and the tactical maps humped their way out of the wreckage and swooped through the air like huge bats.

If the apparition of the centaur guardian had vanished, the insidious effects of his horn call raged on. Stolid field veterans screamed and pounced, or turned tail and sprinted, as their personal belongings went mad and attacked them with stabbing intent to cause mayhem.

'Light save us, we're undone!' screamed the Etarran watch captain.

'We're not,' Lysaer snapped through rolling tremors and murderously clenched teeth. Still on his feet, though the rocks on the hillsides continued to wail, and the ground quivered like a horse with a stinging fly, he ripped his sword from the scabbard. He spun on his heel, determined strides bent toward the collapsed ruin of the command tent.

Sulfin Evend regrouped the bare semblance of self-possession. He scrambled upright, still unnerved and shaking, and surged in a rush to catch up. 'What will you do? The men are in no shape to march, far less handle weapons and fight.'

Lysaer turned his head. His face was chipped marble, his eyes blazing rage to outlast all sane choice or argument. 'First thing, I will run a blade through that redheaded sorcerer's heart! Fiend storm or not, his body will burn. By the Light, I shall raze his remains down to ash that won't keep the name of his memory!'

'And the men?' Sulfin Evend bore up, sobered cold as he realized the Blessed Prince was yet undaunted. Regardless of setbacks, *alone if need be*, he intended to press on and complete his campaign to destroy the Master of Shadow. 'You realize this fiend storm's unlikely to wane? We have no spare iyat banes. Nothing to avert their spree of destruction before the next bout of bad weather draws them away.'

With baleful purpose, Lysaer stopped short. He drew breath. 'You will commandeer every soldier we have standing upright. Regardless of rank, have them winnow the ones who are hysterical or faint.' As a fire broke out amid the wrack of downed canvas, running flares of reflection caught on gold threadwork and the polished steel of his sword quillons. The avatar yet wore the flesh of humanity. If his tone was flat level, his hand jerked and started, the poised tip of his sword as unsteady.

'The scouts on patrol won't be back for two hours, and the rest are nigh unto useless!' Sulfin Evend ran a jaundiced eye over the snarled remains of the camp he had just painstakingly set to sharp order. 'We don't have a fighting force. Not until we've nursed mass hysteria and salved the bruised nerves of every mother's son back to bravado. Don't expect to see discipline before daybreak.'

But the Divine Prince gave emotional frailties short shrift. 'We'll be marching before then. You will slap faces, or else appoint surrogates! Have them clasp these men's weeping, turned heads to their bosoms and croon like their damned mothers until they recover their wits! I don't care what you do, or which method works best. These troops swore their oath to fight minions of Darkness! Once that s'Valerient barbarian's ashes are scattered, I will personally cite for desertion any sniveling wretch who's unfit!'

Stand

Left alone to secure the cleft notch to the Mathorns, Braggen nocked his last arrow. Blinking the salt sting of sweat from his eyes, he drew, aimed, and fired. The shaft hissed out, punched flesh with the ugly, staccato smack that denoted a solid hit. The slavering mastiff charging upslope to attack him pitched head over heels and fell dying.

Through the flung gouts of snow carved up by its final throes, Braggen counted two more. He cast down the bow, ripped his sword from the scabbard, and drew his short knife from his boot cuff. Since boyhood, he had won all the contests when the scouts threw with daggers, left-handed. He gauged his distance, much too aware of his peril if his aim went amiss.

Darkness would lend the brute dogs an advantage. That narrowed his range, meant he must cast his blade at a distance of under ten paces. No margin for error remained. He could gut only one murdering beast on his sword. If another still lived, it would have him.

'Here's eleven, for luck,' Braggen gasped in dry irony. He cocked his wrist, steady from desperate necessity, and watched the paired mastiffs charge in. The wait became punishing. As the dogs closed the distance, their two-legged handlers would discover the disastrous fact that he had spent all his arrows.

Relentlessly trained to make sure of his target, Braggen held off until the last second. The mastiffs hurtled nearer. Their eyes were black pits. Gaping mouths dripped stringing gobs of foam, and their harsh, panting breaths sawed through their fleshy throats. The leading dog had a white blaze on its chest.

Braggen sighted that mark, nervelessly stilled for the lag as the heavy-boned predator gathered its haunches to leap.

The short knife left his hand in a point-blank trajectory; he never saw whether his cast steel struck true. Sword upraised, he braced for the hammering impact as the second dog launched at his face.

His blade pierced the animal from chest to spine and ripped through. Hard impetus slammed its breast against the quillons. Kicking and thrashing its passage from life, it managed to maul his right forearm. Powerful teeth clamped down on his bracer. If the steel studs prevented the worst of the gashing, the creature's jaws locked down strongly enough to bruise. Braggen rammed his knee into its underbelly and heaved to fling the writhing beast off his sword. The blade bound on bone. He had to stamp down, pin the dog's struggling body with his boot while he twisted the recalcitrant steel free.

The maneuver cost him dangerous seconds, and gained him a bitten ankle. At long last, the knifed dog stayed down, gushing blood like sprayed ink on a rumpled page of snow.

Downhill from its whimpering carcass, six enemy survivors broke out of cover and ran hell-bent with drawn weapons to harry him.

Braggen tested wrung muscles, found his grip on his sword slightly weakened, the dog's damage marginal, but enough: the limb was not going to stay trustworthy. The sword's simple, flat cross guard let him change hands, a skill his kind honed through a lifetime of dedication. With the mauled right, he drew his long dagger. Not stoic at all, now the hour had come, he faced his oncoming foemen. A last wish, he begged for the straight courage to die. He must stand his ground, and not falter in pain, or mire his purpose in regret for the kinfolk and close family left to carry his dwindled lineage after him.

For his prince, for a stake in the future for Rathain's feal clansman, Braggen determined to make each hard-fought thrust of his blade cost a life until the Etarran patrol overwhelmed him.

The first pair of enemies came on, enraged for nine fellows already fallen to this barbarian marksman's arrows. They were veterans, too well seasoned to rush blindly in. Braggen promptly marked them as Lysaer's elite field troops. The alert way they carried their round, spiked targes showed at once they were trained to deflect throwing knives. They drew in without haste as they sized up the ground, then measured the attributes of their opponent.

Braggen gave them no favors. He hung back in the cleft where night shadow would mask him, his littlest knives saved for infighting. A late grandaunt of his had been knocked down by headhunters; fatally wounded, she had taken her killer with a leg stab that opened an artery. An enemy lamed meant one less to trail Arithon. Finesse was not going to matter a damn if Rathain's crown prince never lived to reach freedom.

The trackers soon realized the cliffs on both sides offered no trail for ascent. Braggen had already ascertained that no enterprising climbers could be dispatched the long way to flank him. The sole option they had was a frontal assault on a chasm too narrow to admit more than two men abreast. If both tried to rush him, the space was too cramped for the reach of their swords: they would find their technique disastrously hampered, as likely to injure themselves as their enemy in the close press of a mêlée.

Their best men with the short bow were already dead. With shrewd foresight, Braggen had dropped those two earliest. His antagonists were unlikely to appreciate the fresh difficulty. Under cover, in darkness, a bad shot was too likely to gift him with an arrow to pick someone else off at leisure.

The Etarrans grasped the grim pitfalls well enough, their disgruntled talk peppered with epithets as their fellows drew abreast and fanned out.

The thin man in the lead summed up with a nerveless accuracy. 'No way. Can't flush the motherless fox with covering fire while he's pinned down in a fight. Our man with the sword would be far too likely to take a shaft in the back.'

'No choice, then,' said the veteran who replaced the slain officer. 'We'll go one at a time, hand to hand. Back in Etarra, the unblooded survivors can buy his killer three nights with a harlot. As my personal stake, I'll throw in all the beer tonight's hero can drink.'

'Don't send Gery first,' someone jeered, to a companion's snatched cough of laughter. 'If he wins, his new wife will spit him.'

'She'll do worse, I promise, if I spend my month's pay getting one of you oxen rolled in a brothel!' the offended party sniped back.

Lest the banter distract from the bloody work ahead, the ringleader swiftly quelled them. 'Listen up! We draw lots. As the first pick gets tired, the man next in line will replace him. Six to one odds, the hell-spawned barbarian must eventually wear himself down.'

Whatever their method of deliberation, the outcome took but a moment. A man broke away and unsheathed his blade and approached the rock cleft on cat strides. Braggen tagged his light tread and deliberate balance, and knew beyond doubt his opponent was going to be uncommonly skilled. Candidates who earned the sunwheel badge of life service were never less than exceptional. A springing, hot sweat slicked Braggen's palms underneath his thin gloves. He cursed fickle nerves, gently shifted his stance onto the balls of his feet. He faced the grim charge his clan chieftain had asked of him, his last course of action bitter and set, and the life in his veins summer sweet.

He had the advantage of facing an opponent limned against ambient light. By contrast, the Etarran must seek an armed adversary shaded in seamless darkness, half-masked among obscuring rock. A sword thrust would cast a flat line of reflection, thin reference upon which to engage in a bout of lethal combat. The added endangerment made the attacker move in with hair-trigger alertness. He would not strike first, or grope blind for his quarry. Nor would he make the green fool's mistake and work his way in too close. A sharp, seasoned veteran, he came on with care and listened for Braggen's quick breathing.

The thrust he expected shot out of ink shadow with only the soft, warning grate as boot leather ground upon stone. He parried the lunge with a predator's speed, flexed knee leading, and his body in flawless form, presented sidewards. The shorter reach of the clansman's poised dagger was granted no opening to strike.

The urge became overpowering, to release strung-up tension through expletives. Both combatants curbed the temptation to vent. Curses and insults would not hold off death or lessen the fear that stalked in lockstep with the danger. Quick and quiet, they closed in deep earnest, their duel marked by the flurried scrape of fast footfalls, the forced calm of each breath, and the shearing clashes as steel hammered steel amid the pitch blanket of darkness.

Then, as Braggen had dreaded, the backup man crept toward the notch in the rock. His silhouette melded into the outline of his Etarran antagonist and blurred clear perception beyond recourse. The odds traded sides, with the defending clansman hampered by distraction. The bystander's stray noise now overlaid the small, vital clues that matched his offensive to his combatant.

Braggen fell back on his merciless training and the honed edge of his clan hunter's instincts. His first lessons had not been conducted in a closed hall, with waxed floors and candles for lighting, but in the deep wood, with obstructions and roots, and the inconvenience of glaring sunlight. He had sparred by night, even in filthy weather, with the rain a cold sluice in his eyes. A man learned to trust more than sight and hearing, bruised and cut by his betters until he outstripped learned limits, and found he could move in and strike without thought on the prompt of intuitive reflex.

Though the Etarran had endured stringent tests in the field, more than half his secure life had been spent between walls, to the atrophy of the more primitive range of his senses. The next flurried exchange, he found himself pressed by fast steel that licked in and bit out of nowhere. Braggen scored on his shoulder, then again on his flank. The next lunge left him overextended. The dagger stabbed low into his right side, and he crumpled, moaning the name of a loved one.

The blow that dispatched him came fast and clean, and opened the neck just over the glint of his mail shirt. His blood jetted out in a heated, wet rain, sluicing the coffin-close rock face.

'Forgive,' Braggen whispered. He paused, while the man he had felled embraced the Wheel's turning, the life in him drained into final oblivion, and his sightless eyes fixed on the faint ribbon of sky, pricked with cold, distant starlight.

Respite was brief.

'Jolm's down,' the man in the passage informed the companions maintaining the cordon. The one who stood as the patrol's tactician came next in the lineup. Collected, he firmed his grip on his drawn sword, sucked a tight breath, and advanced.

Where a squeamish recruit might have flinched from spilled blood, this man reviewed Jolm's mistakes with stark purpose. The shuddering corpse in his path was likely to spoil his footwork. To clear room to fight, he needed to haze Braggen backward down the black throat of the ravine. Nor would he risk such a task to rank chance, blinkered in treacherous darkness.

Not proud, he begged backup help from his officer. 'Have Kitz bring a torch! Can't spit slinking clanborn while I'm trapped in this Light-forsaken pit.'

Reassurance filtered back from outside. 'Hold, then. We'll send in pitch brands. If you can't find a rock hole or crevice to wedge them, you'll have two bearers. I want that barbarian cut down, he's cost us a damned sight too dearly!'

Braggen blotted a trickle of sweat with his forearm. He could do naught but wait in taut readiness, while the men outside fumbled with flint and battled the sharp gusts to light torches. The wind through the gap raked through shirt and leathers. Shearing cold burnished his overheated body, his damp skin roughened with dangerous chill. Let his reflexes become slowed, he was going to succumb, his worst nightmare made real if an enemy sword managed to drop him, wounded.

The officer's changed mood had served him dire warning: he had plucked off too many Etarrans with bowfire to allow pride to let him die cleanly.

He rolled his tired shoulders, tried to stay loose, while his overstrung nerves rebelled at the creeping delay.

'You could run for it,' mocked the swordsman who faced him, testing his temper for weakness.

Braggen denied him the grace of an answer, nor dropped his raised steel for an instant. He maintained wary vigil, prepared for the opportunistic rush that must not catch him off guard. Second bled into agonized second. He held his strained focus on the enemy before him, while minutes dragged by, and the breeze funneled through the black cleft of the notch slapped and fluttered the soaked cloth of the dead man's sunwheel surcoat.

Fire flickered at the entrance. Braced for the change, struck alert by his peril, Braggen resisted the natural impulse to shift his established vantage. The dazzle of flame did not spoil his night vision on the moment his stance was revealed. He was still settled, even expectant, as his wily enemy lunged for him.

The attacking blade met Braggen's solid parry, a jarring clash that raised belling echoes within the tight stone enclosure. This bout was no tentative, testing affray enacted in covering darkness, but an assault stemmed from frustrated rage, brought to bitter focus by half a lifetime's experience. The Etarran headhunter whose blows Braggen fenced was a cold-handed veteran, gifted with weapons and tempered beyond any braggart's need to flaunt his extraordinary skill. His brassy competence had but one aim: to finish his man without flourish. Bounties were his livelihood, and killing a trade he had mastered with consummate skill. Poor footing did not shake him, nor the sharp blasts of wind that hissed with pummeling force through the gap.

Against brilliance and a gift of unshakable balance, Braggen owned the reflexes of a poisonous snake. He met and matched the man, stroke for stroke, resisting the fast-paced assault that insistently drove him back and back again. Wise enough not to seek to win ground, he chose his attacks to conserve strength and effort. For when this foeman's blistering talent wore down, he would be free to step back and allow a fresh companion to resume in his place.

The seasoned Etarran pressed that binding crux. If he could not kill outright, he would settle for wringing his opponent to a state of panting exhaustion.

Braggen blinked stinging sweat from his eyes; strove not to be dazzled by torch flame. The men kept their brands shining full in his face, a sore setback the swordsman well knew how to use. He had a reach slightly longer than Braggen's, and his lightning touches drew blood with a nettlesome sting. If the tactic provoked fury and won him the match, this bearded clansman refused to succumb.

Braggen had lived with black rage all his life, instilled by the memory of Tal Quorin. He parried the lunges one after another, blocked the whistling blade until his wrists and arms ached from the slamming vibration of impact. In the dark, under hellish, flickering brands, the match crossed beyond a pitched contest of straightforward muscle and steel. Battling contention also encroached on the delicate realm of the mind. An opponent this skilled was accustomed to winning. Etarran, he would also be prejudiced. The fact a contemptible clansman sustained his best form without taking crippling injury must eventually sting him. Provoke that cool poise, and he might be lured into brash risk.

Yet if the Etarran had overweening pride, or a reputation to flaunt in front of admiring fellows, his attack suffered no inconsistency. Time and again, Braggen was forced to defer to the viper-quick strike of his lunges. The clansman was tiring. Neat, solid footwork slipped and slithered on snow. Twice, he almost turned his ankle on the rocks. His right forearm had punctures stabbed through his bracer, and a bleeding nick in the webbed skin at the ball of his thumb left his dagger grip slippery.

Hazed by the smoky flare of pitch torches, the town swordsman came on, his blades casting jarring, carnelian reflections, and his citybred features an inhuman mask of concentration. He had cold, pale eyes, and a punishing, ethereal style that gave him the appearance he was invincible.

Braggen caught himself short of a disastrously wide parry He must not let his disheartenment throw him. Gasping for air, bathed in the rank pong of his trail-beaten clothes and the unwashed blood of dead enemies, he snarled and blocked like a snared fox. Exhaustion had stripped his veneer of humanity.

Hounded and battered, he handled his weapons by the reflex of gut-stripped instinct. Outnumbered before this, he knew the strange landscape that bordered the extreme edge of survival. A handful of times he had fought past the point when better sense said he was beaten. He had surpassed himself then. This bout was no different; except before, he had not been alone.

He had held on for the sake of beleaguered clan brothers, their interconnected dependence a wellspring of inspiration.

Now he faced death for an absent prince, trapped in a place of desolate rock, keened over by mournful, sharp gusts. Fatigue robbed his focus, leaching the urgency from his purpose. The shattering din of steel meeting steel savaged his ears without mercy. More pleasant by far to let go of hard striving, to imagine his daughter, with her long, satin hair being combed by the hands of his wife.

The slapping sting of a graze to his bracer snapped his wandering thought. Braggen parried; again, yet again, his lips peeled back from bared teeth. He saw an opening and lunged. His sword was predictably struck and deflected. But his dagger hand scored, and opened a fluttering rip in the flank of his enemy's surcoat.

Tired as he was, he realized this indefatigable townsman was flagging as well. Heady encouragement rushed through his veins, until he had to rein back to stay recklessness.

No fool, his opponent sensed the turned tide. He shouted, asking the next man to step in and give him relief. 'Change the lineup,' he added, taking the vicious cut meant for his head on the flat of his angled blade. His riposte kept clean rhythm, through a voice wrenched to strain. 'Send in Kitz before Gery. Tell him, play safe. If he's blooded, stand down. This creature we've cornered was born without nerves, and he's strong as a deadly wild animal.'

Braggen held ready, pressing for opening, but the fight did not lag. The two veterans changed places without missing a beat. All over again, with his muscles cramped to burning, and his sight still trammeled with torch flare, the clan swordsman must meet and size up a new adversary. In the speed of sharp action, he must gauge this foeman's style without opening his guard, or succumbing to thought that might stall his response time and lead to a fatal mistake.

Kitz proved a lean veteran with shaggy dark hair, and a cut hard and accurate as a mule's kick. After three slamming parries, Braggen's palm was bashed numb. The punishing ache setting up in his wrist was only going to get worse. This brute's smashing style required well-set feet. Gasping, running sweat from every overheated pore, Braggen gave ground again. He tested the terrain under his soles with a forest-bred hunter's dire patience, and waited. Best to press his attack over loose stone or snow. Then the hammering force of Kitz's traded blows could be robbed of their damaging leverage.

The slipped step that might throw him as he traversed the ground first posed a risk that could not be avoided. Braggen made himself even his raced breath. The disciplined perception that kept him alive required a clear mind, but not too narrowed a focus. Tunnel vision or anxiety would shut down intuition and constrict his physical senses. Tension would force his starved muscles to work harder, further straining his laboring heart.

Parry and riposte, Braggen matched the offensive. Tears of sweat burned his eyes. From block to a high cut, his right shoulder trembled, first warning sign he was losing his war with fatigue. Maddening, to know he could kill this man, if only his stamina was not depleted. As things were, he could scarcely stand off Kitz's rank slashes, far less launch methodical attack. He felt his soles skate on patched ice, then catch in a pocket of gravel. One nearly missed step; Kitz's blade stabbed in at his flank, the thrust stopped on a wrenching parry. Braggen bartered on luck and finessed his way past the pothole that had nearly defeated him. Here lay the advantage he had angled to arrange. If he pressured, perhaps his enemy might rush his form and be lured into misjudgment.

''Ware footing!' cautioned the left-hand-side torchbearer.

Kitz gasped his swift thanks, and stood off for a beat.

Sword poised, the reflected light shot off his blade betraying his unsteady trembling, Braggen panted. He surveyed the faces of the hardened men pressing him and understood that he would be denied any respite. They saw he was failing. Hang back, and someone would just string a bow, and call in a marksman to fell him. Safety lay in renewing the attack, a wicked irony: he must make his move to engage on the same trappy ground he had hoped would defeat his opponent.

Braggen lunged. The fight renewed, to the punishing clang of stressed steel, and the coarse, torn gasps of the clansman. His hair was sweat drenched, and his shirt soaked through. The linen caught on his moist skin and chafed, a binding drag on his shoulders. Now tired enough that his parries were careless, he realized he could not reverse ebbing stakes. He might stay alive, to no added purpose. As his legs shared the same jellied wear as his arms, he could scarcely rally. Only a wrought miracle would let him seize back the offensive.

What gain could ten more minutes' delay serve Arithon Teir's'Ffalenn? Since Braggen had no ready answer for hopelessness, he swung and blocked through sheer stubbornness. If these townsmen wanted his scalp for their trophy, he would not grant them the liberty before he was down and unconscious.

Blind tired, now, Braggen only realized the swordsman was changing when Kitz's pounding strokes reached a lag.

Gery stepped in, light-footed and rested. Braggen flexed his burning shoulders. He noticed he had running blood on both hands as he raised his battered sword to receive the next round of offensive.

No novice, the younger man came in fast. His touch was astute, but without innovation. Against his fussy, classical purity, Braggen needed speed and concentration. If the style was predictable, the drilled perfection of Gery's parries left no slackened technique to exploit. Suffering moments of blacked-out vision, and gaps of distorted hearing, Braggen was aware of almost nothing but the rasp of his own spent breath. The screaming din of struck steel came and went, blotted up by the flitter of torch fire. He fought on by touch, his sloppy feet dragging over rough ground in a manner that swiftly wrecked boot soles.

Through the din, he understood his bystanders made wagers on how long he would take to fall. He parried the next stroke, and the next after that. Slow rage burned through him. Be *damned* to Dharkaron if he would allow a dullard like Gery to take him out, or claim honor in front of his comrades.

For rockhead clan pride, Braggen kept on. He vowed he would die of a burst heart, before he laid his neck bare to a stripling with no imagination.

The futility mocked him, that he would be finished the instant the more polished swordsman reclaimed the assault. Against that one, he could not stand past two strokes. He could but hope the man had the grace not to lay back and toy with him.

Braggen caught the next stroke too near the cross guard, and narrowly missed being disarmed. His dagger hand saved him, a manic bluffing stab at Gery's wrist that made the fool flinch and shy off. Too spent to mock, he fought his sword up, caught the next slamming stroke, just barely.

Unnoticed, through the labor of staying alive, the town officer had realized his men were making a game of the outcome. Through shivering steel, and a snatched moment of clarity,

Braggen caught his outraged, barked order, that commanded young Gery to stand down.

'Now will you buffoons attend to your business!' the Etarran served in sharp reprimand.

Sheer rage born out of twisting despair, Braggen snatched the diversion. He cast down his long dagger, and in a swift move, whipped the small dirk from his sleeve cuff.

His throw followed by seamless reflex.

Then the sharp grief, dousing the sweet triumph of revenge, as the man toppled neck struck, and left his young wife a widow.

'Forgive,' Braggen grated. The needful word chafed at his tortured throat. With no chance to recover the dropped dagger at his feet, he hauled the lead weight of his sword up to guard point. Through eyes glittering with trapped rage and regret, he beheld his own death as his first, rested nemesis came back at him.

This man was not tempted to stall, or waste time. He dispatched his kills by expedience.

Braggen parried the first lightning stroke, a blind miracle.

The next could not fail to rip through his chest. His arm was too sluggish to manage the block. Nor had he the dregs of strength left to deflect the sheer, driving force of an expert swordsman's stop thrust.

Worse, his vision was patchy from prolonged exertion. Half-unconscious, he fumbled to maintain his shambling defense. From outside, very faint, he thought someone shouted. Then a wasp-fine hum creased across his stressed hearing. No doubt his body served up final warning that his overtaxed senses were failing.

He planted numbed feet; and the lunge that he braced for delayed, and then never came.

Rocked forward into a stupefied stumble, Braggen yanked himself short of a fall. Balance gone, utterly, he averted collapse in a jarring drop to his knees.

Before him, torn with agony, the lethal town headhunter lay thrashing. Braggen watched the man's puzzling demise, too numbed to feel curiosity. Stupid with shock, he finally noticed the arrow punched down through the jointure of neck and collarbone. The shaft was clan made, and still quivering.

Braggen blinked. He hurt too much to be dreaming. Still, the sure evidence of his salvation took a moment to reach his stunned brain. For a mercy that stupor did not burden the archer.

The next, seamless second, the dumbfounded torchbearer buckled and slammed on his face. His brand bounced free of his slackened fingers. Sparks spattered and flurried over the snow. Through the sheared hiss of steam as the coals sizzled out, Braggen wrestled the urgent awareness that he should snatch up his lost knife. But sight showed him the officer, already fallen, his cheek in a spilled pool of blood.

The remaining torchbearer dropped his brand, spun, and ran. The flared flag of fire cast a glinted needle of reflection, scribing a descending line through the darkness: a third released arrow whined downward. The steel-tipped shaft of vengeance, it struck the Etarran's sunwheel surcoat directly between pumping shoulders. He tumbled, legs drumming in useless spasm. A last arrow dispatched him, clean through the nape, where his wisped blond hair curled from the rim of his helm.

'Forgive,' Braggen gasped in the killer's behalf.

Undone by fatigue, senses reeling with dizziness, he tipped his chin up in salute. Limned against the faint ribbon of starlight, he made out the form of the archer, a spare silhouette where sky met the scarp of the ridgetop.

'Six,' he rasped hoarsely. 'There was another . . . just at the mouth of . . . the notch.'

'I took him down first,' said his Grace of Rathain. His apology rang terse as his marksmanship with the bow. 'Can you forgive me? The precaution almost delayed me too long.'

Braggen dropped on his buttocks. Stupefied with anger, he slammed his limp fist against the spent flesh of his thigh. 'Damn you!' He squeezed shut dripping eyes. Wrung through by a wave of convulsive reaction, he sucked in a harsh, rasping breath. Then, dogged, he gathered himself once again. Though a useless fury that all but choked him, he cursed with bitterest venom. 'Damn you, my liege, to the black gates of Sithaer! You were to go on without me!'

'Don't be a fool. One dog, or one tracker, and the next wave of pursuit would have run me to earth before morning.' Nettled beyond sentiment, Arithon threw a snowball. His sharp, sniper's aim doused the smoldering torch 'Hang on. Are you wounded?'

Braggen shook his head, speechless.

'Then I'm coming down to round up the strayed horses.' Concern cracked through the pared mask of practicality as Arithon peered intently downward. 'Are you sure you're all right?' Somehow he guessed the stunned clansman was unable to rise to his feet. 'I might be an hour. Can you manage?'

'Find the horses and go!' Braggen snarled back, annoyed to be seen puling weak as an infant. Nor could he stem the frank tears of gratitude that soaked his embarrassed, flushed cheeks.

For answer, Jieret's bearskin cloak floated down, leaving him the autonomous means to keep warm, and gifting him back precious privacy.

Spring Equinox Eve 5670

Visitations

At Whitehaven, in the mountain hostel of Ath's initiates, Elaira breaks weeping from the depths of a dream, while the echoes of her beloved's agonized cry resound without voice through her mind; to the startled adept who asks after her tears, she gives her wracked answer: 'Rathain's *caithdein* just died in Daon Ramon Barrens. The Teir's'Ffalenn was blood-bonded to him, and I hear the raw imprint of his Grace's grief . . .'

Another seer in Halwythwood dreams of Earl Jieret's body run through by the sword, in the hand of Lysaer s'Ilessid; Jeynsa shoots upright, her dark hair in snarled disarray, to behold her father before her in spirit form, his face grave with love, and the sorrow of a forced parting: *'Daughter, forgive me, I can't keep my promise and come home. You now stand as Rathain's caithdein, charged to uphold the royal charter at the right hand of the sanctioned crown prince . . .'*

Fled deep into hiding, Princess Ellaine dreams of her joyous young son, arising unmarred by disfiguring burns from the trilling waters of a spring; then she wakens, torn to fresh, sobbing grief, for her Kevor is dead, and the vision that reached her had held too unearthly a beauty for any place found this side of Daelion's Wheel . . .

XII. Rockfell Peak

Whem the Mad Prophet had last visited the frigid heights of the Skyshiels, he had journeyed through the milder winds and clear sky of early summer. Since ice runged the uppermost tier of the ranges year-round, the voice raised in complaint had been his own, venting his pique to a brace of unsympathetic Sorcerers.

Now, in reverse, as he maintained tense vigil on the ledge near the storm-lashed summit of Rockfell Peak, he was the one being reviled for the heartless behavior of mages. Worry had wrung him beyond grace for tolerance. Burdened by the grave perils he had been sent by the Fellowship to help defray, grown into a broader frame of awareness by the trials of sore experience, Dakar was amazed in hindsight. A stark miracle of forbearance, that Asandir had not pitched him over the cliffside to silence his incessant whining.

In irritating, changed circumstance, he winced for the sharp ring to Fionn Areth's curses, and tried to muffle his ears. Shrewd wisdom would not let him ignore unseen truth: that the knife-edged pinnacle they had scaled with such hardship picked up and pondered the vibrational essence of the ignorant goatherd's rank phrases. Stone was patient; it would unwind the essence of each and every explosively frustrated epithet.

That dissidence, added into the building charge that warned of the approaching equinox, made the very ledge where they sat sing of oncoming danger. Overwhelmed by the sense of mounting stress, Dakar poked his head from the garments that sheltered him, shook unkempt hair from his eyes, and cast a sour glance at his companion. 'You wouldn't malign an innkeeper who gave you free hospitality.'

'This?' Fionn Areth's arm encompassed the bleak vista sealed under the indigo dome of the sky. Rockfell Vale was not visible. The lesser summits framing the view showed only their barren tips. Spurs of jagged, stacked rock thrust through the threshing floor of the cloud line, drifting like combed cotton three hundred feet lower than the comfortless eyrie that seated them. 'You call *this* hospitality?'

When Dakar refused answer, the herder scowled harder. The grimed hood of his mantle slapped at his face, flagged by the fierce wind that battered the black scarp without letup. The monotony rankled, after three days and nights parked in wait for a Sorcerer who had signally failed to show up. 'That's a maniac's fancy. Just look at yourself!'

Hunched like a toad under rucked layers of cloaks and a mismatched assemblage of blankets, the Mad Prophet blotted his dripping, red nose. His streaked beard bristled like a mange-ridden fox brush as he gave his disgruntled contradiction. 'For Rockfell, the weather's been generous, trust me.'

'I can't.' Fionn Areth kicked a fragment of ice from the brink. The shard tumbled, snatched up by the gale, which flung it with redoubled force back toward the flank of the mountain. 'This place would give a stiff corpse the creeps.'

The ice sliver struck. Its glassine explosion showered pulverized bits over an incongruous, carved staircase, replete with brass newel posts and an array of leering, unpleasant statues. A stone gargoyle with mantling wings oversaw the intrusive impact, granite eyes flared briefly red.

'The wise man wouldn't trouble those,' Dakar warned. 'Raise one to anger, you won't like what happens.'

'The wise man wouldn't be here at all!' Fionn Areth snapped. The scream of the incessant wind chafed him raw, with the acidic boredom of Dakar's imposed vigil showing no sign of reprieve. 'What are those things, anyway? They make me feel stared at.'

'And so they should,' Dakar said, his strained note of unease beyond masking. Had he realized that Kharadmon would be unimaginably late, he would have chosen to roost elsewhere. 'Those figures are sentinels.' He huddled farther under his blankets, not just to escape the blasting gusts. Even when the pit's binding wardspells were stable, Rockfell Peak was no place for a man to bide easy. It had stood guardian for too many harmful entities, over the course of two Ages. The experience had stamped an irascible undertone into the forgiving, staid nature of stone. The heart of the Vale sang in sympathy with Athera, with the mountain's preferred loyalty not readily given to creatures whose busy minds carried the ripe urge to cause mayhem.

Dakar suggested, 'If you dislike being watched, you might want to stop pacing. The aimless activity sets the watchers on edge.'

Fionn Areth sat down with resigned bad grace, his elbow braced on the supply pack. Provender had run low. The scuffed canvas held little beyond cookpot and pannikins. Two meager wrapped packets of smoked fish and venison had reduced them to half rations since yesterday. The goatherd turned his glower downslope, all but daring the sentinels to shoulder the blame for his sleepless nights and his hunger pangs. 'Daelion's black bollocks! Only a Sorcerer would go to such lengths to carve follies that drive a grown man to the *grullies.*'

The term in grasslands dialect referred to spooked fear. Dakar's response fell somewhere between a derisive laugh and a snort. 'Davien's works never look kindly on anybody.' Eyes shut, knees tucked up, he nestled his napped head onto his folded arms. 'If such ever changed, I'd find that a likely reason to start worrying. Now bear up and let me sleep.'

Left to his own company, and miserable for it, Fionn Areth jammed restless fingers through his dark hair. He regarded the view he had already memorized, and found nothing redeeming to savor.

Above, a naked fang thrust against sky, Rockfell's bleak summit split the wind. The ledge the Mad Prophet had chosen for his perch held no natural cave or even a cranny for shelter. The opposite, in fact; the site reeked of sorcery. Some working of spellcraft had altered the cornice, razed its split rock to a polish as clean as a slab of black glass. The rare intervals when Fionn Areth had dozed, he suffered unsettling nightmares. Grown peevish and tired, he brooded upon the combed river of cloud that masked the miniaturized scenery below.

For the fiftieth time, he tried to console himself. Storm probably dumped snow in raging billows against the lower slopes. In blizzard conditions, the game stayed denned up. A camp in the lowlands would see their bellies just as pinched, if beleaguered flesh would be warmer. Fionn Areth regarded the clear sky over-head with equally jaundiced gratitude. These desolate heights were continuously pummeled by vicious, razor-edged winds. Nothing garnered a foothold in the cleft rock beyond a few scabrous lichens.

Fresh protest erupted, before he could think. 'If we died here, no one would find our stripped bones.'

Dakar refused answer. The long days of waiting had exhausted his plausible words of encouragement. Nor did he have an innocuous explanation to salve the raw torment of waiting. Nightfall approached, threatening an array of inescapable conse-quence, while the Fellowship Sorcerer they had traveled to meet was irremediably delayed.

If Kharadmon's absence extended past midnight, Athera's magnetic flux would raise the tides of spring equinox. The wardfields holding the Mistwraith confined would be sundered as the lane forces crested.

The predicament posed a potential for disaster beyond Fionn Areth's imagining. His questions left Dakar stubbornly uncom-municative. Left no other outlet for his uninformed apprehension, the young herder struck out with insults or stalked through his fits of taut nerves.

'Rain goat turds on the doings of mages,' he grumbled at length. Rather than sit still and strangle with worry, Fionn Areth rejected advice and began to rise to his feet.

A pink rose fluttered downward out of thin air and struck the crown of his head.

'Be glad,' cracked a voice of silken, barbed clarity, 'that I didn't take your wish seriously.'

Fionn Areth yelped, startled recklessly erect. Only Dakar's timely grab at his collar saved his upset balance. Yanked back on his haunches, he narrowly escaped a headlong tumble over the cliffside.

Once assured the shaken young man was secure, Dakar shed his mantling blankets and stood up. Head tipped awkwardly back, he vented his pique into what seemed vacant sky. 'You took your sweet time! It's equinox eve, and we're sitting on a keg of fermenting trouble. And could you for once try a little consideration? The Araethurian's scared witless of mages.'

'Well he can dive off the ledge, if that's his free choice. I won't stir to prevent him. You promised his safety to Arithon, not me.' A riffling vortex of icy wind marked Kharadmon's free-ranging laughter. 'Don't expect me to turn foolish with sentiment just because a young idiot got himself used by Koriathain, and happens to wear s'Ffalenn features.'

'Meet Kharadmon,' Dakar introduced to the disgruntled herder beside him. 'If you don't let him know that his baiting upsets you, he'll grow bored and leave you alone.'

Fionn Areth bent down to retrieve the dropped rose, which vanished before he could touch it. If he masked his sharp flinch, he was less successful with the reflexive backstep provoked by the Sorcerer's abrupt appearance.

Kharadmon's elegant image unfurled, standing with booted feet planted squarely over the void. His preference ran to flamboyant dress: a green cloak lined in vivid, flame orange, and a black-velvet doublet adorned at the seams with a sparkling band of glass beadwork. His spotless white shirt had lace cuffs and cord points tipped with wired gold emeralds.

Tall, rakishly dapper, his streaked salt-and-pepper hair streaming in the wind, Kharadmon smiled. The expression set off his rapacious, sharp features. Pearl teeth parted a sable mustache and a beard trimmed down to a spade point. 'Well met, Fionn Areth,' he greeted. 'If the company's unsporting, I trust you're enjoying Rockfell's exceptional view?'

'Well, he shouldn't be,' another voice cut in out of nowhere. 'This mountain knows the foul trouble that stirs in its bowels. When stone gets annoyed, it doesn't share your penchant for the ridiculous. You know you've cut the interval too fine? We haven't time to reset the wards before the advent of equinox.'

'Ah, Luhaine!' Kharadmon's narrow features lit to manic delight. 'Still tripping over yourself to pontificate, I see. Did you think I would stall for caprice?'

'Weren't you?' Luhaine retorted. 'That's a novelty.' His formed image crowded the narrow ledge: a short, rotund bald man with a waterfall beard spilled down a scholar's robe of dusky gray. He hooked exasperated thumbs at his girth, belted with a strap as sturdy and plain as a country plowman's ox collar. 'The last time we debated that point, you'll remember, you were flitting about with a summer swarm of cicadas.'

'Not watching them copulate, but learning their language. I remember.' Kharadmon's smile vanished. The image of vexed elegance, he flicked out his sleeves as though stainless lace spun from thought and intent could set into wrinkles before his colleague's distaste. 'Short-lived creatures, cicadas, and wise. An example to careless, ignorant beings who use words before vision and accuse others of wasting irreplaceable time.'

This once, Dakar picked up the nuance of underlying menace. 'Kharadmon? What in Athera held you up?'

The elegant apparition of the Sorcerer stared back, unblinking. When troubled, his eyes wore the same shadowed hue as the spruce-covered foothills. 'Nothing in Athera. Unhappy news that should give you both pause.' He watched the fierce impact of that statement register: Dakar's brosy face turned to whey, and Luhaine's stout image snap frozen in gaping disgruntlement.

'What is it?' Fionn Areth demanded. 'What's wrong?'

His outburst was ignored.

Kharadmon said, not thoughtful, 'Unlike rock, I prefer the grace of my sense of humor kept intact.'

'Wraiths?' Luhaine's exclamation climbed a register above his placid orator's baritone. *'You say that free wraiths have moved out of Marak?'*

'Entangled in mazes, waylaid, and dizzied to blinded confusion,' Kharadmon allowed. 'A pack of two dozen, to be rudely precise. They're questing. By sheer luck, they don't realize the rich prize at the end of the hunting trail.' The Sorcerer advanced a smart step, spanned the chasm of air, and alighted without sound on the ledge. Poised with heels at the brink, in the chilling aplomb given only to bodiless spirits, he awarded Luhaine his weasel's smile, along with a flourishing court bow. *'Now* we waste time. Rockfell's wards must be set under protection, and quickly. As you see, I've a dance left unpartnered that I must return and attend with some urgency.'

Dakar's moon face drained an impossible shade paler. As though his legs failed him, he sat. 'If Arithon finds safety, his Masterbard's talents might help you Name those strayed wraiths.'

Luhaine's flustered image dissolved into testy sparks. 'But his Grace of Rathain is far from uncompromised. We have a pending crisis right here to avert, before we can begin the first step of addressing repairs in the pit. Greater mercy above! With the wards safeguarding the Mistwraith unstable, the timing couldn't be worse.'

'What's happening?' Fionn Areth persisted, the hair prickled erect at his nape by the proximity of Luhaine's distress. Jarred by the ill-suppressed climate of anxiety, he thrust out his chin in belligerence.

'Potential trouble, on a grand scale,' Luhaine snapped. 'Bide still. You wouldn't understand all the ugly possibilities, even if we had an idle hour to explain.'

'Then you flatter yourselves! What makes you believe that I care in the slightest?' Fionn Areth straightened. Cloak clasped to his shoulders with stiffened affront, he withstood the buffeting turbulence shed by the discorporate spirit's irritation. 'Don't think I wouldn't rather be anyplace else but on a mountain in the company of Sorcerers!'

Kharadmon's cat eyes narrowed. He stroked his beard with a tapered hand, his grin agleam with white teeth.

Yet before he could deliver his pungent opinion on keeping the dull company of goatherds, Luhaine reappeared and barged in. 'Boy! If you want to leave Rockfell alive and claim your safe passage to Alestron, you'll need to stay balanced and vigilant.' He shook a finger, admonishing, 'This place doesn't serve mortals a kindly welcome. Dakar's business could extend for a number of days. During that time, you'll have no one to calm your panicky nature. Step headlong into trouble, and heed this as fact, you could quite easily die here.'

As the herder braced up to take unwise umbrage, the Mad Prophet thrust back to his feet. He locked a warning hand on the young man's forearm, sorely tempted to deliver a drastic shaking to chastise such harebrained behavior. 'Trust me, we all wish we were someplace else.'

Fionn Areth glared back, deaf to reason.

Dakar dredged up his lost tact. Confronted by the double of Prince Arithon's face, he often forgot that this stripling's aggression was not heartset, but the reflex of Araethurian ignorance and no small measure of shrinking fear. 'If you're going to pick fights with Fellowship Sorcerers, listen to me, Fionn! The practice is dangerous, and brings no reward, as I learned from harshest experience.'

Before Kharadmon proffered more inflammatory comment, or Luhaine snatched the opening to lecture, Dakar edged the young man to the sidelines. 'Just stay here. You'll witness wonders, not all of them pleasant. Try and remember we'll be free to leave once the wards over Rockfell are refounded.' Through gnawing urgency, and the rattled awareness that the equinox was too close to reliably promise success, the spellbinder strove to placate. 'That basic task has not changed. Only the stakes are much higher. Should you come to harm, I assure you, I'll be dead, and the Fellowship Sorcerers will have failed in their charge. Then address your fate as you can, for no haven on Athera will be safe.'

Fionn Areth folded his arms, black brows knitted into the frown that foreran his worst fits of obstinacy.

Dakar lost his patience. 'Perhaps Luhaine's past impression was right. Arithon should have left you in Jaelot to burn.'

The spellbinder turned his back on the herder. Seized by a bone-deep tremor of trepidation, he shored up failing courage and presented himself to the Sorcerers.

'I'm not ready,' he confessed with wounding honesty. 'Yet I see no option.' If his chestnut hair was unkempt and his clothing rumpled in hagridden disarray, he had inwardly changed: the last time the Sorcerers had required his help, Asandir had needed to drag him by the heels from the stews of drunken indulgence. Though dread for this assignment had not lessened one whit through three months of arduous travel, Dakar expelled a sharp breath. Upright on shaky feet, he led the commitment at Rockfell. 'You have my permission. Go forward.'

Luhaine withheld from disparaging comment, and Kharadmon for once did not mock. They would not offer false platitudes. Better than any, the Sorcerers knew the perils an apprentice spellbinder offered to shoulder in their behalf. Nor could the works of a pending catastrophe be delayed for the sake of human discomfort.

'You'll want to sit down,' Luhaine urged, a suggestion made in bald-faced regret. 'If your body convulses through the stresses of transfer, I can't help. Let's not risk a fall off the precipice.'

Kharadmon's last advice was worse than disquieting. 'You realize your consent to this binding must be extended beyond your mortal survival.'

Dakar swallowed, and ground past the husk in his voice, 'You destroyed your flesh once already in Athera's service. Should I be surprised I might share the same fate? You hold my consent. I suggest you step in, before I lose my last grip.'

'And what, soil your breeches?' Kharadmon laughed. 'Well, don't bet I won't suffer the same lapse myself, if the critical muscle's as abandoned to flab as the rest of you.'

Dakar opened his mouth, his enveloping anxiety flushed by stung outrage; and in that kindly moment while he stood diverted, the discorporate Sorcerer encompassed his unguarded mind like a numbing blast of chill wind. Kharadmon's massive presence flowed in, a building pressure not meant to cause hurt. Yet demands and necessity disallowed compromise. The expansion required by his entry nonetheless strained and stretched assumed boundaries, then wedged rifts through every fixated limit lodged within the spellbinder's awareness.

The Mad Prophet gasped. Seized head to foot by a tingling rush, he fought dizziness, the assault to his senses more potent than the inaugural burst forerunning a tienelle trance. The flux did not slacken as his flesh was squeezed full, but spilled over and flashed outward, respinning the unseen matrix of his aura until every nerve end felt flushed by a blast of raw heat. His body trembled, then quaked. Sight drowned, rinsed into delirious hallucination. Dakar reeled, unmoored, awash in a deluge of color and light that exploded the foundational patterns of cognizance.

'Don't try to move,' Luhaine admonished. 'The changes you're sensing hold peril incarnate. To disrupt the flow for even a second will drive you to madness beyond remedy.'

Dakar locked his teeth to stifle a scream of rank terror as emotions he never knew he possessed tore up from the pit of his stomach. He could not tell whether his effort succeeded. Hearing dropped out next. Felted in deafness, then cast adrift from the feel of the solid rock wall at his back, he panted to recover his breath. The air drawn through his lungs never reached his starved brain. He felt swathed in tar to the point where he could not escape the frantic belief he would suffocate.

'Steady, hold steady. You're not close to dying,' Kharadmon's whisper bridged the maelstrom of battering distortion, but did little to allay the gibbering shadows of fear.

'Steady,' the Sorcerer repeated. He touched something inside of Dakar's core awareness. When pressure and pain stayed his tacit probe, he gently asked for a word of permission.

Half-lost to madness, Dakar yielded a response in beleaguered trust.

Something snapped, sure as the thrust of a surgeon's knife cutting the thread of a cobweb. Dakar shuddered, his dread fallen into eclipse as he felt himself stripped of every reflexive defense. Ripped naked before the devouring unknown, he howled until he was emptied.

He gave way, exhausted; and suddenly found himself deluged in light. Soft as the kiss of spring rain in renewal, the cascade poured into the void that yawned through his ravaged being. The tenderness broke him all over again, that he could be loved and understood, despite his wayward flaws and his failures.

'Kharadmon?'

'I, myself,' the Sorcerer replied. 'Why should you doubt your own worthiness?' A reflection spilled back, of strengths and bright talents dulled behind the false tarnish of potent drink: the fears and detritus amassed through a lifetime spent in shrinking denial.

Reforged in the crucible of Kharadmon's regard, the spell-binder released his self-doubt. Surrender claimed him for one fragile moment, and in the peace of that transient acceptance, Kharadmon asked again. This time as a friend addressing an equal, he requested permission to claim space, and share the seat of the spellbinder's physical consciousness.

'Enter as you please,' the Mad Prophet invited, his third stage of consent given beyond any ties of duty or obligation.

The exuberant influx took him by storm, a bliss so pure every tie of awareness came unraveled before limitless wonder.

Dakar felt routed and reamed, remade from within in ways that defied understanding. He had walked in the presence of Fellowship Sorcerers for most of his life, and apprenticed to Asandir for over five centuries. No experience prepared him. Gripped by an awe that blasted him senseless, he realized he had never come close to encompassing the masterful might of one such being, firsthand. The experience smashed through every veil of preconception, then lifted, and lifted his vantage again until the sensation of such rarefied height left him a stranger unto himself. He heard tones beyond hearing, pure and clear. Sound to make stones shout aloud for sheer joy, had man held the means to share comprehension; he saw color beyond light, and still failed to encompass even a fraction of Kharadmon's broadscale perception.

Possessed by a will that might touch, and smash mountains, or turn thought and respin the vanes of a moth's wing, Dakar wept. 'Sky and earth, Kharadmon, *who are you*?'

'*Far easier to ask who I was in my past*,' the Sorcerer replied, an echo arisen from inside his mind. '*Though if you delve into my deepest memories, you may come to wish that you hadn't.*'

Dakar encountered the core of a human awareness. But like the view seen through the wrong end of a ship's glass, the original persona had long since outgrown limitation. The peppery cast of the birth-born man held the seeds of some qualities he recognized, but vastly diminished, and set against the backdrop of a world nothing at all like Athera.

Snatched glimpses streamed past, of sprawling cities with turrets of glass; a changed vista that encompassed cinders and rubble; then a red-haired woman of ravishing loveliness curled like a jewel amid lavender sheets. Dakar yanked back, singed to embarrassment. Chagrined, he realized that his contact with the

Sorcerer lent him wide-open access to even the most personal memories.

Dismay followed, that a similar encounter forged through magecraft with Arithon had altered his life ever after.

'Oh, you'll be changed,' Kharadmon promised with caustic frankness. 'Like a glove that's been stretched to fit larger fingers, try though you might, you can't quite ever shrink it back to its former shape.'

To bridge the abyss of Dakar's trepidation, the Sorcerer extended his forgiveness. 'The beautiful lady I once loved was Carline, and I don't mind sharing her memory. For the rest, don't worry. There won't be time to expose the lying flattery you use to inveigle your doxies. Since the precious creatures won't bed with ghosts, I've no use for the names of your favorites.'

Since goading humor failed to stem the spellbinder's distress, Kharadmon laid bare his core of sincerity. 'I can't in good conscience suppress your awareness! That would demean the trust of your consent and cross the line out of free partnership. I won't break the Law of the Major Balance. Not even for the sake of securing Desh-thiere. Such use of your body would become an act of outright possession.'

At that, Dakar rallied. Beneath the words, he had sensed the deep currents of a pain caused by losses too vast to describe, when whole worlds had exploded in conflagration. Kharadmon had experienced grief and guilt, raised to torment on a scale unimagined; and had been found by drake-dream, and granted redemption by the grace of Athera's Paravians. The experience had reforged his whole being, mortality shed like dross before flame.

The branding echo of suffering remained, stamped into permanent recall. As eyewitness, Dakar experienced the gifted worth of Athera. He measured the scope of unbearable consequence, should his part at Rockfell fall short.

'If you don't put scruple second, and those free wraiths break through from Marak, the fate of Athera will stand beyond salvage,' he told Kharadmon. 'That's a choice not worth living.' Impelled by the unequivocal truth, not his own, that recalled the wholesale ruin of fully inhabited planets, Dakar added, 'Get on with this. The equinox won't wait. Do as you must, before Luhaine starts to smoke with impatience.'

'Brace up, then,' Kharadmon warned. 'One final adjustment remains before I can work through the matrix of your body.'

A touch at the center of his skull became a tickle; then something physical gave with a snap, as though an invisible membrane had been cut, then peeled from the fabric of his awareness. A dammed-back river of potential broke free, and the isolation of his mind became smashed by a second cascading torrent of bright light. The influx was not gentle, or softened by the polite constraints of bonding friendship; this was a knowingness of unstoppable force, a marriage of self into self.

This tide of beingness *was his own Name*, but loomed on a thread that extended far past the constraints of time and space. Dakar lost his grounding to Rockfell's staid peak. The flux that roared in to reclaim him raged on, stripping out reason and logic. Every template of mortal belief was hammered flat with no mercy, then reforged to support a near-limitless platform. Dakar screamed, unstrung by shock. The sound battered through him, a barrage that took form as senseless waves, endlessly tumbling outward.

Then his eyesight cleared. Given no warning to preface the transition, Dakar sat and blinked, restored to an unnatural clarity that saw far outside the range of visible light.

'How disorienting,' he gasped. The arm he propped to lean on was as tangibly perceptible as the refined layers of his aura. Stone cast an equally manifest energy field. Dakar stared, stupidly trying to sort through an interface of bewildering complexity. Objects and flesh were now overlaid with the energy lines that defined the tracks where light and air interacted. He saw himself melded, rendered at one with the dancing expanse of the sky.

Eyes squeezed shut, or lids open, Dakar discovered he could not close down the broadened band of his altered senses. Awed once again by Kharadmon's equanimity, he said, 'Did you see this way before you were disembodied?' Nausea knifed through him. The spasm was swiftly suppressed by the Sorcerer's expert touch, more efficient remedy than his own crude impulse to clamp his teeth in set misery. 'How did you manage to know what was solid, and how do you steer without hitting things?'

'Experience.' Kharadmon's reply issued through the Mad Prophet's own lips, inflected by his breath and voice.

'Dharkaron wept!' Dakar cried, startled half out of his skin.

He opened his eyes, beheld the intricate patterns of light and sound that *was Luhaine*, and jumped from riled nerves yet again.

Before the other discorporate Sorcerer could proffer an involved explanation, Kharadmon finished answering the gist of the question. 'Some of the senses you're using lie outside the body. The brain still interprets. That's why the perceptions don't respond as you block out your eyesight.'

Dakar glanced aside in searching anxiety, belatedly mindful of his forced promise to Arithon. 'Fionn Areth will surely think I've gone crazy, speaking with myself out of hand.'

'The fool herder's out cold,' Kharadmon dismissed. A raised hand that moved beyond Dakar's volition indicated the young man, slumped amid a haphazard nest of rucked blankets. 'When your body appeared to be having convulsions, the young idiot lost his head. To quiet his shouting, Luhaine sent him to sleep.'

With supreme tact, neither Sorcerer mentioned the irony: that the first time Desh-thiere had been sealed within Rockfell, Kharadmon had performed the selfsame service at need to quell Dakar's intrusive behavior.

The disappointment struck, bitter, that the epiphanies of realigned awareness had not fully released the conditioned shortfalls of a lifetime. Neither age nor maturity quite banished the specter of past terror instilled by that earlier experience at Rockfell Pit. Dakar sensed the reechoed, questing touch, as Kharadmon mapped the source of his apprehension. He shuddered in discomfort, sweating for the residual memories dredged up for examination. Even the fragmented impressions he retained held the stuff of undying nightmare.

'Try not to fight me,' the Fellowship Sorcerer advised. 'I can't help where you won't give your trust freely.'

But to release ingrained fear without trained comprehension was to act on a leap of blind faith. Dakar knew the shortcomings of cowardice too well to stand on false comfort or illusions. 'I told Arithon once, I'm not a hero.'

Kharadmon shrugged. 'You'll have to be, this time, no choice on the matter.' The mental query cast out to Luhaine sidelined his partner's contrary perceptions and his mishmashed muddle of uncertainties. 'How deep does the fracture run through the wards?'

'You have to ask?' Luhaine released a vexed puff of breeze. 'Very deep. All the way down to the innermost ring.' He need not belabor the obvious point, that no saving miracle could buy them more time: the defenses could not be reworked soon enough to stave off the maligned currents of the impending equinox lane tide.

'No choice then,' Kharadmon answered, laconic.

Granted no pause to relapse toward self-pity, Dakar shared the paralyzing resignation: as a Fellowship Sorcerer *who was also afraid* lifted his spread hands and flattened both palms on the mirror-polished stone which concealed Rockfell Pit's outer entrance.

For his opening, Kharadmon sent the presence of the mountain a formal greeting. He gave unflinching acknowledgment that Named who he was, and added a heartfelt apology for delays fallen outside his province to remedy.

Next, with an attentive humility that raised Dakar to amazement, the most impetuous of the Fellowship Sorcerers stilled his perception and *listened*.

A resonance reemerged through the stone, deep and slow, in bell tones rich with harmonics that transcended natural hearing. The voice had striking character. Dakar experienced Rockfell as never before, a being more distinctly defined than a man. The mountain was conscious on more levels than the animate mind could encompass. Its nature of inherent tenderness stunned him, a nurturing born of unsurpassed patience, and strength backed by an integrity that reserved no allowance for hardship. Rockfell was mineral, its structure a statement of everlasting commitment that gave of itself without boundary.

Nor was the mountain without unique preference. Rockfell's record of service framed its steadfast pride. The lament in its appeal to Kharadmon was described in a detailed and poignant delicacy that shattered Dakar's preconceptions. He had always assumed rock was carelessly dull, its endurance rooted in obstinate bulk. The contrast tore him open, for the opposite held true: Rockfell's purview was no function of brute mass. It knew itself down to the tiniest fissure, even to the most delicate vein of formed crystal, whose miniature terminations would seem no more than a sparkle of dust to human eyes.

The mountain's noble scale reflected the reach of a meticulous memory. It had known time prior to the Age of the Dragons. Its consciousness held the linear record of each day, and each second of each bygone hour. At will, it could sing back the tones of sun and rain, for any season or any tempest to fall within the long tenure of its existence. Each change of the wind could be recounted with flawless exactitude. Events were not ranked or attached to importance. The death of a leaf, and the melting of a snowflake were recalled with equal detail. Against such broad scope, the lives of men and beasts became as a fleeting thread set into a tapestry of epochs.

Rockfell knew Desh-thiere. Kharadmon was given the acute rendering of the mountain's distress, that its steadfast guardianship stood compromised. That awareness spanned layer after vertical layer of nested consciousness, fully informed of the consequence should its vested pledge of internment fall short.

The mountain sensed Desh-thiere's malice. It had recognized its dark peril in the rainbow scale of reverberation cast beyond elemental awarenesses. The potential for pain and wrought harm to plants, trees, and mosses came entwined with knowledge of the fish and snails in the riverbeds. Rockfell's taproot communed with the red fires of earth's magma. Through strata of bedrock, and the lisping trickle of groundwater, it knew the distant thunder of surf, where Athera's vast oceans creamed against the stark bastions of the headlands. It understood patterns, and lane flux, and the draw of the stars and the moon. The sink pools where Koriani meddling had backlashed in misalignment reverberated through stone's deep heart, a knell of congested, bruised pain.

The sheer magnitude of all the mountain encompassed bespoke empathy beyond all imagining. The cognizance of its looming failure, once the lane tide crested at equinox, struck tones of sore grief for the sorrows that heartrock might bear through the ages.

At one with Kharadmon's tuned sensitivity, Dakar measured the grandeur of the mountain's petition. The unimaginable scale of its care overwhelmed him. He heard and wept; then received back the reflected anguish of his own tears, as stone shared his distress and responded.

Kharadmon did not weep. Instead, in fluent Paravian, he framed his eloquent promise. 'Rockfell Peak, I have heard. Be it known, let all being stand as witness, that Luhaine and I are pledged not to let down such trust. Stone has not fallen short. Nor shall, as I live. Morriel's wrought malice will not be permitted to sunder the charge of your duty. Accept my commitment by Name, and as Fellowship warden, the crisis at equinox shall be averted.'

The lie was transparent, a deception of such arrogance that Dakar's gorge rose. Entrained into empathy with the mountain's predicament, he exploded in revolted fury. 'What can you do? The critical hour has already passed! Even with all seven Sorcerers helping, you can't hope to refigure the wardings that bind Desh-thiere's prison in less than eight hours!'

No recourse existed. The equinox tide would blast over Rockfell's skewed axis. Roiled energy would leach through the imbalanced ward rings, and Desh-thiere would seize its fell freedom.

'Then the wards will stay flawed,' Kharadmon agreed without rancor; the opposite, in fact, as he bowed to the truth behind

499

Dakar's frantic outburst. 'Since the misaligned axis must be healed second, we'll try for a stopgap remedy up front, and protect warded stone from the elements.'

Given the Mad Prophet's blank incomprehension, Luhaine's windy presence sketched out an explanation. 'We must isolate Rockfell. The faulted bindings inside have been patched. Deshthiere's prison will hold stable as long as the ward rings can be shielded from the direct surge of the lane flux.'

The overweening arrogance of that undertaking struck Dakar utterly breathless. '*You think you can divert the equinox tide at its crest? Sheer insanity!*'

'That's the workable option.' Unlike old stone, Kharadmon had no patience for dissecting esoteric minutiae. 'If you have some genius alternative, speak up. If not, we have a lot of brute conjury to lay down before the advent of sunset.'

Such a working must be unassailably in place, Dakar realized with flattening dread. Once the lane flux arose with the dawning of equinox, there would be no recourse; no pause to remedy inadvertent mistakes, or to make last-minute adjustments. The Sorcerers must foresee every ramification, on all levels, with no detail left overlooked. The task posed complexities of titanic proportion, a challenge to strain vision as broad as Sethvir's, with the Paravian gift of his earth-sense.

'We'll have Rockfell in partnership,' Luhaine pointed out. To Kharadmon, brusque, he demanded, 'Which remedy, a sink for grounding the distressed recoil, or shall we attempt to create an alternate conduit?'

Still in contact with the mountain through Dakar's bare hands, Kharadmon framed his answer in consultation. 'The sink is no option. We have a canted axis, and this imbalance is impelled energy, not meant to travel to ground. To try would fire the veins of magma that run molten under the Skyshiels. We dare not build pressure under the fault line. The risk of cracking a new fissure is too high, which leaves urgent need for a conduit.'

For Dakar's benefit, Luhaine spoke aloud. 'Attractant or bridge?'

'Bridge,' Kharadmon snapped, then added the imperative driving his decision. 'At the crux, we are two to your one.'

The dismayed revelation set the Mad Prophet aback. Now aware he must loan more than his flesh, but also the inadequate discipline of his craft, he recalled his part in the death of a girl child in a lonely Vastmark ravine. Despite Arithon's forgiveness, the shame of Jilieth's memory still rode him. Easier by far to balk in straight fear, like Fionn Areth; to fail as the victim of mishap rather than endure the conscious awareness of becoming the bumbling wretch who fell short.

The equinox forces could not be averted to spare the weak link in a chain. 'I have no discipline to match this demand! Moon and tide, I can't stand in the path of the flux!' Dakar shivered. 'You ask the impossible!'

'No?' Kharadmon's amusement stung fierce in denial. 'Then you'll hold the breach while Luhaine and I do our best to prove you are wrong.'

Neither Fellowship Sorcerer would give any thought to the range of unbearable consequences. Dakar gasped a last, strangled protest. 'If you've gambled badly?'

Kharadmon lifted the spellbinder's quivering shoulders into a fatalistic shrug. 'No remedy left. We all die for it.'

Refusal pinched off, with Dakar's free permission an already irrevocable pledge, the Sorcerers pursued preparation. Luhaine whisked off on a brisk crack of wind. Kharadmon resumed his intense communion with the self-aware essence of Rockfell. His dialogue was too dense to follow, beyond the immediate gist: as the mountain yielded its requisite consent, the spellbinder grasped that the Sorcerer asked leave to unbind the outermost ring of defense wards.

Rockfell's acquiescence tripped off an igniting burst, as Kharadmon's risen power combined in a synergistic flow of cause to instantaneous effect.

Dakar felt the strain. A burning pull jarred through muscle and tendon as his short, pudgy fingers were pressured to match an ephemeral impression, where the effortless reach of Asandir's larger hands had spanned the smooth rock face before him. The masterful tracings of embedded spellcraft imprinted the spellbinder's sweat-drenched palms. The virulent sting as the contact engaged raised his yelp of incensed surprise. Kharadmon paid the disturbance no mind. The vibrations pulsating through flesh and bone spoke a code that his adept intellect could interpret. He responded with precise counterwards, a sequence of runes framed in light, visualized in his mind. Dakar could not fathom their meaning, but only gasp awestruck at the complex shadings of colors and line overlaid in a mapwork of dazzling geometrics.

There were traps. Templates of overriding emotion triggered and burst through mind and flesh at staggered intervals, designed to wreak ruin and break concentration. Kharadmon disarmed each onslaught. Wave after wave, he banished wrought barriers of terror and pain and illusion. The defenses he unwove were not set in place only to deter intruders, Dakar realized. The hedging maze framed a double-edged warding *also intended to repel an escape from within*.

Thought encumbered by mortality could not track the rapidity of the sequence. Kharadmon kept pace with the unleashed torrent by setting his ear to the stone, then extending his awareness into the aura beyond flesh. Dakar captured only the lower register of resonance, as the Sorcerer assimilated the loftier frequencies past the range of his mental agility. Kharadmon's upstepped perception reached farther. His tactile senses pierced through the grand veil, then extended across the unknowable range of the parallel continuum.

Dakar felt his stretched senses flicker and pinwheel. Engulfed by the mystery until he spun, lost, he fought reeling faintness. Hearing and sight juddered in wracked disarray, interposed by null intervals of darkness. Then activity ceased; the warding under his drenched palms lay sundered. Shaken, he shared the moment of transmutation as mirror-polished stone relinquished its guarded secret: how the linkages of fused mineral secured the portal that gave entry to Rockfell's upper chamber.

Kharadmon had unlocked Asandir's primary defenses, an array that could only be addressed by a spirit securely enfleshed.

'Luhaine?' the Sorcerer demanded; then lifted Dakar's head and stepped back.

Their linkage of consciousness extended the range of the spellbinder's faculties. He witnessed the source the discorporate mage raised to unbind the last seal on the portal. The power was not Luhaine's; only the guidance, as he called on the unshielded potency of the elements. They responded, not in submission to need, but through an abandoned and joyous partnership. Lightning cracked and burned, a stiletto of pared might, threaded through the poised lens of Luhaine's request. No breathing flesh could support such raw charge.

Caught in close proximity, Dakar shivered. Every hair on his body lifted erect. Only the support of Kharadmon's seasoned steadiness let him withstand the barrage. Nor did the wonder diminish. The Sorcerer's augmented mage-sight unveiled the consummate delicacy of Luhaine's work, as he wielded the lightning as stylus.

Stroke by precise stroke, the electromagnetic bands of chained light bonding stone to itself became sundered. The sequence itself involved demanding intricacy. No tolerance existed for mishap.

The untamed forces that surged in release as solid matter dissolved were vast beyond comprehension; enough by themselves to batter Athera to a litter of dust and smashed fragments. Luhaine had made disposition. Chains of spellcraft embedded through the mineral matrix recaptured the shed backwash that flared in sharp bursts. Runes appeared in the rock face, infused to cold blue, as the forces were safely channeled off and returned to a source far beyond human recourse to fathom.

A corona of bled heat whipped the air to thermal eddies. The drifting floor of banked cloud billowed upward in recoil, anviled to towering thunderheads. Dakar recalled being scared by the sight, on the hour of Desh-thiere's first confinement. Now, as he beheld the bared forces that raised massive storms from tranquillity, his utter terror escaped speech. He longed heart and spirit to be safe on the southcoast, lolling drunk in an Innish brothel.

'You won't blot out the nightmares, no matter how strong the drink,' Kharadmon pointed out in rough solace. He laughed at the sour curse Dakar croaked back, taking impish delight in the searing, shrill winds whipped up by the play of grand conjury. His unbending will held the spellbinder upright, while the tempest raged and battered their shared stance on the ledge abutting the rock face.

At length, his task finished, Luhaine bid the elements to subside. The runes of discharge faded from harsh blue to violet. Empty space remained where stone had stood, seamless, scarcely minutes before. The uncanny light flickered into quiescence, leaving an incised, rectangular portal cut through the sheer side of the mountain. Dakar regarded the gaping vault, his gut roiled to acid trepidation. Inside, doused in darkness, he beheld the square chamber incised floor to ceiling with patterns and sigils of guard. Their core strength was so virulent, a man felt his teeth ache even at safe remove on the threshold.

'You first,' Kharadmon invited the spellbinder whose shrinking flesh necessity forced him to wear. 'Your knees are shaking like jelly, a frank hazard. Fat as you are, if I have to walk for you, we'll likely fall flat on your face.'

'Fionn Areth!' protested the Mad Prophet, grasping excuses like broomstraws. 'If a storm brews up while we're working inside, he'll certainly die of exposure.'

'A risk,' Kharadmon agreed. 'But there's nowhere else safe we can take him before the equinox tides run their course. The conduit we build to reroute the lane flux must pass through

Rockfell itself. Exposed to such forces, unshielded, human tissue would burn to a crisp. Outside, the hazards of weather will allow your pet herder a chance. He doesn't lack for warm blankets.'

'Remind me never to trust you again,' Dakar groused as he assayed a wobbling step forward. 'You have a mind as crafty as Prince Arithon's, and you keep given promises like a starved crocodile.'

'For which you should be grateful, prophet,' Kharadmon needled, delighted to whet his predatory malice after years of lonely vigil in the star fields. 'Just remember the hunting pack of wraiths left diverted, while I turn your mind to the unsavory business of keeping Desh-thiere confined. We have only a few hours before equinox eve midnight. Believe me, we'll need every one of them.'

Spring Equinox Eve 5670

Testament

The adept keeping watch at Sethvir's bedside in Althain Tower straightened, her shining white robes a soft, varnished gold by the spill of a single candle. Concern stitched a frown line between her silk eyebrows. Despite the masked dread binding her sorrow, she stroked the Sorcerer's limp fingers on the coverlet, her touch a firm reassurance. 'The request you have asked will be granted.' Shattered from calm, her voice shook as she added, 'One of us expected this hour might come. The witness is already summoned and waiting here at Althain Tower.'

The Sorcerer's eyelids returned the barest, small flicker. He hoarded his dwindled strength, while his game heart pushed the blood through his veins, unflagging as time itself. Yet unlike an organ wrought of formed flesh that could be asked to answer his bidding, he could not slow the trickling passage of seconds, or defer the last, waning hours before equinox.

The adept waited, not patient or resigned, but troubled by the entangled coils of the world's fate, a knot far outside her strict provenance to answer. She could succor Sethvir, but not his bound causes; such was the nature of the power she wielded, that sourced itself in the prime life chord.

'Brave spirit,' she whispered. 'As always, we live in the Fellowship's debt.'

Nothing else could she give Althain's Warden. Words fell far short, for her depth of gratitude; the inadequate solace of her patient presence could do nothing to stave off the perils to come.

Desolate, she measured the deep, spaced intervals of Sethvir's breathing, while the fugitive brilliance of the candleflame flickered, its wobbling illumination cast over the wine red carpet. The chamber was stark, in its sickbed neatness, the tipped piles of books and worn bridles put away, and the chairs and side tables tidied. The wicker hamper in the corner was empty, the holed stockings darned and folded into the bronze-studded clothes chest. The adept bent her head, chafing Sethvir's slack palm. Her throat closed, and her shut lids trembled with sudden, upwelling emotion.

'You're weeping?' Sethvir ventured, his speech a thread-slender whisper.

She swallowed, fought up a wounding smile. 'Sometimes tears have a mind of their own, do they not?'

'A diamond is less precious,' the Sorcerer replied.

The silence that followed was grief-struck.

Nor did the brine tracking the adept's dusky cheeks leave space for her rage, or the furious protest that howled inside like the smothered blast of a thunderclap. The Prime Matriarch and the Koriani Order had desired the Fellowship sundered, the guiding covenant of their compact with the Paravians broken. Now, the crisis brewing at Rockfell Peak threatened to finish the objective Morriel's conspiracy had set in train the past autumn.

The Warden the adept guarded might never arise from his pallet. If the worst happened, Sethvir of Althain would not be allowing small spiders to make homes in his teacups again. He could lose the chance to wear out the soles of the new wolfhide buskins Traithe had sent as a gift. Nor would a human successor step forward to inherit the wide-ranging gift of his earth-sense.

Stark tragedy, that the Koriani Prime deemed the price of Athera's survival as a bargaining chip, to leverage back access to the starfaring culture renounced by mankind's destitute forebears.

Too weakened to scry through the thorns of possibility, or to measure the scope of the pitfalls that might lurk in the uncharted future, Sethvir faced the dire worst without flinching. He had made his request to record a last testament. Should Luhaine, Kharadmon, and Dakar fail at Rockfell, and Deshthiere's fogbound entities burst their wardings, he had no hand left to send to avert their inbound brethren from Marak. Athera could be devastated, first by the malevolent sentience in the mists taken captive at Ithamon at terrible cost to two princes; and then by invading free wraiths, voraciously seeking possession. Horror would not end there. Every living spirit on Athera, enslaved or free, would be lost in turn, immolated by the dreams of dead dragons as Sethvir's steering hold on the land's fractured grimwards weakened and finally faltered.

'Keep trust in your spellbinder,' the adept whispered, shying back from the darkening maze of possibilities, each one a bearing landscape of ruin too grim for cool sanity to contemplate. 'Dakar has untapped strengths. In crisis, he may well discover them. Believe in the strictures Asandir instilled over the course of his training. Your Mad Prophet may yet keep his stance through extremity.'

But Sethvir's stilled face showed no flicker of hope in the kindly spill of the candleflame. He held to his wish, unrelenting.

The Sorcerer had begged the service of a witness of Ath's Brotherhood to help seal a record in crystal. As Warden of Althain Tower appointed by the Paravians, Sethvir was insistent. The integrity of his post lay at risk. His last act before he engaged threatened faculties must catalog the cascade of events that might soon write the last lines of Athera's closing chapter. Should Asandir return from his labor to find ruin, he must know in detail what had passed. The great drakes had entrusted the Fellowship of Seven to ensure Paravian survival. An integrity outlasting three ages would not founder; not without leaving clear word of the struggle that could stand as the Sorcerers' epitaph.

At length, a soft tap at the chamber door; the adept called in for his specialized skills had arrived to enact Sethvir's dispensation.

The bursting glitter of silver-and-gold threadwork emerged like a cry from the gloom of the outer landing. The slim figure stepped in and closed the oak panel. Such was his care, the latch fell without sound. Then he pushed back the hood, with its crowning cartouche, the interleaved ciphers of safekeeping and trust framing the seal of the bonded witness. If the man was still young in years, with the beautiful thin hands of an artist, his talent had powerfully marked him. The solemn brown eyes in his beardless face reflected an ancient's deep wisdom, paired with an astuteness that had gazed into world upon world past the veil.

He nodded to the lady on watch at the bedside. His poise could have been a dancer's, a warrior's, or the mold for a sculptor's masterpiece as he knelt at the Sorcerer's shoulder.

'I am here by request to stand witness,' he greeted Althain's Warden, then laid his hand overtop of the lady adept's, still clasped to Sethvir's slack fingers. 'Though I wish that the sorrow of this hour had not come, and that I was not the one called to assay the burden, know you are beloved. As ever, our Brotherhood bides in your shadow. Mine, the honor, to serve your request with integrity.'

The Sorcerer's fingers fractionally tightened within the adepts' linking grasp. A tormented interval elapsed before Sethvir opened his eyes. His speech came with effort. 'In the aumbry under the arrow slit you'll find five wrapped crystal spheres.' His voice sounded stiff as the rust on old hinges as he labored to impart his instructions. 'I ask, leave the amethyst and the citrine. The clear quartz preferred to work with Ciladis, and should stay undisturbed. Of the two smoky quartz, bring the pale one.' His breath exhausted, the Warden explained by sent thought that for joyless tasks that particular sphere was most likely to grant its expansive permission.

'I understand.' As the witness gathered his robe to arise, the lady adept touched his arm in restraint. 'Stay with Sethvir.' She disengaged from the Sorceror's slack clasp and offered her vacated footstool. 'I'll fetch the crystal the Warden suggested.'

Resettled at the Sorcerer's side, the witness bent his head, eyes closed as he readied his faculties. A mind as complex and broad-ranging as Sethvir's would require far more than a long reach. His earth-sense could impose complication and hardship. The scope of the electromagnetic current he channeled, minute to unthinking minute, was vast enough to burn the unshielded mind to a cinder.

Ill equipped to engage such a burden without help, the adept calmed his breathing, then opened the gateways in mind and heart to tap the prime source itself. Power flowed in, gentle and sure, of a force to spin mountains from one grain of sand, or clasp a butterfly without one particle of dust disturbed from fragile wing tips. The chord that first made, then sustained all creation charged the adept's presence with a shimmering corona that washed through the thin glow from the candle. Shining, in his robes of pure white, the thread pattern on his hood and cuffs scintillant as sparks splashed off heated steel by a forge hammer, the adept set barriers of protection to encapsulate his inner self. The rest of his being became as blank slate, empty and clear of all imprint.

'Sethvir, I am here,' he pronounced in soft assurance. 'When you're ready, I'm prepared.'

The cool hand he cradled between his warm palms returned no

response. But deep in his mind, a sure, controlled touch claimed the channel the adept offered up to the Sorcerer. That tacit, first contact was not overwhelming, a ripple of light imagery drawn from the surface current of Sethvir's entrained gift of earth-sense . . . *in the ruins of Penstair, a snowy owl furled silent wings over a killed hare. Southward, in Orvandir, three unsettled crows pecked at glaze ice by a streamside that by now should be swelling with thaw.*

The witness sighed through parted lips, amazed by the masterful, flowing thread of the Sorcerer's shared awareness. He understood resonance. Like a perfect, sustained note pared out of a chord that described every facet of reality, from harmony to cacophony, he sensed the fierce will that embraced the mammoth torrent of Athera's moment-to-moment existence, and, *even pressed to extremity*, stepped its vast torrent down to a delicate trickle.

The ongoing effort such a feat must demand stunned even the adept's illumined cognizance. *While over the Storlains, a new blizzard raged; a field mouse in a burrow in Havistock husked a dry seed, a small wrongness: by this time of year, had the frosts been less deep, the shell should have softened and cracked as the pale shoot inside strained to sprout . . .*

No witness in the dwindled ranks of Athera's hostels could keep pace with a presence refined to such infinite precision as this. First raised to awe, and then abjectly humbled, the adept let the tears seep shamelessly through his closed lids. *'You are needed beyond measure,'* he dispatched through the link. *'Truly, is tonight's course the choice of absolute necessity?'*

Sethvir's answer emerged as a wound skein of imagery, clear-cut as sorrow itself. The sequence opened with sight of the Paravian continent, and its massive, crossed fault lines, whose major array intersected beneath the thermal pools of Silvermarsh. If the Fellowship's effort to isolate Rockfell Peak failed to channel the deranged branch of the lane flux into safe realignment through the Skyshiels, the fragile balance of Athera's crust would be set under stress. Disturbance in one fault was certain to rattle the more active rift through the Thaldeins, disrupting a cycle of quiescence that had lasted the span of an epoch.

'The continent would survive the shaking,' Sethvir sent. A string of images fleeted past, of town buildings crumbled, and sorrowful loss of life. Yet grief and death did not shape the core of the Warden's immediate concern. *'Just one massive quake would shift links of anchoring spellcraft set in place since Paravian times '*

The visions that unreeled after that caused the witness an unpleasant shudder: of wardings released, that kept vile creatures and malevolent sprites under gate and guard, and which human language had no name for. The Fellowship Sorcerers maintained deep protections in steadfast dedication until such time as the Paravian races should reclaim their abandoned place on the continent. Yet the aberrant creatures given form by the impetuous dreams of old drakes paled unto insignificance as Sethvir delivered the shattering gist, of spelled anchors tied into the earth's molten iron core, that would spin out of alignment with an unnatural shift of Athera's crust. A sharp change in the flow of the planet's magnetics would destroy fine-tuned calibrations and *unravel three more grimwards wholesale.*

'*Should those grounding seals be disrupted, I have no more resource,*' Sethvir confessed in bald helplessness. The Paravians were gone, who had sung those mighty constructs into existence. Lacking the strength of his Fellowship colleagues, one Sorcerer would not be enough to instill any patch of remedial spellcraft: the grimwards would break, disgorging rank chaos, and cascading ruin would unleash a cataclysm beyond all imagining.

'*I cannot stand idle and watch as all life on this world is destroyed.*' The Warden of Althain served up his conclusion in stark rage, that refused the bittermost ash of defeat. '*While I recognize truth, I hold power to act. Ath Creator allows us our lives, to spend or redeem by willful expression. In passing the Wheel, I might, perhaps, constrain those lost dragon haunts for just long enough to bear them across the veil with me.*'

The adept paled, appalled. 'You would fail in that sacrifice. Even risk unraveling the pattern of your spirit from the infinite span of existence!'

'*I would merely be first to suffer that fate,*' Sethvir corrected in gentle sadness. '*If the Fellowship falters, you and your white brotherhood, and everything extant would follow. By the end, unless Asandir returned in time to attempt the recall of a dragon, random chaos would devour the whole world, and then the bright, teeming consciousness of all that claims space and order within it.*'

Never mind that the mists of Desh-thiere would escape, and effect damning congress with the questing free wraiths that Kharadmon's mazes had temporarily forestalled. Their unchecked arrival must inevitably open the floodgates, drawing the invasive hordes out of Marak. Those perils would wreak their assault over time. Even a late intervention might curb their worst damage and permit a slow road to recovery; whereas the effect of just one unleashed grimward could unbind the stability of the planet. Such wholesale ruin would find no surcease. Without living dragons to placate the ghosts of their dead, and lacking Ath's gift of the Paravian guardians, *one maddened haunt's dream held the power to unbind the spun thread of creation.*

'Their ghosts can spin form and create without love,' the adept saw, aghast.

Sethvir stirred, the weak trace of a nod his frightening affirmation. 'You do understand.' Words taxed him sorely. Shadowed by looming, explosive disaster, Althain's Warden dispatched his beleaguered conclusion by thought. *'My spirit is bound. Any one breaking crisis might doom the Paravians. The charge the great drakes laid on our Fellowship leaves no recourse. If the warding of Rockfell fails over equinox, I will have no choice but to try for an intervention.'*

A doomed attempt, the adept perceived beyond question, lent knowing insight by a linkage that unmasked the Sorcerer's secret doubts. The glistening tracks of the tears on his cheeks became a gesture of travesty. No word could console such service as this. The young witness in his stainless white robes, wrapped and crowned in the empowered glory of his golden aura, set his face in spread hands and wept anyway.

For tortured moments, Sethvir gave back nothing more than his tacit reassurance, that the world loom his Fellowship endeavored to guard was a force that did not subscribe to the human onus of worry . . . *In the mountains of Vastmark, a kestrel pair mated; a frog in the Salt Fens stirred from hibernation; on the Ippash plain, a pair of cranes danced, while the locust grubs dreamed of their hatching in spring, burrowed beneath teeming grasses . . .*

Too soon, the lady adept returned, her careful hands clasping a gleaming quartz sphere, crisscrossed with fissures like mirrors. Its core seemed to burn, a living, bright play of captive veils and reflected rainbows.

'Warden?' The lady knelt in tender respect. When the Sorcerer's shut lashes flickered in recognition of her whispered warning, she brought the fiery weight of the crystal to rest on the coverlet above Sethvir's heart.

The fine wrinkles surrounding his eyes tightened in stressed response to even that expected influx of sensation. His other hand lifted, frail as a storm-tossed leaf. He fumbled once, then settled the limb back to rest with his crabbed, schclar's fingers spanned over the curve of the sphere. 'Forgive me. I'll also need help with the wakening.'

'Let me.' The witness lifted the slackened limb in his clasp, leaned across, and guided their combined grasp to steady the crystal. Through the Sorcerer's contact, the young man received the stone's Name, followed by the phrase of toned sound that would key its rise into tuned resonance. Joined in grim purpose, he and the Fellowship Sorcerer stroked the stone's gleaming surface. They addressed its smoky heart, teased and warmed it with touch to a state of roused energy that soon quickened, singing, into a presence of heightened sensitivity.

'*I'an, i'anient*,' Sethvir whispered greeting, the Paravian words meaning, 'thou, thyself'.

Recognition flowed back, then an intimate testing as the consciousness imbued within crystalline form surveyed both witness and Sorcerer. Sethvir responded by laying flat his formidable array of defenses. With childlike clarity, he yielded himself to inspection, his courage a breathtaking display of absolute trust.

The sphere responded, unveiling its core self, in turn. Quickened, its watered tea coloring brightened, until the inclusions flared and sparkled, alive with a brilliance too vibrant to arise from the gold-madder glare of the candleflame. The adept's refined vision sensed the stone's opening, as the rock crystal's aliveness responded. Its calming presence emanated a gift of balancing energies, precisely attuned to steady and lift the Warden's exhausted spirits.

The exchange seemed the handshake of two ancient friends, keeper and jewel conjoined in free partnership. This crystal had resided at Althain Tower since Paravian times. Throughout Sethvir's guardianship, its nature had been tendered in flawless respect. Gratitude resounded through the shared moment of greeting. Even to an adept's schooled perception, the upwelling exuberance of the sphere's energies rang meticulously clear and unburdened.

The crystal embraced its service, joyful despite the troubles that prompted its calling. Its sweet chime of permission rang down from the exalted, high frequencies, where the seeded, first concept of form meshed to the template of thought and flowered into existence. Whatever Sethvir wished the quartz matrix to hold, it would imprint within its consciousness.

The adept appointed as Sethvir's witness was well trained to detect that shimmering moment of alignment. He removed his grasp, leaving only the Sorcerer's hands clasped to the wakened sphere. Then he settled at the end of the pallet, his touch tender as he gathered the silken flood of white hair and cradled the Sorcerer's head. 'As you wish, I am ready to proceed.' The adept closed his eyes, settled into a trance state, now poised to engage the trained gifts of his office.

The wisp of a thought framed Sethvir's reply: '*I must fully immerse in the stream of my earth-gift. You'll sense the pulse, though the signal is faint.*' Already engaged holding three distressed grimwards, Althain's Warden lacked the strength to focus his awareness with the requisite clarity. '*You must stand as bridge. I ask that you receive the events I select. Act as a lens. Sharpen them to the intensity needed to inscribe them into the crystal.*'

The adept caught his breath, his head bent to contain his stunned flood of emotion. The sorrow became punishing, that a Sorcerer of Sethvir's stature should ever require such assistance as this, a service most often performed for the dying, too foredone to speak their last wishes.

'*Grimwards,*' came the flicker of Sethvir's fierce irony, the concept tagged by sharp concern for Asandir's health and safety. '*Too taxing a burden for any flesh-and-blood consciousness to grapple without paying a murderous penalty. Small resource or grace is left over.*'

The adept shared the echo: of a roiling force, inexhaustibly powerful, clothed over in alien patterns that sank a ranging, dull ache through his bones. That such energies could exist in the flower of Ath's creation, and not burn through restraint and scorch out teeming life, posed a dichotomy past all understanding. The wisdom of Ath's Brotherhood lacked the terrible scope of a Fellowship Sorcerer, whose first initiation to the mysteries had been ordained by the fire-born minds of the dragons.

'Dakar will not fail you at Rockfell,' the adept stated, as desperate himself for reassurance. 'Let your wish be done, but as a precaution this world will never require.'

Sethvir returned no empty platitudes. Dignified by an austere, tactful courage, he aligned to the deep rhythm of the earth's pulse. One by one, he selected the key images to be preserved as an inviolate record of events.

The adept standing vigil could do no less than attend his office as witness. Steadied at last by the discipline of Ath's peace, he received the sequential stream of visions from Sethvir, and recorded them with faithful clarity. He became the clear conduit for the Sorcerer's intent, to lay down his last testament into crystal.

The transcript contained an unnerving complexity, much of it patterned in coded geometry, curves, lines, and angles framing a language derived from proportional mathematics. What streamed past, too fast for the adept to interpret, another Fellowship Sorcerer could grasp at a glance. At times, Sethvir's sending broke into pictures: fleeted images of snowbound forests, or fallow fields gray-rimed in hoarfrost. The iced tumble of streamlets locked fast to cracked rocks interspersed with impressions of small, starving birds seeking forage. At intervals, the ghost imprint of the future flowed through as an overlay set on the present: the thaw that would come, disastrously late. The adept was shown rivers swelled to thundering flood as pounding rains swept the mountains and lowlands. Deluged by an intricate catalog of detail, he caught only the urgent gist: that the unnatural, prolonged winter was going to breed famine across the four northern kingdoms. Warning must reach King Eldir in Havish. The harvests in Lithmere alone would not fail, and the crown must be charged to make disposition in advance of the inevitable shortfall.

More geometrics: red flares in cold ward rings; in Tysan, Khadrim flew and slaughtered at will across Camris and Westwood. A farmstead burned; a wolf den was savaged. Two necromancers met in warded conspiracy in a cottar's shed outside Erdane. Four dragon skulls smoldered in sealed iron coffers in a brick-walled tower in Avenor. There, also, Cerebeld schooled his coterie of young acolytes to old, unclean practices, forgotten lore garnered from a musty cache of grimoires confiscated from a condemned talent. In Lysaer's absence, the High Priest wielded the reins of Tysan's state policy with hot ambition and iron hands. Cerebeld still found his dearest wish frustrated: patrols in Avenor's crown livery completed their sweep of the roads and the countryside, and returned to the city unsuccessful; while a princess disguised in fustian rags stayed hidden, transferred southward into safe hands.

Scenes shifted, to a dark cave where things chittered and cried, their voices like tormented fox kits. Something bloody and torn struggled in a snowbank, snagged in the coils of its own spilled entrails. South and west, a drought threatened; farther east, new stands of fencing disrupted the game trails in Radmoore Downs. Sethvir left word for a raven by Name, asking a boon, and in prescient consequence, Traithe would come to leave Methisle fortress after spring spawning, to set seals of rot on the oak posts and boards. Another generation of ambitious farmsteaders who thought to found a new village east of Firstmark would return, beset by ruin, bearing new tales of Paravian ghosts, and lamenting the soil was accursed.

Exhaustive maps followed, on the state of the lane flux, and the resonance of certain alignment spells imbued into ancient stone markers. More geometrics detailed a wearing list of ills, from an herb witches' coven fallen to spinning bold curses against the persecution of Tysan's crown policy, to major wardings in need of revitalization, to minor irritations, among them a new mill in Fallowmere whose placement would disrupt the spawning of salmon. Since the slaughter at Tal Quorin, Rathain's clans were too depleted to steward the northern wilds of Drimwood. Although the Fellowship had no hand to spare them, affairs in their territory would require an intervention.

The adept received snatched impressions of undersea ruins he had never dreamed existed: stonework that had been the made lairs of dragons, before some long-forgotten cataclysm left them submerged. He caught glimpses of wardings there, also, and saw other dark caverns far under the earth, where things nameless moved in the dark.

Sometimes he received words, written in flowing light, in a language outside understanding. Another view, commonplace, flowed through the weave like a lumpy splice in smooth rope: fishermen tied nets by stinking lamplight in North Ward. Their talk ran to worry over the prolonged cold, with early fears spoken in whispers, a theme repeated in the songs of the whale who swam on the ocean currents: of bergs torn from the northern ice cap that could make summer seas and the calving grounds deadly with danger.

Rathain's heartland was quartered, the phosphor burn of loosed animal magnetism a smear across hill and thicket. There, wrapped in their fresh shrouding of snowdrifts, lay the ranks of the recently dead, their life force spilled in raw violence. Beyond carbon-seared hills and a ravaged landscape, the busy movement of men: Lysaer and his Lord Commander strove to mend a sunwheel company's shattered morale. With cajoling words and stern discipline, they exhorted listless, weeping men to re-form broken ranks.

Startled, the adept curbed his personal outrage, though the shared sight of Lysaer s'Ilessid driving men to resume war on the heels of a centaur's visitation struck chills through his passive trance. Even sourced as he was in the grace of Ath's presence, he was humanborn. He could not disallow the beguiling pull of the man's astounding charisma.

Here stood falsehood reclothed in dazzling trappings. Lysaer walked and moved enveloped in the shimmering radiance of his birth gift. His façade was not gentle or compassionate, but the clarion cry of sun-caught steel, to spur men's hearts to take up forged weapons and assuage mortal fear through the catharsis of righteous violence. Natural male beauty and fair coloring lent stirring force to the directive of Desh-thiere's curse. Lysaer's eloquence held a fierce and terrifying conviction as he browbeat his dazed and nerve-broken veterans to embrace his warped frame of belief: that the grand harmony that walked in a Paravian guardian's presence was no more than the tainted allure of a demon, conjured up by a clanborn talent.

'What else would blind a man, or lure him from steadfast faith, than a rendition of shining compassion?' Lysaer gripped a steadying hand on a weeping man's shoulder and assisted him back to his feet. 'Stand tall. Are you as addicts, drugged and complacent on the substanceless syrup of joy? Grace arises through sacrifice. Who stands behind me holds to divine light. Will one sorcerer's spun web of fair shadows tempt you from the haven of truth? Will you allow one minion of evil to cause you to abandon the backbone of your sworn purpose?' Blue eyes charged with fury and rhetoric, Lysaer extended his appeal. 'I think better of you! I see you as men, redeemed by your innate human courage! Show me the trust I have placed in your character has not been a mistake.'

The man raised from the mud wiped shamed tears from his cheeks. He fought shaky legs to stay standing, while another beside him did the same. Around those, others blinked, as though kicked from drugged sleep, while Sulfin Evend prodded a sobbing officer to sit up and reclaim his lapsed tour of command.

Sethvir's final outlook came stamped and grim: against natural inclination, in rebuttal of all that was joyful and free, Lysaer's handling was largely going to succeed. *The hardened core of the Alliance Etarrans would be cozened to resume their offensive march. They would leave behind their grim toll of wounded and the dishonored few who failed to recoup shattered wits. The unfit and those stricken to placid stupor would be escorted home in slow stages by the drovers who manned the supply train.*

The adept who stood witness forced himself to bear up. He adhered to his Brotherhood's code of neutrality. Though his heart ached in sore affliction and grief, he continued to receive Sethvir's testament: another succinct burst of geometrics, then sight of an eagle, soaring over the Mathorns by night. The bird kept keen watch on two fast-moving fugitives, while southward, after days of hagridden flight, another clanborn Companion named Sidir reached the safe cover of Halwythwood.

Then, last of all, the sequence defining the stopgap construct of wards laid down at Rockfell Peak by two Sorcerers. They worked in tight partnership, borrowing off the unsteady assistance wrung from a rabbit-scared spellbinder. Here Sethvir grew specific. His exhaustive care mapped the details of rune and seal, and each listed grace of permission garnered from natural forces. The adept beheld the grand axis of power, arrayed to the cardinal points, and invoking the elements, as only Fellowship magecraft could found them. He read the spiraling channels that would serve as the conduit to reroute longitudinal lane forces. East and west, the flux would deflect into alternative paths, just as a great river in flood must circumvent the snag of an island. Althain's Warden unveiled the night's work in its splendor of pressured invention: the courageous innovations Kharadmon conjured at need, laid out like stamped foil and inscribed with needle-fine runes wrought of light; flanking each curve and precise angle like stars were the seals, holding the checkspells of containment. Each one had been fashioned with the fussy, precise patience Luhaine evoked to balance his colleague's impetuous genius.

Laced through by referenced points of concern, Sethvir's sending mapped the weak points where rushed wardspells were horribly likely to fail. Jointures made to stone that lacked enough time to set with the requisite permanence; the cast rings of ciphers their haste had been too brisk to test. Rockfell itself could not keep pace, the consciousness of stone being tied by its innate character, which pursued all it touched with deliberate, exhaustive complexity.

At length, the closing sequence of geometrics played out. The witness was left wrapped in pristine silence, his mind hollow as a flushed conduit.

'It is done,' Sethvir whispered.

The strained words jostled the adept from his trance. Overcome, he bowed his head. As long and as well as his Brotherhood had known the company of Fellowship Sorcerers, the far-reaching scope of the charges they minded outpaced their most wise estimation. Humbled, the witness completed his work, sealing the Sorcerer's codicil into the crystal under the veracity of formal signature: 'Sethvir, Warden of Althain, born Calum Quaide Kincaid.' He closed with a spell to guard the information inside from falling into wrong hands. Last, he impressed the quartz with the energetic pattern of his own Name, and a cartouche that resonated to the prime life chord, to serve as steadfast protection.

As though sensing completion, Sethvir spoke again. 'Once the crystal is wrapped and stowed, I must seal the wards over Althain Tower itself. No free wraith shall be permitted to trespass inside. Nor will any others who might come to seek access be permitted to despoil the Paravian artifacts held here.' A labored breath, as the Sorcerer marshaled his tenuous strength. 'The last cipher I set will be bonded with Shehane Althain's bones.'

The adept understood the gravity of that warning, well aware that few powers could release a binding that invoked the awareness of the ancient guardian spirit. Only a Paravian singer, or another Fellowship Sorcerer in full possession of his faculties, might challenge such warding and survive.

'Forgive me,' Sethvir whispered, as the lady adept approached to retire the quartz sphere. 'I am grateful. The generosity of your white brotherhood has given me cherished comfort, but after this, no more can be done. I would face the equinox alone. You and the other adepts must depart, or else risk becoming entombed.'

The witness glanced up. His young face reflected a matchless serenity as he locked eyes with the lady, who knelt at Sethvir's other side. Her level poise and her dignified silence assured him their hearts lay in perfect accord.

'We stay,' he insisted, steadfast in love. 'Not to intervene with the way of the world, but to stand on our core of belief. We choose our future from the infinite range of probability. There will be a possible path to salvation. This once, may you lean on the strength of our hope. We place our trust in your spellbinder and two colleagues. Since the thread of their lives twines with ours, by Ath's grace, let them not fail in their charge at Rockfell Peak.'

As the Sorcerer's stark silence assumed a dimension of desolate pain, the lady adept clasped his hand. 'Where better to stand vigil? If you should perish, Athera dies with you. In that case, let our bones lie with honor beside yours.'

The witness stroked Sethvir's dampened hair from his temples, while the lady arose, the shine of the candlelight glancing over the ciphers sewn into her sleeve. She lifted the quartz sphere from the Warden's slack fingers, then secured and tied its silk wrappings.

Her office finished, she claimed her place, shoulder to shoulder with the young witness. Here in Atainia, two hours remained before midnight. But eastward, over the channel that carried the sixth lane, the cascading flux would start cresting within the next minute. On station at the summit of Rockfell Peak, a spellbinder and two Sorcerers sealed their stopgap work with the Paravian rune of ending.

Under shuttered wards at Althain Tower, tense vigil began at Sethvir's bedside. Naught else could be done under earth and sky, except cleave to patience and wait.

Lane Flux

A hemisphere away from Rockfell Peak, a scant second slipped past before the sun's disk climbed to the height of its arc. Dakar suffered the tension of that closing instant. His rapid, gulped breaths, acid drawn in pure terror, hissed in the sealed quiet where he stood. His kneecaps quivered to his stifled panic, while around him, the hollow of the mountain's upper vault pressed like a tomb of black ice.

'*Steady, hold steady*,' Kharadmon urged in his mind. '*Die now, or later, the difference is moot. Best rein your fears sharply in hand.*'

'Daelion wept!' Dakar forced out, through teeth clamped to stop them from chattering. 'I can't do this!'

His pleas availed nothing. He had nowhere to run. If he lost nerve and tried, Kharadmon would show no shred of mercy. The Sorcerer's bleak presence would quash natural instinct and lock his legs to paralysis.

Nor would time slow for a faltering heart. Somewhere above the lifeless stone anvil of Kathtairr's desolate landscape, the sunlight blazed down, marking the cusp of high noon. *Contact*: a screaming silence like an indrawn breath, as the fiery disk touched the meridian half a world away.

The seasonal rise of the lane current began, the cool sapphire energies of the flux snapped to instantaneous excitement. A tightening spiral of forces exploded to a burgeoning fire of loosed energy. The frequency climbed, then reached resonance and sang like the pure tone struck off a tuning fork. The north-to-south

520

oscillation of pulses would surge to tidal peak in less than the span of a heartbeat.

The moment brought wrenching disorientation.

Naked at the crux of a Fellowship construct designed to capture and reroute those vast forces, Dakar felt wrung through. His senses wheeled into abrupt disconnection. Perhaps he cried out; if so, he felt nothing. Sound fell away as his hearing faded into dissolute silence. The breath left his lungs as a ghost's might, insubstantial, while his consciousness spun into involuntary expansion. For one distressed second, he felt as though all firm awareness of his body had been jerked through the pores of his flesh.

'Steady,' came Kharadmon's anchoring reassurance. '*Things are as they should be, no surprises.*'

Ruled by the Sorcerer's ironclad discipline, cradled by a confidence that had grappled such incomprehensible forces before, the Mad Prophet felt his being spliced into the staid patience of stone. Bound into eerie sympathy with the land, he *was* a forest of trees, rooted into winter-hard soil. He knew the mineral murmur of ore veins, laid like arteries deep in the mantle of the planet. Then over the surface of wind-whipped hills, at the jointure of moving air and staid earth, he perceived the aberrant flow of the lane flux, which Morriel's wrought construct had hurled out of balance, then wrung from its natural setting.

The onrushing comber of juxtaposed force gathered strength. Dakar saw it as light, or the gush of spilled mercury, licking down the quartz vein under the Skyshiels. Through the steel eyes of Kharadmon's experience, he measured its oncoming flood. The fear in his vitals did not lose its grip. The towering magnitude of the earth's wild forces made him feel insect frail, an ant asked to withstand an avalanche. For shielding, Sorcerer and spellbinder had not much more than a spiderweb: a fine network of spellcraft stitched over the breach, anchored in hope and desperate need, and sourced by a patchworked quilt of permissions garnered from the conscious landscape. As through a template of wrapped and spun wire, Dakar saw his own handiwork laced into the mesh, clumsy weavings like botched snags of string clumped within the fiercely clean elegance of Fellowship crafting.

Thought gave way to overwhelming despair, that such mismatched jointures could never hold firm.

'Hold steady!' Kharadmon cracked in bald-faced command. '*Bear up, or you'll leave me no choice but to numb your wits senseless.*'

The moment had passed, to stand down for incompetence. The rise of the flux engaged their front lines, already beyond any power on Athera to halt. Like the charged edge preceding the storm, Luhaine raced ahead of the oncoming crest. The fanned essence of his spirit combed over the landscape, the faint charge of his presence laid down like dragged scent, scoring ion trails of alignment. Slight though they were, those ordered channels attracted the distorted currents of magnetic flux. These were not tamed energies, but powers dashed to chaos, spitting white spikes and snagged peaks, spun off the disrupted sixth lane, that, unaltered, would become snatched by the conductivity of the quartz vein under Rockfell. If any one burst grazed through the pit's damaged wardings, chain-linked seals would unbind like flung acid.

Luhaine captured and wrapped those disparate coils of loosed chaos. He braided white fire. Eddy by snagged eddy, in their myriad thousands, he married the raging wave into a focused blaze like a spearhead.

The influx flared, then burned, a monstrous, bloated meteor aimed straight for the circle of protection set to isolate Rockfell Peak. Woven across that intricately forged ring, a strung path like a cord, crossing the ring-spell's diameter: the bridged conduit fashioned and held by Kharadmon and the Mad Prophet.

No space remained to plead for reprieve. Entrapped at the cusp of explosive event, Dakar watched the risen lane flux come on. The rampaging maw of raised power exceeded all human understanding. Its annihilating threat made the oblivion of death seem a haven of blessed peace. Unmanageable fright and regret canceled speech and denied the relief of shed tears as the spelled construct arranged to spare Rockfell engaged the roused forces and bloomed.

Cold-struck veins of spellcraft flared active. Fine chains of seals and flowing ciphers ignited, then burned to stenciled ribbons of violet radiance. As though the spells carved through each nerve and bone of him, the spellbinder sensed the recoiling, flash burn of heat. He felt the breathtaking, terrible wrench, as the equinox tide encountered the seals that hooked and then turned the misaligned torrent from the earth-bed of quartz transmission, and hurled the unstoppable impetus down the throat of the alternate conduits.

Then the overwhelming, wild force barreled down Kharadmon's entrenched construct, and plunged his awareness straight to perdition.

Dakar tumbled, awash in many-colored light that beat and swirled like the blast of a rapids. Rainbow swirls rinsed his sight, as though he gazed through the film of an oil slick. The shimmering hues brightened, then blazed, erupted to showers of sparks that grew blinding. Through the dazzle of ranging force hurled against him, the spellbinder dimly sensed Kharadmon's presence, immersed in the diligent work of holding the wards' calibration. Where the scouring currents eroded a weakness, the Sorcerer extended a finger of thought, and patched distressed seals and linked runes.

He grasped strands of fully charged power bare-handed. Using Dakar's dough fists, he twisted new rings of protection, spending reckless strength, again and again, until the shared flesh he inhabited swayed like a gale-blown candle. Kharadmon noticed. He dared not take pause to gauge whether such stress might inflict irreversible damage. Set against the alternative of ruinous consequences, all things within reach were expendable. Burning human resource like a touch match to hot oil, he forged craftworked barriers like linked mail and thrust them, untested, into the roil of the flux. Like the eye of the needle, guiding live thread, the lane's crested power roared over him. Ruled willy-nilly by that hellish partnership, the Mad Prophet became as a plucked stalk of grain, flailed seed from hull on a threshing floor.

Reduced to a husk, then a shred of limp cognizance, he felt even fear fray away. The drug of false peace did not assuage him. Trained spellbinder under Asandir's watchful tutelage, Dakar recognized peril. Vitality was draining relentlessly from him. Another moment, and the drum-taut fabric of selfhood threatened to tear. His core awareness would whip into tatters, swept away and erased by the inexhaustible surge of the lane flux.

Unable to call out or warn Kharadmon, Dakar felt the sudden, rushing burn of the first breach as it happened. A point in the major wardings thinned. Snagged light tore through. The Sorcerer, nerveless, countered by capping the breach with Dakar's naked hand, laid palm outward against Rockfell's granite.

Through that whiplash instant, as Kharadmon dammed the lane's force in check through naught else but singed tissue and brute will, Dakar gasped, 'Disengage! You can't think to contain the flux with *mere flesh*!'

Response was impossible. A breath, a slammed heartbeat, and the Sorcerer lost his fool's grip. The tide of the lane force rammed through, inexorable.

Dakar screamed then, a cry flung back in strained echoes off Rockfell's black stone.

The searing eruption of raw energies coursed through sinew

and bone, scouring his nerve sheaths to fire and scraped agony. Still screaming, Dakar collapsed. Mind and thought were milled under a barrage of barbed sparks that drilled a thousand hot pins through his brain.

And still, the Fellowship Sorcerer who partnered him did not release hold on his body. Thrashed and ravaged amid the raw pulse of the lane force, the spellbinder forgot life and breath. The span of his existence sleeted into a cocoon of strained noise, and sensation became torment distilled into suffering without hope of surcease.

How long could the mind support senseless pain, without tumbling, lost to insanity? How long, before the heart burst, and overstrung muscle unraveled to quivering jelly? Denied the black passage into unconsciousness, forbidden the crossing of Fate's Wheel, Dakar gibbered, entangled in the wracked shreds of awareness. He felt like the butterfly battered by gales. No leverage existed to tear himself free of Kharadmon's shackling demands.

The moment of surcease passed all but unnoticed as the aftershock memory of suffering and horror cast its imprisoning shadow over the future.

Then, framed in white light, a Paravian rune of renewal cut through the clawing pain.

Dakar gasped, whirled dizzy. His overturned senses restored in a rush, leaving him a crushed wad without strength. He recovered himself, folded onto his knees, doubled over with racking nausea. The snagged gaps in his sight shrank to sparks, and then faded, as the lane forces dwindled, subsiding to background quiescence.

'*Midnight lies behind us. The first crest is passed,*' Kharadmon ventured, a gentle, soft touch in a mind still grazed raw, as though every synapse was blistered.

Dakar whimpered. His palms were left scalded. The singed threads of his sleeves stuck to red, weeping flesh. Inside and out, he felt scarred and reamed, as though someone who loved torture had pumped liquid lye through his bloodstream. The air drawn into his overstressed lungs felt abrasive as sand; thought and cognizance seemed dulled to poured lead.

'I can't do this again,' he sobbed through a throat like ripped meat.

Kharadmon's response was inflexible. '*You must, else the world dies. Meanwhile, we have until the next surge at dawn to refit the wards and strengthen the patches holding the weak points.*'

No reprieve; no rest; even for small healing to ease the sting of seared hands. Hazed back onto his unsteady feet by the Sorcerer's driving urgency, Dakar plowed ahead. His spirits stayed low. He could not shake off his creeping anxiety, that the next onslaught would break him past mending. Warning or protest, his admission proved useless. Defeatist thoughts wrung no mercy from the brusque presence of Kharadmon.

'You'll find the dawn tide by lengths less taxing,' the Sorcerer dismissed, impelled to join awareness with Luhaine, and assess how his colleague had weathered the first test. 'With the sun's position squared with the pulse of the lane force, the next crest won't be as defined.'

Yet Dakar was not fooled. He found no haven in false consolation. The dawn surge, *on any day*, was sufficient to fire the lanes. Such natural phenomena enabled the Fellowship to effect their spelled transfers across latitude, or ignite the constructs of conjuries beyond the pale of all other orders on Athera. Seasons created a sine wave fluctuation, with the event of spring equinox framed as a harmonic balance point, raising an exponentially heightened peak resonance.

Suffering, each step, with his muscles whipped slack and a screaming ache stabbed through each unstrung nerve end, Dakar knew the ordeal just endured had been little more than the opener. The inevitable outcome required no genius. If the dawn crest did not test his resilience so severely, the noon surge would bring the high tide mark. All but shattered by the inaugural pass, he now realized *just how far* his personal resource fell short. Barring a miracle, Dakar suspected he was too drained already to surmount the dawn; never mind noon, or the waning aftershocks to follow at sunset and midnight.

The spellbinder hacked in a coarse breath to denounce the endeavor as fool's play. Kharadmon's barbed tone interrupted. 'Quit belaboring the obvious. Everyone knows you're a few feathers short of a turkey. Which point cannot signify, given the dangers. Besides, you've not tapped the last of your resources yet. We're not finished, and won't be, until then.'

Without knowing why, Dakar felt a terrible grue chase down the length of his spine. 'I don't want to go there,' he mewled. 'Ath's infinite pity! Why do I know I'd rather face death, first?'

For answer, Kharadmon mustered his will like a knife, and applied himself strengthening ciphers.

Night Encounters

At Althain Tower, the adepts sitting vigil at Sethvir's side watch him stir from deep trance; blue-green eyes snap open, unseeing and wide, as he gasps in stunned horror, 'Kharadmon, *no! What are you thinking*? How dare we draw on a resource already burdened to breaking? If the world should be lost, I beg you, don't ask Rathain's crown prince to shoulder remorse for another annihilating failure . . .'

Wearied by days of solitary, fast flight, the Companion Sidir at last reaches the clan enclave in Halwythwood; and his news meets with consternation and tears, then the rage of a grief-stricken girl, desperate to deny the Sighted dreams that foretell her accession as Rathain's *caithdein*: 'Jeynsa,' he says, 'I can't ease you with lies. If the High Earl still lived when we last parted, he stayed to face odds worse than dire . . .'

Predawn, in the Mathorns, a wary clan sentry challenges two riders, one upright and alert, and the other, wrapped in a bear mantle, and slumped with exhaustion against his hill pony's neck; and the answer comes back, in old speech royal accents, 'Bless Ath! By the name of s'Ffalenn, I beg succor and sanctuary for Braggen, one of Earl Jieret's loyal Companions . . .'

Spring Equinox Dawn

XIII. Teir's'Ffalenn

To the five wary clan scouts who kept watch from the remote Mathorn outpost, and who found themselves playing startled host to unexpected s'Ffalenn royalty, Arithon made his firm disposition. 'There is no other choice to be made. I must move on, and at once.'

The biting, harsh cold attended a brief silence. Across the windblown rags of the blaze kindled to brew water for remedies, Braggen slept like the dead. His sword cuts had been bathed and bound by his liege's own hands, with his slack, weary body finally settled amid the folds of Jieret's bear mantle. In predawn darkness, huddled in leathers and furs against the cruel chill whose grip lingered on for the season, the three scouts holding parley exchanged unsettled glances.

The fox-haired woman slapped the stick just used to score maps in the snow against an impatient, gloved palm. 'That would cause disappointment.' Her remonstrance snapped through consonants as brisk. 'Braggen will want to go with you.'

Arithon regarded her, features cut to sharp angles by the harried, low fire, and his green eyes hard-set against sentiment. 'He would pose a liability.'

No need to belabor the core of that argument. Braggen had gone three nights with scant sleep, then exerted himself to a standstill. The man the scouts had dragged out of the saddle had verged upon total collapse. If Jieret's Companion suffered no lasting harm, sheer exhaustion must take its due toll. He was not going to awaken refreshed, but raging stiff, bruised, and sore in every taxed joint.

While the woman scout matched her liege lord's level stare throughout a prolonged, tensioned quiet, Arithon saluted her point with the barest, flexed smile. 'Braggen would suffer the punishment gladly, I know. But I must heed my heart on the matter. The news from Daon Ramon is already devastating. With Earl Jieret dead, this Companion's feal duty is now to survive. When he disagrees, and he will, tell him plainly: he is needed. My decision is made for young Jeynsa s'Valerient. For the good of the realm, I urge that Braggen go south and report forthwith to Sidir.'

'You could stand on royal prerogative and make him,' suggested the white-haired scout who supported the cold with remarkable immunity. His bare fingers stayed supple at their task, cleaning and sorting the best arrows from the outpost's scant stock of armament.

'No.' Arithon looked away, perhaps abashed, or else too grief-struck to master his sorrow for the blood just spilled in Daon Ramon. 'Let Braggen choose. He's earned the right. If fortune is kindly, I should be a day's ride to the north by the hour he wakens.'

'Well, you won't go alone, liege.' The woman who held rank tossed her stick down, determined. The clamped set to her features would brook no more argument. She tipped the grounds from the tin mug just used to brew willowbark tea, wiped the residue clean, then tucked the implement away in the rock niche that sheltered them. 'I'm off to fetch remounts.' Arisen, lithe-limbed, she hooked the clasps on her hide jacket. 'The fittest horses we have will be ready before dawn. Machlin, attend the provisions.'

As Arithon bristled for blazing rebuttal, the elder again intervened. 'She's right, you know, liege. These mountains are a maze for those who don't know them. You need to make time against hot pursuit? Then necessity demands that we guide you.'

'You're asking for suicide!' Arithon snapped, goaded to vicious brevity. 'Do you have progeny safe somewhere else? Let that determine the sacrifice.'

In fact, two scouts foisted their presence upon him when the time came to mount in cold darkness. Arithon had paused only to dress his mauled hand, reopened by the pull of the bowstring. He could eat jerky, moving, and his rest was caught up, a surplus benefit of the days just spent in extended spiritwalk.

'Lysaer's Etarrans will be moving by daybreak,' he warned, well aware the woman who proffered the reins of a restless gray gelding was about to exhort with entreaty. 'Fear that. I dare not allow the Mistwraith's curse to overset my last grip on sanity. Distance will save that. *I have to ride now!* Take my blessing in thanks, knowing your generosity has saved Braggen, and quite likely myself as well.'

A flurry of farewells, exchanged in clan dialect as the oldest scout gave his filled quivers to the younger pair chosen to ride. The woman relinquished her best horse, approving, as her prince gave the saddle his expert, fast check. A sharp man made certain her hurried work had not left cloth or girth strap ill set, to chafe the animal sore down the trail. His Grace cared for dumb beasts above human pride; and that ingrained kindness won her over.

'Guard your mauled hand,' she cautioned. 'Promise you'll strap it the moment you reach safety, and rest until it heals properly.'

'Ah, lady,' said Arithon, suddenly beset. For a moment, uncertainty and stark need frayed the firm weave of his voice. 'Trust me, I made that same bond to myself, months ago in the Skyshiels. As soon as may be, I'll bow to good sense.' He sorted the gray's reins, then clasped her gloved fingers and touched her palm to his cheek in rushed salute. Then he mounted. 'I hear your caring most clearly. Take my earnest word that it matters.'

Despite driven haste, regardless of trials that burdened his shoulders with worry, Arithon's handling was silk on the bit, and his heels, a light pressure asking the gelding's compliance.

'Ath speed your Grace,' called the white-headed scout as the three riders wheeled in the darkness. Beside him, the clan woman had nothing to say, beyond the heart's gift of her tears.

Unseen, the fifth scout standing sentry in the forest signaled a clear trail with an owl's call. Then the horses surged away. Night swallowed their forms. The snow-muffled thud of their hooves faded swiftly, leaving Braggen in safe and oblivious sleep before the birch-spiced warmth of the embers.

Given fresh mounts and the scouts' expert guidance, Arithon made rapid progress. The last hours of night wrapped the land in charcoal gloom, splotched by snow-clad ravines, with shadows and trees rendered in shapes of punch-cut black velvet. The burn of cold wind on nose and cheek interspersed with the slap of iced boughs in the thickets. Beneath slab-sided ridges, over winding, sparse game trails, the clansmen pressed for speed and silence. They were well practiced at secretive cunning. Wild-born predators, they knew how to trust the horses' keen sight in rough territory, with moon and thin starlight their sole guidance. Once, they flushed the spotted khetienn stalking for ermine. Another time, set against the silver voile of a snowfield, they spotted an eagle in gliding flight.

'No canny bird, that,' observed one of the scouts through the plaid tied over his chin as a muffler. 'Such don't fly at night, nor in these ranges at all, come to that. Not at this time or season.'

'Sorcerer's shapechange, or a fetch, very likely.' The other scout quelled the uneasy instinct that prompted a reach for his bow. 'If it's spying for Koriathain, won't die of an arrow. Only make trouble if we try.' He shrugged, fatalistic, then used the brief pause to open his saddle pack and dole out a ration of jerky.

But Arithon shook his head. 'No fetch, in this case.' He accepted the dried venison, and the scouts' sidewise glances with pragmatic equilibrium. 'You don't need to believe me. Eagles don't fly by night, I agree. But my bard's ear will discern flesh and blood from worked magecraft. If that creature's a construct, I can't detect any whisper of resonance from the spell seals.'

'Blasted winter's not natural itself, you ask me,' the elder scout carped through a mouthful. 'Cold as the Fatemaster's bollocks, still, and no sign of melt on the south side of Jaire Peak.'

'Fretting won't help such,' the other said, long-faced. He shared out his dried stores, then bowed to his liege's overriding impatience and shouldered his horse to the fore.

Already the stars overhead glimmered paler. The eastern sky showed the first pall of gray. Straight in the saddle, and until now, stark steady, Arithon suddenly gasped. Doubled over his clasped hands, he curled in on himself, racked by a shuddering spasm.

'Your Grace?' The nearer scout sidestepped his horse and steadied his liege's bowed shoulder. 'What's wrong?'

A fleet, wringing shiver passed under his hand. Then Arithon pressed back upright. Disheveled black hair masked clear sight of his eyes. His face in the half-light wore a distressed pallor, and his hands shook, though his stressed equilibrium appeared to be fully restored.

'What's wrong?' the scout pressed.

But the other first broached the dread subject outright. 'Do you fight Desh-thiere's curse?'

'Not that. Not yet.' Arithon raked back fallen hair, puzzled himself as a dwindling frisson stormed through his braced up frame. 'I'm not sure what touched me.' Words could scarcely describe the split-second event, as though a fragmentary chord had been plucked, ringing echoes through the land underfoot.

He tipped a frowning glance overhead. The oncoming dawn brightened second by second over the saw-toothed crests of the peaks. 'Whatever's amiss, the Etarrans won't wait. We had better ride on.'

Upon mounts displeased to be facing the wind, over ridges of stone mottled piebald where clinging snow chalked the cracks, the small party picked their way steadily north. The terrain all the while grew steeper, rougher. Toothed summits scraped a black-violet sky, with the deep vales below shattered by time into fissures of crazed marked granite.

As his gray slithered down a stony embankment, Arithon gave on the reins to let the beast regain its balance. His worry was less easily managed. 'Will horses be able to finish this crossing?'

The scout in the lead glanced over his shoulder, his sharp-boned youth pronounced in the growing light. 'In thaws, they could. Given the cold, the high passes would be mired. The way over the divide must often be finished on foot.'

A steep, zigzagged course through a corrie of stunt fir, where a gaunt herd of deer flushed. The scouts paused. Still stewards of the land, despite centuries of persecution, they allowed the animals to settle and move on without wasting themselves in blind panic.

'Aye, on now,' the clansman crooned to his horse. Red-faced in the wind, he turned back to his prince and resumed the dropped thread of his discourse. 'Won't blister your heels, though. Tomorrow eve, we're going to swing west. There's a narrow track that leads to the coast. On that we'll make time. By then, we think Lysaer and his Etarrans should be well into the mountains. They don't know the country. Zeal should drive them west also, trying to track as the crow flies. Do that, and they'll be in the spurs, sheer ramparts of rock with no crevice for passage. Men would need to swing north to get through, and by then, we should have you a wee boat. You'll be safely away to Atainia, forbye, with your enemies left as lively prey for our raiders.'

The other scout pressed forward, a fair-skinned, middle-aged man whose hawk nose jutted from the shadow of a jaunty wolverine cap. 'Be sure Kesweth will harry them. He'll cheer their retreat with some spring traps, maybe pink a few laggards with arrows.'

Yet his effort at humor raised no grim smile from his prince. 'Not if my half brother hammers these mountains to slag with the frustrated force of his gift.'

'Kesweth's frustrated, too,' the younger scout demurred. 'Damned scalpers got his wife, last autumn.'

They scaled another ridge. Around them, light and sky changed moment to moment, from deep cobalt to the lucent blue of an armorer's burnished steel. Eastward, day would already have broken over the Eltair coast. The high peaks of the Skyshiels would be gilt dipped, their gaunt shadows spiked across Daon Ramon.

For some reason acutely aware of that passage, as night made way for the sunrise, Arithon was raked by a sense of uncanny expectancy. He tipped his head to one side, strained and listening. *Something* grazed his senses. A high note, beyond sound, like the prelude to a chord wrought from a band of wild energy. Touched by a leaping shiver of bliss, he said, startled, 'What's the date?'

'Equinox,' came the answer from under the wolverine. 'There's a centaur's mark, not far distant. Do you sense it? Some say the stone sings at the turn of the season.'

Forced to snatch back his poise as the gray sidled under him, Arithon glanced about, interested. 'We've straddled the lane, then?'

'The fourth, near enough.' At the crest, the wind's blasting shear raked their faces. The horses' flagged tails snapped like streamers. Still speaking, the scout snatched at black-and-white fur, as his heavy cap threatened to whisk off. 'The line runs from the ruin at Penstair through Strakewood, then down the rock ledges with Tal Quorin. From there, she crosses the old dance site at Caith-al-Caen.'

In fact, the ancient marker stone did sing aloud, as herald of the true dawn. Its tuned cry pierced the whining hiss of the wind and raised the hair at the nape. For Arithon, sensitized by a masterbard's talent, the sorrowful overtones bespoke violent death, and fresh blood spilled on Daon Ramon Barrens. Through the hour that followed, he rode, beyond speech, while around him, the high mountain silence became stitched with chirping birdsong. Firs braided the lonely voice of wind with their secretive whispering. The gusts smelled of spruce and scrub pine and scoured ice, and slacking, wore the tang of sweat damp leathers and horse.

Late morning, they paused. The scouts fed and watered their mounts, and the gray, with its pale, snowflake dapples. Arithon sat in solitude, arms clamped over drawn-up knees, the desperate ache for the loss of Earl Jieret swelled into a grief he could not assuage. He tried not to care how the pair of scouts eyed him when they thought his attention lay elsewhere. He detested the need that required their presence, and the lifelong demands of sworn sovereignty. Nor could he argue their bond of feal service. Circumstance rankled, that Braggen's exhaustion and a Sorcerer's blood oath should have constrained all his preferences. He wished no owed loyalties, no more death and striving. Dread rode him, whetted by the urgent, needled warning as Desh-thiere's curse scraped his nerves and informed him that Lysaer was moving.

The dichotomy seared, for the wrench in perception, with the Mathorns' stilled splendor commanding caught breath at every angle of view. Arithon shut his eyes, overcome. His rank, inward turmoil seemed an offense, while the sunlight sparkled gilt-silver and diamond, off snowbank and cornice and mica-veined granite.

Yet the wild upland peaks could not ease his mind, for all of their savage majesty. The rising spate of the equinox lane forces sheared through the ground, charging the bared stone underfoot. The unseen, swift current set Arithon on edge. He felt as though an overcranked string was just plucked, outside the range of his hearing. In odd fits and starts, he glanced over his shoulder. Some presence seemed to stand at his back, or a distant, chill touch threatened to comb through his aura. He did not share his heartache, that once, given mage-sight, he could have scried and found name for what ruffled his instincts.

The hesitant crunch of a boot sole on gravel informed of approaching company. Arithon lifted his head. The younger scout picked his uncertain way toward the boulder where he took refuge. He wished all at once he could duck out of sight. Beyond bearing, that he might be addressed with diffidence, or uncertainty, or worse, even fear; wounding proof, whatever expression awaited, that his reputation had distorted the person he was, underneath the encumbrance of state titles.

Avoidance was nothing if not straight cowardice. Arithon met the young man face on, set to handle whatever hurtful presumption might cloud the discourse between them. He failed to anticipate the crushing, bright pain: First Steiven and Dania, then Caolle had died, with Jieret's fresh loss the most grievous. Arithon pulled in a deep breath, let the chill douse the rise of his anger. He stilled his revulsion, that this eager young man might too easily become the next sacrifice for a crown rule that would first shackle, then suffocate every last precious shred of autonomy.

Fact lent him no quarter. Arithon faced the quandary, that to disown this one would dishonor the others before him. Unstrung as he was, even the slight movement of air hurt his skin. Yet s'Ffalenn compassion and bardic perception allowed him no shield. He could raise no self-determined defense against the exigencies of his own character.

He beheld the young scout in the full light of day, and read in the man's windburned, flushed face a grave sincerity, wrapped thread on thread with pride and desire. Raised to uphold the traditions of heritage, such a liegeman would honor the trust invested in his clan ancestry. Some mother's beloved son, some brother's cadet, he was a brown-haired individual wearing a stained leather baldric, and steel-studded war gauntlets; old enough to take pride in his competence, yet too young to have passed on his gifts, or to behold the legacy of his grown child. He had youth's cocky strength, a matched set of fine weapons, and a flamboyance that led to a silver earring hung with a nugget of turquoise.

Aware in that instant of Arithon's survey upon him, he stopped. Embarrassment brightened the flush lent by weather. Braced wariness squared his trail-wise carriage as he acknowledged the presence of royalty. 'My liege?'

Arithon inclined his head, a considered response he hoped would allow the scout to gather himself. Though the private part of him wished, heartfelt, to eschew royal etiquette, he refused the indulgence as cruelty. If weapons were drawn later, the crown that he stood for would lend courage and meaning to what, in sharp fact, was no better than outright waste. He contained his temper, though every fiber of his being reviled the lie, that defense of his person became a sore tragedy his personal code could not countenance.

Caolle and Jieret should still be alive, and before them, Steiven and Dania.

Mage-schooled to mask the deep bent of his thoughts, locked motionless with forbearance, Arithon waited. Despite his strung patience, the scout glanced away. Discomfort deepened his flush.

'There's some trouble?' the Teir's'Ffalenn prompted.

Reluctant, the young man plunged ahead. 'Maybe. Hewall says there's a place to camp in the next corrie. He's suggested we stop there.'

Arithon's lifted eyebrows showed all of his stark surprise. 'Unwise, for my sake.' He stood, unable to contain his dismay. His hagridden nerves stemmed from no defined source, which unleashed his scalding, quick anger. 'Trust me, Hewall can make camp wherever he likes, but Lysaer s'Ilessid is marching. Let him gain ground, and Desh-thiere's curse will slip my grasp. That's a risk I won't stand for. Tell Hewall, I can't brook the slightest delay.'

The scout shook his head, consumed by frank misery, and dropped his bad news like a stone. 'Hewall comes from a lineage that has Sight. He says you won't ride any farther.'

'He has prescience? *What did he see?*' When the scout could not answer, Arithon strode past to pursue the matter directly.

'You doubt Hewall's vision?' the young scout pursued, his anxious glance sidewards a stabbing rebuke to his prince.

'I doubt no one.' As neat on his feet as any man forestborn, Arithon cut a path for the tree where the resting horses were tethered. 'Camp in the next corrie, or not, I'll know what might possibly arise to prompt such a foolish decision.'

But three steps later, the reason became manifest without need to consult Hewall's talent. Arithon was clouted by what he first thought was a buffeting gust of rogue wind.

The blow staggered him. Knocked to his knees, with the scout's dismayed cry ringing in his ears, he fought and failed to level his whirling senses. The snow under his gloved hands, and the solid, stone presence of the Mathorns suddenly seemed as insubstantial as smoke. He sucked in a breath of bone-hurting cold air. Yet speech would not come through brute effort. Had he not lost his talent by Tal Quorin, years before, he would have attributed his distressed confusion to a nerve storm brought on by mage-sight.

But the imposed state of calm he had trained hard to master slipped through the clenched fist of his will. Faint with distance, he heard his Name spoken in tones like mallet-struck iron. Understanding touched his heart like a finger of ice: he was being summoned, by powers of magecraft he had no defense to withstand.

The next second, all his barriers became hammered flat, down to his innermost mind. The driven will gripping him seemed honed by the fires of destiny that had once forged Dharkaron's Black Spear. '*You are entrained by a Fellowship mandate, and for this, you are called into service, prince!*'

Hit again by a rushing current of force, Arithon gasped. The hands he plunged wrist deep in soft snow failed to anchor his reeling balance. Mazed by an overwhelming impression of power sweeping over the earth like the tides, he lost track of the scout's distressed shouting. The waking vision overrode all awareness of outside sensation. Arithon realized that the wilding currents plaguing him were not wind at all, but the cascading rush of an imbalanced lane flux.

Which should have escaped him, impaired as he was, his mage-sight still deafened and blinded. Not only that, noon lay a full hour away in the steep-walled dell where he sheltered. Lane's crest through the western spur of the Mathorns *had yet to occur by the sun's arc.* Arithon grappled that unsettling truth. Through the hollow sensation that preceded fraught fear, he realized: the aberration he picked up must originate from the east, where the sun would already ride at the meridian.

The worst onslaught lifted. Arithon recaptured his lost breath. Upset senses stabilized; a split-second interval restored the spinning impression of torn clouds and blue sky, with silver-and-black pinnacles folded one on another like serrated rock shards driven through crumpled foil.

He managed to drag words through his mauling weakness. 'I'm not beset.'

Insistent fingers clamped his shoulder and arm, trying to help him stand upright. The scout's urgent speech raised a rattling buzz his ears could scarcely interpret. 'What's wrong? Are you ill? Or does your Grace suffer the onset of the Mistwraith's curse?'

'I don't think so. Not yet.' Arithon groped, caught a boulder, seized just enough presence to sit.

Through wheeling confusion, the second influx drowned out all else, as the voice resumed in thundering command: *'Crown Prince of Rathain! You are called! By your sworn oath to serve, the land has dire need!'* Arithon recognized the touch as Kharadmon's, then received, *'Dakar is at Rockfell, in crisis. The fact he holds your free will permissions has drawn you into the conflict.'*

Open contact with the Sorcerer lent a channel of clarity that provided a flash-point assessment. Arithon shut his eyes. Propped on the boulder by the scout's steady arm, he labored to speak before splintering vision whirled him off-balance again. 'There's threat to the kingdom,' he managed, while Kharadmon sent through a horrific summary of the catastrophe pending at Rockfell.

Arithon felt his shocked blood all but freeze the hammering beat of his heart. 'Merciful Ath, we have trouble!'

His liege's torn note of anguish at last struck the scout's exhortations to silence.

Yet none else but the ward rings binding the Mistwraith were besieged by the imbalanced lane flux. Anguished, Arithon saw how his past transfer from Sanpashir could have exacerbated the problem. He was given no space for regrets or apology. Kharadmon's entreaty showed Luhaine's stressed presence, immersed at the crux of doomed struggle. Yet even the most desperate measures could not stem the solstice tide at full onslaught. Dakar was not going to recover his lost grip. A blind fool could foresee every effort was futile: no resource the Sorcerers commanded at Rockfell could claw back the disastrously slipped balance.

Time itself seemed suspended as Arithon scrambled to encompass the full scope of the problem Kharadmon's message unfolded. Head in his gloved hands, he sat helplessly shivering, while a chill more intense than the bitterest wind reamed him through to his core.

'You are sensing the skewed lane tide as it crests through the Skyshiels,' the Sorcerer sent in raced urgency. 'And yes, if our endeavor fails here, more than Rockfell's protections will sunder. Grimwards will burst free of their ancient, set boundaries. Earthquake and ruin will follow, unstoppable. All of Athera will suffer the brunt of a devastating backlash.'

Kharadmon's terse appeal implied an annihilation utterly without quarter. In bitter despair, Arithon found himself made party to a dilemma beyond hope of salvage. Worse, far worse, than Desh-thiere's release, or the loss of clear sun, or any threat posed by loosed free wraiths, he was shown the chains of linked spellcraft binding the grimwards in Rathain and Melhalla. The mastership rigorously earned at Rauven let him read their threatened configuration. Their seals restrained chaos beyond all imagining. If such bulwarks were to be even marginally compromised, the chaotic forces inside would storm unchecked through the breach.

Arithon saw disaster and trembled with rage. Impaired as he was, *he could not lend direct help using spellcraft.* Denied the intelligent expression of his talent, he became the hapless string puppet to need, so much straw fodder before the raging flame of an irrepressible holocaust. His unconditional permissions to Dakar would let the Sorcerers tap and drain his vitality; *as they must!* To stabilize their construct, Kharadmon required the living shield of a borrowed bodily form. He would have no choice but to draw Arithon's life force to shore up the Mad Prophet's faltering flesh. Either that, or lose everything; bow without fight before apocalyptic failure.

'Forgive!' came the plea, Fellowship Sorcerer to sworn crown prince, for an act of gross usage that would come to cost unimagined torment before death. *'For the world's sake, forgive!'*

Obdurate, Arithon rejected defeat. Torbrand's lineage to the marrow, he refused to embrace the suicidal rush toward destruction. 'Do you not hold my irrevocable bond to survive?' he flung back into Kharadmon's teeth. 'Even for this, I am constrained to fight. Or did your Fellowship accept my grief lightly, on the hour I was asked to swear my blood oath to Asandir at Athir?'

The paired Sorcerers at Rockfell received that raw cry. Before courage and duty that demanded full due, its appeal stunned them to humbled silence.

Arithon s'Ffalenn flung back his head, under torn cloud and chill sky in the Mathorns. Eyes shut, braced against the steadfast presence of a frightened young liegeman, he clamped his fists in bone white denial. Straight logic insisted all prospects were spent. He faced crushing odds, with the fate of the world attendant upon his sure failure. Still, he could not back down. His sworn oath forbade him. 'As you value life, no matter how I scream, keep me upright,' he instructed the scout through clenched teeth. 'Though my clothes catch fire, or flesh burns in your hands, don't dare give way! Do not let me fall unconscious!'

'Ath guide you, my liege,' spoke a voice to his right. The other scout reached him and knelt in support, and a second staunch hand braced his shoulder. 'As long as life remains in our veins, you don't carry the kingdom alone!'

Arithon had no chance to acknowledge such bravery. He had already immersed in the sharpened awareness instilled by his master's training. Against the imperative, breaking disaster, he still owned his store of hard-won experience, tempered and tested through twelve initiations undergone at Rauven. He could not assist by working grand conjury. Yet he retained an exacting knowledge of spell strictures and natural law. By the grace of Halliron's teaching, he also possessed a masterbard's schooled ear for harmony.

Formidable strengths, paired once before, when he and the Mad Prophet had jointly attempted a doomed effort to draw an injured child back to health.

Arithon stood on the presumption that every avenue of straight conjury had already been fruitlessly tried. Music offered the sole, untapped reservoir within his province to lend.

Kharadmon's fleeted thought grasped that untapped potential. In lightning response, the Sorcerer suspended his claim to a Teir's'Ffalenn's life to dam back the breaking breach. Fast as ricochet, Arithon received terms for that stay of reprieve: he could be granted no more than split seconds to shape a successful response.

No moment to spare, for the scouts' rampant worry, no thought, for Elaira's anguish. She would surely sense the sword's edge of peril through the linkage that joined their emotions. Unable to affect any saving last grace, Arithon threw all that he was into action. He was forced to let go, plunge down and down again, deep into his innermost self. There, he sought the listening source of his gifted inspiration. Through cycles of seasons, for thousands of years, the ancient Paravians had once channeled lane force through ritual song and dance. If Arithon could plumb the key phrasing in time, he might sift out the tonal chord that would call the fourth lane's flux to shift resonance. If his mastery *could* match the massive demand of such challenge, if mortal man bearing the title of Masterbard could *perhaps* encompass the thundering scope of that untamed peal of primal harmony, one chance might be pried from the jaws of adversity.

No course, but to try. Arithon surrendered the pure, blank mirror of his intuition into the battering thrust of the lane tide. He allowed sound to rule him, body and mind. Naught else must concern him. He dared not think past that initial step. Nor could he spare thought to question slim odds, that no means in existence could find access in time to use that enabled gateway. A gulf lay between the first capture of melody, and the raw methodology required: to bleed off the raging crest of the equinox, then to bend its rarefied high frequencies into a safely reduced register of vibration.

Arithon drifted. Sleeting noise rushed over, then through him. Plunged into immersion, cast headlong into the shredding dissonance of the fourth lane's skewed forces, Arithon gasped in white pain. The deranging explosion of chaos enveloped him. His sharp, strangled outcry pinched off, unvoiced. At once, he perceived that the current tumbling his thread of freed consciousness was no natural pulsation of earth's magnetics. The flux surge the Sorcerers wrestled at Rockfell bore no resemblance to the clean, lilted flow he had sounded before, one starry winter midnight amid the black sands of Sanpashir.

This scrambling din sliced his awareness like knives. Its cacophony wrecked concentration. Arithon held fast, his teeth set on edge. He endured, flushed and sweating as his mind came unraveled, retuned to the rank beat of turmoil. Fierce training allowed him to spin with the maelstrom. He made no attempt to seek order; dared not grasp after his lost equilibrium. Instead, Halliron's taught wisdom must rule him beyond panic and temper his assaulted nerve ends.

The memory of his mentor resurged, immediate as yesterday: *'You must learn to listen. The practice becomes an art in itself, and first requires that you cast off all ties to identity.'* The sadness returned, woundingly deep, as the graduate apprentice now beleaguered in the Mathorns reviewed the old man's testy admonishment. *'Listen! That means, bide still, so still, sound itself molds the fabric of your whole being. Arithon, you must allow what is there to pour through you, then see what feelings awaken. Heed this well, your open heart reveals everything. Emotion alone will key all the notes and unlock the gateway to genius.'*

Yet these shrieking harmonics scored him bone deep. Still, Arithon clung to his obstinate discipline. He kept access to his perception jammed open, let the scouring pain pour through tissue and faculty unhampered. *Listening*, he let his passive flesh be the tuning fork for the struck peal of the lane's deranged forces. He felt, head to foot, the racing rise through all registers. The devastating crescendo fast approached, that would sweep the bright tides of the equinox lane flux into its seasonal peak.

Disaster for Athera, should he not ferret out the precise range of tonality that once tamed such raging torrent. Mortal man, and alone, he must reclaim the ancient ritual the Paravians had enacted in dance step and song. Somewhere, amid dissonance, Athera herself must recall the fired glory when the old races had walked the earth in strides of pure light and shaped the lanes into pealing renewal.

Arithon held. Mage-schooled to brace himself calm through adversity, to divorce mind and heart from the physical turmoil of pain, he endured, though the lane forces flayed him. A dust mote in a cataract, he cast off his fear, let himself be tossed by the vast power of a planet. His musician's ear encompassed its voice of raw turbulence, but found no more meaning than an insect might, flung headlong down the throat of a gale.

Tumbled, unraveled, flensed thought from flesh, Arithon forced his stance passive. He persisted, though every born instinct urged him to shrink in retreat. Through the eye of an instant, his whole being become a savaged rag. His inward self felt raked into needling agony, and his awareness of body became a flayed remnant dragged through a bed of flint gravel.

He sustained. The inherited grace of Halliron's wisdom became as a spar in the storm sea: *'You will find an intelligence expressed in all sound. Mastery lies in the ability to divine that spark, then to effect a creative translation.'*

The strictures instilled by the Archmage at Rauven yielded supporting insight: *'Since nothing in Ath's creation is truly random, know a thing for itself. That uniqueness is the only signal truth you'll ever touch. You must ever strive to lose your own barriers and allow the pattern to speak to you. No matter how obscure, no matter how far removed from humanity, existence itself affirms the presence of consciousness.'*

Arithon listened. He kept every inward barrier flattened, until the staid boulder beneath him and two clansmen's staunch presence became all that anchored his place in the world. He tuned his receptivity wider, then wider again, until voice answered, and the stone of the mountain itself opened the path to retrieval. Granite possessed a faultless, long memory. It recalled the old measures danced upon the stations of equinox and solstice. From the veined rock, layered beneath the dell's frozen soil, Arithon received the ghost imprint of the chord underlying the fourth lane's magnetics. He picked up the tuned imprint that Paravian singers had once stepped out at Caith-al-Caen.

That wisped fragment must source his inspiration, raw seed for an invention he had only the split frame of an instant to complete.

His gift answered the challenge. A masterbard's heartfelt search for trued sound took soaring flight, bearing those remnants of melody. Arithon rode intuition, entrusted his instinct to fill in the gaps. Were he bound to the physical limitation of rendering song on the lyranthe, he understood he could not do other than fail. At the crux, the interface of hand and wound string would have proved too clumsy and slow to draw half-sensed fragments of dream into full manifestation.

Yet immersed in the unworldly stream of the mind, Arithon could respond on the fleeting breath of tuned reflex. He *knew* when the notes that he groped for were wrong; sensed the instant correction to any disharmonics running counter to the pattern's completion. He saw in advance where the gaps became canceled by harmonics and misplaced resonance. Here, a fifth interval changed to a seventh raised an answering blaze of cleared light. Riding blind on a current of crystal tonalities, he reached, touched, shaped, and observed, until the grand confluence of the chord he sought to restore achieved its masterful glory within him.

The raised fourth lane melodies reached stasis and *blazed*. Fired illumination and tuned power combed through the uprush of wild forces, and spun even Kharadmon's watching presence to awe.

On the trembling brink, with the sixth lane still cresting, Arithon stood on that platform of raised harmony and *reached out, listening again.* Desperation framed the bent of his guidance. To avert the disastrous break through at Rockfell, he must tune the fifth lane, and *not stop there*, but cast outward again. He must re-create in flash-point, perfect recall, the sixth lane chord he had once raised in song to enable the focus circle set under the mayor's mansion at Jaelot.

Yet the axis of extension unreeled too far. Arithon felt himself spread too thin, thoughts paled to the edge of attrition. His frail, human faculties were going to fall short. The overwhelming scope of the task was defeating: his talent, but one thread, when he needed the breadth of a loom to string the warp and weft of a whole tapestry. He sensed, in concept, how to close a bridging conduit, then call the aligned energies into the ancient channels and disperse them like a tonic across latitude. But the structure was too deep and complex for the mind riding on the wings of rushed thought and intuition.

Given time, he could solve this! Despair all but tore him. The millisecond that remained before the flux reached full peak was too scant to raise and align the precise chords to consummate balance, and wed three parallel lanes into harmonic connection.

'Arithon!' Kharadmon cried out in appeal. *'Call on your strength as Rathain's sanctioned crown prince! There was power invoked by the oath you once swore at Etarra. The land knows your Name. Draw on your blood heritage! We all have no choice! You'll have to reforge the connection!'*

At the Sorcerer's encouragement, the flash-point memory resurged: of the hurried ceremony conducted under Fellowship auspices, affirming the s'Ffalenn right of succession . . .

Under chilly spring sky, inside a walled garden, Asandir had gathered a handful of soil. The Sorcerer's invoked blessing had laid a binding upon the Named Teir's'Ffalenn, and a feat of grand conjury had transformed common earth into a silver circlet. Arithon had experienced a swift flash of heat at the moment the metal had been pressed over his brow. Yet the nature of the attunement had been too brief, too ephemeral to grasp at the time he had spoken the crown heir's traditional acceptance . . .

Now, pitched by fraught need, Kharadmon broke the seal that had blurred the full scope of that past initiation. *'Prince, you have married Rathain through the element of earth! Call on that asset! Let the wisdom of that union guide you.'*

Such a move would assuredly reaffirm a commitment, and engage active ties to an unwanted royal ancestry. Yet Arithon saw no option. The cresting currents at Rockfell already hammered the first crack in the guarding ward rings. Stressed seals crumpled and burst. A rain of loosed lane flux laced sputtering static over the link bridging Kharadmon's distant awareness. Luhaine's effort to spin a remedial patch became swept away in the torrent. The Sorcerer who rode Dakar's body flung himself into the breach; and a cataract grown too massive to stem carved onward. Its voracious charge ranged down the irrevocable chains of permission linking the Mad Prophet with Rathain's prince.

Contact touched the nerves like live fire. Arithon experienced a scouring agony that seared flesh and bone from within. Had the breath not been wrung clean out of his lungs, he would have lost hold, all awareness dissolved into shattering screams.

Torment upset the tuned chord in his mind. The next instant would see him immolated by the rampaging conflagration. He fought back. Earth, beneath him, and the iced kiss of snow, became all that secured his stressed grasp upon human awareness. Against the sliding fall toward oblivion, Arithon called on the cast-iron discipline instilled by his grandfather at Rauven. He hardened his will, recaptured the stressed harmonies of the ancient Paravian melody. Pain, fear, raw terror itself were reforged by sheer will into a razor-point edge of aimed thought. Since the land afforded his last hope of deliverance, Arithon yielded to the claim of his ancestry. As affirmed s'Ffalenn prince, he embraced the staid calm in the bedrock spine of Rathain's mountains.

For a split second, the template awareness of his body merged into the pulse of the land. His sovereign oath bound him. He became, all unwitting, the living interface between Rockfell's crisis and the greater territory set under his oathsworn charge to protect. Nerve and bone melted into ley meridian and mineral; and the lane flux, raging wild, leaped the gap.

At Rockfell, Kharadmon's last defenses tore asunder.

In the Mathorns, Arithon screamed under the whiteout barrage as the lane flux roared over him, unchecked. Fire shrieked through his flesh, crested into a vast, searing wave. Its wild force flooded *through him*, into the tuned conduits his bard's gift had reopened across Rathain's winter landscape.

Earth wailed in response, as the staid channels of the lanes stressed and flexed out of balance. Trees would burn, and fault lines flare up into boiling lines of loosed magma; except for one line of flung melody: the pavane recaptured from the mists of the past, where Paravians had danced the old rituals at Caith-al-Caen. The backbone of the hills there slept with the memory. Through the cleared lens of Prince Arithon's gift, the chord resurged, and tempered the jagged flow of chaos to a resonant peal of held harmony.

Ancient patterns held true. Age upon Age, their harmonics had tempered Athera's magnetic flux lines into alignment with the consummate force of Ath's mystery.

Aware of himself as the sole point of catalyst, Arithon poured all that he was into the song he was given. His mind sustained the grand chord, while his ripped-open heart maintained the connection to his ancestral bond to the realm. He was wild earth; and flawed man; and consummate melody; a dynamic balance spinning in glorious triad over the raging void.

Braided into the confluent harmony just retrieved, the land granted him knowledge of others. One by one, the songs of the lanes that crossed through his kingdom were surrendered like silken bridle reins into his trembling hands.

Arithon added them. And lane flux responded to pitch, tone, and timing, exactingly meted out. The bard felt the diverted flow ease and broaden, tamed as its concentrated currents fanned out. Multiple channels absorbed their raw kick, force released into peace like calmed water. Under his cheek, the stone roots of the Mathorns rang out, their vibration lifted to resonance.

He had no breath to laugh, and no mind to rejoice, as the link held, by his desperate, obdurate will, and by nothing less than pure miracle.

Far off, at Rockfell, Kharadmon sank weeping to his knees. Sunk in flesh not his own, in tender remorse, he held Dakar's burned hands clutched to his heaving chest.

Beaten to wisped rags, the spirit of Luhaine knitted torn seals. Then he slackened his work, dumbly awestruck. He stilled to observe through discorporate awareness, as the lane channels raised across Arithon's kingdom flared and burned, released to their glory of exalted healing. White light burst in showers across the sere ground. In cold soil, chilled seeds quickened, straining toward spring germination. Ermine mated, and wolves ran, leaping in revitalized ecstasy. Overhead, the vast vortices of storm winds dispersed. The whipped clouds of cyclone eased and settled. On the Eltair coast, and above the high passes of the Skyshiels, snowfall transformed on a breath into a sluice of warm rain.

Across Daon Ramon Barrens, deer raised inquiring heads from their browsing. Perched hawks roused ruffled feathers and blinked. Other small creatures sunk in warm hibernation stirred and stretched, and dreamed of snowmelt and awakening. The roused lane forces played the chord of grand life force in purling light across latitude. Throughout Rathain, from the eastshore harbors to the coves of Instrell Bay, the iron grasp of an unnatural winter snapped, and at one breath, shattered.

A suspended instant saw the winds dance, exultant.

Then the noon crest of the equinox passed over Rockfell Peak. Its course left the patched integrity of the inner wards still intact. The guarded pit at its heart, where Desh-thiere lay imprisoned, maintained its ring of sealed silence. Where the course of the diverted currents had crossed, no harm to the mountain beyond a few craze marks of slag, and an array of scorched lines on dark rock.

In the Mathorns, slumped under a mottled sky, Arithon received a last, fleeting impression: of Dakar collapsed, his fast, distressed breathing held stable by Kharadmon.

Then the lane flux released him. His overtaxed senses shrank to a pinpoint, then spiraled away into unfathomable darkness.

Arithon did not feel the anxious hands of the scout, shaking, and failing to rouse him. He remained, tumbled senseless, as the other clansman knelt at his side, exclaiming in consternation. The pair raised him from the snow with painstaking care. They settled him over the gray's saddle and, in slow stages, bore him to the next dell, where a small spring bubbled beneath a thin screen of alders. Warmed and tended by his solicitous escort, he did not dream. Soon the first, stirring fevers of backlash stormed through his frame. He shivered, flicked over the high brink of delirium. His blank, opened eyes made no sense of the sight of the golden eagle who perched, unobtrusive and still, in the tree overhead to observe him.

Far westward, a strained hour of wait reached its ending at Althain Tower. A faint flush of rose stained Sethvir's hollowed cheeks where he lay, propped against linen pillows. The adepts who stood vigil maintained their posts to the right and left of his bedside. Then movement returned, a release of cranked tension marked by a long, soundless sigh as the Sorcerer stirred back to wakefulness.

No one rushed him with questions. The lady smoothed out a crease in his blanket, while the younger man standing witness arose, found the striker, and lit a fresh candle.

'It is accomplished,' Sethvir murmured, his syllables slurred as he rose from the depths of a seer's trance that had borne him far outside the veil.

The adepts bowed their heads in the brightening flare of gold light. Man and woman, the pair gave silent thanks for the miracle: that equinox noon had passed over Rockfell, without seeding a widespread disaster.

They waited, braced for the inevitable toll of wrought damage. The Warden presently opened his eyes, their unfocused depths the sheet-lace tinge of sea breakers, rolling shoreward at dawn in midsummer. Still diffused by an awareness spanned over an incomprehensible distance, Sethvir dredged up a thin whisper and pronounced, 'You can stand down. Fate's hand is averted. The peril posed by the equinox flux lies behind us.'

'Blessed Ath!' the woman adept intoned, grateful. 'Then your two colleagues and the spellbinder triumphed?'

'No.' Sethvir gave a fractional shake of his head. The wonder he had witnessed poured through in that moment, and lit him like light from within. 'In fact, they failed.' His gaze dropped, a suspect, moist brilliance masked behind closed lids and a snow-white veiling of lashes.

'Then how?' the young male witness asked, diffident, too awed to expect a clear answer.

For a moment, the stilled chamber held no movement beyond the tremulous flicker of candleflame. Then Sethvir's beard stirred; he smiled, shook his head yet again, this time in bemused, laughing wonderment. 'Kharadmon called upon Rathain's crown prince,' he admitted. 'A step of innovative genius, but bearing a frightening risk. Yet the bold step did not fall short. Arithon's talents as Masterbard found expression through his sovereign tie to the land.'

'Then he stood in the breach in his power as Rathain's vested high king?' the witness filled in, close to speechless before profound startlement.

He received Sethvir's patient refutation. 'Not that. Arithon couldn't.' The Sorcerer mustered his patience and explained. 'Our testy Teir's'Ffalenn has never been crowned. He has yet to receive the ritual initiations of air, fire, and water, that attend a high king's accession. Only the earth bond was made, by tradition, on the hour he was sanctioned as crown prince. The silver circlet marked his oath at Etarra, and sealed a union made with the land. The crux of event forced that rite to consummation. Rockfell was saved by that sacrifice.'

Touched by the first, icy finger of doom, the lady adept ventured the difficult question. 'Sacrifice?'

Sethvir nodded, his wise features saddened. 'His Grace called upon the Paravian ritual. He wakened three lanes through the tones of their primal song. Those flux lines now resonate to the Great Mystery in Rathain. Sundown and midnight, the cry of vibration cannot help but cross over latitude twice more, raising the keys of renewal and healing. Athera may rejoice, but human misunderstanding will shape its double-edged sword of mixed blessing.'

Comprehension dawned. Consternation raised a glance of dismay shared between the adepts. Arithon Teir's'Ffalenn had tapped his bright talent and birthright, and brought an unlooked-for reprieve. There would be green fields, where there might have been famine, and restoration of harmonic balance. But only in the kingdoms to the east. Lanes in Tysan and Havish had not been summoned into the dance, and there, the imbalance of Morriel's wrought backlash would linger. The death grip of winter would not release in time to bring late-sown crops to fall harvest.

The equinox would ride its course through two more crests and surges. As forests and wildlands, and the stressed forces of weather flourished and settled in rebirth, Rathain's towns would be dealt a mixed blessing.

'For today's bright rising, a bitter price yet to reap,' Sethvir allowed, and detailed the opening gist of his point through a shared sequence of imagery . . .

In the city of Jaelot, for the third time, the active resonance of lane forces caused one of the guard towers to crack; the oak window frames of the Mayor's mansion sprouted the shoots of green leaves, and a mad beggar in the square prophesied aloud to passersby that the guard company ridden into Daon Ramon Barrens had met death and ruin at the hand of the Master of Shadow . . .

At Etarra, the staid brick walls trembled and shook as the foundation stone of the mountains screamed aloud. The sustained, belling note burst stoutly locked doors and caused the bounty gold in the treasury to flow molten inside the locked vaults. 'Battle!' the sunwheel priest exhorted the guild ministers, who gathered in chattering fear. 'Call the garrison to arms, for there will be a clash of force in Daon Ramon between the dark powers and the Light . . .'

Elsewhere, a warm, falling rain softened the snow to slush and chill

547

rivulets. Over soggy ground, through gray puddled melt, the army of Lysaer s'Ilessid drove north. Their dedication was not blunted, but reforged by fear for the fact that the black-stone peaks of the Mathorns had rung aloud, an ominous, uncanny chord of wild sound named as an evil wrought by the Spinner of Darkness . . .

At Althain, the male adept closed unsteady fingers over Sethvir's limp wrist. 'Enough. We have seen enough.'

His grief had no words, since the full course of the equinox had yet to reach completion. The grand chord of the mysteries had been raised, with the advent of sunset, then midnight to come. The lane crests would rise in bound harmony through two more rounds of exalted confluence.

That blessed passage, so long denied, could not do other than raise mayhem across every walled city in Rathain, a false testimonial of damning proportions.

The witness clasped his beautiful hands over Sethvir's motionless palm. 'We must hold out hope. Given such gifts of grace and resourcefulness, and the help of loyal clansmen, surely Arithon of Rathain can be spared from the swords and the hatred of enemies. The light of Ath's grace moves within him, as a man born to flesh with such talent.'

Sethvir never moved. His seamed eyes stayed closed, but not in the peace of tranquillity. For Ath's hand was not alone, on that hour, when the course of Arithon's fate cast him into the dark shoals of jeopardy. Althain's Warden did not mention the last image withheld, of the Prince of Rathain tossed by the wracking throes of a backlash that mounted to dangerous severity. Nearby, a golden eagle ruffled broad wings in the rain. The bird cocked his head, his avid gaze watchful, while the soft, southern breezes that heralded spring flung diamond-bright runoff from rock ledge and fir branch and spruce.

First Recovery

Fionn Areth awakened to an indignant slap of cold wind. Bleary with sleep, he grumbled complaint, then snapped open offended green eyes as an intrusive draft whisked off the blankets that covered him. The next gust razed his uncovered cheek, unpleasantly bracing as a facedown tumble into an ice-crusted snowdrift.

'Fiends plague! Not an iyat!' he swore on a steamed breath. He pounced, snagged back the errant wool, then waited through a testing pause to see whether the cloth would turn unruly and try to flap out of his grasp. Unpossessed, the innocuous wool remained limp. Alert despite his better sensibilities, Fionn Areth settled back. Eyes shut, he burrowed into the lost warmth of his bedding, not yet reconciled to the intrusive stab of bright sunlight. Cursed if he would surrender the dark comfort of sleep for another inhospitable day in the forbidding heights of the Skyshiels.

A second gyre of air funneled down, its vexing persistence without quarter. The thick blanket was snatched clean away from Fionn Areth's curled frame. His furious lunge missed.

Then a tart voice addressed through the whistling, rank breeze, 'Roust up, goatherd! You're needed.'

Outraged, Fionn Areth shoved tangled hair from his face. He spat out the strands that had snagged in his teeth and blinked into the glare of midday.

'Piss and white lightning!' he swore in his thick grasslands dialect. 'It's damned well already tomorrow!' Embarrassment mottled his cheeks to a flush. Never since his last sick day in childhood had he snored like a sluggard past daybreak.

Be damned again if he intended to rise in good temper while a Sorcerer's haunt tried to accost him. Flat on his back, he sucked in an offended breath. 'Go away. Flit! I'm not playing the part of your servant.'

Luhaine outwaited youthful rebellion. Poised in sly expectation, he was content to let impatience and curiosity carry the war with recalcitrance.

Fionn Areth hardened his mouth, battling to ignore the enticement of his avid senses. Around him, the air wore the sharp taint of char, touched by a lingering, fresh reek of ozone. He flung a forearm over his face, obstinate enough to reject all morbid view of the immoral doings of mages. 'Why not leave me alone? Or better, kite off through the sky, and maybe butt-hump a moonbeam. I'm tired.'

Yet even after wrestling the equinox tides through a night and half of the day, Luhaine of the Fellowship was no spirit to rise to a baiting framed in crude language. In arctic agreement, he said, 'You can sleep, then, and let Dakar die. If that happens, by my personal request, Davien's sentinel guardians won't let you depart from Rockfell Peak unchallenged.'

Distempered, distrustful, Fionn Areth sat up. 'Save your henchman yourself, and your lost prince as well.' He tossed back his snarled mane of black hair, scratched the stubble erupted like wire from his chin. 'I'm through being everybody's string puppet.'

Luhaine forwent argument. Invisible amid the silver-bright sunlight dazzling off Rockfell's coped cornices, he bided, a pool of frigid calm skirted by the moving play of the winds. A lapis enamel dome of clear sky lay floored in carded fleece cloud banks. The buried valley below, with its blanketing forest, and its secretive life of furred animals, seemed vanished out of the world.

Fionn Areth shrugged his aching, stiff shoulders, painfully aware he had rested too long on chill rock. He disdained to examine the face of the mountain, would not look back to see whether the eerie portal the Sorcerers had opened still existed. First move, the moment he regained his feet, he unbuttoned the flap on his trousers and relieved himself over the brink.

The stream fell a disconcertingly long way, broken like scintillant jewels in the extended plunge down the abyss.

Sensitized to the punch-cut void of permafrost at his back,

Fionn Areth damped back a shiver. 'If Dakar's in trouble, who's to blame anyway? Last I saw, your colleague was driving him into a foaming fit of possession.'

The chill at his back grew strikingly colder, more silent than silence itself.

The barren shelf of rock offered nothing by way of diversion. Fionn Areth pridefully mastered the nagging urge to shed his pride and glance around. He felt smug, to be holding his ground with impunity, until the suspended quiet between gusts let him realize the moan at his back was not caused by natural weather.

Unease turned his head, before he could think.

First sight to greet him was a pair of burned hands, groping and scrabbling in distress. Dakar was sprawled facedown in a heap across the mountain chamber's uncanny threshold. His palms were a weeping mass of raw blisters, and his suffering raised Fionn to fury. 'Your damned murdering colleague has killed him!'

Luhaine corrected with acidic restraint, 'Right now, Kharadmon is the only thing keeping him breathing. We can heal the damage, but not before his body has been given time to restabilize. Which is why I've respectfully asked for your help.'

Fists clenched on his hips, dark eyebrows snarled with distrust, Fionn Areth vented a barked laugh. 'What, no apologies for yesterday's rudeness, or your threats of hurling me over the cliffside?'

'I won't change that opinion,' pronounced Luhaine, as stubborn. 'You have yet to show you're worth much at all, beyond abusing the innocent air for uncivil comments and arguing.'

'Oh, you could puff bladders for floats with such noise!' His rancor dissolved into startled snide humor, Fionn Areth stretched the last kink from his sturdy frame. 'I'm not excited. The clerk who used to tally our chamois spoke the same stuffy way. His big, windy lectures used to tie my great-uncle Poirey in stitches till he rolled like a fish on a streambank.'

'Yokel, I'm not concerned with your mud-wallowed relative,' Luhaine huffed, at last something more than offended. His presence acquired a shaved edge, brittle as frost strung on cobweb. 'Yes or no. Will you help Dakar, or not?'

Fionn Areth glared back, still armed in bristled defiance. 'What do you want me to do?'

He turned on his heel, advanced two mincing steps toward an entry that drove him to gooseflesh and cat nerves. Then he lowered the petrified angle of his chin and gave Dakar's injuries his flinching inspection.

'Salve and bandages, first.' Luhaine was ever succinct, when exasperated. 'Those are strapped in the pack.' The vexation still galled, that existence as a discorporate spirit made even simple tasks difficult. His flat state of exhaustion pitched his tone to cranked worry. 'Also, could you fill both the pannikins with snow? While you dress Dakar's burns, I'll boil the water. You'll find herbs in the Mad Prophet's satchel for tisanes. I'll say which to use. There's also a lichen that's easily foraged at this time of year on the mountain.'

'Well, if I'm not book learned, you won't find me squeamish,' Fionn Areth retorted. Changeable as a weathercock, he could scarcely stem his flooding burst of contrition. Dakar's welted palms were ugly and seeping. The brosy curve of his cheek sagged, dull gray. The fast, shallow breaths rasped through slack lips, sounding distressed as those animals the goat gelders in Araethura always slaughtered as lost beyond remedy.

Luhaine's snappish mood eased. In fact, the young man was good with his hands. His rough, calloused strength held surprising gentleness as he worked salve into Dakar's scoured flesh. He made neat work of the bandages, as well, and managed the snow compress, steady enough under Luhaine's detailed instruction. The brewed remedy dripped into Dakar's mouth with a twist of clean rag slowly eased the dangerous, raced pulse and stertorous breathing.

'You count all this worth it?' Fionn Areth asked later, picking his way in precarious steps over ridged ice and slick rock. He bent, now and then, at the Sorcerer's direction, and pried windburned lichens from Rockfell's seamed face with his knife.

'In fact, yes.' The nexus of cold that was Luhaine came and went at juxtaposed intervals, tacking over the cliffside below, as he selected which plants should be harvested. Now and then, sheeting flares of gold light marked a pause as he worked minor spellcraft to ease stress from the stone so severely tested at noontide. 'If Dakar had given one whit less than everything he had, you would have been left with no mountain to stand on. The whole of this world would have perished.'

Close enough to make Fionn Areth start, Luhaine finished, flat serious. 'We all owe our well-being to your crown prince.'

'Arithon?' Fionn Areth clawed for a handhold as he slid on the unstable footing. Still venting mixed feelings, he inquired, 'Then the Master of Shadow reached safety?'

'That's his Grace, to you. Don't forget, he's your liege,' Luhaine supplied in bracing correction. 'You've been his guest, and he once saved your life. And no, to answer your impertinence. His survival is still in grave jeopardy.'

So grave, in fact, that Sethvir had been reticent with details through the disturbing contact exchanged between Rockfell and Althain Tower. Given tacit awareness of just how precariously hard Kharadmon worked to curb Dakar's raging fever, Luhaine's soulful sigh loosed a vagrant whistle of breeze. Such a severe backlash was inevitable, wrought by energetic imbalance and a massive exposure to the currents of untempered lane force. The Sorcerer feared to speculate upon Arithon's condition. Nor had he dared ask what succor might be found on the isolate, high slopes of the Mathorns, with Lysaer's crack troop of Etarrans bound under Sulfin Evend's command and marching to claim their blood vengeance.

'. . . can leave here,' Fionn Areth was saying. At some point, scarcely noticed, he had sat down to rest. The ice between his tucked-up feet was jabbed into shards, chipped by his knife in a fit of volatile impatience.

Luhaine gyrated down from a vantage point hundreds of feet in the air. 'Is your poke filled?'

'Not counting the gravel bits?' Fionn Areth raised slanting eyebrows, yanked off his gloves with his teeth, and opened for inspection the small sack that Dakar used to store tinder. 'Never mind this ledge, anyway,' he mumbled through wadded leather. 'I *meant*, when can we get off of this Ath-forsaken mountaintop?'

'Take care how you slander the ground where you're standing. No one's going anywhere before Dakar recovers.' Luhaine's chilly presence sieved through the sack's contents, ejecting the hollowed-out husk of a beetle, and something else dubious and brown-colored. 'You can travel anywhere you please after that. No Sorcerer will stop you. But the spellbinder won't be released from our company until the wardings that guard Rockfell are resealed.'

'How generous.' Fionn Areth retied the poke, donned his damp gloves, and scrubbed at the gooseflesh raised on his arms by the Sorcerer's eddying presence. 'By that I expect you think Dakar will survive?'

'He has no other choice,' Luhaine said, glum. A gyrating wind devil of flurried ice, he crossed the sunlit expanse of the snowfield. The dearth of sound options rankled his methodical nature. Verrain was too beset at Methisle to be summoned to stand as relief. Irony of ironies, the brilliance of Arithon's success had exacerbated an already thorny list of troubles. The methspawn contained by the late-winter ice were now at large in the hot springs, restlessly seething to launch in migration the minute the spring melt opened the waters of Methlas Lake. As Fionn Areth lagged, the Sorcerer admonished, 'Hurry on. The lichens you have are sufficient.'

The mismatched pair, spirit Sorcerer and goatherd, picked their separate ways back to the ledge. At the entry to Rockfell Pit, they found Dakar wakeful, and seated inside, enthroned like a toad in a nest made from saddle packs and blankets.

'What took so long?' he inquired in Kharadmon's whetted consonants. 'If you had to pick daisies and admire the scenery, surely *someone* could have stayed to assist?' Ignoring Fionn Areth's high yelp of startlement, the Sorcerer rolled the Mad Prophet's mooncalf eyes. 'If you laugh,' he snarled at Luhaine, 'I shall thrash you to a gibbering wisp! Don't claim you've lived as a spirit so long, you've forgotten the disgusting necessities attending the burden of flesh.'

'Should I laugh?' Luhaine's prim delicacy would have caused butter to transfigure rather than melt.

Over Dakar's ludicrous bristle of beard, Kharadmon blushed virgin pink. 'This body's too weak to stand upright,' he growled. 'That's a problem, since we're also splitting with an almighty need to take a piss.'

Fionn Areth choked and sat down like dropped stone. He crushed mirthful shrieks behind mittened hands, until tears streaked his windburned cheeks.

Kharadmon was forced to wait, fuming, until the young man's paroxysm subsided. The Araethurian arose at due length. Still gasping, he assisted the fat prophet's bulk onto its feet. He had to manage the undoing of buttons as well, and learned more picturesque language through that undignified interval than Dakar had acquired in five centuries of debauch, perusing the dockside brothels.

Bared at last to seek urgent relief, Kharadmon ceased his cursing.

As his strangling impulse to chortle ran down, Fionn Areth demanded point-blank, 'What have you done to Dakar?'

Through a grunt as the Mad Prophet's bladder eased enough to stop hurting, the Sorcerer glowered askance. 'Address me like that, and the wind might reverse and serve you up a good dousing.'

'Not if you still want my shoulder to lean on.' Fionn Areth smiled, his reasonable sweetness all poison.

Kharadmon tipped up Dakar's tangled head, narrowed bloodshot eyes, and glared into the hovering, arctic silence that marked Luhaine's watchful presence. 'Take fair warning, I'll be nursing a festering grudge!'

Then, as Fionn Areth prepared to repeat his nagging question, Kharadmon let fly with sharp venom, 'Dakar's asleep. Yes, and suffering with illness! So be a smart boy and sit us back down.'

When Fionn Areth showed signs of planting his feet, Dakar's features purpled, straitly vexed.

Before Kharadmon could unleash more invective, Luhaine interjected, 'We all overreached our wise limits, no surprise.' He added in judicious explanation, 'We were handling earthforce enough to immolate half of the continent. The lane currents are settled. However, neither Kharadmon or myself have passed through the process unscathed.'

Fionn Areth crossed his arms, stiff-shouldered and still dubious.

Kharadmon provoked with more than his usual savagery, discomfited by pain and sore joints. 'Fool goatherd, why do you think you're needed to fetch and carry and wrap bandages? Were we Fellowship Sorcerers whole in ourselves, we could heal simple injuries without medicines! Dakar himself can do that, on his good days. But being a spirit embodied, just now, he's suffering a physical reaction. This damned raging headache would shame the fires of Sithaer's eighth pit!'

'That means, Kharadmon hurts as well,' Luhaine supplied in salacious remonstrance. His entreaty, 'Stay wise, boy, and don't try his temper,' collided headlong with his colleague's retort.

'Since I need a semblance of peace to recoup, and Dakar couldn't stop bending double to throw up, we agreed. He's better off out of the way.' Kharadmon stopped, wrung out a vehement breath, and shook a damp hank of cinnamon hair from the puffy sills of his eyes. Far removed from his preference for cool equanimity, he fixed his predator's stare on the Araethurian beside him. 'Now, since those lichens you've gathered hold the remedy to lift this crushing headache, will you please unscramble the intelligence Ath gave to live worms? *I need to sit down.* We'll all do very nicely if you could find the grace to follow Luhaine's instructions.'

'I'm not going up to that portal again,' Fionn Areth declared, his hot spurt of fear forced through as belligerence. 'Whatever's inside makes my teeth hurt.'

'Mine, too,' Kharadmon admitted with sudden, limp weariness.

As Luhaine whirled off in a flurry of agitation, the Sorcerer gave up trying to fasten bone buttons with wrapped hands. In response to an unspoken jibe from his colleague, he dredged up the Mad Prophet's most plaintive shrug, and confessed, 'Yes, a new leak has sprung in the ward seals. I was holding it stable, before Dakar's bladder laid siege to my efforts. You think it's grown worse? Then you'll just have to hold the breach stable while Fionn Areth mixes the posset for pain. Soon after that, if the sky doesn't fall, I ought to be fit to resume work.'

Strung to a note of horror and dismay, Luhaine shrieked from beyond the black portal, 'Merciful Ath! That's no minor breach! We're both going to be tied here until Dakar's strength is restored and each layer of the wards is rebuilt.'

As somber, Kharadmon bowed his unkempt head. Unreconciled to the body where he maintained a residence of uncomfortable necessity, he gave his last word in unspoken thought, wrung to grief and impotent helplessness. *'We are shackled, my friend. Chained here by fate and the murdering works of the meddlers we once sent to exile through Southgate.'*

Luhaine's aroused presence spun down. Poised above the swept ledge, to mage-sight a roiled play of interlaced light against Rockfell's gaping portal, he said, *'Now I am worried. You realize, neither one of us can break free to honor Sethvir's request? We can't send help. Prince Arithon could die in the throes of the fever he's bound to suffer in backlash.'*

Kharadmon had no comfort to offer. No condolence crafted in any world's language held the balm to ease that harsh truth.

Luhaine, lead stubborn, ground on to belabor the frighteningly obvious corollary. *'But that leaves—'*

'Don't speak that name!' Kharadmon cut him off. As apprehensive himself, for once stripped of his prankish invective, he shivered against the staunch young man who propped his swaying bulk upright. *'We're too accursedly shorthanded to weep, far less do a thing in prevention.'*

'What's happened?' Fionn Areth demanded. A passing veil of cirrus raked the disk of the sun. Downslope, a transparent cloak of shade swept across the lockstepped mosaic of snowfield and rock. Blurred edges fell out of etched clarity. Suddenly cold, the Araethurian tightened his grip on the shoulder beneath Dakar's mantle. His plaintive tone added resonance to an already cruel despair. 'Something else has gone wretchedly wrong, hasn't it?'

'The whole world's upside down,' Kharadmon snapped. Drained wan, and bitterly disgusted, he left his trouser flap gaping and assayed a wobbling step forward. 'If you'll help this Prophet's ox frame off sore feet, and fix that confounded remedy, we can at least make a start setting one addled patch of Ath's wide creation back to rights.'

Divide

The depths of Arithon's fever-soaked dreams spiraled his mind through featureless darkness. He rode that black tide, wrung by savage desperation, and pursued by relentless, sharp terror. The Mistwraith's curse tore at him in force. Lose himself, let his frail self-possession fray away in delirium, and the legions of enemies stalking his mind through the quagmires of nightmare would have him.

Not formless dream, but relentless reality, the screaming clamor of instinct: Lysaer s'Ilessid invaded the Mathorns, with a troop of armed men, trained for the sole purpose of killing him.

Through the raced beat of blood through his veins, amid the stressed pain of a body unstrung by the recoiling cramps of raw backlash, Arithon wrestled that branding awareness. He resisted the pull of incessant need, strove to turn a deaf ear to the siren whispers that urged him to cease fighting the inevitable. The fickle voice never quieted, but spun him the honeyed promise of peace. He need only give in; embrace the beguiling ease of surrender, turn back, and engage the merciless directive to destroy the cursed seed of his hatred.

Lysaer s'Ilessid was marching.

The spiteful drive of Desh-thiere's cursed enmity battered at the locked gates of identity. Twisted passions flared up and eroded a boundary now fatally undermined by his unshielded handling of wild earth flux. Left miserably sick, Arithon curled into himself, the cool comforts of reason fallen behind. Ahead, the rough waters of uncharted peril pummeled him into the dark.

His set will was reduced to a spluttering flame, overwhelmingly besieged. As the hours passed, the conscious choice holding stark madness in check became worn, a thread strung across the howling abyss that would seal his annihilation.

Just once, through a feat of dogged exertion, he clawed back to wakeful awareness. He lay wrapped in blankets, still dressed, but not armed. Night sky overhead showed clear stars. A wolf pack howled in the distance. He must have cried out, or groaned as he surfaced, for the clan scout wearing the wolverine hat knelt over him, his unsmiling face stiffly anxious.

'Liege?' A cup touched his lips, cold with the mineral tang of water scooped from a puddle of snowmelt.

Eyes shut, suffering gut-wrenching cramps and muscles sucked hollow with lassitude, Arithon wet his mouth. He swallowed, then forced the reserves to frame speech. 'Get me up. Lash me onto my horse.'

The scout withdrew the cup in stark shock. 'But my liege! You're—'

'For mercy, just listen! Whatever the cost, for my life's sake, keep moving!' Arithon subsided against the rough blanket that pillowed his sweat-runneled cheek. 'Strap my sword on me. We have to press northward.' Against the dragging pull of spent strength, and the clamor of curse-stressed awareness, he stayed adamant. 'Or else give the enemy his prize while I fail you. Hold me here, and we die for your pity. The insane designs of Desh-thiere's geas cannot do other than triumph.'

He resurfaced again, jolted briefly aware as competent hands heaved him back into the saddle. Every jarring move pained him. The backlash he suffered bit with fell vengeance, cramps in his belly like twisting, hot knives, and his limbs rendered weak by a nerve storm of palsy that could do nothing except grow worse. Breathing hurt. His lungs and chest felt strapped in hot lead, and his ribs, laced in knots by the fever. When someone's voice pleaded to lift him down, he rejected the sympathy, cursing.

Much later, the crust on his swollen lids cracked. The dazzle of snow glare struck through his eyes and rammed heated rods through his brain. Through the melodious rush of the breaking spring melt, he measured the passage of tormented seconds by the clangor of shod hooves on rock. Wheeling vertigo suggested ascent up a slope of snagged boulders. Arithon assembled painstaking awareness. His flesh felt wrung to a flaccid rag. An ice compress, packed in cloth, had been tied against the burning, tight skin of his forehead. Marred hearing netted him snatches of birdsong, the high notes fallen distorted through the ringing dissonance of his fever.

He struggled, not knowing how long he had drifted, or how far the horse's gait carried him. Not far enough to find quiet or win surcease: the eddying pull of the Mistwraith's curse twisted each thought like hot wire. Moment by raw moment, its hold gnawed away the integrity of his barriers.

The effort required to sustain staunch denial slid him back down into darkness. He refused to let go, even then. The abraded shreds of his will could be bound to the ordered meter of cantrips. He chose the first lines of the prayer of prime law, phrased in the lyric Paravian, and used by Ath's adepts for self-discipline and release. *'I speak peace, I breathe peace, I live peace, for all of my days, birth to death.'*

Over and over, against Desh-thiere's assault of ravening hatred, Arithon affirmed his desperate plea for deliverance and protection . . .

By nightfall, his chanting had come unraveled to ripping, coarse gasps and slurred phrases. The clan scout who walked at the horse's head paused, his fingers clenched hard on the bridle.

'No, he's not raving,' he answered his fellow. The gray horse stamped in the shadow of the firs, while day faded over the bleak scarps of the ridges, and the afterglow of sunset stained high-flying cirrus to bloodred wisps overhead. The clansman listened through the next tortured line. 'His phrasing's still lucid, just barely.' He stripped off his glove, laid the back of his hand against the prince's slack face, then recoiled, stunned breathless. 'Merciful Ath! There are limits.'

The younger clansman wheeled his horse and rode back, readied weapons and flamboyant earring masked in the fast falling gloom. 'Bad news?' While the rising wind fluttered the horses' tucked tails, he snugged down his mantle, and winced at the sting of the sore newly chafed on his knee. 'Do you think we're going to lose him?'

'I don't know.' Hewall jammed down his piebald fur hat, his shrug a cranked gesture of misery. 'He's very far gone. Skin's a dry furnace. Got muscles all tied into shivering knots. You ask me, he can't tolerate very much more. Merciful maker, the helplessness wrings me! I can't stand to watch him slip over the edge.'

'Then I suggest that you stop,' said a crisp voice ahead of them.

Both scouts bounded into a violent start. Spun on matched reflex, with weapons unsheathed, they wildly scanned their surroundings. Yet whoever approached, his presence stayed masked. Ahead, the swept snow lay unmarred as spread silk. No movement strained through the thin stand of firs, nestled into the stony rise of the crest.

'Or not,' the speaker resumed, *far too close*.

A knife might pose problems, except the attacker must break out of cover to throw. A man set in ambush would scarcely talk first, and this stranger's diction was not hostile, or townborn. In phrasing marked out by the antique lilt inflected by fluent Paravian, he added, 'Whatever you choose, I'm no threat to your liege.'

'Speaks like a Sorcerer,' the younger scout whispered.

Less prone to entangle himself sorting out riddles, Hewall snapped out a challenge. 'Who are you? Show yourself!'

For answer, the fellow stepped into view. His light-footed presence emerged quiet as a breath, uncannily detached from the screen of the trees. He approached with no disturbed rustle of needles; no cracked ice spilled from capped branches. He was lean and well made, richly clad for the wilds, in brushed suede leggings and soft boots topped with lynx fur. If he carried a blade, he would not be drawing at speed, with the rest of him wrapped in a russet cloak pinned with a round silver brooch.

Closer, he came, empty-handed. His forthright manner did little to placate the unsettled scouts. He moved like a stalker, his rugged stride easy. Bareheaded, with a shock of shoulder-length hair streaked to white at the temples, he had sharply creased features fitted over ascetic angles of bone. Faint moonlight traced a firm mouth, a hawk nose, but did nothing to illumine his strikingly piercing dark eyes. Stopped at arm's length, his presence screamed power as he offered in unruffled courtesy, 'If you wish, I might lend assistance.'

Hewall expelled a rattled breath. 'You were sent by the Fellowship?'

The man smiled, unspeaking. The understated bow he returned reassured, for its seamless elegance. He gestured toward the bundle of blankets, and paused, closely listening, as Rathain's stricken prince labored through another affirmation. 'His Grace is not in a good way. Shall we see what can be done for him?'

'He's grown steadily worse,' the younger scout blurted, frustration outstripping his innate sense of caution. He felt the instant, bearing pressure of the stranger's regard, demanding as a lover's touch upon him. Sword lowered, he flushed to sweating embarrassment. 'Nor are we versed in the remedies to treat him. What other choice do we have?'

'You can shield his mind from Desh-thiere's geas?' Hewall ventured, his braced stance unmoved, and his raised sword arm too stiff, as he fought to stay sensibly guarded.

'I don't know,' said the stranger. 'For that, I would have to examine him.' He clasped his bare hands, perhaps to contain his impatience. 'I don't wish to press, but his enemies are moving. Every lost second is critical.'

From the gray's back, a jagged tear in the meter as Arithon broke his recitation. His frame convulsed, head to foot, in a wracking, sharp cramp, while the upset horse under him sidled. Though the scout tugged the bridle and arrested the movement, its burden was unavoidably jostled. Arithon gasped in pain, but did not regain waking awareness. Still trapped in the narrows where delirium and consciousness raged in the throes of doomed struggle, he snarled a curse, then fought and regrouped savaged wits. At length, he picked up his dropped line of verse, the words jerked like stones through clenched teeth.

'I can't help him at all if you stall for much longer,' the stranger said, tart. His mood all at once seemed volatile as hazed smoke, to disperse at the whim of the breeze.

'If you're Fellowship sent, we've no cause to distrust you.' Hewall slammed his sword, ringing, back into his sheath and told the young scout to offer the reins of the gray.

But the cloaked man refused him, the corners of his mouth a tucked pleat of graven amusement. 'No need to go anywhere.' His bare hands raised, palm open, he eased closer. 'His Grace overextended his mortal faculties, channeling unrefined earth flux. The worst imbalance in his aura can be cleared by informed touch. You need disturb nothing.' A nod to the young scout, 'If you will, simply steady the horse.'

Arithon's forced recitation snapped off, leaving uneasy silence as the clansman braced his stance and firmed his grasp on the gray's reins.

The stranger stepped past him, his assurance unthreatened. His glance of deep irony acknowledged Hewall, judiciously placed to keep guard on his opposite side. 'Believe this,' he stated, his resonant baritone uninflected enough to seem mocking, 'For the service rendered to Athera this equinox, Arithon of Rathain is due my undying respect.'

He had neat, tapered fingers, adorned with a silver ring

patterned with interlocked crescents. Its glittering citrine setting displayed no arcane powers as he laid his spread hands over Arithon's dark hair. There, his touch lingered, sensuous, as though he enjoyed a sculptor's appreciation for the nuance of texture and form. He cradled the prince's head, his fierce concentration surveying the landscape of Arithon's unshielded face.

'Oh, my leashed wild falcon!' he exclaimed, his let breath of air too soft to overhear. Like the flare of sparked flame, his expression changed, for one fleeting instant aroused to captivated fascination.

The odd moment passed. His features again revealed nothing beyond the wear carved by rugged, long life, and an unruffled detachment.

Through the interval while he stood motionless, the night constellations wheeled overhead. A low-lying cloud bank edged in from the south, its drifting advance moist with thaw. No wind stirred the firs. The night-hunting wolves had finished their chorus under the high-riding arc of the moon. The hole in the silence struck by Arithon's quiet left only the plumed breath of the horses, ephemeral as drifted spirit light.

Then, without warning, Arithon stirred. His unseeing eyes flicked wide open, and he blurted, 'But I don't know you!'

The stranger released him. Hedged by nervous clan scouts, he met their renewed distrust with a bemused headshake. 'No harm done. Your prince is mage-trained. He carries an array of extremely well guarded barriers.' In rueful amazement, his peaked eyebrows lifted. 'Unusually strong ones, to hold past waking consciousness.'

'You can't heal him,' said Hewall, distressed. He shifted stance, his furtive right hand still relentlessly poised to draw steel.

'Not safely, not this way,' the stranger confessed. Lightless black, the eyes in their deep, shadowed sockets swept away and regarded the troublesome s'Ffalenn subject, once more draped obliviously limp. As though two riled scouts were not primed for assault a sword's easy thrust from his back, he kept speaking. 'If I asked, your prince would lower those defenses. But in staying guarded, he's also resisting the draw of the Mistwraith's laid curse. An enemy might risk his exposure. I won't.' He turned, sharp and sudden. '*Do you have a water flask?*'

The vehemence of the question set both clansmen aback.

The younger one answered. Perhaps more attuned to the ripe threat of danger, or perhaps the stranger's self-contained courtesy shot warning like cold through his gut. 'If you're a friend, Hewall bears a horn flask.'

'The water is yours, but you must give your name,' the older scout added, insistent.

Exasperation flexed the man's chisel-cut mouth. 'Asandir could not come. A deranged grimward prevents summons or contact. Sethvir lies ill at Althain Tower. Kharadmon and Luhaine are repairing wards, which are failing, at Rockfell Peak.' Under starlight and the wan gleam of the moon, the set stone on his finger seemed a lit spark, against his anonymous clothing. 'Traithe is too far, and would be endangered. There is no one else, and if I were your liege's enemy, I would not stand here at all.'

'You've not said you're his friend,' the elder scout noted. Aware his companion had all but stopped breathing, he plowed on with mulish bluntness, 'Arithon is sanctioned as Prince of Rathain, whose late crowned ancestor bled and died at the hands of a mob in the uprising. By all means, as you wish, let us not say your name, if you are who you must be, Sorcerer.'

'So do knives cut, and needles pull thread,' the self-contained visitor agreed, no longer equable or patient. 'If I wanted his Grace dead, why trifle? Your Teir's'Ffalenn would have seen his life forfeit the instant the last of his overthrown lineage returned to set foot on Athera!' The gold ember of the ring's stone moved in the dark as he extended his hand for the horn flask unslung from the clansman's shoulder. His steely, bright humor without amusement, he accepted the offered strap. 'Thank you, profoundly. I've been called many things. But never before this has anyone had the effrontery to name me a liar.'

'You don't lie,' the young scout allowed. He had the advantage, not being pinned down by the Sorcerer's sardonic, deep scrutiny. 'You don't murder, either. But history tells us you toy with men's lives. Why should we entrust you with this one?'

'I have no time for your plodding review of the past.' Trapped water gurgled as the Sorcerer changed his grip. He clasped the horn between his opposing palms, then glanced skyward, his shot silk hair tumbling free as a stallion's mane down his shoulders. 'The stakes are too high to waste thought or motion. Always, then or now, I act to forestall the pitfalls that shadow the future.'

No polite word of warning prefaced his burst of grand conjury. Blue light flared and crackled over the flask, a turbulent static that lanced between his poised fingertips. Darkness shattered. Limned in the dazzle, the Sorcerer's face was stamped pewter, his tall form unreeling a ribbon of cast shadow across the glaze-crusted snowbanks. The display flickered out. Ink nightfall returned. Far off, a wolf howled. The sigh of the breeze stirred the fir copse.

Flash-blinded and dazed, Hewall started as the flask was set back into his hands. The silver-capped horn was cool to his touch, its leather cord supple and unsinged. But a shimmer of phosphorescence trailed on the air like spun smoke as he fumbled the strap over his shoulder.

'Within two hours, your prince will awaken.' The Sorcerer crouched. Utterly without ceremony, he scribed a circle in the snow at his feet. Fire burned where his line traced, sheet gold and spitting as the ice underneath sublimated into lashed steam. The figure framed a dizzying view of Etarran headhunters with dogs, then a packed company of horsemen, surging over a boulder-strewn notch.

'That's Leynsgap!' cried the young scout, appalled. 'Blessed Ath! They're all but at our heels. We could be run down before morning.'

The Sorcerer looked up, poised as the arrow nocked to the drawn bow. 'I'll say this just once. Your prince will wake up, because Desh-thiere's curse will finally drive through the disorientation of backlash. When that happens, his Grace will be under assault. He'll have only minutes before his free will is broken down for all time. You must give him that flask. He will hear, through his bard's gift. Harmonic vibration will show him the spellcraft I've laid down for his healing. Let him decide for himself whether or not he will drink. If he does, then give him the fastest horse you possess. Tell him to ride for his life.'

No one interrupted as the fires whirled up. The image of Lysaer's advance line consumed in a crackling burst, then vanished without trace of smoke. The indented circle remained in the snow as the Sorcerer stood erect. 'Only one place at hand has wards of guard that can deter the Etarran Lord Commander. If put to the test, the same refuge might shelter your prince from the ills of Desh-thiere's curse.'

Amid blanketing night, the young clansman's features went ashen. 'No! Never there. Not the Maze of the Betrayer, which leads through Kewar Tunnel!'

The creature whose artistry had fashioned those caverns did not argue; his prosaic shrug skirted the thin edge of insult. 'Your prince's life is not in my hands. I leave you perfectly free to seek help however you can.'

He vanished. No warning, no move, no grand flourish; one

moment he stood, solid and breathing, his brows raised in caustic humor. Then he was *gone* without sound, and no breath of wind to mark his eldritch passage.

'Damned *fetch*!' snapped Hewall, wrung to cranked tension, and enraged by the trembling that spoiled a reliable grip on his sword hilt. 'Probably been spying on us all along, through the eyes of that wretched eagle.'

A sharpened voice contradicted from thin air, 'The eagle is mine, and an ally. As you choose, *if you ask*, he will guide you.'

The younger scout looped the gray's reins and bent over to brace his flushed face with scooped snow. Past the thunderstruck shock of the Sorcerer's parting, he examined the ground where the uncanny creature had stood. 'No fetch,' he said, shaken. 'Look. Those are boot prints. Whatever visitation we saw bore weight, and walked on two feet as a man.'

'The Betrayer was rendered discorporate by the Fellowship!' Hewall tugged his hide jacket close, as though sudden cold had fingered his heart. 'I don't trust the tricksy turn of his spells. Nor this witched water flask either.' He cast a discomposed glance right and left, then, beyond logic, straight upward. No eagle circled. Only stars burned serene over ramparts of bleak rock, and the snow-clad expanse of wild landscape. No voice pronounced reprimand. 'Damn the meddler to the hells of Sithaer's pit, anyway. I see no other option before us.'

'We should move on, and not lose more time quibbling.' The younger scout settled the gray gelding's reins and remounted, ripped to threadbare worry. 'Balefire and fiends plague the name of s'Ilessid! With trackers at Leynsgap, we would need help from Dharkaron's Black Horses to win his Grace free to the coast.'

'Man, take care what you wish for. Davien's visitation was enough!' Even with enemies riding their heels, Hewall could not shed his rattled composure. Stout as nails, he refused to return to the saddle until he had traced the Sorcerer's footsteps back to the stand of stunt firs.

Plain as plain, the trail stopped at the edge of the wood. No marked print went farther. Beyond, mottled snow quilted the ground, pocked with snapped twigs, and small craters where the ice clods had dropped off the wind-battered branches. Nothing alive had disturbed the masked ground, and nothing had walked through that twisted, meshed tangle of tree limbs.

Arithon roused near the end of the brutal, switchbacked climb that crested the great divide. The high, central ridge marked the spine of the Mathorns, and parted the headwaters north from south. The horses by then were sweated to lather, flanks heaving to draw the thin air. Moonset had ignited the stars to fierce brilliance against the black sky of high altitude.

If Hewall missed the shuddering gasp of Arithon's intaken breath, the young scout, behind, had no chance to speak out. The transition came fast, from the limp sprawl of unconsciousness into a thrashing, emergent awareness. The prince convulsed in the saddle, jerked short of a wrenching, failed effort to stifle his whimpering outcry. To keep him astride, his wrists were securely roped around the gelding's damp neck.

The half-stifled outburst resounded with anguish to raise the hair at the nape.

Breath expelled, Arithon shuddered through a knifing cramp. The stresses of backlash intensified with movement and ripped him to gagging nausea.

By then, Hewall had the gray gelding stopped. The pitch of the slope made everything difficult. To dismount would strain a horse's braced balance; to vault off would risk a turned ankle. Hewall wisely chose to stay astride. He unslung the water flask fast as he dared, while the young scout shouldered his mount forward to collect it. The spells had not diminished. A pale haze of light blurred the pendulum swing as the leather strap changed hands.

'Your Grace? Arithon,' addressed the young scout with spare clarity. His skilled handling settled his horse alongside. 'Here's a remedy made by a Sorcerer who may or may not wish you well. At your word, I'll dispose of it. You decide if you're fit to measure the risks.'

Arithon turned his head. His eyes were wide-open. The running sweat strung on skin and lashes welled like tears pressure-forced through taut flesh. His breathing was tortured, every wracked spasm savaged by pitiless conflict. 'Don't cut me free,' he cautioned through locked teeth. 'Just be silent. Allow me to listen.'

The scout, all but weeping, averted his glance. His liege's features had become a wracked animal's, human dignity shredded to rags. His spirit as well had been set under siege, the murderous directive of the Mistwraith's revenge raging like fire through dry brush. The core of fierce strength had long since been spent. Now, the hard-driving urge to wreak violence fast consumed what worn will still remained.

A fraught interval passed before Arithon mastered the self-command for clear speech. 'It's all right. The draught will help, not cause harm. No!' as the scout drew his knife to slash the ties binding his wrists. 'First, help me to drink.'

'Hewall, steady the gray.' The young scout hooked his reins through the crook of his elbow. Surrounded by snow and naked, black rock, and brushed by restless winds that were backing due south, he prayed the mare under him would not startle, or choose the wrong moment to shake dripping foam from her bit. Hollow with unease, he stripped off humid gloves, then worked the cork stopper free. The spelled water sloshed, without odor, but turned unearthly and strange: pearlescent light streamed from the neck of the horn, as though the liquid inside burned cold white.

'Steady,' the scout murmured. 'Here's the draught.' He reached out, touched flesh that recoiled under his palm with the reflex of a trapped cat. 'That's my hand. All right? Keep steady.' Murmuring as he might soothe a whipped animal, he cupped Arithon's cheek. Twisted sidewards in his saddle, the posture was awkward. He had to brace, hard, to damp the shuddering tremors wracking through Arithon's frame. 'Mercy upon us, mercy upon our unborn children,' the scout whispered in age-old clan benison. Then he touched the tipped rim of the horn to his prince's lips.

Arithon swallowed. Eyes squeezed shut, he finished the contents in carefully measured sips. For one queer instant, his form appeared hazed in light. Then the recoiling spasms eased up. A sigh escaped Arithon's rasped throat. Relief smoothed his dripping face into calm. The glance he returned in swift reassurance showed a wounding, sweet moment of gratitude.

'All right,' the scout whispered. 'Don't talk.' He looped the drained flask at his saddlebow, while Hewall observed, his knitted brow critical with worry.

For a drawn-out moment, the Prince of Rathain rested his forehead against the steamed warmth of his horse's neck. He sucked in a steady, scouring breath. Then he spoke, and his voice sounded lucid. 'Very carefully, draw Alithiel from my scabbard. If the sword doesn't glow, you can cut my wrists free.'

This time, even Hewall's stout courage snapped. He could not bear to watch the young scout set his hand to Alithiel's leather-wrapped grip. The black sword sheared free with a whining dissonance that caused Arithon a flinching, shocked gasp. But the sword's silvered inlay gleamed with no more than the chance-caught reflections of stars, whose Named essence the Athlien Paravians had entwined into song to enable her

568

ranging defense spells. A fraught second elapsed. The blade stayed unroused, its forged length parting air like black smoke, sliced by the pearlescent sheen of cold runes. Night quiet still reigned. Tension eased to the hissed gyre of wind over rock, and a sour, rasped clink as Hewall's lanky bay champed the bit.

'Thank you.' Arithon smiled, a fleeting release that scarcely smoothed the marks of a bruising exhaustion. He added a musical phrase in Paravian neither scout had the learning to translate. The untoward familiarity set them apart. Rathain's prince turned away, the unabashed tears falling in ribbons down his cheeks. 'Your service has been flawless. Mind and body, I'm whole. Your care has brought hope for me, after all.'

The strain was straight cruelty, that he dared not dismount to seek rest. Arithon knew. Resignation a palpable weight on his silence, he straightened his worn shoulders before anyone urged him. He asked nothing, but only gathered his dignity, waiting in hard-leashed control while the ties on his wrists were released.

Erect in the saddle, he loosened the gray's knotted reins on his own. The scout talked. His Grace listened, his head inclined an attentive fraction to one side. He did not interrupt the steady address, even through the shattering setback, that the route to the coast was not possible.

Chin turned ahead, his Grace of Rathain did not rail or curse. Only stated, with hammered determination, 'I'll ride on anyway. You both need not stay.'

The scout lost words.

Arithon accepted his sword back. His hand was cool, his grip calmly steady as he rammed the blade home in the scabbard.

'You won't go alone,' Hewall protested.

Arithon shortened his reins. He did not look back, but spurred his gray gelding up to the top of the slope. 'Hewall, not this time. A skilled escort saves nothing. If I lose my wits now, no one alive can react fast enough to deter me.'

Inarguable logic; of one mind, both clansmen jabbed heels to their mounts and trailed their prince over the crest.

At the rushed clash of hooves, Arithon of Rathain spun around. His raking glance measured the bearing of the men who dogged his doomed path out of loyalty, or for a wretched burden of pity. Their faces stayed masked. Perhaps the low-set brim of Hewall's wolverine cap and tight jaw underneath snagged Arithon's empathic instincts. Or maybe the oddity, that the affable young scout with his jaunty earrings shied off from the straightforward contact.

'Dharkaron's Black Spear, what else aren't you telling me?' Presented with helpless, stunned silence from the scouts, Arithon reined in his horse. He forced the pair to narrow, and then close the gap and confront him directly.

Near at hand, the clansmen observed his self-control was not perfect. However he tried, the nettling drive of the curse chafed at his poise without mercy. Even this added moment's delay scalded patience like a dousing of lye on stripped nerves. 'Talk while we ride. What can be so difficult?'

No man rushed to begin conversation. Arithon edged his horse through the washout that forced the trail through a switchback. Far below, the land spread mottled white and dun, tatted to tussocks where yesterday's sun had softened the snow from the thickets. No sped pace was possible until the horses reached the low ground. The lengthy descent would prove wearing. Under the wind-fluttered strands of black hair, the royal face showed the stamped pallor of quartz. Green eyes remained fixed on the vista ahead, as though the hieroglyph tracks of the gulches held meaning that might be unraveled, if only a man studied them hard enough.

An interval passed, tortured, while the horses slid on their hocks down an embankment of rattling scree. Neither clan scout responded, or dredged up the courage to address the source of their clamping dread.

'Well, I'm dead, either way,' Arithon snapped, stripped down to core desperation. 'If that's what we're facing, and you insist you won't leave, then I'll have to ask you to truss me again. When the sword blazes, and I rave beyond remedy, pierce me through the heart. Would you stay the course and render true service? Then hear my bequest! Dispatch me with honor. I ask that decent preference. Don't let me become the bound tool of the Mistwraith's stroke of revenge.'

'There is a path,' Hewall blurted, forced to lay out the unthinkable course that had once, in the past, led to tragedy. 'A choice that's deadly, with the potential to lead you to ruin.'

'A way to evade Lysaer?' Arithon pressed.

They had rounded a cornice. Below, the cleft vale that should have opened his route to the west spread a brocade pattern of hillocks. The furrowed slope rose steeply on the far side, tucked with gulches scoured by glaciers. Here dragons had once launched in languid flight. The massive horns carved from their dorsal spines had been winded by Athera's lost guardians.

Arithon clicked to encourage his horse. Apparently in command, he eased its passage downslope; but his hands on the reins were white knuckled. In the vise-grip, forced calm of a man who endured a sword sheathed hilt deep in flesh, he repeated his hagridden question. 'You believe there's a way to elude my half brother?'

A jerked flash of turquoise, off to his left; the young scout, guiding the blown mare at his side, returned a miserable, curt nod. 'There may be a chance.' He still could not meet his liege's sharp glance, or mention the sad history that had brought Kamridian s'Ffalenn to an unkindly death. 'Not certain, or safe.'

But ahead lay only disaster. 'Then I go on,' Arithon said, beyond hesitation.

The Betrayer's warning had been apt, concerning the dearth of time. Already the pinched lines of his Grace's carriage showed mounting evidence of strain. Both clansmen caught the corrosive, small signs. All too swiftly, the geas upon him sapped the healing of Davien's spelled flask.

As his pitched state of tension unsettled the gray, Arithon soothed a hand down its cable-taut neck. As though, against logic, patent care for his mount might outlast Skannt's best trackers and dogs, or deflect the elite company from Etarra, whipped on by a half brother's fanatical fervor to run him down in cold blood.

'Given the opening to find a clean end, I would at least meet my fate unencumbered.' Arithon shot a glance over his shoulder, then realized the response was cued by the curse. His mouth thinned to savage distaste. He turned forward, sought to anchor his rocked equilibrium by savoring the warm wind at his back. Its sweet, laden scent held the promise of rain, sure harbinger of thaw before morning.

Then, recomposed, he assaulted the clan scouts' reluctance with heartfelt words and quiet force. 'Let me fight. I can die but once. Of all I have done, of all those hapless spirits I've killed in the warped course of my fate, there are worse transgressions yet. I would endure anything not to cross out of life with a brother's death on my conscience.'

However he suffered, if the crux came, he would abjure the cold risks of strategy he had attempted, and lost, in his past. This time, he refused to taunt destiny, and invoke Lysaer's equally curse-bound hatred. He had nowhere to turn. With his own life at issue, and not Rathain's feal clans, he preferred not to end all his music and dreams, butchered by misled enemies.

Compassion ruled him. *If nothing else mattered, he would spare Elaira the agony of sharing his last flight.*

Even still, the scouts' close-mouthed reluctance prevailed. They wrestled cruel doubt, allowing the horses to pick their own way down the seamed slabs of the mountain. Silence, and the caress of spring's breeze, while the slide of hooves against flint-bearing rock spat orange sparks through the darkness. Leading them over the trappy, rough ground was Rathain's sanctioned crown prince, last of his lineage and their oathbound liege.

He abjured power and privilege. A man, self-contained, he no longer pressured them, but guided his gelding through the hazards of descent with settled competence, and no undue risk. His grinding burden of sorrows stayed veiled. The desperation walled behind masking gentleness was that of a man who faced execution with no family at hand, no close friend; no deep word to share, beyond an empty apology, that the hour of ending that would lay him bare must become an embarrassment, exposed before strangers.

He did not, even then, force his will on his escort as a royal command. Arithon Teir's'Ffalenn did not plead. Nor did he need to; the integrity behind his unyielding humility scarred the scouts to intolerable grief.

They felt like his murderers, to send him to Kewar.

Yet, worse, the unbearable mercy he asked if they insistently sheltered him: to grant him his crossing on the blade of a sword, trussed like a rabid animal.

'I'll call the eagle,' blurted Hewall, too miserable to extend the prongs of unbearable quandary. 'Then ride for your life, liege. Where the bird leads you, none of your line who have entered have survived to return. You will be guided to the portal of Kewar Tunnel. If you decide to cross that dread threshold, may Ath Creator stand at your shoulder with every bright power of guidance.'

Lynchpins

Late day at Rockfell, Fionn Areth stands lonely vigil on the ledge, while the Fellowship Sorcerers Luhaine and Kharadmon, who shares Dakar's mind and body, shoulder the arduous task of resetting the ward rings guarding the Mistwraith; while beyond the star wards, questing free wraiths from Marak spin through another maze spell, ever closer to unraveling the defenses laid down to deny their crossing to Athera . . .

The Warden of Althain lies imprisoned in bed, staying the flawed seals on three grimwards; when his earth-sight reveals an eagle in flight over the Mathorn ranges with a lone fugitive following, his fists clench in helpless remembrance of High King Kamridian, who had set foot into Kewar Tunnel, and encountered the Maze of Davien, and died, entangled by the thorns of his conscience, and his born gift of s'Ffalenn compassion . . .

Past Leynsgap, Lord Commander Sulfin Evend weighs up the explosive tension displayed by the Blessed Prince, and the reports of Skannt's expert trackers; then commands the moment to engage the spearpoint of his strategy: 'We send on the squad of fifty light horse, with a hundred more in reserve. Press them ahead. Let them harry the Shadow Master's heels. I want him worn down! Drive him staggering blind with exhaustion. Then we corner him for the kill . . .'

XIV. Hunted

T he clan scouts left their prince the gray gelding for his
willing heart, his sharp turn of speed, but also because of his
color. A light horse's coat would blend with the snowdrifts
and fade into the veiling rain, chased in by south winds at
midmorning. That elusive quality made Arithon s'Ffalenn the
more difficult to trace, by friend and enemy alike. His image
became an ephemeral shadow, embedded in the watery clarity
of the quartz sphere attuned for scrying his covert movements.
Elaira cursed the steamed prints of her hands, sprung to damp
sweat as the Etarran light horse dispatched by Sulfin Evend
closed their relentless pursuit. As wedded to the chase as hounds
coursing deer, they crossed over the great divide in the Mathorns,
their human prey running ahead of them.

Well mounted, well armed, they were fifty men, with double
that number of reserves hauling spare gear and remounts behind
them. Expectation spurred their excitement. Pitched for the end
of an arduous chase, they quartered the low ground of the valley
and knew: their quarry had drawn within range.

Hounds and skilled trackers were no longer necessary. The
riders on point now pursued the fresh-stitched trail of the dappled
gelding's hoofprints. As morning advanced, the marks filled with
puddles of melt under the wisped curtains of drizzle. One rider's
imprint forged onward by then: at Arithon's suggestion, the two
clan scouts dispersed into the brush. Wherever they could, they

set spring traps and nooses at opportune crossings and gulches. Their efforts were shortly defeated. The soaked ground dissolved into slush and patched mud, the slurry too sodden to smooth with a pine switch. In the end, they were forced to seek cover themselves, lest their own furtive tracks upon the sere landscape become too troublesome to mask.

By then, even the most skillfully laid traps posed the enemy too small an impediment. A handful of casualties, and the five unlucky men and three mounts waylaid with snapped bones did not slow Sulfin Evend's chosen veterans. Their risks were well compensated. A death on campaign granted a man's surviving family a crown pension; for the glory of the Light, and deliverance from evil, the elite guard were relentlessly honed for a manhunt over rough country.

Each stage of pursuit passed in agony for Elaira, immured in distant sanctuary at Whitehaven. The quartz sphere traced each brutal development, each barked order from the dedicated troop captain whose vehement manner and driving, sharp spurs permitted no moment of respite. He marshaled his assets and made no mistakes, pressing horses and men to their limit.

Arithon's lead relentlessly narrowed.

Elaira observed each step of lost ground, aching beyond succor or recourse. Ath's adepts gave her shelter, but could not intervene. Lent the use of a quiet tower chamber for her vigil, she stayed the grim course, while Alliance pursuit harried the Master of Shadow ever nearer to inevitable capture.

By noon, the gray gelding had spent its generous reserves. Stumbling tired, without wind and stamina, it had reached the far side of the valley. There, the steep rise in terrain all but brought the brave animal to its knees.

Arithon s'Ffalenn was forced to draw rein halfway up the first hillock. He stroked his mount's steaming neck with apology. Then he kicked his feet from the stirrups. The horse's drawn flanks and painfully rasped breaths left no choice. He must dismount now, or wantonly kill by riding the blameless beast into the ground.

Yet as he shifted his weary weight to vault off, the eagle ahead banked into a tight reverse circle. Screaming indignation, it looped back and stooped out of the sheeting rain. Black talons grazed the horse's hindquarters. The creature bucked into panic-struck flight.

Arithon grabbed a wet handful of mane. Half-unseated, his loose stirrups banging, he clung through the careening gallop over the hilltop, then down the boulder-strewn pitch of the slope.

Rain wet his face, plastered the hair at his nape, and snaked tangled strands at his temples. Soaked leathers had long since blistered his knees. His hands were chafed raw, and the sodden cloth binding his wound wore new bloodstains. That lone splash of scarlet stood out like a cry against the vista of gray slush, weathered stone, and wind-raked stands of bare brush.

The quartz steamed again. Elaira swore as her gusting breaths clouded the ephemeral image. Desperate enough to weep where she sat, she wiped the fogging moisture away. For Davien's intervention, she had painful, mixed feelings, entangled as she was by her empathic link to Arithon's mind and heart.

'Since he can't spare himself, he won't feel any better if he leaves a good horse broken-winded,' she whispered aloud in frustration.

If her entreaty reached the self-assured Sorcerer who sent the guiding eagle's flight, he was no spirit to waver for a dumb beast's reprieve. Must not, in harsh truth; at this jointure of fate, when that smallest of mercies would deliver Arithon alive to his enemies.

Elaira tossed aside the limp square of creased silk, striving again to contain the worry that married her to the crystal. Yet the lamplit shelter she enjoyed at Ath's hostel brought her no semblance of calm. How long could the stout heart endure the unbearable? Her beloved rode for his life in the Mathorns, and she could not act to spare him. Not without invoking a debt that would bind his free fate to the whim of the Koriani Matriarch.

As worn as the faltering mount underneath him, Arithon lacked the brute strength to curb the animal's terrified flight. Rain blinded his eyes. The rocks in his path were half-sunk in pooled melt. The hollows lay choked with the grayed rinds of drifts, under a gauze layer of ground mist. The crystal recorded the stiff set to sore shoulders. It showed every gobbet of foam, flung off the horse's rank bit, and each thorn-ripped tear in soaked clothing.

Stride followed careening stride; the horse trailed the eagle as if nose led by spells. Then a misstep cost its precarious footing. It flung up its head, skating wildly downslope. The right foreleg struck a boulder, and the weight-bearing cannon bone shattered. Horse and rider went down in a violent, threshing roll. Arithon pitched free and crashed in a granular puddle of snowmelt.

Palms clamped to the quartz sphere, Elaira cried out. She waited through agonized, terrible seconds. At length, the Shadow Master stirred. He folded his scraped frame, stood up, and swiped mud and gravel off a grazed cheek. Battered but uninjured, he smoothed a kink in his baldric, then wrung out the cloak hem that slapped at his calves and hampered his need for free movement. No use to pause for the provisions in the saddle pack; the men dogging his back trail would close before nightfall. He would have no chance to fade through starvation. The enemies at his heels would prefer sword and fire to dispatch him to Dharkaron's vengeance.

Arithon bled the horse, out of mercy. Shivering with chill, or perhaps aching pity, he held his gloved hand cupped over its dulled eye as it shuddered through its suffering last breaths. Then he stroked its stilled neck one last time, and spoke his first words since daybreak: 'Little brother, you gave no less than Jieret, or Caolle.' A torn gasp, then the finish, wrung to desperate anguish. *'How in Ath's wisdom will I ever prove worthy, bound under Desh-thiere's curse?'*

Bone weary, hounded against the stark rim of insanity, Arithon pressed on afoot.

Elaira whispered a useless entreaty over the bleak image in the quartz. Her words would not be heard. But her blazing desire to encourage her beloved became the shot arrow, sped on the heart link between them. He must sense her presence amid the rain-swept hills where he thrashed, stride by stride, through clinging thorn and wet gorse. Touched back by the steel in his agonized courage, Elaira scarcely noticed the white-robed adept who came on silent feet to trim the small lamp and leave her mulled cider and currant bread.

The quartz sphere consumed her attention. With the same stark fiber once shown in Jaelot, Arithon rejected defeat. He clawed up seamed gullies of granite, scaled rocks splashed with gushing snowmelt, and plowed through dense brush, choosing the rough ground to hamper the horsemen. If his enemies must close on him through the next hour, he would not fight their onslaught blindly.

Granted her keyhole view through the quartz, Elaira watched, dizzied, as his straight flight tacked a zigzagged, reeling course over a stony crest. The corrie beyond gleamed with leaden, iced drifts. Slipping and tumbling down the steep slope, Arithon planted his staggering trail partway up the next rise. There, he left his stuffed cloak and jacket, collapsed in convincing extremis.

He backtracked, relying on softening snow to excuse the blurred edges as he stepped within his own footprints. By now, he had enemies all but on top of him. Elaira could hear the oncoming jingle of harness beyond the line of the ridge. She observed with stopped breath as Arithon engaged a masking of wrought shadow and concealed himself in a thicket.

Rain fell, relentless. Strung droplets pattered off thorn and twig, and streamed from Arithon's soaked clothes. Such damp chill would settle in aches to the bone, through even the briefest stilled wait. Arithon crouched, gloved hands tucked to conserve warmth. He looked wretched, exhausted and pale. The miniaturized view through the quartz did not mask his incessant shivering.

Elaira pressed her hand to her mouth, too miserably riveted to weep as the Etarran horsemen surged onto the hilltop. They held their formation at a confident trot. If the sunwheel surcoats over their mail shirts were rust-streaked, their weapons and spirits were diligently sharp since discovery of their quarry's dead horse. Cloaked in oiled wool, fortified with spirit flasks and raisins, hard bread, and cheese, they knew they were one short step from their victory, and instantly deadly to a lone fugitive forced afoot.

Arithon kept his head down as the mounted force jingled by. A held screen of shadow lent him the semblance of a rock spur through the shouts of excitement as the lead ranks spotted his false form in effigy. Despite harrowing odds, he kept nerveless timing, withheld his move until the charging riders plunged well down the far slope, with the advance troop's rear guard just breasting the rim of the rise.

As he hoped, there were stragglers. Men grown weary of the brutal, long chase, who, perhaps, did not revel in the death of a fugitive who had drawn them in grueling pursuit across leagues of wind-scoured wasteland. Arithon kept still until the last, stolid horseman drew alongside his thicket.

Then he unfurled his gift of shadow like a lid on a jar, and plunged the corrie in darkness.

The trailing Etarran scarcely felt the crashing blow to the nape that felled him. Unconscious before he struck ground, he gave no outcry in warning. Arithon seized his shying mount's reins. He vaulted astride as the animal spun, and drove it, flat out, off the ridge. His oblique descent carried him away from the corrie his gift had left swathed under darkness.

Elaira swore like a southshore fishwife. The quartz attuned to scry Arithon's movements might as well have been dipped into ink. Sound still came through, faint but distinct. She choked back frustration, straining to discern one horse's rushed hoofbeats from the yammering shouts of the Etarrans doused blind in the corrie. To judge by the bursts of ripe language from the men, and the shearing screams of downed horses, untold mayhem unraveled the pride of the sunwheel troop's vaunted order.

'Mother of chaos, love, what have you done?' Then she realized; might have laughed outright had the straits not been other than desperate. Arithon's shadows had snap-frozen the slope to an impasse of treacherous sheet ice.

A hornet-mad remnant of the rear guard managed to claw its way out. Cast shadow still mazed them. Through bitter complaint, Elaira heard them dismount. They had to grope forward by touch, until the dark thinned to wisps and momentarily lifted. By then, their fell quarry had opened a fresh lead. The best bowman among them attempted two shots, the first a near miss, and the second one fallen short. The minion of darkness had passed out of range, with the best of their troop trapped, milling like trout in a bowl. Escape for them would be impossible. Hours would pass before the flash-frozen slope softened enough to lend purchase.

Elaira resettled the quartz between clammy palms through the pause while the Etarrans retrenched their balked strategy. The shouted parley exchanged with the troop's furious captain could not hold her attention. Whether the five men at liberty would be dispatched in pursuit, or if they would hear orders to stand down until the reserves could send in reinforcements, the fierce wish of her heart ruled the spells of reflection. The scene with its milling men and jostling, panicky horses dissolved, overlaid by another.

Charcoal shadow against gray-felt curtains of falling rain, the quartz unveiled Arithon driving on at a hammering pace astride his purloined mount. Shown his bloodless, set face, and the stripped concentration engendered by breakneck flight, Elaira cried out in tortured understanding. For the Prince of Rathain, the hounding fury of the Etarran light horse was no longer of prime concern. The forced delay to dispatch the mounted troop at the corrie had enabled Lysaer s'Ilessid to narrow the critical, safe margin. Now set under redoubled assault by the pull of Desh-thiere's geas, Arithon rode as though the furies of Sithaer howled and snapped at his heels. Lose his battle of will, and killing madness would drive him to turn and engage in doomed battle with his nemesis.

'For mercy,' Elaira whispered in cold-struck terror. Sliding and careening over unsafe terrain, the pressed horse must surely stumble. 'Arithon, beloved, go carefully!'

He managed a league at that cracking, fast pace before the blown animal forced him to slacken. Dropped back to a ragged trot, the horse flattened its ears as Arithon's heels pressured its choppy stride forward. His determined hands on the reins drove a straight course, with no allowance for clawing, low brush, or snow-patched swales and snagged ground. The Master of Shadow forged on like a wraith, through stands of black firs, their storm-whipped boughs bowed to the ground. He clattered over rock gulches and fissured ledges at a pace not designed to spare horseflesh.

The eagle he followed flew steadily northwest, its wing strokes no less urgent. The hillocks it traversed reared upward into massive stone ramparts. No horse could scale them. The towering scarp sheared in canted, layered stone, patched with glaze ice and rockfalls, and riddled with treacherous footing. Left nowhere to go but into the heights, Arithon slid from the saddle.

He murmured phrases to soothe the beast's rattled nerves, but could not stop its shying from the smell seeped through his right glove as he stripped off the blood-soaked leather. His breathless apology translated through the scrying spell in the quartz sphere. 'Little brother, stand easy. I owe you my life.'

His voice missed the gentle register he required. Elaira winced for the strung note of tension; shuddered as he drew the clogged knife that had dispatched the valiant gray. Yet this time the blade was not wielded for slaughter. Arithon cut only the leather headstall and girth, then jettisoned the stripped tack.

'Go find a wild mare!' he enjoined the dazed horse. Perhaps knowing Elaira's presence stood by him, he loosed a lamed gasp of laughter. 'I'd do as much, if I had your freedom.'

The confused animal regarded him with mournful, dark eyes: nothing like the endless, deep mystery he cherished in Elaira's bright gray ones. The solitary desolation of his straits all but broke her heart, as he slapped the creature's steamed rump, then peered ahead, and shouldered his dogged way forward.

'After you,' he said in stark irony to the eagle, perched above him in ruffled impatience.

The bird snap-turned its head. Its glance harbored no human light of encouragement as it unfurled dark wings and launched into a beating climb up the slope.

By then, the warm rains had slackened to drizzle, touched chill by the increased altitude. Ground fog drifted off the thaw-rotted snowbanks, breathed into white rags of mist. The vales hung under cloud like spoiled lacquer, and the dank air blew raw off the heights. Small sounds fell magnified by close rock and dense moisture, until Arithon moved through a half world defined by the rasp of his own labored breath and the slipped scrape of his steps on slicked rock. At times he clawed upward hand over hand, his fingers grazed raw on the ledges. He suffered repeated, painful delay, his knife needed to chip off loosened ice.

Elaira shared each labored increment of his progress. The empathic link showed the stark determination that forged beset thoughts into focus. Step by step, under siege by Desh-thiere's curse, Arithon scaled the inhospitable face of the mountain. His beloved observed each missed foothold, breath bated through each perilous traverse, over ledges moss rotten and frost cracked. The mulled cider set at her elbow cooled off, untouched, beside currant bread barely nibbled. The adept who returned to collect the small tray knew her will, and scattered the stale crusts for the birds.

In time, the guiding flight of the eagle curved into a lazy circle. The peak where it took station reared up into mist, a jagged shoulder of stone too grizzled and stark to offer a high pass for egress. Cloud cover lidded the summit above, and late afternoon limned the shrouded slope in lusterless gloom and flat lead. The drizzle now slackened, an ominous sign, as the fickle south wind backed and threatened to blow once again from the north.

Wringing worry crushed hope. Elaira whispered helpless endearments over the wheeling scene in the quartz sphere. She fought to contain her crippling doubt, that would only serve Arithon disheartenment. Yet the fickle equinox weather was worsening. Nightfall in the heights was going to bring punishing cold.

Stripped of jacket and cloak, Arithon knew he faced death by exposure. He carried no provisions. His hunting bow had been lost underneath his dead horse, leaving no weapons but dagger and sword. Though the trapper's pouch with tinder and flint remained strung from the strap at his shoulder, the rock crannies grew no fuel but gorse. No comfort could be wrested from that lonely place, even if he eluded the half brother closing steadily from behind.

Elaira heard the shrill cry echoing up from the defile as the Etarran advance scouts encountered the jettisoned saddle and bridle. Her pulse raced, overturned by raw fright as Arithon reacted to the unkind moment of discovery. He knew he posed a defenseless target, exposed on a slope with no cover.

By main strength, he banished the pressures of fear. Without looking, he kept climbing, every shred of his faculties applied to maintain forward progress up the cliff face. He drove himself, even as enemies answered the hail of the scout and gave chase with redoubled zeal. Elaira shut her eyes, unable to stem the graphic flood of her dread, or Arithon's raised pitch of desperation.

He rejected bad odds, that the townborn light horsemen were many to his one, or that the ledges he inched up hold by creeping hold could be scaled at speed, given the advantage of numbers and highly skilled training. Elaira clamped the quartz sphere between paralyzed hands. Her worry distilled into needling anguish, she saw Arithon discard the logical tactic, to haze his back trail under shadow.

'Beloved, why not?' Strain rushed her dizzy as she plumbed the linked contact to fathom behavior that seemed incomprehensible.

Yet Arithon's mind had become a closed vault, his concentration too narrowed. *Nothing* emerged but his pinpoint intent to keep climbing despite all impediment. His headlong sprint drove him heedlessly upward. Such profligate effort must break him down with exhaustion inside a matter of moments.

Elaira, who knew him, felt her damp skin rise to gooseflesh. 'Beloved, where are you going in such haste?'

For of course, *the eagle had granted him purposeful guidance. Yet where, in this vista of untenanted stone, could a hunted spirit look for refuge or sanctuary?* Then logic leaped one drastic step further. That first, reaming chill shot panic down to the bone.

'Arithon, no!' For in the high Mathorns, one dread place existed where Davien the Betrayer had formerly drawn a crowned s'Ffalenn forebear. Where Lysaer's avid troops might indeed fear to tread, since the site held a maze of dire spellcraft, inextricably linked to old legends of terror and death.

Elaira cradled the quartz sphere over her heart, ripped into white-knuckled tension. Ath's blinding glory, *how could she send warning*? To spare Arithon one fate was to leave him as victim to the Etarrans' black hatred and the insanity of Desh-thiere's curse. Act to intervene, and she would invoke the binding obligation of a Koriani oath of debt. The jaws of the quandary were closing too fast, if any safe option existed.

'Dharkaron forfend!' Elaira started to rise, prepared to risk an appeal to Ath's adepts to beg for wise counsel. Too late; the eagle unfolded dark wings. Its brief, gliding flight set it down on the incongruous, carved stone of a newel post set on the side of the mountain. The gray-on-gray image unveiled by the scrying showed the parting of the mist, then the stair of cut marble, fashioned by the eerie precision of a Sorcerer who owned an artisan's genius for masterworked spells. Patterns of knotwork were incised on the blocks that marked the odd, angled landings.

Elaira understood her beloved had been led to the threshold of peril already. 'Mercy, Arithon, no! Not the passage into Kewar Tunnel!'

He could not hear. The scried link was passive, restricted to remote observation. Yet if the quartz would not transmit her cry of dismay, the shared bond of empathy first forged through healing obeyed no such limit. Her explosive distress would flow straight to his heart, a stab of jagged emotion that could only tear him apart.

Arithon looked up, green eyes wide. As though she stood in his path, crying censure, he braced himself mid-climb. 'Elaira?' His speech was lucid, despite breathing torn by exertion. The quartz sphere transmitted his astringent concern with excruciating clarity. 'Beloved, my heart, you fear for me? I ache for your hurt. Yet I would shoulder the unknown danger here.' As her surge of response reached out and touched him, he turned whitened features away. 'Yes, I will take that choice! This before giving myself over to Lysaer, and the blind hatred of Desh-thiere's curse.'

Upslope, the eagle screamed an agitated warning. Arithon snapped back his lapsed concentration; heard the whine crease the air at his back. War-trained instinct took over. He flattened against the breast of the slope, wary enough to recognize the sound of an inbound arrow. The shaft fell short. Its rattling clatter tumbled down the ledge he had scaled scarcely seconds before. Arithon hurled himself onward. His clawing flight upward abandoned all rules, and every small care for his safety. Whipped on by sharp worry, he had to realize one of the bowman's companions might pull a stronger weapon; or another archer might supplant the first, armed with steel quarrels and crossbow.

The base of the staircase nestled above a vertical rock escarpment. No man who set foot there arrived by mistake. Arithon began the laborious last yards of ascent, clinging to the face like a spider. More arrows shrieked into the slope right and left of him, arc shots launched at extreme range. They would wound readily enough, even kill if he suffered an unlucky hit. Arithon grimaced. The taxed muscles in his forearm screamed under strain as he stretched for a handhold over his head. The troops swarming up from below by now realized his flight up sheer rock held the hope of a saving destination. More arrows sleeted in, through an officer's shouting. Then the sound he most dreaded: misted air carried the measured ratchet of a crossbow, cocking. The enemy longbowmen did not let up, but pressed the limits of skill and loosed off more ragged volleys.

Arithon scaled rock, forced to take ruthless risks, his stamina and judgment fast failing. The misstep, the slipped hold he could not afford might as easily dispatch him to a plunging fall down the mountain.

'By Torbrand's name, no!' An end bought by mishap would make ungrateful repayment for Jieret's life, and a clan war band more than half-decimated; would adulterate the desperate murders Braggen had been forced to commit in the name of his prince's survival. For Caolle's sake also, and the sworn oath of debt owed to the Fellowship Sorcerers, Arithon drove his taxed flesh beyond mercy, while Elaira wept for his suffering.

The scried image spared her no small detail. For each creeping foot won from that last rock face, the demands of exertion cost him. His old sword wound reopened. Blood stained the grimed wrap that remained of Jieret's careful dressing. The thin air of high altitude became as a knife in the lungs, until Arithon's head swam and reeled. Spoiled balance bought mistakes. Once, he slid backward, saved by the jut of a stone and one hand. No time to recoup from that narrow escape; lost footage must be won back, while the wasp hum of arrows invited distraction, and the angry smack of the first crossbolt hammered flying chips from the granite. Too close; fragments of stone pelted into his cheek.

Arithon shut his eyes. Reduced to driven flight, he dragged himself upward, and tried to shut out the ratcheting clank, as the weapon was spanned by the marksman.

The next bolt bit into the crevice above him. Arithon's clipped expletive collided with the sawn gasp of Elaira's intaken breath. A sharp marksman's next shot might easily take the Prince of Rathain through the back.

The danger did not escape him. Arithon scrabbled, jammed his toe in a crack, and shoved upward on faith and main strength. The thrust let him catch the lowest carved riser, but only with his left-hand fingertips. A fraught moment, he dangled in helpless extension, while his legs kicked and scraped against icy stone, vainly seeking fresh purchase. Like vengeance unleashed, the next crossbolt howled in. Arithon had no secure footing to move. Need drove him to try, a mistake. His cramped fingers started slipping off the smoothed edge of worked stone.

The bolt struck, *too close*. It pierced through the grimed rag of his sleeve and rebounded, snagged by the flange of its broadhead.

His instinctive recoil cost the last of his balance. Arithon screamed in wordless rage. With the last, fierce scrap of will he possessed, he hurled flesh and bone beyond limits and thrust his legs straight. Off a fugitive toehold wrung from straight friction, he snapped out his right arm and clawed upward.

He hooked the lip of the stair, just barely. Through a gasping interval, he hauled himself up the rough rock. Weathered granite resisted each inch, dragged at his clothing and scoured his flesh. Exhaustion racked him to snarling pain. Arithon forced one forearm and elbow onto the stair, then the other, crossed over the first. Shaking, he clung by his shoulders and chin, then levered his torso until his cheek pressed against the smoothed marble riser. There he dropped, spent. His pumping breaths whistling in graceless gasps, and his feet dangled limp down the precipice.

'Move, oh Ath, move!' Elaira exhorted.

For the next crossbolt hissed on a deadly trajectory, straight for Arithon's exposed nape.

'No!' Her anguished scream rang out, simultaneous with the wakened explosion of Kewar's outermost guardspell, as the inbound quarrel crossed the perimeter.

The quartz crystal in her cramped hands flared stark white. Elaira recoiled, caught short of dropping the sphere, while the newel posts flanking the base of the stair burned and blazed, unfurling a shimmering net of grand conjury. The eagle launched out of that raised conflagration. Its form vanished away into howling light as the shot projectile flared up like so much caught lint. Steel and wood immolated to a burst of sparks just shy of a lethal impact.

'Father and mother of demons!' Dazzled half-blind, Elaira squinted through the starburst of flash-marked vision. The sphere in her hands seemed a ball of white fire, and Arithon s'Ffalenn was not saved. Until he finished hauling himself across Davien's secured threshold, his back was still unprotected.

Sound warned him, perhaps. As the sheeting flare of the wards flickered out, the scried image cleared to show Arithon clawing himself up, wrist and knee. By the time he finally folded his body against the lowest of Davien's carved risers, Elaira blotted away streaming tears. The stairway ahead seemed defeatingly steep. Scarcely master of himself, her beloved lay beaten prostrate, while the frantic shouts of his Etarran pursuit reechoed off the stone ramparts.

'Save us all! There's true sorcery afoot! Somebody! You, yes, take one man and fly! Carry word back to the Prince of the Light! Tell him we need reinforcements!' A clatter, as the frightened messengers departed. The distress catalyzed by the eruption of spellcraft was swiftly marshaled by an officer, whose hardened veterans resumed hot pursuit.

The eagle had flown, leaving Arithon to shape his fate by free choice. Elaira battered back her outright terror, striving to recall scraps of riddle and lore concerning Davien's errant creation. Certainly its history of harrowing peril did not leap to the eye. The uncanny stair zigzagged up the rock face, laid from smoothed marble, and incised with black patterns of knotwork. Circles and angles laced into themselves, with no warning marks or carved runes. The Betrayer's works were subtlety itself. If the spells of outer guard would not admit arrows, the flesh-and-blood consciousness of a man must be permitted full rein in accord with the Law of the Major Balance.

Enemies, even Lysaer, might follow at will. No power would stop them from engaging their quarry. Short of the upper portal leading into the mountain, they could still kill hand to hand, or subdue the Master of Shadow by main force and drag him back as their bound captive.

Arithon must realize he had to reassemble the raw grit to arise and resume his flight upward.

Yet the punishing effort he required to compel weary sinews to contract, and command balance, and bear weight, caused Elaira's staunch courage to falter. She looked away, tear-blind, unable to withstand the cruel cost of necessity. Like a man whipped, or a terror-struck animal, Arithon s'Ffalenn reached his feet. He ripped off his sleeve to divest the encumbering quarrel. Then, in drunken, stumbling steps, took flight the only way possible: up the carved risers of Davien the Betrayer's bewitched stairway.

Behind him, the troop of dismounted Etarrans grappled their way up the cliff face. Well fed, determined, and drilled to seamless teamwork, they swarmed up the same ledges that had left their enemy half-killed. A testing pause at the newel posts soon reassured them that no sorceries would disbar their passage.

Running, the lead scouts pounded up the stairway, hard at Arithon's heels.

He heard them. The wet slap of boot soles chipped echoes off the misted scarps of bare rock. Ripe oaths and the sour jingle of mail, and the metallic scrape of drawn weapons warned of his narrowing lead. Harried to a shambling run, Arithon rounded the first landing. A fleeting glance backward could only slow him; no breath could he spare for the heart-torn appeal of a prayer. His chest felt strapped in wire. The effort of each riser made his thighs burn and his taxed breath whistle through his throat.

Davien had set rows of gargoyles on pillars, creatures winged and beaked and snake-necked, with eyes that watched a man, climbing.

Yet Arithon had little chance to heed instinct, or address the shrill cry of Elaira's unease. He rounded the second landing, fended himself off the snout of a carved gryphon. The cold burned his aching lungs raw. Sweat blurred stinging eyes. Gusts lashed the hair not left drenched by the rain, or slicked by sweat to his forehead. At his right hand, the wild stone of the mountain dripped snowmelt. Runoff streamed down the stairwell, guttered by the seamless marble wall. Beyond the flat coping hung a chasm of air, and a drop that turned the mind dizzy. The penstroke stands of evergreen folded into the valley seemed a raveled assemblage of scrap cloth and burlap and stuck pins.

Arithon slipped on an ice patch, bashed his ribs into the lip of the wall. The arm he flung out caught him short of a fall, but the blow had shocked the wind from him. Elaira hung on the bloodless pallor of his face. Second by second, she agonized with him as he waited for his paralyzed diaphragm to break out of spasm.

The delay lasted too long.

Two landings below, the leading scout shouted. His cry was close followed by an officer's horn, pealing the shrill triumph of discovery. The blaring note rolled down the chasm of the valley, then rebounded, scattering echoes off the high rims of the peaks.

From the vale, another horn answered; then another, a league farther back. The rallying cry of Sulfin Evend's rear guard resounded from farther still. The fanfare was answered this time by a knifing burst of white light.

Elaira raked her cheeks with tight knuckles. 'Merciful grace, don't give in!' For the moment could not have been timed with more cruelty, that Lysaer s'Ilessid should receive confirmation the picked guard dispatched by his Lord Commander had run the Spinner of Darkness to earth.

Lit by the flicker of that distant burst, Arithon snapped straight as though branded. His outcry was wordless, and his face, stripped to shock. He whirled. Lashed on by the fast-snapping threads of his will, he rammed himself breathlessly forward.

Elaira lost words. The quartz sphere felt welded between her numbed hands. Love and sorrow poured out of her stricken heart as the Mistwraith's curse claimed its firm foothold. Arithon's lips curled in an inhuman snarl. Shivers racked him from head to foot. He shook off the assault. As though hazed by wild bees, he gasped out a mangled phrase in Paravian. The light, lilted cadences somehow helped snag the fast-fraying threads of lost reason. No respite lasted. The roused force of the curse redoubled its siege, too inhumanely strong to deny. Arithon battled, regardless, his features contorted as though every nerve had been dipped into acid.

The green in his eyes lay eclipsed, pupils stretched into widened, black wells. Before the force that demanded surrender, he had no name, no mind, no grace of memory. All that he was became channeled will, to mount the stair and lay claim to the final landing.

The third one now visible above, flanked by winged carvings and guarded by a two-headed stone demon perched upon skulls. Another horned face overshadowed a dark archway. There lay the dread threshold of Kewar Tunnel: a place where the natural world ended, and spelled sorcery loomed order into the patterns of peril known as the Maze of Davien.

Yet Arithon had no moment to weigh what good or ill might lie in wait in the passage ahead. The flash-point crucible of Desh-thiere's geas already immolated his identity. Unswerving destruction would rule him within a matter of seconds. He would turn and draw steel, and howl for the blood of the half brother framed as his enemy.

One more burst of light sent by Lysaer must hurl him over the edge.

In a caroming stagger, from wall to rough rock, Arithon battered up the last risers. He drew his dark sword, left-handed, perhaps ruled by curse. Or perhaps, as a futile gesture of fight toward the Etarrans who charged in a yelling pack just behind him. Elaira dashed away tears. Alithiel, in the grasp of her beloved, would do nothing at all to deflect Desh-thiere's curse. The blade's powers could only arise when turned against the evil that locked down to claim him.

Yet a fox run to ground could still snarl defiance. It would use teeth and claws as the hound pack bore in and grappled to tear out its throat. Arithon pressed upward, stooped by cramped muscles as the Mistwraith's directive gained dominance. The urge to turn back raised a clamor of conflict. His sinews were stapled in knots. Compulsion gnawed at him, body and mind, until he could scarcely force one clumsy step after another.

The way he crashed from gargoyle to railing, Elaira knew his eyesight was marred. Perhaps ripped through by the harsh pound of his blood, and the laboring strain to his heart; or perhaps shut down by the unbearable pressure that mounted, second by second. If Arithon saw the brief flare of roused power as the starspell in Alithiel flickered warning, he was too spent to react.

The anomaly posed a riddle Elaira lacked time to consider, riveted as she was by the convergence about to unfold in the quartz sphere.

The last, bending curve of the stair, then four steps; three; two. Arithon tripped. On the impetus snatched from falling momentum, he pitched himself toward the black maw that demarked the entry to Kewar Tunnel.

Below him, dismayed shouting burst from his pursuit. In balked fury, they realized their quarry would pass through; had in fact planned the unthinkable to outwit them. The dread site where his daring had led them ripped their resolve to divisive fear.

Arithon had no moment to acknowledge that irony. He could not spare even one thought for his future. His tumbling fall cast him sprawling against the top stair where the archway loomed into darkness.

Light burst again from the valley, as though Lysaer s'Ilessid somehow understood that his chase would end in futility. The discharge raked open the sky overhead.

Thunder slammed.

Arithon screamed as the Mistwraith's curse ripped through him, skin, bone, and viscera. His body convulsed. Unspent momentum cast him rolling across the threshold to Kewar Tunnel. Nor had the air emptied from his wracked throat before the ranging, dire spells that ruled all who trespassed seized and entangled his flesh. A moment of clarity splintered through chaos, permitting the gift of clean choice: *to go forward, and rise to the Betrayer's dark challenge, or turn back, and succumb to the soulless violence engendered by Desh-thiere's cursed vengeance.*

His decision was immediate, a razor's bright edge held resolute against the unknown.

'My victory, beloved,' Arithon gasped in last salute to the enchantress who watched through the quartz sphere. Then he gathered scraped limbs and thrust to his feet. Firmly and finally, he stepped across peril's gate.

The quartz sphere went dark. The tied link of empathy snapped away also, as the warding forces that guarded the cavern closed over Arithon s'Ffalenn. That severance of contact was utterly irrevocable. His being was claimed, body and spirit, consigned to an unknown fate. Free will had been held inviolate, in accord with the Major Balance. Not even another Fellowship Sorcerer could breach that sealed threshold, now.

Elaira collapsed. Shaking with sobs running too deep to stifle, she scarcely felt the hands of the adept who caught her limp shoulders in support. Reduced to a child's need for blind comfort, she allowed the quartz sphere to be lifted out of her paralyzed grasp.

'Kamridian s'Ffalenn died of his royal conscience,' she murmured, dazed by wild grief, while other hands pressed a clear elixir to her lips, and soothing voices urged her to swallow. She was helped to her bed. Then the calming soporific took hold and eased the circling pain of stunned thought.

The air changed, across the threshold to Kewar. That detail struck Arithon first where he lay, unable to do more than recover his overtaxed breath.

If the spells of protection set over the gateway had broken the drive of the Mistwraith's directive, the ruinous price of exhaustion remained. His strength was spent, utterly. His unsheathed sword rested where she had fallen across the cool flagstone floor. The limp fingers slackened across her wrapped grip could not flex and close with authority. Eyes closed, panting against the trip-hammer race of his pulse, Arithon sampled the astringent, dry atmosphere. In this place, he detected no smell of dank moss, no silted traces of dust. Only the mineral scent of clean stone, against which the sweat-crusted taint of his clothes seemed a bestial intrusion.

Silver-tinged daylight filtered up from the entry, several steps lower than the level that sheltered him. Sprawled in battered prostration, Arithon listened. He strove to recapture the rich chord of the guard ring just crossed, whose fell powers now bought him a haven. Yet the sound had cut off as he reached the top stair. Even the memory eluded him.

He could not discern what unknown fate he had traded, for the known one, so narrowly avoided.

The shouts of the Etarrans seemed excised from existence. No sound passed the archway behind him. Nor could he hear the whine of the wind, or the sullen drip of the melt seeping from thawing drifts. The silence that wrapped him was absolute, cut by the shrill rasp of his breathing. He did not feel cold. Each scrape and scratch that abraded his skin set up a chorus of stings against the deep ache of strained joints. Arithon knew he should move, make some sort of effort to rub down tired muscles before his stressed limbs seized with stiffness. But the effort required to drag himself upright was going to cost far too much.

Easier to languish in total stillness and savor the drugged sweetness of respite. Arithon understood very clearly he could not run any farther. If enemies followed, he could mount no defense. The sword at his hand was too heavy to lift, a point rendered totally meaningless. All sense of danger seemed remote. He felt sealed off by pervasive solitude, which wrapped him like close, felted wool.

The impression followed, distinct as engraving: if threat to his life lay coiled and waiting, it would not arise at the hands of his enemies. No force lay in ambush; he would not be attacked. Not here, where the very set of stilled stone bespoke power beyond understanding.

He longed for mage-sight, then caught back the hurt for the blank, inner barrier that smothered his talent in blindness. The stark pain of loss still cut far too deeply. Unhealed grief ran him through like a sword of regret, and left him trembling with weakness.

Even blocked as he was, the deep quiet touched him. The poised flow of power eluded the senses, not crude or restless, but gently subtle as mirror glass that would show no movement outside of reactive reflection. Arithon lay still, tensed and waiting for *something*. Yet his bard's ear caught none of the tonal harmonics touched off by a chord of grand conjury. He detected no trace of any force moving, felt no tickle of vibration from the high frequencies past the range of sensory hearing. He was too weary to indulge curiosity. Thought and reason bled away, diffused as drifted cloud after hours of pounding stress. He had endured too many months of cranked worry, with every raw nerve end poised for fast flight, and every thought pitched for adversity. His reserves were all spent, with no resource left to plumb riddles of wily complexity.

His drowning exhaustion dragged him under at last, defeating his better intentions. His breathing steadied. Running pulse slowed to rest. Arithon surrendered to lassitude. His eyes drifted closed. Across an imperceptible transition, waking consciousness slipped beyond reach. The last Prince of Rathain finally slept as he lay, prone on the slate floor of Kewar Tunnel; and so lost his chance to turn back.

Soft, silent, more subtle than spider silk, the wardspells wrought by Davien the Betrayer wove him round, as they had every being, humanborn, or Paravian, who had crossed that dread threshold ahead of him. As they had his ancestor, High King Kamridian, who had died here, broken and screaming.

'May Ath Creator stand at your shoulder with every bright power of guidance,' the clan scouts had wished Arithon in parting that morning. Now, in fast refuge at Althain Tower, with tears welling from distant eyes, Sethvir of the Fellowship shaped the same blessing with all his brave power of conviction.

Gone to Earth

The instant after the Spinner of Darkness eluded the Etarran patrol by crossing the entry to Kewar, Lysaer s'Ilessid felt the driving pull of his enemy's presence fray away into nothing. Reined up short by the momentous event, an outcome of appallingly unseen direction, he called an immediate halt to the advance of the Etarran main company and its rear guard.

The sunwheel banners flapped in the shifting, sullen wind. The men stood in stilled formation, uneasily silent, or talking in unsettled phrases. Discipline held them facing rigidly forward, while their Blessed Prince conferred with his officers and issued his change of orders.

After that, Lord Commander Sulfin Evend rode up and down the ranks like a hazed hornet, gathering a specialized, small troop, then selecting the cream of the royal guard. The reduced company went armed, but carried no burden of banners or supplies. Chosen for speed and responsive mobility, they lathered good horses to rejoin the advance guard, sent into the high ground ahead of them.

Amid their sharp company, Lysaer s'Ilessid reached Davien's stair in the late afternoon. Daylight by then had just started fading. The gray scud of cloud lidding the vale had dispersed to streamed tatters, with thicker mists hooding the peaks. The land wore its ragged cloaking of snow in splotches of pearl and gray, interlocked with upthrust stone outcrops. By evenfall, the lucent patches of aquamarine sky would deepen to cobalt and amethyst.

The stair wore the light like watermarked glass, the sheen cast off its cut angles reflective as marbled satin. The effect was eerie, a contrast of masterfully worked stone set against the savage, split rock of the ledges; as though Davien's works had slashed natural law to a razor-cut break in continuity.

Regarding that vista, his hands pinched on his reins while his mount sidled irritably under him, Sulfin Evend thought of his uncle, Raiett Raven, whose shrewd mind and keen insight now advised the mayor's council at Etarra. Even that renowned statesman might lose his objectivity before such an unsettling marvel. In framing his entrance to Kewar Tunnel, Davien had fashioned a bold statement of force that challenged the mind's arrogance and compelled man's separatist nature into a disquieting self-examination.

The first impulse to look away, to deny, became overridden by morbid curiosity. The eye found itself as helplessly riveted as steel filings drawn to a magnet.

'Are you planning to spin cloud wool, or have you decided to take the role of a stone statue?' Lysaer arrived at his horse's head, gold and white and commanding. A diamond flashed, scintillant, as he caught the beast's bridle and restrained its restive pawing. 'Your horse wants its comforts, whatever you choose, and the men require your attention.'

Sulfin Evend dismounted, a wind-ruffled hawk unhooded and deadly. 'If that is the bolt-hole that shelters the bastard, our swords will be woefully useless. You mean to go forward?'

'I'm astonished you think there's a choice in the matter.' Lysaer passed the horse to his hovering squire. The glance that sized up his Lord Commander was sapphire cool, couched in a majestic self-reliance that, against such a setting, seemed the effrontery of a fool's arrogance.

Or else such a bearing of seamless assurance hallmarked an avatar of the divine. 'Have your sharp wits all fled, bewildered by spells?' Lysaer smiled. His kindly humor robbed the sting from a ribbing that could have rankled his wellborn officer. 'Or by chance, have you lost your excellent hearing?'

Sulfin Evend roused as though kicked from a dream, made aware of the distant, raucous noise rebounding amid pristine quiet. 'Father and mother of all coupling fiends!' he ripped out in acid irritation.

For the light horse patrol he had entrusted to run down the Spinner of Darkness appeared to have jettisoned discipline. The whoops, the explosive, bursting laughter of a manic celebration carried downslope to the site where the horses were tethered, and where the small company forming the royal escort had also been forced to draw rein. 'What stark, raving madness has turned them possessed?'

'Fear. Courage too long held, that is trained not to bend, set against the minion of darkness.' In place of self-righteous fury and frustration, Lysaer displayed openhanded pity, and tolerance that granted magnanimous forgiveness for foibles and human shortfalls. 'Left a challenge beyond mortal bearing to face, they may have resolved their distress by assuming the trappings of victory.'

'Well, someone up there better have a dead body triced up for a ritual burning!' Sulfin Evend's snapped gestures masked shame as he adjusted his sword belt for climbing. 'No other cause under sky could give those wretches a reason to slack off their duty, rejoicing.'

'They don't have a dead body,' Lysaer s'Ilessid pronounced. Awarded his Lord Commander's piercing disbelief, the Light's minion was frost and iron, the braced prospect of failure leashed into regal restraint.

Sulfin Evend dispatched a clipped order, and his officer rushed to ease girths and tie up the horses. While other men mustered to stay on as escort, his impatient survey combed over the slope risen in tiers of stepped ledges. 'Do I gather you think the flasks in the saddlebags have been freely shared in our absence?'

'Well, the other alternatives aren't so inviting.' Lysaer kept his tone low as the reduced company re-formed foot ranks within earshot. 'Would you rather your men had been reft of intelligence, spell-touched and maybe possessed?'

Sulfin Evend adjusted his rust-streaked, scaled gauntlets. His grim gesture inviting the Blessed Prince to proceed at the fore-front, he said, 'I suggest we go up and find out.'

The scrambling ascent was accomplished in spare efficiency and silence, the crunch as hobnailed boots cracked through refrozen slush interspersed with terse words of command. Lysaer did not set himself apart from the superb teamwork of the men. As often as not, it was his grip that steadied, or the interlaced fingers of his white-gloved hand, offered to cradle a rank-and-file climber's foot. True to the letter of his earlier promise, he left Sulfin Evend in charge. In tacit deference, the Light's Lord Commander gave his divine liege no demeaning task or direct order.

Yet the punctilious humility with which the Blessed Prince

answered the need of the moment caused his guard to surpass themselves. Inspired by the exalted touch of one they held as god sent, they shouldered each trial with alacrity. Yet their efficiency could not halt time. Day was fast fading around them. Freshened gusts from the north refroze sunken drifts into granular ice, lending a hazardous edge to an ascent already steep enough to be treacherous. Despite difficulty, their progress was swift. The lead climbers reached the self-abandoned party of their fellows with no fanfare to forewarn of a royal arrival.

The light horse patrol whose lapsed quest had unraveled into debauched celebration never noticed. The most aware of them proved scarcely able to stand upright. Their less sober comrades lay in prostrated heaps. Others swayed singing, arms linked over the shoulders of their unsteady fellows. Still others lolled at ease, their surcoats unlaced, passing the dregs of broached spirits between them. Their boasts roused sniggering bursts of drunk laughter. Slurred insults described the minion of evil's tail-whipped last run into the guts of the mountain. Others rambled through wistful dreams of hot women and high living, anticipating the sumptuous crown reward awaiting their honorable discharge.

Sulfin Evend's stunned outburst cracked through the genial mayhem like the thunderbolt fall of Dharkaron Avenger's first spear cast. *'Honorable discharge?* For you lot? That's laughable! Unless you have charge of the Spinner of Darkness as a stiff corpse? Sure as sluts whelp, you're no sort of guard I'd entrust to secure a live prisoner!'

The troop's flushed officer fumbled erect. Spurs jingling, he staggered, tugging at his disarranged surcoat and sword belt in a pitiable effort to restore his parade-ground decorum. He swiped a hand over his smiling face, then slapped his breast in snide imitation of the salute exchanged between clansmen. 'We have no live prisoner, nor even a dead one. Just eyewitness proof. No man need fear the Spinner of Darkness from now to the ending of time.'

His expansive gesture toward Davien's stair head needed no further embellishment. Thought of crossing the archway beyond was a peril no right-thinking man would dare contemplate.

The Blessed Prince proved the exception.

'Show us.' Two whiplash, shaming words of command, delivered in velvet-clothed patience; Lysaer s'Ilessid stepped to the fore. The spun gold of his hair gleamed like sunlight unveiled against the gloom of the Mathorn landscape. His face was wind-burned as any man's, his white surcoat begrimed and creased. Yet amid that trail-weary company, his fired edge of determination bespoke a dimension outside of humanity.

His steady blue eyes showed no flare of censure. Beside Sulfin Evend's rankled impatience, the equanimity cut from such lordly restraint raised the Etarran to livid embarrassment.

He bowed, if not sober, then dignified by a pride beyond oathsworn service or loyalty. 'Lord Exalted, mount the stair. You shall see. This day has brought the Light a great victory.'

'I'm going along,' Sulfin Evend insisted. 'No other,' he declaimed, as the captain of the royal escort moved to join them. Then, wiser than most to the perils of spelled ground, he gently suggested that Lysaer s'Ilessid shed every one of his weapons. 'I'll carry the blade for us both, and shoulder the consequences if bearing steel calls down a sorcerer's penalty.'

Lysaer's attention fixed on him, immediate. The wide-open, blue eyes displayed limpid sincerity, unfailing reassurance that any belief, no matter how strange, would be heard and weighed without prejudice. 'You entertain that possibility?'

'I questioned the guard the light horse's captain left posted on watch at the picket lines.' The pale steel of Sulfin Evend's returned glance was like the wild falcon's, that would strike to defend on pure reflex. 'The man said he saw a crossbow quarrel hammered to sparks by a wardspell. If the stonework carries embedded protections, let me be the one to risk springing the snares we can't see.'

'I am the living Light,' Prince Lysaer returned, his unsmiling correction almost tender. 'Your life rides in my hands, not the other way about.'

Sulfin Evend inclined his head. The thoughtless, bright elegance of the prince alongside stamped him to the acutely discomfited awareness of his own grizzled stubble, and the marring splotches where rust on his mail hauberk had bled into his rumpled surcoat. The owlish silence fallen over the men implied he was no fit figure of command. The finest of his officers seemed a clay martinet, ineffective and silly as his drunken light horse, who had fled Davien's stair without posting even the basic pretense of a sentry.

The cut marble soared upward, an uncanny fashioning. Of the band of tired men gathered beneath, only Lysaer's self-possessed, golden authority seemed a match for its dimension of exalted challenge.

'Lend me your shoulder,' said the Prince of the Light. 'When I reach the first stair, I'll haul you up.'

The Lord Commander masked his own shaken nerves behind the ripe pretense of Hanshire arrogance, well aware that on his own account, he would never be treading anywhere near such a place. Yet in Lysaer's shadow, a man found himself. The core fiber of his being became reforged into something addictively glorious. Whether or not his death lurked ahead, he would not back down before uncanny evil, or quail in the face of adversity.

'Then grant me the folly of kindness, Lord Exalted.' Sulfin Evend squared his shoulders, hapless as the fighting cock tossed into the pit to challenge a mastiff. 'For the sake of my peace of mind, first humor my needless request.'

Still smiling, Lysaer unbuckled his sword belt. Sapphire settings flared in the half-light as he passed the blade to the gaping man at his right hand. 'I, myself, am the weapon sent to drive out the Darkness,' he reminded. 'For both our sakes, don't forget that.'

Sulfin Evend set his jaw, assaulted by memory of seared men and horses, smoking on the razed earth of Daon Ramon. Even so, he stepped forward.

Ahead of his asking, two others offered their bodies as living ladder to assist the Divine Prince up the sheer rock abutment. No easier path granted access to the carved staircase. For the act of trespass upon his most intricate creation, Davien the Betrayer had set his explicit demand: the journey began with an unequivocal act of free choice.

Sulfin Evend stripped off his scale gauntlets, which might hamper his grip on sheer stone. Sweating and pale, he followed his prince, aware as others were not, that threat to his own person might not arise from the Dark, or from dread assault by any Sorcerer's laid wardspells. He alone had stood witness to nightmare, as the brave company from Narms had been shorn down by Lysaer's own Light, set off by a conjured illusion.

Integrity held him, and the bound obligation that the same endowed gift of s'Ilessid had once spared his life. The Alliance Lord Commander set his boot and thrust upward.

'Bless you, Lord, guard his Exalted self,' murmured the captain behind him. 'Light bring you both back unharmed.'

Sulfin Evend returned a curt glance of acknowledgment. The latent talent inherent in his trace of clan ancestry would grant him instinctive warning. He would not shirk his place, standing guard.

The stair had not been fashioned by artisan's tools, the Hanshireman realized as his bare fingers encountered the seamless, slick surface. Nor had woven spells engendered the mirror-smooth polish. Embedded like silk in the grain of the marble, he sensed the touch of its maker: a being who had mastered an unearthly power through a sympathetic bonding with the structure of mineral itself. The Sorcerer and the crystalline matrix he worked had conjoined into physical partnership. The result · had rewritten the bounds of the veil, reshaped the layered slab of stone from its native, wild synergy to something *other*: a creative, new order that struck the mind dumb, and that recognized no man's known boundaries.

Sulfin Evend had handled the cognizant skulls cut from the flesh of unhatched dragons; had experienced terror as Koriani Seniors built constructs through the harnessed matrixes of major spell crystals. He had witnessed the light flickering over Paravian marker stones at solstice midnight and noon. Yet never, even in the oldest of ruins, had he perceived such a working as this.

The stair which led upward to Kewar Tunnel framed a monument to innovation, an unsettling gift of rogue genius that instinctively lifted his hackles.

Lysaer must have sensed the same dimensional groundswell. 'Who was Davien?' he asked aloud, half-startled by the sound of the thought he had given careless voice.

'Who are any of the Fellowship Sorcerers?' Sulfin Evend stood upright on the bottom-most stair, fighting the sense that the stone underfoot was not entirely secure, or in any other way trustworthy. 'No parchment record I've ever seen mentions their point of origin.' He readjusted his cloak against the tug of the wind, then qualified, 'The Seven were here long before men came and settled this world. Koriathain claim their arrival heralded the dawn of the Second Age. That could be truth. The order's archive is not written down. No initiate sister I've met will say how the Matriarch's records are kept. But Koriani knowledge of history survived the uprising more intact than any library spared from the burning that swept the breached towns.'

Side by side, Lord Commander and Blessed Prince resumed their ascent on the stair. Lysaer, bareheaded, seemed serene, until a swift, sidewards glance snapped the illusory veneer of deportment.

His lucent, blue eyes seemed hedged as blued steel, the mind behind a turning millwork of furious thought. 'One town never fell,' Lysaer stated, pensive.

Sulfin Evend raised startled eyebrows. 'Alestron?' Thought of the s'Brydion stronghold raised a queer twist in his gut, as though the supporting logic fell away from every prior assumption of strategy. 'Why Alestron, here and now?'

All patterns of conjecture appeared cast to the wind, the pertinent strands of the weave spun outside of his grasp. Sulfin Evend repressed the hot impulse to swear. Of all men living, his uncle Raiett Raven routinely cast him outside his depth. When he floundered against Lysaer, the feeling he was but a puling babe seemed a thousand times more intense.

Where Raiett would have offered a riddling hint to sharpen the mind to new possibilities, Prince Lysaer kept silence. His fingers, also bare, ran in questing touch over the knife-cut edge of the marble coping that finished the guard wall.

Arrested by the unswerving focus reflected in that sharp survey, Sulfin Evend felt his thought crystallize. 'Not Davien!' His disparate unease hardened into a knot that slammed like a fist in the belly. 'Sithaer's Fiends, the Fellowship of Seven named that creature an outcast! You can't think to try meddling with a spirit so dangerous, or possessed by such deadly caprice.'

'Is he dangerous?' Lysaer asked, his query chasing down the undisciplined lines of a free-running exploration. 'Or was Davien named the Betrayer because he disagreed with his colleagues? Maybe over a matter of ethics, or perhaps an adherence to principle? His trial by his peers was never made public, though all of us hold common ground. Every lord mayor ruling inside town walls owes the new order to that Sorcerer's black-sheep meddling. If he wasn't insane, the rebellion he raised could not have been wayward action.'

'Well, that doesn't presuppose Davien's going to prove a willing ally against Shadow.' Pricked beyond testiness, Sulfin Evend stalked around the first landing.

Overhead, the high clouds wore their last rim of sunlight. Already the mounded snow on the slopes lost depth and crisp definition, flattened by impending dusk. Sulfin Evend flexed his chilled hands, wishing the afterglow would not fade into gloom before they accomplished their unpleasant errand. Ahead, the first ranks of carved gargoyles peered from veiling shadow, motionless, yet inexplicably more alive than any warm-blooded creature.

Wrung by an involuntary shiver, the Lord Commander lost his power of speech until the paroxysm released him. By then, the gap torn through the conversation made his words seem nakedly groundless. 'The assumption could be deadly, that such a spirit would rise out of five centuries of seclusion to cross Fellowship interests again. Yes, Davien's dangerous. Beyond all we know. The stone here screams magic. These bindings appear to run crosswise and counter to currents everywhere else.'

'Did you ever wonder if such a power might have lured the Master of Shadow to its web?' Lysaer's piquant suggestion dangled as he started mounting the next course of risers.

'No wonder Raiett Raven says you think in fiend's knots!' Sulfin Evend snapped. Next to an avatar's unearthly poise, he took on the semblance of a chastened child, tagging a grown brother's footsteps. 'If that's true, then I'll drink myself senseless with the men and entrust all your cities to muddle themselves clear of Darkness.'

Abreast of the first gargoyle, a snake-tailed, winged demon with a forked tongue, scales, and clawed feet, Sulfin Evend glimpsed a sharp flare of red out of the corner of his eye. He spun, sword half-drawn. But his wary stance met only stone eyes, carved with inanimate, sly irony.

'Bleeding death!' Enraged by the caprice of guard spells that seemed to needle the peeled ends of his nerves, Sulfin Evend rammed ahead. His irritable haste collided with Lysaer, who had stopped short, his proud face blanched as fine linen.

'You saw that, too?' the Blessed Prince said without mocking.

Sulfin Evend recovered himself, grimly steadied by acid amusement. 'You're surprised? Don't be. Your s'Ilessid heritage well might include latent mage-sight.'

'Well don't tell Vorrice,' Lysaer said, queerly shaken. He fell back on humor to restore his habitual sangfroid presence. 'The break in rigid dogma would shatter him.'

'He would jump off a cliff,' Sulfin Evend agreed, his answering grin just as shaky. 'But then, you could hardly appoint a man of vision or imagination to the post of Crown Examiner.' Oddly strengthened by Lysaer's stripped moment of weakness, the Lord Commander gestured ahead. 'Go on. Unless you're wanting to see the rest of the sights in the dark?'

Lysaer's grin was a white flash of teeth, lightning swift amid deepening gloom. 'You forget,' he admonished. 'Where I walk, there can be no foothold for Darkness. Come on, or stay as you please.'

Sulfin Evend advanced. At his side, the jangled clash of gold spurs bespoke a step sure and even. Lysaer s'Ilessid mounted the next span of the stair, his hands relaxed at his sides. Perhaps wisely, he restrained the temptation to raise illumination from his gift.

The pair reached the second landing, locked into welded silence. Neither one chose to pause. The breathless, white plumes of their puffed exhalations hung like evanescent fog in the well of crystal, cold air. Up they went, while the warded stone eyes of the gargoyles flared sultry red and chill blue at their backs. Neither one turned a glance toward the feathered watcher who wore the still, perched form of an eagle. Unseen, its living, sharp glance surveyed the son of s'Ilessid from head to foot. Yet that raking, invasive moment of scrutiny did not draw notice as the two men followed the steep stairway upward.

At length, their paired step crossed the third landing. Above loomed the tumbled crags of the mountain, punch-cut against cobalt patches of sky, and streamered in misted cloud. The first stars glimmered through, fuzzed in argent halos. The stairway razed across the sloped crag of the face, its geometrically ruled lines a stubborn anomaly that could not be discerned as separate.

Stopped to recover his overtaxed breath, Sulfin Evend examined the seamless join between a sheared block of marble and the sedimentary layers laid down eons past in strata of primal bedrock. 'The two kinds of stone appear as though fused,' he concluded in whispered awe.

A man could not stand here untouched by awareness of the mind that had crafted this structure; a cognizance that tapped the deepest mysteries surrounding the nature of being itself. A power of understanding vast enough to encompass plain granite and limestone, then transmute jumbled form into stairs, and basic structure into another dissimilar mineral.

'Don't wake your gift, here,' Sulfin Evend warned sharply. 'I have the terrible sense such a move might be taken as meddling.'

'Sooner started, soonest finished,' Lysaer s'Ilessid said, equable. He offered no promises. If he found Davien's prodigious craftwork intimidating, no further trace of uncertainty showed. The firm set of his shoulders and the inborn ease of royal carriage framed the appearance of intimidating strength.

'Why do you not fear to tread here?' Sulfin Evend burst out, a startling break.

Lysaer mounted the next riser, the pale gold embroidery on his surcoat like moving flame in the fast-falling dusk. 'If I turn back, who will go forward?' All at once too humanly vulnerable, he added in clear desperation, 'The issue at hand is not whether the

Spinner of Darkness is dead, but whether his claim to a dangerous sanctuary might garner him a new ally.'

Sulfin Evend felt as though he had reached for a stick and twisted the tail of a snake. 'That's why you wondered whether Davien might not stand in league with the rest of the Fellowship?'

'That's the hope we must lean on.' This time, as Lysaer resumed the climb upward, his frayed edge of unease sawed through. 'Otherwise, to protect the innocent populace, the Light must raise a defense such as this world has never seen.'

Ahead loomed the archway, a carved folly of knot patterns with the horned face of a greenman standing vigil over the keystone. Winged gryphons supported the right and left pillars. Their powerful, taloned forms held a predatory grace, imbued with the virtues of eagle and lion: killing strength tempered by the stern mercy of aggression, which enacted swift end to all suffering.

Yet the portal between was no longer open. The entry that admitted Arithon s'Ffalenn was now sealed off by a slab of seamless, black stone.

'Light save us all,' gasped the Blessed Prince.

The Master of Shadow had bought his escape. Unequivocally, he set himself beyond reach. The helping hands of his friends could not touch him, or the punitive swords of his enemies.

Sulfin Evend regarded that wall of defeat, at first without words to encompass his upwelling explosion of rage. Once, *years ago*, in pursuit of the Master of Shadow, he had entered a grimward with forty brave men. Not a husband, brother, or son among them had survived to return to his family. No bodies were recovered for the widows to mourn. Sulfin Evend remembered each harrowing death; he still suffered sweating nightmares. The far-reaching impact of Arithon's escape left him hollow with frustration.

The debt invoked by his survival still bound him. One step shy of requital, and freedom, the term of service he owed to the Light was rendered unfinished. Here, at one stroke, with no blood and no fight, the release of atonement was canceled. A barrier of spelled stone stood between his father's city of Hanshire and the son's duty still owed to his family.

Sulfin Evend could have hammered that barrier with his bare fists, had he not known the tales the old records held concerning the caverns inside.

'This place is no haven,' he managed at last, his voice a forced note of normality. 'The minion of dark will surely encounter the torment of final destruction. No one enters the Maze of Davien. There is no surviving what lies inside, and no turning back from this entry.'

But Lysaer shook his head. Under feathered blond hair, through the glinting, gold grain of unshaved stubble, the hardened angles of his set jaw appeared graven by shattering setback. 'A mortal might perish of what lies within,' he agreed. 'But Rathain's black prince is a demon.'

In the dauntless, bleak gaze of the Blessed Prince, Sulfin Evend beheld the future. The exhaustive scope of that vision all but crushed him. They would have to go back and bear news to the towns, then prepare in cold cunning for the rebirth of a peril beyond all human imagining.

Early Spring 5670

Respite

On his return to Althain Tower, Asandir was met by a white-robed adept bearing news that the last s'Ffalenn prince had stepped irrevocably into peril. Delivered in the echoing, bare walls of the focus chamber, her grave pronouncement shattered the weary relief he found in his moment of homecoming. 'His Grace of Rathain was hard-pressed. Desperation and Desh-thiere's curse have forced him to seek refuge in Kewar Tunnel.'

The Sorcerer raised a cinder-burned hand to his face, stunned beyond poise by an ill-turned event he had never thought to imagine. 'Not Davien's Maze!' he blurted, shocked as though he had rammed a stone wall. '*Anywhere* else in Athera but there.'

The white-robed adept bowed her head to his grief. She extinguished the candle set into the north-facing gargoyle, the faint golden shimmer of her aura subdued in the fallen gloom. 'I'm so sorry,' she murmured. 'No one of your Fellowship had the free rein to attempt an intervention.'

Asandir let his battered hand fall. Never before had his strong fingers looked helpless, dangling limp at his side. 'Did Arithon's mind-set allow them an opening?'

The adept glanced away. Her innate sense of grace left his question unanswered. In strict fact, the fine point was moot. Any such keyhole of missed opportunity could not be accessed unless the Sorcerer chose to lift the veil of time; and the record of the actualized past made even that possibility forfeit. The license to act had been overturned by free will on the instant the Teir's'Ffalenn made his choice to cross over Davien's dread threshold.

'I have always regretted that the cavern and maze were never destroyed on the hour of Kamridian's death,' Asandir stated with rare vehemence. Haunted by shadows of that tragic past, his weathered features turned sharp with a desolate focus, as though the discernment of exacting farsight carried thought into unpleasant distance. His silver-gray eyes gone bleak as stormed granite, he stood fast, the inlaid geometric of the Althain focus flaring in sheets of smoked light at his feet.

The tenor of his being jangled too close to bitterness for the adept's serene peace of mind. She resisted her instinct to step out of range. Nor would the code of her Brotherhood let her issue a restraint in warning. Quiet, she stood, radiating sympathetic peace. She abided the precarious instant without censure, sensing the vast tides as the Sorcerer's power churned through him, grazing the fraught edge of release.

Yet Asandir did not act. Tall, somber as midnight in his cinder-burned cloak, he reset weary shoulders. His sigh of resignation reflected all the deep shades of sorrow born into the wide, tangled world. 'Knotted are the works of the great drakes, and painful the will they laid on us.'

When his regard returned to address the adept, he was himself: a ghost presence, shielded, the light in him mild as a lesser star, his leashed carriage so tuned into balance, not even a dust mote or a moth would be set off course by his breathing. 'Ath lend the Prince of Rathain grace and strength, and mercy, most of all.'

Arithon would be bound to thread the Maze of Davien. No power on Athera that observed the Major Balance might spare him that trial, or mitigate the perils to challenge his crossing.

Asandir weighed the scar left by King Kamridian's death. The likelihood that the last living s'Ffalenn prince might suffer the same fate transfixed him with distress. The air drawn into his aching, singed lungs cut his heart like obsidian glass. The Sorcerer held, though the stern courage that sustained him through the trials of two Ages had loosened to sand in his grasp. Fears loomed on all fronts. The Sorcerer strove to grapple their enormity, until the pearlescent glimmer of Athera's lane flux seemed branded within his fixed stare.

'Come.' The adept presumed, captured his worn knuckles in her smaller grasp and gently urged him away. 'Upstairs, my sisters have a heated bath waiting. None of your terrible worries will settle until you are refreshed and rested.'

Some other nuance remained that she still refused to address;

Asandir sensed the held tension behind her serenity as he followed her up the worn stairwell. He had the respect not to venture an inquiry.

Yet she was adept; the veiling shadow raised by his tact would show through every trapping of courteous privacy. 'Momentous events have occurred in your absence,' she finally admitted, forthright. 'Sethvir left you records impressed into crystal, and will convey recent details in person.'

Hours passed. The wheeling stars above Althain Tower marked the passage of midnight, their dance the interlocked measure of time. Sethvir's chamber was a wrapped well of gloom, the honey grain of the maple stand at the bedside lit by a flickering candle. Seated on a painted leather hassock once the gift of a Sanpashir Desert tribe's holy woman, Asandir laid aside the smoky quartz sphere that held the Warden's witnessed testament. He retied its shroud of silk wrappings, lifted shaken fingers, and nestled his forehead to his cupped palms to ease his explosive tension.

Since words were beyond him, a light whisper emerged from the pillows cradling Sethvir's head. 'You have come back to a world that still turns. We abide with the compact unbroken.' Drained by the constant, bleeding pull of four unbalanced grimwards, he lacked the resilience to express railing humor. 'As ever, I cannot decide whether to curse or rejoice in the bent of Davien's recent actions.'

Asandir raked back the singed ends of his hair. 'He's abroad in the world again, that can't be argued. If he helped right the imbalance that threatened Rockfell Peak, then we owe him sheer gratitude. None can deny his assistance was a necessity.'

There were no gentle words. 'But Davien made no direct intervention to resolve the crisis at Rockfell.' Sethvir's gnarled hands raked the coverlet in frustration, until his colleague offered an arm and lent him the strength to sit up.

'Then how in creation did we ever prevail?' Asandir encountered the Warden's stark weariness, flesh and bone reduced to the frailty of paper, and the bright spark of irony worn from lusterless eyes. Even their natural color seemed leached, battered to a dulled shade of slate.

Braced yet again for a frightening answer, the field Sorcerer showed disbelief. 'But your earth-sense imprinted in crystal reflected impossible odds.' The combined powers of Luhaine and Kharadmon, run through a mere spellbinder's flesh, had never been close to enough to forestall a cascading disaster.

The inevitable rupture at Rockfell should have called down a catastrophic chain of failures.

Sethvir's sigh scarcely ruffled the fall of his beard.

Asandir filled an unsettled pause, rearranging slipped quilts and piling up pillows for support, while Althain's Warden marshaled his anguished reluctance to speak.

The blow fell with utmost, stunning brevity. 'Kharadmon saved the wards by invoking the crown prince's tie to the land.'

Asandir snapped stiff. He turned his head, shocked, the silver-gray hair tumbled over his shoulders darkened by gloom to the grain of rough, filed iron. *'The world's fate was cast wholesale upon Arithon's shoulders?'*

'We were lost already.' Sethvir folded limp hands in the trough of his lap. The effort pinched creases across his pale forehead and drained his tired eyes almost lightless. 'Kharadmon knew as much. If the lane flux had destabilized the Skyshiel fault lines, added risk to his Grace was not going to signify.' Like a torrent bursting through a broached dam, the Warden dispatched sequential images unveiling the full course of events. Rather than reveal the onerous imprint of the crown prince's subsequent suffering, he summed up with impersonal speech. 'By the time Davien effected Arithon's healing from the energetic imbalance of backlash, Lysaer's Etarrans were too close. Escape to the coast of Instrell Bay was no longer a viable option.'

'Which left Kewar and the maze? Ath forfend!' Asandir thrust to his feet. 'I never imagined the hour straight weakness could leave us so desolate!' Needled at last outside disciplined calm, the field Sorcerer drove into a fit of long-strided pacing. 'Fire and frost! We stand here breathing each moment on *nothing* but borrowed time!'

'Then you noticed the eagle?' Sethvir broached, his whisper glass-edged.

'That the bird was actual bone-and-blood flesh, and not spun from etheric energies? Right away.' Asandir stalked to the table. The drawn jut of his brows seemed chipped out of obsidian, in the whirl and dip of the candleflame. Wolf gaunt and austere as his leather-clad form, his shadow swooped over armoire and clothes chest as he addressed the task of pouring the sweetened tea Ath's adepts had left on a tray.

He crossed back to the bed, the porcelain of an antique cup cradled like a songbird's halved eggshell in his welted, large hands. 'It's all right,' he assured as he settled the vessel into Sethvir's trembling grasp. 'I already understand that Davien has evolved beyond prior limitations. He has drawn Arithon to Kewar, if not through opportunity, then by crafty design. The question of why may well pack a bitter poison.'

Sethvir peered into the depths of his mug, as though some benign remedy for lethal secrets might reside in the rising, wisped scrim of steam. 'Why indeed?' He did not set speech to the shadow that hung, unmentioned in leaden silence: that King Kamridian had died, broken by the magnified burden of self-perceived guilt, as the royal gift of s'Ffalenn compassion entangled him in his conscience.

Asandir fetched a second cup for himself, swirling in a dollop of honey infused with ground cloves and cinnamon. He sat down again, his lanky legs folded, and his bent elbows braced on his knees. 'Where are the sureties? Unless Davien's gone insane, he would be mortified at the thought of retreading past steps and old ground.'

Sethvir sipped his tea, his glance fever bright with exhaustion. 'Well, since he chose not to open free dialogue, like beggars without coin, we can do very little but sit and wait on the outcome.'

'Not a comfort.' Asandir changed the subject, not thrilled by the fact that a blood oath sworn at Athir became the sole straw weighting a negatively tipped balance. 'What of the torn wards at Rockfell?'

'Almost back in hand.' Sethvir sent the sequence of patterned geometrics that defined the ward rings in the mountain. The construct glowed blue, gold, and pulsating, soft purple, where light crossed the extreme edge of vision. At the heart of the shuttling play of live energy, an obsidian core had been wrought of a stuff beyond sensing. Asandir had worked wardings at the site many times. A brief glance assured him that the innermost guard ring was fully sealed, with work under way on the second. The runes of closure could stand complete in a day, maybe two, depending on Dakar's stamina. The outermost ward on the entry itself would not take long after that.

Asandir settled back, the restlessness in him rechanneled to deep thought, and the piercing steel of his eyes masked by steam as he lifted his mug to his lips. Persistent aches gnawed his bones from prolonged exposure to the deranged resonance of the grimwards. No respite lay in sight. Despite sternest discipline, and the pungent, spiced warmth of the tea, disheartened sorrow wore the field Sorcerer through. He felt Sethvir's moth-wing touch brush his knee, responded with a nod, then received the swift stream of images that showed other incidents drawn from across the Paravian continent.

Not all the tidings were bad. A long shot had borne fruit, and Prince Kevor had survived; Elaira still claimed safe sanctuary with Ath's Brotherhood at Whitehaven hostel. Lysaer's Etarrans mustered for their march homeward, while the survivors of Rathain's clan war band limped back into Halwythwood in small groups, exhausted and hungry, bringing joyful consolation to some, and tears of bereavement to others.

If marauding Khadrim still flew and slaughtered in Tysan, Prince Arithon's spectacular orchestration of grand confluence had rebalanced the lane flux enough to bring in the spring thaw in the east. Fields could be sown in time to stave off widespread famine. Asandir stretched out a cramp in his leg, then set his empty mug aside.

'At least Davien left Prime Selidie in a state where she's unlikely to become an immediate stone round our necks,' Sethvir said, raising the kicked ghost of humor.

'I could wish the galley that bears her would founder on its coast-hopping run down to Ithish,' Asandir replied with bad grace. 'The Great Waystone could certainly benefit from a permanent dousing in seawater.' Having just shared the unsavory details concerning the Koriani Matriarch's succession from Sethvir's recorded testament, he looked ready to lapse into venomous temper. 'You could have informed me of Morriel's possession of Selidie sooner than this.'

Althain's Warden glanced up, his eyes the limpid blue of a robin's egg, gilt touched in the uncertain candlelight. 'What could you have done?'

'The same thing I'll do now. Go to refound the seals on the next grimward her mad bout of meddling left deranged. I'll be away just as soon as the dawn tide fires the Paravian focus.' Asandir stood, still bristling, though his touch stayed unfailingly gentle as he lifted Sethvir's finished cup from slack hands. 'Which of the damaged ones drains you the worst?'

'Haspastion's, in Radmoore.' The Warden seemed suddenly dwindled, a wisp of starved flesh tucked amid a bastion of pillows and quilts. 'Though your journey from Methisle could entail complications. Traithe had to take work with a farmer near Ganish to earn the price of a skiff.'

Asandir laughed. The free-ringing sound filled the close chamber like the brisk clash of sword steel in challenge. 'The mud pots of Mirthlvain will be thawing, of course. A few methspawn, poisonous serpents by the vile dozen, or fifty thousand hatched karth-eels with sharp fangs, those plaguing ills I can handle. In fact, after Morriel Prime and Davien, I'll find them a welcome diversion.' Any crawling horror seemed more inviting than standing slow vigil, wondering how Prince Arithon fared, entrapped in the maze under Kewar. 'I'll lend Verrain what help I can as I ride the mire's west border. He'll manage until Traithe comes, rest easy on that.'

'Mind your step on the wall,' Sethvir bade him. 'The harsh winter set frost that has loosened the stone.'

'Isfarenn will look after me.' Asandir bent one last time, laid a hand on the bone-thin shoulder beneath the muffling blankets. 'I'll try to return before the spring orchards reach flower.' The trace flush raised by his brief mirth had faded, erased by concerns he lacked any resource to lift. 'You'll be all right, here?'

Sethvir's eyes drifted closed on the offered imprint of the entangling, stopgap diversions Kharadmon had left spun outside the perimeter of the star wards. The imminent threat of invasion from Marak still dangled, unbroached and dangerous beyond measure. 'Once Rockfell is sealed, I'll have too much help,' the Warden of Althain complained in flippant, brave parting. 'Or do you think a few wraiths can make Luhaine and Kharadmon cease their incessant brangling?'

'Summon Davien,' said the Fellowship's field Sorcerer, spurred on to stabbing, wry irony. 'Sit him down in between, and if we're lucky, that feuding pair might rip him to shred pie instead.'

Early Spring 5670

Sunrise

At Rockfell Peak, daybreak streaks the high clouds in bright crimson; and exposed to the freezing winds on the ledge, Fionn Areth shivers in the whipped folds of his cloak, waiting for the Mad Prophet and two discorporate Sorcerers to complete the harsh wardspells that drill ranging vibrations in waves through his bones, and burn him to raging headaches . . .

At Methisle, roused out of sleep when the Paravian focus flares white, the master spellbinder Verrain descends the dank sandstone stair with a fluttering rushlight in hand, to be met by the scrape of a stallion's shod hooves; then the dark, cloaked presence of Asandir stops him short with a cry of relief, 'Oh bright Ath! Let this not be a figment of dream, here and then gone to leave me alone with the horrors of a waking nightmare . . .'

At Avenor, clad in his robes of high ceremony, and surrounded by twelve of his acolytes, Cerebeld, High Priest of the Light, enters the square and pronounces the Spinner of Darkness driven into the dark maze of Kewar, where no mortal man might walk with impunity, but where a demon might consort with fell powers of sorcery, and emerge with yet more fearsome strength . . .

Early Spring 5670

XV. Peril's Gate

Arithon awoke untold hours later. Featureless darkness met his opened eyes. His ears felt stuffed in a black-cotton silence, and the absence of wind abrading his skin made him feel entombed alive. No trace remained of the portal that admitted him. The smooth-polished stone supporting his body felt chilly, but not winter cold, and the air held no scent at all.

Prickled to a crawling stab of disquiet, Arithon rolled onto his elbow. He sat up. The movement disturbed his unsheathed sword, which loosed a clangor of echoes. As he groped left-handed to recover the hilt, he discovered more: every ache and bruise, scraped cut and strained tendon seemed erased from his body. Leaving the weapon untouched where she lay, he explored his bound hand, but felt only minimal discomfort. Only the knot of lumped proud flesh let him know the disfiguring wound still existed.

Grief cut to the quick for the ruin of his music, the blight of lost hope most cruelly resharpened by that isolate, black well of stillness.

To forestall self-pity, Arithon rose to his feet. His joints were all limber, his mind clear and rested. The neutral stillness around him did not smother, but instead seemed to feed his heightened state of awareness. He listened, unbreathing, but could not detect any lingering vibration from the subtle spellcraft that must have combed through his being as he slept. That singular fact spurred his rising uneasiness. Whatever the potentized forces at work, that gloved, quiet power also muted Desh-thiere's curse. The geas seemed a lodged stone in his gut, unmistakably *there*, but reduced. Its inert, weighted presence did not wear him with pressing compulsion.

Left with no explanation but his unquiet breaths, and the pounding rush of his pulse, Arithon knelt and swept the featureless floor left-handed until his questing touch encountered his sword. He closed his fingers over the wrapped leather grip, and froze.

The Paravian starspells imbued in the steel came alive at his touch, a living thrum of aroused vibration that razed through his bones to the wrist. Light followed, a hazing of actinic flame that licked down the silver-laced runes. For no reason under sky he could name, that pallid glimmer gouged his sight like the vicious stab of a levin bolt.

Arithon gasped. Still poised on one knee, he averted his eyes before he went blind, wincing as busy needles of pain rained length and breadth through his aura.

Yet where was the enemy? Unease consumed him. Never before this had his vision been bothered by the ancient blade borne by his forebears. Arithon squinted, avoiding the disquieting dazzle of the blade. Nothing else stirred in the darkness.

He sensed no one near. The sword's slowly waxing, silver-smoke glow burnished the stone floor, a smooth-polished slate with a merled grain configured into a spiral. The shape snagged his attention, was in stunning fact *not natural*. Arithon examined the rippled striations scattered into gray stone like sparkling grains of cast salt. Distinct as a touch, icy fear lanced him through; *he was staring at minuscule runes interlaced into thousands of braided chains, and binding who knew what spell-charged directive.*

Sweat sprang out on Arithon's skin as he realized the place where he slept had crossed the centerpin of the gyre.

He bit back his impulse to plead for Ath's mercy; stamped back futile longing for unimpaired use of his mage-sight. Sorely as he wished for his sundered gifts, no flicker of talent would answer. He could not pierce the blank barrier imposed by the bloodshed once wrought by the river Tal Quorin, although his life might rely on such access.

Arithon gathered his shaken nerves, forced his trembling legs to bear weight. Standing erect, he lifted Alithiel high overhead, using the brightened flare of the runes to survey his surroundings. As he first suspected, the archway that admitted him had erased, melded back into walls of wild stone. The layers were ribboned with ancient striations, where eons of fire and sediment had birthed their early formation. Arithon turned a full circle in place. No opening appeared. No crack broke the rock, not even a cranny to admit roosting bats or the wings of a night-flying insect.

Yet the place was not sealed, despite seamless walls that appeared to entrap the unwary spirit who trespassed. At each move he made, Arithon sensed the rising tickle of power playing across his damp skin. The sword in his fist waxed brighter, second by second, until he was forced to shield his eyes with the back of his bandaged hand.

'Mercy,' he whispered.

The pain was intense, knifing-bright light now joined by the low thrum of harrowing sound. The sword's song brought no joy. Only a deep, deranging vibration that made his skull ache as though Dharkaron Avenger's gloved fists boxed his eardrums with ringing force.

Then came true movement, a concatenation of elemental forces ignited *from nowhere* behind him.

Arithon spun. He faced a wide archway. The structure, with its queer, twisted pillars *had not been there* when he had examined that wall scarcely seconds before. Across a silled threshold incised with black runes, the sword's glow sliced, muffled, through darkness.

Where prior aspirants had wailed at the sight, Arithon held, braced and silent. No stranger to grand conjury, he had once commanded the veil of the mysteries, lifted. He had knowledge. A master's training still structured his outlook, lending the wisdom to override animal instinct. He required no access to vision to realize he was fully ensnared by powers too vast to grapple.

Warned as well by the blazing cry of his sword, he understood he must move ahead. Cringing thought would not save him. No hope would bring rescue; no chance remained to turn back. Far better to meet unknown sorcery head-on, than to be sought, or much worse, to be hounded along out of forfeited will to a fate magnified by raw fear. Arithon was too well seasoned by experience to succumb to self-blinded helplessness. Weakness that fled the spelled strength of aggression never yielded the slightest advantage.

A Fellowship working of consummate genius, the Maze of Davien was unlikely to prove the exception.

Arithon Teir's'Ffalenn gripped his sword in slick fingers and engaged a decisive step forward.

Two torches sprang into crackling flame, set in black-iron sconces at either side of the archway. Their unsteady light spilled across the carved sill, revealing a high, vaulted ceiling. Another pattern of runes spiraled upward, their reverse image dizzying to the unshielded eye. Arithon wrenched his spinning gaze free, before his trapped mind tumbled senseless into the infinite. More ciphers were set in the walls past the arch, leading downward into a stairwell. The curving rows of interlocked seals had been formed in Paravian script, yet the language framed no words that Arithon knew. Under close scrutiny, they seemed to shine with blue light, too deep and dark to cast illumination, both *there* and *not there*, like the eruption of color caused by grinding clenched knuckles against the lids of shut eyes.

Arithon advanced. His booted step echoed. The tingle of live energies speared through his flesh, and the sword in his hand whined and brightened. *Who was the just enemy, if not himself?* The prospect filled him with terror. Far worse, the alternative: that the construct of the maze held the basic, brute resource to bend Alithiel's imbued virtues. Whichever case faced him, he walked a path of rank folly to believe he could challenge a ward of such potency.

Rathain's prince swallowed back his unease. His master's discipline was *all* he had left. Shrinking back was not going to spare him.

He braved the next step, and the next after that. Stark will brought him up to the archway. More torches ignited on the far side. Their snapping flame unlocked the dread way ahead of him. Shivering to suppress a nerve storm of alarm, Arithon crossed over the threshold.

Alithiel screamed. Her wail of stressed sound razed down his arm, driving a cascading wave of vibration. The dissonance raised pain that knifed into his viscera and threatened to flay living flesh off the bone. Jaw clenched, sweat streaming damascened tracks down his temples, Arithon refused to give way. He did not sheathe the blade, though mounting discomfort threatened to derange his cognitive thought. He could not use mage-sight. Stripped of access to talent, he must cling to bare trust: Alithiel's forging carried the sound-and-light chord of primal creation. The tonal harmony that had first Named a star had been laced through its steel by Athlien Paravian singers, then sealed by the dance of the mysteries called down by the graceful Riathan. The shrill peal of the sword's voice became the only true gauge of the dangers aligning against him.

Changing resonance as the Paravian weaving encountered the worked emanations of the maze provided some semblance of warning. Arithon could trace the ward's waxing or waning. Left nothing else but his limited eyesight, he would have seen nothing more than a stair that led *downward*, and torches that bloomed into flame, lighting the passage of each forward step.

Down, the stair spiraled. Torches blazed up, unveiling what seemed a limitless path to infinity. Arithon walked with Alithiel held upright, one forearm thrown over his forehead and face to ward off the hurtful blaze of the starspells. Raw sound reamed him through, and cast hammered echoes back off the rune-marked stone of the well. In time, the orange glow leached from the torches. Their unnatural blaze crackled as bright as the sword, glaring white against the stygian dark receding without end ahead of him.

He forbore the temptation of meddling with shadow. To win through the maze, he must master its center. A divergent purpose might only exhaust him, or provoke a reaction as likely to set back or weaken him.

'*Never needlessly test yourself against a power of greater self-awareness,*' his grandsire s'Ahelas had cautioned. '*You could incur a devastating backlash, at worst, as countercurrents seek equilibrium. If you did not lose balance, you still might lay open every part of yourself to fine scrutiny. That mistake could set a crippling limit upon every choice you make afterward.*'

Reliable counsel; yet even a high mage's vested guidance carried small consolation. Arithon could not shake the undermining belief that he was a walking sacrifice.

He descended until his legs throbbed from exertion, and the sword's screeling vibration numbed out his mind and senses. The stair shaft delved into the roots of the mountain beyond any concept of depth. Arithon could not have described where he was; knew little else beyond the fixed choice that sustained his will to move forward. He anchored himself to the rhythm of his feet, stepping downward in endless progression.

The stair ended. Unbalanced by the wrenching change as his boot slapped onto a level surface, Arithon flung out his bandaged palm to catch himself short of a fall. Unshielded contact with the rune-inscribed wall hazed his flesh like the kiss of raw fire. He recoiled, swearing. Dazzled by the sword, he squinted past his masking cuff and made out the outline of another doorway ahead.

This portal was framed by two pillars, one black and one white, bearing more chains of spiraling ciphers, and the timeworn sigils representing the sun and the moon. The lintel above was not a keyed arch, nor did it have a guardian statue or gargoyle. The massive beam was a slab of razed granite, of post-and-tenon construction. Its crosspiece was carved. Through the searing glare thrown off his sword, Arithon made out Paravian runes twined into the symbol for infinity, etched above a ruled line of script wrought out in glowing blue characters.

He labored to decipher their meaning, grasped that the words would be known to him. But Alithiel's vengeful resonance burgeoned, risen to a torrent of punishing light and battering waves of shocked sound. The flux swept him under, tore him piecemeal and shattered him. He buckled at the knees, never felt the impact of his fall. The shrieking chord of the Paravian sword's resonance unwove his being and sucked him into a whirlpool of darkness.

Hearing returned first. Cradled in velvet-textured stillness, Arithon came aware lying prone on smooth stone. A throbbing ache bespoke a bruised cheekbone. Opened eyes remained sightless. His limbs would not move. As though all his nerves had been stripped, he sprawled helpless, an inert mass of pummeled meat cased over a deadweight framework of bone.

The uneven rush of air through his lungs suggested he was not totally paralyzed. Against looming panic, mage-trained discipline resurged: granted the tenuous continuity of his breath, Arithon created the anchor to define the rest of his being. He imposed reasoned will, smoothed down raging fear. In abiding calm, he affirmed the rhythm of life, inhale to exhale, until his mental clamor subsided.

Sensation returned. His displaced awareness reintegrated with his body, a tingling surge that racked running tremors from head to foot. Rough return from a spiritwalk sometimes induced such reaction. Arithon kept on breathing, held himself quiet until the disturbance faded.

He lay by the portal, awash in the chilly glimmer of light tracing the lintel's inscription. His dropped sword was not far. The rune-worked length of the blade rested partway over the threshold, the dark sheen of spelled steel gone ominously quiescent. Tenderly careful, Arithon sat up. His shadow pooled underneath him, a darkness as void as the well of primal creation. Everything lit wore the silver-blue flare cast by the carved characters overhead.

Leaving the sword, Arithon stood. He scraped back tumbled hair, raised his gaze to the twined runes that commanded the intangible reach of infinity. This pass, he read what was written there.

The impact of meaning raised a transfixing dread that slammed him through, until he felt pinned on the shaft of Dharkaron Avenger's thrown spear.

'*Siel i'an i'anient*,' the inscription read; meaning, 'Know thou, thyself.'

Stunned by recognition of *just what* he had challenged, Arithon understood how Kamridian s'Ffalenn had met tormented death in this place. He knew, as well, why Alithiel had wakened. No given cause in Ath's wide creation could be so exactingly just: *the enemy he faced in the Maze of Davien was to be the shadow within his own self.*

The truth had been evident, all along, plainly stated by the symbolic gryphons flanking the outer entrance. Mercy. and strength offered the sole powers of deliverance for the trial which lay ahead.

Preparation was impossible. No weapon could stave off the danger. To wait would only engender starvation, and deplete the resilience of courage and will into the turmoil of mental anxiety. By every wise tenet of his upbringing at Rauven, Arithon realized he must forge ahead. Yet the knife-edged range of consequence that move must entail robbed the impetus from firm initiative. He hesitated, shaken to clammy sweat.

He fell back, yet again, on the words of his grandsire. '*Arithon*,' the old man had said, when a mishap had half drowned him while learning to swim, '*our fears play us like string puppets.*' While the high mage spoke, his brusque fingers had bundled up his dark sleeve cuff to dry a small boy's disturbed tears. '*There is no terror so powerful as the one you never faced. That sithaer, that hell, must not rule your mind. The man who makes the water his friend is the master who breasts the current and learns how to tame it through partnership.*'

Then again, years later, as a callow apprentice, Arithon recalled the day he believed he had slipped and omitted a line of protection. A shadow of nightmarish force had slid cold and dank through his construct, and his splintering scream had brought his grandsire running.

Mak s'Ahelas had not been as tender, that time. '*Boy, your wards were well sealed! That terror was not outside, but in fact within. You encountered a reflection of yourself!*' The high mage bore in, overriding his grandson's blustering claim that the threat just dispelled had surely been separate and alive.

'*Were you frightened, boy? Oh, then by all means, hide the fact. Shove it down! It will not be gone, but run wild and nip at your heels. You'll have a lurker haunting your dreams. Your belief you are helpless now* feeds its existence, and it grows, sucking off your self-trust. Now, that energy you've left to itself will evolve, unchecked, and yes, as you say, even kill. Not with teeth or claws, but by the much slower poison of leaching your innate free claim to existence. Though you go on and enact all life's motions, you will be worse than dead. That fear never faced becomes a parasite that will not respect any ward. It will slide through the best-laid protection, unbanished, for you have given it leave by quitting the arena without contest. You cannot pretend you don't know you were vanquished. The self cannot mask from the self and stay whole. Left to bide, fear will never relinquish its hold, but forever possess that lost bit of vitality you surrendered to endow it with being.'

Far from his childhood at Rauven Tower, embroiled beyond help in the Maze of Davien, Arithon s'Ffalenn repeated the high mage's counsel to breast insurmountable terror. '"Go back in. Die once. Let the fear be the part of yourself that does not survive through the crossing."'

Yet what bracing words would Grandfather Mak have advised for the wretched encumbrance of Desh-thiere's curse? The spontaneous answer arose, fresh as the kiss of changed wind from the mind schooled to self-disciplined mastery. 'Die once, and be done. Let Fate's Wheel turn, quick and clean.'

Stripped of false consolation or comfort, Arithon scrubbed his damp palms on his forearms. He sucked in a final, unsteady breath, bent down, and retrieved Alithiel's dropped length from the floor. Spelled steel did not rouse. The blade remained black and utterly inert, even as he assayed a trembling, reluctant step forward.

The Paravian characters scribed in the lintel flared brilliant white, and snapped out.

Darkness descended, a pall of absolute jet that stabbed the eye to behold. Left to grope his way forward, Arithon sheathed his sword. Between one bold step, or two shuffling, short ones, he chose the first, and crossed over the darkened threshold ahead of him.

A trace prickle of force shimmered over his skin, lifting the hair at his nape. The sensation raised a fresh sweat on his brow. No other sign of distress marred his person, where other mortal predecessors who had threaded the maze in willful self-conceit had been forced to duck, or crawl through that portal, or worm belly down in ignominious shame.

No sconces flared alight on the other side. Arithon's arrival roused a flat, directionless illumination that unnaturally threw off no shadow. He found himself in a narrow corridor. The walls were stone, still, but strangely polished. Their silvery sheen wore the same glaze of reflections found in a tarnished mirror. Other small changes rattled the nerves. Arithon found his wide-open eyes utterly unable to blink. Nor could he muster the self-command to stand down as he saw a living replica of himself approach from the opposite direction.

He quenched rising panic, which urged him to run; resisted the impulse to unsheathe his weapon. To flee would just bind his consent for the nightmare to hunt him down from behind; to attack would certainly wound his own flesh. A bold forward step was the only option. Arithon advanced on his uncanny double, *and the floor changed beneath*: his leading footstep set him down at the heart of an intricate pattern inlaid into seamless obsidian. He recorded the flash-point impression of the quartered cross and circle of Daelion's Wheel, the centerpoint cut by the diagonal slash that signified the axletree of fate. Then upending dizziness routed his mind. His senses reeled under a storm of wild power like nothing ever encountered in life, or the brutal, hard course of his training.

If he cried out, his scream became swallowed. The mirror-smooth walls blurred, then shattered ahead of him. He saw his doubled image split asunder, repeated until he beheld himself as a multitude, face after face alike as his own, regarding him with accusation. Then vision dimmed. He discerned no surroundings. The surge of incomprehensible power withdrew, rewoven into a seamless webwork of insubstantial, poised force. The subliminal sense of its confining pressure lurked just beyond reach of his outstretched hand.

Given nothing, again, but his harshly rasped breathing, Arithon mustered a semblance of disciplined calm. He made his way forward, surprised by his own steadiness; and the featureless twilight around him balled up and gave birth to a scene from his childhood . . .

Sunlight silvered the slab granite stair at Rauven those days when the westerly wind blew. The crash of the surf at the spring's high tide showered over the landing. At three years of age, a black-haired boy sat huddled with his arms wrapped over his knees.

'She's not coming back, bastard,' mocked his cousin's voice from above.

Arithon tucked his chin into his sleeve, eyes wide-open and stinging with spray as the waves crashed and unraveled themselves one after the next against the rock-studded shoreline.

He would not close his lids. If he did, the unbearable memory surged back, of his mother's remains cloaked in red flames, and the chanting of the Rauven masters speaking her spirit across Daelion's Wheel. She had gone to Athliera beyond the veil, never to be returning.

Water conquered fire.

Arithon set his jaw. Perhaps if he stared at the ocean long enough, the hurt in his heart might wash clean.

'*She's dead!*' goaded Jorey. Clever and blond as his s'Ahelas father, the older boy was already affirmed in his talent. He would start with the apprentices next year, the hour he passed his tenth birthday. 'Do you hear, bastard? You're not wanted at home. My mother won't let you stay.'

Young Arithon kept his fixated gaze on the sea, not turning to acknowledge the baiting. He knew his cousin would get angrier still, and probably throw a stone.

The expected missile cracked on the stair, missing Arithon's tucked form by a hairsbreadth. He flinched, but refused to take to his heels. Here he would stay, though the spindrift soaked through his clothes and the brisk wind set him to shivering.

'You can mope and wait for a ship till you rot!' Jorey yelled, 'but your pirate father won't come for you! By now, he will lie with another mistress, and she doesn't want you, either.'

But Arithon expected no brigantine flying the leopard of Karthan. Instead, he longed to be gone, *just disappear*. Become wet and still as the stone of the landing, inert until the thundering brine rinsed out the shame of being a child abandoned. The wish burned, focused into a savage intensity as Jorey's next pebble stung the small of his back. Arithon bit his lip and *wanted* with all the balked force of the tears he had no safe place to shed.

His gift of shadow answered. Avar's bastard son felt the inward surge of his talent, but not, this time, to bring darkness. His whetted desire to fade into stone, *to be not seen*, re-formed through his latent, raw power.

Jorey's shrill shout of surprise brought Arithon to his feet. He stared at his cousin's flushed, frightened face, and exulted: he realized some unforeseen twist of worked shadow had let him grant his own wish. He had turned invisible. For the first time, he saw his big, loudmouthed cousin shaken to white-faced uncertainty.

That moment, the dammed-up emotions burst. Balked rage and grief flooded in with the unstoppable force of the tide. Arithon saw red for the countless times he had suffered Jorey's prodding taunts. Always, before this, he had been too small, too afraid to stand up and fight back. Thoughtlessly spurred by his own wild hurt, Arithon picked up a sharp flake of granite and threw.

His aim would strike true, he remembered, and Jorey would bleed. But now was not then; he did not stand as a three-year-old boy on the sea-drenched landing at Rauven, but as a man grown in the Maze of Davien, under the roots of the Mathorns.

In the cavern of Kewar, Arithon Teir's'Ffalenn gasped as the stone hurled in childhood hammered his own exposed forehead. He felt the hot blood streak down his adult cheek. In intricate, exacting detail, he experienced Jorey's wild panic; all of his cousin's confusion and pain, as the boy took to his heels in screaming distress. No longer the enraged, invisible child, Arithon became the victim of his past action. His heart raced in fear, while stone after vengeful stone cracked around him, and he stumbled up the winding stone stair, skinning his shins and his knees.

'Stop!' he gasped. 'Enough.'

None heard. The reliving did not end until Arithon had suffered the sting of his final, thrown pebble, and wept the last drop of his cousin's hysterical tears. He was not released until he understood, heart and mind, that Jorey's cruelties stemmed, *every one*, from the fear that one day, his own mother might succumb to a fever. She could waste and die just as horribly as Talera, and he, *himself* might be left with no home and no loving comfort . . .

Arithon s'Ffalenn recovered full awareness of himself on his knees, in the shadowed deeps of Davien's Maze. The stone underneath him was no weathered stair, but inland granite cut to a mirror polish by the dauntless spells of a Sorcerer. The corridor of Kewar stretched ahead with no turning, its darkness alive with the too-vivid specters of a past summoned back in reliving. Arithon straightened. He climbed back to his feet, his pulse still unpleasantly pounding, and raised shaken fingers to his sore brow. Yet no gash met his tentative touch. The scar he experienced was impressed on his innermind, damning proof of a bygone brutality that now lashed him to poisoned remorse.

The inexorable knowledge *he could not turn back* forced his unsteady step forward . . .

The beautiful dyed carpets that graced Rauven's lower halls did not soften the high-tower aerie where the high mage kept his study, or the cramped, book-lined chamber he liked to use to dress down his errant apprentices. Mak s'Ahelas preferred floors of bare slate, which could be easily marked with chalked ciphers, then scoured with sand when his constructs required a ritual dispersal. Led onto that comfortless space by his aunt, then left there to face his due reckoning, Arithon stood shaking in salt-damp clothes.

Small fists clenched together in rigid dread, he endured while the deep, dark eyes of the high mage surveyed him without quarter.

Mak s'Ahelas had been tall, forbidding, his hands with their thin, blue mapwork of veins as starkly cut as chipped marble. His presence commanded the silence. If his black robes breathed the haymeadow scent of sweetgrass, the air when he moved shed a charge of pent power, and sometimes, the unnerving, raw tang the wind wore after a lightning strike.

'Boy,' he said finally. 'Arithon. You have broken the tenets of responsibility and used your talent to cause harm to another. Have you anything to say?'

The child held his ground like a frightened deer, eyes wide and black with distress. He shook his head, scarcely able to speak for the terror of having displeased no less than the high mage himself. 'Nothing, grandsire.'

'That is well, boy.' The high mage stepped in front of the lancet window. Backlit by the glare of the afternoon sun, his stern features dissolved into gloom. 'No excuse can absolve such behavior. Are you sorry?'

Arithon raised his chin, the move an open defiance; *so slight*. But the gesture was truthful. Mak s'Ahelas took note. He waited, cat still, to see whether his daughter's wayward offspring would also be tempted to lie.

On that day at Rauven Tower, the youngster had spoken no falsehood. In defense of his cousin's torment on the stair, he had said no word at all to his grandsire.

Yet his grown counterpart in the Maze of Davien did not feel the stricken shame of the child summoned forward for his misbehavior. Instead, *Arithon experienced the helpless, stifled pain of the high mage*, who had looked on in love, but dared not show mercy.

Not to a boy born to such immense gifts.

A grandson alone, newly orphaned, understandably angry and hurt, but one with an unmeasured talent and intelligence. Though Mak s'Ahelas felt his heart twist, he had forced himself to stand firm. Wisdom must come before kindness on this day. However he ached to gather his daughter's child into his arms, he recognized the pitfalls that too often destroyed the prodigiously gifted.

To give way, to cosset this wayward child might allow his tender burden of grief to sow the first seed of cruelty. Young Arithon's resentment must not, at any cost, be given the false foothold of adult indulgence. First and foremost, as high mage, the s'Ahelas patriarch could not condone a misuse of wild talent, one just exploded with formidable force, into startling, spontaneous development.

Aching, his throat tight, and his face a mask of severity, Mak s'Ahelas addressed his grandson. 'Arithon, today you have transgressed the first law with your talent. If you can cause harm to another, then it follows, you are also strong enough to learn the respect such gifted powers are due. You will begin your training with the apprentices this moment. Report to Master Krael. Tell him you have broken the prime stricture of restraint. You will say I expect him to treat with you as he would any other boy under his charge.'

'Grandsire,' said Arithon, his whisper twisted with wrenching apprehension.

The boy left to do as he was bidden. *Yet reliving did not end as the high-tower door clicked shut upon his departure.*

The power of Davien's spelled maze reached back into time, spanned the space between worlds, and raised a subsequent scene, when Master Krael had stormed into the high mage's study, appalled to unprecedented outrage. 'Your grandson is three!' he cried in appeal. 'How can he stand up to the course of study expected of boys who are ten years of age, even twelve? The solitary contemplation you've commanded for today's act of cruelty just last week left a girl of fourteen in hysterical tears! Mak, forgive me, but Arithon's mother just died. Give him the time he needs to grieve! If you don't, let me say, you risk breaking him.'

'Then break him!' Mak s'Ahelas rammed to his feet, faced the window to the sea to hide the pain that ripped him bone deep. 'Better that than to see the boy mocked as a bastard, tormented by peers, and poisoned through by the vengeful misfortune that gave us his birth! He is the most gifted child ever born to s'Ahelas lineage! Do you realize what that means?'

Master Krael's censured silence allowed he did not.

The High Mage of Rauven hardened himself against the weakness of humane argument. 'I'll say this just once. My grandson starts his apprenticeship. If Arithon's talents are ever to reach flower, then he *must* learn, and learn now, how to handle his rage. Or his born gift of shadow will lead others to fear. If that happens, he will never in this life find his balance. Let him languish and train older, and the spontaneous opening he provoked this morning will lead to another, tomorrow. He will realize the prodigious extent of his gifts. If he grows more resourceful, even his teachers will be forced to shy off! He will become the embittered victim of loneliness, and no one I know has the bare-handed strength to reach through if that boy should build walls against us!'

'No, please no,' Arithon s'Ffalenn begged as a man; yet the maze permitted no respite. As a three-year-old orphan, he reembarked on the arduous course of his training under the mages at Rauven Tower. A small child among boys, he was compelled to adapt, to react, to stretch and engage his born talents without causing harm, until the taunts of his older peers taught him how to respect himself. All over again, he endured the harsh lessons, the disciplines tempered to engage his inner awareness and make him seek his own truths. He must not be swayed by the other apprentices' mocking laughter, or their scorn, or their envious fear as he groped through his sorry mistakes. On his own, under solitary discipline, he created his first measure of success.

The study he completed for harming his cousin was no punishment, but a teaching of ruthless expedience. Confined by himself inside a small room whose walls were spelled mirrors, Arithon could not rage at Jorey without seeing his own fury reflected; then behind that, his pain, then the puppet strings of fear, breathed to life by his secret terrors. He could not run from himself, or throw stones, or cast blame, but only arrive at the weakness ingrained in his innermost being. Trapped in abject misery, the young child threw tantrums. He beat his fists until he bloodied his knuckles, but could not run or hide to find surcease. No one came to offer him comfort. The mirrors that reflected endless views of himself forgave no cover of illusion. At tender, young age, Arithon endured day and night in confinement until he faced his own hate and fear, and learned to temper the loneliness and grief that were his undying companions.

Yet as the reliving unfolded and cast forth the tempestuous bursts of infantile emotions, Arithon did not retaste the salt of his tears. He did not experience the anguish of boyhood hurt and confusion.

*Instead, the Maze of Davien gave him back that child's raw screams,
as they touched on the sore heart of his grandsire.* An old man
bereaved, who had just lost his daughter. The sole legacy she
left was her bastard, begotten by Avar of Karthan as an act of
rage and defiance. Yet the pirate king's relentless compassion had
transformed her ill-starred act of rebellion into spontaneous love.
In agonized loss, Talera had left the man, had come home to her
father to give birth to her son inside warded walls at Rauven.

'To keep them both safe,' she had said, weeping in the high mage's
arms, while the brigantine flying the leopard banner had scudded
hull down over the seaward horizon. 'Let my s'Illessid husband
empty his treasury sweeping the wide seas. His revenge will elude him.
Had I stayed on Karthan with a newborn child, Avar s'Ffalenn would
be bound to the shore to defend us. He knew, as I did, the cost in shed
blood would lead his people to ruin. Such a war would grant Amroth's
king the outright gift of a sitting target.'

Talera's deathbed fever had left a boy too gifted for a grandfather's coddling. For each night young Arithon cried himself to
sleep, Mak s'Ahelas had listened, and wept also. Alone in his high
tower, pacing slate floors, he had matched tear for tear, aching,
knowing, that to answer the need of his lonely old age would
destroy the independence of mind such a rare talent required to
fledge.

'You will not praise him,' he commanded Ornison, the benevolent master who instructed the child of five to weave his
first chain of spelled ciphers.

'Your grandson's good!' the kindly mage protested, set aback
by the admonition. 'Didn't you see –'

'Oh yes, he's good! And indeed I saw.' Mak s'Ahelas did not
relent, though he bled inside for necessity. 'He's strong-minded,
as well. Not being blind or deaf, my grandson certainly knows
how well he achieves. Leave him free! Let him make his own
comparisons, and hard as it is, allow him to choose for himself
how to handle them. Don't insult his intelligence! Arithon will
not thrive if he's trained like a dog, good boy this, nice boy that,
until he loses his way. Don't blur the distinctions that lead him
to seek his own happiness.'

'But he has no father, no mother, no family!' Ornison argued,
his laughing humor shocked still. 'Who's left to take pride in his
progress?'

'He has no family,' the high mage agreed, leaving his vantage
at the seaside casement. The brass loops of the armillary reflected
his haunted pacing as he resumed his unbending diatribe. 'That's

Arithon's greatest setback, one he must rise to overcome. Praise will draw on that weakness most powerfully. He's an unformed boy! He'll seek to please you, then bend his opinions to earn your favor. Just to feel less alone, he will lose the ability to listen to his innate inner balance. How will he, how can he *ever* manage to master the vast scope of his talent if he forgets how to think for himself?'

'I had not thought,' Ornison confessed, chastened, his dough features sagged to distress. 'Of course, the boy will be managed as you ask.'

The High Mage of Rauven withheld his approval, bound by the tenets of merciless wisdom. Black-robed, gaunt, and silent, he observed from a distance, while the boy learned the harsh lesson *to act for himself, to see and discern through clear eyes, the shifting template of his evolving belief unbiased by outside opinions.* That course of teaching alone would let Arithon develop the clarity of mind he required to stay the difficult course of a mastery so gifted, the mages who taught him at times could not hope to keep up . . .

Looped in the spelled coils of the Maze of Davien, Arithon s'Ffalenn suffered his childhood twice over: once for the solitary boy he had been, and again for the High Mage of Rauven, who, unseen, unheard, had cherished each brilliant stride of his grandson's achievement. Yet he could let no man or woman see his care lest he spoil the boy's developing consciousness.

Fragments of recall broke and receded, bright-edged and vivid as experience. Arithon tasted the dust and sweat of the tiltyard, *again*, as Rauven's one-eyed swordmaster made his slender, boy's hand hard with callus on the grip of a practice stick. In sharp, twofold echo, Kewar Tunnel re-created the bruises of learning, alongside the sharp sting of each blow he had dealt his opponents in the course of rough sparring.

Again, he relived the banged shins and scraped knees in the trials that strengthened his developing mage-sight, when he had been asked to cross room after room mazed with obstacles masked under darkness. Once he commanded the more subtle landscape of his delicate, inner senses, he endured testing of more punishing exactitude, when self-trust had been paired with live danger.

Again, he relived the tense, panting terror of the hours he had drilled with bare steel in the black pit of Rauven's dungeons. He was given no torch to augment his senses. In blank, dusty darkness, the master at arms drew his blood, cut him day after day, until he learned to retune his perceptions and maintain that heightened state of awareness by ingrained reflex.

He learned archery, then accepted the blindfold again, and loosed repetitive arrows. His task was to sense the grass target through mage-sight, then progress to shooting down thrown knots of rags until he could hit them, ascending or descending, or strike them on command at the tip of their arc before falling.

Again, he relived the pranks he had played, the tarts filched from the kitchen to the cook's fist-shaking dismay, and the redoubled workload laid on the baker's boys brought by dishonest indulgence. Arithon shared the distraught anxiety of the searchers, the night he had gone wading for shiners at low tide, and foolishly cut himself off on a rock when the rip currents roared in. He grew older, stung by remorse for the least word of thoughtless unkindness. He gained skill with his fists in the fights provoked by those peers whipped to rage by his quick mind and his excellence, until the day came when the hurt he inflicted overtook the scuffling bruises received. Such times, the Maze of Davien rewove recall: his opponent's blacked eye became as his own with exactingly unbiased restitution.

His past came alive, each act of misdeed accounted. At odd intervals the compassionate drive of s'Ffalenn birthright wove a net of resilience to shield him.

Fledgling birds he had nursed to first flight, a deer he had healed of a broken leg, the elderly seeress who had befriended him – all walked at Arithon's side. Their protection of him in return lent some measure of mitigation. He retrod his own footsteps to ten years of age, when the high mage himself instilled the lessons that readied the mind for the perilous initiations that opened the keys to grand conjury.

Past warnings reechoed with the resonance of summer thunder. *'Before you access the gateways that cross through the veil, before the quest of the spiritwalk, where you link with the forces that weave Ath's creation, you must comprehend the raw impact of your mind. Every thought creates shape. Every feeling, no matter how passing small, precipitates the spin that unleashes event. To tread the way of power, you must waken the intense self-awareness that permits you to clear and harness the stream of your inner being.'*

Again, Arithon stepped across the tuned rim of the circle laid down by his grandfather's hand. Yet this time, the trial that led him through the nethermost pit of his fears was not guided. At Rauven, the high mage had steadied his past steps. His wise presence had stood as bulwark and shield to guard against youthful uncertainties. Firm admonishments had steered each misstep through the quagmires of imbalanced thought, and the entanglements of false beliefs. On Athera, alone in the Maze of Davien, Arithon s'Ffalenn performed the same trial, stripped naked.

He did not revisit his boy's fears again. Those phantoms had been conquered, reforged, or put to rout through the ceremonial cleansing of each battle of self enacted within the spelled circle. No longer the carefree, untried youth, the man who walked Kewar's Maze trod the more shadowy thicket of his adult expectations: the bad thread set through the cloth of his being that still bound him to self-induced error. Through the unblinded eyes of compassion, he wept for his deepest shortcomings. *The young girl who had feared him because, deep down, he felt flawed; the hollow cry that insisted he could not trust himself. The very power that flowed through him was double-edged, a moving peril that could touch and raise beauty, yet still carried the dire potential to wound.* In green youth, Arithon had survived on naive expectation, that he could keep such dark passions in check.

Yet the Maze of Davien did not mask the unrecognized truths under beguiling innocence.

Unbuffered, Arithon became stalked by his future: *knowing* that his later experience in Karthan would brutally rip through his dreamer's pretense. Exile had not freed him. A crown prince's oath on Athera would see his unfounded presumptions shattered in one day, a sentence written in running blood on the spring green banks of Tal Quorin.

'No!' His scream pierced the reliving, made bare stone ring with the echoes of horror to come. But no sound and no agony could stave off the flaying knives of his conscience. Through the eyes of the Spinner of Darkness in Kewar, Arithon saw the forged pillar of self-worth that had founded his master's integrity crumble, then winnow away into dust.

The lens of the maze realigned his perspective. The music that founded his emotional mainstay, the surrogate outlet for the love and close family he never had as a child, rang hollow. Forced to retrace his past step from the trial of the high mage's circle, Arithon was no longer blind to the fissure shot through the weave of his character. His ears were not deaf to the seed of rank discord soon to sour his untrammeled happiness.

Lessons in ancient language and lore, the arduous study of spellcrafting, the respite he wrought through his skill on the lyranthe, every hour of reflective contentment he enjoyed in the company of animals passed him by, a cascading flicker of imagery.

Again, he stood red-faced, as his grandfather upbraided him for letting the kitchen maid lure him into the hayloft for a bout of giggling dalliance.

'Boy, you're born with talent!' The old man tapped a white heron's quill against his creased palm, while the migrating geese streamed past the window, and autumn breeze wafted, sharp with the scent of the apples being pressed to make cider in the yard. 'You have sight well beyond the dullard's vision that Ath granted to men born with two eyes! Did you use it today, boy?'

Arithon maintained a desperate, locked stillness, his snarled shirt laces still half-undone, and his sable hair caught with straw. He stood straight as iron, too embarrassed to cringe. 'No, grandfather.'

Mak s'Ahelas arose. 'You will, then. Right now. Terik will escort you down to the harbor. You will visit the sailhands' brothel, not to indulge, but to observe what occurs in the aura when a man and a woman lie down in the act of coupling.'

Arithon paled, then flushed in shrinking humiliation.

But his grandsire showed no shred of masculine mercy. 'Sex creates an energetic binding, you'll not forget. You will accord women your deepest respect, whether or not they grant themselves the same reverence. Use your body as a spiritless object of pleasure, and you'll tie up your strength and bleed off your power with more subtlety than an addiction. You will go to the brothel, and perceive the cost, and know not to undertake such things lightly. Done without love, any congress between man and woman degrades the creative intelligence that graces your humanity.'

The maze granted no quarter. Young Arithon saw the past lesson through, by the end of the night brought back weeping with mollified pity. He avoided the kitchen maid after that, and later, threw silver to the sad-eyed harlots who accosted him on the street. 'For your comfort,' he told them, not accepting even one grateful kiss on the cheek for his blessing.

His last years at Rauven streamed past in a blur of marred happiness.

Arithon shrank from the heartbreak to come. In step-by-step traverse down Kewar's narrow corridor, he suffered the past, strapped to the pain of his future losses. Each revived memory arose resharpened by the untempered lens of blithe innocence. *Again*, he reenacted his learning to transmute the poisons of tienelle. From trance, he retraced his first spiritwalk, striding the limitless stream of the mystery whose wellspring lay past the veil. Still gloved in flesh, he learned to split his perception at will. The indescribable thrill of wild ecstasy rode him, as he first read and mapped the energy signatures of Name woven from the living elements, fire, earth, water, and air.

Once, all of those things had been effortless.

He had never questioned their permanence; never thought to imagine that the solid foundations of self could be cast to the four winds and jeopardy.

The foreknowledge of pain all but shredded his being as, *again*, Arithon watched himself make the decisions that *would come* to unravel his core of integrity. The ephemeral expectation of triumph slammed his heart like a physical blow on the day he completed his final initiation, and his grandsire bestowed the earned accolade of full mastery.

Every particle of will, of good sense, of learned wisdom, wished for opening to remake the past. Yet the maze forced one foot to follow the next. Arithon could not change his cognitive memory, or alter the choices that unstrung his fate. All over again, with bruising awareness of consequence, he answered his father's request to shoulder the heirship of Karthan.

Then, as now, the decision cut like a sword's edge. The inherited drives of farsight and compassion unraveled his peace until he could not escape. The needs of a people must ever overshadow the cry of his burgeoning talents.

Yet this time, as Arithon repeated the impassioned words that sealed his decision to depart, vision widened. The maze forced him to share in an aged man's heartbreak. This pass, he was shown his grandfather's frail hands, locked in whitened anguish on the wooden desktop to mask their grief-stricken trembling. The dark, intense stare and inviolate stillness, then mistaken for censure, became cruelly unmasked as the High Mage of Rauven heard fully and finally that he would be losing his daughter's beloved son.

The most gifted master he had ever trained stood tall before him, and pronounced his intent to voyage to Karthan and rule a sandspit of marauding pirates. In measured, firm words, Mak s'Ahelas saw his years of restraint bear the fruits of triumph and punishment. Arithon had indeed learned to think for himself. The irony came barbed, that the relationship a wise grandfather had expected to cultivate with the young man he had tenderly guided would not ever flower under his roof at Rauven.

'Avar is fortunate,' Mak s'Ahelas had said, honoring his grandson's independence. By then a weary, lonely old man, he had been great enough to allow his young protégé the gift of his heady freedom.

The maze replayed every wretched detail. *Again*, Arithon s'Ffalenn knelt at his father's feet and swore his oath of peace over the bared blade of Alithiel. To the cheers of Karthish sailors, and the high mage's stifled sorrow, he set sail from Rauven, into blue waters and the very wreckage of his youthful hopes and dreams.

The barren fields encountered on that distant shore were no less an offense against nature, for the fact they were revisited in memory. The hunger of babes and the tears of the widows whose loved ones died at sea marked the heart with no less wrenching a sorrow. Arithon settled among the villagers of Karthan. Sharing poverty and rags, he engaged his deep talent and strove to transmute salted soil back to grain-bearing fertility. He engaged his mastery, used every trained resource at his command to assuage the devastation of generations of feud that had shackled a proud kingdom to garner subsistence through piracy.

The knowledge of his inevitable failure turned his words of encouragement to bitterest ash on his tongue. The maze did not forgive, or soften the outcome. Arithon *now* could not apologize for the defeat of his high aspirations.

His appeal died, broken to echoes between Kewar's unyielding stone walls. He could make no redress for the promise of hope that would be irremediably broken.

In wounding, inexhaustible detail, he retraced his path through battle and fire to the hour of his father's death, then his exile to distant Athera.

As the white static forces of the Worldsend Gate hurled him from Dascen Elur to the Red Desert, he screamed like the damned, to no avail. No ears heard. No help came. The Maze of Davien allotted its victims no mercy. Ahead, inexorable, lay the curse of Desh-thiere, then ten thousand dead in the field of blood on the banks of the river Tal Quorin. Arithon knew, *oh, he knew*, he could not repeat the violence of that reliving.

The wardspells allowed no deliverance.

'No!' Arithon walked, milled to abject despair. He could not face the consequence of the horrors he had wrought, bound by oath to the Kingdom of Rathain. His misuse of grand conjury to save lives would not spare him the vicious lash of full consequence. The spells in Kewar Tunnel were bound by their nature to mirror the past with strict clarity. He must experience the unspeakable toll of atrocity with no saving shield of separation. Every death, every wound, every shed drop of blood that already savaged his conscience would be replayed in clear empathy upon the stripped cloth of his mind, and the bound, naked flesh of his body.

Gyre

Protected in sanctuary at Ath's hostel at Whitehaven, the Koriani enchantress Elaira slept undisturbed as the night stars wheeled, and the stately turn of Athera led in the moment of midnight. Across the world from the point where she rested, the blazing noon sun touched the zenith, conjoining the balance of opposition. The waxing half-moon notched the eastern horizon, dragging the sea's tides, and the twining dance of the subtle energies of creation marked and measured each moving change of alignment.

Ath's adepts lived and breathed the awareness of such currents. They walked through each day, attuned to the harmonies of the spheres, adroit at reading angularities and patterns. In that late-night hour, as the vortex of tuned energies unlocked the electromagnetic signature that keyed the dimensional gateways across dreams, the male adept assigned to keep guard and watch sensed the forewarning of threat. He spun off a formed thought, then charged its ephemeral image with the gist of his focused intent.

Deeply asleep, Elaira's breathing acquired a slower rhythm. Her quickened thought traveled the corridors of dream, inevitably steered by the living flame of her steadfast love for Prince Arithon. The empathic linkage between their paired minds had been forged amid the quickened flux of a grand conjury. Such a binding ran outside of time and space, a marriage of consent between their two spirits sealed across the veil of the mysteries. No posset could quell those aspects of self that transcended the bonds of the flesh. In longing, in need, in tacit awareness of Arithon's raised state of distress, Elaira's footloose thoughts traveled. Her seeking journey unfolded, tracing the barriers of Davien's wrought wards, testing the force of each balking construct down multiple parallel avenues. Until midnight, crossed by the tide of sun and moon set in angular alignment, the tangential energies sprang into resonance. Led by the dance, her questing mind at last encountered the one opening that could grant her untrammeled admittance.

Wrapped in the raiment of lightbody awareness, the enchantress pursued her core of desire. She reached the pillars that framed the etheric entry to the grove of Ath's mystery. Beyond lay the heartcore of the hostel at Whitehaven, a well of bright power established and tended by generations of resident adepts.

Waiting on that threshold to meet her was the messenger of the male guardian, diligently standing his watch. 'Brave lady, beware. If you should cross this particular threshold, you will enter Ath's grove, but through a passage that will not answer to our directives. No one of us can extend you protection. The sacred grove lies outside the veil, and the gyre of forces therein will answer what lies in your heart. The strength of longing and passion can fuse. You can shift the framework of esoteric ideas into experienced form on the wings of your breath and pure thought.'

Her urgent awareness of Arithon's peril had no patience for sensible precautions. Yet Elaira forced the restraint to rein in her impetuous need. 'What are the dangers if I should go forward?'

The spun image of the adept bowed his head. Gold and silver ciphers entwined on his hood gleamed, a flare of bright radiance against the unformed shadow of dream. 'There are three. First, Davien's wards themselves forbid entry, once the powers of the maze have been raised. You would travel to Kewar through the gateway of Arithon's heart, in plain fact, your presence admitted as a breathing, inseparable part of him. If he dies there, the cord to your body would be cut. Your unmoored spirit would cross the Wheel along with him, while the flesh left under our care would slowly wither and finally stop breathing.'

'If I chose life?' asked Elaira, more wise than before to the nuance of the greater mysteries.

The adept's thought construct regarded her, gravely still. 'At that moment of crux, you could break your ties and claim separation from him.'

As Elaira started in surprise, the imprinted messenger nodded, his demeanor subdued with sorrow. 'Yes, brave lady, you can walk a path that does not twine with Arithon's. Choice gives you the inarguable right, but what then? You would stand naked in the Maze of Davien. Even the founding tenet of Ath's law could not intervene to avert the dire consequence. The act of laying claim to your fate would spare you the Wheel's turning, but leave you exposed, made vulnerable to the powers that hold Kewar inviolate. The protections there would destroy you without quarter for trespass upon warded ground.'

Listening, undaunted, Elaira spoke after scarcely a second's thought. 'You mentioned three perils?'

The adept's sending yielded in sad acquiescence. 'The last pitfall, the most obvious, concerns the ties to your order enacted by Selidie Prime. If you help your beloved, if you extend yourself by thought or by word to lend him support through your presence, you would bind him. As you fear, Prince Arithon would become entrained to obligation by a Koriani oath of debt.'

'I understand,' Elaira said in level earnest. 'If I don't go, Prince Arithon has one less chance to emerge from Kewar Tunnel alive.'

'Does he, in the harshest light of full truth?' The adept's messenger regarded her, his penetrating survey not unkindly, while the gray mists of moonbeams drifted through myriad ghost shapes about them. 'Your prince is s'Ffalenn born, tied to compassion as well as the gifted farsight of his matrilineal ancestry. The trial of the maze might snap his endurance, despite everything you can give.'

Elaira faced the bittersweet challenge, unblinking. 'I won't know that answer if I stay behind. Better, I think, not to abandon a man's fate on the basis of timid assumption.'

The adept's sending bowed. 'Brave lady. Believe this, whatever comes, the love you bear is not wasted. Go in grace, and may Ath's greater mercy walk beside you.' White robes seemed to shimmer as his form stepped aside, clearing her path to the portal.

Yet Elaira made no immediate move to advance. 'Have you other advice to assist me?'

Her request raised a blinding smile of relief, the outright acknowledgment her greatness of heart held to unselfish character and rare depths. 'Bless your wisdom for asking, yes. The entry must be carefully handled if your arrival is not to draw notice. When you pass these pillars, go straight to the spring. Look neither right nor left. Reach the water, wet your hands, and close your eyes. Do nothing more than imagine your beloved. Let the water absorb the fullness of your feelings. Allow the transfer to happen through love, with no stake set on the outcome.'

Elaira returned his smile in salute. 'Thank you, wise one. Rest assured, I shall do as you say.' She stepped forward then, her commitment made firm by the irresistible cry of her heart. The adept's reserved warning had simply reechoed the augury once given by no less than the Warden of Althain: that if she failed Prince Arithon, or he failed her, the result would call down disaster.

Elaira did not pause to reflect or look back as her step crossed the portal, and the sacred grove's gyre of wild energies closed down, and irrevocably swept through her being.

The icy splash of clear springwater sluiced through her, transmuted into a maze of overlaid images. Multiple views blurred one into the next, their kaleidoscopic spiral spun down to sequential memory . . .

Elaira experienced the green eyes of Arithon Teir's'Ffalenn meeting hers in the gloom of a seeress's garret. Amid split-second contact, the still, small shock of awareness closed the gap between minds. She knew beyond doubt that here sat a man fully trained in the ways of the mysteries . . .

Then fleeting contact melted away, submerged by the tumbling bedlam of a taproom brawl. The moment came back, resharpened to living immediacy, as Arithon fell to the blow from a pastry roller. Dropped at her feet, his harried consent reechoed with laughter, as he allowed her wrought sleep spell to claim him . . .

Renewed recall yielded the chilly night gloom of the innyard stable loft. Elaira breathed in the dust of old cobwebs and the meadow-sweet scents of mown hay. The piercing eyes this time reflected a rage that blazed in adamant rejection of a crown prince's inherited fate. *Karthan's griefs were all too hurtfully recent, and the temptation, refused, though just barely, when love and loyalty had sorely begged the false steps of engaging wrongful acts in requital! Arithon had not turned his knowledge of grand conjury to spare a father from dying.* He had not killed by causation. The wardings of shadow engaged for defense against Amroth's fleet had been cast with intent to dispatch the confused enemy into a harmless retreat.

Ships had burned; men had died in steel and fire, but *only* because overriding aggression had mistakenly caused frightened captains to turn in attack on each other. Arithon had not done willful murder. But the razor's edge of awareness borne away from the poisoned crux was that, *so easily,* he could have . . .

Then tumultuous emotion dropped into eclipse as the juxtaposed layers of images resolved down to *one,* stamped into pristine clarity: Elaira felt Arithon's warm palm cup her cheek. His other hand stroked wisps of hay from her hair with a touch of unnerving tenderness. Dream and longing merged into resolute form: he was there with her, *all of him,* self laid bare in the vital charge of a moment's restructured symmetry. Elaira was Koriani, exactingly trained to interpret the nuance revealed by a face. The contact purloined through the Maze of Davien exposed the intimate feelings replayed through a man's being. This time, the empathic link wrought in Merior lent her the leverage for full understanding. Not the shading of conjecture she expected, evinced by the subtle tensions reflected in carriage and expression; instead, the unveiling took her by storm as the door between two separate minds opened without clouding pretense.

Arithon s'Ffalenn was mage-schooled to evince the exacting self-discipline of mastery. He lived and breathed, attuned to a reflexive state of rigorous mental clarity. Therefore, the bolt of fierce passion that shot through him scribed its response on his vulnerable heart. He resisted the hitched breath, *let the feelings flow in unimpeded.* His spontaneous reaction, by conscious design, became wholly turned inward, self-questioning.

Never denied, that surge of attraction raised no marring defense. Not even a whisper of rejection arose to reflect signs of conflicted interest.

Elaira now shared his stunned self-acceptance. Merged with his thought by the powers of the maze, she experienced the wonderment permitted to flower, spontaneous in beauty as a wild rose surprised into bloom out of season. She sensed Arithon's unflinching acknowledgment of her being as total and real, then followed his untrammeled review of probability. S'Ahelas farsight perceived the potential of a love profound and deep. Arithon found a joy beyond trifling attachment in Elaira's insightful wry humor. The magnetic allure posed by an enchantress who clearly saw through to his core framed a rarity demanding his absolute honesty.

The Maze of Davien unveiled the grand depths. Because the connection might be lastingly real, respect for the independent woman she was invoked Arithon's considered restraint. He would take measured pause before he unleashed the heedless, sweet rush of desire.

Here, as in the past, they met interruption. The Koriani initiate assigned to keep lane watch broke through the delight of enchanted discovery.

'*Sithaer's furies, not now!*' Elaira had cried then, venting frustration with a shockingly filthy epithet.

Arithon's response, '*I beg your pardon?*' showed contrite confusion, that he might have caused her inadvertent distress.

'*You did nothing,*' Elaira repeated in memory, the moment charged with crystallized dread for an upcoming round of harsh consequence. As emotionally volatile, her current awareness cried out to explore the exposed intimacy of Arithon's reminiscence.

The absence of barriers posed seductive temptation. Elaira longed for *nothing* but to let instinct rule, her being and Arithon's granted the unprecedented opening to meld into seamless accord. The honeyed promise of union beckoned her onward, forgetful of caution or danger.

A thorn prick of warning snagged her impulse short. Jerked back from the dizzying brink, appalled to discover how narrowly close she had come to unmasking her illicit presence, Elaira seized on the grace of her beloved's past flush of confusion. She spun subtle barriers using new knowledge gained through her study with Ath's adepts. In the split second before the Teir's'Ffalenn recovered his mage-schooled aplomb, she masked her incursion behind a delicate circle of concealment.

For better or worse, she now shared his fate. No course remained, except to endure the trial of Davien's Maze alongside him. If Arithon won free, no harm would befall. If he faced defeat, she would be there to offer him Selidie's tainted bargain in last resort to spare him his life.

Time unreeled. Joined in lockstep with Prince Arithon's experience, Elaira encountered the raised powers of Alithiel, when he once drew the sword against an attacking Khadrim in the heights of the Thaldein passes. At his side, she experienced the blade's weighty history, and with him, ached in bone-deep longing for escape from the yoke of royal destiny. She burned with his need smoldered like banked fire, to pursue to fulfillment his endowed aptitude for music. She knew the fast silence of Althain Tower, and as Dakar before her, lost her breath to the consummate, tuned edge that Arithon evinced in his handling of mage talent. She saw the true depth of his gifts brought to bear through the hour he had ceded his resource to Fellowship use to suppress an outbreak of venomous methspawn.

For the first time, since Merior, she grasped the full scope of his sacrifice at Tal Quorin. No moment was given to measure the pain. Time was granted no stay in the maze.

She wept Arithon's tears, watching the spirits of unicorns dance on the bare hills of Caith-al-Caen. As his heart bled, she tasted the whiplash of irony, as he suffered the hurtful brunt of Rathain's shattered legacy at Ithamon. Amid the ruined walls and the ringing, bright purity of the towers raised by the Paravians, she heard his scathing rebuttal of crown heritage, hurled down like a gauntlet to Asandir.

There came no release. The days unreeled, autumn to winter, in brute labor and windy turbulence, as Arithon twined his birth-born mastery of shadow with Lysaer's command of light to drive the Mistwraith into captivity. The adroit touch he used to weave mage-sighted conjury into the limitless fabric of spun darkness could not do other than leave her awestruck. Since his teachers at Rauven had never made an issue of him as a prodigy, Arithon used his gifts quietly. His rapport with the deep mysteries carried a forthright acceptance that moved Dakar to fury, and Asandir to well-guarded respect.

The result was a living masterwork. Grazed by scalded air as Lysaer's light bolts sheared aloft, buffeted by ripping gusts and chill as the mist slammed and cracked against an ink bulwark of wrought shadow, Arithon tempered the dark with fine spellcraft, spun to a precision that seemed outwardly effortless. Inside, he stifled the cry of his heart. His free spirit yearned to throw off the constriction of the crown rule that awaited at Etarra. He transmuted the bitterness, day after day; rejected the urge to wield his gift in raw violence to release his tied rage and the pitfalls of maudlin depression.

Through the exhaustive reliving as Desh-thiere was subdued, Elaira suffered Arithon's stress as the mage-sight he was born and raised to entrain jarred against the countercurrents of savagery inherent in any joined field of conflict. Since Karthan, Arithon had struggled to assimilate the hard lesson of tragic experience: in blood, he had learned the demands of high kingship could not be reconciled with the clean strictures that founded grand conjury.

The Maze of Davien forgave no uncertainty, glossed over no slip or incompetence. Arithon was dealt forced review of smashed dreams, the prismatic linkage of cause and effect replayed to the least stinging nuance. The visions laid bare the warp thread and the weft, as thought and emotion spun out the choices that sourced his personal experience. Though Elaira kept her shielded presence well grounded, the buffeting journey left her winnowed like chaff threshed in the wake of a squall line.

Nor did she have warning to brace for the moment when, in the throes of his labor to restore open sky, the Prince of Rathain detected the subtle presence of her own personal signature.

Appalled, Elaira first presumed her masking protections had slipped. As she reached in struck panic to seek out the breach, Arithon's mage-sight identified the source: no error on her part, but a separate event within the context of his past.

Unstrung by relief, Elaira belatedly recalled the fragment of gossip taken from Traithe, that Morriel Prime had once contrived to dispatch Lirenda into a scrying trance as her cat's-paw. The bald-faced attempt had been made to pierce through the Paravian wardings the Fellowship had entrusted to stand guard on affairs at Ithamon. The Matriarch had engaged the Skyron aquamarine, then used its recorded imprint of Elaira's unconditional, new love to garner admittance through the sealed rings of ancient defenses. Thrilled to wicked fascination, the enchantress now observed the course of events as the brazen ploy unfolded. She savored the piquant, inside awareness, that the foil to mask the Prime's covert prying had been tried without knowledge of Arithon's mastery.

A mistake that wrought backlash: the Teir's'Ffalenn maintained too keen an awareness not to realize the touch was no passing thought of his own. An intrusion set on him from outside, then, not necessarily unwelcome *except* that the sense of an irreconcilable imbalance lifted the hair at his neck. Trained reflex responded. Arithon set the intuitive imprint of Elaira's presence in Erdane against this moment's spurious contact. In splintering clarity, he saw the paired template of experiences *did not match*.

This touch of caressing, sweet tenderness was not based upon innate potential, but sprang from the aroused passion of a woman entrained by response to him in return.

Stunned yet again by the striking precision of Arithon's compassionate insight, Elaira recalled: *in strict fact*, her acknowledgment of an emotional attachment had resolved days after their fateful first encounter, when a formal Koriani interrogation had forced her to examine the issue in depth. Indeed, her conscious acceptance of Arithon as beloved *had never surfaced throughout the scene in the hayloft*.

That hour in Ithamon, bristled to forewarning, Arithon traced down the intrusive contact. His rage towered as he grasped the bloodless framework of Morriel's manipulation. Beyond question, he would permit no such meddling interference. Nor would he accept the implied violation, that Elaira's feelings had been shaped and used as a tool, without her informed consent. His testing probe measured with blinding speed, weighed the range of harmful probabilities, then extracted the tacit word of collusion which ensured that the Mad Prophet would turn a blind eye. Still charged to wild fury, *but not uncontrolled*, Arithon shaped his rejection. He revised the guiding intent behind the forces of shadow held poised to receive Lysaer's next inbound light bolt.

Each stage of enactment, from reflexive reaction to a genius command of fierce impulse, Elaira witnessed the mapped artistry of Arithon's rebuttal. She saw the charged powers raised to rip another breaching tear through the mists deflect in mid-course, to wreak havoc on Morriel's construct.

Nor did the maze allow one shred of quarter for the effects of constrained vindication. In simultaneous rebound, Arithon experienced Morriel's pall of alarm, for an upset arranged by a dazzling intellect she could not raise the spontaneous innovation to counter. As merciless in interconnected detail, the break in the Prime's unilateral competence became the hook that engaged Lirenda's twisted fascination with Arithon's character. The defense meted out in Elaira's behalf ripped past secure barriers, feeding the needy insecurity that drove the former First Senior's voracious ambition.

One moment's vengeful facet of brilliance, dispatched from Kieling Tower in Ithamon, became precursor to a dark future.

Elaira surveyed the changed landscape of repercussions, aghast at the brutal scope opened up by the maze's expanded vision. She watched, in stark heartbreak, as Prince Arithon shuddered to the chill shadow of his own making: that Lirenda would not accede to strength in a man she could not use spelled force to control. Her lurking fear must now evolve as blind hatred, lending impetus to her insatiable drive to seek outright domination. The lashing round of verbal humiliation she received from her distressed Prime further hardened Lirenda's denial. The latent love already stifled by terror, her vulnerable need to embrace pure compassion and rekindle the light of her lost self-acceptance was unlikely to find the gentle redemption a bard's gifted touch might *perhaps* one day have awakened.

The maze was a lens that unmercifully exposed: a branch in Arithon's life path slammed closed, more of his cherished freedom of movement irrevocably rendered forfeit. Tumult and tragedy, as the barb of satisfaction chosen that fateful, past moment at Ithamon presaged the unconscionable abuse of a herdboy named Fionn Areth . . .

Arithon paused, wrung to gasping remorse. The next step forward would not bring reprieve, or the next, as the coils of Desh-thiere were bound under seal and ward. Victory here would but lead to further imprisonment. Ahead loomed the upheaval surrounding his crown oath at Etarra, then the first breach of his inviolate will under the curse of the Mistwraith. That fracture of self would birth all the horrors of Tal Quorin, and the ultimate loss of the prodigious, sighted talent that stood as his raised shield against Morriel Prime's deadly enmity.

In the dark of the maze, Arithon uttered his threadbare plea to sustain. 'Move, damn you! No fear can be worse. It's just a reliving. The fiendish embellishment is nothing but truth, and truth, of itself, does not kill.'

But conscience could, and had, in this place, where Kamridian s'Ffalenn had died screaming.

Elaira held fast, her empathy crushed silent, as her beloved mustered his strength and mastered another step forward . . .

The sequential impressions raked like cut glass, as Asandir arrived on the scene and exchanged brisk words of chastisement. Arithon retreated to seek solace in solitude. Alone in the ruin, he was hounded first by Ithamon's endowment of haunts, and next by his half brother's misguided effort to seek his counsel in private. The hour wrought consequence: the Master of Shadow, too ridden by anguish, and Lysaer, too ignorant to realize the perils of speaking outside, on unwarded ground. The Mistwraith launched a vicious attack and caught them defenselessly exposed.

Elaira shared the bursting crisis firsthand, as Arithon raised talent to counter. She tasted his rank fear as his efforts to set wards became jangled; each construct unbound before his seals could be joined into stable completion; tearing breaches that erupted across his fixed barriers with no more finesse than a chalk line erased by the feet of a trampling multitude. Although Elaira had been born on Athera when the mists still enveloped the sky, she had never sampled the nature of Desh-thiere's underlying malevolence. No record existed, for what she beheld in the maze-wakened stream of Arithon's recollected experience. The nightmare terrors that surrounded and tore at him had no form. They expressed through no framework of flesh. Pure spirit, they swirled, fragmented faces with leering, fanged mouths, and empty, vicious, starved eyes. Hands plucked, one touch seductive and insistent, and the next, raking with claws to rip life essence out of the aura. The wraiths were not one, or a dozen, or a hundred, but a mass mind too vast to encompass. Teeming millions of entities had fused over time, awarenesses knotted and tangled into a vortex of virulent hatred. Their amalgamate presence was malice distilled, a more dangerous net than any spider could weave to entrap its diet of hapless small insects.

The influx Arithon strove and failed utterly to grapple was a massive gestalt, cognizance loomed into an insatiable thirst to consume and assimilate life.

Elaira shuddered to acknowledge the colossal misapprehension, that Morriel Prime, and after her, Selidie, had neither understanding nor experience to measure the broadscale threat posed by the entities the two princes had subdued at Ithamon. Koriani lore held no concept to encompass the malevolence, live and seething under ward beneath Rockfell. Otherwise, no Prime would dare the audacity to meddle, or play Arithon as a live pawn in their age-long struggle to disband the Fellowship's compact.

The horror defied description, as Desh-thiere's attack side-stepped Arithon's invention with alarming speed and agility. Its lancing, swift contact stabbed like needles of ice, razing through spell-wrought shielding with numbing force. No work of man seemed enough to counteract a barrage of such sustained ferocity.

Demoralized by what seemed an inevitable slide toward defeat, Arithon still fought. He ceded no ground. His mulish, inventive resistance served breathtaking rejection to the overpowering force ranged against him. He would not stand down, though every barrier he raised flashed to ruin like spark-touched lint. Against landsliding despair, the Master of Shadow held to his obdurate belief: that an avenue to stave off annihilation *must* exist. The intelligent complexity of Ath's creation was not bound by limitation. Some untried combination of wards must be possible to wrest back the chance for salvation. He clung to hope, mustered bare-handed resource for as long as he could stay upright.

More than his own life lay at risk. Lysaer had collapsed. Arithon dared not break, lest the half brother slumped in his arms become the shared victim of his incompetence.

Yet against the brewed horde of Desh-thiere's wraiths, one man's self-determined refusal to yield was the wish of a feather exposed to a gale. Arithon felt wrung through. He reeled, milled under and hooded by probing darkness. His lost senses were buffeted by incomprehensible movement and noise until his knees gave way underneath him. He sought to cushion Lysaer from harm as he swayed and lost his balance. Then agony sliced through and splintered his mind to a thousand glittering fragments.

Just as trapped by the maze's projected reliving, Elaira heard Arithon's harrowing scream resound through Kewar's sealed passage. For a moment, elusive, *something* of cold purpose flicked and passed like a snake through his mind. She felt it questing, gathering, absorbing his core being with a ransacking turn of intelligence. Then a crackling force of purple-white light snapped down like a shining cleaver. The shadowy presence retreated, its tainting influence there and gone without trace.

Elaira grasped after the memory, concerned an impression of vital importance had somehow escaped her awareness. But she lost the ephemeral sense of its essence. The encounter receded, unformed as the shimmer of heat lightning glimpsed and then lost into distance.

Then Asandir's voice cried, *'Let go. Dakar has hold of Lysaer.'*

Through Arithon's spinning vertigo, and a nausea that grabbed like sloshed sand in his gut, the ugly, rifling presence escaped memory, obliterated by thundering torrents of bared force as the Fellowship Sorcerer unleashed his might in protection. Merged at one with the Shadow Master's mind and memory, the enchantress lost herself to awe, that a spirit in command of such power as this should still walk as unassuming humanity.

Elaira saw nothing, felt nothing beyond the dazzling constraint in Asandir's bridling of raw power. Forces that *by their wild nature could have unstrung the grand arc of the veil, and banished all substance to chaos.* Such was the depth of the Sorcerer's resource, *he could have expunged the most rigorous Koriani protections from the face of Athera on the spin of a moment's defined thought.*

That his Fellowship had not countermanded free will; had not crossed outside the bounds of the Major Balance to blunt the pricking thorns of the Prime Matriarch's meddling bespoke a tolerance beyond comprehension. Recast to such scale, the order's belligerent challenge of the compact seemed an act of desperate insanity.

Reluctant to examine the reach of such insight, Elaira regarded the troubled conference that followed the Mistwraith's attack.

Asandir led the questions. His mage-sighted survey of the surrounding countryside touched every leaf, stone, and briar like a probing interrogation.

That Arithon could track the Sorcerer's mental agility by now came as no surprise. Yet the heartsore regret he experienced in the maze wounded all the more deeply set against the concurrent awareness that access to talent was closed to him.

He could not turn back. The last days in the battle to contain the Mistwraith unfolded, inexorable, the glass edge of danger braided through the close-woven thorns of a jagged despair. Each step unwound time; carried him closer to his accession at Etarra, and the horrific reckoning meted out on the banks of Tal Quorin.

Arithon plowed ahead. His progress was accomplished by ingrained determination, and the steel-cased awareness that to stop, or to languish, would buy him no grace of relief. Davien's web of spellcraft held no mercy for the man who could not face his actions head-on. Past the harrowing hour of Desh-thiere's captivity, Arithon endured his ceremonial presentation as the Fellowship-sanctioned crown heir. *Again*, he knelt in the chilly spring earth of a rose garden to receive affirmed right of succession from Asandir.

The antagonistic hatred and distrust of the townsmen surrounded him like a caul, day and night. He breathed and moved through their webworks of intrigue, slept and walked under strong wardfields entrained to deflect the knives of their covert assassins. Hampered in strangling cords of obligation, Arithon traversed the last days leading up to his disrupted coronation. Hindsight let him see the Fellowship's tension; telltale signs embedded in words, and in the consummate handling of masked reactions. The Sorcerers had been forewarned of a reckoning to come on that fateful day in Etarra.

Freely sweating, arms crossed tight at his chest as though mortal strength could restrain the cry of his captive heart, Arithon made his way forward. By the cascading complexity of his emotions, Elaira saw how the Fellowship's awareness cast disturbing, fresh light over the shape of events yet to come. *The Sorcerers had known, and not acted.* The reason for such a momentous betrayal stayed maddeningly veiled beyond reach. In pursuit of that mystery with all his sharp wit, Arithon reached the inevitable crux of the hour he became cursed by Desh-thiere.

Elaira sensed his shrinking trepidation. Beside him, she experienced the blackout dread that threatened to sap his fixed will.

Here lay the dire crossroad. The next step forward must refire the moment that had fully and finally unstrung the course of his life.

Arithon's whispered cry of appeal was addressed to his absent grandfather. 'Mak, when I said I could not accomplish what's asked, you told me, by all means, start dying at once.'

'Shrink yourself down to a shadow, a ghost, because you fear to make a mistake? Mistakes are life, boy! They teach strength and character. Back down from the contest, and you cast to the winds the best part of your given potential.'

But had Rauven's high mage ever foreseen such a challenge as Desh-thiere's stroke of revenge?

Elaira held fast, pressed to uttermost sorrow, as Arithon s'Ffalenn mustered his courage. She heard him speak the forlorn phrase in Paravian, *'Iel drien i cadiad duerung undai sied ffaelient,'* meaning, 'Light for the path leading into rank darkness.' Then he gathered himself and stepped unresistingly forward.

Again he was fleeing through packed throngs of people, seeking Fellowship assistance, and *again*, the hands of two merchants detained him with self-righteous force. His half brother's cast light bolt arced over the packed square, with himself held as captive target. Arithon had no time, no chance for evasion. Traithe's raven, extended in flight overhead, became his sole hope to draw help. In his desperate fear, he ripped his right wrist from the townsmen's encumbering grasp. Only one split second of freedom, and one narrow opening for choice: he had snapped off a shadow laced through with spells to protect the Sorcerer's winged messenger.

Elaira gasped, knowing as Arithon had, that the brunt of Lysaer's offensive must now strike his naked hand.

At the crux of reliving, he had curbed all fear. Yet his past grounds for trust became poisoned, in hindsight: that his trained talent and his skilled handling of darkness could still intercede and effect a recovery after the moment of impact.

Superbly prepared, his balanced mind braced to withstand searing pain, he turned his palm upward. By the first jolt of contact, he had already engaged shadow. The lethal force of wrought light was strained off on effortless reflex. Then the stunning, stark horror that served warning, *too late*: as a power embedded within the assault burst through his defenses unblunted. Spiraled energies pierced *through* his wards in a half twist, and wrapped his exposed flesh like hot wire.

Arithon screamed. Wrenched out of mental alignment, he was

slammed to his knees by a blistering influx of agony. His torment was not born of blinding light, nor charring heat, but the cleaving bite of spellcraft aligned with devastating thrust to cause harm. The construct was not random. Its design had been specifically tempered to access the range of his shortfalls. In one stabbing thrust, weeks past, at Ithamon, the Mistwraith had mapped out this strategically tailored attack.

Beyond help, the shocked victim discerned his misjudgment. *Lysaer's light bolt had been no more than the carrier to enact Deshthiere's vengeful malice.*

Arithon fought, wrung breathless as the jagging, red coils of the curse closed over him, mind, heart, and spirit. His banishing wards were deflected straight back at him. He dodged, and encountered the vibration of Name, his own image the raised snare to entrap him. The Mistwraith's incursion ripped viciously inward. He felt its prongs pierce his inviolate core and invade, threading an inextricable geas of compulsion: *for as long as he held to life and breath, he would seek to destroy his half brother.* Arithon contested each coil of the pattern. His countermeasures met defeat. All his raised barriers crumbled. As a whole being, he could not be divided against himself. Yet to thwart Desh-thiere, he must try. A string of laid snares anticipated, then blocked his attempt to cut away the taint entwined with his essence. The Mistwraith had learned guile. The innovation that once had saved Traithe from possession became most cruelly forestalled. Not even self-destruction could wrest back the firm ground for Arithon to seize back his will and stay free.

Rathain's prince sensed the moment as his doom settled over him. Conquered from within as though self-betrayed, he set his last resource to mitigate a defeat that lay beyond reach of salvage. As Desh-thiere's core hatred supplanted his will, he applied his whole being to thwart its directive and to resist its rank clamor for bloodshed. The backwash of shed energies hurled down the merchants. They died where they fell at his feet. Arithon snatched up his dropped sword. Even as the Mistwraith's curse wakened the scalding desire to kill, he stretched ingenuity to maintain his denial. Mage-trained to full mastery, he knew how to govern the templates of mind and emotion. Destructive thoughts could be bent onto tangents. The venom of murderous intent could be stalled, outwilled through doubleblind logic and feint. Arithon chose a strategic retreat and unleashed his power of darkness over Etarra. Against that apparent capitulation, he thrust the sealed rune of limitation. Shadow descended, dense enough to blinder his enemies' vision, but reined short of the freezing blanket that might inflict lethal harm.

A shuddering half instant of recoil ensued, as the curse slackened slightly, appeased by his hedging subterfuge. Arithon snatched back initiative and took flight. Lashed to blind pain, he could do nothing else but impel himself from Lysaer's presence.

His crazed dash to the stables, the soft warmth of his horse, then his ill-starred effort to release the clan children enslaved by the knackers – the reliving passed in a blur of ripped motion and noise. Holding the curse's directive at bay was like treading live coals, possible if he kept moving. If he thought about *anything else,* the raging urge to slay Lysaer could be checked and redirected into manageable bounds.

Arithon had schooled for long years at Rauven to instill the discipline required by grand conjury. That endowment alone let him find Etarra's gate. He managed to ride out, through a scattered lack of planning. Distance bought him a measure of reprieve. The curse lost full strength the farther he moved away from Lysaer's proximity.

He chose the north road because he had been driven, and because south, there lay only Ithamon . . .

Tal Quorin

The copper brown bed of last autumn's beech leaves felt no less damp in the reliving invoked by the Maze of Davien. Once again, Arithon s'Ffalenn poised on bent knee under the dappling gold of spring sunlight. On that past day, a hawk had flown, crying, and he had been chilled through and shivering. *Just as before*, he spoke the oath that affirmed him as sanctioned crown prince. *'I pledge myself, body, mind, and heart to serve Rathain, to guard, to hold unified, and to deliver justice according to Ath's law. If the land knows peace, I preserve her; war, I defend. Through hardship, famine, or plague, I suffer no less than my sworn companions. In war, peace, and strife, I bind myself to the charter of the land, as given by the Fellowship of Seven. Strike me dead should I fail to uphold for all people the rights stated therein. Dharkaron witness.'*

A binding promise made to a kingdom whose honesty he would see broken; *he was curse-flawed*. Worse loomed than dishonor. Ahead, he would face the betrayal of self. The legacy of his mage-trained talent must pitch him into inevitable conflict under the shadow of coming war. Imprisoned in vision, he felt reviled, never so aware of the *caithdein* standing guard at his back, the naked length of Alithiel unsheathed in a trusting and steadfast hand.

The Maze of Davien showed no mercy, in hindsight. This hour's raw grief tasted bitter as poison, with suffering and bloodshed looming; a stamped record of atrocity unsoftened by years, that far exceeded the past's nerve-wound mantle of unformed, anxious foreboding.

Wracked in mind, sore of heart, the invested prince who lived then reenacted his royal blessing over each clansman's offered pledge of sword or dagger. On his feet in Kewar Tunnel, his tears of remorse ran unchecked, while in Deshir's greenwood, under stainless spring sunshine, the ancient ritual ended. The last weapon was duly returned.

In reliving, Rathain's crown prince arose. He received back the cold grip of his Paravian blade from Steiven s'Valerient's hand.

'My first act,' he said then, 'will be the rending of that oath.' For in fact, on that hour, he still planned to abandon the burdensome legacy of his ancestry. No imaginable cause might justify the peril of risking his mage talents to the compulsion of Desh-thiere's curse. The ethical simplicity of that past resolve now returned to haunt him unbearably. Then, Arithon could not bear to meet Earl Steiven's eyes, dead set as he was to enact the part of the craven, leaving Deshir's clans with the lesser betrayal of facing entrenched feud with Etarra. War and death, please Ath! An ugly enough future, but one kept untainted by the warped evil ruled by the Mistwraith's design. Let his name be accursed by man, woman, and child, before he risked a whole people to usage as the weapon of geas-bent enmity.

S'Ffalenn compassion could weep for the doomed; yet s'Ahelas farsight and the obligations of crown oath demanded one last step. Arithon would shoulder the task of scrying the future to test his decision for surety.

In Kewar, his beloved marked his care for integrity. Wrapped under sealed wards, Elaira endured in silenced misery as she matched the bias of actualized circumstance with the wrenching confession Arithon had once cast at her feet in the night solace of a tropical greenwood. He had made passing mention of a cast augury. Now, she saw the enactment revealed, and the shock of full clarity harrowed her.

Rathain's invested crown prince slipped away from his oathtaking. As a master of magecraft, the most assiduous trial he could bring to bear upon his planned course to break faith would be the prescient vision born out of a tienelle trance. Dangerous work, since the narcotic herb used to open the mind was also a fatal poison.

In solitude, standing on unwarded ground, the perils that Arithon shouldered entailed a frightful array of sharp risk.

Touched by shrinking terror, Elaira realized too late that the vigil she kept might leave her overfaced. Nor was Arithon scatheless. She tasted his fear, felt the clammy kiss of sweat at his temples. Firsthand, she experienced his ironclad resolve as he forced his mind steady, then packed the stone pipe he had filched from the stores in Sethvir's satchel. One with her beloved, Elaira partnered that bleak night's forecast, an agonized search through alternate futures that traversed the landscape of nightmare. She saw death, and death again, horrific visions of unrequited human suffering. The shock did not lessen, for the thousand desecrations of the body brought down untimely by weapons of war. With Arithon, weeping, she witnessed atrocity, repeated with brutal invention, as each thread of happenstance revealed Deshir's clans massacred to the last man. *And not only men, but children, young boys, cut down by steel and arrow, and worse: the executioner's clotted blade in the packed public square in Etarra.*

Elaira understood, as never before, the net of dilemma that had closed down on that lonely night in the glen of a northland forest. Arithon had languished, his sensitized nerves unstrung, against the trunk of an ancient oak. No ghostly twist of imaging had prepared for the scale of disaster unveiled by his augury. He had waited in forced patience, while the lingering aftertides of drug-induced vision subsided. In strict solitude, he sifted the spurts of hazed fantasy from the unpleasant bones of hard evidence. He could still run, leaving Steiven's staunch clansmen to die. Or he could stay, wield his talent in killing defense, and face the brazen risk of Desh-thiere's curse. Perhaps, *given no unseen turn of ill fortune*, he might keep a third of them living . . .

The toll of mute slain would burden his conscience, whichever choice he enacted.

In the night clearing, while grief and dire poisons cramped his wracked body with sickness, Elaira shared Arithon's heartrending vigil. She felt every shiver course through him, as he agonized over his future. This was not Karthan, where restored peace could be bought through the healing of salt-ravaged fields. Here, in Athera, the burdens of crown oath were most likely to entangle his integrity with the direct violation of killing. Desh-thiere's curse forged that high probability into near-devastating certainty. Etarra's armed host would be marching already. Prince, or mage, which facet of self to betray? And what savage reckoning would remain to be paid on a field ruled by feud, if the flaw in his being wrought by enspelled vengeance overwhelmed his restraint and claimed triumph?

The safest course, damnably, was to tuck tail and run. Self-contempt seemed cheap coin to deter the Mistwraith's unclean design. Leave Deshir, reject royal heritage, and never look back, and he might escape being the string-puppet tool to wreak murder upon a blood kinsman.

Yet whether Arithon could have cast off his doom, if he might have seized one last opening to reshape the coil that bound him, his birth-born legacy of compassion undid him. The reliving unspooled with damning, bright clarity and exposed the moment the snare had snapped shut.

Again, young Jieret s'Valerient invaded his solitude, and triggered the fateful precognizance: *the vivid image of Deshir's women and girls lying slaughtered in the moss by Tal Quorin.*

'Ath, oh Ath!' Elaira gasped, stormed and shattered by rending pity. 'Cry mercy, beloved, you could not let them go!' The brutal exposure of Arithon's trial broke her heart and her mind, the grievous awareness lent bitter edge, since the tragedy he would have stayed to avert already lay beyond salvage. The stark echo of her pain, matched to his, remained warded. Nor was the past walked in lockstep with Arithon's in any one facet still mutable. Tal Quorin's massacre must be reenacted. The powers of the maze would spin out the events with detailed and hideous ferocity. Arithon was foredoomed to feel each death singly, retracing the course of his footsteps.

Trapped in the cognizant, shocked mind of the present, Arithon relived the hour he had weighed the untenable horror of girls and women, torn bloody and violated. He could not turn aside. Just as he had been unable to suffer the widows left weeping in Karthan, he took willful charge. He would stay on to brave every vile consequence, and stand to Deshir's defense.

Arithon s'Ffalenn sustained the nerve-stripping distress. He stepped forward, consumed by the colossal irony, that his sacrifice would be made futile. At Merior he had spoken his inadequate summary, a trusted confidence given to Elaira as he struggled to reconcile the damning pain of the aftermath: '*More than two hundred clansmen survived the fight at Tal Quorin. But there is no settlement to be found in such victory. I can't sort past the deaths and the bloodshed to say if their lives matched the cost.*'

Alone in Kewar Tunnel, he would plumb the vested truth of that statement: he would know in full measure the savage impact of the choice he had taken, the torment and loss of eight thousand dead played through on his living flesh.

'Cry mercy,' Elaira whispered. She choked down the sympathy that urged her to let down her barriers. To watch was unbearable, a violation of all of a man's guarded privacy. Yet in love, for survival, she must hold fast. Stilled to awestruck silence, she watched Arithon measure the abyss and muster the rags of his courage.

Eyes shut, he trembled. Sweat sprang and rolled down his temples. 'This is not punishment, but knowledge of what a man, a woman, a child have all borne,' he entreated in ragged unsteadiness. In anguished effort to brace up his nerve, he exhorted in the musical cadence of Paravian, '*Anient fferet i on arith*,' the broken phrase meaning, 'All action must beget consequence.'

At Tal Quorin, his hand had shaped spells that killed. He had wielded a sword and done murder. Fear strangled resolve, for the reckoning the maze would mete out, a lash to inflame the already bleeding wound of s'Ffalenn conscience. Compassion could never be reconciled with suffering. Reluctance became weakness that threatened to unman him, and for one dire moment, he faltered.

The embedded power of the maze reacted.

Arithon's form shuddered, shimmered, lost definition at the edges. Through a second of suspension, Elaira beheld his fractured being, split off into alternate images: the past self, which had no other choice but move forward, and the present, ripped out of itself by remorse, that shrank back from owning the burden of an unbearable destiny.

Koriani awareness awoke the shrill instinct of danger. Elaira fought panic, well aware that such separation must open Arithon's defenses. Divided against himself, he would face annihilation. Anything less than whole being would rend his awareness into fragments that could not sustain breathing life. He would perish, tormented as his ancestor Kamridian, first condemned, and then shredded apart by the poisoned storm of his self-hatred.

Braced to act, poised to rip down her wards, Elaira was stopped by a movement. Caught short, she beheld the spun-silver wraith of a girl, standing staunch at Arithon's back. The child had a horrible gash in one hand. Her face was carved into piteous hollows by the ravages of fever and starvation.

Elaira recognized the little one. This was the clanbred child, sickened from gangrene, who had been delivered out of slavery from the horse knackers' sheds at Etarra. The girl who had died free, her last breath drawn in the shelter of Arithon's arms. Because she had been too ill to walk, he had taken her onto his mare in the course of his harrowed flight out of the city.

Now, in the stifling darkness of Kewar, the girl's smile emerged like the play of light, dancing over clear water. 'For your kindness,' she said, and closed her small fingers over the limp hand of the ghost trace of Arithon, who now faltered. 'My liege, look forward.'

In split form, Rathain's prince turned his head. He beheld the one moment of forgotten grace that occurred in advance of the carnage. *Again*, young Jieret, son of Steiven s'Valerient, knelt with a boy's knife for carving. Flushed by excitement, he cut his palm and completed the formal binding of friendship with the man who was sovereign prince. *A blood oath bound and sworn by a mage set its ties to the living spirit* . . .

Merged back into one with a shuddering cry, Arithon stumbled, caught by other strong hands: Steiven's, wrought of silver-spun light, and after him, an ethereal, sweet touch that bespoke encouragement from his lost wife, Dania. 'For your sacrifice,' they whispered, 'for the continued survival of Deshir's old bloodlines, and for the cherished life of our son.'

Arithon drew a ragged breath to entreat them, to explain that Jieret had been murdered by Lysaer s'Ilessid after all, quartered and burned as a sorcerer. 'He was taken captive in my place, then butchered like a dog in Daon Ramon Barrens.'

But his voice went unheard. The ephemeral shades of Rathain's lost *caithdein* and his lady already stepped back and faded. Arithon was left standing upright, shivering in clammy sweat, surrounded by biting, cold darkness. Saved. He had only to move forward again and face the full reckoning that waited in Strakewood Forest.

'Cry mercy,' Elaira whispered, still shielded. Shaken by wretched tremors of dread, she watched her beloved reach into himself and muster the will to press onward. Just as the past he had lived had not allowed him to abandon Steiven and Dania, Arithon could not fall short in the Maze of Davien. As Rathain's crown prince, he had sworn the Fellowship Sorcerers his blood oath to survive; nor could he cast away Jieret's brave death, that had set him free of Desh-thiere's triumph, and his half brother's armed trap in Daon Ramon.

Arithon stepped forward, and died first as a horse, down and rolling with the agony of a javelin shaft impaled through the gut. Thrashing, his throat opened in a scream of animal pain, he pressed on, and died again, as that mount's fallen rider. Paralyzed and neck-broken, he choked out his life with the taste of green moss and mud mixed with blood on his bitten tongue. Death did not release him. He suffered the lingering, penumbral shadow: the bereaved ache of that man's aged mother, and two brothers; of sister, and wife, and three fatherless children. Their tears and smashed dreams hammered nails of pure sorrow into his laboring heart . . .

'Oh, cry mercy!' whispered Elaira. Ribbons of tears coursed down her dreaming cheeks. Far removed from Whitehaven and the sheltered, secure couch of her body, she felt nothing of the hands that cradled her head, and brought towels as her pillow grew sodden . . .

She walked Kewar, as Arithon died, again and again, uncounted assaults of wounding steel; of arrows; of drowning; of maceration under thundering tons of unleashed current and logs, and razed trees. He died of spring traps, moaning from the ripping cut of sharpened branches that disemboweled. After a hundred contorted falls, he lay sprawled amid the spilled steam of his organs, whimpering for nonexistent mercy. He gasped out his life with crushed lungs, pinned under the weight of a bloated, dead horse. He drowned in his own vomit, facedown in black mud. He died trampled by panicked companions, and of threshing plunges into cunningly masked deadfalls, where he writhed impaled upon pointed stakes. He died of a cut throat by the hands of a furtive child. He died, weeping for his mother, his father, his young sons; for babes orphaned and wives abandoned to the miseries of unmarried childbirth.

Over and over and over again, the Wheel's dark crossing claimed him. Worse, sometimes he lived, croaking in fevered delirium from the slow agony of suppurating wounds. He begged in the gutters of Etarra and Narms, without legs, or a hand. Other times he endured in wasting neglect, in the care of impoverished relatives. He exhaled Gnudsog's last breath, gagging bile and silted water, and lay broken on a rock in a river as a girl child shot down by a quarrel. As a woman, he drowned in a river of hot blood while the bright sunlight faded to dark.

He died, raped and screaming, as Jieret's young sister. Of a sword thrust in the belly, he died yet again as Steiven's violated wife. He died as a babe, torn from the breast of his mother and spitted. He died, an old man, hacked like carrion; and the same, in eight thousand sickening variations, again and again, a progression of visceral nightmare that skinned his throat raw, leaving him voiceless. He pleaded in a scouring whisper, and still died, without water, without succor, without hope or mercy, while the repeated assaults of shattering pain hounded him to the threshold of madness.

When he could not walk, he crawled. The steel-poised awareness he sustained through mage training yet clung to a battered understanding. The spells that entrapped him allowed no relief; to stop would only prolong an already untenable suffering. He died of burning, of freezing chill shadow, of arrows that sleeted down through ripped leaves, and out of the dazzle of sunlight. He died to the frenzied, shrill clamor of steel, and then of a crossbow whose metals were sundered by an unspeakable, warped twist of spellcraft.

His ugly work; even mage-blind, he sensed his own patterning. For that act of transgression, young Jieret had survived; even still, conscience howled. He heard his grandfather at Rauven, words quiet and scornful with censure, then the thunder of Dharkaron's condemnation, a shriek that lashed with edged lightning, denouncing him in Paravian that no end ever justified the foul means.

Steiven's Deshans survived; *the act had to mean something*. But surcease was not granted in deliverance.

Arithon clawed forward by tortured slow inches, and died: of sword thrusts, of quarrels, of jabbing, sharp steel, snared in the slow sap of a tree's dreaming, his mind and his agony filtered in the muffled fall of snow and the whisper of leaves through midsummer. He died, slammed in the back by a javelin as he fled other clansmen wrought of illusion.

Then the moment of reliving he most dreaded overtook him, etched out in unnatural hatred. Arithon fought to rise up on one knee as he beheld the past vision of his half brother Lysaer, and reexperienced the smashing assault of Desh-thiere's curse. He howled in despair. No one answered. *Again*, his humanity was lost, milled under a riptide of black, burning passion. He felt mind and heart consumed by fell fires that tore away all restraint.

Again he opposed Lysaer, reforged as the Mistwraith's claimed instrument of destruction.

The horror returned, magnified, venom-sweet, as the ecstasy of surrender raked through him. *Again*, he blazed with the ripe triumph of the moment when he had mustered his shadows and raised his bared steel to annihilate his half brother.

One split second, in the maze, Arithon felt the inward recoil: *sensed the lashing response as the curse awoke in him, no stripped vision of reliving, but as an excruciating storm of live force that bludgeoned his exhausted grip on identity.*

Then young Jieret blundered into him with wrenching force, and tore him back into his past. *For this, the boy lived. Always to call him back from the brink, and for what purpose under Ath's sky?*

The suffering and death were ever destined to recur. The damning proof would compound, seeding holocaust at Minderl Bay, at Vastmark, and Daon Ramon Barrens . . .

Broken, weeping, Arithon crumpled.

He died, seared by fire and light, and died again, as a thousand trees, burning. He lay for uncounted hours in pain, tortured breaths puddled in rivers of shed blood, then met death again as a friend on the sharp, skilled knives of his kinsmen.

Grief beat him down. He languished in mourning for loved ones slain, and for others lost to nightmares and madness. He moldered as hacked bones beneath a stone cairn, under the singed trees of Strakewood. He blew on the winds as dry ash, and he cried as the rain falling on the slagged rock of a grotto.

At the end, lying flat on the slab-cold granite that floored the Maze of Davien, he wept for the beauty of a single voice. The bard was his lost self, immersed in the guidance of mage-sighted singing, that called on compassion and used woven harmony to settle the riven shades of the slain who wandered Tal Quorin, bewildered.

'You have to arise,' urged a gentle voice. A hand firmly tugged at his shoulder.

Arithon turned his head. Sucked clean of strength, he regarded the sad ghost who knelt over him, bearded and kind in the starlight. Tears clogged his throat. He unlocked his tongue and gasped a mangled utterance that resurrected a name from the past. 'Madreigh?'

'For the gift of your care,' the clansman admitted. His soothing quiet drowned the fading last clamor of Strakewood's red toll of slaughter. 'I breathed through the sunrise, and was laid to rest alongside my sons. For your effort, a brother survived me.' Madreigh reached out again. His touch was silvered mist, and his hands, healing light, as he bore Arithon's battered flesh up in his arms. 'Let me carry you through the crossing. As you did for me, let compassion free you from the pain as you meet your hour of reckoning.'

One step, two; Tal Quorin fell behind. The ghost of Madreigh embraced his liege, cradled like a child in his arms. Then he set his royal burden down, and on soundless footsteps, departed.

The nightmare horrors receded, leaving the bright-graven memory of eight thousand deaths, bound in chains of guilt and the withering ironies of Desh-thiere's entrenched geas of vengeance. The legacy lingered, no less cruel in reliving: Arithon felt the blank caul of blindness settle over the marvel of his gifted talent.

Set back on his heels, alone with searing grief and the ache of a loss beyond words, the man who was Master of Shadow and prince leaned gasping against the smoothed stone of the tunnel wall. He begged the still air for the grace to bear his bruised spirit onward.

No one answered; nothing stirred.

But in time, under starlight, a soft spray of lyranthe notes emerged and buoyed his flagging resolve. In music, he bought consolation, if not healing. On world-wearied feet, he assayed the next step, and the next, and the next, after that.

'So, prince, are you guilty?' Asandir's voice lashed at him from the darkness.

The harsh answer condemned.

Arithon shivered, still punished by the unequivocal truth forewarned by his tienelle scrying; that now, beyond the pale of his knowing, an enchantress he cherished shared also: *had he broken his crown oath to Rathain and fled, had he not stood to Deshir's defense using talent, the toll of dead would have numbered half of the eight thousand who had passed beneath Daelion's Wheel. But of the four thousand he might have left standing, who could have marched back to Etarra triumphant, no single one would have been clanbred . . .*

Deshir would have sheltered no standing survivors. The legacy of Jieret's people would have been utterly destroyed, lost to memory and land forever after.

'Cry mercy,' Elaira said, her shielded whisper scraped raw by sorrow. 'Beloved, I never knew.'

Hour of Darkness

Told by Ath's adepts that Elaira has dreamed herself passage to join her mind with the fate of her beloved, the Warden of Althain closes tortured eyes; for although the news brings him strong affirmation of Arithon's continued survival, he views probabilities, caught into recoil by an evil stab of foreboding: 'Cry mercy,' he murmurs, grief-struck and subdued, 'she's likely to break before he does . . .'

Met by Whitehold's seeress as her galley docks, and informed of Arithon's attempt to seek sanctuary inside Kewar Tunnel, Selidie Prime lends her view to the forecast that Rathain's royal lineage must be irretrievably lost: 'We know, since we once used a fetch to provoke Desh-thiere's curse, that the binding responds to ephemeral stimulus. Davien's Maze will grant Arithon no mercy. On the outside chance he can emerge alive, he will not retain grip on his sanity . . .'

During a catnap snatched on the crumbling wall in the midst of Mirthlvain Swamp, Asandir is touched by a true dreaming: *again* on the night sands of Athir, he accepts the fresh-blooded blade that Arithon Teir's'Ffalenn once used to swear his oath to survive; but the rending cry cast through time and space to the Sorcerer's listening presence on this hour frames a scream of unending agony . . .

XVI. Path of the Damned

Within the reactive spell-wards of the maze, the oath sworn at Athir changed everything. Immersed in the coils of reliving his past, Arithon knelt upon salt-damp sand, the knife cut beneath his freshly dressed wrist stinging like Dharkaron's vengeance. The full-throated scream torn out by his anguish slapped diminished reverberations down the corridor of Kewar Tunnel. The echoes rang still in his dreaming mind, though above, vision showed him a tranquil night sky, cloudless and jeweled with stars. Waves unraveled their white-lace petticoats against ribboned sand, glistening like old, tarnished silver. The dune grasses whispered of breezes.

Arithon ground his knuckles against his closed eyes, but could not erase the overlaid memory imposed by the powers of the maze: of the moment of oathswearing, when Asandir's vision had bled into his awareness, smashing across the blockage that blinded his mage-sight.

For one reeling interval, he had shared the breadth of the Fellowship Sorcerer's perception, the structural imprint of present experience underpinned by its etheric array of probabilities. Through Asandir's eyes, Arithon had watched the unloomed thread of creation spinning the course of the future. At the instant he pledged, while the searing, white lines of his binding promise became sealed by let blood to his fate, he had glimpsed the jagging red cords of Desh-thiere's curse, nipped like tight stitches through all he had done; and far worse: all he would strive to accomplish in the days and the years yet to come.

If Arithon had successfully thwarted the drive to pursue his half brother's murder, one glimpse through the Sorcerer's clarified perception revealed that his acts had not been untainted. Desh-thiere's geas might not have broken him to fully consenting collusion, yet it had still managed to rob him. In vicious small increments, its whispering currents sapped his autonomy. Creeping influence stained even innocuous thought, and slipped barbed hooks through his weaknesses, until the fragile balance he maintained between incidents abraded clear thought like the burn of salt rubbed in a blister.

Unmasked, as the blood oath tied him to life, Arithon reeled under the certainty that such secretive incursions must increase over time. The curse gained force and momentum at each subsequent encounter with Lysaer. Even the accreted memory of conflict sharpened the impetus of its pattern. The constant trickle of subtle manipulation must eventually swell to a current that would burst his last barrier and flatten him.

Arithon saw beyond ambiguity: within Davien's Maze, *each subsequent reliving would refire the geas, invoking the additional increase in virulence raised by a live encounter.*

'Cry mercy,' Elaira whispered.

She knew mortal terror. The trial her beloved shouldered in Kewar cast him beyond all concept of peril. Laid over the threat of his personal shortfalls, the ranging force of Desh-thiere's revenge could not do other than ruin him.

Arithon howled, heart and spirit, for release. But if any Sorcerer possessed the power of intervention, no stay of mercy was granted. Nor did the exacting weave of the maze let its victim take false shelter in mage-blindness. Initiate, now, to a masterbard's arts, Arithon could not deafen his wakened awareness as the rapport with Asandir faded. He now sensed Desh-thiere's curse as a continuous, buzzing dissonance, razing across his leashed thoughts.

Davien's Maze smashed illusion with diabolical thoroughness. Arithon bled on the thorns of fresh grief, too aware he would find no escape. He must carry his pernicious cognizance forward. Through the rending distress of the bloodbath to come, he would be forced to unvarnished acknowledgment of the manipulative twists his cursed nature had spun through the train of events.

The stark effort he required to arise and assay his next step drove Elaira to riveted anxiety. The dread in him gained over powering force, as his resharpened vision caught the stamp of Desh-thiere's design on his shipbuilding interest at Merior.

Again, Arithon returned from the north to find the yard's works damaged by fire. The cruel discrepancies this time stood exposed, a self-damning truth, that with unblighted mage talent, he would have set wardings. The ill will of the disaffected sword captain whose torch had engendered the sabotage would have been easily deflected. Recrimination tortured, that the curse itself might be fueling his guilt to ensure that his talent stayed shackled. Each step, each choice, each small tie of friendship came under the blighting venom of reassessment. Reviled by integrity set into question, the Teir's'Ffalenn traversed the maze, touched bitter by self-condemnation.

How much had the Mistwraith tempered his loyalties to a widow and her blameless children? Arithon stumbled, sucked by riptides of doubt. Had he in fact sworn Jinesse his oath of protection to excuse his involvement against the hour his presence must draw Lysaer?

'Forward,' he whispered. 'Don't think. Just move on.' He had but one grace to sustain him: on the night he had sailed, leaving Merior defenselessly open to Alestron's inbound war fleet, Elaira had gone far away. His beloved was blessedly sent outside his influence, safe under vows to her order.

'Cry mercy,' the listening enchantress whispered on the wrung rags of her breath. The unveiled pitfall yawned under her feet with acidly punishing clarity. For the heartrending phrases that Arithon had once spoken, imploring their separation at Merior, never showed a more vicious coil of truth: *'Give me torture and loss, give me death, before I become the instrument that seals your utter destruction,'* he had said. *'Of all the atrocities I have done in the past, or may commit in the future, that one I could never survive.'*

She must not lose her grip. Arithon's fragile hold on self-trust had never in life been more threatened. The unwelcome exposure, that she had dared step into jeopardy alongside him, might easily become the telling stroke that sealed his destruction. His trials in Vastmark still lay ahead, an entangling chain of events that must preface the most brutal encounter of all.

Sealed inside her warded circle, Elaira watched Arithon retrace the year's late spring and early summer, each facet of activity replayed with spell-stripped clarity. There had been joys to temper the sorrows of Merior's forced abandonment. Notes for

667

gold, written in unshaken faith by friends at Innish; a young boy rescued, to mitigate the tragedy of a six-year-old shepherd girl's fatal wounding on the claws of a wyvern. The thrill as the brigantine *Khetienn*'s completion raised a flush of pride and accomplishment. The untamed night splendors of the Vastmark sky lifted spirits, and the rough, chafing humor as the tribesfolk worked their herds of recalcitrant sheep. Afraid beyond words for the violence to come, Elaira ached for Arithon's braced recoil as he encountered the fresh stings of bared truth. For the sinister weaving of the Mistwraith's intent had indeed been laced through his most stringently guarded planning.

Ground down by that ongoing backdrop of devastation, Elaira cherished the rare moments of warm, human contact, blessing those acquaintances who had lent her beloved their affections, or steadied his moments of uncertainty. During the months the Alliance host mustered, Arithon had applied himself, unstinting, to life. The enchantress tasted his exhilaration in the archery contests, and again in the madcap pranks played to manage the cross-grained clansmen sent to handle Shand's raided livestock. She tracked her beloved's dizzying invention, then the inspired flight of planning that had arranged his daring abduction of Princess Talith.

Elaira's laughter, unheard, tracked the piquant contest of wits as Arithon proceeded to raid Tysan's ransom gold. Yet as the summer days lengthened, such byplay lost its savor. Grief shadowed the razor's edge of awareness, that the ending brought Talith to tragedy.

The princess's marriage would come to founder. The taint left by Arithon's wily handling would finally lead to her death, arranged by the machinations of conspiracy that riddled Lysaer's inner cabal at Avenor.

The small hurts struck deepest for being unexpected. Elaira suffered the backstab of the widow Jinesse's distrust, and the needling pitfalls of Dakar's virulent hatred. She watched, awed, as Arithon met the Mad Prophet's undermining interrogations with stark truth. Hazed in the smoke of a summer night's campfire, he had once admitted, bald-faced, the self-damning possibility that Desh-thiere's machinations might color each facet of his affairs. Davien's Maze saw that bleak probability confirmed, making a razor's nest of past hope.

Self-determined, Arithon sustained. Though the darkening trial of his planned defense, and the unforeseen snares wont to snag him, each footstep, he relied upon Caolle's gruff and unfailing support.

Too soon the freedom of Vastmark was exchanged for the tense court setting at Ostermere. At each turn, the maze affirmed Arithon's effort to maintain his core framework of honesty. The proofs stood like stars: in his unvarnished confession to Sethvir, that the insidious grasp of the Mistwraith's curse deepened its stranglehold at each encounter; then through the dance-step reenactment of diplomacy, as he rebuffed Havish's courtiers through the due public process of restoring Princess Talith to her husband.

The deep, hidden wounds were relentlessly exposed. Elaira shared Arithon's grief-struck rage at the stunning news of Captain Dhirken's death, hurled down in petty revenge as the ransom in gold was accounted. She endured the bleak hour of Arithon's recrimination, as he reboarded the *Khetienn* and drove under spelled winds back to sea.

On that hour, no friend stepped forward to help lift his leaden depression. Elaira resisted the sting of her pity, lent no grounds for interference. She had seen her beloved sustain worse as his nerve snapped at Minderl Bay; when at his royal orders, Earl Jieret had been compelled to break him at sword point, then force him to complete the hellish strategy that provoked Lysaer to destroy his own fleet. She clung to belief, and begged fate the next stage of reliving would not hold the unseen barb that would cripple. Given the clear winds and the freedom of seafaring, surely Arithon could use the delay to regain his fractured resiliency.

No succor came to him. The maze retraced his past, unremitting, and the hour delivered its freighted burden, a poisoned interval of self-condemnation suffered inside the locked privacy of his cabin. The ongoing strain compounded since Tal Quorin at last shredded Arithon's restraint. Nothing prepared Elaira for his suicidal risk, as he embarked on a maudlin and desperate bid to wrest back the slipped reins of his fate.

The method he chose courted outright disaster: to force the locked wall of his blinded talent by attempting a tienelle scrying.

Davien's Maze could only exacerbate the danger as the narcotic smoke of the herb expanded perception. The sudden, drawn tension in Arithon's carriage reflected his redoubled apprehension. A decision once made in isolate security, surrounded by leagues of salt water, must inevitably strike a more plangent chord in the course of a spell-forced reliving.

The volatile, fresh contact with a past, high-stakes crisis must provoke Desh-thiere's curse in live concert. Arithon shuddered, jabbed to unchecked terror. The next step might see his free will thrown irrevocably into forfeit.

Beyond any doubt, he had acted the fool, that unpleasant night after Ostermere.

The coils of the maze would redraw the penalty against irrevocable stakes. Arithon held no illusions. He confronted a passage of harrowing traps. To emerge intact, he must hold the Mistwraith's geas in check through raging madness: brave the unclothed nightmare of drug-induced visions, with no counterbalance of reason to temper his visceral reaction. This trial would hurl him outside known limits, a live testing in fire *made after subsequent encounters had strengthened the impetus of the curse.*

Arithon bore up under sweating dread. His strength now relied on his unassailable belief that he walked the maze in strict solitude. If the wretched worst happened and Desh-thiere's will triumphed, the bleak comfort remained, that no others would be doomed alongside him.

'Cry mercy,' whispered Elaira. Her resolute confidence ebbed to a flicker. Woe betide her if she came to break, and Arithon's peace became shattered by the signal unkindness, that her presence *in fact* rode the unmalleable risks laid against his fight for survival. The maze forgave no inept fumbling, no blunder of fatal ignorance. Like Arithon's rash move to drive fate through tranced consciousness, the enchantress could not reverse her decision. She could not escape the dread consequence of commitment as her beloved steeled himself and advanced.

Again, in the tossing dimness of the ship's cabin, Arithon lifted a spill from the candleflame. He ignited the bowl of the packed stone pipe with trembling fingers, set the stem to his lips, and drew breath. Like the seed of damnation, the spark ignited the silver-gray leaves of the tienelle. The stinging tang of toxic smoke spread throughout his filled lungs. The herb's effects followed, a swooping, spiraling rush that upended and shattered the senses. In transfixing fear, hung on the thread of agonized hope and the rage of rebellious exhilaration, Arithon rode the first wave of expansion.

Resolve from his past had welcomed the chaos. He could no longer tolerate life as the storm-tossed victim of fate. Stung by his forced abandonment of Merior; aggrieved by the unjust deaths of Lady Maenalle and Captain Dhirken; just that evening dealt a Fellowship Sorcerer's word that divisive ruin would sour Lady Talith's royal marriage, Arithon raged at his shortfalls. For far too long, he had left himself hobbled, unable to set the most basic of safeguards around his day-to-day movements. Trained talent had once accorded him mastery. He refused to handle the trials ahead, shackled by crippling helplessness.

Friends suffered for even his innocent acts. Acquaintances who enacted his business had *died* for the curse that beset him.

Arithon sucked down another rash breath. Confronted by pending invasion of Vastmark and the might of his half brother's war host, he saw no alternative but to try and wrest back his mage-sight. Hurled without anchor into the tienelle's rush of expanded awareness, he must wrest back the foothold to force the locked doors to his talent. In the past aboard *Khetienn*, at the crux of the crisis, he had rejected the likely alternative, that he might kill himself in the attempt.

Davien's Maze ripped away that tissue of delusion, laid bare his self-blinded dismissal. Impelled to the precipice, Arithon stayed chained to the instant as drug-fired vision unreeled out of control. He battled sharp terror. Amid thundering chaos, already lost, he wrestled the tide to cling to bare-bones survival.

Then nightmare dropped like a blanket and swallowed him. Fragmented visions flooded his mind. Deaths at Tal Quorin came indiscriminately mixed with the fatalities of sailhands, burned and drowned with the fleet at Minderl Bay. Their thrashing torment and their screams yanked him down. Arithon shuddered, unable to stay upright as the agony of a thousand unendurable wounds pulped his body and mangled his awareness. *Not again*; the maze had already extracted its due for those victims his actions had slaughtered. Yet Arithon failed to subdue his flayed nerves. Hurled to visceral revolt, he reeled, helpless, as his curse-driven violations of integrity touched off an explosion of drug-induced chaos.

No discipline saved him. The strictures to restore calm tore through his flayed grasp, and his access to mage-sight stayed darkened.

Arithon lost his anchoring contact with the present. The fixed stone of Kewar seemed fallen away, dissolved to a well of oblivion. Unmoored amid tumbling torrents of dream, he thrashed screaming, the horrific fragments of experience shredding thought to an abattoir of white pain. He was many men, dying to the red plunge of steel; he was the tears of women raped and widowed; he was a child, burning with fever instilled by a septic hand; he was a young girl, lying broken on rocks, bleeding out life from a crossbow bolt.

'No!' Arithon gasped. 'Not again.' But drugged vision cast up random memory like jetsam, and the maze, uncaring, reclothed unending deaths in the torment of pitiless detail.

'Cry mercy,' Elaira murmured, unheard behind her sealed ring of wards.

For this reliving augmented by tienelle exceeded the concept of punishment. Resharpened senses snapped each experience into still more ruthless a focus. Emotion expanded. Suffering and fear and blinding agony came refigured to a barrage of magnified emotion. The mind lost its boundaries. Imagination seized on distortions and ran rampant, until quivering flesh balked at mapping the scope of an ordeal driven amok. Ripped apart under the heightened influence of narcotic smoke, Arithon felt himself savaged. His talent stayed blocked. Each access he attempted pounded into blank emptiness, congealed over mind and heart. No method availed him. *He could not break through.*

Yet in contrary malice, the flares of unruly vision skittered past every stay of encumbrance. Etheric perception opened his sight in raging fits and starts. The effect made each battlefield a stark nightmare. Over pulped bodies lying churned in wet silt, Arithon watched the contorted flares of loosed energy shred into streaming smoke. Here, in the wake of violent death, animal magnetism bled off in a spilled miasma. The impact as spirit was torn from dazed flesh ranged outside the physical senses. Arithon felt each passage arise as a cry, marring the grand chord that inflamed the realms past the veil. He was a mote in a gale, flailed and winnowed as the destruction of massacre wailed across the living web underpinning all conscious creation.

The battered intellect languished, assaulted on levels beyond mind or heart. Drug-honed perceptions smashed identity and reason, until shocked flesh, torn asunder, defined breath and life. Arithon shivered and wept for release. Easier, to let go. So simple, to lie back and die of the next arrow or sword wound, to embrace a battering fall from a yardarm torched into crackling inferno. To surrender life, shed the mangle of crushed tissue, and let the turn of Fate's Wheel mill him under. The temptation to surrender himself to Daelion's judgment beckoned with the honeyed syrup of oblivion.

Yet the oath sworn at Athir forbade him that grace. Binding spells set over freely let blood strapped him to suffering survival.

Arithon plowed forward on hands and knees, long past mourning his gutted integrity. He was the sword, slaying; he was the arrow aflood in the stream of arterial bleeding. He was the cold brine of Minderl Bay, filling the lungs of a rat trapped inside a foundered vessel.

Davien's Maze had long since immolated the threadbare remnants of pretense. No refuge existed as the tienelle visions unfolded full view of his wretched, curse-driven destiny. The birth-born mold of s'Ffalenn compassion left him a wrung rag in the trapjaws of self-condemnation. Arithon dragged himself onward, his knuckles skinned raw against the stone floor of the cavern. He owned no more recourse beyond brute resistance. He could not evade culpability. No cursed act of violence could ever be justified under the Law of the Major Balance. His bruised conscience accepted expiation as meaningless. The dead would stay killed. An ocean of tears would not restore them. Arithon endured that assault of futility through bare-handed, dogged persistence.

And nightmare spurred him, each forced inch of progress achieved to the rake of steel through his heart. He was the fire, voraciously feeding until entrails and flesh crisped to paper. He was the tears of a grandfather's lonely despair. He was a clansman, gasping in leaked blood, perpetually caught at the crux of a mortal wounding. At next breath, he was an innocent babe, flash-burned by the levin bolt hurled down by Lysaer into the grottos of Tal Quorin.

That single death, in the random deluge of thousands, wakened the sleeping dragon.

Arithon bristled as the blaze of Lysaer's unleashed talent roused the coils of Desh-thiere's curse.

This, the true enemy whose handling could unstring him. Arithon howled in abject terror. No wall he raised might shelter the opened well of his mind. The geas rammed like a knife through the gaps torn by the tienelle visions. The cold-cast force of compulsion blazed uncontested through and through his whole being.

Stripped naked amid the surge of the torrent, Arithon planted his will in denial. Just as well ask the sand to reverse the riptide. Intact resistance had crumbled *long since*. For years, he had moved and breathed the insidious taint of Desh-thiere's spell turned corruption. Each year, each encounter, eroded him further; Davien's Maze even now battered the footing that grounded his failing stance.

Tienelle vision refocused truth with unflinching, painful clarity. Arithon owned no untouched bastion within, no clean space to guard his self-worth.

No choice, but to strangle in sighted awareness, tugged this way and that by the strings of the Mistwraith's revenge. The lockstep rape of choice that plundered his joy could only give birth to more acts of self-damning violation. Arithon groped forward. He wormed on his belly, confronting the mockery of a resistance that came to mean nothing. Brute endurance might sustain him for an hour, or a day, or a minute, all to no meaningful purpose. He must finally break down. His abraded identity would wear away, until he was sucked to a hollowed shell, directed by the string-puppet pull of the relentless evil he carried.

'No.' His whisper cast back flurried echoes. '*I will not go down.*' Over and over, he repeated the words to stave off crushing surrender. Nor would the Mistwraith have the least part of himself, uncontested. He would hold on, as he once had in Riverton, until the mind came unmoored from the last frayed tie holding sanity.

Yet even so brave, he could not sustain.

Elaira wept for inconsolable pity as the tienelle visions fell as a scourge upon Arithon's conscience. Better that his refined talents had never been born to Talera; that a world beset by Desh-thiere had never known the rarefied light of his talent. The loss would darken Athera for all time, that the exalted grace of her Masterbard's empathy should be cut down to mute struggle by suffering.

Elaira cursed the spelled works of Davien as Arithon shuddered into collapse. At any moment, the Mistwraith's cursed geas must finally shatter him. Well braced for this hour, worn sick by necessity, the enchantress readied the ritual runes of unbinding. Before she watched her beloved give way, she would cast off her concealment and dare intervention. Lent her strength and her balance, buoyed by her undying love, Arithon might find the grace to stave off final ruin. Debt to the Prime Matriarch seemed a small price to pay, if her joined presence could defer Desh-thiere's triumph.

If compromised, his will might be salvaged intact.

Yet her move to react was cut short.

An outside assault of rough magecraft hurled in, smashing like a dropped boulder through the churned visions of backlash. Elaira's bursting hope, that her need had drawn rescue, became instantaneously dashed. The disturbance was only another reliving, drawn out of Arithon's past. Exasperation struck next as she realized the mangling invasion could not be a Fellowship working.

The rash of taproom swearing that followed tagged the unlikely culprit. Kicked from his rut as the complacent wastrel, Dakar had embarked on the startling effort to draw Rathain's prince to safe haven. Only a fool would undertake such peril lightly. Arithon's blinded talent had not stripped out the trained patterns instilled during childhood. Dakar's clumsy effort provoked a defensive response out of hair-trigger reflex.

Arithon's explosive rejection lashed out like a hurled sheet of balefire. Witnessed at second hand, its natural force left Elaira shaken. Even while shocked outside his right mind, Arithon's guard could unbind the Koriani sigil of command.

Dakar caught the full brunt, whimpering in misery. By the martyred whine of his curses, the enchantress derived that the fragmented horrors of the tienelle vision had bled through his attempted contact. Smashed to reeling retreat, Dakar understood any subsequent effort to help would be hammered down with the same vengeful finality.

'Cry mercy,' Elaira whispered, wrung to sorry distress for the fact she was just as wretchedly helpless. Her own resource fell just as woefully short to scale a barrier of such vicious magnitude.

Yet where prudent talent should have known to step back, the Mad Prophet returned like a terrier. Again his attempt was mauled to lame shreds. Battered numb, hazed dizzy, well aware his slipshod technique was outmatched, the Mad Prophet hauled himself up by his bootstraps and rashly refused to give in.

Elaira tracked the decision, incredulous. 'Ath's deathless grace! Dakar, don't try. The next strike must surely shatter him!'

Yet the past was not mutable. Bound to the chain of enacted event, the fat spellbinder gathered himself, weeping, and launched off a third attempt.

The insidious progression would not stay before breaking crisis. Elaira shared Arithon's beleaguered recognition *that the reliving was going to unstring him*. His defenses *had* crumbled, that ill-fated night aboard *Khetienn*; Dakar's reenacted response was going to tear him wide open. For that crucial instant, he must stand as he had, inwardly stripped of protection. *Past and present would intersect in Kewar Tunnel*. His core self would be stripped naked and exposed to possession by Desh-thiere's curse.

Frozen to horror, Elaira looked on. The grief all but savaged her, that her power fell short to stave off the fall of disaster.

Dakar's strike shocked through vision like thundering storm, *the brutalities of Tal Quorin and Minderl Bay seized and turned back as the edged weapon to stun Arithon's mind to paralysis*. The tactic was deployed with icy forethought, as Arithon's awareness spiraled unchecked, entrapped in the throes of drugged nightmare.

Elaira gasped, shocked dumb as the blow fell. She scarcely tracked the surgical follow-through, made on the moment the

Master of Shadow flinched into agonized recoil. Dakar attacked in dead earnest, his spearpoint the most reviling scenes ripped from his victim's cursed past.

'Oh beloved.' Bleeding with sympathy, the enchantress shuddered with each smashing impact as the Mad Prophet punched roughshod through Arithon's beleaguered identity. She could but watch, slapped numb by stark suffering, as the corrosive remorse became excised from each field of slaughter. The Mad Prophet stayed the course of that lacerating history, sealed against scruple or pity. He smashed privacy wholesale. Memory for ugly, reprehensible memory, he cut through with locked runes of binding and laid claim to Arithon's innermost mind. Each contested sequence of raw recollection, the Mad Prophet closed into the circle of his own being. There, as he hoped, a mage trained to mastery would hesitate before daring trespass.

That night in *Khetienn*'s stern cabin, Arithon succumbed.

A stunning victory for Dakar in the past, one that had wrested Arithon's salvation from the seizures of tienelle poisoning. Yet here, relived in the Maze of Davien, embattled by the roused threat of Desh-thiere, the exposure flung wide the gates to disaster.

The balance of the world rocked in that moment.

Elaira could do nothing, *nothing at all*, except hide her useless presence; a shaming, sad epitaph, to leave her beloved no more than his false belief in her safety.

Yet as Desh-thiere's curse rose in force to flatten its helpless prey, Arithon's *current* lack of response struck a shrilling note of discrepancy.

'You have a plan?' gasped Elaira, incredulous. *Limp surrender made no sense from a man who never accepted defeat, even when he was beaten.*

Elaira held herself braced, too much in pain to hang her hope on a straw. Hard as she tried, she imagined no course that could buy any last-ditch evasion.

Yet as the red coils of the curse flared into blinding coruscation, the Mad Prophet *had not taken wise charge as a mage, to steer Arithon's drug-inflamed consciousness back to safe harbor.* Instead, swamped by inept uncertainty, Dakar relied on the absence of guilt to lift the block over Arithon's mage-sight.

All unwitting, the enchantress was caught by surprise, still linked to Arithon's consciousness.

The explosive unfurling of his restored talent struck her wards like an unshielded blast of white light. Spun into the firestorm,

Elaira sensed his empowered awareness meet and grapple the curse's bid for possession. As the garroting coils of compulsion closed down, choking his access to self, the battering exchange of attack and defense came on too fast for her to assimilate.

The Mistwraith's geas had its victim stripped naked, *but no longer helplessly vulnerable*. On set course with his past, Arithon wielded the untrammeled gifts of his mastery; *as well* his maze-bound awareness redefined the event, granting unilateral vision into the crystalline web of earned consequence. He fell back on leverage and genius. His pulsed burst of rage threw wracking strain against Desh-thiere's curse-bound compulsion. Arithon engaged talent in affirmation of private identity, lent borrowed force on the strength of a Fellowship seal set under blood oath at Athir. His focused will blazed and struck through.

Final possession was narrowly denied, but not without unforeseen backlash.

The mage-trained, rigorous survey he launched to cleanse and balance his aura raked Elaira's stilled spells of concealment like the actinic slam of a lightning bolt. *In present awareness, Arithon perceived the circle masked under her wards*. Given unshielded vision, his bristling assessment cut through her set runes of concealment on the speed of furious reflex.

Stunned shock limned the moment in pristine silence.

On the stopped cusp of time, strung on the synapse leap between startled, first contact and the irrevocable step of conscious recognition, Arithon grasped the instinctive premonition he had stumbled against lethal peril. Davien's Maze was a Fellowship warding, a framework of spellcraft far outside his strength that would suffer no act of trespass. He realized also: only *one* presence in all of Athera might touch on his inner boundaries without ruffling his reflexive protections.

Arithon's reaction arrested instinct, shattered every rule of time and progression. Pressed by agonized need, he burst limitations and ripped past the veil, claiming the simultaneous intersection of past and present in the higher-range frequency of synchronous existence. Once there, he accessed grand conjury and slapped down the wardings that circled Elaira's self-contained presence. Even as Dakar had done to shield a snatched store of punishing memories, Arithon embraced his beloved's linked consciousness and enclosed her within the self-aware current of his vitality.

He wedded her at one with the inviolate love he cherished within his heart. One thread and one mind, Elaira felt herself claimed as an inseparable part of him. Not trusting such acceptance to shield her from harm, he infused her with himself, poured the inner grace of his being through her spirit in turn, until even the maze's exacting, cold wards could not unspin his meshed weave and define her autonomous existence. Within that sealed haven, that core of free will that no Fellowship Sorcerer would venture to violate, poised over a well of stopped time, Arithon took pause. Shuddering yet from his jolt of raw fear, he marveled. His care for her bloomed, illuminating the exquisite jewel of a consummate, vulnerable intimacy.

'I'm not sorry,' Elaira ventured at brief length. 'Sorry's too small a word for what's happened. Since I didn't destroy us, I can only find space to be glad. Can you ever forgive me?'

'You are here,' said Arithon, still dizzied to wonderment. His stunned joy turned wry. 'And anyway, what's between us to forgive? By this I presume the chase is still on, with my carcass decried as the Prime Matriarch's prized trophy?'

'They'd prefer you caged living,' Elaira admitted, her riposte touched to acid chagrin. Cocooned in his presence, the connection between them was wholly without shadow or subterfuge.

Arithon perceived her naked self just as clearly. She need not fear misunderstanding. In the maze, joined as one, he must unequivocally discern that her loyal priority lay with him. Given his attentive, searching focus, he had already mapped the extent of Prime Selidie's clever bind; how the treacherous release to exercise autonomy let Elaira's presence in love become the made tool of Koriani machination.

'You aren't Fionn Areth,' Arithon pointed out, stung to fraught apprehension as he further explored the extent of her vulnerability.

She chose to dig back, knowing razor-edged wit sometimes eased his shattering concern, 'Well, you smashed their last trap and made off with the bait.'

Yet this time his maudlin mood did not break. If the stakes carried too charged a peril for mirth, he matched her in lockstep for wit. 'The lesson didn't stick. A hatchling crow has better memory.'

'Crows have more brains than to peck at a wildcat, far less try the deadly trick twice. Should I trust you?'

'Ahead of your order?' Now Arithon did laugh. 'I would, but for having the Mistwraith in tow. What blandishment would entice Prime Selidie to give up?'

'She won't,' said Elaira in levelest honesty. 'It's a two-legged trait, to meddle with wildfire bare-handed. And Jaelot blistered. A shaming performance.' In fact, Arithon had played a Senior Circle selected for reliable experience for a pack of rank fools, no sort of behavior to make a proud, female order tamely tuck tail and give up. *'Though it costs blood and death, the Matriarch wants her finale.'*

'Quite. It's the bitch without the bone.' Arithon's inner smile reflected his bitter recrimination. *'I've regretted that, often, in hindsight. Beloved, I'm sorry. Jaelot was a botch-up. Can you accept my apology? I would have spared having you stuck as the lynchpin turning the crux.'*

'Well, there hasn't been leisure to invent another script.' Squeezed dry of humor, Elaira fell back on immutable truth. *'You are loved. That counts far more. I would rather stand at your back and do nothing than suffocate elsewhere in safety. Nor will I extend any help unless you ask me.'*

Arithon shut his eyes, struck speechless with gratitude. Then he turned his head, his unseeing regard trained once again down the tunnel in wide-lashed, forced concentration. *'I would suffer any indignity of Selidie's before I allowed myself to fall prey to the curse of Desh-thiere. If I lapse into madness, take my permission here and now. Should my life become threatened, don't lie, beloved. Even had I not sworn my oath to the Fellowship, I could no more watch you die than cease breathing. My love for you will not suffer false promises. Honor my preference, but only if you are able. For myself, in plain truth, I lack the fiber to hold firm and see you take harm.'*

Which meant he must live at all cost or sacrifice. More than a seal set in blood tied his life. To spare her, he would indebt himself to the Koriani Prime Council a hundred times over. Cruel hardship still confounded his best-laid intent. Kewar's maze might defeat him, regardless. *'We have Vastmark ahead. Then an affray at Riverton that made a mockery of my oath as a crown prince. Merciful Ath! I can't do a thing to spare you from sharing the raw worst!'*

'Don't try,' Elaira returned, her admonishment gentle. *'You survived both. So can I. Please remember.'*

He swallowed again, forced down the rogue panic, that he could not manage to make his wracked body stop shaking. *'You know I can't keep my talent to shield you. I'll be blind once again, after this phase of reliving plays itself through.'*

'You will endure,' said Elaira. *'You must.'* Then, anguished, she let him explore the bleeding roots of her pity. *'Oh, beloved! Can you not weep and be done? Further suffering is useless, a meaningless punishment. Have you not paid enough for the deaths of the innocents you could not prevent at Tal Quorin?'*

Arithon drew in a tortured breath. He lifted his bracing hand from chill stone and crossed both forearms over his breast. Yet no gesture could rebind his torn heart, or refound his worn store of courage. *'Guilt offers no haven, since payment and suffering can never put right any loss that has already happened. Remorse can't bring back even one child. Asandir's question is answered.'* He paused, buried his face in scraped palms, then stated in sorrowful, stripped anguish, *'Yet where lies the reprieve? Desh-thiere's curse will not answer the release of self-forgiveness, or any other Ath-given grace allotted to our human spirit!'*

Elaira had always suspected his lost talent was self-inflicted, a defense to ensure his aptitude for grand conjury could never again be turned as a weapon to kill. *'Choose to try,'* she exhorted. *'Above anyone living, I trust you. My Prime's trap has now been unmasked by your hand. Therefore, my order cannot charge you with debt. If my presence now strengthens your will to survive, the advantage comes as the consequence of your own actions.'*

Which words fell short. If she came to harm through a failure of his, she saw all too clearly the blight would destroy him. Nor had he the power to unbind Davien's Maze bare-handed, or set her free of the strangling ties of a Koriani vow of life service.

'Reset your wardfield, beloved,' Arithon said, grim. *'The guard seals on this place will not forgive, and I don't trust Prime Selidie not to claim intervention if I take the first step joined to the sweet joy of your contact.'*

He was right to move on. Delay would spare nothing; only make the needful but harsh separation all the more difficult to complete. Elaira could not ease his dread for the trials to come, but only release him to address his demons without grinding him down with the misery of additional forethought. *'When you master this maze, when you see sky again, I'll indulge my bound orders and find my way to your side. Surely between us we can contrive stirring escapades to balk Prime Selidie's will? In fact, the bait's willing. We might actually drive her to hair-ripping fury if you wish.'*

'Kiss under the moon till the stars fall?' Arithon smiled, the tenderness in him a radiance clean as new morning. *'My dear, my heart, for your order's comeuppance, I'll bow to your pleasure on all counts. Consider the promise as done.'*

Yet to hold his word true, he first must surmount the ordeals that awaited ahead.

Still wrapped in the shelter of Arithon's protection, Elaira rewove her tight ring of wardspells. *'You will triumph,'* she whispered, steady as she brought an end to an intimacy fast becoming too hurtful to sustain. By the gift of a miracle, her will remained firm as she shaped the last rune of closure. The circle joined. A flare of searing light severed her awareness back into desolate separation.

Easier, surely, to rip out her heart, than to bear the set apprehension whitening Arithon's features. Now alone in the spell-charged gloom of the cavern, he shied back from measuring the testing to come. Reflection would but tear him to lethal uncertainty. Forced by exigency to secure Elaira's safety, Arithon stepped forward with no pause at all to regroup.

The past reclaimed him, thrusting him back into the *Khetienn's* locked stern cabin at the moment when Dakar's stopgap sacrifice had restored his access to mage-sight. *Again*, he would spurn the safe course of escape. *Ruled by the fist of unmalleable expediency, he rejected the decision to transmute the tienelle's potency and stand down* . . .

His choice reached Elaira within her sealed wards like a dousing shock of thrown ice water. Her dismay rivaled Dakar's, as she shared recognition that her beloved intended to take up the dropped reins of his purpose, and scry the cycles of probability that attended the hour Lysaer's war host would march into Vastmark. As committed as he had been on the eve of Tal Quorin, Arithon would not meet that armed invasion blindly. He engaged his talent and single-mindedly pursued sequential auguries, each grueling course of posited choice tested to define the best tactics to grind down and starve out the enemy. Each combination was replayed, many times, at each repetition revised to bring the toll of lives down, and to ensure that the tribal archers he had hired as marksmen would not become decimated or run from their ancestral territory.

The posed course of each future unreeled as running waves of searing impressions: of men caught in traps, or shot down in passes; of townborn patrols lured onto weathered stone ledges, to perish of falls as the unstable footing gave way; of men hazed up impassable gullies, then cut off, for bowmen to shoot down at leisure. She watched her beloved test substitute tactics: to spare *this* shepherd an end, trapped and tortured for information; to dispatch toward safety *that* encampment of mothers and young children; to deflect those advances that could not be stopped. Arithon worked the disparate threads of his resource from all angles, ferreting out every method to unravel the discipline of seasoned troops. He spun out unspeakable, ugly strategies designed to break nerves and devastate tight-knit morale. Where relived experience had shattered the mold for brutal ambush and massive casualties, the Maze of Davien unveiled one thing more.

At first, Elaira thought she glimpsed a ghost imprint – the sudden, unlikely shimmer of movement brought on by overcranked tension. As adept as she was at wielding her inner senses, she found this ephemeral disturbance eluded her focused skill. Arithon's initial attempt brought no better success. Yet the next time a phantom slipped through the weave, he was on wary guard. On lightning reflex, he snapped down a ward and froze the flow of the augury in midstream.

And there, damningly inscribed, he uncovered the masked face of tragedy. *Spellcraft derived from his signature style had been worked like snarled knit through his scrying*. Here, strung in cobweb fine patterns, he read subtle runes of shading and masking; there, a seeded impulse to waylay the eye, as though by chance met distraction. Arithon pulled up short with stopped breath. *Here*, he encountered the deft nets of spellcraft he had once wrought to protect young clan children in Deshir on a carefree spring morning spent carving toy whistles.

The maze stripped away pretense. That same innocuous chain of ciphers now obscured a more sinister activity. Proof stood, unequivocal: *Desh-thiere's furtive workings had in horrid fact infiltrated his mind and skewed the results of his augury.*

'Cry mercy!' Elaira gasped in a soundless, stunned whisper. Her tears flowed then, for a grief beyond mending. *For alternative pathways of future event had existed, no doubt ones with changed outcomes*. The insidious compulsion of Desh-thiere's geas had slipped them from Arithon's grasp in vile and secretive cunning.

In the heart of the maze, the Master of Shadow faltered between ragged steps. His face blanched bone white. Sorrow and guilt all but unstrung him, as he viewed the dawning horror of past judgments made on the basis of a false assessment.

'Thirty thousand deaths,' he ground out, punished by abject revulsion. Rage drained him, that *perhaps* probability had contained the unseen thread of happenstance that might have spared Lysaer's war host from subsequent, sweeping carnage.

Elaira choked back the cry of her heart. She could not reach through, or dare to point out that logic argued against such a likelihood. Given the preset array of raw circumstance, no ending could evolve with such wishfully clean simplicity. The Mistwraith's covert meddling just as likely masked lies, well designed to entrap its victim's sensitized conscience. A sequence of viable futures might lurk behind those insidious, spelled wisps of diversion; or the barriers might have been set as blank decoys to inflame an already tormented mind.

Too easily, the gift of his forebears' compassion might draw Arithon to lose himself in the mire of his past, endlessly seeking improbable reprieve on the lure of unfounded suggestion.

The Teir's'Ffalenn must have perceived that potential pitfall. Despite reeling distress, he turned aside, left the invidious snags without giving way. He abjured the temptation to salve his past agony through futile exploration. The maze forgave no man who refused the soured fruits of even his misled past action. To stop, to shy back and glance sidewards would be construed as a willful avoidance. *Whether or not a bloodless solution had existed to resolve the battle plan gone awry at Vastmark, the path he had taken must run straight through the cliff-walled cove of the Havens . . .*

Cry mercy.

Elaira had heard the damning accounts attributed to that spree of slaughter. For the wanton butchery enacted on that shore, Avenor's judiciary council still held a sealed arraignment for black sorcery. Their case, heard in absentia, had hung on a disaffected sailhand's account and conjecture, founded in scholarly diatribe.

Unreconciled to town law, the clans had not shirked the horror of plumbing the truth. Rathain's vested *caithdein* had been charged with the unsavory burden of conducting formal trial under the justice of kingdom charter. Earl Jieret had named the event as forthright murder, excused on the grounds of war and expediency. His sentence had been incontrovertible, with the prime testimony given by Arithon himself, bound under a blood oath laced through with truth seals, and with an unwilling Dakar forced to stand horrified witness.

Still other voices had damned by omission. The Fellowship Sorcerers gave no opinion at all. Caolle, who had been second-in-command to his crown prince, had kept as stony a silence. Of the clan liegemen who had served in Vastmark, all returned changed; Sidir, who was closest, had wept.

When challenged by a peer Koriani on the subject of Arithon's guilt, Elaira had allowed him testy defense, saying, *'I would ask him. Whatever his Grace of Rathain did, then or now, he will have had his own reason. I have never seen him lie for convenience. Nor have I known him to break from the sound tenets of his character.'*

Mearn s'Brydion, a clan duke's brother with an uncanny, sharp mind, had said almost the very same.

Now, in Davien's Maze, at the cusp of reliving the unplumbed depths behind Arithon's core of reserve, Elaira noted his expression of chiseled dread. The trapped quality to his stillness, captured between steps, scraped her nerves to quailing unease.

Some truths perhaps were best locked away beyond even a loved one's shared sight.

The thought chafed like scaled iron, that his fear ran bone deep: she might not find the endurance to stomach the darkness he kept wrapped in obdurate privacy.

'Oh, beloved,' she cried, though he could not hear.

For of course, if he halted, Davien's wards would close down. Inaction on his part would kill her. 'Give me torture and loss, give me death,' Arithon forced out in a ragged, tight whisper: a repeat of the words he had spoken in Merior, when he had denied his love rather than author the cause of Elaira's certain destruction. He finished in fluent Paravian, *'Llaeron iel tiriannon an shar i'ffaeliend.'*

'Send light, to ward off the shadows,' Elaira murmured in desolate translation.

Arithon s'Ffalenn closed his eyes. From a heartcore of tempered strength he never knew he possessed, he summoned the grace to step forward.

The scene in the *Khetienn*'s cabin resumed, launching the final sequence of tienelle auguries into full-bodied reliving: seed plan for the massacre Arithon had deployed from the rock inlet at the Havens. No thought could prepare, and no rote forgiveness withstand the visceral violence of the onslaught.

Elaira encountered, face on, a savagery without parallel. She recoiled, appalled, as the pattern unfolded for a bout of killing no spirit-born human might reconcile. Sickened through, weeping for release, she shared Dakar's pealing cry of distress. *For the explosive indulgence of cruelty was not random.* Pinned to a crux of horrendous expediency, the enchantress watched Arithon hammer down compassion, stamp back his bardic sensitivity. Over his most ruthlessly trampled sensibility, he mapped a cold course to disown every moral tenet of his character. Here, in the scalpel-cut clarity of tranced scrying, he tailored a bloodbath with nerveless intent to revolt the most battle-hardened nerves.

Stunned beyond word, wrenched outside thought, Elaira saw him design one brutal, sharp strike, to be enacted with heartless forethought. The wards of the maze permitted no secrets, but laid bare the hideous framework. Arithon engineered violence on a large enough scale to ensure no mistake, and to waive any possible grounds for ambiguity.

His premise sprang out of soul-chilling mercy: if five hundred men were cut down without quarter, the ploy might provoke the living retreat of Lysaer's remaining thirty thousand.

'Cry mercy,' Elaira murmured, her aghast litany a plea to ward off the shattering vista of final disillusionment.

Unfounded fear; upon the next step, the maze reaffirmed steadfast proof of Arithon's intact compassion.

He had not launched his course of premeditated massacre with no tested proof on the outcome. Before the influence of the tienelle faded, he embarked on his closing round of scrying to establish rigorous sureties. He sifted futures one after another, until he garnered his promised reprieve: a scene showing Lysaer broken in sorrowful distress, commanding the war host's withdrawal. And there, in exacerbating viciousness, the resharpened vision of the maze exposed an insidious, fresh twist: *the geas of Desh-thiere had not been quiescent.* Flicked to flash-point life by the brief view of Lysaer s'Ilessid, the curse had been wakened, its touch invisibly subtle. A masked flare of static had sheeted through Arithon's being, invidiously timed to break Dakar's guarding hold over his guilt-ridden conscience.

The spellbinder's protective wardings had snapped *by Desh-thiere's provocation*, with the flattening burden of self-damning remorse fallen back onto Arithon's shoulders.

Just as before, the resurgence of blindness smothered his access to mage-sight. At the edge of defeat, as his born talent failed him, the Master of Shadow saw his work irretrievably cut short before he could cross-check his result.

Nonetheless, he had not yielded tamely. Wrenched from the fast-fraying threads of his mastery, Arithon had grasped his last shred of awareness to effect a practiced unbinding. He saw Dakar freed. If his truncated augury brought a misstep in Vastmark, he could at least make sure the Fellowship spell cord that shackled the importunate prophet to his service would not tie another victim to his doomed company.

The reliving ground onward, while the maze refigured yet another excoriating thread of repercussion: before the shattered scrying went dark, a fragmented incident had been swept aside, masked under the cascade as Arithon's mage-sight subsided to blankness. The moment of faulted memory was no accident. The deep-seated influence of Desh-thiere's design had effected another intervention, hazed under blanketing spellcraft. In chilling exactitude, Kewar's spells revealed *one last, lost sequence of augury*. The scene unveiled a clandestine exchange in the field quarters of Lysaer's war host. Now dredged up intact, its contents became incontestably damning: *under tight secrecy, Lord Commander Diegan signed a writ of execution that ensured the handpicked survivors of the Havens never lived to report the atrocity to Prince Lysaer*. The Light's army had marched into Vastmark *unknowing*. Their proud companies advanced and attacked, fatefully ignorant of the warning Prince Arithon had designed to dispatch them safely homeward.

'Oh, cry mercy,' Elaira gasped in devastated shock. Five hundred murdered spirits at the Havens had died, each one, in unforgivable futility.

The crucial flash of augury that cast doubt on the outcome had been hidden by Desh-thiere's spelled geas. An indispensable gift of uncertainty *that would have changed Arithon's subsequent choice of action. Surely, without any cursed stroke of meddling, the campaign at Vastmark would have left a less brutally damning legacy.*

At what point does the strong heart fail? How many sliding falls into treachery, before the visionary mind must shudder off its set track, and seek the surcease of ungoverned madness? Hands braced to the narrowing walls of the corridor, Arithon attempted the next step. The pain slashed him, anguish sharpened tenfold. He buckled to his knees, bruised under a crushing, harsh grief that hounded him past reprieve.

Cry mercy.

His body rejected his will to arise. *'Iel dediari,'* light forgive, he could not go forward, could not face again those five hundred premeditated deaths. Not struck to cold knowing that his premise had been warped by the poison of Desh-thiere's manipulation.

Cry mercy.

If he broke, if he faltered or stopped, his dearest beloved would be destroyed along with him. 'Elaira, I was wrong. You are more than my life. Never, ever forget that.'

Cry mercy.

He strove again to recoup his shattered initiative. Shuddering against the forced pressure of sobs he would not let break from his throat, his flesh failed him. He sank, bowed onto crossed arms. Nausea racked him. Crumpled to the stone floor, he shuddered, wrung by sickness. His stomach had nothing inside to expel. He retched, gagging bile. The dry heaves came on with overpowering savagery, and would not permit him to stand.

Cry mercy.

He could not face this, could not repeat the horror of the order to burn a ship laden with wounded; could not walk again those bloodied, wet sands, in silenced distress choosing which wounded man should survive, and which would be dispatched on the brutal, swift cut of the knife's edge . . .

Cry mercy.

Willed initiative became as a black-glass wall, high and bleak and insurmountable. The blood and the fire, the shrill screams of the dying would grant him no quarter at the Havens. Lysaer's massive advance would close in, inexorable. *Thirty thousand deaths*, and a war host milled under by the calculated, loosed force of a shale slide. Arithon wept, flattened under the pain of a reliving too massively vicious to contemplate.

Cry mercy.

The feather-light touch that brushed his hunched shoulder ripped him to a raw scream of recoil. Prone on the tunnel floor, limp as a shot animal, he lacked the bare strength to flinch in retreat. If the darkness seemed lessened, the raw ends of his nerves scarcely recorded the difference.

A minute passed, filled by the rasp of his breath, before his shocked gaze registered the impression of a woman standing over him. She was not Elaira, but another, her form limned in the ephemeral blue fire of spirit light. Her shoulders were mantled in the coarse cloak of a Vastmark shepherd. She had fair, wind-wisped braids, tied off with soft yarn and the chiming, sweet clash of bronze bells.

Arithon ripped out a gritted croak. 'Dalwyn.'

Elaira recognized the name on a flood of relief. Lane watch had once shown her the woman, warmed on a chill night by Arithon's tender embrace. At the time the enchantress had wept, grateful for a release granted to her beloved on the heels of their desolate parting at Merior. Arithon had let Dalwyn importune him for comfort. In wise, female instinct, Elaira held that union beyond reach of possessive hurt or petty jealousy. Love made allowance for Dalwyn's raw need, and gave grace for any small kindness that might ease Arithon's deadlocked distress. Upon such small gifts, hopeless pain could find surcease.

Now, in the clotted gloom of the maze, Dalwyn's offered solace cast a circle of radiant light. As he had done in her moment of mourning, a light touch soothed his suffering in kindness. 'For the caring you granted to support me through my trial of sorrow, your Grace, look ahead.'

For a miracle, Arithon listened. He unclosed his fist, braced himself on one forearm. His glance turned forward as she bade him.

Even as Dalwyn's form faded at his back, another arose, this one a small girl standing on planted feet. Arithon recognized the departed child named Jilieth, lost to a mauling by wyverns. In the depths of a ravine, by a winter-chill stream, his Masterbard's talent and Dakar's healing spellcraft had failed to restore her to vitality.

'Little one, forgive me,' Arithon whispered. 'You were heart set to go. Did you wish I had broken the stricture of free will? Should I have struck darker notes of compulsion and played other music to hold you?'

She gave him laughter. Her brown eyes alight with bold merriness, she offered Rathain's prince her small hand. 'Come. There is no horror in crossing Fate's Wheel. The dead are beyond suffering, as you will see. For the song that eased my passage, let me guide you. Together, we will walk until you win clear of the shadows that bind you to Vastmark.'

Arithon bowed his head. His shoulders quivered. The tears falling and falling in silvered drops off his cheekbones, he reached out and clasped Jilieth's extended, ghost fingers. At her urging, he arose. Leaning in shameless need on her courage, he reforged the lamed strength to go forward.

Cry mercy.

Again, a red-streamered arrow snapped off his bowstring. The shaft arched into the vault of the sky above the cliff walls of the Havens. The signal descended, past fate to recall, and a picked band of marksmen loosed bows.

Spelled wards spun their maze of insidious retribution, *and Arithon died*, ripped off sun-baked rocks as a broadhead whistled down and slammed through him. *Again*, he knew the tears of a widow and her orphaned child, a brother, a mother, and two unmarried sisters, keening unending lamentation . . .

Cry mercy.

For thirty thousand deaths, there would come no respite. Only a small girl's unquenchable courage, insistently tugging him onward. Arithon stumbled ahead. At each dragging step, a broken corpse stayed him. He waded through let blood, deafened by harrowing sound, and the dying screams of a multitude. He was the cry of the wounded earth, the violated peace of whole mountains torn down to serve as his ready weapon. He was terror and pain, hammered over and over by the gut-ripping shock of all manner of lethal injury.

Unseen, unheard, with no tender child to take her wrung hands, or to ease the edge off her suffering, Elaira endured all that Arithon must. She flanked his fraught passage as the horrors of the Vastmark campaign flowered into a nightmare of vivid reliving.

Cry mercy. Cry mercy. Cry mercy . . .

Adept

Cold morning and deep frost clasped the rock islets at Northstrait in a mantle of crystalline white. The brine broke and scattered like jewels over the rimed shore, and sunlight touched the outcrops to sequined platinum under a sapphire sky. That same pristine light flooded through the tower windows of Ath's hostel, where the latched-back shutters admitted the scoured east wind. Pale stone walls captured the booming thrash of the breakers against a backdrop of silence, undisturbed as the field of snowy linen spread over the pallet, where a motionless figure reclined. The faultless, clean lines of hands and face might have been a master's crafting of marble, but for the glint of red touched through fair hair and the unhurried rhythm of breath.

Morning after morning, dawn had brightened the stark chamber, with the elements little changed. At one with the bleached-bone colors of winter, a fair-haired adept clad in gilt-and-white robes kept patient watch to one side. Through a passage of days piled up into weeks, she had measured her time to the change of the tides and the wheeling turn of the stars. Yet on this day, stirred by a current of imperceptible change, she raised her head, and at last saw an end to her vigil.

For the first time since his flesh had been scorched by Khadrim fire, Kevor s'Ilessid opened his eyes.

The orbs in their sockets were unmarked, a piercingly clear porcelain blue. New-grown hair fringed his unmarred brow, and his hands, tucked in a drift of clean bedding, showed not a trace of a scar.

'Welcome back,' the adept murmured, then settled, attentive, and waited for his reaction.

Kevor licked his lips, blinked, drew in a roused breath. In total stillness, he allowed his restored consciousness to explore the healed miracle of his body. The transcendent cleansing he had experienced in the spring at the heart of the hostel's sacred grove had been far more than a dream. All pain had departed. His damaged flesh was renewed. Yet if nerve and muscle and joint had found ease, restored to functional harmony, nothing else was the same.

He was no longer the boy he had been, but a spirit annealed and reforged by the powers that had lifted him out of suffering.

'My eyesight is blinded,' he admitted at due length. The lapsed burden of speech held an awkwardness, grained to a rust-flecked whisper. As though use of words had turned strangely coarse, he resumed in halting impatience, 'Yet everywhere I look, in my mind, I see light. You sit beside me on a cushioned stool. Your hair wears the colors of ripe wheat in summer and your robes are a river of molten silver, cascading under the moon. I don't know your face. But even without making the effort to look, I perceive the rainbow weave of your spirit.'

'A more accurate vision than the illusion of shadows our mortality values as eyesight,' the lady adept admitted. 'The change is quite rare, and considered by some to be a most blessed gift.' Her smile of encouragement fingered his heart, more tenderly distinct than any physical sensation. 'If you have been touched in this way, you will know your travels raised you far beyond the earthly side of the veil. A part of you still resides there. Is that troublesome?'

'It should be, but no.' Kevor found, with surprise, that he need not dwell on the matter. In hindsight, his childhood life at Avenor seemed a busy, constricting tangle of noise, cluttered with meaningless trinkets. Under the gilded trappings of royalty, the honeyed falsehoods, and the poisoned plays of intrigue that riddled the court and high council, a few genuine threads yet held meaning. Among them, he continued to value his love for his mother, a tie strong enough to have drawn him back across the divide and into the wellspring of life.

Awake to the rush of blood through his veins, he felt reborn into heaviness. He sensed the poised stillness of the adept at his side, and knew that she understood: his tentative binding to recumbent flesh might not be sufficient to hold him. Ellaine's grief at his loss all but shrank to insignificance before the undying glory he had experienced in his freed flight past the veil. The unreconciled dichotomy burned like rare fire. His heart seemed too small to encompass the absence left imprinted in waking memory. 'I don't want to return to Avenor. If my father wishes a high king for Tysan, he must find another heir to assume the crown.'

Touched by the plangent note of desolation struck through his measured words, the lady adept reached out and closed his loose fingers into her own. Their joined touch was warm, unaffected by the icy wind swirling throughout the chamber. 'No one expects you to return to Avenor.'

Kevor turned his head. His air of remote beauty all but stopped thought and breath as he tipped his face toward the streaming east light admitted by the tower window. His expression showed a longing beyond words, as though he found even sunlight diminished, or his hands had held something precious, now irretrievably lost. 'If I am released from the burden of royal inheritance, what is left?'

'There is work for you in this world, if you choose,' the lady assured, ever patient. The sewn ciphers on her hood flared to her movement as she released his grasp and sat back. 'When you wish to arise, I will show you.'

Slowly, tentatively, Kevor flexed one arm. No discomfort marred the movement of muscle and joint. No twinge of agony flashed down quiescent nerves. If regeneration had not restored his mortal eyesight, the loss caused no grief. The rest of him responded like oiled silk, strong and seamlessly functional. He gathered himself, though long unused to the heft of his own weight, and with distinct, fragile care, sat up. A slight frown marked the effort, as though he had forgotten the intricacy required to manage physical balance. The sheets slid away from his torso. Underneath, he was naked. The fact left him unabashed, an oddity he scarcely paused to examine.

Once, he would have burned red to arise unclothed before the eyes of a woman.

A faint smile curved his lips, an amusement. Such emotional tumult now seemed meaningless. He swung his legs clear of the bedding and stood on the frost white stone of the floor.

The bracing wind buffeted him, tossing the bright ends of the hair that had grown back, unsinged. Kevor did not feel the cold. Remade by the mystical powers of the spring, he paused to laugh, as though drinking in the unaccustomed sensation of air flowing over his skin. Without embarrassment, he stepped to the window and looked out. If his eyesight was blind, the moving force of the breakers dashing themselves on sharp rock revealed a patterned play of energy, a tapestry limned in pastel colors fired through with delicate rainbows.

He would not walk in darkness, wherever he went.

Kevor tasted the thrown salt of sea spume. He stayed lost to reverie, while the clear, northern sunlight painted over a perfection of form that would have wrung tears of awe from a sculptor.

'The world is still beautiful,' he marveled at last. His spontaneous smile showed wounding delight, that one cherished fragment of joy seemed unexpectedly restored to him. He savored a last breath of the ocean air, then faced the lady adept, who had risen to wait by the open doorway. 'I am ready.'

Since he did not ask, she did not send for a robe, but matched her pace to his increasingly confident step down the light-shafted gloom of the stairwell.

'You're taking me back to the grove,' he observed.

Unsurprised that he could divine her intent, the lady led him across the outer threshold into the courtyard. 'We'll begin there, yes.'

Kevor stepped barefoot into the ankle-deep snow fallen during the night. Untroubled by chill, he glanced down, moved to unexpected curiosity. The kiss of the ice crystals, melting, seemed to speak. Their whispered phrases formed in a language he knew, if only he would stop to listen.

'Time for that later,' the lady adept said, laughing. Her touch at his shoulder gentled him onward. 'All the days left to the world, if you wish. The pleasure is yours to decide.'

Kevor raised sightless eyes, absorbing the shimmering light of her presence directly into his innermind. 'You have something needful to show me first?'

'I do.' She accepted his offered hand. Though he required no guidance to find his way, she led his steps to the courtyard's south door, then inside, through the polished-stone halls of the sanctuary, and between the pillars that marked the threshold of the sacred grove.

Kevor s'Ilessid paused in the dew-drenched grass. Some of the strung tension flowed out of him, bled away into peace as he savored the aromatic scent of balsam, and the subtle fragrances of night-blooming flowers. The trickle of springwater over quartz stone braided into a soothing melody, and the silence between spoke of the grand chord that sourced all creation. He did not need eyesight to sense the flight of the snowy owl, who folded broad wings and perched on the bough of an oak. He discerned the essence of the field mouse in the grass, and the stilled graceful strength of the mountain cat which padded past his knee to lap at the pool.

Cradled within the grove's living serenity, Kevor felt the unassuaged core of longing inside him rise up, and almost receive its true match. The heartbreak, that something still fell indefinably short, lit a restlessness in him that could never be quenched by the banked embers of earthbound contentment. Touched to tears by the unnamed loss that raged through him, he trembled, his emotion resharpened to unblunted potency, and his grief, too poignant to bear. 'Ath, oh Ath,' he appealed, 'should I not have come back? What is left here that does not seem dulled, or reduced to a poor, shadowed echo?'

A white-silk sigh of movement, the lady adept squeezed his forearm and collected his scattered attention. 'Come.'

Where she guided, a hidden path opened through the towering trees. Leaves rustled. Spritely breezes frisked through the boughs overhead. Small stones sparkled, star-caught, with mica. The cool majesty of the forest enfolded them, alive with an air of green mystery. The mountain cat tagged playfully after their heels, while a woodthrush trilled its lyric arpeggios under the velvet mantle of twilight. Soothed by the wise endurance of the trees, Kevor settled. Uncaring of nakedness, unmindful of sightless eyes and the altered contours of his inward vision, which revealed the surrounding landscape as a tapestry spun from pure light, he made his way to a second clearing, where a low, mounded hill arose, crowned by night sky and a diadem of turning stars.

At the crest, a circle of white-robed figures stood with joined hands, immersed in silent concord.

'They are Ath's adepts,' the lady explained with hushed anticipation. 'Go forward, if you wish. They have invited you to join their circle. Permission is given to share in their dreaming.'

'They are all from this hostel?' Kevor inquired, a bit distant. His attention had snagged in rapt fascination upon the play of golden light shimmering and falling like a misted rain over the adepts' convocation.

'All hostels send them,' the lady explained. 'Each sacred grove has a path that leads to this place, for ones who know where to find it. Will you accept the experience?'

Carefully as she guarded her intonation, Kevor's altered vision detected the strained edge of possibility, that if he refused, he was likely to retrace the steps of an untold number of predecessors and lose his fresh foothold on life. The vitality brought back from his exalted sojourn of healing would fade with disinterest, until the awareness required to maintain health slipped away, replaced by prolonged periods of sleep. In gradual stages, his mind would drift into unconsciousness, then past the Wheel's turning into death.

No adept of Ath's Brotherhood would argue his free choice to depart. The lady waited quietly on his answer, wrapped in seamless tranquillity. She made no mention of pitfalls. In the unwritten way of her kind, she would not ply him with blandishments.

Yet the deep-buried cry of the world's pain touched through her presence, striking as a spark of scribed fire against Kevor's altered awareness. He grasped the sense that his decision would matter. He listened between the notes of the night-singing birds, and the crickets' chafed song in the grasses, and heard in them the shared echo of the adepts' muted urgency. The quiet plea moved him. In fact, *he was sorely needed*.

Nor could the mores of a prince's upbringing be fully and lightly cast off. Kevor's smile held the steadfast promise of his ancestry as he touched the lady's hand to his lips in an abandoned gesture of court courtesy. 'Show me the mystery you speak of.'

Together, they waded through the lush grasses and climbed toward the top of the rise. Delicate white flowers wafted perfume, and the young crescent moon fired the dew to strewn diamonds. At the crest of the hill, no word was spoken. No one cared that Kevor was unclad. Two hooded figures amid the gathered company stirred and parted linked hands. Their circle expanded, then seamlessly rejoined, an elderly grandfather and a smiling woman admitted the younger man and his fair-haired lady attendant. The rustle of white robes fell still. The soft flames of spirit light wove through the round, burnishing sparks off the thread worked ciphers stitched into pearlescent silk.

Then, as one, the adepts drew breath and chanted the word for the Paravian prime rune. Their raised voices melded into a chord, sealing their company into a sweet, running torrent of joined sound. Kevor felt pierced through and through by that current, until his heart spiraled upward in joy. His mind took flight, arose, unfolding in bursting exultation. Propelled on a fountainhead of burgeoning vibration, he felt as a bird, with white-feathered wings outstretched. Soaring, now, effortless, he took wild flight: up and up, *until once again, he sailed on the rivers of pure light, which spun through the realms past the veil.*

In wonder, he bore witness, while the adepts who sang him back to ecstasy dipped into that quickened stream. As they had, many times, they gathered unharnessed power in looping coils. Their deft handling braided the energies into a rope, then guided the living current back down, through their linked minds, into the heart of the circle.

There, the power surged, made gently captive to the wisdom of their intent. Into the cataract of drawn light, they dreamed, and their thoughts spun the fires of energy into form, ephemeral and unearthly fair.

Kevor cried out, his spirit raised to an explosion of exquisite delight. He beheld the living mystery, whirled into the dance of pure light as the adepts interceded, calling down the singing powers sent forth by Ath Creator. He witnessed the alchemy of transmutation, as their Brotherhood invoked unity and blessing, and allowed the wild forces to adorn the heartcore of their sacred groves. The limitless creativity of their dreaming sustained their liminal forests, and brought forth the water to endow the deep wisdom embued in their welling springs.

Here, the hoop of the cosmos was joined, sunfire and moon-beam and love bent to earth and cradled there in tender care, to engender undying celebration.

At first hesitant, then with an unleashed, bursting confidence, Kevor joined into the summoning. He had walked that far place, where the power was drawn from the limitless flow of abundance. He had seen and touched patterns that others had not, in the course of his convalescent sojourn. From those far horizons, the thread of his gathering flowed into the weave, and the colors of twilight flowered in joy, as the first new voice in a hundred years joined into the circle's chanting . . .

The moment was marked.

Far southward, in Ath's hostel at Scimlade Tip, an adept named Claithen opened his eyes, aroused from his hour of contemplation. He stretched as though touched by a fresh breath of wind, though no breezes stirred the dead leaves, gathered in brittle drifts at his feet; nor had, for a quarter of a decade.

'Oh, blessed,' he whispered, as the burgeoning awareness touched him and powerfully infused his wearied spirit. As though heavy darkness saw the first blush of dawn, he straightened. *Almost*, he thought he heard the tentative trickle of water splash over the dry stones of the spring.

'Oh bravely blessed, let me bear the truth.' Afraid that his aggrieved longing might have tricked his sore heart, he looked up just in time to behold the blighted tree overhead burst into a fragrant shower of white blossom.

'Oh blessed!' His shout rang. 'We are given a savior and the gift of rebirth.'

His trembling smile melted into tears of gladness, and the echoes of his cry brought the dusky-skinned lady, who alone had remained at his side to attend the withered wreckage of a grove that had once been made green through thousands of years of devotions.

'Who?' she asked, ripped into laughter as the joy burst from her throat. 'Who has accepted the white robes of adept and brought us the first breath of healing?'

'You don't recognize the voice of this miracle?' Claithen caught her slender brown hands, his dark eyes shining with wonderment. 'Life has wrought another full circle. His birth name was Kevor s'Ilessid.'

Crucible

Exhaustion was a blanketing weight, dragging him down into darkness. The draining ordeal of Vastmark behind him, Arithon sank to his knees in Kewar Tunnel as Jilieth's determined grip faded and left his limp hand. He realized he must not give way before weariness. Must not lie down in prostrate surrender, or succumb to disorientation.

Yet the traumatized nerves that suffered the impact of thirty thousand violent deaths were by now numbed past response. Emotions tormented by a surfeit of grief had wrung dry, scorched beyond reach of desire. The screams of the lost had pummeled Arithon's mind until he would have been grateful for deafness. He had cried aloud for heart-torn remorse, until his voice wore away, leaving a ringing, blank silence. To feel nothing at all seemed the very haven of peace. Pummeled half-witless by the experienced trauma of repeated battering wounds, his shrinking flesh clung to the false safety of stillness. Ingrained reflex insisted the least effort to walk forward would unleash the floodgates of punishment.

Arithon battled that visceral recoil. Blood oath had been sworn to the Fellowship Sorcerers. No less than Elaira's life lay cradled between his two hands. He dared not succumb to the leaden weakness dragging him down into lassitude.

'Respect my free will,' he husked through a throat skinned from incessant screaming. 'I have not broken down in consent.'

Yet will by itself could not master the overwhelming weight of spent flesh. Beaten limp, rendered half-dead by the bleeding rags of s'Ffalenn conscience and the unruly drive of the curse, Arithon sank toward collapse. Pressed to the reeling edge of unconsciousness, he sprawled on chill stone, one aching breath drawn after the next. The sorry truth scourged him, that his last mustered strength seemed insufficient to drag himself back to his feet. A reviling shame, if Davien's Maze claimed him with an unbroken will, through an outworn body unable to marshal the brute resource to stand upright.

Touched by the first sense of numbing diffusion as spelled powers crept through his being, beginning the process that would unspin his mind, Arithon extended his arm. He forced the lamed effort, wormed another inch forward on his belly.

'That's it,' encouraged a vibrant male voice, just ahead of him. 'Now reach!'

Arithon opened his bandaged right hand, strained outstretched fingers to their trembling limit.

A hard grasp closed over his blood-slippery wrist, stained wet from the killing at Vastmark. A man's sure grip pulled, and the floor rolled underneath him, transformed at a breath from cold stone into sun-heated planks. The smells of warm tar and oakum rode the bracing east wind, salt tanged by the booming rush of blue water cleaved by a brigantine's stem post.

Arithon shut his eyes, overwhelmed by sheer gratitude. The draw of filled canvas and the thrum of taut rigging bespoke the last freedom he owned in the world. The mercy of another unknown savior had delivered him onto the decks of his own vessel, *Khetienn*.

'Sail with me,' invited the speaker, a voice he recognized at last. 'They say that Ath's ocean holds all the tears in creation. Man need shed no more. Only allow the rocking of waves and the cry of the wind to ease the sore grief from his heart.'

Arithon unsealed shut lids and looked up, disbelieving. 'Father?'

Spinning vision showed him Avar s'Ffalenn, his sturdy stance braced against the toss of the swell. Brash and bold as the day he raised *Saeriat's* sails, charting the course that had carried a son from Rauven to a prince's inheritance on Karthan, the sire did not appear royal born. Dark hair was tied back in a sailhand's braid. A fighting man's breadth of shoulder, as always, wore sun-faded linen spun from second-rate flax. The rough fibers would have been pulled and spun by Karthan's women, who wrested their living out of the saltmarshes and bottomlands too poor for raising cattle or barley.

The gray eyes whose compassionate clarity had once won Talera's love regarded the grown son, now sprawled on the planks at his feet.

'Your Grace, why are you here?' Arithon ground out. For this ocean voyage aboard *Khetienn* had not been launched on Avar's homeworld of Dascen Elur. She had sailed the uncharted deeps of Athera in vain search for the vanished Paravians.

The pirate king who had once ruled in Karthan flashed a smile of even, white teeth. Laugh lines scored across the old scar of a cutlass crinkled his weathered features. 'I'm here because I fathered a man with great heart. You once renounced all the gifts of your upbringing to bring succor to a people who needed you. There is pride in the heritage of our ancestry. Will you stand for it? Or will you languish and let yourself die as a sacrifice to the cause?'

'What cause was worth this?' Arithon regarded his dripping hands, still wet with the heartsblood of the slain: both friend and enemy who had marched onto the field to die because he existed. 'Some who paid sacrifice were my sworn liegemen, and mine, the cruel purpose that killed them.'

Avar raised dark eyebrows, gravely astonished. 'The dead are beyond pain. You alone suffer, now.' His grasp upon Arithon's wrist only tightened. His seafarer's strength raised his son up from prostration, with no thought at all for the bloodstains wicked up by his cuff. 'Where is the evil? Show me *one man* you coerced into war. Find me one child you forced to wield the knife. Name the one enemy you killed out of hatred, or the one woman who was despoiled under your orders. Arithon, you never once compromised the first Law of the Major Balance. You have never misled friend or enemy, or beguiled them from free will.'

Arithon shut his eyes, the bile of self-hatred like a coal on his tongue. 'I have done worse.' Seared to a whisper, he added, 'I have used magecraft to kill, not once, but many times.'

Ahead, still ahead, lay the field at Daon Ramon, and the passing of Jieret, who had been his sworn blood bond, and dearer to him than a brother.

'The violation of murder is a human error.' Avar gave him a slight shake, the censure a man might deal a beloved dog who cringed, expecting the whip. 'A man wreaks harm because he forgets to love peace. He kills because of self-blinded fear, that imagines no other protection.'

'I am cursed!' Arithon cried. 'Desh-thiere's geas –'

Avar cut him off. 'Arithon, no! To pronounce yourself condemned in this place is to die. Abandon your own grace, and the maze will tear you to pieces.'

'What else is my life, but a cipher that upends the peace?' Arithon locked stares with his father. Silver-gray as the luminosity of sunlight through fog, Avar's direct gaze encompassed him. As Talera had done, just as anguished before him, he fell and fell, into those fathomless eyes. Their compassion absorbed his jagged-edged pain until the hurt was left no place to rest, except one.

'I gave Karthan my pledge for peace, your Grace, and then watched you die of an enemy arrow aboard *Saeriat*,' Arithon resumed, torn rough by his sorrow. 'Your realm was abandoned, a kingless prize lying ripe for the vengeance of Amroth.'

'Yes, I passed the Wheel.' Avar shifted his grip, eased his son's stumbling balance to rest against the support of the ship's rail. The brigantine tossed, the frisky wind driving her close-hauled. Shearing foam boiled up from her rampaging passage. Leaping and splashing against *Khetienn*'s black strakes, the frothing blue swell of the Cildein carved up into lace and dashed foam.

As the healing of the elements worked its slow magic, Avar resumed the snagged thread of conversation. 'Amroth's arrow killed me, but Karthan was not conquered. After your exile, the high mage himself interceded. Rauven forced the peace. The treaties bear the seals your grandfather wrought of grand conjury. His mages came and saw your dream realized. Our island realm is made green again. That is the legacy you left Dascen Elur. In your memory, the heirs of s'Ahelas have pledged their trained talent to stand surety that the long feud with Amroth stays ended.'

As Arithon, who had thought himself emptied of tears, bent his head to crossed forearms and wept, he felt his father's embrace cradle his shaking shoulders.

'My son, you are loved. Accept the gift and find respite.' Avar's plea took fire, became passionate appeal. 'Sail with me, prince. Celebrate life for the people of Karthan. They raise no more children, crying in hunger. Nor will they send brothers and husbands to sea, bearing a sword to win plunder.'

Time passed. The calming influence of spring sunlight, sea wind and spray worked their gentle restoration. Arithon settled. His legs bore his weight, and gradually ceased trembling. Uplifted by the surge of sail-driven wood knifing over the ocean, he straightened at last. He found that his fouled hands had washed clean. As he straightened to give thanks, he felt Avar's steady presence fading to filmed smoke beside him.

'Father,' he pleaded, heartsore with regret. 'Must you leave? I always felt as though I had just found you. If our days in Karthan were too brief, I would not stand here without you.'

The rough-cut s'Ffalenn king who had steered his last landward course smiled fondly. 'On that point, my son, you are most wrong.' His expression reflected a tenderness perhaps only Talera had witnessed. 'Arithon, use your perception as you were taught at Rauven. You will then see the truth. It is I who would not stand here without you. My presence in this maze was admitted by yours. It is ever your own virtue that guides you. *Remember that!* You are your own lamp, through the darkness.'

'Then what light will guide me past Caolle's death?' Arithon cried on a split note of dread. 'Desh-thiere's curse claimed my reason in that hour. Where will I turn if the drive of that binding grows too overpowering to control?'

Avar raised his eyebrows, his outline thinned to an iridescent shimmer. 'Well, there's one tactic left that you haven't tried.'

Caught dumbfounded at the rail of his own command, Arithon stiffened. 'Ath's earth and sky! I swore my blood oath at Athir to survive!'

In that wry, vicious cunning that had endlessly confounded Amroth's best-outfitted fleets, Avar laughed. 'Oh, but death is too obvious, a coward's trick well beneath your s'Ffalenn name and lineage! Are you not my son? Did Karthan's outmatched plight teach you nothing?' The last trace of the pirate king's form wisped away, leaving only his voice, a challenge flung back on the wind. 'Desh-thiere's spells wage a feud, boy! Don't rely on control! Can't fall back and negotiate! Take hold of the hell-spawned geas that gnaws you. *If you cannot run, you must master it!*'

Arithon stared, sightless, at the rolling swells, surging unbroken toward the horizon. 'Master the curse? Merciful maker!'

For if means existed, why had the combined wisdom of Fellowship spellcraft not found the path to release?

Arithon jabbed savage fingers through his hair, goading his stumbling intellect. The maze collapsed time, caused memories to flow one into the next without regard for scale or proportion. Davien had designed this trial to test a man's conscience. The thrust of spelled seals held no investment in reward. The victim who had lived all his days in tranquillity could pass through at one stride, without suffering.

The snags came where willed choice threw the mind out of balance. Restored to a measure of healed equilibrium, Arithon felt the respite of seafaring drain away. Now, when he most needed a clear interval to think, vision faded. The confines of the tunnel closed back in. Another breath, one last kiss of sun and salt wind on his cheek, and he faced the inevitable step that must carry him into the reliving at Riverton.

No mercy would be shown, should he stall to think. The maze would allow him no planning. No choice, but to apologize through hard-shut teeth, begging grace from the shade of his father.

Arithon strode forward.

His foot came down, setting him back into the blustery chill of that fateful westshore springtime. *Again*, he played as the bard in residence at the Laughing Captain Tavern. The languorous days spent winding lyranthe strings, and the deeper threads of subterfuge laced through the works of Tysan's royal shipyard, were not seen as harmless, in retrospect.

First came the fever-bright dreams, running tracks through his restless sleep. He had tossed in damp sheets, plagued by suggestive whispers, or lured into visions of blood and killing. The nightmares had eluded precise waking recall, eroding his spirit like slow poison and leaving him snappish during the days. Next came the tossing, wakeful nights, battling down the sweating desire to bolt, sword in hand, for the stables. The hours in solitude when he burned like vengeance unleashed to ride flat out toward Avenor. He had flinched like a man ambushed at queer moments, when Lysaer's image fleeted into his thoughts, striking him to rage like the brutal, swift jab to a nerve.

He quelled the spurious flare of such feelings. Dismissed the stray incidents, or shoved them down. Absorbed in single-minded determination to wrest away Tysan's ships and spare the clan bloodlines of Camris, Arithon lived and acted his belief that the drive of the geas could be managed.

He rationalized. He argued with Dakar. The Alliance advance guard would not guess his identity. In all of Riverton, only three others knew that a screening of shadow had altered his natural face. The subliminal friction relentlessly mounted, until that last evening, two days before the planned launching.

Again, Arithon sought his bed, dressed to ride. He kept Alithiel at hand, grimly prepared for the possibility he might need to take evasive action. Against the restive pull of the curse, he trusted his fast wits, his hard-set self-control, and his absolute commitment to winning the clans their chance to secure their survival.

In hindsight, he watched the seductive, slow dance, while the curse's manipulation played him straight into vulnerable blindness.

The maze held to that damning course of events. Arithon struggled to stem rising panic. No power could answer his need for more time. *Too soon*, his doom overshadowed him. Night led in the fogbound hour before dawn, bringing the Mad Prophet to his bedchamber door. The spellbinder slipped the latch, inflexibly drawn by self-righteous belief that Desh-thiere's geas had already laid claim to the Teir's'Ffalenn's mind.

Too driven to sleep, caught fitfully pacing, the Master of Shadow again took his quiet stance behind the door panel, now swinging open. His ambush, and the bared blade of his sword touched against Dakar's nape: the damning, first pieces fell as they must, into refigured alignment. Another step down the tunnel unfolded the burgeoning tension as Arithon sought to recover the broached grace of his privacy. Alone, undistracted, he could yet subdue the building force of the curse's raised currents.

Then the watershed moment arrived: Dakar's fateful, brash courage as he stood stubborn ground sparked the s'Ffalenn gift of compassion. For the one, fateful instant, Arithon saw himself waver. His resolve became flawed, to wrest back the clarity of solitude. Deflected by the Mad Prophet's earnest concern, diverted to a self-doubting review of his intact defenses, he had lapsed. The spelled pressure of the geas was left unwatched *for only an instant*. Yet that mental misstep opened a chink through Arithon's tight-kept inner guard.

Compulsion closed on him with wrathful force. Then that strike was lent impetus by Dakar's disastrous challenge: '*I won't move aside. To get past, you'll just have to kill me.*'

On that fatal split second, Arithon confronted no one else but the enemy.

Spelled forces consumed him in a red tide, snapping through all conscious ties *except one*: he had been forced into thrall, not claimed by willing consent. That grace alone let him cling to survival. Where the grim past at Riverton had seen his defeat, in present reliving, he suffered the event as observer, beset: for the curse woke in resonance. Its active bid to claim mastery set him under redoubled attack. Only now, stirred by the stress of his passage through Kewar, the spelled cords through his being noosed tighter, invincibly strengthened by the insightful course of retracing each prior event.

Arithon had already plumbed the extent of his mage lore trying to seek mitigation. He had savaged the uttermost depths of his spirit, breaking more of himself at each trial. Since the initial defeat at Etarra, he had attempted a thousand combinations of tricks. Neither cleverness nor strength had affected the outcome. Always, he lost. By inexorable increments, the Mistwraith's geas drained more of his will to resist.

Only one wild-card tactic had not been tried. Arithon had never attempted the unconscionable risk of a passive retreat, made to seem like surrender: to give with the storm as the willow will bend, yielding rather than break.

Driven down by main force as the geas tore into him, already cornered beyond remedy, Arithon measured the abyss. The course he confronted seemed little different than an outright plunge into suicide. No advance assurance, that he owned the resilience to snap back from the dangerous brink; no way to measure whether the curse would simply snatch its opportune opening to grind him down into oblivion. He might be crushed outright. Worse, he might find himself caged inside the ring of his shrunken defenses. The husk of his awareness might stay imprisoned, helplessly pinned under siege.

He held nothing beyond the sorrowful list of past failures. Rather than tread a known path to defeat, Arithon chose not to fight. He tapped every shred of wise training from Rauven, casting himself into a diffuse passivity that would appear to spring from exhaustion. He yielded, becoming the emptiness of vacuum, or the mirror-clear reflectivity of stilled water, smoothed under rippleless air.

He had no instant to reconsider, no second to reset flattened barriers. The force of the curse leaped howling through the breach. Uncontested, the channels of his mind became thrashed into a thousand smashed fragments. His foothold for cohesive resistance ripped away, dissolved beyond hope of salvage. Arithon let his dispersed identity drift free. Passive, *inert*, he dared not draw notice. Nestled amid the false semblance of vacancy, he could do nothing else now except wait. The next minutes would resolve his hung fate. Either he would stay lost, bearing the burden of Elaira's death to the scales of Dharkaron's reckoning, or his field of sealed quiet might see him through and buy him a desperate reprieve. He had only to pass unnoticed amid the harrowing of Caolle's downfall.

Arithon stamped down every flicker of distressed thought. A man walking the razor's edge, he dared not glance right or left. He must suffer the coming reenactment, unmoved by the horrors Davien's Maze would configure to provoke his revolted senses. With wide-open heart and unshielded mind, he must endure without flinching as Desh-thiere's workings inflamed him. As the fires of spell-turned, bridleless hatred drove him to insanity and murder, *he must raise no resistance. Nor could he succumb to distressed emotion.* To express any human feeling at all would expose his unconquered awareness.

False hope could not comfort him. To accept the atrocity of his own warping madness must demand the most callously rugged endurance. Arithon faced the truth. The ruthless detachment this trial might demand could well prove impossible to reconcile. All too likely the compassion aligned through the s'Ffalenn bloodline would outmatch his most desperate will.

Then the next stride was upon him. The powers of the maze unfolded the shift in ruthless detail, and Arithon saw himself on that past night at Riverton, reforged to the Mistwraith's laid pattern. The caring light of perception left first, chilling his eyes to the gleam of snap-frozen ice. His expression hardened over to unprincipled ferocity as he firmed his grip on his sword.

'*Stand me down at your peril*,' he had said in ultimatum to Dakar.

Across a gathering darkness, the words came touched through by a note to wring bone-chilling dread from the sensitized ear of a masterbard. Arithon quelled his first shudder of revulsion. He held, yet unflinching, while Davien's spellcraft respun the threads of past nightmare. *Again*, as he had in the Riverton tavern, he angled his blade and attacked.

Unable to ache, denied the expression of natural horror, Arithon watched his ferocious, trained talent slash into Dakar's inept defense. Bound to his right mind by the test of the maze, he endured the breathless entreaties the Mad Prophet cried out in stressed effort to snag back his departed reason. No word touched his heart, no appeal wakened mercy. In reliving, he came on with bared steel, reduced to soulless savagery.

Past and present entangled on that ripping crux. Feeling the clamp of Desh-thiere's geas drawn like stitched wire through his vitals, Arithon forced himself *still*. The howling clang of unsheathed steel shattered hearing, strike after desperate, balked strike. He strangled back the gut impulse to recoil, while the murderous blows he had directed to wound shredded flung cloth, and splintered through marquetry furnishings. The battle raged, beyond stopping. All mercy stood forfeit. Dakar's improvised, beleaguered defense seized on whatever object lay to hand, to be snatched up and thrown against the barrage of snake-fast lunges.

Present time self-control came at lacerating cost. Mangled by the silenced cry of his heart, Arithon marshaled the harsh tenets of mage training.

He would not break.

The rampaging rise of his outraged pity must be ruthlessly deflected. Where he could not sustain the ache of distress, he narrowed his focus, fixed his sorcerer's concentration on the minutiae of visual detail. Anything ordinary and innocent, to bleed off the impact of event; watch anything else that was not flying steel: *here*, the moving cloth of his shirtsleeve, or *there*, where direct avoidance was impossible, the rippling play of caught light, sliding over the polish of Alithiel's inlaid runes. When the rasp of Dakar's stertorous breaths broke through refined concentration, Arithon fastened his hearing around the harmonics cast off of belling, stressed steel.

That stopgap diversion proved a mistake. The spelled seals of the maze would stand for no respite where a victim's past action caused pain. Thrown into the expanded insight of mage vision by the powers of Davien's artistry, Arithon was made witness to the stained shimmer cast through his aura. Still disbarred from direct use of his talent, he saw the scorching tendrils of hatred overmaster his being. In damning clarity, he discerned how his weaknesses made him the flesh-and-blood puppet to mow down any fool who balked his intent to kill Lysaer. Truth laid him bare: the workings that turned him *had in fact been laid down through his own knowledge, and the rigorous trappings of mastery*. Rauven's learning had limits. He could not diffuse spells that learned strictures insisted lay beyond the reach of his resource. Nor could Fellowship power intervene, since the curse was no outside force. Its warping reflection stemmed from flawed beliefs, those personal shortcomings he had not faced, lacing their unseen cracks through his core image of self.

A forced break to excise Desh-thiere's influence would violate free will, also fragment the inborn integrity of the evolving spirit. Any being so abused would pass Daelion's Wheel, reflexively crossing through death to restore its disrupted wholeness.

Arithon grasped the diabolical irony. The insights of Rauven's knowledge stemmed from Ath's law: the self could not be made to disown the self. Desh-thiere's works neatly strangled the avenues of growth and change that might set him free. The necessary step of claiming a flawed idea as his own, and thus acquiring the power to master it, had been set under seals by the curse to engender his own self-destruction.

To snap its binding chain would inflict instant suicide, against his oath at Athir, and to the ruin of the enchantress whose innocent life relied on his continued survival.

Stymied by the bitter fruit of his own brilliant talent, Arithon snatched to steady his rocked foothold on self-confidence. He struggled to settle his rising gorge, that he had helped author his own downfall. Desh-thiere's geas was active, its coiling vigilance like trip wires strung to snag his unwary thoughts. The least flare of self-recrimination would signal rebellion, and call down immediate destruction. Arithon stilled out of desperate need. He let the raging despair rip him through without raising a whimper of protest. Limp and yielding before the disfiguring root of his own baneful evil, he watched himself dance in lockstep to the drive of Desh-thiere's geas.

Again, Arithon employed deadly, sharp swordplay to batter Dakar to a gasping standstill. The poisoned moment of triumph replayed: *again*, he watched the fat spellbinder burn his own life force in reckless extremity, a fool's effort to stave off the ruin of a friend gone insane. *Again*, Arithon pressured to snap through the warded permissions given over in foresighted trust; and now the sole stay that harried his geas-bent course to attack Lysaer. *Again*, the explosion of balked fury, as he cut Alithiel downward to gut the Mad Prophet like a rabbit.

'In Earl Jieret's name, leave that spellbinder be!' For unbearable horror, *yet again*, the unholy slaughter was deflected by the jarring stroke of a longsword wielded by Caolle's steadfast hand.

Cry mercy! Elaira was made to stand witness to this. She must share the inconsolable atrocity that had seen this tough liege-man destroyed. Arithon choked back his wretched self-hatred. Dragged through an exposure that left every nerve scraped over by glass-edged distress, he held on, *made himself passive*, though the lashing storm of raw shame battered at his heart like a cataract. He saw nothing, heard nothing, felt nothing. Only the venom of bestial bloodlust, which drove him to honorless slaughter.

Nor was Caolle the soulless obstacle that the dross of curse-bound madness had once made him seem. Davien's Maze unwound all illusion. Arithon, passive, suffered every stressed parry of his liegeman's desperate defense. He heard each tortured breath. Endured Caolle's whimpering gasps of rank terror, as the older man matched cruel blows with an unprincipled creature *who was also his oathsworn crown prince*. The last Teir's'Ffalenn he would have to vanquish unharmed, for the sake of the clans' future liberty.

The struggle had been doomed from the outset. The veteran who had stood thirty years as Deshir's war captain understood killing odds, had an uncanny, keen instinct for timing and battle-field tactics. Caolle's strong arm was tiring. His fixed expression showed he had already reconciled the horrific recognition that a clean victory was not going to be possible.

Arithon squelched his shuddering denial. Exposed by the maze, cornered and pinned down under Desh-thiere's curse to the point where he dared not weep, he *stayed still* through the shattering moment as Caolle firmed the decision that let in the tragedy. His parries retreated from active defense. He did not fight to save himself, now. Only to bring Arithon down, in sacrifice buying the desperate hope that the curse's fell grip might be broken.

Caolle's life, laid down in loyal crown service at the last, his oath of fealty acquitted to the man who must sire the next heir for Rathain.

Reviled by the torment of facing the ugly finish, Arithon felt his self-control waver. Stroke by unmerciful stroke, the wound tension splintered the restraint that stifled him silent. *How could he watch, and feel nothing at all, as his own hand struck Caolle down? How could he allow Desh-thiere's geas its triumph, with no effort of token defense? How could he dishonor Caolle's brave stand, without grief, without tears, without protest?*

Wrung white by a lacerating hurt he dared not birth into expression, Arithon held. Unblinded, *passive*, he relived the stroke that disarmed him. He allowed the ghastly, unbearable follow-through of his left-handed defense. Felt the stabbing thrust of his main gauche sinking hilt deep in the flesh of Caolle's exposed flank. Where the choke hold of the curse had admitted only flushed victory, the flaying spells of the maze slammed him down with the full impact of terrible grief.

He held, burned and blighted by self-loathing. He held, unable to wrest solace from the assurance of Elaira's survival. He held, riven through by revulsion, as the *worst of himself jerked back the knife in sickening ecstasy*. A twisted aberration owned by Desh-thiere's obsession, he felt himself revel in the warmth of bursting, let blood that *soon, very soon, would be Lysaer's*.

Blistered by a wave of a corrosive triumph that would scar his self-image forever, Arithon fought. He battered back the cleansing fires of compassion, *that insisted such a creature as he had become should not be permitted to live*. His sworn oath at Athir slammed headlong against the heritage of his s'Ffalenn bloodline. He struggled, rejected the schism that had ruined Kamridian, but *still* felt his iron grasp slip.

Hope died in that moment.

Arithon saw, beyond recourse, that he was not going to win through. Laid open by empathy, then pummeled through that breach by his remorse for the profanity of Caolle's murder, he sensed his cohesive purpose slowly shredding apart. All his love for Elaira *was not enough*. The forced state of permissiveness he upheld to protect her tore like tissue before the malevolence of his reprehensible past.

'No, Ath no!' the protest burst from him. Not to endure was unthinkable. Yet to live with the blight of the curse was atrocity. *No one he cared for was safe from his hand*. Like Caolle, each one might be sacrificed. Survive, and they died. Die, *and she who was his heart's only beloved would perish, her life extinguished for the craven cry of his mercy.*

Arithon screamed. Pinned at the crux, ripped apart by the irreconcilable halves of his nature, he found the torment too massive to bear. Though aware he was beaten, he still wrestled to stay his worst nightmare, unfolding.

Frayed on the sword's edge between past and present, he scarcely noticed Dakar's coarse cry, relived from that fell night in Riverton. Arithon heard words, but scarcely registered meaning, until the Named phrase woke the Paravian starspell imbued in his black sword, Alithiel.

The bright chord once sung to Name the winter stars scored the air like light unleashed.

The explosion of pure joy smote against the breaking circle of his conflicted resolve. Bright ecstasy hammered that schism, smashed his already crumbling passivity to irretrievable fragments. He could not withstand this, the absolute purity of tone caught from the harmony that underpinned the majesty of creation. Snatched into celebration by unbridled bliss, Arithon did as any other mortal man must, when caught within listening range: he lost himself to the dance.

While in the past, the hold of Desh-thiere's geas became sundered, Arithon's present self in the maze stayed under siege.

He had yielded up too much raw resource, even if, stunned

beyond breath and thought, he could have wrested his presence of mind from the exultant peal of Alithiel's unearthly harmony. Whipped like a tossed straw between the black blight of the curse, and the keening sweet tones struck from the grand chord of the mysteries, Arithon Teir's'Ffalenn lost his way. As he foundered, unmoored, he was able to frame *nothing* more than the gossamer wisp of one thought: that as the curse ground him under and bound him into slaved hatred, he would not go down as the Mistwraith's consenting accomplice.

On the brink of the fall, that glimmer of defiance opened a keyhole through time.

A resonant voice rolled down Kewar Tunnel, exhorting an apprentice with fond clarity. Through rushing darkness, caught in a snap-frozen circle of calm, Arithon heard: and memory answered the summons.

Once in the past, when his impossibly high aspiration had crashed in a fit of frustration, Halliron Masterbard had bestowed wise advice by the late-night flutter of candlelight. Softened into the fragrances of rose and patchouli, and the citrus-oil tang of the wood furnishings in the musicians' gallery of a wealthy patron's grand ballroom, Arithon recalled . . .

'No, my dear man, that assessment's not strictly accurate,' the elderly bard had admonished in straightforward pique. 'Your performance tonight never once fell short of perfection.'

Arithon's exasperated glance earned Halliron's wry laughter. 'In fact, such rigid polish fashioned its downfall.' Standing, his veined fingers still straight despite his advancing years, the bard gathered up the fleece cover, intending to wrap his lyranthe. Yet his hint was not taken. He saw at a glance his scowling protégé was not going to take his defeat to an unsettled bed.

Aching for his apprentice's passionate disappointment, Halliron deferred his own weariness. 'True art is not cut from the cloth of predictability. Rather, it's an ephemeral brilliance snatched from the chaos of unformed inspiration. The ear for such nuance cannot be forged from mechanical practice.' Sympathetic tawny eyes turned a chiding glance toward the young hand, snapping out scales in a soundless, sharp dance up and down the lyranthe's fretted soundboard.

'Arithon,' the bard said in exasperated tenderness, 'let go. You have to set trust in your inherent talent and goodness. You won't find those treasures, berating yourself. Every musician who would unlock true genius must cast himself free of self-censure. Forget the literal truth. Throw away your belief that the wood and strings of your lyranthe are separate. The instrument must become an invisible extension, and your fingers, outside conscious awareness. When that threshold is crossed, all the physical barriers dissolve. What happens is like alchemy. The bard rises above matter. He flies on the clear insight of the mind and heart, and the body serves him as invisible conduit . . .'

The gem-cut fragment of vision snapped out. Reclaimed by the tumult of reliving, Arithon awoke, his lost shreds of consciousness dashed over and over by the crested paean of Alithiel's unleashed cry. He heeded Halliron's wise counsel because he could do nothing else. The relived chord of grand harmony still fired his being into uncontrolled bliss, even as the locked jaws of the curse dragged his fading awareness of self into enveloping darkness. Wrung by mangling defeat, a part of him also stayed thralled to the Betrayer's sealed spells, pinned as a captive observer.

Past events still unfolded. Even as the ranging harmonics of the sword's unleashed cry shattered Arithon's compulsive insanity at Riverton, the clear vision of the maze showed the moment in acid-marked depth, recast to an intricacy without parallel. Tone for pure tone, Arithon witnessed the sequence: failing, he saw Alithiel's outpouring rapture of sound shiver and snap the sunk barbs the geas had wound through his aura. He marked the precise resonance of the grand chord that disrupted Desh-thiere's embedded seals: *an effect very like the tuned threnodies for fiend bane that released inert objects from possession.* Such lore had been given deep study in the course of his masterbard's apprenticeship.

Yet no moment was given to examine that finding. The maze demanded its due step ahead. While the last, binding coil of the curse sheared away from the past self embroiled at Riverton, Arithon lost all thought, all conscious grasp on the present. *Again*, he fell, transfixed by the stab of overpowering grief as reliving delivered the shock of restored wits, and the shattering discovery of Caolle's bleeding, felled body.

'Caolle! Ath's mercy on me, Caolle!' Again, he dropped to his knees, hands stained to the wrists in his feverish need to stanch the red spurt welling over the sunk steel of the knife. 'Dharkaron strike me, it's death I have dealt for your service!'

Too disoriented to sort past from present, Arithon lost his last grip. Dakar's blow to the back of his neck, redelivered in vivid force, hurled him beyond reach of all bearings. Sick unto himself, utterly consumed, he foundered. Stunned limp in the corridor of Kewar Tunnel, he was unable to command his revolted nerves or recover the will to drag himself upright.

The maze, spell-driven, did not forgive. Unless Arithon regained self-command and moved onward, the broadscale vision of Davien's crafted seals would relentlessly tighten its strangling grasp. Yet even one infinitesimal, saving grope forward might have been the impossible distance between earth and moon.

Caolle's last spoken words to Dakar filtered through, sharp reminder of damning obligation: *'Say to Prince Arithon, when the Fellowship Sorcerers crown a s'Ffalenn descendant as Rathain's high king at Ithamon, on that hour, he will not have failed me.'*

Arithon stirred. His feeble effort strained to throw off the mantling weight of the darkness. If he failed here, he would dishonor far worse than Caolle's charge to uphold his oath to the realm. Yet his last striving thought crashed into a wall of resistance.

Racked across time, hung on the cusp between the grim past and the untenable present, Arithon encountered the curse, still aroused, its winding web closed upon him in final conquest.

The absolute suffocation of defeat slammed him to reflexive recoil. Trapped like a caged, wild beast, he exploded in manic rage. *Not again!* The horror of Elaira's peril was visceral. He would not yield, would not give himself over to usage. If Davien's Maze released him alive, but possessed, he *would not* endure the desecration of taking the knife into his already bloodstained hand. No more, after Caolle, would he permit living madness to strike down another who loved him.

Driven by instinct, his fury the elemental spark struck between hammer and anvil, Arithon reacted. If the grand chord of the mysteries belled out of ensorcelled Paravian steel could not be re-created by the human voice, he was a trained master. He could, as he had the past equinox in the Mathorns, encompass that fullness of sound within the rich discipline of his mind. Those tones above hearing could be fired through harmonics, driving raised energy into the far, upper registers where earthbound vibration became reclothed as light.

Arithon slammed beyond inspiration, lifted himself on the wave of bursting epiphany. *He was Halliron's last legacy, and Mak s'Ahelas's most gifted, born talent.* The telling fact struck him, *that the spellcraft invoked by the geas of Desh-thiere did not encompass the legacy of his combined heritage.* Only his lore from Rauven had been suborned, a purloined store of knowledge that must have been garnered through the questing assault the Mistwraith had launched at Ithamon.

'*Ban i'ent*, no more!' Arithon recast all that he was into sound. He became the chord that once Named the winter stars, that lost eon before time began. That harmony lifted, hurled him through limitation and into the grand dark of the void. He infused that stilled force; tapped the limitless depths that existed before the spun seeds of consciousness that became the Paravians answered their first calling as Ath's gift, to walk Athera as quickened flesh.

Ripped into light, flying free on the wings of refired inspiration, Arithon sang the harmonies of creation, tone by tone, inside the trapped realm of his mind.

One by one, he raised the harmonics of joy. Masterfully deft, he tuned each register, resharpening purity into a razing, bright force. In the fullness of his power as bard, he tested and refined intensity and pitch as a duelist might wield a shining blade of forged steel through the dance of riposte and parry. The expanded clarity of the maze lent him vision to see. Weeping, undone by the ecstasy of his own making, Arithon s'Ffalenn slashed, one by one, the hooked barbs and spelled seals that shackled him in possession.

The garroting force of the curse lost its choke hold, and slowly, grudgingly slackened. Arithon sensed the way open before him to snatch back his forfeited freedom. Wholly unmoored by the rainbow currents called forth from harmonic creation, he sang. The grand chord rang out, its swelling peal igniting the unbridled flame of pure majesty. Arithon soared on its primal, clean force, tuning selected vibration at will to shape the known patterns for fiend bane.

The last tie let go, a sharp sting to the heart, which slapped him to quivering stillness.

Desh-thiere's geas was not undone, not gone; yet its rooted effects had lost their unbreakable purchase. Curse-bound cords of compulsion could not set false ties, or twist any knot through his being, that sound of his making could not tear their vile urges asunder.

Arithon recovered himself, dropped facedown on chill stone. Sweat-drenched, racked limp, he lay still, scarcely trusting the triumph of bought silence.

For long moments, his stunned consciousness seemed to revolve to the rhythm of his panted breaths. Then wonder touched him.

Spun out of reliving, cast free of cursed hatred for the first living moment since the light bolt had arced down at Etarra, Arithon s'Ffalenn at last found his hour of release. Curled in the lonely, chill caverns of Kewar, he bent his head to rest on the cradle of his crossed forearms. There, overcome by shaken reaction, he wept in lament for Caolle's dying. Nor could he choke down his sobs of relief, that his love for Elaira had sustained the raw worst, unscarred by a forced self-betrayal.

Wardings

By the Prime Matriarch's relentless order, twelve senior enchant-resses spend a trying night, engaging scrying spells through a grand focus crystal; as dawn breaks, they are forced to report their defeat: every effort to lay a sigil of influence on Elaira has failed to cross the warded walls of the Brotherhood's hostel . . .

Deep in the vacuum black void between stars, an insatiable pack of questing wraiths unstrings the masterful layers of Kharadmon's series of mazes; and a tissue-thin ring of guard spells flares red, early warning that the grand ward itself now lies in danger of invasive assault . . .

Within the five-sided chamber cut into the base of Rockfell Pit, the Mad Prophet huddles in aching exhaustion, while Luhaine, of necessity, weaves the last sequence of primary wards with dire energies whose vibrational frequency would sear away living flesh; the defenses mesh to a crackle of whipped air, leaving only the seals on the shaft itself, and the outer stone entrance, incomplete . . .

XVII. Second Recovery

Dakar dreamed. In the visions, his eyesight was seared by a million pinpoints of light. The flecks endlessly shuttled in coiling spirals that twisted his guts to sharp nausea. Though he shut aching lids, he could not lose the imprint: of haloes of blued light, tinged with a deadly corona of black-violet that beckoned his thoughts toward ravening madness. He spoke summons in a language his mind could not translate, then watched as his sweat-clammy fingers shaped intricate knots of spelled runes. The forces he handled had no mercy in them. Contact hazed his skin to scraped pain that stung worse than a raging sunburn.

Strive though he might, he could not awaken. His cries for release went unheard. At times, the focused intensity of his nightmare seemed destined to eat him alive. The powers he annealed into balance coursed through him in manyfold layers of complexity. Their sharp focus crossed dimension and transcended matter, ripples interlocked into chains of wrought forces that commanded the weave of creation. The bound edge of such grandeur caused Dakar to cower. He touched concepts that ripped him to abject terror, and still he did not awake.

The hold binding his mind wore Kharadmon's voice, unbreakable as welded steel shackles.

There came no relief. As one pattern of torment came to an end, the process was wont to repeat itself, some cycles climbing at intervals of fifths, others set into sevenths, with the octaves firing the refined harmonics too rarefied for mortal cognizance. Sureties were unfailingly woven in triplicate, with coils that pierced the grand tapestry affirming their anchors within time and space. Familiar sensation was surpassed as well. The spellbinder knew heat with a subtlety that altered the blood, and cold beyond concept of freezing.

The horrors he endured outstripped mere entrapment. Hearing delivered the whispering voices, beating against the throb of his heart and whispering pleas through his mind. They exploited the pinhole cracks between thought. They begged. They whined. They promised and wheedled, then resorted to viciousness, invoking threats with ghastly invention. Had Dakar been given reprieve for a meal, the descriptions would have caused him to render his gorge.

'*You can't listen,*' Kharadmon admonished in response to his mewling misery. '*The wraiths find their foothold by preying on fear.*'

Kneeling within a five-sided pit that *was* darkness, the Mad Prophet whimpered, harrowed as he watched his inept flesh weaving patterns of shuttling light. That vision broke sometimes, its intricate, spelled circles smashed like a plate of dropped glass. The gaps between shards unveiled the star-strewn black of the void, where more voices gibbered, crying of insatiable hunger.

Called back to lift Rockfell Pit's massive capstone, and yelping from a bruised finger, Dakar lost himself again, immersed into chanting strung couplets that only a Sorcerer's mind understood. He held an extended conversation with the mountain, then traced mazes of cold wards through stone.

The dreaming peace that descended like a benison proved wrathfully short-lived. The exhausted rags of Dakar's awareness exploded in bursting red pain, as though, all at once, every nerve he possessed had been drawn through his skin like hot wire. The top of his skull felt torn away by a rocketing thrust that scrambled his brainpan to jelly.

Immersed in his misery, undone by his foolish word of consent, Dakar scarcely noticed the moment that insistent hands started shaking him. The sensations of cold wind and iced rock seemed unreal before the delirium that routed his being like limp flotsam.

Again he was spinning runes in bright light, tying them off into endless, chained rings of spellcraft . . .

'Wake up!' someone shouted. The snarling vowels of a grass-lands insult described an act of rude congress with a goat.

Adrift in oblivion, Dakar failed to respond.

Whoever harangued him yelled louder. 'Damn your fat bulk, Luhaine says he can't heft you! Or do you truly intend to freeze your bollocks to marbles? Just keep on playing the limp sluggard. We'll let you stay like a corpse on a slab in the teeth of the coming snowstorm.' The hand with the wringing hold on his collar shifted grip, then delivered a slap on his cheek.

The Mad Prophet watched the explosion of sparks gyrate across darkened vision. After dense cogitation, he discovered he still possessed a furred tongue and somewhat slurred powers of speech. 'You don't have to hit me,' he mumbled, offended. 'A man can fall prostrate from strong drink, time to time, and not perish under the aftermath.'

'This wasn't a binge!' cracked his tormentor. 'You can't sleep off a backlash exposed on this ledge, and Sorcerer or not, a ghost can't help you sit upright.'

Dakar unstuck stinging eyelids, blinked, and absorbed the whirling gray view of a sky fogged under wool batts of cloud. He tried to swear. Yet the word that emerged from between his chilled lips came out in actualized Paravian. Before he could retract that horrific mistake, the air flashed with bursting streamers of light.

'Have you gone mad?' Luhaine chastised, a shrill gust of urgency. 'Rockfell's grand wards are already sealed! You don't have the restraint to speak in that language now that Kharadmon's presence has left you.'

Dakar's subsequent groan was interpreted as a question.

'You didn't see the state of the star wards yourself?' Luhaine huffed, amazed, then supplied his miffed explanation. 'Kharadmon left in haste to forestall an incursion of free wraiths.'

Dakar dredged up a blank stare, too drained to his dregs to assemble the list of threatening implications. Even if he had wanted to think, Fionn Areth switched tactics and tugged. The jostling stoked the fires of agony in each joint and overstrung ligament. Dakar mumbled. This time his brain had unscrambled enough to use sailor's vernacular in king's tongue. Pleased to discover he could swear as he chose, he decided to study the drifting snowflakes that settled into the eyes.

Luhaine allotted such dreamy recalcitrance short shrift. 'Really, Fionn Areth is only trying to help. You honestly do need to move.'

Skin and bones, Dakar ached as though stretched on a rack. A sulfurous aftertaste fouled his mouth. No evil penalty brought on by drink had ever left him so wretchedly sick. Against the resistance of air in his lungs, the Mad Prophet made his pronouncement. 'Never mind wraiths, Kharadmon was remiss. Next to him, Jaelot's rotgut gin was a kindness.'

'Say so when he's present, he'll steam-clean your ears,' Luhaine pointed out with no sympathy. 'Not least, you'll need something more bracing than rough language if I have to help Fionn Areth force you back to your feet.'

Dakar turned his head in martyred injury. 'I thought I was asked if I'd rather freeze solid. At least then I'd escape maceration.'

Luhaine would not bend his dignity to answer; a glance showed the contrary Araethurian herder was unwilling to back his rash statement, implying a state of free choice. In fact, his green eyes looked a bit *too much* like Arithon's, pinched by an impatient frown. The frayed muffler he wore snapped in the gusts, making him shout to be heard. 'You'd rather be slid down sheer rock on your arse?'

Not Arithon's style, except for a tone that bespoke nasty promise rather than threat. Breath hissed between his clenched teeth, the Mad Prophet mustered his assemblage of joints and plaintively shambled erect.

'There's a cave lower down,' Fionn Areth added more kindly, as vertigo set his charge swaying. 'Bear up that far, you can sleep in dry blankets or stuff yourself on stewed deer.'

'Rockfell's sealed?' Dakar asked, his eyesight rinsed blank by a rolling riptide of faintness. In vaguely sketched fragments, he recalled resetting the capstone over the pit. A bruised finger attested the memory was real, though the rest of his mind seemed corroded away by attrition.

'The wards are refounded,' Luhaine reassured from his vantage above the abyss. Beneath his windy presence, the cliff sheered away, the vertical drop hemmed by frost-broken stone left heaped by the force of past slides. 'Desh-thiere is secured, and none too soon, considering the invasion that threatens the star wards.'

No lecture followed, an ill omen, from Luhaine. Trouble of unknown proportion descended, freshly arisen from Marak; Dakar himself was too spent to measure that worrisome turn of event. Since he lacked any power or resource to help, he applied what remained of his botched concentration toward the hazards that menaced his balance. Each wobbling step down the spell-crafted stair served up the evil reminder: Davien's works always held the unkindly penchant for tripping his unwary feet. Dakar would have paid gold for the chance to sit down. Fionn Areth's sharpened temper aside, he knew if he settled, he would never again recover the brute will to stand upright.

'Not much farther,' prodded the herder, no doubt concerned as Dakar's slipshod steps seemed ready to give at the knees. Huffing under the stout spellbinder's braced weight, he hastened his pace, unable to suppress his uneasy shudders each time they passed the eldritch regard of the Betrayer's sentinel statues.

Even to Dakar's overplayed mind, the creatures appeared more than usually watchful. For some reason that anomaly bothered his nerves, even moved him to make tired comment.

The wind moaned across the swept ledges of Rockfell, but carried no Sorcerer's answer.

The Mad Prophet stopped short. 'Sithaer's breeding fiends! What's happened to Luhaine?'

Fionn Areth stared at him. Given Dakar's blank bafflement, he grudgingly said, 'The Sorcerer left a few minutes ago.' As Davien's carved stairway came to an end, the Araethurian visibly relaxed. 'You didn't notice when he flitted away to look in on Sethvir in Atainia?'

Not about to admit the Betrayer's queer works had unsettled him, Dakar let the younger man steer him off the last of the uncanny risers. Panting and slipping amid the dense snowfall that sifted over the scree, he ventured the question the Fellowship Sorcerer had certainly been avoiding. 'Did Luhaine leave word about Arithon's safety?'

'He said you were free to pursue your affairs.' The herder plowed through a drift, then, more slowly, flanked his charge's gimping progress toward a cornice of fractured rock. 'The haunt added that his Grace would keep his planned rendezvous with *Khetienn* in spring, if he could.'

Dakar damped back an involuntary shiver, praying the paroxysm arose from the cold. Just now, the fiend packs of Sithaer could not make him embrace his errant talent for prescience. Weary as he was, and suffering raw backlash from Kharadmon's murderous usage, he had no wish to set off the tranced fits that delivered his auguries. Whatever rough scrape still embroiled Prince Arithon, the Mad Prophet knew he was in a useless state. If he assayed as much as a cardinal-point scrying, he would assuredly set slipshod wards and unleash a fumbling disaster.

Arrived at the rough cave where Fionn Areth had made camp, Dakar resisted the overpowering urge to sink to his knees where he stood. Once off his feet, he was likely to tumble headlong into unconscious sleep. Since the howling descent of Dharkaron's Black Chariot would be unlikely to rouse him, the thorns of integrity demanded a reckoning. He could not let go until he vouchsafed his promise to see Arithon's double to safety.

'You're willing to remain in my company to Alestron?' he pressed Fionn Areth. No way to guess how the opening was received, with the uncanny likeness of spell-changed features blurred by the pervasive gloom. 'I have to know. Will you accept a secure place in Prince Arithon's service and discharge your debt to him fairly?'

'I'll finish the trip to the coast as he asked,' the young herder allowed after scarcely a moment's hesitation. The experience at Rockfell had seeded a change. No longer green with the uncertainty of youth, Fionn Areth's carefully tempered reply showed the flint of adult determination. 'After that, who can say? I don't plan to raise goats. The s'Brydion loyalty is allied with the Light. Perhaps I'll enlist with Duke Bransian's field troops.'

'Well, for that you won't suit,' Dakar said in rejoinder. He sat all at once, choking down ripe laughter that might rankle the Araethurian's stiff pride. Nevertheless, the hilarious irony raised the Mad Prophet's sly humor. 'The duke picks his men for their silent tongues and their unquestioning obedience.'

'I can learn, you stuffed tripe sack,' Fionn Areth sniped back. 'At least, watching you hump your fat arse off this mountain will teach me unbreakable patience.'

Too weary by half to sling back biting insults, far less delve into the thorns of subversive truth, the spellbinder curved his bearded lips into his best mooncalf smile. He knew, none better, that Alestron's clan lineage could not stay aligned with town interests. In rich fact, the s'Brydion had been Arithon's active spies since an hour's incisive exchange in a shepherd's hut back in Vastmark. If Lysaer's sunwheel fanatics should levy for troops, Alestron's crack companies were most likely to answer the muster by arming against them.

Yet that vexing snag must be broached in due time. Helpless to do more than snatch rest in false peace, the Mad Prophet rolled into his blankets. Inside of a minute, he was dreaming again, this time of drinking mulled wine in a brothel, sprawled across perfumed sheets. Best of all, the bed was not empty. A lush pair of doxies stroked his back with sweet oil and murmured suggestive endearments.

In a striking departure from methodical propriety, the discorporate Sorcerer Luhaine deferred his departure for Althain Tower and his planned consultation with Sethvir. Gale winds and snow posed his self-contained presence no ruffling inconvenience. The morbid unease that distressed his staid mood did not settle, though at first, the Sorcerer had tarried on the pretense of ensuring that the Mad Prophet was escorted to shelter. Yet even after the rash goatherd delivered his promise to finish the journey to Alestron, and through the interval while Dakar slept off the rough worst of the backlash Kharadmon could not stay to avert, Luhaine continued to linger. A tight-laced, trim vortex, he whirled unseen in the storm above Rockfell Peak.

Recurrent anger plucked at his thoughts and rankled his prosaic nature.

The rock ledges beneath sensed the Sorcerer's distress, and in patient empathy, concurred: seldom had the world of Athera been threatened by perils of such wide-ranging potency. Sun might still shine while the living earth turned, yet who knew for how much longer? Wraiths inbound from Marak could endanger all life. Between imbalanced grimwards, and Khadrim flying free, Luhaine gloomily tallied the seeds of disaster that lay primed and ready to germinate. Ever and always the cheerless pessimist, he spun in tight circles and fretted. His obstinate sensibility balked at the raw fact that his overmatched Fellowship lacked the resource to manage the next crisis.

The gestalt labor of resealing Rockfell's triple ward rings had exposed their appalling deficits. Unlike Kharadmon, who delighted in mayhem, Luhaine was left irritable and depleted. Rather than loose his vile temper on Sethvir, the Sorcerer coalesced to a pinpoint of chiseled awareness. He drifted earthward with the settling snow and alit on the stairway carved into the flank of the mountain by Davien's intransigent artistry.

Gargoyles watched him. Crested heads capped in drifts, and cold eye sockets scalloped with crusts of rimed ice, the carvings aligned their uncanny awareness and sampled his stalking presence. Stone wound in spells did not stay inert, but flared into a surly corona.

'Listening, are you?' the discorporate Sorcerer snapped in rancid distemper. 'You've spurned Sethvir's queries for long enough. I, Luhaine, do summon you here! This world stands in peril. Your choice to retreat can't excuse shirking dalliance as Athera falls into jeopardy.'

A moment passed, filled by whirling flakes, hard driven by keening winds.

'Don't pretend you don't hear me,' Luhaine accosted, tart with impatient asperity. 'You'll surely know Sethvir's flattened with weariness, minding the world's deranged grimwards. The way you eavesdrop, you're surely aware that Kharadmon's gone alone to divert a migration of free wraiths.'

'Luhaine, how boring if the world falls to ruin, and you, poor sod, never change,' the carved statue pronounced in reply. 'Must you always bear in like the jaws of a pit terrier when you lose your self-righteous temper?' The voice was Davien's, and the awareness just arrived, knife-edged with dissecting sarcasm. 'Since I won't hear your lecture, you can't go away? What an unimaginative stalemate.'

Luhaine's churning presence spat ruffled sparks. 'Where will your vaunted complacency be on the day an invasion from Marak descends on your lair in the Mathorns?'

Davien's bent of humor roused a diamond-hard gleam within the stone eyes of the gargoyle. 'Such gaudy melodrama! The bit part's not like you. And who claimed, about free wraiths, that I've chosen to lounge at Kewar in frivolous solitude?'

Touched by a bolt of stark apprehension for that fox-subtle change in tonality, Luhaine punched an agitated gyre through the horizontal lash of the snowfall. Already he sorely regretted his impulse. Sheer folly, not to have consulted Sethvir to ask for the current news. 'Don't claim you've left to assist Kharadmon.'

The gargoyle's mocking leer seemed to change, sculpted eyebrows raised in astonishment. 'That's assuming your henchman would want me along to share his labor in unreconciled partnership? Don't, please, die laughing. We're sticklers for truth.'

Had Luhaine still been embodied in flesh, he would have flushed deeply scarlet. 'He named you Betrayer. On good days, the rest of us usually agree, the delicate question's still dangling.'

'Perhaps not,' said the carving that spoke for Davien. 'The verdict might fall with me out of favor, depending what happens to Prince Arithon.'

That instant, full force, Luhaine felt the chill wind, and the roaring dark of the abyss. '*What have you done?*'

'Despoiled the lynchpin that upholds this world's promise,' the Betrayer replied with a bite that invoked outright challenge. 'Or else forged you the weapon you can't do without to stave off the throes of invasion. The hours ahead will determine the outcome.'

'What have you done?' Luhaine repeated, though the gargoyle cast back a statue's blank silence, and in truth, *he already knew*. Clear as a spearcast, Arithon's flight would have led to the entrance to Kewar Tunnel.

'Mercy, brave heart,' Luhaine whispered, as wild with sorrow as the keening gusts that lashed over Rockfell Peak. 'Bitter, the hour that brought your Grace to shoulder Kamridian's trial, and woe to this land should your spirit fall short in the course of that sorrowful testing.'

As always with Davien, ethics tangled with necessity, until even the enlightened among Ath's adepts might be sorely beset to discern the fine line between meddling choice and the justifiable dictates of crisis.

Arithon struggling to survive passage through Kewar bespoke a crushing potential for tragedy; but against threat from Marak, Athera would require all the help and straw hope the Fellowship could wring in support.

'Fires of eternity!' Luhaine hissed in vexation as his presence shot aloft and veered west to resume his deferred passage to Althain Tower. 'Let me not be the one sent to tell the Mad Prophet if Arithon Teir's'Ffalenn fails his oathsworn charge to survive.'

Bound by the coils of Kewar's forged spells, Arithon mustered frayed nerves and committed another step forward. Behind, sprawled the corpses of Baiyen Gap, and the unburied dead from Jaelot and Darkling dispatched to their doom in Daon Ramon. He had shared their suffering struggle for last breath; had wept, as their widows in mourning. Exhaustion remained, a shuddering weakness that burdened his frame like dipped lead.

Ahead, he still faced the last battle by the Aiyenne, and the fates meted out to Lysaer's sunwheel companies as they closed to engage Jieret's war band. A few hundred casualties, when laid against the slain thousands undone at Tal Quorin and Dier Kenton Vale. Yet in Kewar, no loss by armed conflict was a pittance. Each bereaved mother and each orphaned child scored the heart with their signal patterns of tragedy.

Such sorrows could be endured, mourned in suffering, and finally atoned by forgiveness.

Less easy to reconcile were those clanborn fallen who had perished to break the Alliance's cordon. Braced for the savage toll wrought by their sacrifice, Arithon stepped into the maelstrom, and died.

He knew the eviscerating rip of the spring trap, and the mangling crunch of the deadfall. He was a horse, tumbling head over heels, a snapped foreleg snagged in a noose. He died of arrows, of quarrels, of cold steel thrust deep into shuddering flesh. He was the hot spurt of blood on cold ground in the screaming mêlée of battle. Clanblood or townborn, the battering shock brought an agony alike to the very bone. Arithon died, of a warhorse's battering hooves, of an axe cut that severed his spine. He fell, weeping, beside slaughtered comrades at arms, his croaked prayers to the Light left unanswered.

He was Eafinn's son, shivering out life facedown in a snowdrift. He was Theirid, lying maimed in thick brush, screaming to draw fire from enemy bowmen to spare other men pinned in a thicket. He was an officer from Etarra, choking on vomit in the thorny waste of a gulch. He was a widow sobbing in a sad, empty bed, then a child scourged by nightmares no pension in gold could restore a lost father to assuage.

Another step, his foot dragging with unreconciled dread: Arithon encountered Earl Jieret's untenable conflict. He saw mage-sighted conscience clash with brute will, then ached with remorse as an unfailing heart shirked the charge of a bloodborn heritage.

'Oh, my brother, forgive!' Arithon's apology scattered echoes down the confines of Kewar Tunnel. Yet the sorrows of Jieret's shame did not lift. The *caithdein*'s dark destiny stayed excised to exposure by Davien's entangling spells.

Arithon shivered, arms wrapped to his chest, for an ache beyond consolation. 'My brother, you have suffered my sorrow at Minderl Bay, but with no stalwart hand to uplift you.'

Unspoken, the useless, hagridden protest: *that the man standing vigil beside the ninth acorn before Lysaer's advancing vanguard* should have *been Braggen, well hardened for war by his festering grudges, and unburdened by initiate mage talent.*

The maze ceded Arithon no ground for the fact his tailor-made orders had been spurned; that Earl Jieret had shouldered his fate by free choice, against the will of his crown prince. The Teir's'Valerient had already passed over Fate's Wheel. Now bound to stand as unreconciled witness, Arithon brazened through shrinking cowardice, one shaken step after the next.

Reliving burgeoned in lurid detail, and a crossbow bolt flew, striking Jieret high in the shoulder. A triumphant Sulfin Evend strode forward to claim the trophy brought down by his marksmanship. Disregarding the fallen *caithdein*'s croaked warning, he ground the frail shell of an acorn under his contemptuous heel. The shards scattered. A string of ciphered spellcraft unreeled and spread with the winnowing wind.

Jieret's full-throated howl of regret could not stay that unleashed construct.

Nor could Arithon's remorse, as spellbound observer, do aught to reverse the course of determined consequence. The diabolical impact of his own design bloomed over that sere, winter hilltop. Woven shadow and illusion invoked Desh-thiere's curse, whipping Lysaer to berserk ferocity.

Earth and sky rained white fire. The percussive blast of uncounted levin bolts sheared over the hapless landscape. The strikes hammered down, on and on in blind reflex, but brought no consummate release. Geas-roused passion would not answer to reason. No power of light could defeat the wild wind, or the blighting provocation of set banespells. The Narms field troop who marched on the strength of their faith were immolated where they stood. Arithon learned their Names to the last man, his flesh razed from bone in a shrieking deluge of agony.

Bound to their pain, Davien's Maze saw him burn through three hundred hideous deaths. In manyfold horror, he felt crisped skin blister, then blacken to paper, and peel. He could not weep through eyes torched to carbon. A throat choked by flames could not scream. Nor was the scope of his suffering confined to the fate of two-legged humanity: Arithon was the brush, razed stem from root. He was the hare, and the deer, and the field mouse, torched as he foraged the sere thickets. Lashed by the terrible, indiscriminate ruin released by the sweep of his strategy, he endured measure for measure in destruction. No mercy was shown as Jieret's chains of rote spellcraft reaped a swath of wholesale slaughter.

Graven in mind and flesh, Arithon bore the furious brunt. As his half brother's attack recoiled in blind fury through the acorns imbued as his fetch, he was old stone, heat-split as the snowdrifts boiled skyward. He was the tortured disharmony of the land, raped by manic rage and the hostile misuse of the elements.

No recourse, for guilt, but to keep moving forward. Arithon lost count of his stumbling steps. Aware he must walk the full course of the holocaust, he held no saving hope. Dogged endurance must see him through. Lysaer's rampant fury added peril to hardship. As the wakened response of the curse clawed his mind, Arithon called upon mage-trained resilience and raised music to stave off insanity.

Each note that he forged was a victory snatched from the closing jaws of disaster. Through grief, through sorrow, through the horrors of scourged flesh, he must frame without flaw the ethereal chords extracted from Alithiel's grand harmony. The toll of such effort came at punishing cost as the screams of the dying and the moans of the burned unstrung concentration and poise. Time and again, he was forced to start over. In lockstep perfection, with no drift in tone, he reordered his mind and raised the exalted harmonics that dissolved Desh-thiere's geas-bent drive to shed blood.

The music itself laid him open. The suspension of unbridled joy shattered thought, set against a raw backdrop of violence. Arithon made his way, scorched to branding remorse for the choices his botched fate had presented. Savaged by inconsolable grief, he fought to bridge shattering dichotomy: while binding his cognizant mind to the sound that had seeded the glory of creation, *he died*: over and over, he fell, screaming other men's curses amid the base terror of war. Star song woke the earth. He *was* the lane energies flowing through boulder-strewn slopes, the spun force of magnetics ripped out of true by hatred and ruin and strife. Remanded to peace by the keys of rebirth, the torn heart could not be reconciled. Let blood stamped the shadow of desecration on a land once cherished by unsullied majesty: the frost-silver grace of Riathan Paravians, running wild under spring moonlight.

Another step; another; Arithon pressed onward. Each cycle of death exacted its forced reckoning, until the one wound that could not be absolved. Kewar's maze forgave no affliction. As the last victim's suffering faded behind, the gnawing ache of the crossbow bolt remained sunk in Earl Jieret's shoulder.

'Mercy on us both, how did you survive?' Raked over the coals of his unresolved sorrow, Arithon saw Lysaer's Lord Commander crest the hilltop and bind Rathain's *caithdein* captive.

'Jieret, no! You can't have lived through this, not for me, not even for the sake of the realm!' Arithon braced himself, shaken, against Kewar's unyielding stone wall. The appalling penalty set on the next step hurt too much for his bruised heart to bear.

Memory blazed back, a lacerating truth drawn from one of Jieret's past arguments. *'What is left in this world after us, liege, but earth and sky, each bearing the imprint of our living stewardship?'* The words brought fresh pain, graven with the straightforward affection the clan chieftain had shown during life. *'The legacy of your lineage must survive all our choices, and all of our failings, your Grace.'*

Another fragment of recall surfaced, as sharply damning, from another dispute with Erlien s'Taleyn, affirmed as the steward of Shand. '*That's how it's given for* caithdeinen *to test princes . . .*'

Arithon finished the stricture aloud: 'to lay down their lives, if need be.' First Steiven, now Jieret; wrenched to bristling abhorrence by his ties to royal birthright, the Master of Shadow reeled onward. Yet no cry of scorched conscience stayed the brutal reliving as the Alliance Lord Commander dragged his injured clan captive downslope.

Spurred on by his outrage, Arithon stayed upright. 'There are limits!' he accosted the spell-charged air. Yet if Davien was listening as hidden observer, no plea for succor was granted. The vision unreeled, showing Jieret's doomed effort to drive Lysaer and Sulfin Evend to disparity. Rathain's crown prince wept. Doubled with dry heaves, he watched Steiven's grown son lose his bold tongue to the knife.

'Avert and forgive!' Arithon gasped in wracked protest. The injustice stopped thought, that the maze shaped this trial with invasive disregard for an intensely proud man's guarded privacy. No worse humiliation could have befallen Earl Jieret. He would never have condoned such a legacy as this: a prince loved as a brother forced to experience the sordid ignominy of his suffering.

'Enough!' shouted Arithon. Surely, the Betrayer's shackling spells weighted the scales too severely. Sworn as Rathain's protector, a crown prince must answer for the welfare of his pledged liegemen. Yet the inhumane handling that brought Jieret's death had occurred outside choice, beyond reach of his royal justice.

Unrelenting, the bared truth rescinded his plea. At next step, Arithon received the heartsore reminder he had abdicated his will *without reservation* to a *caithdein* bound to serve the inflexible dictates of duty. Stumbling to meet the array of strict consequence, Arithon cursed the black hour his spirit had been drawn from his flesh and merged with the spelled steel of a sword blade.

He could beg no mercy for the whiplash reprisal bought by that act of submission. The sole route to survival must scribe its straight course through the nightmare of Jieret's captivity.

Arithon clenched his jaw, hackled to revolt. In self-honest reflection, he understood that his willed choice on the staircase had framed his consent to this challenge. Yet to endure the low drama of a friend's degradation abrogated the fabric of human decency. Warned that his path through the maze could not deviate, Arithon poised his inner awareness and reached, sounding the well of spell-textured silence above the range of natural hearing. He strained every limited resource of talent, seeking to access the vortex that aligned his course to the stream of past conflict.

He heard nothing; felt nothing; encountered no more than the mirrored image of himself, entrapped by the riddle engraved on the black-stone portal that admitted him. The enemy before him, behind, and against him was still himself, and no other.

Impelled by the blaze of a scorching, bleak rage, Arithon rammed his way forward. Helpless to intervene, he watched Jieret's flesh become cosseted coin, held for barter to draw in the proud clanborn. Brutality made a mockery of honor and cause. The price paid to enact a royal escape surely came at too high a cost.

'Was the future worth this?' Arithon gasped, as vision showed his *caithdein* dragged like stunned game off the back of a steaming horse. He shared shaming pain, every futile recrimination as Deshir's clan chieftain was installed in drugged stupor within the Alliance campaign tent. 'Would you have heeded my pleas by the Aiyenne if you knew you'd be trapped for a public maiming?'

For answer, a raven's spread wings rustled out of deep darkness. The tips of her primaries flicked Arithon's cheek as she passed to a breeze of sliced air. The sealed deeps of Kewar roiled like smoke in her wake as her passage tore open the gateway to Ath's greater mystery.

Arithon staggered, whirled into the exalted perception of mage-sight.

Expanded sensation unleashed his awareness. More than just light, he experienced heightened sensitivity to sound. The vast chord that arose from the heart of the mysteries came alive to his bardic discipline. He saw form rewoven as ribbons of light, orchestrated by waves of grand harmony. Stone yielded its secretive dance of wild energies. Arithon felt reborn into wonder, the reforged access to his lost mastery a gift that restored balanced strength.

Drawn past the veil by the guidance of the raven soaring ahead on stretched wings, the Master of Shadow understood his fresh insight could be nothing else but shared dream, derived from Jieret's past journey. *This uplifting spiral of wild talent arose from the spontaneous unfolding of the* caithdein's *innate gift of Sight*.

Once, before this, Arithon had perceived the land through a Sorcerer's eyes. A brief bond of shared resonance had let him track Asandir's refined survey of Daon Ramon Barrens. That reaching glimpse had shown rolling hills wrought in the silver-foil tracks of wild lane flux, the ephemeral fires that licked each swept summit underscored by the shining patience of bedrock. Deft touch had tracked the underground water seeping through the hidden strata of the earth, with the upwelling springs of the virgin flows like glistening spills of jet glass. The beauty had surpassed any language to describe. Arithon had traced the spirit-light prints of the fox, and known the huddled sleep of the hare. His mind had danced with the sylph currents of the wind, shuttled across by the combed streamers inscribed by the hunting flight of an owl.

Yet where his snatched insight from Asandir had parted the gateway to wonders, the gift of a raven and Earl Jieret's unvanquished determination carried the questing mind farther. Arithon was shown unity beyond human life, his crown prince's oath interlaced through his being like a webwork of sparkling cord.

He was the land, and the land was himself.

Individual as one wrapped thread in a tapestry, Arithon was aware of himself in the whole, and of Jieret's being, inseparably braided within the breathing miracle of his life: a joining of purpose made out of love, before oathsworn duty or loyalty. The clean grace of that partnership, shown in shining balance against the grand arc of creation, broke Arithon's rage, left him weeping. Brought to his knees by stunned awe and amazement, he knew a joy that shattered all concept of beauty; felt the limited bounds of mortality burn away, reforged in the fires of primal song and its higher octaves of infinite light.

Shown the unsullied splendor of Athera's existence, the glory of myriad consciousness interwoven on the tireless loom of the elements, a man who was crown prince could but bow his head and give way in exalted surrender.

Even blinded, even maimed for the cause of Lysaer's alliance, Earl Jieret had not been diminished as a man in any fashion that mattered. Beyond earthly life and transient flesh, his being shone untouched, richly vibrant with the radiance of his character. The resented weight of a burdensome guilt that Arithon had begged not to carry lifted away like a mist.

'I forgive you the choice to change places with Braggen,' he whispered, each word delivered with tears of unadulterated sincerity. The release set him free. Braced for wracking loss, expecting the barren stone passage of Kewar Tunnel, Arithon dragged himself back to his feet and assayed another step forward.

Yet the vision that bared the true glory of the land did not dissolve at his back. Instead, the starred flow of the lane's pulse waxed brighter, raised to untamed exaltation. The rainbow shimmer shot through his reliving, transcending the thresholds of sound and light. The inevitable, plunging fall into bloodshed came presaged by refigured horror, as the intertwined ribbons of conscious life shivered to the blast of a war horn, mustering men to take arms.

'No!' Arithon slammed short, reviled by the lash of assaulted instinct. He refused the desecration, a clear-cut violation of Rathain's sacred balance that demanded a crown prince's appeal for redress. 'No more killing in my name, or for the sake of the old, feuding hatreds!'

.Yet where spoken words could do nothing to heal the festering wounds of past conflict, Earl Jieret's freed spirit could act on the strength of his unvanquished free will. His courageous triumph would not go unsung, or become lost to the annals of history: for the act of humility that had admitted acceptance of his sorry part in the sacrifice, Arithon s'Ffalenn was granted the gift of observing his liegeman's last deed.

The land's tapestry blazed, raised and wakened by command of Jieret's empowered signature. His voice was the self-aware cry of his Name, shaped as a shout against silence. The sound reverberated through sky and earth, loud and full with the reclaimed resonance of a being whose vision discerned his ancestral ties to the chord of Ath's infinite creation.

A miracle answered that wounded appeal.

Another horn call swelled over the first. This note, winded on the whorled spine of a dragon, came ranging, freed, across time. Its resounding, deep echo rocked the roots of the hills. All clamors subsided before shuddering awe. Some indefinable quality to the belling, rich overtone made the heart yearn to pause and show reverence. Arithon resisted. He still walked the trial of Kewar Tunnel, where delay carried fatal penalty.

Head up, eyes wide-open, somehow he forged onward. Bound to his forced step, spells of cause and effect gave birth to uncanny vision. He was made witness to an event such as no sanctioned crown prince had seen for five centuries, as the soil of Rathain answered a *caithdein*'s last plea. Night burned and wind gentled. Stars and moon welcomed a towering presence, whose flesh-and-blood hooves trod the ground of a bygone age, yet whose manifest form cast its solidified consciousness into the convergence of Jieret's summons.

Vulnerably mortal, Arithon lost his breath as the centaur guardian entered the Alliance war camp.

The Paravian's arrival transcended all boundaries. The beauty, the wild grace, the shining, immortal majesty stunned thought into poignant stillness. To mage-sight, the creature was blinding light; to the ear of a bard, a peal of ethereal harmony that lifted old pain into ecstasy.

Unable to stand upright before such a beacon of truth, Arithon s'Ffalenn let his trembling limbs fold. Kneeling, he felt himself immolated. The blazing presence of the Ilitharis Paravian burned him down to a core of absolute parity. Recast in pure light, Desh-thiere's curse seemed a cobweb of shadow. The distressed cries of the elite Etarran troops became raucous noise, of no more concern to the vast, turning earth than the shrilling of squabbling gulls. Nor were the forged weapons men carried for war bound to such usage as mute objects. Sword steel thrummed and rang in an outcry for peace. Lance shafts dreamed with the roused awareness of trees, while sheaves of arrows keened into vibration, their fletching yearning for feathered flight, and their forged broadheads recalled to their silent beginnings as ores in the veins of the mountains. Man's purpose was transient. Where a guardian walked in command of the mysteries, the resurgence of natural order *must* prevail.

Caught up by wonder, Arithon forgot fear. All driving needs lost their urgency. In the span between heartbeats, death and sorrow were subdued, the sting of grief drawn from their memory: except one. That single loss swelled into a festering sore, a scourge branded into quickened flesh with a burning, indelible urgency.

The unabashed tears coursing down his bared cheeks, Arithon cradled his face in his hands and cried aloud without thinking. 'Oh most brave, Ath's beloved! Why did your kind ever leave us?'

Enormous, warm hands grasped his wrists; gently raised him. Their tender touch was immediate: *real*. Kewar Tunnel's interlaced wheels of spellcraft had bridged space and time through a crown prince's unleashed passion of longing. *Standing foursquare, wrapped in the swelling chord of grand harmony and his matchlessly regal splendor, the Ilitharis Paravian had* in fact *materialized in Kewar's cavern to meet him.* 'That riddle was not written, the day I greet my death,' the centaur apologized, his bass voice towering above.

Within the cramping confines of the corridor, the creature's direct presence overwhelmed. His horned head should have scraped the vault ceiling overhead; yet did not. Before such a being, stone itself must give homage.

Ripped open to mage-sight, Arithon could not discern the guardian's detail or form. He beheld the centaur as a pillar of fire and light, felt his touch as a shower of refined illumination more subtle than the glimmer that presaged spring sunrise. Dazzled blind by the creature's shining, pure aura, wrung ecstatically deaf by the unfolding shower of pure harmony that lilted like song through his being, Arithon addressed the incomprehensible. 'How have you come here?'

'I was called, truly. Fate's forger, you were Named. There lies your destiny, ripe for the hour when you finally embrace the full reach and strength of your power.' For a moment, the guardian's massive palm brushed a feather's touch across the crown of Arithon's head.

A rippling tingle swept Rathain's prince into tremors from head to foot. The thrill both defined and uplifted his awareness. Recast by that play of resharpened force, he experienced a range of emotion that surpassed any word to describe. He reeled, mind and senses overset. The shattering wonder that deluged his spirit whirled him into a sublime peace that seemed chiseled from infinite light.

'I give you my memory,' the centaur pronounced. Each word rang with crystalline overtones, wild and free as his horn call had been, ranging over the vales of Daon Ramon. Sound spoke, drawn out of the silence of mystery. The echoes awakened remembrance: of a beauty that burned, as Riathan danced, liquid silver under the moonlight. 'Henceforth, you'll recall your *caithdein*'s last deed. Through my eyes, behold his final triumph. Masterbard! Hear the charge of your calling. When you write the ballad to commemorate Jieret's passing, craft each note and each line without mourning. Your Earl of the North abides now in joy. Let his memory inspire your world without bitterness.'

'The sword of my half brother killed him,' gasped Arithon, aggrieved as he surveyed the detailed, harsh fact, then amazed to find his sorrow undefiled by the answering spark of his hatred. He trembled then. Humbled beyond words, he discovered even Desh-thiere's curse had been silenced.

'Your *caithdein* did not suffer,' the centaur replied from the peace that encircled his presence. 'The sword and the fire that dispatched his flesh have no power to mar his true spirit. If your oathsworn brother crossed beyond Fate's Wheel by the

734

murderous act of your kindred, heed my word, the broken husk of his flesh felt no pain.'

'He'll be missed, nonetheless,' Prince Arithon said, moved by imperative truth. 'I can't let his priceless companionship go without feeling the burden on my heart.'

'Walk on, go free,' the centaur said gently. 'Remember the gifts without sadness.' He removed the exalted benediction of his touch.

The withdrawal engendered a desperate, fierce absence that darkened the mind like suffocation. Cast back toward the dimmer frame of his mortality, Arithon screamed in recoiling pain. Unable to endure the descent into darkness that must attend his next step through the maze, he cried out in abject appeal, 'Mercy upon me, I am not yet free!'

Davien's trial still bound him. A short step ahead, more horrors awaited. The coarse prospect of suffering written into maimed flesh posed a contrast the uplifted mind could not bear; not hard-set against the scalpel-sharp purity of a centaur guardian's live presence. Arithon suffered the burn of his conscience more acutely than ever before. Peeled to raw nerves by his birth-born compassion, he sensed the dense knit of the spells, still poised to extract every hurtful stroke his past would demand in redress.

He could not walk, could not return to the mire. Life meant desecration, burdened down by the leaden sorrow of more deaths. How could he condone even a dog's severed life? A survival bought by the premeditated butchery Braggen had committed to preserve s'Ffalenn lineage became an offense before the living gift that Ath's grace once bestowed on the world. Sorely anguished, that his hands were going to run red with the blood of more hapless victims, Arithon bowed down in humility.

'Let me take Jieret's death.' He could no longer shoulder his burden of shame before the Paravian's shimmering presence. Nor in self-honesty could he pretend that the shreds of his courage could outmatch his own rankling weakness. Trusting Elaira's transcendent love would find a way to forgive him, he said, 'Some sorrows have embedded too deep for reprieve.'

'Then receive absolution,' the Ilitharis replied. 'Stand tall and walk at my side.'

'You ask this?' Lent hope beyond horror, offered comfort amid the black wasteland of his despair, Arithon straightened. He could do nothing else. The centaur's compassion was too commanding a force. Before such sovereign grandeur, every shadow of uncertainty must dispel, resolved by the light of the infinite.

The guardian's massive strength caught and steadied his lost balance; and again, the uplifting tingle of ecstasy razed like a balm through worn flesh. The centaur said gently, 'What is a flaw but a human mistake, or an ignorance that sees without options?'

'My grandsire tried to teach much the same thing.' Arithon shivered, contrite. 'How sorely I failed, as his living example.'

'Failed?' Liquid movement embedded in a fountain of gold light, the Ilitharis bent his horned head and gazed downward, his regard as distinct as his touch. 'Daelion himself would not judge you so harshly. Come ahead. Let true meaning unveil your self-worth.'

Under the Ilitharis's shielding protection, Arithon assayed a next step. The inevitable fall nonetheless struck him breathless. With utmost, dark cruelty, the spellcraft of the maze hurled him back into reliving.

Underfoot, now, the deep drifts of the Mathorns, shadow black and salt white beneath the thin gleam of a waning moon. The rock summits echoed with the belling of hounds, and the shouts of pursuit from armed enemies.

Yet this time, the harrowing vista contained the flame of a living splendor: the centaur guardian walked one step behind the man sanctioned as Prince of Rathain. If gold-feathered hooves left no trace of tracks, the creature's arrival was acknowledged within the broad tapestry of Ath's creation. Time became meaningless. Space shifted, rendered fluid as thought. In the stately reach of Paravian presence, the stone, the trees, and the cloudless night sky upheld the natural order of a world that remembered its first, pristine peace. Under the shining glitter of starlight, the movement and noise of striving men seemed diminished to a puppet play of illusion.

Arithon recovered the resilience to face forward. Erect, his eyes clear, he reforged the confidence to claim his marred past, as the way through the notch yawned before him.

He stepped forward.

Braggen's arrow hissed downward out of the dark, and an Etarran tracker fell screaming.

'Am I worth this death?' Arithon gasped, his voice wrenched into strangled distress. He braced for the pain by raw reflex. But wrapped in the spun gold of the centaur's aura, the shock of the broadhead piercing the man's breast passed him by with no further suffering.

'What does your worth and this death have in common?' the

736

guardian stated in tender remonstrance. 'If this stranger's harsh end for a misled cause and a sorrowful muddle of hatred brands your greater life as unworthy, why does his delusion matter more than another who knew you with intimate clarity? Your Jieret crossed the Wheel for your sake as a gift born of love. His regard for you sprung from a trusting heart, just as his sacrifice stood surety for your character. If you argue that the vision of mankind is clouded, the land of Rathain herself is aware. For the risk you assumed on the solstice alone, this world of Athera upholds your good name as a Fellowship-sanctioned crown prince. I came here, Arithon Teir's'Ffalenn, because I was called. I stay at your back on my free choice to answer! Claim as fact your irrevocable right to survive, or else choose, if you dare, to disown me!'

Arithon recoiled. Slapped short by rebuke that shamed his adherence to shortfalls as arrogance, he cried out. Then he squared his trembling shoulders. Stripped bare by the eyes of the guardian's truth, he confronted the horror of his own making.

Sickened, still upright, he addressed the agony of the Etarran who writhed in his grave of stained snow. 'If your strength stands beside me, great one, as a gift, I still can't condone this man's pain.'

A harsh truth: he could not pass without stepping over the throes of an arrow-shot victim's last suffering.

'Then help him die,' the Ilitharis said, unequivocal. 'Strike down your limiting belief that you're powerless!'

Arithon knelt. Snow chilled his scraped knees. He tugged the trailing, torn hem of his sleeve from the hand not encumbered with bandaging. 'Easy,' he soothed as he touched the stricken man's chest. He was aware with glass-sharp, terrible clarity, how the damage of such a wound felt. He had died *many times* through the spasming jerk as torn heart muscle labored, stabbed through by the flange of a broadhead. 'Lie back. Relax, and the numbness comes quickly.'

The Etarran choked, gasping through welling fluid. His filled lungs were rapidly drowning. He peered up, confused by the indistinct form of the stranger arrived to bend over him. 'Who are you?'

Arithon swallowed. He spoke the truth gently. 'Arithon Teir's'Ffalenn.'

'You?' The man jerked backward, racked by a hacking, wet cough. 'The bastard-born Master of Shadow?'

'I am not what you fear,' Arithon replied, the empathy in

him at last granted outlet through the grace of his Masterbard's training. 'At least tell me your name, that your passing will not go unsung.'

The tracker spat foaming blood; gave his answer, defiant. Then he winced through an agonized spasm. 'What's my name, to a demon?'

'Very shortly, you'll see.' Granted the musician's insight he required, Arithon sang the first phrase to distance the pain. His talent responded. Relieved by the sigh as contorted flesh eased and settled under his fingers, he added, 'Who do you wish to hear your last words?'

The man mentioned a sister, his mother, a son. He asked that his wife understand that he loved her. Weeping unabashed, as a voice like spun gold sang lyric lines in Paravian over him, he subsided into a haze of regretful puzzlement. 'I wanted to kill you. May Ath and Dharkaron forgive! Your life could have been the one wasted.'

'Does that matter?' asked Arithon, heartsore, as slowly, with tenderness, he built on the phrasing to loosen the life cord.

Slack in the snow, the pumped spurt of blood from his chest a stilled puddle, the man coughed, then struggled to look up. More than starlight gleamed in the distanced depths of his eyes. He knew who he was, saw where he was going. The bard's inspired singing had opened the way for his spirit to ease in transition across the veil. Already, the Wheel turned. His attention diffused, near the moment of release as he struggled to impart the last of his life's garnered wisdom. 'It matters, your Grace.'

'You owe me no title, no sworn word of fealty!' Arithon said, overset by the acknowledgment of rank.

The man's breath spasmed, caught, then eased once again as the flawless phrases of melody resumed. He closed weary eyelids, still aware of the face of the bard, clear as stamped quartz under starlight. 'Then is the kindness you offer an enemy a lie? Is such compassion not the land's hope for peace, that may one day nurture my grandchildren?' The tracker resumed, labored. 'We marched for a false light. Don't you see?' The smile that eased his gruff face at the end smoothed over the lines pinched by trauma. 'I lost my life for embracing delusion. But your death would have made me a murderer.'

Suffering passed into final peace. Arithon settled the corpse in the snow, then arose upon unsteady feet. Ahead lay the rock-strewn slope to the notch, where eleven more deaths would extract their toll of due reckoning. Behind, a fired brilliance of unsullied light, the centaur guardian awaited.

Arithon Teir's'Ffalenn regarded his hands, smeared with the blood of the Etarran tracker whose honest last testament had finally silenced his conscience. 'What did that man see, on the moment he left us?'

'That's not yours to ask, or my will to answer,' said the Ilitharis Paravian, his quelling, deep tone hushed with mercy.

Arithon bowed his head, at the last unable to disown his core self, or the unmasked face of his gratitude. 'I accept absolution,' he whispered, contrite.

He felt the radiant warmth of a touch at his back, impelling his final step forward.

'Go in grace, Teir's'Ffalenn.'

The reliving shattered. Blasted apart by the flare of burst spellcraft, Arithon caught himself short of a stumble as his boot sole came down upon Kewar's unyielding stone floor. He cried out, disoriented. Through and through, like a sword's thrust, he ached with the awareness: *the centaur was no longer with him.*

Better men, before him, had gone mad from such grief: high kings and clan chieftains, whose brief rule had ended when the lacerating toll of such parting drove them to unreconciled agony.

Arithon shuddered. Cast back to the obdurate dictates of training to bind closed the rifts in his being, he swayed. When his groping hand met no corridor wall to steady his spinning balance, for one draining heartbeat, he thought he had been torn, whole spirit from dissolute flesh.

Then flash-blinded eyesight cleared all at once.

The tunnel's close confines no longer imprisoned him. Arrived in a doorless, five-sided chamber, Arithon beheld juxtaposed views of himself, the myriad reflections a mirror image of his snarled hair and torn clothing. His composite forms detailed each harried breath, each jerked move, from across a scribed circle incised with Davien's intertwined spirals of runes.

Arithon shut his eyes. 'Elaira,' he whispered. Binding his love to the iron of his oath, sworn on his let blood at Athir, he regathered his will and kept his pledged word to the vanished centaur guardian. 'I will choose to survive.' Unburdened and gasping, too worn to contemplate what consequence might spring from the impetus of forward motion, he completed his final step.

No further reliving ripped his mind into visions. He had brought himself home to the center of the maze. Here, the multiple facets of himself were reclaimed, merged back into autonomous awareness by the empowered acceptance of humanity's right to embrace the full impact of free choice. Quittance came as a tingling, sharp play of energy.

Spelled power fell away, of no more import than a gyre of spent sparks.

Utterly drained, Arithon regarded the jointures of polished black walls. Each unmarked one was lit by a sconce spiked with a burning wax candle. 'I may be free, yet this trial is not over!' he pronounced in a shaken voice.

When no listening presence answered his challenge, he gave way to need, sank to his knees, then curled up in shivering exhaustion. Within seconds, he fell into a blanketing sleep that, mercifully, brought him no nightmares.

Challenge

Deep under the caverns of Kewar Tunnel, far below the polished corridor of the maze, with its spiraling arcs of carved spellcraft, a sealed cylindrical chamber nestled close as a secret within the heart of the mountain. The arched ceiling described a perfect parabola, a shape to refigure the least murmur of sound into cutting, razor-sharp focus. Walls and floor were drilled out of satin-smoothed marble, the raised pool at the center a master-work fashioned by wayward, rogue genius and grand conjury.

No tool of man could enact such precision. The round ring of stone containing the spring had been carved without seam from veined bedrock. Its basin was inscribed with the overlaid lines of a faultlessly patterned geometry. Entwined loops of interlace and locked chains of ciphers became source and channel for a gyre of energies that flowed in perpetual motion. Virgin water welled from earth's underground source, spilling a silenced, sheeting flow across that meticulous construct. The play of its current across spelled designs raised flares of electromagnetics. The rainbow outbursts waxed and subsided, a display not unlike winter's dance of boreal light.

Here Davien the Betrayer had fashioned his sanctuary, a haven shaped for his personal use through his years of discorporate isolation. An enclosure without access or entry, except through the live signature of its creator, the rock chamber was not empty in the stilled hours before dawn. A spark of light burst out of the air at the focal point under the curved ceiling. Falling as though on a plumb-line descent, the illumination met the pool's surface.

Fire and water touched with a snap of conception, their merged forces birthing an image: *of a dark-haired survivor lying curled on his side under the sweet-burning glow of five sconces.*

Affirmation, at long last, that this Teir's'Ffalenn had surpassed his ancestor's failure. Arithon had mastered the first trial of the maze.

The unseen presence of the Sorcerer in the chamber whirled into cogitation. His activity cast no disturbed ripple across the image burned onto the water. Davien assessed the tucked form of the man, asleep across the grand axis inscribed on the floor of his Chamber of Midway. From Arithon's soft breathing, to the slowed pulse of blood through the veins threaded under the skin, to the most minute change imprinted in his subtle aura, the Sorcerer's survey missed nothing.

No doubt remained: the maze had shifted the balance.

Davien's reaction was not relief, not triumph or gratitude, but the whetted steel edge of a relentlessly trained fascination. His declarative statement threw off flurried echoes, inside the cylindrical stone vault. 'In truth, you are Teir's'Ffalenn, a spirit worthy of crowning.' Irony struck his tone to grained rust, as he weighed the trace spike of dissonance that arose in response to his use of that name. 'Your Grace? You still object to that title, I see. How you would detest my acknowledgment.'

The first stage of the passage had been severe, as much could be read in the protective, motionless posture. Weariness blanketed a mind without dreams. A snarl of black hair masked the face, tucked behind sheltering forearms.

Out of delicate respect, Davien did not pry.

The interchange of events that transpired within Kewar Tunnel would stay spun in a dense veil of privacy. The grand arc of its wardings forbade outside eyes. Although his hand had fashioned the maze, Davien himself could not open the sealed record of Arithon's trials inside. Despite his entangled, contentious history, the Sorcerer had never been known to sully the word of his given promise.

Though the stone of the earth by its nature retained the broad-spectrum imprint of energies, in Kewar, the patterns from Arithon's passage had been promptly polished away. The tunnel's vast and impartial forces reigned with unchecked authority. The walls of the maze would already be restored to a state of pristine blankness, cleansed and recleansed until no strayed wisp of nightmare could linger to disrupt the course of another aspirant.

By reflex habit, Davien checked his work. His outflung awareness seined through the layered stone where his conjury struck
through the mountain, sampling the whispers that ran through
the quartz veins.

Pattern and light came rebounding back. Davien froze. Stunned
to stark disbelief, he sharpened his questing touch and received
the same stunning result. *A jumbled imprint of outside activity still
rippled from Kewar's sealed corridors.*

'Dharkaron's blind vengeance!' the Sorcerer exclaimed. Chamber
and pool blazed up in white fire to the charge of his total astonishment. 'How has the devil begotten the very devil himself?'

Spurred by bristling unrest, Davien extended his awareness.
His care was meticulous as he marked and measured the scope
of an unprecedented turn of event.

At once, he realized not one, but *two* other entities had managed to gain entry to Kewar. *The sealed wards of guard had not been
breached*: each separate presence had been granted its access from
inside the bounds of Arithon's inviolate being.

'The devil has in fact begotten the fiend!' Davien snapped.
He was scarcely relieved to discover his grand arc of spells
still intact. The seals had not failed. No loophole of omission
had seen their integrity compromised. If anything, the sigils for
cleansing and erasure had accomplished their task much too
thoroughly. The Sorcerer found himself confoundedly blind to
an exchange *that should never have happened*; yet had, through a
strikingly unprecedented turn of strength.

For a breathless half second, Davien almost chuckled. 'Merciful
mother!' No doubt pompous Luhaine would fly into a rage if he
saw how his worry had nurtured the snake.

No probe could recover the lost content of Arithon's personal
interactions. The stone walls were restored to blank realignment.
The telltales that lingered had been retouched by the air, no more
than a ghost imprint of the two vagrant visitors' identities.

One had been a woman, her access seized through the gateway of dreams, and a love that bonded her Named being to
inseparable partnership with Arithon. Davien ascertained, in one
blasting, swift cross-check, that no lasting harm had befallen
her. Once Arithon had released the entrapments of conscience,
Elaira's wandering spirit had spun free. She would slowly drift
into waking return, well secure under the guiding wisdom of
Ath's adepts.

The other intrusion had been wrought by a force no Fellowship Sorcerer would have gainsaid. Summoned, *living*, that

presence had crossed the veil by free will, straight out of bygone history.

Once Davien addressed the astounding loose ends and dispelled the residual energies, his awareness whirled back into singular focus, transfixed by the image set on display in the shimmering gleam of the rock pool. By now scarcely able to contain his exuberance, he resurveyed the spent form of the prince arrived in his Chamber of Midway.

'Far from tamed, my bold falcon!' Davien mused, entranced. 'Unleashed, I see. You've shown us the strength to have mastered your past. The present is now yours. How will you handle your future?'

When Arithon awoke, the wax candles still burned without showing a sign of time's passage. Either their flame had been fueled by spells, or else he had slept no more than a handful of minutes. That outlook seemed skewed by his sense of well-being. He sat up, not stiff, feeling thoroughly rested. Except for a lightness brought on by fasting, he was well poised and clearheaded. Beneath the stained dressing, his hand did not ache. Beyond a raffish growth of new stubble and hair caught in sorrowful tangles, he judged himself fit. A Sorcerer's trial was no state tribunal, to be swayed by rough grooming or the disheveled state of a man's trail-worn clothing.

Arithon stood and reviewed his surroundings, unshaken to find changes invoked as he slept. Of five featureless walls, four now contained doorways, each one matched to a burning sconce. The three standing open before him dropped away into featureless darkness. The last one was barred by a shut panel, marked with black ciphers, and a pattern spell strung with Paravian runes.

'Three invitations and a challenge?' Arithon asked aloud, his determination ironically amused. 'Or else three temptations, and the proverbial double-edged puzzle? Lure the rash fool to rush to his death, or mete out a brute test, and perhaps reward the wise mark with bliss and long life. Or here, since we're likely to rattle the querent, one might find an encounter designed to trip up the arrogant.'

The chamber gave back only silence for answer. No surprise; Davien's works eschewed the obvious. Rathain's prince flexed his hands, rocked by discovery that his meddlesome injury showed no trace of residual soreness. He considered a moment. Feet set in a swordsman's alertly poised balance, he resumed speaking, affirmed in his conviction an unseen presence was listening. 'Given my cozy experience with dying, I won't dance. Not again! As the mouse with the tail well pinched by the trap, by strict preference, I'd rather cheat.'

No sound; no movement; yet the transparent air gained a charged sense of stillness, as though some invisible power had shifted.

A slight smile firmed the line of Arithon's mouth. 'You do hear.' His eyes held a concentrated steadiness, the pupils wide set with the untamed dark preceding an ocean tempest. 'Be warned. I am coming.'

He gathered himself, discarding his tight apprehension. Thrusting past his deep barrier of conditioned fear and his shrinking trepidation, he engaged the balance point of his mind, reached inward, *and talent answered*.

His access to trained awareness slid open. The wire-strung tension in braced shoulders loosened. Arithon settled. In gradual stages, he eased his guarded self open, allowing the ranging quiet beyond senses to deepen into the enveloping calm of the mysteries. Lost perceptions wakened. A retuned rapport with the elements embraced him. Then the powerful acknowledgment of his being returned, clear and bright as the flare of new light over an unsheathed sword's edge.

Sharpened back to a state of potentized harmony, Arithon gasped through his own springing tears. If this was a dream, he wished never to waken, as the birth-born power he had schooled to high mastery settled back into his hands.

The uprush of uncontained, joyous relief nearly shattered his equilibrium. He held on, engaged the stern arts of his discipline, and steadied his mental balance. Gently, with the reverence of testing a wellspring after a punishing drought, he immersed himself into mage-sight.

The signature glimmer of mineral met him, patient as rooted endurance. The light-dance of energies that founded all form held its resonance, unchanged, throughout eons. Ripped to a shiver of unwonted delight, Arithon picked up the pure, tonal song that nurtured all being like the pulse of a mother's heartbeat. His masterbard's arts tracked his vision, partnered in light, unveiling a unified balance. Arithon felt his former limits expand, as smoothed granite yielded the heart of its secrets as never before. Such innocent trust framed a gift that both stunned and appalled him.

Acceptance followed. He would not deny his self-worth, or

flinch back from bowing to his achievement. Kewar's maze had reforged the foundations of his identity. Arithon touched the vulnerability of earth's stone, *and knew beyond doubt*: he had earned gifted right to that guardianship.

Shaken though he was, as wildly touched by explosive exultation, he adhered to his chosen task.

He extended his awareness, tacitly testing. The chamber around him was actual stone, not some glib frame of illusion. The dark portals appeared blank, impenetrable to vision, sure sign they were held under warding. The shut door contained no detectable cracks. No breath of draft crossed its barrier. Even where the closed panel touched the stone jamb, his sweeping search found no seam. Arithon detected no shimmer, no resonance of altered energy. The chiaroscuro play of subtle frequency adhered to primordial patterns. The mineral planes spun their ordered, geometrical array, the sheen of earth consciousness shuttled within the sturdy lattice of mountain granite.

Arithon backed off, well warned that he tested a guard spell of binding, laid under masterful seals. Or else his review met a masking illusion, and no portal existed behind that closed doorway at all.

The restored gifts of mastery lent subtle means to explore Davien's provocative riddle. Already set to unravel the veil cast over the Sorcerer's creation, Arithon knew he must act before creeping dread undermined his determined initiative.

First thing, he summoned four streamers of shadow. The thin scraps of darkness called into his hands assumed form with unwonted reluctance, as though in this place, Davien's wardings suppressed basic aspects of structural creation. Arithon refined his concentration, persisted. He annealed his decision in the fires of raw will, set his template of desire, then flicked a back-spinning twist of barbed thought through a rune to cut through obstruction. Fueled by invention, his crafted pattern of thought punched outside time, across space, and returned, slick as a hot needle through tar.

He divided that essence. With rune and seal, Arithon braided his ephemeral construct into the weave of his shadows. He attached a permission asked of the air. The completed formation of energy was minimal, and vengefully elegant, little more than a spell-charged field of awareness spearheaded into a geas of seeking intent.

Arithon paused once his work stood complete. Sweat sprang in drops at his temples. The fingers of his left hand cradled the fruits of his crafting, while the right, in stained linen, hung limp. 'Fly true,' he whispered. With fixed deliberation, he cast his first shadow down the portal immediately before him.

It encountered the match of his heart's desire. The assault on the senses snagged his unwary mind and slid past his deepest defenses.

Desh-thiere's curse was a memory, all bloodshed behind him. He could abandon both crown and sword without guilt and reassume the pursuit of his music. Elaira's voice called him. Her open arms promised him peace, and the delights of unimpaired freedom. Together, they would build a bright future. Immersed in the rapture of her tender love, Arithon beheld a shared life made full. Together, they could study the grand confluence of the mysteries and raise a family of gifted children.

Drawn forward, unwitting, Arithon took one stumbling step, then wrenched himself short with a cry. His denial extracted a harrowing cost. Stopped, gasping, he slapped down the raw yearning of his musician's sensitivity. Stormed by the fires of raging thirst, he strangled the passionate wave of desire evoked by the dream of Elaira's sweet touch. He stifled all clamor, all human need. The effort required pierced his heart to sore grief, making him shiver like an addict deprived for a beauty that dazzled him witless.

Yet the promise enticed like the bait of a trap, set too perfectly close to the bone. Like a windfall apple dropped ripe to the hand, the haven the portal presented would carry rot at the core. No enchantment could reclothe naked truth. Elaira was vowed into lifetime service, and Davien's known works were not kindly.

Eyes shut, his frame quivering, Arithon reminded himself of the proof. He had already run afoul of the Five Centuries Fountain. The Betrayer's grant of longevity already exacted its toll of afflicted sorrow. A man must live on while his closest friends aged. Over time, the relentless shadow of loss must poison an isolate future.

'Keep on,' said Arithon in gritted rage to the unseen Sorcerer's presence. 'You'll just scour out every weakness I have, until nothing remains to exploit.'

Steadying the shadow back on its course required sharp use of his resources. Breathless, sorely shaken, he braced his core will, then summoned the courage to cast his inquiry deeper. His probe snagged, then burst through a veiling ward; and paradise dissolved, torn apart like burst silk. The colors that beckoned bled off, mere illusion. Elaira's form melted like evanescent wax, and the music dissolved into the plink of cold water, seeped from an underground spring.

'Avert!' Arithon snapped. A sick shudder racked him. Pricked by a threat like blown smoke at his back, he intoned the word for the Paravian rune of ending and freed his spun shadow to disperse.

Bruised by the riptides of aftermath, he considered setting an anchor in stone. If he secured his stance, he might guard against being duped into thoughtless folly. At second thought, the hint of a smile turned his lips.

'Ah, no.' A whisper of laughter beneath his caught breath, Arithon raked the stuck hair from his temples. 'Much too easy.'

The mind that had fashioned the core spells of the maze was unlikely to try repeat tactics.

Arithon turned a half step, widdershins, then dispatched his next probe through the portal lying adjacent.

This one arrowed straight as a spear's cast under the roots of the Mathorn Mountains. Unencumbered, it emerged on the northern slopes. Arithon received an untrammeled view of bright snowfields, scoured under clean wind where the freewheeling stars turned over the Plain of Araithe.

Startled wordless, he cried out. Braced as he was for entangling, difficult trials, the clear passage all but unmanned him. Ahead, if he chose, lay the grant of his freedom. He might take his release from Kewar Tunnel. Whole of mind and limb, he could reclaim the dropped threads of his life and resume his disrupted affairs. Instinct, or perhaps the assurance of magesight, let him know he would draw no pursuit on his back trail. Farther north lay the trackless forests of Deshir. A hardy few scouts still maintained a clan presence. Hardened raiders, sworn to the realm, they guarded the land through their handful of outposts, tucked deep in the glens of Tal Quorin. Restored to his former ability to scry, Arithon could find their encampments. Spring already loosened the ice. Once the thaws broke, he could seek passage by boat and make his safe crossing to Atainia.

Sethvir would grant him his right to claim sanctuary. Arithon could rest at Althain Tower and eventually send summons to rejoin his crew aboard *Khetienn*.

Yet he stilled the leaping thrust of raw longing, fought longer to quell common sense. Gut instinct warned him of Davien's caprice. The offer posed by the second portal might be cruelly rescinded if he paused for a second thought.

Arithon tightened his jaw, resolute. He dispelled his sent shadow, braced against disappointment. He *would not* return to the world on the pretext his ordeal in the maze never happened. Crown prince, or pawn, he would make that change serve him. Neither Sorcerer, nor Mistwraith, nor meddling Koriathain would gainsay his choice to forge his own destiny henceforward.

Cleared of past guilt, released from tortured conscience, he refused to embrace the old life of attrition, set running before Desh-thiere's curse.

Arithon firmed his nerve. Straight as hammered iron, he stepped widdershins again, then launched his next streamer to plumb the secret beyond the third portal.

His shadow knifed into the impenetrable dark, struck a wall like black glass, and wavered. Resetting its deflected course rocked him dizzy. Arithon prevailed by main force, only to watch as his construct became swallowed. Guard spell and shadow, his sending was erased by a featureless well of oblivion.

Only his charged field of awareness remained. Arithon whispered a cantrip in beleaguered effort to shore up its failing linkage. Cold silence enveloped him. His probe became savaged by an unutterable blankness that refounded the concept of emptiness. Past the door lay a gap more desolate than the void, a stark well of *nothing*, untenably barren, with no living matrix of consciousness. The prison he sounded held no content but absence, a sterility stripped of even the unbirthed potential that demarked the far deeps past the veil.

This emptiness consumed. Within moments, the tracking spell's delicate cohesion tore asunder. No pattern could withstand such a well of blank entropy. Arithon's set runes of binding dissolved, leaving behind the echo of unending despair.

The insight arose with unbidden clarity, that the horror just experienced had not been aligned for humanity.

Arithon bristled, wrung to antipathy as he realized that the prompt which deflected his thought might arise from an outside intrusion. Yet his reflexive effort to unmask the origin passed through air without trace of resistance. He encountered no presence to grapple. The fleeting touch he had sensed scattered out, dispersed like water into dry moss.

'Why not show yourself plainly?' he provoked, spiked to taunting derision. 'Only a fool would presume you aren't watching. Surely a power of such stunning audacity could have designed more inventive torments than a portal to smother out hope.'

Arithon reexamined his contempt, suddenly chilled by a specious revelation that destroyed every precept of mercy. *Who was Davien, to toy with live beings, as though they were no more than game pieces?* For the lurking bane in the last open corridor surely described a trial to test a Paravian.

Once broached, the idea fit the concept too well. *The old races did not die unless mishap befell them.* Yet Desh-thiere's invasion had shown how their spirits could fade out of worldly existence. Althain's archive preserved the tragic accounts, compiled from Second Age history. Paravians could succumb to relentless sorrow. Against prolonged grief and unending loss, the clear light of their vision must languish. Sethvir had explained that their farsighted wisdom could not sustain the least veneer of delusion. They were Ath's gift, born to shine with the unity that brightened the realms past the veil. Their hearts could not sing to the promise of false hope, which let mankind endure in the face of certain mortality.

Arithon stilled his fast-rising revulsion. Carefully, coldly, he contained his visceral revolt, then set the inflaming lash of emotion into perspective against reasoned experience. The blurred facts that survived as long-winded ballads all converged with unsettling consistency. According to myth, Davien had once thrived on the habit of demolishing his arguments through provocation.

'*"Oh, bold wicked beast!"*' Arithon quoted, snatched breathless and almost enjoying himself. '*"Chase the sly fox, the hunt will be merry. Course the wolf, greet cold death or be wary!"*' For icy hindsight exposed the third portal's darkness as no less than a diabolically elaborate feint to splinter his balance through anger.

'Betrayer!' Arithon shouted, not needing the prickle of lifted hair to warn that he courted a disaster. In Kewar, a huntsman would lose more than hounds if he let his brash instinct mislead him. 'Why not come out? I don't plan to be sidetracked.'

A stir of amusement swirled through the chamber, there and gone in the flash of an instant. Arithon could not grasp its thread, though he tried. The current he chased might be no more than the echo of his own self-mockery. As though in reproach, the portal that offered the northlands, and liberty, remained open as invitation.

Yet Arithon confronted the final barred doorway, spurred by his mulish resolve. The veiled insult galled him, that any Sorcerer's shade should presume he was irresolute, or that his choices were fickle and changeable. The Prince of Rathain cast off his last shadow, a thrown gauntlet that spurned every blandishment to turn back.

The construct slammed against arcane barriers and returned, inscribed by the record of the blood oath sealed under Fellowship auspices at Athir. Nor was the rejection of trespass light handed. Dizzied by the punitive burn of a self-inflicted backlash, Arithon rubbed stinging palms, and asked, 'Why?'

No voice gave him answer. Only a feather touch of awareness instilled thought with respectful clarity: *his Grace of Rathain had sealed that last doorway by choice*. The closed portal contained the straightest path of them all: the promise of crossing into the light that graced the realms of Athlieria. No whim of Davien's, but a crown prince's pledge to survive ruled the force that denied him passage.

Arithon stood, unexpectedly swayed by a wave of fierce desolation. Had he not sworn, that threshold would lie open, offering the bloodless departure from life through the gateway to Ath's greater mystery.

'No.' Preference resurged, the valued part of himself that anchored his love for Elaira. Arithon would not abandon her; could not, without destroying the balance that buttressed his inner identity. After the grace of a centaur guardian's absolution, he would not spurn his burden of steadfast dead, fallen to buy his survival.

'An offense!' Arithon snapped, needled to rage as he rejected the portal's profligate temptation. He would not deign to challenge its well-guarded lock. Whether or not he could break through the wards, no promise of paradise could erase the charge of the heirless bloodline he carried.

Arithon pressed shaking hands to his face, mortified that such a backhanded trick had even raised a reaction. Though the portal that led to the Plain of Araithe presented the sensible option, he turned one last step. The fifth wall of the chamber remained, its surface innocuously blank. The wax-fed flames in the sconces burned unnaturally still, casting his form in unwavering shadows.

One weighted second flowed into the next. Arithon maintained fixed concentration, then swiftly averted his gaze. No change. Opaque stone remained solid as striated glass, glistening with flecks of mica.

Too solid, perhaps; a spasm of gooseflesh roughened Arithon's skin. 'Who spits against heaven, it falls in his face.'

Davien was listening. Touched by the feeling that the uneasy silence seemed to be holding its breath, Arithon Teir's'Ffalenn stepped forward. The wall he confronted mirrored his advance, imposingly dense and massive. Inside arm's reach, he did not raise his hand. He refrained from exploring touch. Instead, he pronounced a reviling satire against the name of Kewar's creator.

Nothing happened. No wrathful presence descended to retaliate. Arithon whistled the opening notes of a jig. His collar rustled to the whisper of stirred hair as he cocked his head to the side. No sound, beyond the rasp of his breath. Yet in listening, he received his oblique confirmation: the wall deflected no echoes.

'First fall, to the wolf.' Arithon's hint of a smile turned feral. 'The lock on that portal was an affront I've chosen to redress in person.' The Master of Shadow strode up to the wall and, with no hesitation, stepped through.

The illusion admitted him without sensation. Nothing solid stood in his path. A six-sided chamber waited beyond. Each wall was lit by a wax-candle sconce, and inset with a jeweled doorway. The frenetic shine of gold-wire inlay and the brilliance of faceted gems burst against refined mage-sight, raising a scintillant dazzle of rainbows. Arithon looked aside. Since the blare of rank opulence muddled his mind, he unfurled a stifling shadow on impulse and extinguished one burning wick.

All of the candles in the chamber flicked out.

The doors underneath proved a construct as well, their form ripped away to lay bare seamless slabs of rough-hewn mountain granite. Closed in drowning darkness, Arithon locked sweating hands. He tried and failed to curb his unsettled nerves and quell his uncontrolled shaking. The unorthodox spellcraft that had granted his impulsive entry had already faded behind him. He had exposed the true Maze of Davien, and beyond doubt, his brash challenge was accepted. Now, he must grope his way forward. If the limits of knowledge and training fell short, no outside resource could save him.

Arithon stamped down the first jangle of panic. Since his concrete senses could not be trusted, he shut his eyes, stilling the nagging impulse to speculate over what might have befallen had he succumbed to the lure of those queer, jeweled doorways. The disturbing possibility could not be dismissed, that he might become endlessly diverted, exhaustively sounding through spells of illusion until his body gave way in collapse.

Dwelling on worry would earn the same end. Arithon released his strung tension, deliberately slowed the ragged edge from his breathing. One by one, he channeled his resources inward. As he had learned as a child at Rauven, he achieved centered balance, then diffused his attention through the poised well of his mind. Inner stillness immersed him. Awareness dissolved, erasing the boundaries of separation until his subtle senses embraced the layered stone of the mountain. He reached from that still point, allowing what *was* to infuse his listening silence. Slowly, he sounded the chamber, entrained into a communion of etheric rapport drawn from the natural elements.

The signature configurations of air and earth revealed the six walls to be solid. The ceiling showed him a smooth, groined vault, unbroken by shaft or skylight.

Arithon deferred apprehension through patience. Persistent, he measured the expanse of the floor, and there, the room yielded its secret. The exit lay scarcely three paces ahead, a shaft that plunged steeply downward.

Tacitly careful, Arithon reopened his eyes. He had solved the next riddle. Now unveiled to mage-sight, a staircase descended from an oblong vault in the floor. Testing each cautious step, he worked his way downward, though the prospect of delving into the mountain ran hard against better instinct. He could not determine how far he had come since he had left daylight behind him. Fellowship spellcraft could bend time at will, or extend the body's vitality. If he felt the slight pinch of hunger and thirst, he had no means to tell whether the deprivation had extended for days. Anxiety hounded him. He might wander too long and finally perish, ground down by Kewar's inexhaustible invention.

The stairwell ended abruptly. No lighted sconce appeared to relieve the pall of featureless darkness. Arithon worked through mage-sight and painstakingly traced the walls of another sealed chamber. This room had seven sides, and dishearteningly yielded no sign of a hidden exit. The stairway behind had predictably vanished, and the air wore a textured, velvety thickness, its presence burdened with spells.

Arithon countered bewildering complexity by choosing the simplest option. He groped, found the shoulder strap hanging the wallet that contained his tinder and flint. As he drew his small knife for striking a spark, the pressure surrounding him tightened. *Any* slight move apparently shifted the balance of unseen forces. Since delay seemed just as likely to spur a reaction, Arithon twisted a spill from a rag, then struck a tremulous flame.

His brave pool of light sheared into the darkness, birthing a rustle of movement. Arithon started. A yearning circle of wax-pale hands reached for him out of the shadows. Unveiled by the wildly flickering brand, he glimpsed a circle of anguished faces steadily closing around him. He could not step back. Old men, grandmothers, women and boys, *more people crowded behind him.*

That moment, his glimmer of flame light snuffed out. The blanketing dark that returned was not empty: the gathering of specters his presence had wakened remained plainly visible to mage-sight. Arithon stamped down the fool's impulse to recoil. He had nowhere to run. Whether or not the fell creatures had form, their presence ringed him like jackals. They suffered all manner of hideous affliction: limbs with weeping sores, twisted bones, or the ghastly deformities caused by old scars that had atrophied to shrunken tendons. Other folk were emaciated and starving. Man, woman and toddling babe, they jostled against him, pleading relief from their suffering.

Arithon reeled, choking down his distress as the crowd continued to press him. He smelled the musty, diseased pall of flesh. Mournful wailing tugged at his heart. He could move nowhere, for the pressing crush of such need, or shake off the plucking grasp at his clothing.

Worst of all, the creatures raised a fell chorus of voices that called him directly by name.

Accosted no matter which way he turned, Arithon saw no one he recognized. Some people were rich, others raggedly poor. Their dress came from all walks of life. No singular clues identified which kingdom or world held their origins. They might have been victims of Kewar itself, trapped in eternal confinement. Or they might have derived from the unlived future, sickly harbingers of some misfortune to come, arrived to demand retribution in advance for unmade choices that would come to ruin them.

Arithon had no succor to offer, no balm of healing or hope. He could not answer their beseeching questions, or promise to seek their release. Disaster in Kewar might wear many guises. If these people were living at all, *their presence in this place would be nothing else but another form of entrapment.*

Yet his inborn compassion would not be ruled by the dictates of hard-core logic. Tears poured down the blanched planes of Arithon's face for the harsh fact he dared not show pity. The least intervention to try and ease pain might invoke the consent for a tie of commitment. Yield out of kindness to just one lost child, and the Teir's'Ffalenn knew he might bind his fate to the plight of these hapless victims. He could ill afford the mistake of misjudgment. Act without caution, and his next step could seal his permanent downfall.

Arithon muffled his ears, to no avail. His bard's gift woke him to empathy. Undone by fresh grief, he battled for callous will to tug free of beseeching fingers. He turned back raw suffering with unblinded eyes, shouldered ahead, and threaded his beleaguered way forward. Yet this time his movement brought no relief. The maze responded by raising another obstruction. The chasm that opened ahead of his feet was no less real for the fact that his vision could not perceive it.

Only the hollow whisper of air gave him warning, its sibilant consciousness picked out by mage-sight. Where the staid tones of earth should have spoken the deeper-toned language of stone, air described the lip of an unseen abyss. Arithon stopped. The jostling press of the maimed barged into him, threatening to stagger him forward. He must not fail to concentrate, even bled as he was by the abrading pull of emotion. Such pity might kill, if he lost firm grasp on the requisite balance to pierce through the veil of the maze.

A triumph of entropy, if he died for a tearful child whose existence was likely a spell-turned trap to snare him through moral integrity. Arithon grappled to silence the cry of his heart, while his nerves became slowly scraped raw. He felt strained and guilt-ridden, as though he ought to be able to disarm the snare that enacted such dreadful suffering. *For mercy, he dared not even raise art through song, to ease even one grieving grandmother's sobs.* His swift, testing effort to call down a banishing recoiled in slamming backlash.

Arithon set his teeth, ripped off-balance as pain shot needles of fire down his nerves. He could not dispel such power as this. The mere effort to stay the sad wretches who pressed him wrung his senses to gray and left him dizzied by the searing scourge of a headache. Shoved a stumbling step by a man with a crutch and a woman with two whimpering children, Arithon confronted the horror of a death by cold sorcery that could conceivably extend past the veil. Should he pass Fate's Wheel still bound by the maze, he might remain trapped as a wraith. Another few moments would see him pulled down unless he tried desperate measures.

'Might as well choose damnation in style,' he gasped through a shudder of nausea.

A mage of his stature could not hope to subdue the vast reach of the forces ranged against him. But through errant recklessness, and novel use of an ill-set combination of ciphers, Arithon could loose the powers of chaos to unbind. Once, at Tal Quorin, he had entrained such a spell and unmade a steel quarrel shot by a marksman to kill him. The impact had caused ruin on a scale unimaginable, and damaged the use of his mage-sight.

Wisdom argued against the repeat of that measure. To wreak an unmaking was a violation of Ath's law, though the bounds of that stricture correctly pertained to the energetic ties that strung matter into formation. Davien's Maze was no solid form, but an entrained mesh of spells worked through the stone of the cavern. In bold theory, the rune string to wake primal fire *might* be tempered. If Arithon directed that force to break nothing more than Davien's lines of intent, only the linked continuity of the spell seals would succumb to annihilation.

Stone and natural flesh would be spared, but the driving ciphers that ranged their substance against him would fly into shreds and unravel.

Logic and theory might not hold true. Arithon had never pitted his mastery against a Fellowship Sorcerer's grand construct. The audacity of *thinking* to meddle on that scale set his heartbeat racing with dread. Yet delay was no option. The crowding horde of injured spirits snatched and pushed him, their needy cries growing more desperate. The wrist exposed by his shredded sleeve already bore bleeding scratches. Though armed with Alithiel, Arithon saw peril in drawing the Paravian steel. These folk might have existence outside Davien's Maze. If some sorry facet drawn from his future created their miserable plight, the cause he defended would not be just. The chance was too real that a wounding in Kewar might cause actual harm somewhere else.

Little use, to jab elbows and fists and push back. The packed mass of supplicants would just tear him down. Alone against many, he would become trampled, or shoved off the brink of the crevice.

Arithon sucked in a swift, harried breath. He must narrow his focus and shut out distraction, subdue the demons of sorrow and fear. *Survive, and perhaps, he could make Davien answer for each of the horrors he witnessed.* Yet first, he must banish all thought from his mind. The rune sequence he had resolved to engage was ugly and unforgiving. The chain could be dangerously swayed by emotion, lending a disastrous twist to its already pernicious function. *He must become the blank page to hold contrary ciphers, lay each delicate stay of protection without slipshod error or omission*. One mismatched seal set against a rune catalyst, and the wretched chain of spellcraft he fashioned would sour and turn in his hand.

No time to prepare. He dared not take pause to review his tight bindings, or test them for deadly mistakes. Jostled and pinched by imploring fingers, pursued by the wail of the damned, Arithon braced his beleaguered stance. He gasped out a breathless apology to Elaira, for the chance his attempt might buy failure. Then he enabled the last rune and tripped the release, unleashing a primal unbinding.

A roaring wind assaulted his ears. Sound exploded to pealing thunder. The flesh-and-blood specters surrounding him frayed into nothing, *not real*, their blemished bodies spun from who knew what arena of unconscious nightmare. Yet the forces his stopgap desperation had loosed did not subside to quiescence. The fires of summary annihilation never paused. Voracious, lent recombinant fuel by wild magic, they raged on and unstrung the structural stone supporting Arithon's feet. He cried out as he tumbled, ripped to awed incredulity. *All that he sensed had been nothing else but another spelled layer of the maze*. Davien's craft had encompassed an artistry that ran outside the pale of natural limitation. *Nowhere* had Arithon encountered an illusion that could replicate stone firm enough to support moving weight. Spinning in free-fall disorientation, he shrank to imagine the enormity of his challenge, or the wrath of the snake whose tail he had tweaked with such obstinate effrontery.

Yet Kewar's creator became a moot threat if he fell as the victim of his own countermeasure. Around him, the edifice of Davien's skilled conjury continued to whirl into discontinuity. The maelstrom battered mind and flesh with a fury that threatened dismemberment. No solidity remained, *anywhere*, no fixed point upon which to orient. Arithon found himself at a loss. He could have unknowingly opened a pit between dimensional reality. No sense of gravity supported him. The explosion of chaos that savaged his awareness adhered to no pattern or law.

He spun, stormed by kaleidoscopic turmoil. To grapple the incomprehensible mass was to risk being shredded to insanity. Shadow would no longer shape to his bidding. Mage-sight was snagged to distortion. No stay of reason could order the flood of bone-hurting, dissonant sound. Arithon grasped in vain for the discipline to steady his ragged breath. Random forces pinned him under assault. Within seconds the threads of his self-awareness became stretched to the verge of snapping. He battled the morass, sought to find his way back to safe refuge inside of himself. The explosive dissolution frustrated his effort to restore his core of identity. Hurled beyond reason, he lacked proper grounding to reestablish a separate awareness.

Every protection instilled by trained reflex seemed utterly blasted away. He had lost all the requisite ties to sensation that maintained his housing of flesh. A mote in a torrent, he would be swept away, flesh and bone razed to final destruction.

Denied other recourse, whirled past reach of help, Arithon decided to sing.

Music had thrown back incoherence, before. The living force of a masterbard's art could break fights, even settle the raging insanity of mob violence driven to riot. Arithon fused his art to the scattered threads of his cognizance, found and formed the imperative notes to forge peace. He stretched past his limit, made his Named voice the honed blade of his naked desire. His straits were desperate. The measured progression of tempo became his last hope to restore the reflex that governed his breathing. The melody he built was an ancient Paravian round, severe in simplicity, five spare lines composed with a consummate, lyrical purity. Note for note, the innate balance of melody described the antithesis of disorder. Arithon matched breath and heartbeat to music, retuning the shattered seat of his being to the strict dictates of pitch and timing. He persisted, added refinement, until he was the song, and the song became the ruled line affirming existence. Whole in himself, but lost in the infinite, he had nowhere else left to turn. He would inevitably tire. No matter how determined, the singing must falter and diffuse, leaving his imperiled consciousness open to invasion.

Arithon s'Ffalenn rejected defeat. He mustered his resource with adamant patience. Walking the knife edge of grim desperation, he delved into his talent, spinning the web of his dreams into an artistry welded beyond compromise. From self-willed authority, he shaped his insistent command, that his surroundings submit to his cadence. He grappled with voice, shading tone with emotion. He subjugated uncertainty. On the memory of the centaur guardian's love, he denied fallibility, then uplifted the dragging pull of the dark with the fires of clear inspiration. He tamed light by harmonics, steered dissonance to resonance. Line by line, he imposed his masterful will. Note for note, he bound the unleashed energies of Davien's Maze to replicate the multiple parts of the round.

The harshness became tempered. The untenable, nerve-rasping wall of raw sound yielded to softening, then gentled. Sweet clarity emerged as pure, rounded tones that converged to the dictates of harmony. Arithon sang louder, notes that soared and dipped like a needle through cloth, quilting the unmoored forces of chaos into the wheeling dynamics of his melody. Stepping through measure for overlaid measure, he augmented the range with his mind. He reforged random motion into burning chords that danced to his bard's ear for subtlety.

In time, five-part harmony soared and took flight, tight as plaited gold through the misaligned shards of rushing noise and burst rainbows.

Arithon wove the grand cipher of peace. Casting off sound as though song were a lifeline, he extended the dictates of self-imposed discipline to the shapeless morass surrounding him. Riotous color gradually ceased its disjointed gyration. Sound spiked the first suggestion of form, like ring ripples caused by a pebble cast into a tempest. Arithon bound the circle. He sang the center point to secure his anchor. To the burgeoning dance of orchestrated sound, he reforged dimensional geometry. Step by slow step, each stage affirmed by the templates of established harmony, he laid down the cardinal cross to restore the foundational stance of the elements.

Arithon smoothed out the last whine of dissonance. He ordered the final bleeding breach that blurred color out of alignment. As the power of his art built toward a crescendo of scintillant harmony, he stumbled, restored to himself, but undone at last by exhaustion.

He had burned himself dry, given until no reserve remained for recovery. Weak as a babe, he sprawled headlong amid the consummate form of his construct. As song died on his final wisp of spent breath, the pattern held strong, self-sustaining. Above him, within him, as solid structure beneath, the beauty he had spun from raw chaos crested and achieved the rarefied pinnacle of balance.

The thundering force of its presence stopped thought. For one awestruck instant before strength gave out, Arithon laughed, consumed by ecstatic victory.

Then his last spark of consciousness flickered and went dark. Oblivion swallowed the undying perfection he had plucked from the weave of Davien's perilous artistry.

Match

Awareness returned, a slow flooding warmth with no harsh edge of stone-enclosed darkness. Yet the habit of caution became ingrained reflex when a man had been hunted too long. Arithon s'Ffalenn opened his eyes to a tapestry hanging. The intricate, stitched floss showed a forest just turned, twigs and branches alive with diminutive sparrows and the dusky brown plumage of thrushes. Candles burned. Their mellow light glazed a knot carpet patterned with stylized beasts sewn in the colors of autumn. Several bronze-studded chests lined the wall past his feet. Wrapped in a state of intoxicating lassitude, Arithon noted he lay on a couch. Piled down pillows supported his head, their loomed softness unreal after unending months of open-air flight and privation. The coverlet over his body was wool, expensively lined with raw silk.

The cosseting folds wrapped his limbs like a dream of long-forgotten comfort. Arithon languished. His drifting thoughts still rang with the echoes of the grand harmony he had laid down to dispel his unbinding conjury. Restfully settled, he had no wish to move. The imperative ache of desire all but broke him, to cling to the beguiling sensations of peace without concern for the danger. The prod of wise caution seemed unwontedly cruel. Too much to expect, that such quiet could last; this was Davien's Maze. Safer to roust slackened faculties and begin the necessary task of unmasking the thorns behind this cocooning pitfall of luxury.

Someone had apparently taken his clothes. His sword had gone missing with them. Arithon found it an effort to care, far less to muster suitable concern. Exhaustion waylaid him. Heavy eyelids slid closed. If the cozy security he now experienced shaped another of Davien's traps, then he must regretfully succumb. He lacked the active will to resist the battering demands of more hardship.

Someone's baritone chuckle answered his thought.

Slapped alert by the sense of an alien presence hanging poised at the edge of awareness, Arithon shot tense. A firm hand restrained his sharp thrust to sit upright.

A male voice of polite, velvet consonants observed, 'Your royal Grace, you have smashed through every illusion Kewar's maze has to offer.'

The touch lifted and freed him. The speaker resumed, his tone of asperity shaded toward a derisively faint self-amusement. 'If you know peace, the reprieve has been earned. My works never foster the illusion of triumph, only the deserving reality.'

Arithon turned his head, awake now, all his languid ease ripped away. With guarded alarm, he surveyed the being who sat, stilled as forest oak, on a felt hassock next to the couch. The face revealed in the fallow flood of the candle showed mild reproof, directed inward as well as toward the wayward royalty installed amid cushions and blankets. Russet hair salted white at the temples lay swept back, tumbling in roguish disorder from the Sorcerer's broad, wedged forehead. The nose was narrow and straight, flaring into the cleft creases that framed an inquisitive mouth. The chin was clean-shaven, the lean jaw, ascetic. The deep-set, dark eyes regarding him back stayed well veiled in cynical shadow.

'You *are* Davien,' Arithon tested at length.

The Sorcerer raised his brows with corrosive interest. 'Has my portrait been removed from Althain Tower?'

Arithon met and held that striking, sharp stare. 'No,' he said carefully. 'But when your name was spoken, the reference held you as discorporate.'

The artisan's hand in Davien's lap recoiled into a fist. 'So I was,' he admitted, his short bark of laughter alive with private amusement. Just as suddenly, he was struck thoughtfully sober. 'Yet who can set limits on determined creativity? I disliked the state intensely.'

He surged to his feet, his charged carriage spilling a tiger's fraught energy. The clothing he wore suggested the same, hose and doublet of walnut-dyed wool neatly bordered with ribbons of gold-and-black interlace. His waxed, outdoor boots had linings of sable, turned back in neat cuffs at mid-calf. As though circling wit goaded him to lithe movement, the Sorcerer paced end to end on the carpet.

Arithon looked on with stalking fascination. Here was none of the self-contained power of Asandir; not the wise patience of Traithe, or the vast, ranging mind behind Sethvir's daft air of distraction. Davien seemed a force of spring-wound energy. His neat, mercuric steps reflected a mind that would question, and question again, discontent with the static answer. Arithon wondered whether the isolate centuries of retreat stemmed from deep-seated bitterness.

At that musing thought, Davien stopped and spun. 'I bear my colleagues no malice for what happened.' His lined features alight with innuendo and a paradox whetted thin as a razor, he shrugged. 'Quite the contrary, though I maintain that I broke the monarchies for a sound cause. Since time will stand as my final spokesman, I choose to reside here in Kewar.'

Arithon pushed erect and swung naked feet to the floor in piqued effort to break the Sorcerer's fixation with the bent of his private thoughts. Davien's inquisitive gaze tracked each move as he stood. No objection arose as he retained the coverlet, its masking warmth mantled over bare shoulders, the heaped folds at the hem draping the scars that disfigured his ankles.

'I have been watching,' the Sorcerer observed. 'You make the mighty of Athera more than a shade nervous. You and I are a bit too much alike to give anyone full peace of mind.'

This time, Arithon himself flashed the smile of provocative insolence. 'So I was told by Dakar.' After the shortest, agreeable pause, he added, 'The comment was meant as an insult.'

'Is that so?' Davien snatched one of the pillows aside and sat on the vacated couch. He did not laugh this time as his hands came to rest, the long fingers adorned with a cast-silver ring nested into his lap. 'Insults show truth, more often than not.'

'And flattery covers the deficit?' Arithon did not disparage by qualifying his question, but waited, arms folded, the coverlet spilled to the floor in the unwitting majesty of a high king robed in state, arisen to administer crown justice. Davien's quick intelligence could be trusted to know he referred to the maze, and the delicate issue of whether his late experience had been a cleverly wrought fabrication.

Davien's stillness turned suddenly profound. 'Did you look at your hand?'

'Healed,' Arithon allowed. He had already tested the scar. No marring damage stiffened the tendons; his skill on the lyranthe would stay unimpaired. Yet whether the Sorcerer had noticed how narrowly close that discovery had brought him to weeping, no sign showed. 'The centaur's touch perhaps wrought a miracle?'

'How fast you are to belittle yourself.' Davien's accusation was not made without kindness. His dark eyes stayed candid as he continued to measure the wary survivor sharply drawn against the flame hues of the tapestry before him. 'Everything you experienced was real. All of the miracles were wrought by your merit. When you have privacy, check for yourself. Your access to talent is not spun from a dream. Can you stand in my presence and not trust that?'

'I could sit, fully clothed, with my weapons returned,' Arithon remarked, too spent to shepherd his temper. 'Is this awkward? Unlike Kamridian, I refused the convenience of death?'

Davien's spare features showed evil delight. 'Do you know you are the only man, ever, to master the first trial of the maze who had the harebrained *audacity* to challenge me? You ask, *is this awkward?* For the Fellowship and the Koriani Order, the issue's beyond any doubt. For myself, I would sit entranced at your feet, sword or not. I have full respect for your outrage, Teir's'Ffalenn. It's your talent that's frankly unsettling.'

Arithon lost his breath, taken aback.

The Sorcerer's laughter rang out, fluid as springwater tumbling through sudden sunlight. 'Oh, my wild falcon! Can you fly, and not know? You are probably the most gifted individual ever to try the influence of the Fellowship of *Seven*.' Perversely confounding that blistering sarcasm, Davien raised a congenial foot and slid the felt hassock toward Arithon.

'How does that signify?' Far from relaxed, Rathain's prince conceded and sat.

'To the Fellowship? Endowed as you are, they would never dare to approach you. Dakar's no liability. Despite his excesses, his idiot vices, and his ungovernable passions, he will achieve the stability of diamond, though a thousand years may be needful to mold him.' At once gauntly brooding against rich autumn hangings and the shine of bronze fittings on the clothes chests, Davien propped his chin on his thumb. 'Ah, but you! Yours, the one quality no teaching can bridle. Men call it arrogance. Koriathain see pride. But a Sorcerer looks deeper. What you have is an unequivocal self-honesty rooted in a poet's perception.'

Arithon tightened his death grip on the blanket, flushed to find himself under dissecting discussion.

'My revenge. You delivered your satire, first,' Davien stated, artfully bland. 'Since you can't fight me naked, I'll say what I think.' His regard seemed to savor his victim's red face as he resumed his prodding discourse. 'Given certain conditions, such developed sensitivity could subject you to pressures no human being should be asked to endure. You would react exactly as you did today, and bid Dharkaron Avenger's Five Horses take the hindmost. No power on Athera could sway your course. In violation of the Law of the Major Balance, you could only be killed, which sets the stinging thorn in the rose. To marry you with wisdom, you would have to be inflamed until you mastered your rebellion. The Fellowship would never cozen such risk. They can't. The brute conflict might shatter the compact.'

Arithon cut through the diversionary rhetoric. 'Then as Teir's'Ffalenn pressured to accept the high kingship, surely the explosion would be contained. I can't smash the world's order while burdened under crown duties. Your impressive list of my threatening tendencies ought to be kept neatly hobbled.'

Davien's assault remained bluntly direct. 'My colleagues would say you owe a debt to Rathain.'

Arithon dropped the pretense of light sarcasm. 'And you think otherwise?'

'Well, you are the issue of generations bred to rule.' Amid the unrippled fall of the tapestry, the tiny songbirds seemed trapped, unable to break from their vulnerable, perched stillness and explode into lifesaving flight. The Sorcerer seated before them seemed more like the wolf than the fox. 'Deny that you bear the stamp of Torbrand's lineage, or that the gifts of s'Ahelas were not passed on at birth, through the errant grace of your mother.'

Arithon swore, the fire that spiked his glance a dire warning. 'Is this why you lured me? To settle the unfinished work of the rebellion, here and now? Then try. I'd fight you naked. I've never liked being the target for other people's principles. You could have predicted I'd resist to the end.'

Pillows went flying as the Sorcerer drove back to his feet in nettled amazement. 'Has the whole world gone mad? What do you and Luhaine believe? That I would bloody my hands as your self-appointed executioner?'

Perhaps not the wolf; Arithon shivered, touched by a frisson of unwonted empathy through the lens of his Masterbard's gift. Sensitivity tossed him the sharp revelation, that small birds were caged for their inventive singing. A Sorcerer of peerless genius and vivid creativity had passed hundreds of years, sealed into a self-imposed isolation under the roots of the mountains. His motives would not be simplistic.

The silence extended, a drawn wire of distress that could not endure without snapping. Arithon resisted the impulse to speak. Moved to tentative sympathy, he listened.

'The rebellion was my personal version of the Havens,' Davien revealed, point-blank. He flexed restored fingers, as though the assurance of quickened flesh smoothed an uprush of unpleasant thoughts. 'No more successful a tactic, I might add.' Irritation broke through, emphatic denial that his plight had arisen from injustice or misunderstanding. 'You're not here to salve my unrequited past.'

'Or your colleagues' unrequited future?' Arithon snapped, lashed into bristled, rash temper. The trials of the maze were too recent, too raw. Weaponless, naked, he rejected the role of the pawn.

'Listen well,' Davien said, pacing again. 'The Seven are ancient. Their beginning lies so far distant, mortal thought cannot conceive of their origin! For a cast of mind that has seen whole worlds reduced to a dust smear against dying stars, five hundred years is a passing trifle.' Citrine and silver, the odd ring on the Sorcerer's left hand flashed through a warning gesture. 'Take superb care, if you would resist. My colleagues think in the language of epochs. Their plans won't drift astray for one man's recalcitrance. When the Fellowship stirs to intervene, you cannot imagine you'll stay the course of their collective displeasure.'

'Their resources are otherwise occupied, just now,' Arithon returned, restored to consummate blandness.

A spasm of quelled startlement crossed Davien's face, the wry twist to closed lips recognizable as suppressed laughter. 'The Mistwraith!' A chuckle escaped despite his best effort. 'Your salvation and your bane. A murderous paradox, mark my words, Teir's'Ffalenn. Savor that sorry advantage at your peril. Some paths to victory are not worth the cost, or did the maze of your conscience teach you nothing?'

Arithon shrugged to arrest the slow slide of the coverlet, the silk lining of which had a maddening tendency to slip. 'I'll have to return to my half brother's game of live chess soon enough. Or am I now your captured player?'

'You are a weapon,' Davien avowed. Equanimity returned, he

bent and unfastened the latch on the nearest clothes chest. 'But in my keeping, one with free will.'

The Sorcerer raised the lid, sorted the contents, then pulled out a plain shirt and dark tunic, both cut for his taller frame. His fleeting grimace admitted the embarrassment: the hem was going to trail below Arithon's knees. He piled a fawn pair of trunk hose on top, the garments extended as a peace offering. 'Your own clothes were too ragged and soiled to save. Mine must serve until we can find you replacements. Your sword is stored in my armory. The door has no lock. Go armed if you wish, but no enemy can reach you in Kewar.'

Arithon let the Sorcerer stack the clothes on the couch. He made no move to accept them.

Set on notice he was being challenged again, Davien crossed the rug and shut the trunk. Disarmingly informal, he perched on the lid, apparently content to curb his combative inquisitiveness.

'The Wheel turns. All princes born to a high king's lineage are not equal, this you have proved. You'll not find me sheltering talented foundlings to further my political preferences, like the Koriathain. But I can offer you this.' A fast move, and he hooked something tucked in his cuff and tossed the small, shiny object through the air.

Arithon fielded the catch, but did not open his fist. 'Is this another trial?' When Davien gave no immediate reply, he plunged on. 'If it is, I want no part of it. Your sorceries are like marsh grass, soft and lush to the eye. But they have a cutting edge. I'm done with bleeding for your private amusement, to try my royal mettle or otherwise.'

Davien presented his hands, the upturned palms guilelessly open. 'You vanquished the maze, and found your strength to master Desh-thiere's curse. What other challenge could be left? Unless you're burning to live in the wilds of Deshir until the ice breaks on Instrell Bay. Your ship won't put in to the eastshore for months. How do you plan to sustain yourself in the meantime? My wards here may not be as exotic as the ones guarding Althain Tower, but they're sufficient to discourage your enemies. At least you won't bleed as the quarry set after by Etarra's frustrated field troops.'

'What are you offering?' Arithon asked, tacitly listening, intrigued by the implied suggestion of sanctuary, but afraid to trust that the Sorcerer's generosity might in fact be an overture toward lasting friendship.

'Guest welcome and the key to my library, which is kept

locked.' Davien's biting humor resurged, as though he also hedged to stave off the sting of rejection. 'Doubtless I'm moonstruck to extend such a gift. Knowledge in your hands is quite apt to breed peril. Accept and have done, lest I reconsider. Where you're concerned, I've already had Luhaine expounding at length on my folly. Sethvir will be next, and then Asandir will feel bound to carve into my hide with rough language. Your Grace of Rathain, if you stay, on demand for the trouble you'll cause, I would ask you to match my sincerity.'

'My satire already gave you the truth,' Arithon insisted, bemused. 'You've a mind to wind Sithaer's fiends into knots. If your hellish round of trials hasn't demolished my worst flaws, the tradition of guest oath demands plainspoken honesty. A meal would be nice, with hot mead for the ritual. Since you're eager to sharpen your wits in my company, I accept. Just don't ask me to stand through the final embarrassment. I've fasted too long. The goblet we empty to swear mutual brotherhood is damnably certain to overset my light head.'

Closures

At Sethvir's bedside, glad tidings affirm the Teir's'Ffalenn's survival, and his wayward choice to remain with Davien for the duration of his recovery; pale as a wisp against piled pillows, the Warden of Althain whispers, 'You still don't approve?' and Luhaine replies, 'I'd hazard the incursion of wraiths out of Marak will pose us less grief than that pair, bound into alliance . . .'

Put in at the quay to reprovision her galley, the Koriani Matriarch's entourage meets stark rebuff by Jaelot's armed guard, until she presents the order's formal apology for the blunder that permitted three fugitives to escape: Lirenda is led forward, helplessly raging, and the evident severity of her punishment wins Prime Selidie the reprieve of a cordial audience with the mayor and his inner counsel . . .

The dirge of the bells resounds from Etarra and Darkling for days; but the echoes that roll off the Mathorn ranges fail to reach Narms on the Instrell coast; late word of the losses in Daon Ramon Barrens comes by sunwheel messenger, followed by Lysaer himself; the bereaved meet his arrival, softened by gold, and braced by consoling speech: 'No man died in vain The demon's been dispatched through Kewar Tunnel. Unless the fell powers of sorcery can bring an unnatural resurrection, no one expects the Spinner of Darkness will survive . . .'

768

GLOSSARY

AFFI'ENIA—the name given to Elaira by an adept, meaning dancer in the ancient Sanpashir desert dialect, but carrying the mystical connotation of the 'water dancer', the wisewoman who presided over the ritual for rebirth, celebrated on the spring solstice.

    pronounced: affee-yen-yah

    root meaning: *affi'enia*—dancer

AIYENNE—river located in Daon Ramon, Rathain, rising from an underground spring in the Mathorn Mountains, and coming above ground south of the Mathorn Road.

    pronounced: eye-an

    root meaning: *ai'an*—hidden one

ALESTRON—city located in Midhalla, Melhalla. Ruled by the Duke Bransian, Teir's'Brydion, and his three brothers. This city did not fall to merchant townsmen in the Third Age uprising that threw down the high kings, but is still ruled by its clanblood heirs.

    pronounced: ah-less-tron

    root meaning: *alesstair*—stubborn; *an*—one

ALITHIEL—one of twelve Blades of Isaer, forged by centaur Ffereton s'Darian in the First Age from metal taken from a meteorite. Passed through Paravian possession, acquired the secondary name Dael-Farenn, or Kingmaker, since its owners tended to succeed the end of a royal line. Eventually was awarded to Kamridian s'Ffalenn for his valor in defense of the princess Taliennse, early Third Age. Currently in the possession of Arithon.

    pronounced: ah-lith-ee-el

    root meaning: *alith*—star; *iel*—light/ray

ALLAND—principality located in southeastern Shand. Ruled by the High Earl Teir's'Taleyn, *caithdein* of Shand by appointment. Current heir to the title is Erlien.

    pronounced: all-and

    root meaning: *a'lind*—pine glen

ALQWERIK—dragon whose haunt is contained by the grimward at Athir in the Kingdom of Rathain.

    pronounced: al-quer-ick

    root meaning: *alkwerach*—sky bolt, from Drakish

ALTHAIN TOWER—spire built at the edge of the Bittern Desert, beginning of the Second Age, to house records of Paravian histories. Third Age, became repository for the archives of all five royal houses of men after rebellion, overseen by Sethvir, Warden of Althain and Fellowship Sorcerer.

pronounced: al—like 'all', thain—to rhyme with 'main'

root meaning: *alt*—last; *thein*—tower, sanctuary

original Paravian pronunciation: alt-thein (thein as in 'the end')

AMROTH—kingdom on West Gate splinter world, Dascen Elur, ruled by s'Illessid descendants of the prince exiled through the Worldsend Gate at the time of the rebellion, Third Age, just after the Mistwraith's conquest.

pronounced: am-roth—to rhyme with 'sloth'

root meaning: *am*—state of being; *roth*—brother 'brotherhood'

ANIENT—Paravian invocation for unity.

pronounced: an-ee-ent

root meaning: *an*—one; *ient*—suffix for 'most'

ARAETHURA—grass plains in southwest Rathain; principality of the same name in that location. Largely inhabited by Riathan Paravians in the Second Age. Third Age, used as pastureland by widely scattered nomadic shepherds. Fionn Areth's birthplace.

pronounced: ar-eye-thoo-rah

root meaning: *araeth*—grass; *era*—place, land

ARAITHE—plain to the north of the trade city of Etarra, principality of Fallowmere, Rathain. First Age, among those sites used by Paravians to renew the mysteries and channel fifth lane energies. The standing stones erected are linked to the power focus at Ithamon and Methisle keep.

pronounced: like 'a wraith'

root meaning: *araithe*—to disperse, to send

ARITHON—son of Avar, Prince of Rathain, 1,504th Teir's'Ffalenn after founder of the line, Torbrand in Third Age Year One. Also Master of Shadow, the Bane of Desh-thiere, and Halliron Masterbard's successor.

pronounced: ar-i-thon—almost rhymes with 'marathon'

root meaning: *arithon*—fate-forger; one who is visionary

ASANDIR—Fellowship Sorcerer. Secondary name, Kingmaker, since his hand crowned every High King of Men to rule in the Age of Men (Third Age). After the Mistwraith's conquest, he acted as field agent for the Fellowship's doings across the continent. Also called Fiend-quencher, for his reputation for quelling iyats; Storm-breaker and Change-bringer for past actions in late Second Age, when Men first arrived upon Athera.

pronounced: ah-san-deer

root meaning: *asan*—heart; *dir*—stone 'heartrock'

ASYA—Koriani Senior from the Highscarp sisterhouse.

pronounced: as-yah

root meaning: *ahs-yah*—a purple wildflower

ATAINIA—northeastern principality of Tysan.

pronounced: ah-tay-nee-ah

root meaning: *itain*—the third; *ia*—suffix for 'third domain'
original Paravian, *itainia*

ATH CREATOR—prime vibration, force behind all life.

pronounced: ath—to rhyme with 'math'

root meaning: *ath*—prime, first (as opposed to *an*, one)

ATHERA—name for the world which holds the Five High Kingdoms; four Worldsend Gates; original home of the Paravian races.

pronounced: ath-air-ah

root meaning: *ath*—prime force; *era*—place 'Ath's world'

ATHIR—Second Age ruin of a Paravian stronghold, located in Ithilt, Rathain. Site of a seventh lane power focus. Site where Arithon Teir's'Ffalenn swore his blood oath to survive to the Fellowship Sorcerer, Asandir.

pronounced: ath-ear

root meaning: *ath*—prime; *i'er*—the line/edge

ATHLIEN PARAVIANS—sunchildren. Small race of semimortals, pixielike, but possessed of great wisdom, keepers of the grand mystery.

pronounced: ath-lee-en

root meaning: *ath*—prime force; *lien*—to love 'Ath-beloved'

ATHLIERA—equivalent of heaven/actually a dimension removed from physical life, inhabited by spirit after death.

pronounced: ath-lee-air-ee-ah

root meaning: *ath*—prime force; *li'era*—exalted place, or land in harmony; *li*—exalted in harmony

AVAR s'FFALENN—Pirate King of Karthan, isle on splinter world Dascen Elur, through West Gate. Father of Arithon; also Teir's'Ffalenn 1,503rd in descent from Torbrand, who founded the s'Ffalenn royal line in Third Age Year One. Died of an arrow in the feud with Amroth.

pronounced: ah-var—to rhyme with 'far'

root meaning: *avar*—past thought/memory

AVENOR—Second Age ruin of a Paravian stronghold. Traditional seat of the s'Ilessid High Kings. Restored to habitation in Third Age 5644. Became the ruling seat of the Alliance of Light in Third Age 5648. Located in Korias, Tysan.

pronounced: ah-ven-or

root meaning: *avie*—stag; *norh*—grove

BAIYEN GAP—the trail built by the centaur guardians through

the pass that crosses the Skyshiel Mountains, connecting the Eltair coast to Daon Ramon Barrens. Twice the site of a drake battle, once between rivals in the Age of Dragons, and again, in the First Age, against a pack of greater drake spawn. One of the old rights of way, not open to mankind's use.

pronounced: bye-yen

root meaning: *bayien*—slag

BARACH—oldest son of Jieret s'Valerient, and older brother of Jeynsa. Successor to the title, Earl of the North.

pronounced: bar-ack

root meaning: *baraich*—lynchpin

BITTERN DESERT—waste located in Atainia, Tysan, north of Althain Tower. Site of a First Age battle between the great drakes and the Seardluin, permanently destroyed by dragonfire.

pronounced: like bitter

root meaning: to sear or char

BRAGGEN—one of the fourteen Companions, who were the only children to survive the battle fought between Deshir's clansmen and the war host of Etarra beside the River Tal Quorin in Third Age Year 5638.

BRANSIAN s'BRYDION—Teir's'Brydion, ruling Duke of Alestron.

pronounced: bran-see-an

root meaning: *brand*—temper; *s'i'an*—suffix denoting 'of the one' 'the one with temper'

CADGIA—Koriani seeress of senior rank who was temporarily assigned to Lirenda's service.

pronounced: cad-jee-ah

CAITH-AL-CAEN—vale where Riathan Paravians (unicorns) celebrated equinox and solstice to renew the *athael*, or life-destiny of the world. Also the place where the Ilitharis Paravians first Named the winter stars—or encompassed their vibrational essence into language. Corrupted by the end of the Third Age to Castlecain.

pronounced: cay-ith-al-cay-en, musical lilt, emphasis on second and last syllables; rising note on first two, falling note on last two

root meaning: *caith*—shadow; *al*—over; *caen*—vale 'vale of shadow', link with prime power. An old Paravian colloquialism for unicorn

CAITHDEIN—Paravian name for a high king's first counselor; also, the one who would stand as regent, or steward, in the absence of the crowned ruler.

pronounced: kay-ith-day-in

root meaning: *caith*—shadow; *d'ein*—behind the chair 'shadow behind the throne'

CAITHWOOD—forest located in Taerlin, southeast principality of Tysan.

pronounced: kay-ith-wood

root meaning: *caith*—shadow 'shadowed wood'

CALUM QUAIDE KINCAID—the individual who invented the great weapon which destroyed the worlds of humanity, and caused the refugee faction, including the Koriathain, to seek sanctuary on Athera.

pronounced: calum kwade kin-cade

root meaning is not from an Atheran language

CAMRIS—north-central principality of Tysan. Original ruling seat was the city of Erdane.

pronounced: Kam-ris, the i as in 'chris'

root meaning: *caim*—cross; *ris*—way 'crossroad'

CAOLLE—past war captain of the clans of Deshir, Rathain. First raised, and then served under, Lord Steiven, Earl of the North and *caithdein* of Rathain. Planned the campaign at Vastmark and Dier Kenton Vale for the Master of Shadow. Served Jieret Red-beard, and was feal liegeman of Arithon of Rathain; died of complications from a wound received from his prince while breaking a Koriani attempt to trap his liege.

pronounced: kay-all-eh, with the 'e' nearly subliminal

root meaning: *caille*—stubborn

CARLINE—Kharadmon's beloved, before the dream of the dragons drew the seven men who became the Fellowship Sorcerers to the world of Athera.

CARLIS—man-at-arms from Jaelot.

pronounced: car-liss

CATTRICK—master joiner hired to run the royal shipyard at Riverton; once in Arithon's employ at Merior by the Sea, now shipwright for Duke Bransian s'Brydion at Alestron.

pronounced: cat-rick

root meaning: *ciaitiaric*—a knot tied of withies that has the magical property of confusing enemies

CEREBELD—Avenor's High Priest of the Light, formerly Lord Examiner of Avenor.

pronounced: cara-belld

root meaning: *ciarabeld*—ashes

CIENN—clan scout and Companion in Earl Jieret s'Valerient's war band, smith who shod their horses.

pronounced: kee-in

root meaning: *cian*—spark

CILADIS THE LOST—Fellowship Sorcerer who left the continent in Third Age 5462 in search of the Paravian races after their disappearance following the rebellion.

pronounced: kill-ah-dis

root meaning: *cael*—leaf; *adeis*—whisper, compound; *cael'adeis* —colloquialism for 'gentleness that abides'

CILDEIN OCEAN—body of water lying off Athera's east coast.

pronounced: kill-dine

root meaning: *cailde*—salty; *an*—one

CILDORN—city famed for carpets and weaving, located in Deshir, Rathain. Originally a Paravian holdfast, situated on a node of the third lane.

pronounced: kill-dorn

root meaning: *cieal*—thread; *dorn*—net 'tapestry'

CLAITHEN—an adept of Ath's Brotherhood in the hostel south of Merior.

pronounced: clay-then

root meaning: *claithen*—garden, earth/soil

DAELION FATEMASTER—'entity' formed by set of mortal beliefs, which determine the fate of the spirit after death. If Ath is the prime vibration, or life force, Daelion is what governs the manifestation of free will.

pronounced: day-el-ee-on

root meaning: *dael*—king, or lord; *i'on*—of fate

DAELION'S WHEEL—cycle of life and the crossing point which is the transition into death.

pronounced: day-el-ee-on

root meaning: *dael*—king or lord; *i'on*—of fate

DAENFAL—city located on the northern lakeshore that bounds the southern edge of Daon Ramon Barrens in Rathain.

pronounced: dye-en-fall

root meaning: *daen*—clay; *fal*—red

DAKAR THE MAD PROPHET—apprentice to Fellowship Sorcerer, Asandir, during the Third Age following the Conquest of the Mistwraith. Given to spurious prophecies, it was Dakar who forecast the fall of the Kings of Havish in time for the Fellowship to save the heir. He made the Prophecy of West Gate, which forecast the Mistwraith's bane, and also, the Black Rose Prophecy, which called for reunification of the Fellowship. At this time, assigned to defense of Arithon, Prince of Rathain.

pronounced: dah-kar

root meaning: *dakiar*—clumsy

DALWYN—a clanswoman of Vastmark; aunt to Jilieth and Ghedair; friend of Arithon's.

pronounced: doll-win

root meaning: *dirlnwyn*—a specific aspect of misfortune; to be childless

DANIA—wife of Rathain's former regent, Steiven s'Valerient. Died by the hand of Pesquil's headhunters in the Battle of Strakewood, Third Age 5638; Jieret Red-beard's mother.

pronounced: dan-ee-ah

root meaning: *deinia*—sparrow

DAON RAMON BARRENS—central principality of Rathain. Site where Riathan Paravians (unicorns) bred and raised their young. Barrens was not appended to the name until the years following the Mistwraith's conquest, when the River Severnir was diverted at the source by a task force under Etarran jurisdiction.

pronounced: day-on-rah-mon

root meaning: *daon*—gold; *ramon*—hills/downs

DARKLING—city located on the western side of the Skyshiel Mountains in the Kingdom of Rathain.

pronounced: dark-ling

root meaning: *dierk-linng*—drake aerie

DASCEN ELUR—splinter world off West Gate; primarily ocean with isolated archipelagoes. Includes kingdoms of Rauven, Amroth, and Karthan. Where three exiled high kings' heirs took refuge in the years following the great uprising. Birthplace of Lysaer and Arithon.

pronounced: das-en el-ur

root meaning: *dascen*—ocean; *e'lier*—small land

DAVIEN THE BETRAYER—Fellowship Sorcerer responsible for provoking the great uprising in Third Age Year 5018, which resulted in the fall of the high kings after Desh-thiere's conquest. Rendered discorporate by the Fellowship's judgment in Third Age 5129. Exiled since, by personal choice. Davien's works included the Five Centuries Fountain near Mearth on the splinter world of the Red Desert through West Gate; the shaft at Rockfell Pit, used by the Sorcerers to imprison harmful entities; the Stair on Rockfell Peak; and also, Kewar Tunnel in the Mathorn Mountains.

pronounced: dah-vee-en

root meaning: *dahvi*—fool, mistake; *an*—one 'mistaken one'

DESHANS—barbarian clans who inhabit Strakewood Forest; principality of Deshir, Rathain.

pronounced: desh-ans

root meaning: *deshir*—misty

DESH-THIERE—Mistwraith that invaded Athera from the splinter worlds through South Gate in Third Age 4993. Access cut off by Fellowship Sorcerer, Traithe. Battled and contained in West Shand for twenty-five years, until the rebellion splintered the peace, and the high kings were forced to withdraw from the defense lines to attend their disrupted kingdoms. Confined through the combined powers of Lysaer s'Illessid's gift of light, and Arithon s'Ffalenn's gift of shadow. Currently imprisoned in a warded flask in Rockfell Pit.

pronounced: desh-thee-air-e (last 'e' mostly subliminal)

root meaning: *desh*—mist; *thiere*—ghost or wraith

DESHIR—northwestern principality of Rathain.

pronounced: desh-eer

root meaning: *deshir*—misty

DHARKARON AVENGER—called Ath's Avenging Angel in legend. Drives a chariot drawn by five horses to convey the guilty to Sithaer. Dharkaron as defined by the adepts of Ath's Brotherhood is that dark thread mortal men weave with Ath, the prime vibration, that creates self-punishment, or the root of guilt.

pronounced: dark-air-on

root meaning: *dhar*—evil; *khiaron*—one who stands in judgment

DHIRKEN—lady captain of the contraband runner, *Black Drake*. Reputed to have taken over the brig's command by right of arms following her father's death at sea. Died at the hands of Lysaer's allies on the charge of liaison with Arithon s'Ffalenn, Third Age Year 5647.

pronounced: dur-kin

root meaning: *dierk*—tough; *an*—one

DIEGAN—once Lord Commander of Etarra's garrison; given over by his mayor to serve as Lysaer s'Illessid's Lord Commander at Avenor. Titular commander of the war host sent against the Deshans to defeat the Master of Shadow at Tal Quorin; high commander of the war host mustered at Werpoint. Also brother of Lady Talith. Died of a clan arrow in the Battle of Dier Kenton Vale in Vastmark, Third Age 5647.

pronounced: dee-gan

root meaning: *diegan*—trinket a dandy might wear/ornament

DIER KENTON VALE—a valley located in the principality of Vastmark, Shand, where the war host thirty-five thousand strong, under command of Lysaer s'Ilessid, fought and lost to the Master of Shadow in Third Age 5647. The main body of the forces of light were decimated in one day by a shale slide. The remainder were harried by a small force of Vastmark shepherds under Caolle, who served as Arithon's war captain, until supplies and morale became impossible to maintain.

    pronounced: deer ken-ton

    root meaning: *dien'kendion*—a jewel with a severe flaw that may result in shearing or cracking

DORIK—officer of the Alliance, sunwheel division from Etarra.

    pronounced: door-ick

DRIMWOOD—forest located in the principality of Fallowmere, Rathain.

    pronounced: drim-wood

    root meaning: *driem*—fir tree

DURMAENIR—centaur, son of the armorer who forged the twelve Blades of Isaer. Sword Alithiel was fashioned for Durmaenir, who died in battle against Khadrim in the First Age.

    pronounced: dur-may-e-neer

    root meaning: *dir*—stone; *maenien*—fallen

EAFINN—one of the fourteen Companions, the only children of the clans of Deshir to survive the Battle of Strakewood. Served Prince Arithon at the Battle of Dier Kenton Vale in Vastmark. Died at the hands of headhunters in Third Age Year 5669. Survived by a son.

    pronounced: ee-yah-finn

    root meaning: *liaffen*—pale yellow hair

EARLE—Second Age ruin located in West Shand, south of the Salt Fens. Fortress where the Mistwraith's first incursion was fought, until Davien the Betrayer caused the uprising; also, where Seannory bound the four elements to conscious presence, in event Athera had need.

    pronounced: earl

    root meaning: *erli*—long light

EASTWALL—city located in the Skyshiel Mountains, Rathain.

ECKRACKEN—king drake who died by the Salt Fens in West Shand; his bones are guarded by a grimward located on the peninsula in West Shand near the ruins of Earle, and his mate's remains rest on the waste continent Kathtairr.

    pronounced: ack-rack-in

root meaning: *aykrauken*—scorcher

EDAL—next to youngest daughter of Steiven and Dania s'Valerient.

pronounced: ee-doll

root meaning: *e*—prefix, diminutive for small; *dal*—fair

ELAIRA—initiate enchantress of the Koriathain. Originally a street child, taken on in Morvain for Koriani rearing.

pronounced: ee-layer-ah

root meaning: *e*—prefix, diminutive for small; *laere*—grace

ELDIR s'LORNMEIN—King of Havish and last surviving scion of s'Lornmein royal line. Raised as a wool-dyer until the Fellowship Sorcerers crowned him at Ostermere in Third Age 5643 following the defeat of the Mistwraith.

pronounced: el-deer

root meaning: *eldir*—to ponder, to consider, to weigh

ELLAINE—Erdani woman, became Princess of Tysan when she married Lysaer s'Ilessid, mother of the heir apparent, Kevor.

pronounced: el-lane

ELTAIR BAY—large bay off Cildein Ocean and east coast of Rathain; where River Severnir was diverted following the Mistwraith's conquest.

pronounced: el-tay-er

root meaning: *al'tieri*—of steel/a shortening of original Paravian name; *dascen al'tieri*—which meant 'ocean of steel', which referred to the color of the waves

ERDANE—old Paravian city, later taken over by Men. Seat of old princes of Camris until Desh-thiere's conquest and rebellion.

pronounced: er-day-na with the last syllable almost subliminal

root meaning: *er'deinia*—long walls

ERLIEN s'TALEYN—High Earl of Alland; *caithdein* of Shand, chieftain of the forest clansmen of Selkwood.

pronounced: er-lee-an stall-ay-en

root meaning: *aierlyan*—bear; *tal*—branch; *an*—one/first 'of first one branch'

ETARRA—trade city built across the Mathorn Pass by townsfolk after the revolt that cast down Ithamon and the High Kings of Rathain. Nest of corruption and intrigue, and policy maker for the North.

pronounced: ee-tar-ah

root meaning: *e*—prefix for small; *taria*—knots

EVENSTAR—first brig stolen from Riverton's royal shipyard by Cattrick's conspiracy with Prince Arithon. Currently of Innish regristry, running merchant cargoes under joint ownership of Fiark and his sister Feylind, who is acting captain.

FALGAIRE—coastal city on Instrell Bay, located in Araethura, Rathain, famed for its glassworks.
   pronounced: fall-gair—to rhyme with 'air'
   root meaning: *fal'mier*—to sparkle or glitter
FALLOWMERE—northeastern principality of Rathain.
   pronounced: fal-oh-meer
   root meaning: *fal'ei'miere*—literally, tree self-reflection, colloquialism for 'place of perfect trees'
FATE's WHEEL—see Daelion's Wheel.
FELLOWSHIP OF SEVEN—Sorcerers drawn to Athera in the Second Age by the dreams of the dragons, and bound to the charge of upholding Paravian survival. Keepers of the compact, they stand surety for the points of concordance made with the Paravians which permitted human refugees to settle on the continent of Paravia. Authors of charter law, which governed the balance of natural law, and the justice of the high kings. Since the departure of the Paravians, the Sorcerers also shoulder the charge of minding the weal of the land. They act in accord with the Law of the Major Balance, which honors the law of free will, and which demands that no consciousness should be imposed upon without permission.
FEITHAN—wife of Jieret s'Valerient, Earl of the North, and *caithdein* of Rathain.
   pronounced: faith-an
   root meaning: *feiathen*—ivy
FENNICK—man-at-arms from the royal guard of Avenor, assigned as bodyguard to the heir apparent, Prince Kevor.
   pronounced: fen-nick
FIONN ARETH CAID'AN—shepherd child born in Third Age 5647; fated by prophecy to leave home and play a role in the Wars of Light and Shadow. Laid under Koriani spellcraft to mature as Arithon's double, then used as the bait in the order's conspiracy to trap the s'Ffalenn prince. Rescued from execution in Jaelot in 5669.
   pronounced: fee-on-are-eth cayed-ahn
   root meaning: *fionne arith caid an*—one who brings choice
FIRSTMARK—city on the coast of Rockbay in Radmoore, Shand.
FORTHMARK—city in Vastmark, Shand. Once the site of a hostel of Ath's Brotherhood. By Third Age 5320, the site was

abandoned and taken over by the Koriani Order as a healer's hospice.

    root meaning not from the Paravian

GACE STEWARD—Royal Steward of Avenor.
    pronounced: gace—to rhyme with 'race'
    root meaning: *gyce*—weasel
GANISH—trade city located south of Methlas Lake in Orvandir, Shand.
    pronounced: rhymes with 'mannish'
    root meaning: *gianish*—a halfway point, a stopping place
GERY—man-at-arms in Etarra's sunwheel company.
    pronounced: gerry
GREAT WAYSTONE—amethyst crystal, spherical in shape, the grand power focus of the Koriani Order; lost during the great uprising, and finally recovered from Fellowship custody by First Senior Lirenda in Third Age 5747.
GRIMWARD—a circle of dire spells of Paravian making that seal and isolate forces that have the potential for unimaginable destruction. With the disappearance of the old races, the defenses are maintained by embodied Sorcerers of the Fellowship of Seven. There are seventeen separate sites listed at Althain Tower.

HADGE—scout tracker, with Etarra's sunwheel field company.
    pronounced: hadj
HALDUIN s'ILESSID—founder of the line that became High Kings of Tysan since Third Age Year One. The attribute he passed on, by means of the Fellowship's geas, was justice.
    pronounced: hal-dwin
    root meaning: *hal*—white; *duinne*—hand
HALLIRON MASTERBARD—native of Innish, Shand. Masterbard of Athera during the Third Age; inherited the accolade from his teacher Murchiel in the year 5597. Son of Al'Duin. Husband of Deartha. Arithon's master and mentor. Died from an injury inflicted by the Mayor of Jaelot in the year 5644.
    pronounced: hal-eer-on
    root meaning: *hal*—white; *lyron*—singer
HALWYTHWOOD—forest located in Araethura, Rathain. Current main campsite of Earl Jieret's band, predominantly survivors of the Battle of Strakewood.
    pronounced: hall-with-wood
    root meaning: *hal*—white; *wythe*—vista
HANSHIRE—port city on Westland Sea, coast of Korias, Tysan;

reigning official Lord Mayor Garde, father of Sulfin Evend; opposed to royal rule at the time of Avenor's restoration.

    pronounced: han-sheer

    root meaning: *hansh*—sand; *era*—place

HASPASTION—ghost of the dragon contained in the grimward located in Radmoore.

    pronounced: has-past-ee-on

    root meaning: *hashpashdion*—Drakish for black thunder

HAVENS—an inlet on the northeastern shore of Vastmark, Shand, now known as the site of the massacre enacted by the Spinner of Darkness, preceding the Battle of Dier Kenton Vale, Third Age Year 5647.

HAVISH—one of the Five High Kingdoms of Athera, as defined by the charters of the Fellowship of Seven. Ruled by Eldir s'Lornmein. Sigil: gold hawk on red field.

    pronounced: hav-ish

    root meaning: *havieshe*—hawk

HAVISTOCK—southeast principality of Kingdom of Havish.

    pronounced: hav-i-stock

    root meaning: *haviesha*—hawk; *tiok*—roost

HENLYIE—herb witch who makes amulets in the city of Highscarp.

    pronounced: hen-lee

    root meaning: *han'lion*—light-handed

HEWALL—clansman serving as scout in the outpost in the Mathorn Mountains in Rathain.

    pronounced: hugh-ell

    root meaning: *huell*—one who protects

HIGHSCARP—city on the coast of the Bay of Eltair, located in Daon Ramon, Rathain. Current headquarters for Selidie Prime, Matriarch of the Koriani Order.

ILITHARIS PARAVIANS—centaurs, one of three semimortal old races; disappeared after the Mistwraith's conquest, the last guardian's departure by Third Age Year 5100. They were the guardians of the earth's mysteries.

    pronounced: i-li-thar-is

    root meaning: *i'lith'eans*—the keeper/preserver of mystery

INNISH—city located on the southcoast of Shand at the delta of the River Ippash. Birthplace of Halliron Masterbard. Formerly known as 'the Jewel of Shand', this was the site of the high king's winter court, prior to the time of the uprising.

    pronounced: in-ish

    root meaning: *inniesh*—a jewel with a pastel tint

INSTRELL BAY—body of water off the Gulf of Stormwell; separates principality of Atainia, Tysan, from Deshir, Rathain.

    pronounced: in-strell

    root meaning: *arin'streal*—strong wind

INWIE—lady-in-waiting to Princess Ellaine.

    pronounced: in-wee

    root meaning: *yanwi*—a sweet made from berries

IPPASH DELTA—river which originates in the southern spur of the Kelhorns and flows into the South Sea by the city of Innish, southcoast, Shand.

    pronounced: ip-ash

    root meaning: *ipeish*—crescent

ISFARENN—etheric Name for the black stallion ridden by Asandir.

    pronounced: ees-far-en

    root meaning: *is'feron*—speed maker

ITHAMON—Second Age Paravian stronghold, and a Third Age ruin; built on a fifth lane power-node in Daon Ramon Barrens, Rathain, and inhabited until the year of the uprising. Site of the Compass Point Towers, or Sun Towers. Became the seat of the High Kings of Rathain during the Third Age and in year 5638 was the site where Princes Lysaer s'Ilessid and Arithon s'Ffalenn battled the Mistwraith to confinement.

    pronounced: ith-a-mon

    root meaning: *itha*—five; *mon*—needle, spire

ITHISH—city located at the edge of the principality of Vastmark, on the southcoast of Shand. Where the Vastmark wool factors ship fleeces.

    pronounced: ith-ish

    root meaning: *ithish*—fleece or fluffy

IYAT—energy sprite native to Athera, not visible to the eye, manifests in a poltergeist fashion by taking temporary possession of objects. Feeds upon natural energy sources: fire, breaking waves, lightning.

    pronounced: ee-at

    root meaning: *iyat*—to break

JAELOT—city located on the coast of Eltair Bay at the southern border of the Kingdom of Rathain. Once a Second Age power site, with a focus circle. Now a merchant city with a reputation for extreme snobbery and bad taste. Also the site where Arithon s'Ffalenn played his eulogy for Halliron Masterbard, which raised the powers of the Paravian focus circle beneath the mayor's palace. The forces of the mysteries and resonant harmonics caused damage to city buildings, watchkeeps, and walls, which has since been repaired. Site where Fionn Areth was arraigned for execution, as bait in a Koriani conspiracy that failed to trap Arithon s'Ffalenn.

pronounced: jay-lot

root meaning: *jielot*—affectation

JAIRE PEAK—mountain near the great divide in the Mathorn ranges, located in the Kingdom of Rathain.

pronounced: jayr

root meaning: from *jieri*—spike

JERIAYISH—sixth-rank initiate priest of the Light who has a seer's talent.

pronounced: jeer-ee-ah-yish

root meaning: *jier'yaish*—unclean magic

JEYNSA—daughter of Jieret s'Valerient and Feithan, born Third Age 5653; appointed successor to her father's title of Steward of Rathain, or *caithdein*.

pronounced: jay-in-sa

root meaning: garnet

JIERET s'VALERIENT—Earl of the North, clan chief of Deshir; *caithdein* of Rathain, sworn liegeman of Prince Arithon s'Ffalenn. Also son and heir of Lord Steiven. Blood pacted to Arithon by sorcerer's oath prior to battle of Strakewood Forest. Came to be known by headhunters as Jieret Red-beard. Father of Jeynsa and Barach. Husband to Feithan.

pronounced: jeer-et

root meaning: *jieret*—thorn

JILIETH—girl from a Vastmark shepherd tribe who died of a mauling by Wyverns in Third Age Year 5647.

pronounced: jil-ee-eth

root meaning: *jirlieth*—to be stubborn enough to cause pain; a thorn of worry

JINESSE—widow of a fisherman, mother of the twins Fiark and Feylind; formerly an inhabitant of Merior by the Sea, now married to Tharrick, a former guardsman of Alestron. The couple reside at Innish in Shand.

pronounced: gin-ess

root meaning: *jienesse*—to be washed out or pale; a wisp

JOLM—swordsman in the sunwheel company from Etarra.

pronounced: johm

KAMRIDIAN s'FFALENN—Crowned High King of Rathain, a

tragic figure who died of his conscience under the fated influence of Kewar Tunnel, built by Davien the Betrayer into the Mathorn Mountains.

pronounced: cam-rid-ee-an

root meaning: *kaim'riadien*—thread cut shorter

KARFAEL—trader town on the coast of the Westland Sea, in Tysan. Built by townsmen as a trade port after the fall of the High Kings of Tysan. Prior to Desh-thiere's conquest, the site was kept clear of buildings to allow the second lane forces to flow untrammeled across the focus site at Avenor.

pronounced: kar-fay-el

root meaning: *kar'i'ffael*—literal translation 'twist the dark'/colloquialism for 'intrigue'

KARTH-EELS—creatures descended from stock aberrated by the *methurien*, or hate-wraiths, of Mirthlvain Swamp. Amphibious, fanged, venomed spines, webbed feet.

pronounced: caar-th eels

root meaning: *kar'eth*—to raid

KARTHAN—kingdom in splinter world of Dascen Elur, through West Gate, ruled by the pirate kings, s'Ffalenn descendants of the prince sent into exile at the time of the Mistwraith's conquest.

pronounced: karth-an

root meaning: *kar'eth'an*—one who raids/pirate

KATHTAIRR—landmass in the southern ocean, across the world from Paravia. The land was left sterile by drakefire during a far-reaching conflict in the Age of Dragons.

pronounced: kath-tear

root meaning: *kait-th'era*—empty place

KELHORN MOUNTAINS—a range of shale scarps in Vastmark, Shand.

pronounced: kell-horn

root meaning: *kielwhern*—toothed, jagged

KESWETH—scout from the outpost in the Mathorn Mountains whose wife was killed by headhunters.

pronounced: kez-ith

root meaning: *kesieth*—small clam found in freshwater streams

KEVOR—son and heir of Lysaer s'Ilessid and Princess Ellaine; born at Avenor in Third Age 5655. At age fourteen, in his father's absence, he exercised royal authority and averted a riot by the panicked citizenry of Avenor, earning the enmity of High Priest Cerebeld.

pronounced: kev-or

root meaning: *kiavor*—high virtue

KEWAR TUNNEL—cavern built beneath the Mathorn Mountains by Davien the Betrayer; site of High King Kamridian s'Ffalenn's death.

    pronounced: key-wahr

    root meaning: *kewiar*—a weighing of conscience

KHADRIM—drake-spawned creatures, flying, fire-breathing reptiles that were the scourge of the Second Age. By the Third Age, they had been driven back and confined in the Sorcerers' Preserve in the volcanic peaks in north Tysan.

    pronounced: kaa-drim

    root meaning: *khadrim*—dragon

KHARADMON—Sorcerer of the Fellowship of Seven; discorporate since rise of Khadrim and Seardluin leveled Paravian city at Ithamon in Second Age 3651. It was by Kharadmon's intervention that the survivors of the attack were sent to safety by means of transfer from the fifth lane power focus. Currently guarding the star ward to guard against invasion of wraiths from Marak.

    pronounced: kah-rad-mun

    root meaning: *kar'riad en mon*—phrase translates to mean 'twisted thread on the needle' or colloquialism for 'a knot in the works'

KHETIENN—name for a brigantine owned by Arithon; also a small spotted wildcat native to Daon Ramon Barrens that became the s'Ffalenn royal sigil.

    pronounced: key-et-ee-en

    root meaning: *kietienn*—small leopard

KIELING TOWER—one of the four compass points, or Sun Towers, standing at ruin of Ithamon, Daon Ramon Barrens, in Rathain. The warding virtue that binds its stones is compassion.

    pronounced: key-eh-ling

    root meaning: *kiel'ien*—root for pity, with suffix for 'lightness' added, translates to mean 'compassion'

KITZ—man-at-arms in the sunwheel company out of Etarra.

    pronounced: kits

KORIANI—possessive and singular form of the word 'Koriathain'; see entry.

    pronounced: kor-ee-ah-nee

KORIAS—southwestern principality of Tysan.

    pronounced: kor-ee-as

    root meaning: *cor*—ship, vessel; *i'esh*—nest, haven

KORIATHAIN—order of enchantresses ruled by a circle of Seniors, under the power of one Prime Enchantress. They draw their talent from the orphaned children they raise, or from daughters dedicated to service by their parents. Initiation rite involves a vow of consent that ties the spirit to a power crystal keyed to the Prime's control.

pronounced: kor-ee-ah-thain—to rhyme with 'main'

root meaning: *koriath*—order; *ain*—belonging to

KOSHLIN—influential trade minister from Erdane, renowned for his hatred of the clans, and for his support of the headhunters' leagues.

pronounced: kosh-lynn

root meaning: *kioshlin*—opaque

KRAEL—master of magecraft at Rauven Tower, on the world of Dascen Elur; one of Arithon's early tutors.

pronounced: krayel

root meaning: *krial*—name for the rune of crossing

LAW OF THE MAJOR BALANCE—founding order of the powers of the Fellowship of Seven, as written by the Paravians. The primary tenet is that no force of nature should be used without consent, or against the will of another living being.

LEYNSGAP—a narrow pass in the Mathorn Mountains in the Kingdom of Rathain.

pronounced: lay-ens-gap

root meaning: *liyond*—corridor

LIRENDA—former First Senior Enchantress to the Prime, Koriani Order; failed in her assignment to capture Arithon s'Ffalenn for Koriani purposes.

pronounced: leer-end-ah

root meaning: *lyron*—singer; *di-ia*—a dissonance—the hyphen denotes a glottal stop

LITHMERE—principality located in the Kingdom of Havish.

pronounced: lith-mere

root meaning: *lithmiere*—to preserve intact, or keep whole; maintain in a state of harmony

LUHAINE—Sorcerer of the Fellowship of Seven, discorporate since the fall of Telmandir in Third Age Year 5018. Luhaine's body was pulled down by the mob while he was in ward trance, covering the escape of the royal heir to Havish.

pronounced: loo-hay-ne

root meaning: *luirhainon*—defender

LYRANTHE—instrument played by the bards of Athera. Strung with fourteen strings, tuned to seven tones (doubled). Two courses are 'drone strings' set to octaves. Five are melody strings, the lower three courses being octaves, the upper two, in unison.

pronounced: leer-anth-e (last 'e' being nearly subliminal)

root meaning: *lyr*—song; *anthe*—box

LYSAER s'ILESSID—prince of Tysan, 1,497th in succession after Halduin, founder of the line in Third Age Year One. Gifted at birth with control of Light, and Bane of Desh-thiere. Also known as Blessed Prince.

pronounced: lie-say-er

root meaning: *lia*—blond, yellow or light; *saer*—circle

MACHLIN—clan scout from the outpost in the Mathorn Mountains.

pronounced: mock-lin

root meaning: *miach'luin*—cat kept for watch purposes, since cats can see etherically

MADREIGH—senior scout, Deshir clans. One of the eleven who stood to Jieret's defense in the battle of Strakewood Forest.

pronounced: mah-dree-ah ('ah' is near subliminal)

root meaning: *madrien*—staunch

MAENALLE s'GANNLEY—former steward and *caithdein* of Tysan; put on trial for outlawry and theft on the trade roads; executed by Lysaer s'Ilessid at Isaer, Third Age 5645.

pronounced: may-nahl-e (last 'e' is near subliminal)

root meaning: *maeni*—to fall, disrupt; *alli*—to save or preserve; colloquial translation: 'to patch together'

MAENOL—heir, after Maenalle s'Gannley, Steward and *caithdein* of Tysan.

pronounced: may-nall

root meaning: *maeni'alli*—to patch together

MAK s'AHELAS—High Mage of Rauven on the splinter world of Dascen Elur, father to Talera, and grandfather to Arithon and Lysaer.

pronounced: mock s-ah-hell-as

root meaning: *miach*—a form of mage-sight

MARAK—splinter world, cut off beyond South Gate, left lifeless after creation of the Mistwraith. The original inhabitants were men exiled by the Fellowship from Athera for beliefs or practices that were incompatible with the compact sworn between the Sorcerers and the Paravian races, which permitted human settlement on Athera.

pronounced: maer-ak

root meaning: *m'era'ki*—a place held separate

MATHORN MOUNTAINS—range that bisects the Kingdom of Rathain east to west.

    pronounced: math-orn

    root meaning: *mathien*—massive

MATHORN ROAD—way passing to the south of the Mathorn Mountains, leading to the trade city of Etarra from the west.

    pronounced: math-orn

    root meaning: *mathien*—massive

MEARN s'BRYDION—youngest brother of Duke Bransian of Alestron. Former ducal emissary to Lysaer s'Ilessid's Alliance of Light.

    pronounced: may-arn

    root meaning: *mierne*—to flit

MEIRIS—one of Princess Ellaine's ladies-in-waiting at Avenor.

    pronounced: marys

MELHALLA—High Kingdom of Athera once ruled by the line of s'Ellestrion. The last prince died in the crossing of the Red Desert.

    pronounced: mel-hall-a

    root meaning: *maelhallia*—grand meadows/plain; also word for an open space of any sort

MELOR RIVER—located in the principality of Korias, Tysan. Its mouth forms the harbor for the port town of West End.

    pronounced: mel-or

    root meaning: *maeliur*—fish

MERIOR BY THE SEA—small seaside fishing village on the Scimlade peninsula in Alland, Shand. Once the temporary site of Arithon's shipyard.

    pronounced: mare-ee-or

    root meaning: *merioren*—cottages

METHISLE—small body of land in Methlas Lake, site of Methisle fortress in Orvandir.

    pronounced: meth

    root meaning: *meth*—hate

METHLAS LAKE—large body of fresh water located in the principality of Radmoore, Melhalla.

    pronounced: meth-las

    root meaning: *meth'ilass'an*—the drowned, or sunken ones

METHSPAWN—an animal warped by possession by a methuri, an iyat-related parasite that infested live hosts. Extinct by the Third Age, their crossbred, aberrated descendants are called methspawn, found in Mirthlvain Swamp.

    pronounced: meth

    root meaning: *meth*—hate

METHURI—an iyat-related parasite that infested live hosts, extinct by the Third Age.

pronounced: meth-you-ree

root meaning: *meth'thi*—hate-wraith

MINDERL BAY—body of water behind Crescent Isle off the east coast of Rathain. Also reference point of a battle where Arithon tricked Lysaer into burning the trade fleet.

pronounced: mind-earl

root meaning: *minderl*—anvil

MIRTHLVAIN SWAMP—boglands located in Midhalla, Melhalla; filled with dangerous crossbreeds of drake spawn. Guarded by the Master Spellbinder, Verrain.

pronounced: mirth-el-vain

root meaning: *myrthl*—noxious; *vain*—bog, mud

MISTWRAITH—see Desh-thiere.

MORRIEL—Prime Enchantress of the Koriathain since the Third Age 4212. Instigated the plot to upset the Fellowship's compact, which upset the seven magnetic lanes on the continent. Her death on winter solstice 5670 left an irregular succession.

pronounced: more-real

root meaning: *moar*—greed; *riel*—silver

MORVAIN—city located in Araethura, Rathain, on the coast of Instrell Bay. Elaira's birthplace.

pronounced: more-vain

root meaning: *morvain*—swindlers' market

NARMS—city on the coast of Instrell Bay, built as a craft center by Men in the early Third Age. Best known for dyeworks.

pronounced: narms—to rhyme with 'charms'

root meaning: *narms*—color

NORTH-WARD—fishing town on the north coast of the principality of Fallowmere, Rathain.

NORTHSTRAIT—narrows between the mainland spur of northern Tysan and the Trow Islands.

ORNISON—master from Rauven Tower who taught Arithon his early lessons in magecraft.

pronounced: or-nee-son

root meaning: *ornia'san*—a blackbird with a crested head

ORVANDIR—principality located in northeastern Shand.

pronounced: or-van-deer

root meaning: *orvein*—crumbled; *dir*—stone

OSTERMERE—harbor and trade city, once smugglers' haven, located in Carithwyr, Havish. City where High King Eldir received his coronation, before moving his court to Telmandir.

pronounced: os-tur-mere

root meaning: *ostier*—brick; *miere*—reflection

PARAVIAN—name for the three old races that inhabited Athera before Men. Including the centaurs, the sunchildren, and the unicorns, these races never die unless mishap befalls them; they are the world's channel, or direct connection, to Ath Creator.

pronounced: par-ai-vee-ans

root meaning: *para*—great; *i'on*—fate or great mystery

PENSTAIR—Second Age ruin on the northern shore of Deshir, Rathain.

pronounced: pen-stair

root meaning: *pensti'era*—watchpoint, place for beacon fires

PESQUIL—Mayor of the Northern League of Headhunters at the time of the battle of Strakewood Forest. His strategies caused the Deshir clans the most punishing losses. Died of a clan vengeance arrow during the crossing of Valleygap in Third Age 5646.

pronounced: pes-quil like 'pest-quill'

root meaning not from the Paravian

POIREY—Araethurian herder, great-uncle to Fionn Areth.

pronounced: pear-ree

root meaning: *paereia*—salmon

RADMOORE DOWNS—meadowlands in Midhalla, Melhalla.

pronounced: rad-more

root meaning: *riad*—thread; *mour*—carpet, rug

RAIETT RAVEN—brother of the Mayor of Hanshire; uncle of Sulfin Evend. Considered a master statesman and a bringer of wars. Currently serving as High Chancellor of Etarra, ruling in the absence of the mayor.

pronounced: rayett

root meaning: *raiett*—carrion bird

RANNE—royal guardsman of Avenor, assigned as honor guard to the heir apparent, Prince Kevor.

pronounced: rahn

root meaning: *ruann*—a fledgling hawk

RATHAIN—High Kingdom of Athera ruled by descendants of Torbrand s'Ffalenn since Third Age Year One. Sigil: black-and-silver leopard on green field. Arithon Teir's'Ffalenn is sanctioned crown prince, by the hand of Asandir of the Fellowship, in Third Age Year 5638 at Etarra.

pronounced: rath-ayn

root meaning: *roth*—brother; *thein*—tower, sanctuary

RAUVEN TOWER—home of the s'Ahelas mages who brought up Arithon s'Ffalenn and trained him to the ways of power. Located on the splinter world, Dascen Elur, through West Gate.

    pronounced: raw-ven

    root meaning: *rauven*—invocation

REIYAJ—title for the seeress who inhabits a tower in southern Shand near the city of Ithish. Her oracular visions are based on meditative communion with the energy gateway marked and measured by Athera's sun. Although born sighted, practice of her art results in blindness. The origin of her tradition derives from mystical practices still extant in the tribal culture of the Sanpashir Desert.

    pronounced: ree-yahj

    root meaning: *ria'ieajn*—to touch the forbidden

RIATHAN PARAVIANS—unicorns, the purest, most direct connection to Ath Creator; the prime vibration channels directly through the horn.

    pronounced: ree-ah-than

    root meaning: *ria*—to touch; *ath*—prime life force; *an*—one; *ri'athon*—one who touches divinity

RIVERTON—trade town at the mouth of the Ilswater river, in Korias, Tysan; once the site of Lysaer's royal shipyard, before the site burned in Third Age Year 5654.

ROCKFELL PIT—deep shaft cut into Rockfell Peak, used to imprison harmful entities throughout all three Ages. Located in West Halla, Melhalla; became the warded prison for Desh-thiere.

    pronounced: rock-fell

    root meaning not from the Paravian

ROCKFELL VALE—valley below Rockfell Peak, located in principality of West Halla, Melhalla.

    pronounced: rockfell vale

    root meaning not from the Paravian

SAERIAT—name of the brigantine captained by Avar of Karthan, defeated and burned in engagement against seventeen warships of Amroth on the splinter world of Dascen Elur.

    pronounced: say-ree-at

    root meaning: *saer*—water; *iyat*—to break

s'AHELAS—family name for the royal line appointed by the Fellowship Sorcerers in Third Age Year One to rule the High Kingdom of Shand. Gifted geas: farsight.

    pronounced: s'ah-hell-as

root meaning: *ahelas*—mage-gifted

SANPASHIR—desert waste on the southcoast of Shand. Home to the desert tribes.

pronounced: sahn-pash-eer

root meaning: *san*—black or dark; *pash'era*—place of grit or gravel

SAYTRA—Koriani Senior in charge of making talismans and fiend banes at the Highscarp sisterhouse.

pronounced: say-tra

root meaning: *saer'tria*—one who joins circles

s'BRYDION—ruling line of the Dukes of Alestron. The only old blood clansmen to maintain rule of their city through the uprising that defeated the rule of the high kings.

pronounced: s'bride-ee-on

root meaning: *baridien*—tenacity

SCIMLADE TIP—peninsula at the southeast corner of Alland, Shand.

pronounced: skim-laid

root meaning: *scimlait*—curved knife or scythe

s'DARIAN—family name for a line of centaurs who were master armorers in the First and Second Ages. Most renowned was Ffereton, who forged the twelve Blades of Isaer, Alithiel being for his natural son Durmaenir.

pronounced: dar-ee-an

root meaning: *daer'an*—one that cuts

SECOND AGE—Marked by the arrival of the Fellowship of Seven at Crater Lake, their called purpose to fight the drake spawn.

SELIDIE—young woman initiate appointed by Morriel Prime as a candidate in training for succession. Succeeded to the office of Prime Matriarch after Morriel's death on winter solstice in Third Age Year 5670.

pronounced: sell-ih-dee

root meaning: *selyadi*—air sprite

SELKWOOD—forest located in Alland, Shand.

pronounced: selk-wood

root meaning: *selk*—pattern

SETHVIR—Sorcerer of the Fellowship of Seven, served as Warden of Althain since the disappearance of the Paravians in the Third Age after the Mistwraith's conquest.

pronounced: seth-veer

root meaning: *seth*—fact; *vaer*—keep

SEVERNIR—river that once ran across the central part of

Daon Ramon Barrens, Rathain. Diverted at the source after the Mistwraith's conquest, to run east into Eltair Bay.

pronounced: se-ver-neer

root meaning: *sevaer*—to travel; *nir*—south

s'FFALENN—family name for the royal line appointed by the Fellowship Sorcerers in Third Age Year One to rule the High Kingdom of Rathain. Gifted geas: compassion/empathy.

pronounced: s-fal-en

root meaning: *ffael*—dark; *an*—one

SHAND—High Kingdom on the southeast corner of the Paravian continent, originally ruled by the line of s'Ahelas. Device is falcon on a crescent moon, backed by purple-and-gold chevrons.

pronounced: shand—as in 'hand'

root meaning: *shayn* or *shiand*—two/pair

SHEHANE ALTHAIN—Ilitharis Paravian who dedicated his spirit as defender and guardian of Althain Tower.

pronounced: shee-hay-na all-thain

root meaning: *shiehai'en*—to give for the greater good; *alt*—last; *thein*—tower, sanctuary

SHIP'S PORT—city located on the Bay of Eltair in the principality of West Halla, Melhalla.

SIDIR—one of the Companions, who were the fourteen boys to survive the Battle of Strakewood. Served Arithon at the battle of Dier Kenton Vale, and the Havens. Second-in-command of Earl Jieret's war band.

pronounced: see-deer

root meaning: *i'sid'i'er*—one who has stood at the verge of being lost

s'ILESSID—family name for the royal line appointed by the Fellowship Sorcerers in Third Age Year One to rule the High Kingdom of Tysan. Gifted geas: justice.

pronounced: s-ill-ess-id

root meaning: *liessiad*—balance

SILVERMARSH—mire located south of Daenfal Lake, in the principality of West Halla, Melhalla.

SITHAER—mythological equivalent of hell, halls of Dharkaron Avenger's judgment; according to Ath's adepts, that state of being where the prime vibration is not recognized.

pronounced: sith-air

root meaning: *sid*—lost; *thiere*—wraith/spirit

SKANNT—headhunter captain, served under Pesquil.

pronounced: scant

root meaning: *sciant*—a lean, hard-run hound of mixed breeding

SKYRON FOCUS—large aquamarine focus stone, used by the Koriani Senior Circle for their major magic after the loss of the Great Waystone during the rebellion.

pronounced: sky-run

root meaning: *skyron*—colloquialism for shackle; *s'kyr'i'on*—literally 'sorrowful fate'

SKYSHIELS—mountain range that runs north and south along the eastern coast of Rathain.

pronounced: sky-shee-ells

root meaning: *skyshia*—to pierce through; *iel*—ray

SORCHAIN—Etarran trade minister with a long pedigree.

pronounced: sore-shain

root meaning: *soershian*—a method of tempering steel

STEIVEN—Earl of the North, *caithdein* and regent to the Kingdom of Rathain at the time of Arithon Teir's'Ffalenn's return. Chieftain of the Deshans until his death in the battle of Strakewood Forest in Third Year 5638. Jieret Red-beard's father.

pronounced: stay-vin

root meaning: *steiven*—stag

STORLAINS—mountains dividing the Kingdom of Havish.

pronounced: store-lanes

root meaning: *storlient*—largest summit, highest divide

STORMWELL—Gulf of Stormwell, body of water off the northcoast of Tysan.

STRAKEWOOD—forest in the principality of Deshir, Rathain; site of the battle of Strakewood Forest, where the garrison from Etarra marched against the clans under Steiven s'Valerient and Prince Arithon, in Third Age Year 5638.

pronounced: strayk-wood, similar to 'stray wood'

root meaning: *streik*—to quicken, to seed

SULFIN EVEND—son of the Mayor of Hanshire who holds the post of Alliance Lord Commander under Lysaer s'Ilessid.

pronounced: sool-finn ev-end

root meaning: *suilfinn eiavend*—colloquialism, diamond mind 'one who is persistent'

s'VALERIENT—family name for the Earls of the North, regents and *caithdeinen* for the High Kings of Rathain.

pronounced: val-er-ee-ent

root meaning: *val*—straight; *erient*—spear

TAERLIN—southwestern principality of Kingdom of Tysan. Also

a lake, Taerlin Waters located in the southern spur of Tornir Peaks. Halliron taught Arithon a ballad of that name, which is of Paravian origin, and which commemorates the First Age slaughter of a unicorn herd by Khadrim.

pronounced: tay-er-lin

root meaning: *taer*—calm; *lien*—to love

TAL QUORIN—river formed by the confluence of watershed on the southern side of Strakewood, principality of Deshir, Rathain, where traps were laid for Etarra's army in the battle of Strakewood Forest, and where the rape and massacre of Deshir's clan women and children occurred under Lysaer and headhunter Pesquil's command in Third Age Year 5638.

pronounced: tal quar-in

root meaning: *tal*—branch; *quorin*—canyons

TALERA s'AHELAS—princess wed to the King of Amroth on the splinter world of Eascen Elur. Mother of Lysaer s'Ilessid, by her husband; mother of Arithon, through her adulterous liaison with the Pirate King of Karthan, Avar s'Ffalenn.

pronounced: tal-er-a

root meaning: *talera*—branch or fork in a path

TALITH—Etarran princess; former wife of Lysaer s'Ilessid. Died of a fall from Avenor's tower of state.

pronounced: tal-ith—to rhyme with 'gal with'

root meaning: *tal*—branch; *lith*—to keep/nurture

TALVISH—a clanborn retainer in sworn service to s'Brydion at Alestron who was sworn into the service of Prince Arithon as a point of honor.

pronounced: tall-vish

root meaning: *talvesh*—reed

TEIR—title fixed to a name denoting heirship.

pronounced: tayer

root meaning: *teir's*—successor to power

TERIK—servant at Rauven Tower on the splinter world of Dascen Elur.

pronounced: tear-ick

root meaning: *tiaric*—an alloy of steel

THALDEINS—mountain range that borders the principality of Camris, Tysan, to the east. Site of the Camris clans' west outpost. Site of the raid at the Pass of Orlan.

pronounced: thall-dayn

root meaning: *thal*—head; *dein*—bird

THARIDOR—trade city on the shores of Bay of Eltair in Melhalla.

pronounced: thar-i-door

root meaning: *tier'i'dur*—keep of stone

THARRICK—former captain of the guard in the city of Alestron assigned charge of the duke's secret armory; now married to Jinesse and working as a gentleman mercenary guard at Innish.

pronounced: thar-rick

root meaning: *thierik*—unkind twist of fate

THEIRID—one of the Companions, the fourteen children who survived the Battle of Strakewood Forest. Best known for his stalking and hunting skills.

pronounced: thee-rid

root meaning: *thierent*—wraithlike

TIENDAR—Paravian word invoking the tie between spirit and flesh.

pronounced: tee-en-dar

root meaning: *tiendar*—spirit tie

TIENELLE—high-altitude herb valued by mages for its mind-expanding properties. Highly toxic. No antidote. The leaves, dried and smoked, are most potent. To weaken its powerful side effects and allow safer access to its vision, Koriani enchantresses boil the flowers, then soak tobacco leaves with the brew.

pronounced: tee-an-ell-e ('e' mostly subliminal)

root meaning: *tien*—dream; *iel*—light/ray

TIRIACS—mountain range to the north of Mirthlvain Swamp, Midhalla, Melhalla.

pronounced: tie-ree-axe

root meaning: *tieriach*—alloy of metals

TORBRAND s'FFALENN—founder of the s'Ffalenn line appointed by the Fellowship of Seven to rule the High Kingdom of Rathain in Third Age Year One.

pronounced: tor-brand

root meaning: *tor*—sharp, keen; *brand*—temper

TORNIR PEAKS—mountain range on western border of the principality of Camris, Tysan. Northern half is actively volcanic, and there the last surviving packs of Khadrim are kept under ward.

pronounced: tor-neer

root meaning: *tor*—sharp, keen; *nier*—tooth

TRAITHE—Sorcerer of the Fellowship of Seven. Solely responsible for the closing of South Gate to deny further entry to the Mistwraith. Traithe lost most of his faculties in the process, and was left with a limp. Since it is not known whether he can make the transfer into discorporate existence with his powers impaired, he has retained his physical body.

pronounced: tray-the

root meaning: *traithe*—gentleness

TYSAN—one of the Five High Kingdoms of Athera, as defined by the charters of the Fellowship of Seven. Ruled by the s'Ilessid royal line. Sigil: gold star on blue field.

    pronounced: tie-san

    root meaning: *tiasen*—rich

VALLEYGAP—pass on the trade road between Etarra and Perlorn in the Kingdom of Rathain, known for shale slides and raids. Site of Pesquil's death.

VASTMARK—principality located in southwestern Shand. Highly mountainous and not served by trade roads. Its coasts are renowned for shipwrecks. Inhabited by nomadic shepherds and wyverns, non-fire-breathing, smaller relatives of Khadrim. Site of the grand massacre of Lysaer's war host in Third Age 5647.

    pronounced: vast-mark

    root meaning: *vhast*—bare; *mheark*—valley

VERRAIN—master spellbinder, trained by Luhaine; stood as Guardian of Mirthlvain when the Fellowship of Seven was left shorthanded after the conquest of the Mistwraith.

    pronounced: ver-rain

    root meaning: *ver*—keep; *ria*—touch; *an*—one; original Paravian: *verria'an*

VHALZEIN—city located in West Shand, shore of Rockbay Harbor on the border by Havish. Famed for shell-inlaid lacquer furnishings.

    pronounced: val-zeen

    root meaning: from Drakish, *vhchalsckeen*—white sands

VHANDON—a renowned clanborn war captain of Duke Bransian s'Brydion of Alestron, assigned to Prince Arithon's service as a point of honor in Third Age Year 5654.

    pronounced: van-done

    root meaning: *vhandon*—steadfast

VORRICE—Lord High Examiner of Avenor; charged with trying and executing cases of dark magecraft.

    pronounced: vor-iss

    root meaning: *vorisse*—to lay waste by fire

WARDEN OF ALTHAIN—alternative title for the Fellowship Sorcerer, Sethvir, who received custody of Althain Tower and the powers of the earth link from the last centaur guardian to leave the continent of Paravia in Third Age Year 5100.

WERPOINT—fishing town and outpost on the northeast coast of Fallowmere, Rathain. Musterpoint for Lysaer's war host.

    pronounced: were-point

    root meaning: *wyr*—all/sum

WESTWOOD—forest located in Camris, Tysan, north of the Great West Road.

WHITEHAVEN—Hostel of Ath's Brotherhood located in the Skyshiel Mountains near the city of Eastwall.

WHITEHOLD—city located on the shore of Eltair Bay, Kingdom of Melhalla.

WORLDSEND GATES—set at the four compass points of the continent of Paravia. These were spelled portals constructed by the Fellowship of Seven at the dawn of the Third Age, and were done in connection with the obligations created by their compact with the Paravian races, which allowed Men to settle on Athera.

Fugitive Prince

The Wars of Light and Shadow Volume 4
First Book of the Alliance of Light

Janny Wurts

Where there is light, there must always be shadow . . .
The long-awaited continuation of Janny Wurts'
epic fantasy saga.

The schism began with two half-brothers empowered to subdue a Mistwraith. In revenge it cursed them a life of perpetual conflict. Each believes absolutely in his cause, and loathes the other for opposing it . . .

Lysaer, Prince of the Light – a charismatic leader sworn to set humanity free from sorcerous oppression. He claims divine power to safeguard his people from an enemy he is convinced will destroy them.

Arithon, Master of Shadow – a trained mage who wishes for nothing but to defuse war, and search out the vanished old races who hold the key to restore the world's shattered peace.

When Koriani enchantresses join forces with Lysaer, new intrigues upset Arithon's hard-won autonomy. Faction is set against faction, heart against heart, and the scene is set for an explosive recurrence of war. The curse of the Mistwraith echoes eternal . . .

'Astonishingly original and compelling . . . A gifted creator of wonder'   RAYMOND E. FEIST

ISBN: 0 00 648299 6

Krondor: The Betrayal

Raymond E. Feist

From the endlessly inventive mind of one of fantasy's all-time greats, comes a spellbinding new adventure featuring old favourites Jimmy, Locklear and Pug.

It is nine years on from the aftermath of Sethanon. There has been peace awhile and it's been needed. But news is feeding through to the people of the Kingdom of the Isles that deadly forces are stirring on the horizon. The bringer of the latest tidings is Gorath, a moredhel (dark elf).

The bloodletting has started. Nighthawks are murdering again. Politics is a dangerous, cut-throat game once more. At the root of all this unrest lie the mysterious machinations of a group of magicians known as The Six.

Meanwhile, renegade Tsurani gem smugglers, a rival criminal gang to the Mockers led by someone known only as The Crawler, and traitors to the crown are all conspiring to bring the Kingdom of the Isles to its knees.

ISBN: 0 00 648334 8